BREACH OF PROMISE

TWO BOOKS IN ONE

PRESUMED GUILTY

James Scott BELL

Breach of Promise

Two Books in One

Presumed Guilty

ZONDERVAN®

ZONDERVAN.com/
AUTHORTRACKER
follow your favorite authors

ZONDERVAN

Breach of Promise / Presumed Guilty
Copyright © 2010 by James Scott Bell

Breach of Promise
Copyright © 2004 by James Scott Bell

Presumed Guilty
Copyright © 2006 by James Scott Bell

Requests for information should be addressed to:
Zondervan, *Grand Rapids, Michigan 49530*

ISBN 978-0-310-32973-2

Cover design: Curt Diepenhorst
Cover photography: Jon Feingersh Photography / Corbis / Getty Images
Interior design: Christine Orejuela-Winkelman

Printed in the United States of America

10 11 12 13 14 15 16 /DCI/ 20 19 18 17 16 15 14 13 12 11 10 9 8 7 6 5 4 3 2 1

BREACH OF PROMISE

For Allegra

I have walked through many lives,
some of them my own,
and I am not who I was ...

—Stanley Kunitz, The Layers

MOON DANCE

Halfway through Twister, when Helen Hunt was about to run down another relentless force of nature, I turned to Paula and said, "Please don't do it."

"Shh." Paula put her finger to her lips. She was really into the movie.

I hadn't been able to concentrate on the film since the first tornado. In fact, I felt like a tornado was churning inside me, destroying all my fixtures, and I knew I had to get Paula's answer.

"I really mean it, Paula."

I saw her turn toward me, her face reflected in the glow of the movie screen.

"Why are you talking about it now, Mark?"

"I can't stop thinking about it."

"We already talked it out."

"You talked. I went along."

A shush issued from in front of us, like a snake hiss.

"Can't this wait?" Paula whispered.

"No." I surprised myself at my own insistence.

"We're coming back to see this," Paula said emphatically, then got up and started for the exit. I followed her out.

The bright lights of the lobby and the smell of popcorn—that odd theater smell, somewhere between fresh popped and yesterday's laundry—hit me. So did Paula Montgomery's glare.

"Do you think," Paula said—her hands were in front of her, palm to palm, fingers pointing at my chest like a spear—"that this is an easy decision for me?"

"No, of course not." I was only vaguely aware of the old couple shuffling into the theater next door, showing the Tom Cruise movie Mission: Impossible.

"Then why bring it up again?" Paula said. Her eyes suddenly filled with tears. They gathered on her lower lids like rain on lily pads. I hugged her, burying my face in her midnight hair, which smelled like honey and cinnamon. Her shampoo. Which I loved.

"I'm sorry, baby," I said. Baby. "But I want it. I want our baby."

"Please. Mark."

"And I want to marry you, Paulie. I do."

She pushed me away and cursed at me. The old couple stopped in the maw of the theater doors and the woman's mouth dropped open. Paula turned and ran away.

I found her crying at Pretzels Plus in the heart of the mall. I hardly knew how to approach her. There was a big, fat pretzel lying under the glass, dotted with chunks of salt. Another twister, of a sort. Everything was twisted now.

It wasn't fair to spring this on her in the middle of a movie. She had struggled hard with the decision. I knew that. I knew pregnancy wasn't good for her career. Not at this point. She'd have to be written off the soap if they couldn't get her pregnant in the story. Maybe she could sue them, like that one actress who sued Aaron Spelling. But Paula didn't want to sue. She wanted a career. And hers was just starting to take off. She'd gotten a cover on Soap Times. "Up and Coming Vixens" was the title of the article.

Abortion was the logical thing. I had accepted it. For about a day.

But it gnawed at me until I had to say something. I didn't want her to do it. But not wanting that probably meant I had lost Paula Montgomery for good.

"I'm sorry," I said.

Paula was leaning against the yellow tile wall next to the pretzel glass. "All right," she said, her voice a thin reed.

I touched her shoulder. "All right what?"

"I'll marry you," she said.

Half my heart filled with new life.

"And the baby?" I said.

She looked at me, eyes red and wet. "Do you know what this is going to mean?"

"No," I said.

"Well, you better learn." She hit me in the shoulder as hard as she could, then threw her arms around my neck and held me like I was now her tether to earth.

＊

One would have thought that a Christian wedding would have pleased all concerned, especially Paula's Bostonian matriarch mother, Erica. After all, I was "doing the right thing" by marrying Paula. But Erica the Red, as I called her only to myself, did not like me. Never had. Not good enough for her daughter. I had the feeling no one ever would be.

The Christian part of the wedding was Erica's choice, too (Paula's father, Franklin, had died two years before). I was not a Christian yet. I worshiped at the altar of Brando and James Dean. My view of Jesus was that he would be a good role to play if Steven Spielberg or Antonio Troncatti directed me in it.

Paula was not a Christian, either. She had some sort of Buddhist leanings. But we both enjoyed the pomp and circumstance that attended us in the big church in Hollywood. The Presbyterians might have been a mystery to me, but they sure had themselves a good land deal and a wonderful architect.

And Paula Montgomery was stunning in her wedding dress. I couldn't believe she was walking toward me.

We had met at a party a year and a half before, thrown by my crazy friend Roland. Roland was a gifted jazz musician by night and a writer of jingles by day. He could sit at the piano and create an ad line for any product you cared to name, right on the spot. He was doing just that when Paula walked in the door.

And knocked me out. As she did maybe half a dozen other guys there. She had hair the color of a Malibu night and violet eyes that ran on their own electricity. I had to do a lot of broken field running to get to her. But I finally managed to get her out to the balcony for some air—sweetening the deal by snagging a bowl of peanut M&M's—and I had the chance to work my magic.

Which she didn't fall for. After my few, fumbling attempts at charming small talk, she looked me in the eye and said, "Why don't you put a hold on the fluff and just tell me what you're passionate about?"

Her eyes were not just hypnotic, they were intelligent. I told her I loved acting, old movies, and baseball.

She smiled, and my heart pounded for mercy inside my chest. "Me, too."

I was so in love my mouth refused to work. I'm sure she thought I was a babbling idiot.

So the next night, when I called to ask her out (I practically assaulted Roland for her phone number), the Yes I heard from her was a shock on the order of holding a winning lottery ticket.

I took her to Micelli's, where working actors liked to eat. It gave hope.

"Too bad LA is not a theater town," Paula remarked at dinner. "I'd love to do Rosalind someday."

She was a serious actress, in other words. Shakespeare was not something a lot of young actors attempted anymore. It's scary to do the Bard, but also the best feeling when you carry it off.

"I'll do Orlando," I offered.

She laughed and said, "It's a deal."

I fell more deeply in love. It was like Shakespeare had written the scene for us, in modern lingo. I promised myself we would do As You Like It someday. As husband and wife.

And now I was marrying her. When it came time to promise to love, honor, and all the rest, I said I do with more intense joy than anything I'd felt before in my life. And then she promised the same. It was too much like a dream.

The nightmare was still five years away.

———

Throughout her pregnancy, Paula continued to act on the soap. Her character was having an affair with the respected town doctor, who was pressuring her to have an abortion. I wanted to go into the TV and slug the guy. It felt good to want to do that.

Paula did have her moments of disquiet about the upcoming birth. I was often not very helpful.

Once, after our Bradley natural birth class, we went to Ralph's Market to pick up a few items. I grabbed a straw from the deli counter and then went to the produce section and selected a big, ripe cantaloupe. I took the items over to Paula.

"See," I said. "All you have to do is pass this—" I held up the cantaloupe—"through this—" the straw. "It's easy!"

"Shut UP!"

– 2 –

When Paula went into labor, I was auditioning for "young father" on a Lucky Charms commercial. It was not a cause of great celebration in my heart. I was twenty-nine and not ready to be listed as "young father" on the casting sheets in town. My agent had not told me she approved the change. I found out when I walked into the audition with my headshots and the C girl said, "You need to update these." I looked too young in them.

So when the call from the hospital came on the cell phone, I did not hang around. I was about to become "young father" in real life. How could Lucky Charms compete with that?

Paula was in labor for eight hours. It was not smooth sailing. There were times when this beautiful woman took on the face of Lucifer's less attractive sister, glaring at me with knives, because I was responsible for getting her into this.

When I told her I had given up a Lucky Charms spot to be here with her she said, "Get me drugs."

They gave her an intravenous injection of Demerol, which at least softened her back into the beautiful wife I knew. And she was beautiful, even without makeup, even with sweaty strands of ebony hair stuck to her forehead like wet string.

We knew we were going to have a girl, and we had decided to name her Madeleine Erica Gillen. The Erica, of course, was for Paula's mother. I didn't fight her on that, because one does not do battle with the Montgomerys and survive.

The Madeleine, though, was my idea, something I just hit on one day, reading through a baby name book. For me it had a classic quality to it, but also suggested just a little bit the madness that I felt for Paula. As in madly in love. As in the woman of my dreams.

The Demerol did not last, and finally an anesthesiologist gave Paula an epidural with a needle the length of California.

That's what I remember most, up until the time Madeleine's head slid out, followed by the rest of her, into the hands of Dr. Malverse Martin.

I began to believe in God at that moment.

***

The next few years passed like a montage in a family movie, complete with musical score. The bad scenes—the tensions, the arguments, the pressures, the finances, the auditions, the juggling of two careers and one baby — these ended up on the cutting room floor of my mind. I kept the good shots on the front of the reel:

The baths. Maddie's skin so soft and my thumbs nearly the length of her tiny head.

My skill as a diaper changer. How I could wad a used Pampers up into a ball of almost impossible density.

Holding Maddie all night in a recliner, because she was so stuffy with a cold she could not breathe when lying flat.

Bringing her to Paula for midnight feedings.

The early, fuzzy sprouts of Maddie's hair.

Her first word, Dada, which really upset Paula. Her third word, Kaka, which to her meant cookie, and cracked me up completely.

The big day we bought Maddie her own potty, and she decided it would be a bed for her bear. Much discussion ensued.

When she was three, we announced we were taking her to Disneyland. Even at that age, a child in Los Angeles knows what Disneyland is. It seeps into their heads while they sleep. When we told her, her blue eyes got huge and she said, "My heart is beautiful!"

I still can't think of a better way to express happiness than that.

And then the time we were watching It's a Wonderful Life on TV one Christmas. Maddie was four. Donna Reed and Jimmy Stewart started singing "Buffalo Gals" as they were walking home from the high school dance. I glanced at Maddie and she seemed mesmerized.

Aaaaannnd dance by the light of the moon.

Jimmy and Donna, singing.

Maddie looked at me then. "Can we do that?" she asked. Paula was on the phone in the kitchen. I alone had to field this one and knew from experience that Maddie's questions sometimes threw a bolo around my head.

"Do what, honey?"

"Dance by the guy in the moon?"

"By the light of the moon."

"Whatever, Daddy."

"You bet we can."

"Now?"

It was one of those things you don't stop and analyze. I think God implants a certain instinct in fathers (who are somewhat slow on the uptake) that tells them to heed their children without extensive cross-examination.

"Sure," I said. I lifted her off the couch—she in her soft cotton PJs with rabbits and me in my cutoffs and Dodger T-shirt—and went to the kitchen to tell Paula we were going up on the roof of the building. Paula, phone at her ear, put her finger in the air, telling me to be quiet.

I carried Maddie up to the roof.

The moon was almost full. It seemed huge. It cast a glow over the hills, where million-dollar homes gawked somewhat incredulously at the apartment buildings below. The kind of homes I dreamed of living in, with Paula and Maddie and a big, fat $20 million contract to star in the next Ridley Scott movie.

But tonight I did not care that I was on an apartment building roof. Maddie had her warm arms around my neck, and I held her and swayed, swayed, swayed. Time went completely away as we danced by the light of the moon.

BAD THINGS

- 1 -

I can pinpoint the start of the bad things.

The three of us were dining at Maddie's favorite restaurant, Flookey's. This was an establishment on Ventura Boulevard serving a selection of hot dogs and chips. It had an outdoor patio. Maddie liked to eat outside so she could say hi to all the people.

At five she was already networking. She'd make it in this town for sure.

Paula's cell rang and she picked up. I half watched Paula and half did a hand game with Maddie.

After thirty seconds Paula looked as if her mother had died. She was silent, her face draining of color in the fashion of an old ghost movie. Just before I asked what was wrong, her face transformed into an incandescent smile. Then the tears came.

She said something and put the phone down.

"That was Phyl," she said. Phyl was Paula's agent.

"Good news?"

"Look at me, honey," she said. How could I not? She was in the grip of something. She put her hand on my arm and with her other hand grabbed Maddie's fingers.

"Antonio Troncatti wants me for his next film," she said.

The name, the news, hit me like a rolled-up Variety across the face. Antonio Troncatti was the director of the moment, the new anointed one. A thirty-five-year-old Italian whose first movie had been nominated for Best Foreign Film. His next project had been for TriStar, a portrait of Napoleon starring Sean Penn. It was a huge international hit. That caught everyone by surprise because it did not contain the action elements usually required for big foreign box office.

The rumor now was he was in preproduction on a major thriller to be shot mostly in Europe. And every actor in Hollywood wanted to work with him.

"Wow," I said in a half whisper.

"Wow!" Maddie screeched. She had no idea who Antonio Troncatti was, of course. She just wanted to be part of the fun.

"I can't believe this," Paula said, her voice and face otherworldly.

"How did he happen—"

"To pick me? Phyl says he wanted an unknown for the role, but a certain look. I guess I have it."

"What about—" I nodded my head toward Maddie.

"What do you mean?" Paula said. I could tell I'd just deflated her a little.

"I mean, are you going to be in Europe, shooting?"

"I don't know, Mark," she said sharply. "I don't know anything yet. Can't you just be happy for me right now?"

I recovered quickly. "Yeah. Sure. Of course. You're going to be a big star. You hear that, Maddie? Mommy's going to be a big star!"

"My heart is beautiful!" Maddie said.

―――

But my heart was not beautiful. To be perfectly frank, I was envious. Acting couples are that way. It's a competitive business, and when your spouse gets the big break you have been hoping for yourself, it's one of those good news/bad news things.

I have to admit that, when we got married, I thought I was the real actor in the family. Paula was on a soap. Not a bad thing. The money is good, the work steady. But it's like the minor leagues of media. I never wanted to be on a soap, just in films or a solid TV series.

My unspoken plans were for me to get into feature films, starring roles, and Paula to follow along afterward. Maybe make her big splash in one of my own movies.

Call it male pride. Ego soufflé. That's the way it was.

Paula could sense it, too, on the drive home. She gets quiet when she's upset, and a little line forms in the flesh between her eyebrows. I call it the John Gruden line, after the Tampa Bay football coach whose sneer is now legendary among followers of the game.

Maddie, happy in her car seat in the back of the Accord, looking at a picture book, ignored us.

"When's it supposed to start?" I asked.

"I don't know any of that yet." Paula looked straight ahead. "Phyl will fill me in."

"Phyl you in? I get it."

Paula did not see the humor. Neither did I. I had done stand-up comedy for a while, on open mike nights, and I knew when a joke was lame. That was lame.

"Troncatti," I said.

"What's Troncatti?" Maddie asked from the rear.

"An Italian pasta," I said. "You make it with Alfredo sauce."

"Daddy's joking, honey." Paula turned around, protecting her child from the bad jokes of the driver. "Antonio Troncatti is a famous moviemaker. Mommy's going to be in his movie."

"With sauce?" my daughter said.

"Good call!" I slapped the steering wheel. "Alfredo sauce and pretentious dialogue."

Paula spun around to look at me. "What are you doing?"

"What?"

"Why are you putting him down like that?"

"I'm just joking."

"It's not funny."

Maddie said, "Not funny, Daddy."

"Look at your book," I told Maddie. "Mommy and Daddy are talking."

"Talk, talk, talk," Maddie said.

We drove in silence along Ventura. It was crowded tonight, and I hit every red light. Each one was like a little slap in the face.

Finally, I said, "Look, I'm sorry. All right? I want you to succeed. I really do. This is great news. I just feel, I don't know—"

"Jealous?"

"Honest? A little."

Paula put her hand on my arm. Her hand was hot. "Mark, you're a great actor. I really think that. I think you should be getting your break soon. I want it to happen for you. I know it will."

Back at the apartment I waited until Maddie was asleep before stirring up some hot chocolate for Paula and me. I took it to her with a big swirl of whipped cream on the top. She was watching a movie in the living room—All About Eve, one of her all-time favorites. She smiled as she took it and gave me the first sip.

"You know, I like being a man," I said.

"And why is that?"

"Because when I retain water, it's in a canteen."

"Oh please."

"And a phone conversation takes thirty seconds, max."

"Very funny."

"But the thing I like most about it?"

She looked at me.

"I get to be married to you."

Two weeks later I had a knock-down-drag-out with Paula. She had officially signed on to do the film with Troncatti. There was still a part of me that hoped something would go wrong. Film cancelled. Change of mind on the casting. Selfish, I know, but I couldn't help feeling it.

When the contract was signed, the reality was like a refrigerator dropping on my foot. Paula was going to be doing interviews, preproduction promotion, media stuff. She had a hundred other things to do trying to get ready to go. One night in the apartment, she asked me to help her go over her list, see if she'd forgotten anything.

"Yeah," I said. "Maddie."

She gave me her signature roll of the eyeballs, which only ticked me off.

"I mean it," I said. "You're going to be in Europe for what? Four months?"

"Give or take," she said.

"And when are you going to see your daughter?"

"Mark," she said, pulling off her glasses — they were black-framed and she never wore them in public, but when she pulled them off she seemed like my fifth-grade teacher about to chastise me — "four months is not a big deal."

"To you maybe, but what about Maddie?"

"Bring her over."

"Right. And meanwhile I quit auditioning."

"What's wrong with that?"

The way she said it entered my pores like an arctic wind. She might as well have said, Your career isn't exactly taking off, like mine, and you haven't had a paying gig in eight months, so how can it be wrong to have you fly over where I'll be making myself into a legend?

"That's just like you all of a sudden," I said. "You're the center of the universe now."

"Maybe I am. Maybe it's my time."

"You sound like George Segal in Look Who's Talking."

"Huh?"

"When he cheats on Kirstie Alley and tells her, 'I'm going through a selfish phase.'"

"That is so mean."

"Comparing you to George Segal?" I can be nasty when I want to be.

"You don't want me to succeed, do you?"

At that precise moment I was not sure if I did. I could feel her star ascending like it was launched by some heavenly Cape Canaveral, while I sat here back on earth, a boulder in Death Valley.

I did want her to succeed. Part of me was so proud of her. She was going to become a major star, I had always believed that. And she was my wife. I never felt so good as when I walked into a party with Paula on my arm. Everyone would stop what they were doing and just stare — at her — and then they'd look over at me, thinking Who is that lucky guy?

But I also didn't want her to go away. And I yelled at her about it.

Paula yelled back. She had a good, strong voice. Great for theater work.

My voice is stronger, however, and I used it. Paula got so mad she started to cry and took off one of her shoes and threw it at me as hard as she could. She missed and I laughed. (To this day I am sorry about that. It was a cruel and ugly thing to do, and I did it because I wanted to win. That was all that mattered.)

And then Maddie came into the kitchen where World War III was commencing.

"Guys!" Maddie said emphatically, "this is not what you do!" We looked at Maddie. I looked at Paula. Paula looked at me. Then Paula started to laugh. And I started to laugh. Maddie put her hands on her hips and said, "This is not funny."

– 2 –

"Mark, I've been thinking."

Paula and I were in bed. I'd just finished getting Maddie settled by letting her read Dr. Seuss to me. I chose Marvin K. Mooney Will You Please Go Now! All the way through I was thinking about Paula. She would be going soon.

"Good," I said. "A woman who thinks is very sexy."

"Not about that."

"Can I change your way of thinking?"

"Will you listen?"

"I'm listening." I folded my hands on my stomach and looked at the ceiling. It had a brown water spot in the corner. Funny, but I hadn't noticed it before. Did it come after the last rains?

"It's about you and Maddie."

"What about me and Maddie?"

"I think maybe we can work something out while I'm gone. To help."

"Help?"

"You know."

I got up on one elbow, looked at Paula. "No, I don't know."

Paula sighed. "About taking care of her."

"What, you're saying I can't handle the job?"

"You said so yourself."

"When?"

"When you were bagging on me going to Europe. All that about your career suffering."

"What are you, an elephant? Never forget?"

"It was three days ago. It's not like last year."

"Why are you bringing this up now?"

"Duh, because I'm about to leave."

"Forget about it. We went through this."

"No, you went through this."

"Then you said okay."

"When did I say okay?"

"When you didn't say anything. That was a silent okay."

She shook her head. "This is starting to sound like a bad Seinfeld script. I'm telling you I've got an idea. You want to hear it, or do you want to bat around lines?"

With a hand to her shoulder, I said, "Or something else?"

She pulled away from me. "Stop it. I'm serious. I've been talking to Mom and she's willing to come out here."

The dreaded M word. "You want your mother to come out here for the entire time you're shooting?"

"She says she doesn't mind. She'll lease a house."

"A house?"

"That's not a problem."

"I guess not. But I've got a problem."

"Mark, you—"

"No." I rolled off the bed. My feet hit the floor like asphalt pounders. "I don't want your mom taking care of Maddie."

"It's only to help, while you're—"

"It won't stay just helping. Your mom will try to take more and more—"

"Maddie will still live here."

"Well, thank you."

"This is for Maddie."

"You don't think I can do this? Take care of my own daughter by myself?"

When Paula didn't say anything I got mad. "I don't want your mom within five states of this apartment."

Paula got up, so she could face me. Fighter to fighter. "That is so unfair. She is Maddie's grandmother."

"And about as fond of me as, what? A rash? A festering boil?"

"Stop."

"That's what she thinks."

"You won't give her a chance."

I pounded my chest with an open hand. King Kong. "What chance has she ever given me? Huh? She thinks her precious daughter got hooked up with a loser!"

Before Paula could say anything we heard a pounding on the wall, coming from Maddie's room. And then her voice, muffled but emphatic: "Hey, some people are trying to sleep around here."

Now that should have been funny. Coming from a five-year-old with perfect timing. But I didn't so much as smile. Neither did Paula. We let a chill settle between us, silent and misty.

"Paula?"

"What."

"Don't worry about Maddie and me."

She did not reply.

"Hey," I said.

"What now?"

"Remember when we went to see Doctor Zhivago? At the Dome?"

"Yes."

"Remember the part where Lara's leaving the hospital? After Zhivago's fallen in love with her? And the cart pulls out and watching it go, you can see on his face he thinks he'll never see her again?"

"Yes."

"And he walks back in and that yellow flower is starting to die—"

"I remember, yes. What about it?"

"That's how I feel right now."

I felt the bed move, and then she was up against me, her breath on my face. "Dope, this isn't a movie. I'm just shooting one, okay?"

"Don't make me go to Russia looking for you."

"Deal," she said.

– 3 –

And then, sooner than I could imagine, it was time for Paula to go make her movie. We—Maddie and I—did not take Paula to the airport. The studio sent a driver around. For some reason that made me feel like a forgotten man. But I kept a smile on my face, for Maddie's sake.

Paula kissed and hugged us. Maddie cried a little, but tried to be brave. Paula promised to phone her a lot.

The last thing Paula said to me, after a final kiss, was, "Be good."

In a morbid, ugly, horror movie sort of way, that is funny.

After Paula left, Maddie was very clingy. She had hold of my jeans and wouldn't let go. I walked around the apartment with this five-year-old growth on my leg.

"Don't go away, Daddy," Maddie kept saying.

"No, cupcake," I said. "I'm here. I just have to go to a meeting this afternoon."

"No!"

"Honey, it's for my work. Mrs. Williams is going to watch you."

She pulled my jeans hard. "No! I wanna go with you."

"It'll be boring. I'm going to have to wait around and—"

"I can color."

How could I argue with that? We packed up a couple of her coloring books—SpongeBob SquarePants and Powerpuff Girls—and hopped in my Accord for the ride to CBS on Radford.

The gate guard, a skinny old guy in a dark jacket (even though it must have been ninety outside), gave Maddie a scowl as I checked in.

"She's not on the list," the guard said, looking at his clipboard like it was incriminating evidence.

Before I could open my mouth, Maddie said, "That's my daddy!" She had a look on her face that was not to be trifled with.

I smiled sheepishly at the guard. Who broke out into a toothy grin. "Go on," he said. Maddie the charmer had done it again.

My audition was in a production office next to Studio C. In the reception area, in between potted plants and ostentatious urns, sat about half a dozen guys roughly my age.

The competition.

I recognized one of the guys from my acting class, Steve Monet (pronounced like the painter). He gave me a half smile and wave, the kind that said, I know you're up for this, old buddy, but I sure hope you drool during the reading.

The receptionist handed me my "sides," the two pages of dialogue I would be reading in order to land this national spot for Colgate. I sat in the one empty chair, put Maddie on the floor in front of me, and started reading the lines.

"That's pretty desperate," Steve said.

"Huh?"

"Bringing your little girl to the audition. Going for the sympathy factor?"

"Funny." I went back to my sides.

"I mean, you really going to bring her in with you?"

"She wanted to come with me."

"Oh. That's right."

"That's right what?"

"I read about Paula. She's doing the Troncatti film."

"Yeah."

"Making you Mr. Mom?"

"Something like that. Hey." I held up the pages, a signal that I needed to get back to business.

"Troncatti's a wild man," Steve said. His half smile slid from one side of his face to the other.

That was too much. He was playing with my head, I was sure, because he wanted me to flub the audition. But his ploy worked. My mind created a picture of Paula and Troncatti, laughing it up on the set, having a good old time. Too good?

Snap out of it. This is Paula's break. Yours is coming. Read the lines.

"What's the kid's name?" Steve asked.

"You mind?" I said. "I want to get ready."

"Take it easy, man."

Maddie looked at him. "My name is Madeleine Erica Gillen and I'm five years old."

"Whoa," Steve said, throwing up his hands in mock surrender.

Maddie went back to coloring Powerpuff Girls.

When my turn came to read, Maddie wanted to go in with me. I got a cold eye from the casting director, a man, and a tepid smile from the producer, a woman.

"Nice touch," the producer said.

I read my lines to the camera and got the traditional "We'll call you" from the casting director. It sounded like a door closing and being locked from the inside.

Actors are paranoid, but then again, everyone is out to get us.

— 4 —

I wouldn't be Oprah's first pick as the model of fatherhood.

My own parents met dropping acid in San Francisco in 1968. Mom got pregnant, and I guess the two of them decided this was groovy. They were never officially married, though I think someone chanted at them one night as they sat on a bed of flower petals and bayed at the moon.

I was born into a commune outside Santa Cruz, one the cops broke up not long after my birth. I was not the cause of the dispersal. A thriving marijuana field maintained by my dad (who had taken to calling himself Kalifornia) was the real reason.

Dad ended up doing some time in a California prison, by the way. I think I wrote to him once. He never answered.

Mom, whose real name was Estelle Gillen but who preferred to be called Rainbow, returned with me to her mother's home in Chatsworth, a suburb of Los Angeles. My early memories are of my grandmother, Joyce Gillen, a widow who worked reception at Hughes Aircraft. Even when I was six or seven, I saw her as the mother figure in my life.

Mom was trying to come back from her years as a brain-fried flower child. She hooked up with another man, a guy named Barza who ran a Harley shop in Canoga Park. Mom, in photographs from the time, is very beautiful in a natural sort of way. I suppose she thought he was the epitome of groovy. That must have been the reason why she announced one day, to me and Gram, that she was taking off for a ride across the country, "like in Easy Rider."

Someone should have mentioned that Easy Rider didn't turn out so good for the guys on the bikes.

We got the call at night. Gram took the phone while I was in the living room watching Dukes of Hazzard. I heard her wail "Oh God, no!" I ran in and saw her collapse onto the floor. I was eleven years old.

Later we found out that Barza had tried to outrun a trooper in Alabama and skidded off the highway into a split-rail fence. He survived. Mom did not.

It shook me in a way I could not understand at eleven. But I would always feel a punch in the stomach whenever I saw a rainbow after that.

Gram did her best with me. But not having a father or mother in my life, or even a grandfather, was not the best thing that could have happened to the spawn of LSD-induced passion.

I started shoplifting, smoking, hanging out with the people I thought would help get me in the most trouble. If you were to look at me at twelve, you would see a poster boy for Future Skinheads of America. I stayed away from the house as much as I could. I loved Gram and did not want to see her hurt.

But the cops dragging me home after I stole beer from a 7–Eleven did that well enough. And so did the vice principal at school who suspended me for selling cigarettes on campus. Gram cried a lot over both of those things and I hated myself for that. But I didn't stop doing what I could to catch the slow train to state prison.

It was baseball that saved my life. Literally. I believe that to this day.

I'd always been good at the game, never taking it seriously. Mom put me in Little League for one season when I was ten and I ripped up the opposition. I was wild with the bat but usually made contact. Hard. My average was .782 for the season.

I also had a cannon for an arm. I was usually put in right field, because my glove work was not the best. Yet. But there was many a time when a hard one to the deep corner turned into a spectacular out as I gunned the guy down trying to stretch a double into a triple.

I was named to the All-Stars and had a great postseason, too.

The next year Mom died and I lost interest in Little League.

But one of the dads from that Little League year remembered me. He coached at Chatsworth High, and when I got there he sought me out. Got tough with me, got me back into baseball. My life got a little straighter after that. Much to Gram's relief.

I rose through the ranks, and by the time I was a twelfth grader I was among the top prospects in LA. I was named first team All-City.

The Red Sox offered me a contract. I had an agent and everything. Off to the minors I went, ready to embark on a glorious and highly paid future.

Then, in a game in Omaha, I blew out my arm. I was trying to make another legendary throw from deep right. The players were much faster up there than I was used to. I gave the throw everything I had and could almost hear the tearing of muscle and cartilage. It was like someone had napalmed my shoulder.

Coupled with the fact that I was still a wild swinger and could not catch up with a professional curveball, my baseball career came to a sudden and inglorious end.

At the age of nineteen I was out of baseball, out of work, out of options. Alcohol seemed like the traditional way to dull the misery. I went for it. That was the start, too, of what they now call anger issues.

At least I gave up drinking when I found out Paula was going to have our baby.

The anger, though, was about to have a field day.

– 5 –

We had a game, Maddie and I, that was her all-time favorite. I called it Maddie's Buried Treasure.

I did not simply give her gifts, or candy, or something fun. I put it in a little box or bag and hid it somewhere in the apartment. Then I'd tell her, in my best Long John Silver voice, "Treasure is hid, ahhrrrr, and ye best be lookin' for it."

Which would make her giggle and scurry all over the apartment. I had to get more and more clever about finding good hiding spots.

One time I bought a box of Nerds, her favorite candy, and a little squish ball and left them in the Rite-Aid bag along with the receipt. I just rolled the bag up and put it on the middle bookshelf, behind a copy of Respect for Acting by Uta Hagen and John Grisham's The Pelican Brief.

And promptly forgot all about it.

Three days later Maddie let out a scream while I was in the kitchen burning some toast. I ran to her, thinking she'd cut herself or something.

But she was jumping up and down, delighted. Holding the Rite-Aid bag in her hand.

"I found it!" she yelped. "And you didn't even tell me it was buried!"

"Ahhrrr!" I said. "Ye must be the smartest pirate on the seven seas!"

"Silly," Maddie said. "I'm a ballerina!"

The other ritual we had was when I gave Maddie a bath. I loved doing that. When I shampooed her hair with Johnson's Baby Shampoo (she could do this herself but I always wanted to, and she'd let me), I would lean her back in the water to rinse and her face got this beatific look. She'd close her eyes and smile. It was complete trust in me and pure enjoyment of the moment. Her hair would float like kelp in a calm sea, and I'd be thinking that I was really doing something here — making my daughter clean and fresh. I loved the smell of Maddie after a bath.

Our ritual was this: Maddie could ask me any question she wanted to.

So, one evening, she came up out of the water and said, "Do you like God?"

I laughed. "Yes, I like God."

"What does he look like?"

This was just a bath, but all of a sudden we were in deep theological waters. When your daughter starts asking questions about God, even if you're fuzzy on the concept, you tread lightly, because you think one wrong answer could start her down some strange path. You see your child, twenty years hence, hanging out in some waterfront dive as the piano plays, cigarette dangling from her mouth, telling sailors the funny story about what her dad said God looked like.

"I don't think God really looks like anything," I said. Good. Introduce a concept she won't understand and you cannot explain. Not look like anything? How can anything not look like something?

"I think God looks like you," Maddie said.

Perhaps I ought to take this more seriously, I thought, though I did appreciate the compliment.

So I told her the only Bible story I knew about God. I didn't have a Bible background, so I was running on fumes. I tried to make it exciting.

"One day," I told Maddie, "there was this big war going on and one side had a giant named Goliath fighting for them. It was really unfair."

"How big was he?" Maddie asked.

"Oh, I'd say about one hundred feet tall."

"How big is that?"

"Like a telephone pole."

"Wow."

"Yeah. And he would growl at the other army, which happened to believe in God, by the way."

"Cool."

"But they were all afraid of this giant, see? But there was a boy named David who was not a soldier, just a kid."

"What did he look like?"

Richard Gere? Nah. No way. "He was good looking, let's put it that way."

"I don't like boys."

"That's a conversation for another time, okay? Listen. This kid David doesn't have any armor or swords or anything like that. All he has is a slingshot."

"Like in cartoons?"

"It was more of a thing that you whirl around your head with a rock in it, and it throws rocks real hard."

"That's dangerous."

"You're telling me? But this big giant Goliath has a big old sword and spear."

"And a gun?"

"Maybe he's hiding a gun in his pocket, who knows? But he marches out and starts making fun of the army of God, calling them names and laughing at them. But no one wants to go out and fight this guy."

"He was too big."

"You got it. But David says he'll do it."

"Was he short?"

"Yeah."

"Was he scared?"

"Nah. He believed in God, see? And he knew God was stronger than any old giant any day. So David marches right out there with his slingshot, see, and some rocks. And that big old Goliath starts laughing at him. And David puts a rock in his slingshot and zips it and BAM!"

Maddie yelped, then giggled.

"Right in Goliath's head."

"Owie."

"Big-time owie. It killed him."

Maddie's eyes got big with wonder.

"So David became a hero and a king and got to have his own castle and everything, because he believed in God."

"Wow."

"Big-time wow."

I kissed her freshly shampooed head and knew that I needed some boning up on God. Because if I knew Maddie, she was going to ask for more stories just like this one.

After getting Maddie to bed I went to the computer to check out an industry website. It was my way of keeping up on the business I had my little toe in. While I was scrolling around I saw a link to an item that mentioned Antonio Troncatti and some "wild times" in Rome during the shooting of Conquered. Naturally I headed right for it.

As I did, I could feel my heart pulsing in my chest, like I knew what I would find. It had the feel of something inevitable and bad.

Here's what I read.

La Dolce Vida Redux

Fireworks are apparently breaking out on the set of Conquered, the new Antonio Troncatti opus starring Blake Patterson and Paula Montgomery. Shooting on the set has featured some outrageous behavior by Patterson, well known for his rather unconventional approach to life, the universe, and everything.

Cast and crew were seen drinking it up at a hot Rome nightspot. Meanwhile, Troncatti and Montgomery were cheek to cheek on the dance floor until the wee hours, according to reports, until heading off together for parts unknown.

A helpless, hot, grinding suction set to work on my guts. My hands and arms almost felt numb. And pictures formed in my mind, Paula and Troncatti. Couldn't help it. I imagined the worst.

Shaking, I got up, looked at the clock. Figuring as best I could, I made it nine in the morning in Rome. I grabbed the kitchen phone and called the contact number I had for the set. I got the voice-mail message of Sting Ray Stephens, the PR person. I didn't leave a message.

I called Paula's hotel. The guy at the desk barely understood English. I said I was Paula Montgomery's husband.

He said something in Italian and hung up.

I wanted to start an international incident right then.

I went to the computer and e-mailed Paula. I need to talk to you right away. Can you call me on the cell ASAP?

That was it.

Then I sat staring at the monitor for I don't know how long, chewing my thumbnail. It even bled, but I kept right on chewing.

No call.

I think I fell asleep around three A.M., watching an old Barbara Stanwyck movie on AMC.

– 6 –

Maddie knew something was up as I drove her to her day camp.

"Why aren't you talking, Daddy?"

Because your mother is eating my heart, honey. Because Mommy is probably in bed with a sleazy Italian director while I'm here taking care of you. Wanna Happy Meal?

"Sorry, cupcake."

"Your eyes look scrunchy."

I tried to unscrunch them, but it didn't work.

With Maddie safely at camp I drove around the corner from the park (somehow having Maddie close by, even though she couldn't see me, helped). I called the hotel in Rome again and had to leave another message.

I tried to keep the anger out of it. Maybe there was an explanation to all this. Imagination can be a terrible thing.

Looking at myself in the rearview mirror, I thought I'd be ripe for a remake of The Picture of Dorian Gray. The bags under my eyes were like suitcases. There would be no need for makeup.

A star in the making.

"You look tired," Nancy said.

"Ya think?" I said, trying to sound like I had some energy left for acting.

"Darling, you have an audition at two."

"Is it a vampire role? I'm ready."

Nancy Radford, my auburn-haired, middle-aged agent, pursed her lips. She was not in the mood for jocularity. She wanted to get me work.

Nancy herself worked for Talent Across the Board, a boutique agency in Encino. I was not a big-agency guy (as Paula soon would be — Variety said that Phyl was going over to AEA and bringing Paula with her).

Nancy had taken me on when I was hardly more than an ex-jock with all my teeth. She apparently saw something in me, enough to suggest acting lessons from a guy, Marty North, who has a studio in the Valley.

It was a good move, and I learned my stuff from Marty, who was a graduate of the American Academy of Dramatic Arts. I got some things going after that, some commercials, some income. The rest of my income came from waitering jobs, the best at Josephina's in Santa Monica, where Roland worked. He got me the gig.

"Listen, kiddo," Nancy said, "this is for a Showtime Movie, a great supporting role, and they're not insisting on a name."

Most casting lists for good parts insisted on "name only." In other words, an actor who wasn't me. An actor people had heard of.

"What kind of role?"

"Cop," Nancy said. "Here's the description."

She handed me a copy of a fax. On the sheet it gave a one-paragraph sketch of a guy named Dex Wainright — thirty-two, burned-out cop, alcoholic, dealing with family stress.

"I can play this part," I said, as if the casting fairy had dropped the perfect role in my lap.

"That's why I'm sending you up."

Just before I left, Nancy said, "How are things at home?"

Had she been reading the same gossip pages about Paula? Was this story all over town? Was I being whispered about in cafés and behind closed doors?

I looked at her with a cocked head. "Why?"

"Just asking. I haven't seen Maddie in a while."

"Maddie is Maddie. She's a survivor."

"Who's watching her?"

"She's at camp."

"What about after? Will that ever be a prob?"

"Prob?"

"Reason I'm asking, it's got to be hard, with Paula gone. You managing all right?"

Don't I look it? Don't I look like the bloom of youth?

"Sure."

"You know," Nancy said, "maybe now's a good time for you to think about what you really want to do."

"What's that supposed to mean?"

Nancy shrugged. "The business is tough enough. You have to really want it, more than anything."

Putting my fists on her desk and leaning over, I said, "Nancy, I want this. I need this. I am an actor. That's what I do. I'm not going to stop."

She smiled. "Just what I wanted to hear. Go and make me proud."

❦

The call finally came at 1:12 P.M.

I remember looking at the time on the phone, as if I needed to get it exactly, as if Jack Webb would come out of the grave as the Dragnet guy and ask me for the facts. I was in Starbucks on Franklin because my audition was just down the street at a studio on La Brea. I took the phone outside so it wouldn't cut out. Also so I could yell if I needed to.

"I'm so sorry," Paula said, her voice sounding remarkably clear. "We were shooting in the country for a few days and the whole crew was out there."

"How'd it go?" I was keeping my voice as placid as possible. I wanted to get verbal cues from her.

"Oh, fine," she said. The verbal cue I got was discomfort. Something was definitely up.

"Great," I said.

"You don't sound too excited."

"Neither do you."

"Mark, it's late. I'm really tired."

"That makes two of us. I didn't get much sleep last night."

"How's Maddie?"

Slick change. "Maddie's great. Maddie's wonderful. I've been spending a lot of time with her, as you may well know."

"Mark, what is going on?"

Should I let it all out now? In one big torrent? Here outside a Hollywood coffeehouse so the ratty-looking guy at the bus stop could hear me?

"You know, the Internet's great," I said. "I can't be there with you, but it's the next best thing. I get reports on the movie, how it's going."

Long silence. "You saw it."

"Of course I saw it. What, were you going to keep it a secret from me?"

"No, Mark. This is so stupid."

"What's stupid?"

"This whole thing. We should both be happy, shouldn't we?"

That seemed like a pretty loaded question. She was preparing me. "Tell me straight up," I said.

"Tell you what?"

"What's going on with you and Troncatti?"

She whispered a curse, the kind that signals defeat. Or getting caught.

"We shouldn't do this over the phone," she said.

The guy at the bus stop was looking at me, like he could overhear the conversation. He couldn't, of course, but it seemed like there was a spotlight on me and all the cars were not stopped because of the red light, but because they wanted to watch me lose control.

"No, let's," I said. "Let's do it right now. Did you sleep with him?"

The silence was my answer.

"How many times?"

"Mark, please. For Maddie's sake, for our sakes, let's just wait until I get back. We need to talk."

The Mayans, I once read, used to cut the hearts out of their human sacrifices while they were still alive. That way, the high priest could hold up the heart while it was still beating, showing the people the power of life and death at the same time.

I punched the End button and powered off the cell. I had an audition. It was time for my big break.

~ 7 ~

There are times when an actor sees something in the eyes of the casting people. A mixture of scorn and pity. A look of absolute amazement that here is a person who thought he could act, who thought he might have a future in this business. The room becomes an orchestra of forced smiles and coughs behind closed fists.

"Thanks for coming in, Mark," the director said. But it sounded like some guy saying, Abandon all hope.

Funny thing was I didn't really care. All I could think about was Paula. Losing her. Feeling like a prize chump. Wanting to kill Troncatti. Wanting to die myself.

Fighting traffic back into the Valley I almost got in a couple of road-rage confrontations. It wasn't me driving; it was some version of Mr. Hyde. Only the thought of Maddie, waiting to be picked up, kept me from totally freaking out.

I was half an hour late to the park.

"We do not appreciate this, Mr. Gillen," the matronly gestapo agent with the Camp Sunshine T-shirt said to me through the car window.

"I'm sorry," I said. "Traffic."

"We're not being paid to babysit, you know." You vill obey!

"Yes, again, very sorry." My voice was vacant, far away, like one of the pod people in Invasion of the Body Snatchers.

Maddie was getting into her car seat in the back. She did not look pleased.

"Where were you, Daddy?"

"I'm sorry. Let's go home and eat."

"I want to go to Wendy's."

"We had Wendy's yesterday. How about I cook us up something nice at home?"

"I want to go to Wendy's."

We were pulling onto Laurel Canyon now, into traffic. A black Cadillac Esplanade, regal and shiny in the late afternoon sun, cut in front of my Accord without signaling. I honked. Hard. The driver, some yoohoo with a cell phone to his ear, momentarily pulled the device from his head so he could give me a one-fingered salute.

"I said Wendy's, Daddy."

"No."

"Yes!"

There is a famous newsreel clip of Benito Mussolini, fascist dictator over Italy during World War II, looking at a cheering crowd. He folds his arms, juts out his chin, and protrudes his lower lip. I am your master, he seems to be thinking. Bow down to me.

I mention this only because that is the pose Madeleine Erica Gillen took whenever she wanted her way. Like now.

"We are going home," I said.

This time Maddie screamed, as loudly as she could. "NOOOOOOO!"

I almost hit a kid on a bike when she did that. Adrenaline blasted through my body, mixing with all the anger and hurt and lack of sleep that had been pooling up in me for hours.

Without a thought between scream and act, I half turned and slapped my child's arm. Hard. It made a crisp popping sound, like a gunshot.

The pause that followed was the worst part. In that silence I could feel Maddie's shock, her sense of betrayal. Never had I struck Maddie, not even the time when she was three and refused to use the potty and deliberately peed on the floor in front of me.

In that long, haunting pause I thought I had lost the last thing on earth that loved me.

And then she wailed. She cried like I'd never heard her before.

―――

Our apartment was on the second floor of a building on Archwood, around the corner from the Department of Water and Power building. It had a reasonable rent for the space, and was close to the freeway. That made it convenient for Paula to get to Burbank for her soap and me to get to auditions in various parts of the city. I could reach Hollywood in seven minutes, the west side in fifteen to thirty, depending on traffic.

As soon as we walked in, Maddie ran to her room, slamming the door. I waited a minute, then poked my head in her room.

"Maddie?"

She did not look up from the floor, where she was working on a coloring book.

"Maddie?" I knelt down.

"I'm coloring."

"Can I talk to you?"

"I'm coloring."

"I see that. What are you coloring?"

"This." Still not looking up.

"I did something terribly wrong," I said.

Half a look.

"I was angry and I hit you."

"It hurt, Daddy."

"I know. I was so wrong. And I'm so sorry. Do you think you can forgive me?"

Now she looked full on, confused.

Forgive. Something her little five-year-old brain had not yet taken in as a lasting concept. A word, I realized, I had not used around her or Paula. Now I was asking her to understand it.

"When somebody does something wrong or bad to you and wants you not to hate him, you can forgive that person. That means you sort of decide not to be mad about it and pretend everything is okay again."

Pretend? Was that the right word?

"I don't hate you, Daddy," Maddie said, looking at the coloring book and the sienna crayon in her hand. "But it really hurt."

Enough reasoning. I picked her up and held her close. She let me. I tried not to let her see my tears. Her arms were tight around my neck.

I walked her to our sliding door, and onto our little balcony. It was too early for the moon, too late for the sun. So I swayed with her in the dusk, and that was enough.

DEMONS

When the urge to drink hit me, it was always like a Randy Johnson fastball to the ribs. It would take the breath out of me, crush some bone, leave me staggering toward first. If you're a problem drinker, you never really get rid of all the urges.

But it seemed I was getting hit more and more by the urges, knowing about Paula and Troncatti. And Maddie. The hitting incident really knocked me flat. Nor did it help that Steve Monet was the one who got the Colgate commercial. He called me up to tell me, and I wanted not just to drink a whole bottle of vodka but actually eat the bottle.

Though Maddie seemed to have forgotten all about it, I couldn't. I kept seeing myself in the newspaper as some awful dad, nabbed by the police before I did more harm.

Drinking seemed a great alternative to the demons. I almost did it, too. I almost left Maddie with Mrs. Williams so I could go out to a bar and get soaked.

It hit me hard Sunday morning and that scared me. The morning? This was bad.

Without much thought, I knew I had to do something drastic. And when Maddie walked into the kitchen, rubbing her eyes, I knew what it was.

I took her to the same big church in Hollywood where Paula and I got married. Part of my thinking was that this would be a goodwill gesture to God on my part.

Hey, God, I'm here, see me? Remember the wedding that was right up this aisle five years ago? That was me, and here I am and you can do that miracle thing they say you're always doing.

For Maddie, there was a full-on Sunday school program, which she did not want to go to at first. I couldn't blame her. All these kids who were not her kindergarten class, who were not her day camp troop. Strangers. Threats.

She held on to my leg like I was the last life preserver on the Titanic.

"I don't wanna go in there," she said. I had managed to get her this far, to the church building. She'd even seemed somewhat excited about a new place to play.

But now that we were here, and all these kids she didn't know were walking by, she didn't want to leave me.

Then Mrs. Hancock came.

There are some people who really deserve the word saint attached to themselves. Mrs. Joyce Hancock was one of those people. She had a smile that made her eyes crinkle, so you knew it was genuine.

After introducing herself to me — I must have had a neon sign around my neck that flashed Lost Father: Help Wanted — she bent down and said, "And who are you?"

Mussolini stuck her lip out. "Madeleine Erica Gillen," she said, tightening her grip on my leg.

"That is a fantastic name," Mrs. Hancock said. "Do you know where it comes from?"

"No," I said. Maddie whipped a disapproving look at me for answering the question.

"Magdala was a village on the sea of Galilee in Bible times. It means tower in Hebrew. Mary Magdalene was a woman from Jesus' time who was called that because she was from Magdala. And guess what?"

"What?" Maddie said, loosening her grip on me a little.

"She became a great friend of Jesus."

Maddie broke into a big smile.

"I'm going to tell some more Bible stories today," Mrs. Hancock said. "Would you like to come hear them? Your daddy will be close by if you want him."

And then my little Mussolini became as soft as new snow. She let go of my leg. "Bye, Daddy."

The church service felt weird to me.

Maybe it was the surroundings. Stained glass windows and polished wooden pews and a choir with robes and everything.

When people sang, they stood up.

The minister was a trim guy with slate-colored hair and a great speaking voice. Looked like he could have been an actor at one time. Maybe he was. This was a Hollywood church, after all.

"This morning," he began, "I'd like to continue our series on prayer. Specifically, how God hears and answers prayer."

That got my attention. I could use a direct line to God right now, I thought. I'm all ears.

The preacher read from a Bible. "'Ask and it will be given to you; seek and you will find; knock and the door will be opened to you. For everyone who asks receives; he who seeks finds; and to him who knocks, the door will be opened.'"

I'd heard that before, somewhere. It always seemed a little like mumbo jumbo.

"Now people will do all kinds of things to gain God's favor and receive his blessings, especially when they are in great need or in extreme danger. You know: God, I'll do anything if you'll just save me from this. They make all sorts of promises. But while people are often willing to do great things in return for God's blessing, things God has not asked and does not want, they are unwilling to do the one small thing that he actually requires, which is to pray."

Made sense. Duh.

"So how do we receive God's blessings?"

Bring it on, preacher dude.

"We ask in faith. We cannot come to God with an attitude of, Well, I'll try praying to God, and if that doesn't work, I'll try something else. That isn't faith. That's just covering your bases. God is not willing to be just one option among many. He will not be satisfied with a piece of our love, a piece of our devotion, a piece of our trust. He wants all of it. He claims his rightful place at the center of our lives. He demands that we trust in him, and him alone."

Now I started to squirm around a little bit. I think my mind was telling my body that God was certainly not in the center of my life, not the very center.

"God is not willing to be put on the shelf with all of the other deities, to be installed as part of our personal pantheon of gods. Maybe I'll try praying to God to meet my needs, and if that doesn't work, I'll try a little Zen Buddhism, and if that doesn't work, I'll try wealth and power, maybe some self-actualization. It's like asking five women to marry you, and then waiting to see which one says yes."

Paula had said yes. Once.

"It's an insult. On the contrary, we must place our faith and trust in God alone, with no backup and no contingency plan. The key to answered prayer is not the amount or strength of our faith, but the object of our faith. 'I tell you the truth, if you have faith as small as a mustard seed, you can say to this mountain, "Move from here to there" and it will move. Nothing will be impossible for you.' The power doesn't come from our faith; the power comes from the One in whom we have faith."

I didn't quite get that yet, but the thing about the mountain got me curious.

He finished off the sermon by talking about praying in Jesus' name. Frankly, that sounded a little like a magic formula. And I couldn't quite connect it all up. But when it was over, I felt like I was glad I came.

And Maddie didn't want to leave, she'd had such a good time. Why couldn't it have lasted? Why didn't I just take her home? Did the thing in the park have to happen? What would the preacher man say about that?

– 2 –

Serrania Park is in the Woodland Hills area of the Valley, next to a development of some of the most expensive homes in town. It's a place you get a better class of parent and kid, not to mention dog. Maddie liked the swings at Serrania, because you could go so high.

A daredevil, Maddie.

We — Paula, Maddie, and I — had come here three or four times. I remember trying to teach Maddie how to throw a Frisbee here, when she was four. She got the hang of it real quick, as Paula applauded my efforts from a bench under a tree. Best applause I'd had in years.

Today there was some good activity in the sandbox, like a toddlers' convention, along with some kids Maddie's age taking to the slides and swings. Since the good high swings were taken, Maddie headed to the digging part of the convention. She is a natural conversationalist and immediately invited herself to join a boy's shoveling near the stone camel.

I took my flip-flops off, sat on the far edge of the box, and wiggled my toes in the sand.

And started to think about what Maddie would be when she grew up. I didn't see her going into acting, like her parents. Too unstable a profession — unless an Antonio Troncatti picks you out of thin air for a major flick.

I thought Maddie would make a good lawyer. She knew how to argue, could dig in her heels when she had to, and was already gaining a fine appreciation of the art of charging outrageous sums of money for her efforts. One day she asked me for a twenty-dollar bill.

"Twenty dollars? What for?"

"I cleaned my room."

I laughed. "But you're supposed to do that."

"Okay." She thought a moment. "Then give me ten dollars."

Smiling at the thought, I watched my daughter negotiate the plastic shovel out of the boy's hand.

"Yours?"

It was an attractive woman about my age. She was looking at Maddie and the boy.

"Yes," I said. "She's five."

"Mine's four," the woman said. "But big for his age."

"Yeah, he is. A middle linebacker, I'd say."

"His father was. Played in college. Really."

"Mark Gillen," I said, standing.

"Kay Millard. You live around here?"

"No, I'm from the land of the studios. Maddie just likes this park."

"Maddie? Short for Madeleine?"

"Yeah."

"I always liked that name."

"What's your boy's name?"

"Duncan."

"Scottish, isn't it?"

Kay Millard smiled. "Very good."

"I know that from the Scottish play."

"Ah, Macbeth."

"Shh!" I said. We were having fun. Not many people know the actor's superstition about Shakespeare's most notorious play. You're never supposed to mention the title, so the belief goes, or something will go wrong during the production. Like a set falling on an actor.

"You must be an actor," Kay said.

"I've been accused of that."

"You seem too nice to be an actor." She sat on the concrete next to me, her Reeboks in the sand.

"I don't know if that's a compliment or not."

"It is. I know a lot of actors. My husband's a director."

"Oh really?" I tried to keep my voice calm and nonthreatening, even as my actor's insides began to quiver, like a hungry dog hearing the supper dish being pulled off the shelf. Out-of-work actors are trained to pick up every possible vibe that might mean a connection to a job.

On the other hand, you can't jump all over every person you meet who has some foot in the business. The two unbreakable rules for actors are Don't be dull and Don't be desperate.

Even though I was feeling desperate, I was not going to show it. But I sure wasn't going to let this one go, either. Breaks come every which way, but never in a predictable fashion. Lana Turner, they tell us, was sitting in a tight sweater in Schwab's Drug Store in Hollywood when a talent scout went gaga for her. All my sweaters were at home.

But I had Maddie. The point of reference. The chip. She had opened the door for me to talk to this woman, whose husband was —

"Would I know any of his films?" I said.

"He's done some independent work, and now for cable."

"Hey, some of the best stuff is on cable."

"He had a movie on earlier, The Tin."

"The cop movie?" I let the excitement grow in my voice. "That was really good." I hadn't seen it, but I'd heard of it. Heard it was very good. And knew that this is a guy I would love to work for sometime.

"Thank you," Kay Millard said. "We're proud of it."

"And you should be." Okay, enough of the schmooze juice. Just play it loose.

"He working on anything new?" I said.

"He's in preproduction now."

Preproduction! Casting decision! Loose, baby, but not too loose.

"Very cool," I said. "Good to have something going on."

Idiot, you sound like you've got NOTHING going on. Desperate!

"It's a crazy business," she said, in a transitional voice, indicating she was ready to change the subject.

No, not yet, not yet.

"Yeah," I said, homing in on her. "I keep getting calls from Spielberg."

"Spielberg?" Sounding impressed, if just a tad skeptical.

"Milt Spielberg, down at the deli. He wants me to settle the account."

She gave me a (polite?) laugh, but I was still in the ballgame. A little joke to keep the industry talk rolling. Maybe she'd think I was funny and charming enough to introduce to her husband, whoever he was.

"Where's she going?" Kay Millard said. I remember that clearly. She said it, looking past my shoulder. But it was like the voice came from across the street somewhere—white noise, inconsequential—because I had already formed my follow-up question and asked it the moment she stopped talking.

"Actually, I'm sort of connected to Antonio Troncatti. You'll think this is funny, but—"

Kay's eyes widened and she shouted, "Look out!"

I turned just in time to see it.

Maddie was running through the sand, head down, full of purpose. She was two steps from the front of the swings.

She was oblivious to the boy on the first swing, who was already beginning his descent from a huge arc.

Two steps ... and I could barely open my mouth before it happened. The outstretched legs with the red tennis shoes—something else I will never forget—rammed into the side of Maddie's head.

The impact was like a tennis racket smacking a ball. The physics of it were unequal, unforgiving.

Maddie lifted from the ground, her body turning like a flipped baseball bat.

I was on my feet, not knowing how I got there, as Maddie hit the sand.

She did not move—my eyes were locked on her as I raced forward. In my peripheral vision I was aware of other adults closing in, while children stood by in silent watching.

A woman was already kneeling by Maddie when I got there. I heard a boy's voice saying, "I didn't mean to!" and a chorus of other voices muttering expressions of shock and sympathy.

"She's mine," I told the kneeling woman, partly as confession, and in part, I think now, to keep anyone from taking her away from such a negligent father.

"I'll call emergency," the woman said. "Don't move her."

Don't move her? Because her neck might be broken? Because she might not ever move again?

A sweat came over me as I dropped down in the sand and put my hand on Maddie.

"Don't move her," the woman commanded, fishing in her purse for a cell phone.

Maddie's pink overalls over a lighter pink T-shirt weren't moving at all, and I wondered if she was breathing. An ugly, red stamp was deepening on the left side of her face, the imprint of a tennis shoe becoming clearer.

"Maddie Maddie Maddie," I repeated in a whisper, my lips close to her ear. "You'll be all right you'll be all right." And then she moaned, low and soft. And I almost cried out with relief.

Someone else, a man, put a towel over Maddie, and then the waiting began. All the activity in the park had ceased, the crowd gathering. Even people walking dogs stopped for a look.

"It hurts," Maddie groaned.

Oh God, give that hurt to me! Take it away from Maddie and let me take it instead, please please.

I stroked her hair and told her to lie still.

"I want to dig," she said.

"We will. Later. We'll go to the ocean and dig up the whole beach, would you like that?"

"Yes."

And we stayed like that for about ten minutes until the ambulance came. A nice paramedic checked her out, and decided Maddie could be driven to the hospital—there was one about a mile away—and she wouldn't have to be taken in the ambulance.

I picked Maddie up and carried her out of the park, sure that the eyes of every parent there were on me. There goes the guy who was so into trying to schmooze a gig that he lost track of his daughter. There goes a guy who doesn't deserve to be a father.

The drive to the hospital was bad, Maddie moaning all the way, tears falling. But the waiting in the emergency room for a doctor was worse. I had to go muck around with the desk over insurance, Maddie screaming at me not to leave her alone.

When I got back to her bed, a doctor was there. He looked like a humorless Bob Newhart. He spoke in a monotone and only registered an expression when I told him what happened. The expression was a raising of the eyebrows.

He asked Maddie some questions, looked in her eyes with a light, touched her head in a couple of places. Maddie, my little trooper, hung in there, and I was proud of her.

"Mild concussion," the doctor told me. "Should be okay. Watch her for a couple of days—" like I wouldn't—"limit TV and reading. If she gets nauseous or vomits or gets numbness in her arms or legs, bring her back in. And no physical activity for at least two days. Any questions?"

Yeah, where do I go to get flogged?

"No. Thanks."

When we got back to the apartment I told Maddie to lie down, but she wanted me with her. Truth to tell, I wanted to be with her just as much. I flopped on the sofa and she got on top of me, resting her head on the soft spot underneath my shoulder. I stroked her hair. And as I did, I silently thanked God that it hadn't been any worse.

Even as I did, though, I had the strangest feeling, really weird, that worse was about to make a great, big entrance.

HOMECOMING

Paula came back on August 3, my birthday.

She did not come home.

Over the previous month I had tried everything to remain sane. I had developed the sweats. My pits and hands would break out in little moist bursts when I thought of seeing her again.

Paula and I had talked on the phone, and she said she wanted to get together as soon as possible. I asked her if she wanted to see Maddie. She said, "After the meeting."

Meeting. It sounded like a Hollywood deal. I knew it was going to be bad. Just how bad I couldn't have known.

She chose a sidewalk café in Beverly Hills, just off Rodeo Drive no less. Why here? Probably many reasons. It was public, so I couldn't make a spectacle of myself. It was social, to soften the blow she was no doubt going to deliver. And it was Beverly Hills. Paula's new stomping ground, after her meteoric rise to stardom.

Feeling out of place, I parked my Accord in a lot next to a Bentley and a Mercedes and walked to the place.

Paula was already there.

Sitting outside, she had sunglasses on and wore a red and gold scarf around her neck that complemented perfectly her coat and blouse. She looked like a catalog model, only better because she breathed.

What hit me then, like a doctor telling me I had only three months to live, was this thought: She is out of your league now. She has left you behind.

"Mark." Paula waved her hand at me like I was a waiter.

I entered through the black, iron gate that separated the pedestrians from the diners. As I did I saw Goldie Hawn at a table, yakking it up with another woman. Beverly Hills indeed.

There was a lily in a vase on the table where Paula sat. Aren't those what the cartoons always have on dead people?

Paula did not smile as I sat in the other chair, also made of iron.

"You look good," Paula said. It was a lie. I didn't look anything like good.

"You look great." That was not a lie.

She did not remove her sunglasses. "It's good to be back. It was a tough shoot."

"But worth it, I guess, huh?"

"The dailies were spectacular. Tony is such a—" She let her voice trail off in a self-conscious Doppler effect.

"Yeah," I said. "He sure is."

A waiter younger than myself, and twice as good looking, presented his million-dollar teeth to us and asked if he could bring us a drink. I almost ordered a double shot of tequila, but in keeping with the atmosphere made it a San Pellegrino. Paula ordered chai tea.

"I don't think I'll be eating anything," I said. "But you go ahead."

"No, I don't think so either."

"Your stomach bothering you too?"

"This isn't easy for me."

"Why should it be?" I let more acid drip from my words than I'd intended.

Paula took a deep breath. "I thought it might be a little easier than this. I didn't intend this to happen."

As if that made everything okay. "Well, it did. So what are you going to do now?"

"I think we have to start talking about divorce."

"You think?"

"Mark, please, I'm trying to be very even about this."

"So that's it? The decision's been made?"

Paula nodded slowly.

"Don't I get a say in this?" I said.

"I wish it hadn't happened the way it did."

There's a famous scene in the old James Cagney movie The Public Enemy, where his girlfriend wishes something. Cagney looks at her the way only he can and says, "I wish you was a wishin' well. Then I could tie a bucket to ya and sink ya."

Then he pushes a half a grapefruit in her face.

That scene came to me in a flash, and I knew I could have played the Cagney role to the max right then.

The waiter returned with our drinks and asked if we would like to hear about the specials.

"No," I said.

I didn't like doing that to a fellow waiter, but there it was. He took the hint and said he'd check back with us in a few minutes.

"I don't want a divorce," I said. "I want you to get over this thing with Troncatti and come home to Maddie and me. I don't like what you did and I want to have ten minutes alone with Troncatti. But I'm willing to forget the whole thing."

Could I ever forget it?

"I've already made the decision," Paula said.

"I'm trying to talk you out of it."

"Don't try."

"Why shouldn't I?" My voice was loud enough to make the couple at the next table glare at me.

"Because it will just make it harder."

"I want it to be hard. I want it to be hard on you."

"This is not helping."

"I don't want to help, either."

"I was afraid you'd do this."

I started to feel prickly heat on my neck, like a noose made of coarse rope had been thrown around it. Paula reached for her purse, which was hanging on the back of her chair.

"You're leaving?" I said.

"I have a lawyer," she said. "He told me not to talk to you, but I thought we could be nice about it."

She stood up and, with a certain flair, dropped a ten-dollar bill on the table. It was crisp and new, just like Paula. And it sent me over the edge.

"Sit down!" I pounded my fists on the table.

Goldie Hawn looked at me, as did everyone else in the place.

"Don't yell at me." Paula slung the purse over her shoulder. "Don't ever yell at me. I'll be coming over to pick up Maddie tonight."

She turned her back and walked out. I was so blinded by rage I couldn't formulate any words. Picking up Maddie?

The San Pellegrino bottle sat openmouthed on the table. My hand grabbed it, lifted, and threw it down on the sidewalk where Paula was now walking. It shattered. Paula screamed.

In acting class, they teach you to go for the emotional moment. It's safe to do in class, because there are no wrong answers. You go for it.

Sometimes actors forget they live in the real world and end up doing stupid things. Like I just did.

Paula's look said to me that any hopes I had of stopping her from divorce were now shattered, just like the bottle on the sidewalk.

- 2 -

I found it hard to breathe on the way back to the Valley. It was like the car was one of those crushing chambers in the old horror movies, the walls slowly closing in. My chest felt knotted and hot.

When I got home and rounded up Maddie from Mrs. Williams, I knew I wasn't going to let Paula waltz in and snatch Maddie away from me.

"How would you like to go to the beach for a few days?" I asked Maddie.

"Oh yeah! Can I wear my new swimsuit?"

Paula had bought Maddie this nice little blue-and-red suit right before she'd left for Europe.

"Yeah," I said. "New swimsuit and everything."

"Is Mommy coming?"

Maddie knew Paula was supposed to be home soon. She'd been pestering me about it for days. But I had mastered the art of being vague.

"Mommy won't be coming just yet."

"When will she?" Her little voice was pleading.

"Let's pack," I said.

Roland's folks had a beach house in Ventura, about a forty-five minute drive north of LA. They used it as a vacation place. Roland liked to go up and pound the keys on the weekends.

I called and begged him to let me use it for a couple of days. I told him I'd explain when I got back. Roland, my buddy and pal, said okay. The only other thing I had to do was sweet-talk Shelly, the manager at Josephina's, to give me the weekend off. Fortunately, one of the newer waiters wanted in for the weekend, and that was that.

We got up there by four o'clock, before sunset, in time to play a little on the beach.

Maddie shrieked with delight as she ran down toward the ocean. She loved the ocean. Loved to stand with her feet in the wet sand as the waves came up around her ankles then ebbed, sucking some of the sand with it. It tickled her feet. She would always laugh.

We played in the water. At one point I picked her up and waded out to chest level. Maddie held on to my neck tightly. She laughed every time a swell swept past us. When a wave came I'd jump up as it broke. It would splash us, and Maddie would laugh some more.

We built a sand castle. Maddie got sticks and beached kelp and did all the design work. I was the brawn, scooping up piles of wet sand and forming it into walls and turrets.

Must have been an hour that we worked on it. Maddie carefully placed her sticks in the mounds, making sure they were evenly spaced.

When it was all done both of us stood back and looked at it. Maddie took my hand.

"That's the best castle ever," she said.

And soon it would be washed away. Just like the marriage I once thought was the best ever.

"How about ice cream?" I said.

"Yes!" Maddie said, pumping her little fist.

We got some at a little snack cart by the public parking lot. We sat on a bench looking out at the blue Pacific. Way off in the distance we could see the outline of one of the Channel Islands.

"Pumpkin?"

Maddie looked at me, her mouth around an Eskimo Pie.

"Can I tell you something?"

She nodded.

"You know your friend Jenna?" Jenna lived in an apartment in our building. Maddie had been to her birthday parties for the last two years.

"Jenna's six."

"Yes, she is. Her mommy and daddy are divorced, aren't they?"

Maddie shrugged.

"You know what divorce means?"

"Where a mommy and daddy don't live in the same house."

"Right. That's what Jenna's parents are, divorced. But Jenna gets to see them both, just not at the same time."

"That's weird."

I had been rehearsing this little speech in my mind for the last five hours. The words were like heavy chunks of concrete in me.

"But Jenna is pretty happy, isn't she?"

"She has five Barbies."

"Yeah." My own Eskimo Pie was melting on my hand. I took a big bite of the soft ice cream. Half of it fell on the ground.

"Oh, Daddy!" Maddie rebuked. Then she softened. "You can get another one if you want."

I got up and threw what was left in a trash can. Then I sat down with her again.

"Maddie, if Mommy and I ever got a divorce, you'd be able to see us both, too."

Her eyes clouded. If I'd thought I could soft-pedal this, I was sorely mistaken.

"Don't do that, Daddy."

"But sometimes it happens."

"Uh-uh."

"If it happened, is all I'm saying. If it did, you'd be okay. You'd be with both of us." The irony of my being here to keep her away from Paula was not lost on me. If we were going to share custody, it would be on my terms, not hers. She was the adulterer here, not me.

"No, Daddy. Promise me you won't do it."

"You've got to be okay if it happens."

"No."

How I hated Paula at that moment. For making me have to spoil the innocence of a five-year-old child. How I hated and longed for her at the same time.

I looked out at the ocean then. A pelican was skimming across the water, looking for lunch. When I turned to Maddie again she was starting to cry.

"Baby," I said, picking her up and setting her on my lap. "Baby." I held her close.

Somebody knocked on the front door. My heart slammed. Who could that possibly be?

It was our third day. Afternoon. Maddie and I had done some beach time, and now she was taking a nap.

I'd been reading a David Morrell thriller, the perfect beach book, allowing myself escape from the nightmare down south.

The knock again, more insistent.

I got up and looked out the window.

A young man in a uniform looked right back at me. He was about twenty-five years old. His hair was short, like a Marine's.

I unlatched the chain and opened the door.

"Mr. Gillen?"

"That's me."

"I'm Deputy Tim Wise of the Ventura County Sheriff's office. We got a report of a missing child."

Stay cool. She's your daughter.

"Nobody's missing," I said. "Maddie is right here taking a nap."

"She's with you?"

"Of course she's with me. We came up here to spend some time at the beach. Who sent you?"

He pulled a folded document out of his rear pocket. "I have an order here demanding that you produce Madeleine Erica Gillen at ten o'clock tomorrow morning. In Los Angeles."

My hands were shaking like leaves in the wind. The document was coldly official looking.

"This," I said, "is unbelievable."

"I'm sorry, Mr. Gillen."

"How did she find me?"

Deputy Wise started to turn around.

"I'm her father," I said. "She can't do this." I threw the order on the ground.

"I'd advise you to cooperate, Mr. Gillen."

I kicked the document, sending it sliding off the front porch. The deputy closed the gate behind him.

"What's the matter, Daddy?" Maddie was rubbing her eyes.

I looked at her, wanted to whisk her up in my arms and run away with her. Take off in a boat or something, sail to Iceland where Paula couldn't find us, and I'd raise sheep and ...

"I guess maybe it's time for you to see Mommy," I said.

"Cool!" Her face lit up and my body shook.

— 4 —

I drove Maddie to Brentwood the next day. The address where I was to go was on the court order.

Hold the anger, I kept telling myself. For Maddie's sake. You're an actor. You are supposed to be able to turn emotions on and off. Do it. Don't let her see that things are blowing up all around her.

Maddie was singing a little song to herself. Mommy, Mommy. Gonna see Mommy.

I gripped the steering wheel so tightly my wrist muscles started to hurt.

Add to that the traffic on the 405. I knew I should have left earlier, but something held me back. A fight for some sort of control maybe. This court order thing was making me jump through a hoop, like a trained dog. Well, this dog was going to make a little noise.

I still held onto this crazy hope that everything would clear up. Like a Valley fog, it would soon melt away, letting in the sun again.

You think a lot of stupid things while driving in LA traffic. So I decided to switch to something else. I started thinking about God.

Just a little bit, but enough to make it more than a passing thought. If there was justice in the world, then God had to be in charge of it, right? When you got into deep water, you were supposed to call out to God, right? No atheists in foxholes, that sort of thing.

Well, if I wasn't in a foxhole yet, I was sure sinking. So maybe I'd send up a real flag to God soon. I'd been going to church with Maddie. Wasn't I supposed to get some benefits?

I got off at Sunset, hit more traffic, then reached the address in Brentwood at 10:37.

It was a huge place. I could see some of it through the iron gates that protected the premises. I didn't need a neon sign to know this was Troncatti's southland residence.

A black limousine with darkened glass was parked in front of the gate. I pulled my Accord to a stop on the street.

The limo door opened on the driver's side and an olive-skinned man with a shaved head and goatee got out. He had a white shirt and black pants. He opened a rear door. Paula got out.

She looked like an international movie star. Dressed, once again, to the nines.

Maddie jumped out of the Accord and ran to her. "Mommy! Mommy! Mommy!"

I watched them like some prisoner on Devil's Island looking at the mainland.

Paula lifted Maddie and hugged her, spinning her around.

The driver glared at me, his eyes saying This is Brentwood. Get that hunk of junk off the street.

Instead, I walked toward Paula. The driver stepped in between us.

"Come on," I said to Paula. "This is ridiculous."

Paula was unmoved. The driver had muscles. I could see them under his tight shirt.

"Do you mind?" I said to the driver, who I called Igor in my mind.

"Is far enough," Igor said. He had some sort of Middle Eastern accent. Maybe he had been one of Saddam's bodyguards.

"I want to talk to my wife." I took another step, but Igor got chest to chest with me.

"That's Daddy," I heard Maddie say. She was trying to help.

"Farid, it's okay," Paula said.

Grudgingly, Igor (I was not about to give him the dignity of a real name) allowed me to pass.

Paula put Maddie down and bent over to talk to her. "Honey, I want to talk to Daddy a minute. Why don't you hop in the big car? We're going to go for a ride."

"Really?" Maddie said.

"Shopping," Paula said. "For toys."

Oh, how smooth. Maddie turned to me, waved with a big smile, and practically dived into the back of the limo. Igor walked a few feet away, his version of giving us privacy.

"What are you doing?" I said.

"Don't fly off the handle, like you did at the restaurant." Paula's tone was clipped and cool.

"A court order? You tracked me down?"

"You knew I wanted to see Maddie, but you took off with her."

"What gives you the right to order me around?"

"I'm her mother, remember?"

"You sure work quick." I was fighting my feelings like crazy. I wanted to choke her. I wanted her to fall into my arms. "What'd you do? Call Roland to find out where I was?"

"My lawyer did."

"Oh. Right. Silly me. I thought you and Roland were friends."

Paula sighed and shook her head. "This isn't accomplishing anything."

She was right. I tried to calm down. "We have to talk about this."

"I tried, remember? You threw a bottle at me."

"I threw it at the sidewalk. I'm not stupid." The breeze must have switched then because suddenly I could smell Paula's hair.

Honey and cinnamon. And then my whole body changed. From anger and anxiousness to a sense of falling, away from light and hope, into some pit. In a few seconds I was going to bust out in tears. But I didn't want Igor to see that, or Paula. I clenched my teeth and took a deep breath to keep it from happening.

I had felt this way before, and knew immediately when it was. Back when the call came about my mom. She was dead and suddenly everything was wrong and ripped up and bad. And would never be the same again.

"Can we try again?" I said. "Can we maybe get some counseling?" That was supposed to be the thing to do, wasn't it? Find some professional and the broken pieces would be put back together again?

"We have to talk about what's best for Maddie," Paula said. "If we can do that in a way that doesn't upset her, then let's."

"What about the two of us?" I said, feeling like a movie cliché. Feeling like the guy who loses the girl to Clark Gable.

"I'll call you." Paula turned toward the limo.

"Wait. When? When do I get Maddie back?"

Paula's head was disappearing into the limo. "I'll call you."

That wasn't good enough. I stepped toward the door as it closed. Igor took the cue and got back into character.

"No more," he said. He had his hand in the air like a traffic cop.

I stood there as he got in the limo, fired it up, and pulled out of the driveway. I wondered if Maddie was looking at me out of the darkened windows.

– 5 –

"You told him?"

"Hey, man, I didn't want to. But he was a cop."

Roland seemed genuinely sorry. And who could blame him for being wary of cops? As an African-American in LA, he'd been pulled over more than once for DWB — "driving while black."

"I didn't know they'd send somebody up there," Roland said. "The cop just said you could be in a lot of trouble, and all I gave him was the phone number."

"They got the address from that." I threw myself on his couch. Roland rented a little house in Silver Lake. "Paula is playing for keeps."

"Come on, man. Let me play you a little Brubeck." Roland sat at the piano. "A little 'Blue Rondo a la Turk.'" His fingers started to fly over the ivories. It was delicious.

I'd met Roland Turner at a place in the Valley about ten years ago. When I found out Roland loved baseball like I did, we hit it off. Turns out we liked the same player best — Frank Thomas.

And we had the same sense of humor. The Simpsons was funny. Roseanne was not.

Roland played more Brubeck ("Kathy's Waltz") for me. I stared at his ceiling. Suddenly he stopped.

"You need to see a lawyer," he said.

When he said lawyer, something went off inside me. The reality of it. I saw the pictures in my mind again, the memories I had on that movie reel. Maddie as a baby, growing up; Paula beautiful, loving me.

I couldn't help it. I started crying and covered my face with a sofa pillow.

Next thing I knew Roland was sitting there on the edge of the sofa. "Hey, man, I know."

That's all he said. He squeezed my shoulder. I was glad he was there.

My cell phone bleeped. That brought me to a sitting position as I quickly wiped my eyes. I had this crazy hope it was Paula, ready to come home.

It was Nancy, my agent.

"You ready for some good news?" she said.

I almost laughed out loud. "You have no idea."

"They want you for a callback on Number Seven."

It took me a moment to sort this out. Number Seven was a major new dramatic series about firefighters, being developed at NBC. John Hoyt, the veteran actor, was already attached, playing the chief.

In other words, this series had major hit written all over it, and anybody in the ensemble had an almost guaranteed shot at a major career boost. I'd read for it a month ago, along with every other actor my age in town, and thought nothing more of it.

"Are you serious?" I said.

"As a heart attack at Disney," Nancy said. "Your call is at 10:30 in the morning, tomorrow. Make me proud."

When I got off the phone and looked at Roland, I felt like I'd been put through several spin cycles.

"Life truly stinks," I said.

❦

Next morning, Monday, Paula still hadn't called me about Maddie. Though I knew Maddie was happy to be with Mommy, I also knew I didn't want her staying up there while Mommy and Troncatti played house.

A callus was starting to form in me with regard to Paula. Maybe it was a natural defense mechanism, but I was sort of glad it was there. Especially since I had to concentrate on the biggest news my acting career had ever received.

I had a real opportunity for television stardom. Emmy Award city. On the couch with Jay or Dave. Cover of People. Real money rolling in for the first time in my life.

All through the morning I psyched myself up. In the shower, I became Vance, the macho firefighter with a heart. That was the part I was up for.

I did some of my acting exercises, the ones Marty North had drummed into me. How would Vance take a shower? How would he move? Marty disdained pure Method acting, which was only concerned with feelings. The outside was just as important.

So I showered like Vance, toweled off like Vance, drank coffee like Vance. I remembered what I could of his background. There wasn't much in the script, but I'd done another Marty thing and invented a whole past for Vance for my own use.

Driving to the studio in Burbank, I began to talk like Vance. Out loud. To myself. It did not matter that people in the other lanes were looking at me. This was LA. That's what people do here. Stand on the corner and talk. Ride in cars and talk. Talk, even if no one else is around.

I had a parking pass waiting for me at the gate, and when I walked into reception, it was like I was royalty. This was no cattle call. The office wasn't stuffed with dozens of versions of myself. I was here because they were really interested. In me.

The receptionist, I was happy to see, was Lisa Hobbes. We'd done a showcase scene together a few years back, something from a Mamet play.

"What are you doing here?" I asked.

Lisa smiled. "I gave up the acting thing. I'm going for the producing thing."

"That's a good thing."

"As things go. Hey, you want anything? Cappuccino?"

This was almost too good to be true. "Water's fine. Thanks."

Lisa came back with a bottled water and a few pages of a script to read. I was the only one in the reception area. A framed poster from On the Waterfront faced me. One of my all-time favorite movies. I looked at the big picture of Marlon Brando and nodded at him. You and me, Marlon.

Lisa and I talked about old times for a while, and then her phone buzzed. She walked me down a hall and suddenly I found myself in a conference room with six other people—and John Hoyt.

I was about to read with an Oscar-winning actor, a man with one of the great careers in Hollywood. I tried not to shake.

I am Vance. I am Vance.

The producer, Barbara DiBova, made some small talk, introduced me to everybody. Their names went in one ear and out the other. She explained the scene to me. Vance was confronting the chief for reprimanding him over an incident where Vance had rushed back into a burning house to save a little girl's pet iguana.

Whenever I was ready, she said, I could read with Mr. Hoyt.

In baseball, I learned there were days when I just didn't have it, no matter how hard I tried. The ball would look like a white pea coming at me at two hundred miles an hour. My legs felt like they had sledgehammers in them. And all my mental tricks couldn't get me out of it.

And then there are days when everything falls into place. Players call that being in The Zone. Everything seems effortless. The ball is as big as a watermelon, and you get the fat part of the bat on it every time.

Most of baseball, and life, is spent somewhere in between these two places. But when you have the most important audition of your life, you pray that you are not in the pits but in The Zone.

As soon as I started reading with Hoyt, I knew where I was. All my training and desires and hopes came together, and everything else disappeared for a few amazing minutes as I read that scene for all it was worth.

When it was over, Hoyt smiled and extended his hand. "That was fantastic," he said.

Everyone else in the room said something to the same effect.

All I could think was Wow. And I didn't want to leave. I wanted to keep reading with Hoyt. I wanted to start work on the show.

Barbara DiBova walked me outside. "I wasn't going to say this until later, but you were our number one choice on the callback list. We have more people to see today, but I just wanted to tell you that was one great reading you gave in there."

"Thank you."

"Stay by your phone," she said.

– 6 –

I sailed through work at Josephina's, smiling at everybody. Got good tips as a result, even from the lunch crowd.

And I wanted to celebrate. So that evening I went over to hear Roland play some jazz at Club Cobalt in North Hollywood. NOHO had become something of an artists' quarter in recent years. There were small theaters, art galleries, cafés, clubs.

I sat in a little booth and drank Coke, with a plate of jalapeño poppers as my meal. Very bad for the stomach, but it tasted oh-so-good. And with Roland wailing on the ivories, I was feeling better than I had in months.

The whole Maddie mess was still there, of course, sitting inside me like a ball of deep-fried grease. But at that moment I had hope. My trend line was heading up. Maybe the momentum would carry over into my dealings with Paula.

After his first set, Roland joined me, as did Milo Ayres. Mr. Ayres owned the club, and I'd met him before. He was an affable guy of unknown ethnicity, at least to me. He might have been Greek or Italian or some mix in between. He wore a goatee and always dressed sharp. He had assorted rings on his fingers and gold chains around his neck. Very old school, if by old you mean the 1970s.

"Good to see you again," Ayers said in his accent of unknown origin. His handshake was strong and sure.

"Likewise," I said.

"Mark here just got some good news," Roland said. "Big part on a new series coming up at NBC."

"Not final yet," I said. "But it's very close."

Milo Ayers rubbed one hand on his lapel. "Very nice. Congratulations."

"Mark needs a good lawyer," Roland said.

I looked at him like he'd mentioned I wore Barney underwear.

"Oh?" Ayers said.

"It's nothing," I said.

Roland put his hand on my arm. "Mr. Ayers knows some of the best attorneys in town. You need a referral."

"What's the problem?" Milo Ayers sat down. Now I had to come clean. I would break Roland's fingers later.

"I may have a family matter coming up," I said. My words told me I was still clinging to that thin reed of hope.

"Divorce?" Ayers asked.

"Yeah."

"You go see Gregory Arsenault. He's the best."

Not wanting to get more into this, I said, "It really hasn't reached that stage yet."

Milo Ayers took on the look of an understanding uncle. "Mark, you listen to me, eh? Speaking as one who has been through the mill myself. Divorce can get ugly very fast, and if you don't have somebody looking out for you, your ex will have the shirt off your back before you know it. You gotta know she'll be doing everything she can to squash you."

I couldn't believe that about Paula. Yeah, she had a lawyer and she had Maddie and she was serious. But squash me? No way. For one thing, she loved Maddie and wouldn't do that to the daddy our daughter adored.

"I still have a shot to talk things out," I said.

But Milo Ayers shook his head. "That's naive, my friend. You got any kids?"

"A daughter."

"How old?"

"Five. Almost six."

He reached inside his coat for a business card and pen. He wrote something on the back of the card. "You call Arsenault. It can't hurt to talk to him. Tell him I sent you his way, he'll give you a free consultation."

Ayers finished writing and slid the card across the table to me. "Believe me," Milo Ayers said, "you need protection."

~––~

At the apartment I just could not shake the whole lawyer thing. I hated lawyers. All of them out for a buck, only making life worse for everybody. The thought that Paula would try to bury me with a lawyer was inconceivable.

Okay, maybe she'd had an affair, maybe she was going to divorce me. But that didn't mean all that we'd had together was squat, did it? How could she possibly look at her daughter's father as someone to crush?

The cliché popped into my head: If only she'd listen to reason.

Or her mother, I thought.

Erica Stanton Montgomery was not my biggest fan, but maybe that was the way to get to Paula. Her number was programmed in my cell phone.

I should have checked the time. It was ten thirty on the West Coast, one thirty back East.

Erica's voice was groggy. "What on earth?"

"It's Mark," I said. "Sorry, but this is important."

"What could possibly—"

"Do you know what's going on?"

Pause. I imagined Paula's mother in her huge bedroom in Darian, Connecticut. Her house was as big as a soundstage. "In what way?"

"Come on, Erica. What has Paula told you?"

"She has told me there is going to be a change in her circumstance."

Change in her circumstance? Cold as ice, Erica was.

"Is that all you can say?" I was pacing around the apartment, going by my bedroom and Maddie's, willing someone to be there.

"What is it you wish me to say, Mark?" Her voice was gaining its normal tone—haughty indifference toward her only son-in-law.

"Something besides her marriage to me being a circumstance," I said.

"That is between you and Paula."

"Oh, come off it. You're her mother. You can give her your opinion."

"My opinion is that she is doing the right thing."

"By divorcing me?"

"Yes."

No beating around the bush by this woman. If I thought I would get her to talk Paula out of her impending decision, I was dreaming.

"You approve of her sleeping around?" I wanted to hit Erica with the biggest guns I had.

"That is not what happened," Erica said like some eyewitness.

"How can you say that? Were you there? Are you even aware?"

"Don't take that tone with me."

"I'll sing opera if I have to, to get you to listen."

"I don't care for—"

"We got married in church, remember? Because you wanted a Christian wedding, right? So now that your daughter starts sleeping with a man not her husband, what's your answer? That she should go ahead and divorce me? Is that your idea of Christianity?"

"I will not go on with this—"

"And what about Maddie? Have you thought about her?"

"Maddie is a survivor."

"She's five years old!"

"She has her mother in her. And me."

"Now there's a horror story for you." I shouldn't have said that. But there was no sock around to stuff in my mouth.

"You will not call me again," Erica said.

"That's it? Forever?"

"As far as I'm concerned, yes."

That hurt, even though no love was lost between us. But I tried my best to be civil to Erica Stanton Montgomery. She was Maddie's grandmother, the only one she had. For that alone I did try.

"Why didn't you ever like me?" I said.

"Because you're a child, and you don't have it in you to grow up."

My instinct toward self-defense flew out of me. I was speechless. Erica filled the void. "And you coerced my daughter to marry you, against my wishes."

"Coerced? How?"

"You got her pregnant and then took advantage of the situation." My chin was shaking. "Paula wanted to get married."

"That's what you think."

My breath left me. Did Paula really feel that way?

"Thanks, Erica. You've been a great comfort."

I threw the cell phone across the room.

I couldn't fall asleep that night. Not until about two in the morning. Instead, I just lay in the dark, remembering voices, remembering when Paula and Maddie used to live here.

In the darkness of our bedroom I ask Paula, "What is the greatest movie scene you ever saw?"

"Greatest movie scene? From any movie of all time?"

"Yes. Silent, modern, whatever you want. What scene was it that moved you the most or is stuck in your head?"

She thinks a long time.

"If I had to choose just one," she says, "I think it would have to be the party scene in All About Eve."

"Oh yeah. Where Marilyn Monroe shows up?"

"Yeah, but of course the best line in the whole thing is where Bette Davis goes up the stairs, stops, looks at everybody with those big eyes, and says, 'Fasten your seat belts. It's going to be a bumpy night.'"

I crack up. Paula does a great Bette Davis.

"So what about you?" she says.

"My favorite scene of all time? That's a tough one, but I think I've got it."

"So?"

"It's got to be from Shane."

"I haven't seen Shane."

"You never saw Shane?"

"Keep your voice down."

"You never saw Shane?"

"No, I never saw Shane."

"And I let you marry me?"

"So what's so great about Shane?"

"Shane, man! He's riding into this valley from some mysterious past, see?"

"Okay."

"And he's got no home, but he happens on this homestead, where Van Heflin lives with his wife and son."

"Van Heflin?"

"Will you listen? Heflin is chopping at this big old stump in the ground, and he lets Shane have a drink of water. Then the bad guys ride up and he thinks Shane is one of them, so Heflin tells Shane to get lost."

"Makes sense."

"Be quiet. But then Heflin sees Shane isn't one of them, and he's sorry and asks Shane to stay for dinner."

"This is your favorite scene?"

"Listen! So Shane gets the first good, home-cooked meal he's had in who knows how long, right? When it's over, he stands up and walks outside."

"He eats and runs?"

"I'm gonna clock you one if you don't be quiet."

Paula giggles.

"Now listen, please," I say. "This is really important to me. Shane goes outside and picks up an ax and starts chopping away at the stump. See, that's his way of saying thank you. Van Heflin grabs an ax and the two of them go to work on the stump together. By evening they're almost through. They're both pushing the stump, but it's not coming out easy. The wife comes over and says, 'Hey, why don't you hitch up the horses and pull it out.'"

"Seems reasonable."

"But Heflin says no way. He's been battling that stump for two years. If he gives in now, the stump could say it beat him."

"He really says that?"

"He says sometimes nothing'll work for a man but his own sweat and muscle. So he and Shane go at it again and together they push out the stump."

"That's your favorite scene?"

"That's it."

"You are such a guy."

I prop myself up on one elbow in the dark. "But see, they came together, and they got the job done. And then they have to get together again later in the movie to fight the bad guys who want to take over the valley. It's like the guys who fought World War II. It's like what made America great. Can't you see that?"

"Why don't we rent it?"

"You want to see it?"

"Of course," Paula says, leaning over to kiss me. "If that's your favorite scene, I'd like to see it, too."

"You got a date."

A shaft of light falls across the bed then, and the door is opening. It's Maddie, all of four years old.

"I could hear you," she says.

"Sorry, honey," Paula says. "Come here."

Maddie, in her fluffy pajamas, crawls up on the bed and gets under the covers between us.

"I'm really sorry," I say, kissing Maddie's hair. "Daddy was getting excited about movies."

"I like movies," Maddie says in a sleepy voice. "I like The Little Mermaid."

"The Little Mermaid is good," Paula says.

"Great," I say.

We lay there in silence for a long time. I'm feeling the warmth of Maddie's body and smelling the Johnson's Shampoo in her hair and holding Paula's hand outside the covers.

And then Paula whispers, "I think she's asleep."

I listen to Maddie's breathing, slow and rhythmic, like soft waves lapping on a distant beach.

"I was wrong," I say.

"Wrong?"

"This is my favorite scene."

LAWYERS

"Hello, Daddy."

Maddie's voice sounded quiet over the phone, almost formal. A horrible thought hit me. She sounded like a little version of Erica Stanton Montgomery from last night's conversation. Maybe it was just the weirdness of the situation for her. But it chilled me.

Paula had accepted my call and given Maddie over to me immediately. I took that as a positive step.

"How are you, pumpkin?"

"Fine."

"Great. Whatcha doin'?"

"Watching TV."

"Uh-huh. Cool." Why was it so hard to make small talk with my own daughter? Because I wanted her in my arms, not in Troncatti's house. And I did not want to upset her.

"Are you coming over here?" Maddie said.

"I don't think so."

"How come? Tony has a big house."

The name, the familiar way she said it, was a hot knife.

"Wow, great," I said. "Hey, you want to go to the ballgame with me?"

"And get a Dodger Dog?"

"You betcha."

"Okay. When?"

"Soon. Let me talk to Mommy, will you?"

"Okay."

"I love you," I said, but I guess she didn't hear me. Paula came on.

"So?" she said.

"When will you bring Maddie back?"

"I'm not sure," she said.

"Well, that doesn't help me," I said, trying not to snap. "You don't have the right to keep her from me, if that's what you're thinking."

"We have to work all that out."

"Fine. Let's start by you telling me when she's coming home."

"Stop trying to force me into things, Mark."

A tongue of flame lit inside me. "Like I forced you to sleep with Troncatti? Come on, Paula, stop this right now. Come home and let's work this thing out."

In the short silence I indulged a vision — of Paula in torment about her actions and a real inner struggle. But for the good of Maddie, she'd see it my way and come home. At least to talk. At least to bring Maddie back.

That vision quickly vaporized. "I can't talk to you anymore," Paula said. "Talk to my lawyer. His name is Bryce Jennings and he's in Century City."

"Wait."

The line went dead.

My heart went dead, too, like someone had flipped a switch and cut the life out of it.

It was really happening. Milo Ayers was right. She was going to try to take everything, including Maddie. I started to sweat.

I fished out the card Milo had given me. I didn't want to do this. This was a bad soap opera story line. Wife runs off with Italian movie director. Hires lawyer. Dumb husband is standing there, phone in hand, as the music goes up and the camera closes in on his perplexed face.

I must have stood like that for ten minutes, waiting for someone to yell Cut. No one did. Instead, I dialed the number on the card.

The law offices of Gregory Arsenault were in the largest building in the Valley, on Ventura Boulevard. Spacious and done up in dark wood and brass, with expensive-looking leather-bound books in perfect order on floor-to-ceiling shelves, the office had the feel of money. Not chump change, either.

The receptionist was a tall, sleek woman who asked me to please be seated. There were some magazines on a glass table. I picked up Forbes. Maybe I could find a tip on how to make enough money to afford Mr. Gregory Arsenault.

A few minutes later a tall, angular man with penetrating blue eyes opened the big door next to the reception desk.

"Mr. Gillen? I'm Greg Arsenault."

I stood up and shook his hand. His grip was firm, like a Brinks guard holding the cash bag.

"Thank you for seeing me on such short notice," I said.

"Anything for Milo."

I followed him down a long corridor, past some workstations and inner reception areas, file cabinets and a kitchenette, to the very last office. It was in the corner of the building (we were on the thirtieth floor) and it had a breathtaking view of the San Fernando Valley.

"Have a seat," Arsenault said.

The chairs in his office were made of leather and wood, with arms and legs that had fancy curlicues. Arsenault's desk was large and organized. Absolutely nothing on it looked out of place.

Arsenault sat himself in a big executive chair and leaned back. He wore a crisp white shirt and patterned tie with a dark blue vest. A gold watch chain made its way out of his vest pocket and a watch fob—looking like a gold nugget—dangled from a vest button in the middle of his torso.

"So your wife wants a divorce," he said.

I'd told him a few preliminary things over the phone. "Right."

"What do you want?"

"I don't want the divorce."

"You want money?"

"No."

Arsenault blinked a couple of times. "Interesting. Children?"

"A daughter. Madeleine. She's five."

"You want custody?"

"Of course."

"Don't say of course," Arsenault counseled. "Not just yet. Does your wife have a lawyer?"

"Yes. Jennings something."

"Bryce Jennings?"

"Yeah."

Gregory Arsenault put his head back and laughed. I did not like the sound of that. When he looked at me again he said, "She is quite serious. Do you know anything about Jennings?"

I shook my head.

"Jennings is known as The Destroyer to the Stars. He has made a name for himself, and millions of dollars I might add, representing celebrities in divorce and palimony cases. He is ruthless."

My chest was beginning to tighten as my mind formed images of a lawyer I'd never seen.

"You are definitely going to need representation," Arsenault continued. "Otherwise Jennings will rip your head off and spit down your neck."

For a long moment I sat there, shaking my head slowly. "Why can't Paula and I just settle this thing?"

"There are alternatives. Have you tried marriage counseling?"

"Not yet, but I don't know if she'd go for it."

"Hiring Jennings is not a good sign, no. There is something called Family Conciliation Court. It's informal, confidential, and free. It's mediation, is what it is, and to work it requires that the two parties try to reach solutions without the blood of litigation. Again, the hiring of Jennings is a sign that your wife wants this to be handled with drawn swords. That's where your lawyer comes in."

"Why does it have to be that way? It seems so stupid."

"You're not the only one who thinks so," Arsenault said. "The whole purpose of the Family Code, if you look at the intent of the legislature, is to foster cooperation between the parties, to actually reduce the adversarial nature of the proceedings."

"You're kidding."

The lawyer shook his head. "But there is no area of the law that is nastier, meaner, as full of brass knuckles and raw hatred as family law. Defending child molesters is a walk in the park by comparison."

"But Paula and I were in love."

Arsenault nodded with understanding. No doubt he'd heard variations on this theme countless times. "Why don't you tell me exactly what happened. Don't hold back. Everything you say to me is held in confidence."

"Where should I start?"

"Why does your wife want a divorce?"

"Oldest reason in the world, I guess."

"Another man?"

"You ever heard of Antonio Troncatti?"

Arsenault's chin dropped just a little. "That's the other man?" I nodded.

"No wonder Jennings is involved," Arsenault said. "When did all this happen?"

"Over the last few months," I said. "She got a part in his new movie and went over to Europe to shoot."

"You never went over there?"

"No. I was taking care of Maddie."

Reaching into a drawer, Arsenault took out a new yellow legal pad. He jotted something on it.

"All the time your wife was in Europe, you stayed home and took care of the daughter?"

"That's right."

"What type of work do you do?"

"I wait on tables, try to get acting work."

"Two actors in the family? How's that going?"

"Better," I said. "I just landed a great part in a series."

"Did you?" Arsenault brightened and wrote some more. "That's very good news. It pays well, I'm assuming."

"You can assume that, yes. John Hoyt is in it."

He scribbled. He asked me a series of questions, probing into more areas of the marriage. It was like having a dentist drilling me. Not much pleasure in it, but it had to be done.

Finally there was a long pause while Arsenault surveyed the notes he'd made. Five pages of legal paper. He flipped them back and forth a couple of times. "The only thing left to discuss," he said, "is the fee arrangement."

I tried to swallow. My throat constricted. "Sure," I said, waiting for him to give me the bad news.

"I will need twenty thousand up front."

"Twenty thousand? As in dollars?"

"It is a retainer," he explained. "If things are settled the final bill won't be that much. But if they aren't—"

"I haven't got anywhere near that much."

"Perhaps you have some resources."

"I don't own any property, if that's what you mean."

"Friends or family?"

"Can't we work out some sort of payment plan?"

Gregory Arsenault's face changed from understanding to hard reality. "You have to understand that Bryce Jennings is a $600 an hour man, and that's exactly what your wife—or your wife's lover—is paying for. If this thing proceeds, we can move the court for attorney's fees, but we can't count on that. My hourly rate is $450. As a friend of Milo's."

Suddenly the disparity of the situation hit me. I was still in the same economic shape I was when Paula left for Europe. But in the meantime, she had hooked up with a multimillionaire director; she would have no problem paying The Destroyer.

"I'll, um, see what I can do," I said.

"That'll be fine. My assistant will give you a client agreement form, and we can talk later. Meantime, you have some homework."

"Homework?"

"I have an information form for you to fill out. All sorts of questions on assets, your child, your work, your references, all that. It's self-explanatory. I also want you to make a list of positives and negatives. First, your positives. Then her negatives."

"Why?"

"That will be important when it comes to custody."

I shook my head. "I don't want to do that."

Arsenault's eyes got serious. "Do you want joint physical custody of your daughter or not? Because Bryce Jennings is going to do everything he can, with your wife's help, to get her sole custody. Of that you can be sure. And to do that, he's going to try to make you look bad."

"But I'm not. I mean, I'm not perfect, but—"

"Which is why I want to know your negatives, too."

"What for?"

"So I can anticipate what Jennings will be using."

I felt sick. Arsenault looked at his watch and stood up. The signal our time was at an end. "Last thing," he said. "Do not discuss these matters with anyone. If you do, the other side may claim that you have waived the confidentiality privilege. Capice?"

"Oh. Yeah. Right." Zombie like, I got to my feet. "She has Maddie," I said. "Can she keep her from me?"

"We can file an Order to Show Cause if there's a problem." He opened the door to his office. "I'll give Bryce a call, as soon as all this is official."

As I staggered by he said, "And try not to worry, Mark. We'll get this thing straightened out."

Sure. No worries. This was going to be a walk in the roses. For a mere twenty grand.

~ 2 ~

I called Nancy from the car. "When will the contract for Number Seven be here?"

"Whoa there, Lightning," Nancy said. "They haven't even made a formal offer yet, but I understand your reading was a killer."

Practically panting now, but trying not to sound desperate, I said, "Is there any way to speed the process along?"

"Hey, I'm just as anxious as you are, but this is not something we need to worry about. I'm sure it's going to be a great offer, and I'll do the agent thing and see how much higher we might be able—"

"I'm not concerned with the amount, but the timing. I need some money."

Silence on Nancy's end. Then: "Why?"

"You don't want to know."

"Loan sharks? Mark, tell me you're not into gambling."

"No, Nancy." I was on the freeway and realized I'd missed my off ramp. Not caring, I just drove. "It's Paula. She's hired a lawyer."

"Oh no."

"I went to a guy today and he wants twenty grand, up front."

"Twenty! My lawyer only charged five when I divorced Frank."

"Paula's apparently hired some big lawyer."

"Not Bryce Jennings, I hope."

"Ding ding ding."

Nancy cursed. "Look, my advice is to get out of this thing as quickly and quietly as possible. Maybe you can find a less expensive attorney, someone young and hungry who'll—"

"Roll over and play dead?"

"Not what I meant."

"Can I get some sort of advance on the money—from the agency maybe?"

"A loan? I wish you hadn't asked me that. We just can't—"

"I'm desperate here." Oops.

"I know, I know. Look, let me give a call over to Barbara DiBova and see what the time frame is. But the way this works, don't count on it. Meantime, take it easy. Try to relax. If Bryce Jennings is on this thing we don't want to upset him. That would mean negative publicity."

Her warning was well taken. I was not name enough to survive negative pub.

"You still there?" Nancy said.

"Yeah."

"You hear what I said?"

"Sure."

"Good. I'll call you."

Traffic had slowed to a crawl, and I saw why. A major car wreck on the side of the freeway. A silver Mercedes looked like an accordion and a Ford pickup was overturned. There were CHP cars and an ambulance there, lights flashing and all.

And on the ground, attended by paramedics, a man was sprawled, looking dead.

———

I don't know why I decided to get off at Gower. Maybe, looking back on all that's happened, it was God directing me. I sure didn't make any conscious decision.

The Presbyterian church where I was married, where I'd attended with Maddie, was staring me right in the face.

Was it a sign? I realized I was looking for one.

I parked on the little street by the freeway, adjacent to the back of the church grounds. It had a security gate, which was understandable. This was Hollywood, after all. But for some reason the gate was not fully closed.

Another sign?

I walked in.

No one was around, as far as I could tell. There was a complex of rooms, some offices, a stairwell. It was quiet. I kept listening for a voice.

Hearing none, I wandered toward the big church building. Someone looking like a maintenance worker came out of the side door. He nodded at me, like my presence didn't surprise him.

I nodded back and entered the door. I was in a corridor, again with no one around. Turning down a hallway, following my instincts, I saw another doorway and went through.

And found myself in the empty church.

The lights were off, but enough sun came through the stained glass windows that I could see just fine. The big pipes of the organ gleamed.

I don't know exactly when I knew I was praying. I wasn't down on my knees. My head wasn't bowed, my eyes were open. But I was talking in my mind.

There's a play called The Ruling Class, where the lead character becomes convinced he's God. When asked why, he says that when he prayed, he found he was talking to himself.

That bit occurred to me as I sat there. But I did not at any time feel I was talking to myself. There was a sense that a presence was there. And I laid it all out.

Can you cut me a break on this one? All I want is my family to be together again. I want Paula and I want Maddie and I want to live in the apartment and I want to buy a house with the money I'll be making on the show—which by the way thank you for—and Paula's going to be a big star and I want to enjoy it with her, together. Can you do something please? I'll do whatever you tell me to do, but I'm asking for this. I want to be with Paula and I want my daughter and whatever you want from me, you've got it.

I stopped when I realized I was crying. Not anything big, but a steady, warm pouring out of the soul. God was there, I believed that much. And the preacher said prayer worked. Well, it was time.

I stayed for a few more minutes, just to show God I didn't pray and run, then slipped quietly out the back.

- 3 -

"There was a guy asking about you," Julio said. He did work around the apartment building, landscaping, some handyman stuff.

"What guy?"

"Don't know. Ask when you be home."

"He didn't give you his name?"

Julio shook his head. "And I didn't say nothing. Didn't feel good."

"What'd he look like?"

Julio shrugged.

"How old?"

"Fifty maybe."

That would have ruled out my immediate circle of friends.

"Did he say he was going to come back?"

"Didn't say nothing. Just walk away."

Creepy. A guy asking about me, not leaving a name. Anger flaming up, I charged up to my apartment and called Paula. Surprisingly, she answered. I'd expected her voice message.

"What is it?" She sounded tired.

"Can I ask you a question please?"

"If it's about Maddie, I told you—"

"No, not about Maddie. Yet. Just between you and me." I was struggling to keep my anger in check. My theory might not even be right, so I had to give her the benefit of the doubt. Also, I was hoping—again—that we could talk about things.

On the other hand, my rage was something I could not fully control. "Did you hire a private investigator?"

No immediate answer.

"Did you?"

"You are supposed to get a lawyer," Paula said.

"That's not an answer."

"My lawyer says I'm not supposed to talk to you, Mark."

"Are you a puppet on a string?" Another thought hit me. How much was Troncatti involved in this? Was he telling Paula what to do as well?

"I just have to do what's right."

"This isn't right, Paula. This is so wrong. Maddie needs both of us. She needs us together. I don't care what people think they can do when they divorce. The best thing is to have us together under one roof."

"No."

"Please. Will you just call this thing off for a while? We can get counseling, or we can try something my lawyer suggested—"

"So you do have a lawyer."

I sighed. "We don't need to do it this way. There's a free service we can try. Why bring lawyers into it?"

"I have to do what's best for Maddie."

"What are you talking about? How is this good for her?"

"I can't talk to you right now, Mark. I was told—"

"Come on!" I was ready to yank the phone cord from the jack. "Don't turn this into a thing with investigators and lawyers and all that. We can work this out."

There was no answer, but some fuzzy sound. "Paula?"

The next voice I heard was male. With an accent. "Don't you call her again!" it said. Then the line cut out.

Troncatti. The great Antonio Troncatti himself. Ordering me around. Had to be.

I did rip the cord out.

—◦—

Next morning I walked to the bank, a couple of blocks away, to see what I could possibly borrow. The very nice woman at the desk tried not to sound completely disheartening, but I had nothing to secure the kind of loan I needed to get my lawyer his retainer.

I called my life insurance company. They reminded me I had term insurance. Nothing to borrow against.

Duh, they must have thought.

Credit cards. I had a Visa and MasterCard. Or, rather, I shared them with Paula. Digging out our last bills I saw that there was roughly $8,000 available on the Visa and $4,500 on the MasterCard.

So back to the bank lady I went. I asked her if I could get a cash advance of $12,000. She told me to wait. When she came back she had that same look on her face from before.

"No available funds," she said.

"What? How can that be?"

"You have a joint account on both cards. There's been some sort of activity to stop advances. This sometimes happens."

"Why?"

She shrugged. "In divorce cases."

Must have been written all over me.

I walked out of the bank into a bright, hot afternoon. It had now been three days since I'd seen Maddie, and I could feel it. We'd not been apart for more than a matter of hours in a long time. As I walked down Ventura Boulevard, feeling a little sick, I remembered the time a few weeks ago when Maddie got sick herself.

We'd been to the movies. I took her to see the new Disney animated feature and splurged on candy. We made it through the movie and into the car.

But as soon as we were in traffic Maddie said, "Daddy, I don't feel good."

She looked so little in her car seat. "What's the matter?"

"My tummy."

Right. Good old Dad had done it again with the diet. "Hang on, pumpkin, we'll be home in a—"

At which point my lovely daughter spewed all over the back seat. It was no small act; it was operatic in its scope.

She started crying.

"Oh, pumpkin, I'm sorry—" Then the smell hit and I knew that I would have to get about fifty air fresheners for my car mirror.

I carried her up to the apartment and promptly got her into a bath. She was subdued. No talk about Bible characters or cartoon shows or the latest kindergarten scandal. All she wanted was to feel better.

After she was in her pj's I gave her what Gram used to give me when I had a similar ailment—a little 7 UP. Then I put her in bed and read her a Dr. Seuss.

With that done I turned out her light and started preparing for an industrial cleanup job on my car.

"Don't go," she said.

"You want me to stay awhile?"

"I want you to sleep in here." She put her hand out and touched my arm.

"There's no bed," I said.

"You can sleep on the floor," Maddie replied, and then with sudden concern for my well-being, she added, "with a pillow."

"But I have to — " I stopped myself. The car could wait. I'd make it a hundred air fresheners if I had to. "I'll get a pillow and blanket," I said.

And so I had a little slumber party with my daughter. We talked for about an hour, on all sorts of things. She especially wanted to hear about some of the trouble I got in when I was little, which is a vast reservoir to draw from.

When I realized she wasn't talking anymore, but breathing rhythmically, I switched off the lamp. I stayed there a long time, listening to her breath. No amount of money could have coaxed me out of that room at that moment. Eventually I fell asleep.

Now, walking down the street without aim, I kept that picture of Maddie and me in mind. No amount of money — Now money was very much what I needed.

At the corner I stopped by the bus stop and casually looked back behind me.

That's when I saw him.

He was dressed in jeans and a blue Hawaiian shirt. His hair was grayish and long. Behind his sunglasses I imagined two eyes looking directly at me.

There was a good distance between us, maybe fifty yards or so, but I had no doubt this was the guy Julio had mentioned.

Now what? Should I go up and confront the guy? Get in his face and tell him to leave me alone?

Maybe that's what Vance, my character on Number Seven, would do. But I quickly reminded myself this was life, not TV. I'd never had anyone tailing me before (at least not that I knew of).

And what if I was just paranoid? This could be some guy just looking up the street, waiting for a ride.

One way to find out. I continued on up to the corner and turned right, picking up my pace past the little strip mall on the right. The twenty-four-hour laundry, where I'd spent some time in the past, was doing a good business. As I looked past the laundry to the sidewalk, I noticed the guy was not in view.

All this was my overactive imagination, I told myself. But I'd started this little game and might as well play it to the limit.

I walked down the side street, past the Taco Bell, and turned down an alley, heading back toward my building. On my left was a block wall, behind which was a residential area. On my right were the backs of buildings—offices, a Thai restaurant, Jiffy Lube. It was like being in a concrete canyon.

Behind me, no sign of the guy. I laughed a little. Urban paranoia, nothing else. It showed me just how much I was on edge.

Which left the question open, who was asking about me at the building? By the time I reached the end of the alley, my mind was full of sneaking suspicions again. The only thing I was sure of was that it had to be someone Paula had hired. Or The Destroyer.

When I turned down my own street I was not anywhere nearer the money I needed than I had been before. My thoughts were just a merry-go-round of repetitions, with no new revenue sources turning up. I must have been pretty deep in my own mind because I actually let out a yelp when I saw him again.

The guy in the Hawaiian shirt stepped off the front steps of the apartment building and smiled at me.

"You ditched me," he said.

I took a step back and glared at him. "Why are you following me?"

"Mark," he said, "don't you recognize your old man?"

– 4 –

Of course not. How could I recognize someone I had never known?

Still, there was a resemblance. Or maybe it was just a projection on my part. I only knew I didn't want this to be my father. One major upheaval in my life at a time, please.

"Come on, who are you really?" I said.

"I really am," he said.

"No way."

He took off his shades. I almost gasped. I could see my eyes in his. "Your mom's name was Estelle. When I knew her she liked being called Rainbow."

My heart almost kicked its way out of me.

"I know this must seem bizarre." He had an easy smile. "How about I buy you a cup of coffee and we talk?"

Every corner in LA now has a Starbucks. In a daze I let this gray-haired, smiling stranger buy me an upscale cup of joe. We sat outside under a green umbrella.

"I know it's weird," he said.

"You got that right. What's your name, anyway?"

"Ron Reid."

That was the right name. Mom had talked about him a few times to me before her death.

"So why are you showing up now?" My body felt like a sack of wet laundry, weighted down by the liquid of mental strain. I had no idea how to deal with this. Part of me wanted to lash out.

When you grow up without a father, you're always aware other kids have something you don't. Not that all kids had dads at home, but all of my friends at school had dads somewhere and got to see them.

And when Mom died, I put some of the blame on my father, wherever and whoever he was. If he had been around, things might have been different. And maybe there wouldn't have been this hole right in the middle of me.

"It took me a long time to work up the courage." Reid looked down at the white lid of his coffee cup. "I wasn't exactly a dad for you."

"Did you ever try to see me?"

He shook his head. "Your mom made it clear she wanted me out of both of your lives."

"So what happened to you?"

Reid leaned back in a little. "I did some serious federal time at Terminal Island. I'm an ex-con, just so you know."

"I knew that."

"Which follows you around the rest of your life. Hasn't been a smooth ride for me. I've been all over the place, done a lot of different things. Welder. Carney. I was even a DJ in Tuscaloosa for a while."

"Looks like you have trouble holding a job." My tone was not warm, understanding, or talk-showy. What I wanted to do was grill him. A churning of resentment was roiling around inside me.

"Boy howdy," he said. "Part of it was just getting bored. If I'm not engaged, I can't stay with something."

"Engaged?"

"With the Wheel." He smiled at my perplexed look. "Have you heard of Mahayana?"

"Is that a resort or something?"

"No, it's a form of mysticism."

"Then the answer is no."

"I was a religious studies major at Berkeley. I don't know if you knew that."

"Nope."

"That never left me. I went to India for a while."

"Didn't the Beatles do that? I read it in a history book."

"Ouch, man." He laughed. There was something laid-back and easy about him. He might have been a typical Southern California surfer, but one who hadn't grown up. His body was lean.

"But of all the world religions, Buddha was the one who got it right. You ever read Siddhartha?"

"No. Variety."

He blinked, then nodded with understanding. "Right. You're an actor. You should be into this. Mahayana is a form of Buddhism that is positive, not negative. Instead of saying that one finds salvation by escape from Samsara, which is an endless series of rebirths, you find it the other way, in the Wheel of Becoming."

"This sounds seriously weird."

"Only because you're of a Western mind-set. If you experience it, you know it makes perfect sense. Nirvana, see, is not found through the extinction of desire, as in older Buddhism. Nirvana is found in the self to be attained, not the self to be stamped out. This is how you can make each day a divine experience."

What was I doing here, I suddenly thought, listening to an ancient hippie and his riff about wheels and Nirvana? That he could be my father was disturbing.

"Why were you following me around?" I said.

"Good question," Ron Reid said. "I'm not sure I have a good answer from your perspective."

"Then give me a good answer from any perspective."

"I guess I wanted to know you a little first without you knowing me. I was nervous."

"How did you find out where I lived?"

"Not hard to do these days," he said. "Computers and all. Did I mention that I was a private investigator for a while?"

"Apparently not."

"Unlicensed, because of the felony thing. It didn't last long. But I've always been a good student."

So far, nothing he said seemed real. But it didn't seem entirely far out, either.

"So where do we go from here?" I said.

For a long moment he sat in silence. "I just thought maybe we could try to reconnect."

"Why?" It sounded cold, but I was still defensive.

"Because," he said, "I found out I have a granddaughter."

He was staying at a cheap motel not far from me. He didn't have much money (never had, since prison, he explained) and didn't have a job. He'd come down here as an act of faith, "faith in the Wheel."

So I told him he could stay a while at my apartment.

My thinking was this. If he was my father (and I was going to check it out further), then I guess I owed it to myself to find out about him. I didn't feel like I owed him anything. He was the one who'd run out on me.

But if I could understand him a little, maybe I could understand some things about myself. Like the sudden rages. Or the urge to drink.

And there was another reason, too. He was Maddie's grandfather, and that gave me an added arrow in my quiver. Paula had Erica on her side. This was a grandparent for my side. Even though he appeared to be stuck in the sixties and had a criminal record to boot, he'd done his time. Maybe I was hoping a court would eventually take that into account, though I wasn't naive enough to consider this a great bargaining chip. I was just grasping for anything that might help me.

Since I'd gotten into acting, I was always observing people, trying to pick up on what they were about. I did the same with Ron—I wasn't going to be calling him "Dad," that was too strange—as we moved his stuff from the Wagon Wheel, with its free HBO, to my apartment, with its free macaroni and cheese.

Ron seemed genuinely grateful. And mellow, that old Southern California word for all-around peaceful and laid-back. Whatever his beliefs about religion, he appeared to have found some sort of respite from the bad road he'd been down over the past thirty years or so.

"So when do I get to meet Maddie?" Ron said when we'd moved him in, which consisted of throwing his duffel bag next to the sofa.

"That's a question that can't be answered just yet," I said.

He looked at me, confused.

"Paula has not been cooperative regarding Maddie. And I've got to get a lawyer to help straighten things out. Problem is, I haven't got the money to pay for one."

"Lawyers are slime," Ron said. His eyes reflected bitter experience.

"Maybe, but I need some slime right now."

"What's the beef?"

I shrugged. "It all comes down to Paula hooking up with another man. She won't talk to me. Maybe that's understandable."

"Why?"

"I threw a bottle at her."

Ron laughed. "That seems like regular domestic bliss."

"I was out of control. I blew it. Now she won't talk to me."

"Hey, don't take this all on yourself." He made a circle in the air with his index finger. "All you have to do is connect with the Wheel."

"Look," I said, "you can stay here for a while and we can talk. But I'm not interested in your mojo."

"That's cool. Just trying to help."

"When I want help, I'll ask."

"Right on. You're not religious at all?"

"I believe in God."

"The Christian God?"

"Something wrong with that?"

Reid shook his head. "Nah, Jesus was cool. He was one of the enlightened ones."

He was really interested in Maddie, so I got out the photo album.

Bad idea, it turned out.

Going back to when Maddie was a baby, every photo was like sharp glass jabbing me. I'd see Paula in there, smiling. Or the two of us with Maddie, when somebody else took the shot. Arms around each other. Group hugs.

Ron would stop every now and then and ask about a picture.

There was Maddie, clomping around in her mom's shoes.

At the beach, Maddie's two-year-old buns to the wind.

Disneyland. Just outside Pirates of the Caribbean, Maddie wearing a pirate hat from the expensive gift shop. She's glaring at the camera, like a real pirate.

"In her non-girly phase," I said.

Maddie in the kitchen, making her favorite food, buttered toast, all by herself.

And then the one that made me clutch: Maddie right in the middle of Paula and me, arm around both our necks and a determined look on her face. It looked like she was trying to pull her mommy and daddy together. It was taken at a surprise birthday party I threw for Paula.

"You know what I see here?" Ron said.

I shook my head.

"Hope. I see hope here. It's gonna work out, my man. Don't ever give up."

I did not know this man who was my father. Truth be told, I still felt very strange about his being here. But that was a nice thing he said and, considering the day I'd had, I was appreciative.

The receptionist's eyes were wide and impatient.

"Mr. Jennings does not see anyone without an appointment," she said, as if this rule were inscribed on a stone tablet. It was Thursday morning, and in my mind a perfect time to interrupt a hot LA lawyer.

"Tell him anyway. My name is Mark Gillen and I'm not leaving until I see him."

The office was on the fortieth floor of a gleaming building in Century City. The minimum rent had to be on par with the gross national product of Paraguay.

"Will you excuse me?" the receptionist said with stiff formality. She looked like a model.

I scoped the reception area. It was about three levels above Gregory Arsenault's office in terms of snootiness. Some sort of African artwork was the theme of the place, with ebony statuettes and exotic plants taking up most of the space.

An ornately carved spear hung on one wall. I wondered if that was what The Destroyer used in court.

The receptionist returned, an angry look on her face. "Mr. Jennings will see you, but you'll have to wait."

"No prob," I said. "I'll just hang here in the jungle."

Turns out I waited an hour and a half. I was sure he kept me waiting in order to tick me off. It worked. But I wasn't going to let him know it.

The receptionist finally walked me to a corner office that was, once again, bigger and richer than my nonretained lawyer's. In the middle of the ministadium, standing stiffly like some general, was a fiftyish man with a full head of perfectly coiffed black hair. His white shirt had no wrinkles. His silk, burgundy tie was perfectly knotted. But he was shorter than I'd expected. I thought anyone named The Destroyer would have to be six feet at least. This man was just over jockey size.

He stood there for a moment, unsmiling. Sizing me up. In my Nikes, jeans, and Lakers T-shirt, I did not fit in his world.

But then his white teeth showed and he stepped forward to shake my hand. "Bryce Jennings," he said. "And before we say another word, do you have a lawyer?"

"Gregory Arsenault."

"Ah, Greg. Good man. He's the one I should be talking to. We can't—"

"All right," I said. "I haven't retained him yet because I haven't got any money."

His eyes narrowed a bit. "Sit down."

"Look," I said, "by now you know all about my assets, or lack thereof, and probably all my personal habits as well. Did you know I sometimes snort when I sleep?"

Jennings said nothing.

"Yep, sometimes, for no reason I can think of, I snort and wake myself up. Paula used to laugh about that."

Tapping his lower lip with his index fingers, Bryce Jennings waited for me to make a point.

"Anything else you want to know about me?" I said.

"Yes," Jennings said. "I'd like to know if you want to save an enormous amount of pain and time and money and help your little girl, too."

"What am I supposed to say to that? No?"

"Some people do."

"What's the catch?"

That got Bryce Jennings to smile. "No catch here, Mark. And despite what you may have heard, Satan is not a named partner in my firm. I know I have a reputation as being something of a—"

"Destroyer?"

"I detest that name, but what can you do? If pushed, I push back for my clients. But I would much rather settle a case without stress or strain. It's best all around."

"I only want what's best. I'd like to sit down with Paula and talk this out."

Jennings looked pained. "I'm sorry, but that's not going to be possible at this point. Paula has made it perfectly plain that —"

"Paula or Troncatti?"

"I'm not sure what you mean."

"Who's paying your bill?"

"I can't discuss that, of course."

"What can you discuss?"

"Terms."

Folding my arms, I waited for him to continue. No harm in listening, was there?

"What Paula would like is the least pain for you, believe me. These things happen. People fall in love, then fall out, we don't know why. But we can't change our feelings."

"Then I guess marriage vows don't mean anything."

"It's a different day and time," Jennings said. "Marriage used to be enforced by the church, but that institution's largely faded. We now recognize there's more torture in sticking to a bad marriage than there is in divorce."

"So my marriage was torture for Paula?"

"Sorry, Mark, that was just a metaphor. My point is, divorce is easier now, as it should be. We have to work to make sure it stays easy for all parties concerned."

"All right, here is how we can make it easy. I want to go to counseling with Paula. I want her to give this a chance. I don't know if she's willing to do that or not —"

"As I said —"

"Let me finish." I was feeling heat. "If she's still going to press this forward, then maybe there's nothing else I can do. I'll have to move on. But I want Maddie. I want her living with me, not Paula and that jerk Troncatti."

Jennings put one hand in the air. "Let's not let personal animosity ensue here."

That did it to me. "Animosity ensue? Why don't you talk like a human being? This is my daughter I'm talking about. I want Maddie living with me. If you want to write that up in a paper and have me sign it, fine."

Silence.

"Well?"

"Mark, I'm afraid that's not going to happen."

The chill in his voice was like something from the frozen north. The temperature in the office seemed to drop.

"Just what is that supposed to mean?" I said.

"It is Paula's desire that Maddie live with her. Physical and legal custody would be required. You would get to see Maddie, of course."

"Oh yeah? How often?"

"That's to be determined."

"And what if Paula and Troncatti decide to move to, say, Rome? What then?"

Jennings shrugged. "Relocation does happen, of course. People learn to deal with it."

I couldn't take this anymore. I stood up. "I'm not going to agree to that. You must think I'm nuts."

He gave no immediate response, which ticked me off all the more.

"This is ridiculous," I said. "If she thinks she's going to take my daughter from me—"

"Her daughter as well."

"—and live with Troncatti, it's not going to happen. I'll tell her that myself, right now."

As I started to go, Jennings said, "Don't call her."

Turning on him, I tried to keep myself from jumping across his desk. "I'll call her when I want to."

Now Jennings stood. "This is your notice, under Penal Code section 653, that any further phone contact by you with my client will be dealt with as a harassment offense by the office of the District Attorney."

When I finally got outside again, it felt like my arms and legs had been cut off. Like I was powerless to move, could not do anything.

God, I kept repeating in my mind. God help me.

On the street I found a phone with a phone book dangling and looked in the yellow pages under Attorneys—Family Law. I just had to get a lawyer, but one that would take this case without a whole lot up front. If that meant me calling every lawyer in the book, so be it.

I scanned a few of the ads and decided not to call these first. If they could afford to advertise, they probably charged the most.

Using my finger like a desperate guide dog, I scanned the page until something jumped out at me. Father's Rights, it said.

Gee, did I have rights? Not if I listened to Bryce Jennings. I put in two quarters and called the number. A guy with a Brooklyn accent answered the phone. I told him what was happening.

"Get in here," he said. "Now."

THE SYSTEM

They've tried to put a whole new face on Hollywood. At the corner of Hollywood Boulevard and Highland they built this huge monstrosity of a shopping mall next to the famous Chinese Theater. The monstrosity also has a theater, The Kodak, where the Oscars are held.

To me, the whole thing is like a doily on a dung heap. There's just no covering up the truth. Hollywood still has the homeless and the hustlers, the beggars and the bag ladies. It is just a little bit cleaner on the sidewalk is all.

At least it was clean just outside the tiny walk-up near Cherokee. The Father's Advocacy Group office was a small, musty space with yellowed windows. About as far from the lofty status of Bryce Jennings as Beverly Hills is from South Central.

"You the guy on the phone?"

The New York voice was instantly recognizable. He was a small, sweaty man with a bad comb-over, maybe in his late forties. He spoke from behind a messy desk.

"That's me," I said.

"Sit down. Name's Joe Pfeffer. One P, a whole lot of Fs."

"Mark Gillen."

We shook hands.

"Glad you came in. Coffee?"

"Sure."

"Came out of my car battery just this morning." Pfeffer spun around in his wooden chair, which seemed 1950s vintage. The ancient springs squeaked. He poured some coffee from a little maker into a Styrofoam cup.

"Take anything in it?" he asked.

"Black is fine."

"Good," Pfeffer said, handing me the cup. "Take it straight to the gut. Get used to it."

"Used to what?"

"Getting it straight to the gut. Your first divorce?"

"Yes," I said. "Though I'm hoping she won't go through with it."

"Then why are you here?"

"Because her lawyer said she wants full custody of our daughter."

"And she'll get it, most likely."

My breath left me in a rush.

"Sorry for the jolt," Pfeffer said. "But I'm from New York. You know what New York CPR is, don't you?"

I shook my head.

Pfeffer looked down at an imaginary victim. "GET UP OR YOU'RE GONNA DIE!"

When Pfeffer laughed, I forced a little chuckle. Was this gallows humor?

"Look," he said. "Here's the harsh reality. Eighty-five percent of the time, the mother is awarded physical custody of the child."

"Eighty-five?"

Pfeffer nodded. "Now I ask you, are 85 percent of the fathers out there bad? The way the courts go about it, it seems so. Judges must have a rubber stamp marked MOM on the bench."

"Isn't there something anybody can do?"

"We're trying. Trying for legislation in the courts to get rid of the prejudice against fathers."

"Any luck?

"It's tough. You got some very powerful groups opposed to changing the system."

"Like who?"

"National Organization for Women, various trial lawyers' associations. I can see why the lawyers don't want to change it. Child custody fights are a cash cow. You know what happens if a mother keeps a child away from a father with visitation rights?"

"What?"

"Zip. Nada. Unless the father goes back to court. Cops don't care. Social services don't care. Dad has to shell out thousands more bucks to a lawyer, wait for a court date. So yeah, the lawyers always win in the end, don't they?"

"Great system."

"What I don't get is NOW's opposition. I mean, whenever you stick it to a father, you're also sticking it to other women."

"How?"

"Grandma. Aunts. Sisters. All people the child has formed relationships with. They're gone from the child's life. How is that good?"

"This sounds like a horror story."

"You don't know the half of it. Ever heard of a guy named Derrick Brainard?"

"No."

"Shot himself outside the San Diego courthouse earlier this year. He shouted his last words, 'You did this to me.' In his hand he had an order denying custody."

"Sounds like he wasn't too stable."

The wooden chair creaked as Joe Pfeffer leaned forward and put his elbows on the desk. "Tip of the iceberg, my friend. Surgeon General says suicide is the eighth leading cause of death in America."

"But what does that have to do with—"

"Men are now four times more likely to kill themselves."

"Why is that?"

"Guy at U.C. Riverside did a study. The rise coincides with the increase in divorce and the discrimination of family law courts against dads."

"There's a study on this?"

"Oh yeah. And the stories we get." Pfeffer dug around in the papers on his desk, pulled out a sheet. "Guy in the Valley gassed himself because he was denied access to his kids. A cop in New York hanged himself because his ex-wife charged him with child abuse, and the court bought it. After the guy died they found out the ex-wife was lying all along."

"Man—" My gut, which Pfeffer had warned me about, was feeling punched.

"See, not only are fathers being denied custody, they also have to pony up alimony, even if the wife lives with someone and is being supported."

Even if the wife has some rich, powerful director paying for her every whim?

"There's even a group on Yahoo," Pfeffer said, "called Ex-husband Is Now My Slave. All sorts of advice from ex-wives on how they stuck it to their former spouse and get away with it."

"You're kidding."

"My friend, about this I do not kid."

I rubbed my forehead. "My wife has this big-time divorce lawyer, and I can hardly afford to pay for gas. My daughter is five. They want to take her away from me." The hand on my forehead was trembling. In fact, my whole body shook.

"I know how it is, Mark," Pfeffer said softly. "Believe me, I know, having been through the wringer myself. First thing you got to do is take care of yourself, you hear what I'm saying?"

My eyes met his.

"Everybody thinks the man should have it all together," he said. "Not true. I want you to talk to somebody, a lawyer. No charge up front. How's that sound?"

———

I hoped the lawyer—Alex Bedrosian, the card said—was an ex-soldier from the Armenian Army or something. Someone who would not be intimidated by the fancy attorney Paula had hired. And someone who would take his time getting his money.

I parked in front of the small office building on Cahuenga, which backed up against the 101 Freeway. A car dealership with all sorts of balloons flying was next door. Across the freeway, the giant presence of Universal Studios reminded me of the old saying: You look under the façade in Hollywood, and you find more façade.

I walked into an office that was small but neat. A pleasant-looking woman of sixty or so was dusting in the tiny reception area. She looked like someone's nanny. My heart sank a little. I was so used to high-powered lawyers with beautiful receptionists.

"Hello," the woman said.

"Hi," I said.

"Are you Mark?"

I blinked. "Yeah."

"Joe told me you were coming over."

"Great."

She offered her hand. "I'm Alex Bedrosian."

There is a fake smile one puts on when faced with shattering disappointment. That was what I plastered between my cheeks as I shook her hand. Some soldier.

"My receptionist is home with a sick dog," she said. "Come on in."

She led me past the reception area, down a little hallway. We passed a bathroom-sized room that wasn't a bathroom. It had a shelf of books and a computer terminal. The world's smallest law library, I gathered.

We got to the back office. Small but homey. The faint strains of classical music—something Mozarty—gave the room a pleasant feel. But I did not want a pleasant feel. I wanted war marches.

"Can I get you a cup of coffee?" Alex Bedrosian asked.

Thinking back to Joe Pfeffer's brew, I declined.

She sat at her desk. A small, potted flower adorned one corner, like a dainty Good Housekeeping seal of approval. "Joe didn't tell you I was a woman, did he?"

"Uh, no."

"That stinker. He's always doing that. New Yorker, you know. What are you going to do?"

What indeed? Bolt out of there was one option. But that left me with exactly zero alternatives.

"Now, Joe gave me a little of your story over the phone. Suppose you—"

"Look, Ms. Bedrosian, I have to tell you this up front. I'm not rolling in bucks at the moment. To be fair, you should know that."

She smiled, and it was warm. I could not for the life of me picture this woman in a court of law battling the likes of Bryce Jennings.

"If I take your case," she said, "I will ask for a retainer. The rest of the payment I will take as awarded by the court. Under California law, the family court judge may assign payment if he sees inequality in the parties."

"Well, how much of a retainer?"

"Can you come up with $1,200?"

I almost burst out laughing. Before she could take it back I blurted, "Yes!"

"Then why don't you tell me your story?"

So I did. For the next half hour I poured it all out, feeling it gush forth like water from behind a broken dam. In the middle of it I realized I felt more comfortable with this woman than I had with the much higher priced Gregory Arsenault. And it wasn't just because of the money aspect. I felt like she was listening to me, almost as if I were her only client.

Maybe I was.

When I finished, she looked briefly at her notes. "I will file for an immediate adjustment of the ex parte order, so you can see Maddie. It may or may not happen. But we'll push hard toward the hearing, on the Order to Show Cause, and I'll do what I can to speed things along. I don't believe Paula is going to give in on any point."

"But why?" I said. "How can she do that to her own daughter?"

"Because she has hired Bryce Jennings," Alex explained. "Jennings practices family law the way Colombian drug lords practice kidnapping. No mercy."

At that point I started to have some doubts. Could I fight for Maddie by paying $1,200 to a lawyer who looked more like a favorite grandmother than a lawyer?

"Could I ask you a question?" I said.

"Of course."

"How did you get into this line of work?"

The knowing smile told me this wasn't the first time she'd been asked that question. "Because I went through the nightmare of it myself."

"Would you mind telling me?"

She seemed to sense that I was looking for some sort of comfort in my choice of lawyer. She began fiddling with a rubber band on her desk. "I suffered for many years from bulimia. What I know now, that I didn't know then, was that a huge psychological hole inside me drove me to men who were wrong for me and finally into an abusive marriage. At the time, of course, I thought I had found the perfect man. We had two kids. The bulimia did not go away. I got a Ph.D. in behavior psychology, and I was more messed up than ever."

Alex told all of this in a matter-of-fact way. No sign of self-pity at all.

"When my husband filed for divorce it was because he'd fallen for another woman, whom he eventually married. But in the divorce fight, his lawyer made me the villain."

She looked at me, as if in warning. "All the secrets I had about my behavioral problems became public record as I was dragged through the meat grinder of the family court. Of course, my fitness as a mother was issue number one. I was portrayed as a combination of Lizzie Borden and the Bride of Frankenstein. This was in Miami. I was grilled by Miami human resource agents, by psychotherapists who knew less than I did about everything, by a judge who was clearly biased, and by local reporters who couldn't get enough of this juicy story. My lawyer fought hard, but we lost. It was a slaughter. My ex-husband got everything he asked for, including full custody of the kids."

"Did you get to see them at all?"

"He moved them out here, partly out of spite, I think. I saw them only rarely. It turned out well, though. I now have a good relationship with both my sons, who have, unfortunately, grown to resent their father. I wish that hadn't happened."

"Why not?" It seemed just to me.

"Because children should have both parents in their lives, unless it's clearly destructive. Matt, my ex-husband, was not an evil man. But he got caught up in an evil system."

"So you went to law school?"

Alex nodded. "Came out here to be closer to my boys and went to night school. I've been doing this now for ten years."

"How?" I said, shaking my head. "It would drive me crazy."

Alex nodded. "You have to have something inside that gets you through it."

"What is that for you?"

"Since you asked, I'll tell you. It's the same thing that got me through the bulimia. I have a strong religious faith."

Please don't let it be the Wheel.

"Mind if I ask you what it is?" I said.

"Christian."

"I believe in God, too."

"I'm glad, Mark. That will help."

To blow off steam I went to an acting class at Marty's. He was thrilled about my Number Seven part and announced it to the class. I got the usual tight smiles of affirmation—tight because actors' envy induces a certain lockjaw that can't be completely hidden.

After a couple of hours and some improv work, I actually felt refreshed. So much so that I decided to defy Jennings' threat and called Paula. I left this message:

"I'm not supposed to be calling you, according to your lawyer. So I won't do this anymore. I just wanted to have one last shot at asking if we can't sit down together again and try to talk this out. I know that didn't go so well last time and I'm sorry. I really am. I don't want this thing to drag out and be bad for everybody. You should know something pretty mind-boggling. My dad showed up. After all these years. Can you believe it? He saw something about us on the Internet and tracked me down. It's very strange, but he seems to have mellowed out with age, and he is very interested in seeing his granddaughter. Might that be possible sometime soon? I miss Maddie. When can I see her again? Call me if you want, I won't make a scene. Thanks."

When I walked into my apartment I was assaulted by a familiar odor, one I hadn't been around in years.

Out on the balcony, his feet up on the rail, Ron Reid was smoking a joint.

I practically tore the screen door off its rail.

"What are you doing!"

My voice startled him into an upright position on the chair. He held the marijuana cigarette daintily, like a lady at tea.

"You scared me," Ron said.

"You're smoking weed in my apartment?"

"I came outside."

"That's not the point!" I slapped my hips, making a popping sound. "I'm in a custody fight for my daughter here! I don't need you doing this! And where'd you get the money for dope?"

Ron remained terminally laid-back. "I had this with me. You want some?"

"No, I don't want some. You want to stay here, you get rid of it. Can you imagine what'll happen if I got busted for this?"

"Will you relax?"

There was a scratching sound from the balcony next door. Mrs. Williams, my very pleasant neighbor and Maddie's sometime babysitter, stuck her head out. "Everything okay out here?"

I stepped in front of Ron, to block him from being seen. "Fine, Mrs. Williams. Sorry I got a little loud."

"You having a party?"

"No, nothing like that. I'll keep it down."

"You tell Maddie I said hello now, you hear?"

"Yes, Mrs. Williams."

"You bring her on over sometime real soon."

"You got it."

She went back inside. I looked at Ron with fire in my eyes. "Listen, this is my place, okay? My rules. You want to stay here, you do what I say."

With raised hand, Reid said, "Okay, okay." He licked his fingertips and dampened the end of the joint. Then he popped the whole thing in his mouth and swallowed it. "Enough said?"

"Just don't do it again," I said.

Before he could respond, my cell went off.

It was, surprise of surprises, Paula.

"I got your message," she said. "Is your father really there?"

"Right here," I said.

"Unbelievable. What's he like?"

"Maybe I should go into that another time."

Pause. "There probably won't be another time. I really can't talk to you. My lawyer just called me. I guess you hired another lawyer, huh?"

"News travels fast."

"She called Bryce, to see what was up."

"And what is up?" I asked.

"You can't see Maddie right now, not until a court rules. You are going to be served. I'm sorry."

She sounded stiff and formal. It was almost worse than having her angry at me.

"So it's come down to this, huh?" I said.

"I have to go now."

"I'm not going to let you have Maddie."

The line clicked.

"Everything okay?" Ron said.

"Don't talk to me," I said.

— 3 —

"So much depends on the judge," Alex said. "If we get a bad one, a pro-Mommy judge, or someone who just doesn't trust men, it will be very bad."

"There's nothing we can do?" I had come into Alex's office on Friday to show her the papers that had been served on me. It was three days after my last phone conversation with Paula. I had seen little of Ron. He was out looking for work, he said.

"We have one peremptory," Alex said.

"What's that?"

"It's a 170.6 motion. Either party can reject a judge, one time, and the judge has to step down from that case. He can't inquire as to the reason. It's automatic. Problem is you might get one who's worse. The presiding judge, who makes the assignments, might try to figure out why you made the move, and get you to a judge who's just like the last one. We won't do this except as a last resort."

"It's pretty much a crapshoot then? The judge?"

"Pretty much."

"I'm so thrilled. So what's going to happen at the hearing?"

"Jennings will try to convince the judge you are not the right parent for Maddie to be with, pending an evaluation."

"Evaluation?"

"A mental health evaluator will be assigned to make a recommendation to the judge."

"Mental health? Am I going to have my head shrunk or something?"

"If he or she wants to shrink your head, you let them. The judge almost always follows the recommendation of the evaluator."

"Who are these people?"

"It varies. You have Ph.D.s in psychology, social workers, licensed evaluators fresh out of grad school. But they're people above all. Some have great judgment and insight into what kids need. Others are houseplants in shoes. Some are good-hearted, some are little Darth Vaders."

"Man."

"Exactly. We will cooperate with these people. You will treat them very nicely. You will not get angry, or you will not pass Go and collect your daughter."

"What else can I do?"

"Pray."

"That's not a very comforting thought."

She narrowed her eyes. "If you look at it right, it's the most comforting thought of all."

MEMORIES

That evening I went to a Mexican restaurant with Ron. My treat. He'd landed a job with a car repair shop on Vineland. Good news. I was going to tell him to move out. I just didn't know how to relate to him. And after the smoking incident, I didn't think it was a good thing to have him around. But where did that leave us?

"Good news about the job," I said as we went at a basket of tortilla chips.

"Yeah," Ron said. "I'm a productive citizen again."

"I'm glad."

"Thanks for not throwing me out."

"You thinking of getting a place?"

He nodded. "Soon. I promise."

"You have any friends out here you can stay with?"

"Not really. Maybe some guys I could look up." He crunched a couple of chips. If that can be done thoughtfully, that's the way he did it. "Listen, is there anything I can do for you, Mark? I mean, I feel like I owe you."

"Nah, you don't."

"But I do. I made some bad choices."

"We all do."

"Yeah, but you were my ... you are my son."

I still didn't know how to take that. "That's all past, Ron. I mean, I don't think of you as my father. How can I? I don't hold any bitterness toward you."

He looked skeptical.

"All right," I said. "Maybe I do. I didn't have a dad around and that bothered me. It bothered me that you never wrote. But maybe I was better off."

"How so?"

"You're a pot-smoking ex-con."

For an instant Ron looked stunned, then suddenly laughed. "I guess I deserve that."

But now I wanted more. "What are you like?"

"What do you mean?"

"I mean, what makes you up? What was your own father like?"

"Dad? He was a World War II vet, Navy. Man in the gray flannel suit type. Ran our house like a tight ship."

"Where was this?"

"Indianapolis. I couldn't get out of there fast enough. Got to San Francisco in time for the summer of love in '67. It was some scene."

"You did the whole drug deal?"

"It wasn't like that," Ron said, leaning forward. "It wasn't ever drugs for drugs' sake. We were looking for a higher reality to tune in to. It was like waking up from a deep sleep, which is what the fifties was like. We didn't want to grow up to be Ward Cleaver or Ozzie Nelson. Would you?"

I shrugged. "When you have a child, your ideas about that change."

"But it was an amazing time," Ron said.

"A lot of brains got fried, didn't they?" My mom, I remembered, had trouble holding a job. Gram always spoke about Mom with sadness, like Rainbow had been lost to her years before her actual death.

"Tell me about Paula."

"What about her?"

"What's she like?"

For a long moment I thought about it. "I don't know anymore. I thought I knew her. I loved her. I thought she loved me. Then she heads off to Europe. Maybe I was being naive."

"Stuff happens."

"That's very profound."

"The Wheel goes round and round. You have to accept that, just accept it."

"No," I said. "I'm not going to sit back while this happens. I have to fight."

"For Paula?"

"For Maddie."

"You still love Paula?"

"I don't know anymore." And at that moment I honestly didn't. You don't have the kind of love I had for Paula and just kick it out of your system.

"Hang in there," Ron said. "Just remember, the—"

"If you say anything about that stupid Wheel again, I'm going to throw the salsa at you."

At night, when alone in bed, memories of Maddie swirled around like gnats. I couldn't ignore them or get rid of them, so I let them come, even though they keep me awake.

I am sitting in the living room of the apartment, practicing some lines for an audition the next day. I'm supposed to be a young father with a kid. Typecasting. I can nail this.

Back and forth I walk, spouting line after line. ("Now don't you go out in the water unless I'm watching you!" my character dad says. "You stay where I can see you!")

And then I hear a CLOMP CLOMP.

Did Maddie drop something on the floor?

I stop and turn.

CLOMP CLOMP.

Maddie clomps in wearing a pair of my dress shoes. And a pair of pink underwear.

As I stand there trying to make sense of this new performance artist, Maddie holds her head up proudly.

"I am Queen of the Underwear," she announces.

Which cracks me up. I almost fall on the floor laughing, all the while wondering where on earth that had come from.

Maddie CLOMPS around some more and sings, "I'm Queen of the Underwearrrr."

That's when my dad voice kicks in and tells me to get some control. "That's a very funny song. Now what would you think about becoming Queen of the Clothes?"

"But I'm Queen of the Underwear."

"All right. I'm King of the Apartment. So I get to tell you to put on some clothes now."

Her Mussolini lip sticks out. "Do you have a duhjen?"

"You mean a dungeon?"

"You know, where you can put people."

"No, I don't have a dungeon."

She folds her arms. "Then I can still be Queen of the Underwear!"

I kneel. "Your highness, if Daddy really, really wanted you to put some clothes on, would you do it?"

Maddie considers this a moment, smiles, nods. "I am a good queen." She CLOMPS off to her room.

A short time later she comes out, having dressed herself in a shorts and a SpongeBob T-shirt. She puts her arms around my neck and kisses me.

"That was a fun game," she says. "What else can we play?"

– 2 –

I called Nancy at home the next morning. Technically, I shouldn't have. It was Saturday. But I didn't care from technically. And I was suddenly hot. Or maybe warm enough to break a sweat. That meant Nancy wouldn't be bothered so much to hear from me. I hoped.

"Any word on the contracts?" I asked.

"Working out some details," Nancy said. "You're going to be pleased."

"When?"

"A couple of days, no more. Then we'll get you a big fat check to cash. How's that?"

"That would be great."

"And what about you?"

"Me?"

"How you doing?"

"Fine."

"I mean really."

Really? I was not so good. I'd gone to the market earlier and saw something that almost flattened me. A father and his daughter holding hands, walking along the cookie aisle. The girl was about Maddie's age. The father was a young guy, younger than me, and he was having a conversation with the girl.

"Where was I before I was born?" I heard the girl ask.

"You were inside Mommy," the father said matter-of-factly.

"Before that where was I?"

The father thought a moment. Fascinated, I followed them. "You were a little egg and a little ..." He stopped himself. "You just weren't here yet."

"Where was I?" the girl insisted.

"You were in God's mind," the father said, pointing to his head.

And I felt a crushing inside me. It was the kind of conversation I used to have with Maddie. We'd had a bunch of them. She was so full of curiosity about things, always asking me questions. Now I realized the big silent void in my life was there because Maddie wasn't with me, asking questions.

To Nancy, who was my agent and not my psychotherapist, I said, "Really, I'm fine. I'll be just fine. Just show me the money."

She laughed. "Spoken like a true star in the making."

— 3 —

Two days later, Monday, I was in the courtroom of a judge named Harold J. Winger.

"Fair man," Alex had told me, which offered just a modicum of relief.

But any good feeling I had got sucked away when Paula entered the courtroom in the company of Bryce Jennings. Nor did it help that a train of reporters flowed in behind her. Paula was good copy now. I was just a subplot in her ongoing story.

Paula did not look at me. She wore sunglasses into the courtroom and was dressed like a star.

Bryce Jennings was dressed in a dark blue suit and a double-edged smile. He nodded at Alex. Alex nodded at him. Choose your weapons.

Paula sat down at the table near the jury box. I was seated at the other table, looking at her. She kept her face forward. She took off her sunglasses. Her beauty was breathtaking.

Alex patted my arm. Today was supposed to get me some time with Maddie. According to Alex, there was little chance I'd be denied it. Even if it meant being supervised, I'd get some sort of bone thrown my way. Then we could prepare for the big fight over custody to come later.

Fight. Just what I didn't want. But Alex said Jennings and Paula were taking a hard line, and we would have to do the same. And let the court sort it out.

Judge Winger walked in at precisely nine o'clock. He looked experienced. At least the lines in his face and gray hair indicated that. I hoped Alex was right, that he was a fair man.

He called our case immediately. Alex and Jennings stated their appearances for the record.

"We're here on a motion to modify the ex parte order entered by this court on August 5," Winger said. "The mother apparently has the daughter living with her, is that correct, Mr. Jennings?"

"Yes, Your Honor."

"All right. The issue is immediate sharing of custody, pending a final disposition. The father wants to see his daughter. Is that it, Ms. Bedrosian?"

"It is, Your Honor," Alex said.

"According to your moving papers," the judge shuffled something in front of him, "the last contact the father had with the daughter was on ... August 6?"

"Correct. Eight days ago."

"Any phone contact with the child?"

"None. And Mr. Jennings threatened my client with a harassment charge under the penal code, of all things, for any phone calling."

The judge looked at Jennings for a response.

"Mr. Gillen was calling my client constantly," Jennings said, "and she is feeling threatened."

Threatened? That was absurd! I may have let my voice get a little heated, but Paula knew I would never try to hurt her.

Winger pressed his little finger to his lip. "Is that really an accurate characterization? The word threat is pretty loaded."

Go judge, I was thinking. Tell him. Lay him out. Give me my daughter.

Bryce Jennings looked as cool as a Brioni-suited cucumber. "And we do not use that term lightly. This is all in the context of Mr. Gillen's assault on my client."

There was an audible gasp in the courtroom. And then I realized it came from me. Maybe Alex joined in, because she flashed a look my way that was both surprised and accusatory.

"You're alleging an assault?" Winger said.

"I can have my client testify if need be," Alex said.

"Maybe you'd better."

Alex said, "Your Honor, may I have a moment to confer with my client?"

"Go ahead."

Leaning over like an angry mother, Alex whispered, "What is this all about?"

"I guess I didn't mention it." My face was flushing. I was sure the reporters could see this.

"No, you didn't. Is it true?"

"I didn't throw the bottle at—"

"Bottle? You threw a bottle?"

"It was only water."

"At Paula?"

"No, at the ground. I was frustrated. It got out of hand."

"Why didn't you tell me?"

There was no good answer. Maybe I was just too embarrassed. Maybe I thought it would just go away. "I'm sorry."

"Is there anything else you want to add?" Alex said. "Any other skeletons rattling around?"

"No, honest."

Alex sighed and turned toward the judge. "May we approach the bench?"

The judge waved her up, along with Jennings. There was no jury, of course, but I think Alex wanted to keep something from the reporters. There was some spirited discussion, then the lawyers returned to their respective corners. I could tell from the look on Alex's face that she had come out on the short end.

Which meant Paula took the stand.

After she was sworn, Jennings started to walk her through the testimony. It was very clear to me that he had set this up, that he was planning to have Paula get on the stand and testify all along. It would make great copy.

"You met with Mr. Gillen on the afternoon of August 3, is that correct?" Jennings began.

"Yes," Paula said.

"At a restaurant in Beverly Hills?"

"Yes."

"And at the time, Mr. Gillen met you and—"

"Objection," Alex said. "Leading."

"Preliminary matters," Judge Winger said. "Overruled."

"Mr. Gillen met you and you sat at an outside table?"

"That's right."

"Can you tell us briefly what you discussed?"

Paula, looking both beautiful and vulnerable, said, "I suggested that, for Maddie's sake, we should discuss the divorce in a friendly way."

"What was Mr. Gillen's emotional reaction?"

"Objection," Alex said. "Speculation."

"Overruled," Judge Winger said. "The witness's state of mind is the issue."

"Angry," Paula said. "He was in denial and very antagonistic."

I almost jumped out of my chair. Finally I understood the meaning of the phrase raked over the coals. I started writing some notes on a legal pad.

"What led you to believe he was antagonistic?"

"Well, first he said he didn't want anything to be easy for me. He said he wanted to make things hard on me. When I finally saw there was no reasoning with him, I got up to go and he slammed his fists on the table and screamed at me."

Paula paused and Jennings said nothing. Letting it all sink in, I thought. The judge looked intensely interested.

"And then," Paula added, "he threw a bottle at me as I walked out."

Another dramatic pause. Like it had been rehearsed.

"What sort of bottle?" Jennings asked.

"I think it was a bottle of sparkling water."

"Did it hit you?"

"No, thankfully. It hit the ground and shattered."

"Were you hit by glass?"

"Some, yes. But mostly I was terrified."

Jennings nodded. "That's all, Your Honor."

"You may question the witness," the judge told Alex.

My lawyer rose, took my meager notes, and walked to the podium between the counsel tables.

"Ms. Gillen—"

"Excuse me, Your Honor," Jennings said. "My client's professional name is Montgomery. We request counsel to address her accordingly."

At that moment, for some reason, Paula looked at me. I couldn't quite read her face. But my eyes cried out to her. Why are you doing this?

She looked away.

"Proceed," Winger said.

"Ms. Montgomery," Alex said, "the bottle you say was thrown at you was actually thrown at the ground, was it not?"

"I didn't know that."

"That's not my question. The bottle hit the ground, not you, isn't that correct?"

"Technically."

"What does that mean, technically?"

"He threw the bottle toward me."

"That's a little different than at you, isn't it?"

"I don't know."

"You know your husband was once a star baseball player, don't you?"

Paula looked as surprised as I was. "Yes, of course I know that."

"Don't you think if he was going to throw a bottle at you he would have hit you with it?"

For a moment Paula was silent. She shrugged.

"Please answer out loud for the court reporter," Judge Winger said.

"I don't know," Paula said.

"Well, if you don't know," said Alex, "then you can't make this accusation about Mark throwing the bottle at you, can you?"

"The bottle shattered at my feet."

"Please answer the question."

"I have."

"Yes," Alex said. "Perhaps you have. I will leave that to Judge Winger." She turned to the judge. "No further questions, Your Honor. This has been a bald-faced attempt to sway you in your decision. I trust you will see through it."

"The court appreciates the trust of counsel," Winger said.

Jennings smiled. A couple of reporters in the gallery laughed. Everyone, it seemed, was amused. Except Alex and me.

– 4 –

During the recess Alex took me down the stairs to the cafeteria on the second floor of the courthouse. We bought coffee and she took me to a corner table where we could talk without a reporter listening in.

"Is there anything else you need to tell me?" Alex said. "Think hard."

"Honestly, I don't think so," I said. "I'm really sorry about the bottle thing. I just wanted it to go away."

"Instead, it sticks. If I'd known about it, I could have brought it up first and lessened the impact. But they did, and the judge looks at it as something we were trying to keep from him. Honesty, even if it hurts, is the best policy when you talk to your lawyer."

I was suddenly aware of someone standing next to the table. It was a young woman with short, styled hair and glasses with black frames.

"Excuse me," she said. "I'm Jan Solomon, LA Times. Mind if I—"

"I'm sorry," Alex said. "I'm in conference with my client."

"If I could just get a statement."

"No statements at this time."

The reporter looked at me. "Don't you want to tell your side?"

"He is telling his side in court," Alex said.

"About the bottle-throwing incident?"

"We really have nothing to say."

"Because it looked pretty bad in there."

My chest tightened. Alex got a look in her eyes like a tiger. That heartened me. What I needed was someone to fight for me, in and out of court.

"No statements, Ms. Solomon. Now if you'll excuse us?"

Alex's expression worked wonders. The reporter, without another word, walked away.

"Thanks," I said.

"You will not talk to reporters without my say, understood?"

"Understood."

"Back to business. The judge seemed impressed with the abuse allegation. Throwing the bottle made the difference."

"Can I get on the stand and explain?"

"It won't do any good. We agree you threw the bottle, even though not at her. What we're going to ask for is an emergency screening."

"What's that?"

"When one party is withholding custody the judge can order an evaluation to take place immediately. Within twenty-four hours. The evaluator will interview you, Paula, and most likely Maddie."

"Then what?"

"He or she makes a recommendation to the judge, who will more than likely follow it. It can be anything from full custody to no contact at all, pending a complete evaluation."

"And how long can that take?"

"A month, sometimes more."

"More? You mean I might not see Maddie for over a month?"

"It's possible."

"I want to know how possible." I could feel my face flush as I tried to process the thought of not seeing or hugging my daughter for that amount of time. How could they do this? I was beginning to understand what was behind some of the things Joe Pfeffer told me. Dads going a little nuts.

"It all depends on you and the evaluator," Alex said, "and I want you to be very aware of that fact. You are to be truthful and calm. Hostility is something they are going to look for in you. Do not show it. We'll talk more later when—" Alex's look swept past me. "Who is this?"

I turned around and saw Ron Reid, all smiles in his Hawaiian shirt, jeans, and sandals, striding towards us.

"The clerk upstairs said I might find you here," Ron said. He put his hand out to Alex. "I'm Ron Reid, Mark's father."

"I'm Alex Bedrosian, his lawyer."

There was no doubt at all who was the more important person in my life.

"I just wanted to show up and be a support," Ron said.

"Thank you," Alex said. "That was very nice."

She was sincere. But I also heard an edge in her voice that was meant to be a subtle signal.

"Anything to help," Ron said.

"Mr. Reid, I need to talk to Mark about a few more things."

"Mind if I?" He grabbed a chair from a neighboring table and slid it to ours.

"Ron," I said quickly, "this needs to be private."

"Oh," he said in mid squat. "Sorry. Sure. Hey. I'll see you later then, huh?"

"Right."

Looking embarrassed, Ron Reid left us. All part of the Wheel, I wanted to say.

Alex brought us back to the moment at hand, laying out what would happen when court resumed, preparing me.

I assured her I got it, that I was ready. And for a small moment in time, sitting at that table, I thought maybe things would start to turn my way a little bit. Get this screening over with, get to see Maddie again, maybe in a couple of days.

But I wasn't ready. How do you get ready for a landslide that buries you?

– 5 –

The first boulder knocked me down the next morning.

Ron was snoring away on the sofa when I went downstairs to get my LA Times. The front page had a headline about a speech by the president the night before. His picture was there with the American flag in the background.

I flipped the front page over to see what was below the fold. Something about an earthquake in Guatemala killing a few thousand people. A possible medical breakthrough for balding men.

Same old, same old.

But then, just before I started back up the stairs, I saw it.

On the bottom of the front page the Times runs some highlights of what's inside. Paula's name jumped out at me like a neon sign. A gossip bit about the child custody fight. And a father going berserk.

My hands started sweating as I pulled out the Metro section. Page two. And there it was, for all the world to see.

Like Father Like Son?

Paula Montgomery, who is hotter than hot after nabbing a role in the latest Antonio Troncatti film (and Troncatti himself, we might add!), was in court yesterday, trying to convince a judge to let her keep custody of her daughter, Madeleine, pending divorce proceedings. She is repped by none other than Bryce Jennings, which is not good news for the father, sometime actor Mark Gillen. Add this to the plotline: Gillen's own father, Ronald Reid, is an ex-con who has suddenly turned up on the scene. We don't know if this complicates matters or not, but it may explain one thing, the bottle Gillen threw at Montgomery in Beverly Hills. During what was supposed to be a civil meal to discuss Madeleine, Gillen threw a bottle of sparkling water at Montgomery. The bottle shattered on the sidewalk, injuring no one, but putting Montgomery in fear for her well-being — and that of her child. Gillen and his attorney, Alex Bedrosian, refused comment. But Reid had his own opinion: "Mark's going through a tough time right now. I'm just trying to help him through it, keep him from erupting." Maybe Gillen's next role will be that of volcano.

Stunned is too weak a word for what I felt. And like it or not I couldn't keep down a very real eruption bubbling up in me.

My face was burning by the time I slammed back into the apartment.

"Wake up!"

Ron was groggy under the blanket on the sofa. I yanked off the blanket. Ron was in boxer shorts. "Huh?"

"You talked to a reporter?"

"Oh." He rubbed his eyes. "Yeah."

"And told them I'm going to erupt?"

"Huh?"

I shoved the paper at him. "Look at that!"

He took the paper and sat up. I gave him time to read it, thinking I could get my breathing back down to normal range.

Finally he said, "It's not that bad."

With an angry swipe I ripped the paper out of his hands. "Not that bad? The judge is going to think I'm a walking time bomb or something."

"Well, aren't you?"

I gawked at him.

"I mean," Ron said, scratching himself, "you've been uptight ever since I've known you. I was just hoping ..."

"Hoping what?"

"I could help a little, you know?"

"By flapping your yapper?"

"No, by being a father for once in my life."

He looked down at the floor. And my anger started to subside a little. What was I looking at, anyway? A man whose life had pretty much gone down the toilet and maybe was looking for some self-respect. Problem was, it was at my expense. The way the cards were dealt, I just happened to be his son. That was nobody's fault.

One thing you don't want to do is take away a man's last shred of dignity. I saw that happen to a friend of mine, a forty-year-old character actor, who got ripped one day by a producer, a twenty-five-year-old New Yorker. The kid told my friend he was not a has-been but a never-was and a never-would-be. And I stood there and watched it. Nothing I could do consoled my friend, who later tried to kill himself with sleeping pills. He recovered, but left town for parts unknown. I don't know what happened to him.

So I stopped short of telling Ron Reid he was a boil on the backside of my existence.

"Look, I appreciate the attempt," I said. "But it didn't help. I don't want you talking to reporters, or showing up to court hearings, okay? Or living here. You've got a job now, maybe you can go out and get a place today."

There was a look of hurt on his face for a second. Then he said, "I'll try."

I sighed. "Let me give you some money to tide you over."

"You don't have to."

"You'll pay me back. If you need somebody to cosign for a place, I'll do that, too. But Ron ..."

He looked at me.

"No more trying to help on the custody thing. Okay?"

– 6 –

The bad part was I did not get a call from Nancy.

Usually, following good news or bad, I get a quick call from my agent. That's the good part of Nancy Radford. Unlike a lot of Hollywood agents, she keeps in touch with clients even if they're not "hot." There were times I had been in the ice tray and she still called me.

She always read the Times—both LA and New York—in the morning, and then the trades. She would have spotted the item about Paula and me. She should have called to buck me up a little.

Maybe she was sick. Maybe she had some emergency.

Or maybe she was really upset with me.

An actor's mind plays all sorts of tricks when his agent doesn't call. Mine did.

So I was not exactly in the best frame of mind when I arrived for my meeting with the court-appointed evaluator.

Her name was Sheila Bonner and she looked about thirteen. Her office was in a bank building in Encino. She was one of four names on a door on the third floor. Marriage and Family Counseling was the designation.

She did not smile once during our meeting.

"We're here for an emergency screening," she said. I thought of that Monty Python skit, I'm here for an argument, but kept my mouth shut as she closed the door to her small, inner office.

There were a couple of diplomas on her wall which, I trusted, meant she knew what she was doing.

"I'll ask you some questions, Mr. Gillen," Sheila Bonner said. "But I'd like to encourage you to open up as much as possible. Give me any information you deem relevant."

"Sure."

"Now, the court has asked me to discuss the relative merits of the two, distinct living situations. There is a slight burden upon you to justify a return of the child pending final disposition. Is that clear to you?"

"I guess."

"You guess?"

"What I mean is, I'm not sure why that should be, but I'll answer any questions you have as best I can."

She went for it without a flinch. "What assurances can you give me about your relationship with your daughter?"

I told myself to relax, feeling my jaw tense as I did. "Well, my relationship with my daughter, when I had it, was great."

"In what way?"

"Every way."

"Isn't that a bit of an overstatement?"

"I don't think ..." I stopped. Quick analysis. Alex had told me to be honest and objective. Yeah, of course I was overstating it. Making myself look good.

"You don't think what, Mr. Gillen?"

"I don't think there was any big negative with Maddie. There was the normal stuff a kid does that irritates the parent."

"Can you give me an example?"

I thought a moment. "A month or so ago she decided the funniest thing in the world was to make a fart sound on her arm."

Sheila Bonner said nothing.

"You know," I explained. "Putting her lips right here—" indicating the elbow crook—"and blat."

"This was an irritant to you?"

"After about the hundredth time."

"You didn't view this as the child's exercise of expression?"

"Yeah, of course I did."

"But you didn't say that."

I felt my right hand clenching. "You asked me about something that irritated me."

"Yes, and that's what we're exploring."

Who are you? Lewis and Clark? "I mean, if it keeps going on and on, you tell her to knock it off. And when she doesn't, you get a little ticked."

"Were those your words? 'Knock it off'?"

"I don't remember my words exactly. No, I don't think I said that to her. I was saying that to you." And whatever I was saying was coming out wrong. Not the way I wanted it to sound.

"Do you get irritated easily?" Sheila Bonner said.

Like now? "I don't think of myself that way."

"What about the bottle-throwing incident?"

"I didn't get a chance to explain in court."

"Go ahead."

"Yeah, I lost my temper there. I just wanted to get through to Paula. She's my wife. She left me for another man. She wouldn't listen."

"So you threw the bottle at her?"

"No. That wasn't it. I threw it at the ground. I just wanted to be heard. Like now."

"Do you think I'm not listening to you, Mr. Gillen?"

What was she doing? Trying to bait me? Then it occurred to me that's exactly what she was trying to do.

"I'm sorry," I said. "I'm just a little upset at this whole thing. You would be too if someone wanted to ... do you have kids?"

Wrong question. I could tell by the look on her face she didn't, and resented my asking.

"Let's keep the focus where it needs to be, Mr. Gillen."

"Sorry."

"Are you sorry? Or are you saying that just to please me?"

Oh man! "All I'm trying to say is that I love my daughter, I would never hurt her, and I want to be with her."

"Do you want to be with her because it's a way of getting her away from your wife?"

"No, that's not it at all."

She pushed her glasses up on her nose.

"Tell me about your father," she said.

"My father has not been part of my life."

"Why is that?"

"He was never around. He went to prison."

"What for?"

"I'm not sure. Something drug related."

"But he's back now?"

"A surprise to me."

"Is he living with you?"

"Was. He's out getting a place even as we speak."

"His status is a bit unfortunate for this case."

"He seems to be okay now," I said. Funny, but I was jumping to his defense without qualm. "I mean, he did his time. He's looking for work."

Sheila Bonner scribbled a note to herself. I wanted desperately to see what it was.

"Please," I said. "Please let me see my daughter. With everything in me I'm telling you I am not going to do anything wrong. I just want to hold her again. I miss her ..." My voice choked. I felt embarrassed.

"Let's take a short break," she said.

— 7 —

Powerlessness. That's how I felt when I finally got out of the wringer that was Sheila Bonner.

The rest of the grilling had gone pretty much the same way. Now Ms. Bonner held my immediate future in her hands. A future with or without Maddie.

I could hardly stand the wait until tomorrow, when we'd be back in court.

I drove over to Jerry's Famous Deli, where industry types like to eat. It boosted my ego a little. As an out-of-work actor I'd come here and eat the pickles. Now I was, at least, going to have a regular part on a series. I could afford a sandwich.

I ordered a pastrami on rye and looked at a copy of Variety. Couldn't focus on anything. My mind was playing a movie.

⸺〜⸺

Fade in: Troncatti's massive home. Maddie wakes up in a big, fluffy bed, surrounded by a whole bunch of new stuffed animals.

She goes down for breakfast in the huge dining room, overlooking a pool in the backyard.

"Can I swim today?" she asks Antonio Troncatti. "Tony" is reading Variety and sipping espresso.

"Of course-a you can, bambina," he says (my movie has clichés and Troncatti's voice sounds like he's from The Godfather).

Paula wanders in, kisses Troncatti. "Maybe we can take Maddie to Disneyland today, huh?"

"You want-a Disneyland?"

"Yes!" Maddie says.

"You got-a Disneyland!"

After Troncatti goes off to do his hair and nails, Maddie looks at Paula. "When will I see Daddy again?"

Paula gets very serious. "Honey, Daddy doesn't want to see us anymore."

"Huh?"

"Daddy tried to hurt me, you see. And he might do the same to you."

"But Daddy wouldn't ever —"

"Daddy's not the same person he was. That's why I brought you here, to live with Tony and me. You're safe here, and you'll have everything you want."

"But won't Daddy be lonely?"

"No, honey. Daddy doesn't like us anymore. He told me so."

Lies! I almost shout it out right there in Jerry's. Am I going crazy now? Is that the way it's going to be? Will I ...

"Are you okay?"

I looked up and saw a woman, about twenty-five, with silky blond hair.

"What?"

"You looked like you had a pain there," she said. "I'm sorry, I just wanted to say hi to you."

She looked vaguely familiar.

"I'm Nikki McNamara," she said. "From Gower Presbyterian."

I did recognize her. We'd passed each other the last time I was at church. I asked her to have a seat.

"I'm supposed to meet someone," she said. "So don't think me rude if I get up."

"Hey," I said, "at this point rude would be a step up."

She looked at me quizzically, but then she smiled. It was a great smile, too.

"You're an actress," I said.

"Is it that obvious?"

"Just a hunch. You could throw a dart in here and odds are you'll hit an actor or a screenwriter."

"I'm in the theater company at the church. Actors Cooperative. Heard of it?"

"Yeah. You get some great reviews."

"We have good people."

"Are all of you members of the church?"

"Not all of us. We're all Christians, though."

"Christian actors? You don't hear that term much in this town. Sort of like honest lawyer."

She laughed. "Before I do any more confessing, you didn't tell me your name."

"Mark Gillen."

"Nice to meet you."

"Likewise."

My sandwich arrived.

"Can I buy you lunch?" I said.

"Oh, thanks. I'm meeting someone."

"Right." I found myself hoping it wasn't a man.

"Are you getting involved at Gower Pres?"

"Well, I sort of go sometimes. I'm leaning in that direction."

"Going to church?"

"God and things."

"That's good. God is a very good thing."

"I'm hoping."

Nikki cocked her head, waiting for me to explain.

"Just for personal reasons," I said.

"You an actor?"

"My SAG card says I am."

"Cool. Why don't you come by and hang with us?"

"Really? When?"

"We have a Wednesday night Bible study and play reading. Down at the church. Hey, tomorrow. Come by about seven."

"Yeah," I said. "Maybe I will."

"I hope you do."

"Hey, Nikki." A dark-haired woman, a little older than Nikki, came over to the table.

"Here she is," Nikki said. "This is Cheline Lester. Another of the gang. Cheline, this is Mark."

We exchanged pleasantries. Nikki stood up. "Thanks for the chat."

"Sure."

Off they went. And I found myself surprised at how glad I was Nikki had not met a man.

At 2:30 I called Nancy and got her assistant.

"She's in a meeting, Mark," Rachel said.

"Can you have her give me a call on my cell?"

"Sure thing."

I drove over to Tower Records and spent a little time listening to sound tracks. Movie scores are my favorite kind of music. I love the classic Maurice Jarre scores to movies like Doctor Zhivago and Witness. And Bernard Herrmann, who made the Hitchcock experience so much more memorable. I also like the haunting, lyrical quality of some of the new ones, like Mark Isham, who did October Sky and A River Runs Through It.

It's the sort of music that can transport you.

Around four I went to the newsstand at Van Nuys and Ventura and got a USA Today. My attention span could only take in nugget-sized chunks. McNewspaper was perfect.

I was reading about a bombing in Tel Aviv when my phone went off.

"Sorry I couldn't get back to you sooner," Nancy said.

"A busy agent is a good agent."

Silence.

"You there?" I said.

"Mark, can you swing by?"

"Now?"

"Yes."

"I suppose I can. Why?"

"Just come in."

I knew then it was bad news. An agent always tells you the good stuff over the phone.

"What is it, Nancy? Tell me now."

"Mark—"

"Please."

"I'd rather you come in."

"Is it about Number Seven?"

"Yes."

"Tell me. Tell me now."

Pause. "They dropped you, Mark."

VISIONS

Of course I knew it was not a good thing to curse at God. Did I care?

No.

My curse took the form of tears at first. I cried hard, for the first time in a long time. I sat in my car so people on the street couldn't see me unless they looked real hard. No one did.

Offing myself entered my head for a moment, making an appearance like a ham actor with two lines. That scared me a little. But the thought didn't hang around, and I chalked it up to the stress of the moment and yelled at myself for being such a wimp.

The next option seemed better. I drove down Ventura looking for a LIQUOR sign. No way I was going in to see Nancy. Not in the mood I was in. Changing my mood is why I wanted a liquor store. I found one a few blocks away and pulled into the parking lot.

And sat there for about fifteen minutes. My legs wanted to walk in and buy a bottle of Jack Daniel's. My throat thought it was a great idea, too. But I fought it. For some reason I was thinking of that old movie, The Lost Weekend, where Ray Milland does a great job showing the horrors of drink. He goes a little nuts, sees terrible visions.

An argument started in my head, like when the little angel and the little devil sit on opposite shoulders in a cartoon. The devil was saying this would be a one-time thing, and where was the harm if you're alone and responsible? The angel kept saying Maddie's name, over and over.

I didn't buy the booze. And I was mad about that, so I screeched into a Jack in the Box and ordered four — count 'em, four — spicy chicken sandwiches. I wolfed one down as I got on the freeway, so I could drive fast. I wolfed down another one as I tore down the Santa Monica freeway and then up the 405.

My stomach was full but I managed to stuff a third belly bomb down my throat, not caring if it came back up.

At 6:45 I saw I was coming up on Universal Studios. The big black tower where the suits make all the decisions hovered over the freeway like some glass King Kong. Up on the hill, Universal City Walk, a neon jungle of overpriced tourist stores and restaurants, was getting ready for the evening rush. Colored lights would be evident soon, turning the sky into some sort of artificial impressionist canvas—the color of LA hip.

And for one second I almost felt better. Despite all the crud that happens here every day, I actually like Los Angeles. It's my home, where I grew up, and I know it well. I've had dark days when everything seemed pointless turn into warm, pleasant memories in various places in the city—going with friends to the Hollywood Bowl; sloshing in the surf at Zuma Beach; kickin' it with Roland and some cool jazz.

All of that hit me at once under the shadow of Universal, and I was just about to let all the bad stuff melt away.

That's when the kid in the truck cut me off.

Weaving in and out of lanes is almost a sport in LA, especially if you're a punk with a pickup. More and more of these testosterone-laced, backward-baseball-hat-wearing dweebs are being handed trucks by Mommy and Daddy so they can race around at ninety miles per hour and show how macho they are.

Any pleasant change got yanked away from my spirits, as if chained to the guy's bumper. And anger flared.

So I chased him. Flashing my lights. Honking.

Road rage. Another urban sport.

What was I doing? People get shot over this stuff. I didn't care. There was no justice in the world, so I was going to bring a little to the blacktop.

I changed lanes without a signal, cutting off a guy in a Toyota. He honked at me, and that added more fuel to the chase.

Traffic slowed, and the truckster got pinned up ahead, giving me the chance to really lay it on his backside with my horn. He cut over a lane, almost nicking a Mercedes.

I followed, gunning the gas. No thoughts at all in my mind, just a blind desire to make life miserable for someone besides myself.

It felt good to be mad. It felt good to have all other thoughts run away and hide in fear of my all-consuming rage.

The pickup found an opening that let him get a good lead. I was hemmed in for the moment, but it wouldn't be for long.

I changed lanes again, in front of a Ryder truck, the driver of which added to the fun by blaring his horn at me.

A little VW got in my way, slowing for no good reason, so I gave it a good rebuke from my horn. The driver, an Asian woman, looked back at me, confusion on her face. I honked again.

On I went, keeping the truck in sight. Not knowing — not caring — what I'd do if I ever followed it off the freeway. Crazy time.

Then I noticed the flashing lights behind me.

My nerve endings erupted. That couldn't be for me. No way was I being told to pull over by the California Highway Patrol.

No, no, no, no, no, no!

Yes. He was on my tail. And the jerk in the truck was getting away.

Come on!

The Chippie blared his siren. I was toast.

I took the next off ramp, driving as carefully as I could. Staying within the lines. Maybe I could act my way out of this one. After all, how bad could this be? I hadn't hurt anyone. It was not my fault!

I pulled to a stop across from a tire store.

The CHP officer was not a he. It was a woman. Tough looking. But somehow this gave me hope. Call me a chauvinist, but I was sure I'd get through this okay.

"May I see your driver's license please?" Her chest pin said MEADOWS.

"Was I speeding?" A cliché was all I could come up with.

"License, please."

Right. And after countless cop encounters on TV, I knew I had to remove it from my wallet. I tried to keep my hands from shaking too badly. So far so good.

Officer Meadows glanced at my license. "Mr. Gillen, did you know you were weaving on the freeway for about three miles?"

"Weaving?"

"Yes, sir."

"Oh, I may have been a little distracted."

"Distracted?"

"Did you see that guy ahead of me?"

"All I saw was you changing lanes without signaling, weaving in and out. That's reckless driving."

"Wait." I put my hands out like a kid caught in the kitchen before dinner. "There was a guy who cut me off and I ..."

"Wanted to teach him a lesson?"

"Officer, come on."

"Have you had anything to drink?"

"What? No!"

"Do you mind stepping out of the car?"

Stepping out? What was this?

"Am I under arrest? Don't I get to talk to an attorney?"

"Please step out of the car, sir."

Something happen, please. An earthquake would be good. A nice California 6.9 shaker ...

I got out, on solid ground.

"I am going to ask you to perform a test," Officer Meadows said.

"I am not drunk! I have had nothing to drink!" The injustice of the accusation really hit me, especially after I'd talked myself out of the Jack Daniel's.

"Listen to my instructions, sir." Meadows removed a pen from her pocket. "I am going to ask you to keep your head straight and follow the movement of this pen with your eyes. Is that clear?"

"This is ridiculous."

"Are you refusing?"

"Let me level with you," I said. "I need a break here. I'm in a big-time battle for custody for my daughter. She's only five, and I think she is getting hurt, and I'm getting hurt, and this doesn't make one bit of difference to you, does it?"

Officer Meadows shook her head.

"Then give me a test," I said. "I want you to take me in and have me pee in a cup. I want to see your face when the test results come back. Just do it, Officer Meadows."

What she did was write me up for reckless driving, right on the spot.

Then she actually said, "Have a nice day." Sometimes Los Angeles is a sprawling city of clichés.

Ron was watching TV when I walked through the door.

"Good news, Mark. I found a place."

"Great."

"Yeah. Little studio. Not the nicest, but I think I can make it work."

"When do you move in?"

"Tomorrow. That cool?"

"Groovy," I said, tossing out a word he might appreciate. Truth be told, I was getting annoyed at the sight and sound of him. He was a graying longhair who seemed to have missed the reality boat. He was still living in the age of Hendrix, whose music I could do without.

Ron looked at me. "Only ..."

"Only what?"

"I hate to ask."

"Money?"

Ron Reid shrugged.

"I just gave you a hundred," I said. "Where did it go?"

"I didn't spend it."

"You didn't score some dope, did you?"

"Hey, man."

"Hey nothing."

"Whoo. Something happen today?"

"Forget about it."

"Come on. Let me help you get out of this reality."

"Ron, do me a favor."

"Yeah?"

"Put a cork in it."

– 2 –

The next day I was in a daze so thick it was like I had a brain disease. This did not help my tips at Josephina's. I worked lunch and messed up just about every order. I dropped a tray of linguine on the floor; I knocked a lemonade onto the dress of a business-woman who had the sense of humor of Dr. Kevorkian.

All the while I kept thinking about the time Maddie took care of me.

It was a day I was fighting a horrific cold. I'd been out on an audition, for Pepsi, and just couldn't give it anything. When I rounded up Maddie from Mrs. Wilson's, I was pretty much thrashed.

I'd promised Maddie we'd have hamburgers, the way I make them. I put little bits of onion in the meat, and Maddie likes that. But all I could do was plop down on the sofa.

Instead of talking to me, Maddie went into the bathroom and wet a washcloth, came out, and put it on my forehead. Even though I didn't have a fever, it felt right. And Maddie sat by me and stroked my hair.

She wanted to make me feel better, she said.

If only she could have made me feel better about working the lunch crowd. But my shift was ruined. Afterward I called Alex. We were due back in court tomorrow, and she said there was nothing else I needed to do—except not get arrested.

Funny.

I called Nancy, partly out of a wish to see if this was all just a bad dream. Maybe yesterday never happened. Maybe I was going to wake up like Dorothy, back in Kansas, looking at Barbara DiBova standing there with my contract. I had this terrible dream, and you were there ...

But I didn't wake up in Kansas. Nancy was sympathetic, but something cool had drifted into her voice. You learn to pick that up with agents. It was the sort of chill that announces a client is about to become too much trouble.

With nothing to lose, I plowed right through it. "Did you ask DiBova why they dropped me?"

"Best to leave it alone, Mark."

"Don't we deserve some sort of answer?"

"It's their show."

"I want to know."

"Leave it alone."

"I'll call her myself."

"Mark," Nancy warned, "don't do that. You had a setback, but you don't need to stir up more trouble."

"Why not? Maybe that's just what I need to do."

"I'm telling you. Don't."

"Whose side are you on?"

"Cool off, Mark."

Click.

And suddenly, here I was again. About to blow up. Not what I needed to do with Maddie's future on the line.

I remembered it was Wednesday.

Nikki McNamara.

Bible group.

But mostly, Nikki McNamara.

When I got there, she was the first one I saw. She rushed over, welcoming me with a big smile. "You made it!"

"I'm here." I felt like the new kid in school.

"I'll introduce you around."

There were about forty people there, mostly actors. I didn't know there were that many Christian actors in LA. A couple of them I recognized from auditions. One of them, Tom Starkey, was pretty big now. He had a great ongoing role in an ABC drama. He also led the Bible study.

Which was out of Romans. We sat in a big circle on folding chairs. The room was large but warm. A big portrait of an older woman—looking like anyone's favorite grandmother—beamed down at us. I found out later it was a woman named Henrietta Mears, a famous Bible teacher from some time back.

Starkey had people open their Bibles (I shared with Nikki). And we read from chapter 8.

"Therefore, there is now no condemnation for those who are in Christ Jesus, because through Christ Jesus the law of the Spirit of life set me free from the law of sin and death. For what the law was powerless to do in that it was weakened by the sinful nature, God did by sending his own Son in the likeness of sinful man to be a sin offering. And so he condemned sin in sinful man, in order that the righteous requirements of the law might be fully met in us, who do not live according to the sinful nature but according to the Spirit."

Whoosh. That just blew right by me. I had no idea what this all meant. Sin offering? Condemning sin in sinful man? It sounded weird.

Starkey, though, was good at explaining things. His voice was easy and his enthusiasm obvious. He wasn't acting. He really was into this stuff.

Bottom line, he said, Jesus was indeed a sacrifice in the Old Testament sense, when they used to sacrifice animals all the time. Jesus was different. His sacrifice was for everyone. Once and for all.

I still didn't get it all, but it sounded better by the time Starkey was finished. It made me want to come back for more.

Afterward, several in the study went for coffee at a little café on Franklin. Nikki asked me if I wanted to tag along.

It was fun. For the first time in a long time, it was actually fun to hang out with some people. They were into movies and theater and music. Topics flew around like birds. I laughed and let the troubles drift to the back of my mind for a while.

When I talked to Nikki, they went away almost completely.

She was from San Diego, had been a theater major at the University of California down there. "Got to LA about three years ago," she told me. "Been knocking on doors ever since."

"How's it going?"

"I've been up for a few things, nothing big yet. Doing theater with the co-op has been a godsend."

"Too bad it doesn't pay."

"It does in other ways." She took a sip of coffee. "Acting for the soul can save your life."

"How so?"

She smiled. "I'm a preacher's kid. You know what happens to them?"

I shook my head.

"We usually start rebelling around fourteen, fifteen. Smoking after school. Hanging out with the wrong boys. I put my dad through what must have been a meat grinder for him. One reason I went to UCSD was to party. Actually didn't talk to Dad for three years."

She said all this with a certain sadness and took a breath. "Came up here more or less lost. Knew I was running away from God. Also knew I wanted to be an actor. Didn't care how or what.

It was rough for the first six months. I didn't get a single thing. And then I was looking through Back Stage West and saw Actors Cooperative was having auditions for The Hasty Heart."

"Great play."

"You know it?"

"Sure. Great movie, too. With Ronald Reagan and Richard Todd."

"Yes!" Nikki smiled. "I got the Patricia Neal role. And that's what did it for me."

"Did what?" I was intensely interested.

"My friend, Cheline, you met her at Jerry's? She has this saying about great art. It doesn't preach at you, but it makes you homesick for heaven. There's that part in all of us that seeks God, even if we choose to ignore it. The play opened up that part of me again. It brought me back to God. And that's how acting saved me."

We sat in silence for a moment. Nikki looked momentarily embarrassed that she had opened up so much. Without thinking about it, I put my hand on her arm.

"Thanks," I said.

She looked at me and I melted into her eyes.

"I needed to hear something like that," I said. "I got dropped from a new TV show that I was supposed to get."

"Oh no."

"Old story, different tune. I just need to regroup, figure out why I'm an actor." I took a sip of coffee. "I wonder if I could join," I said. "The theater group and the church."

"Really?"

"Think I can?"

"Church, of course. There's a new member class. And we have auditions every quarter for the company. If you want, I can set one up."

"You would do that?"

Nikki smiled again. "All you have to do is prepare a scene."

My mind clicked like a well-oiled machine. "Would you do one with me?"

"Me?"

"Only if you have time."

She looked at my left hand. "What would your wife think?"

It was like an ocean wave hitting me square in the face.

"That's kind of a difficult question right now," I said.

"I'm sorry."

"No, you're right to ask. She's living with another man. She wants a divorce."

Nikki's face reflected sympathy. She didn't have to say anything.

"I'm just trying to lead a normal life," I said, "in the midst of all this. Which means trying to be an actor."

There was a long silence. "Okay," Nikki said.

"Okay?"

"I'll do a scene with you. As a favor to a fellow actor."

I could not have begun to tell her how good that made me feel. We spent another hour or so chatting it up, laughing with the others, talking movies and theater and the bottomless pit of TV.

I left feeling good. It was a feeling that would last exactly nine hours.

– 3 –

"The court has taken into consideration the report of the evaluator," Judge Winger said the next morning, an unseasonably cold Thursday. "I have also considered the testimony offered in this matter, and the court rules that the respondent, Ms. Montgomery, shall retain physical custody of the child, pending final resolution. The court will allow two supervised visits by the father, Mr. Gillen, on the following two Tuesdays, for two hours each, with a third party present ..."

His words faded in and out of my brain. Paula had custody? But I was going to see Maddie?

" ... as appointed by the court. Costs for the monitor to be paid by Mr. Gillen. We'll set this matter for hearing September 25 if that is acceptable to both parties."

And just like that it was over. Head swirling, I followed Alex out of the courtroom. (Paula didn't appear at the session. At least I was spared that.)

"So I get to see Maddie?" I felt like a kid asking about going to Disneyland.

"Yes, supervised," Alex said.

"Why? The judge thinks I might do something?"

"He went along with the evaluator."

"That thirteen-year-old? Bonner?"

"This is just temporary. Now we go to work on the formal custody hearing."

"When do I get to see my daughter?"

"I'll call you."

"Alex, please."

She grabbed my shoulders, looking at me as much like a parent as a lawyer. "Mark, this is the first round. I told you to be prepared for a tough fight. Here is the good news. You will get to see Maddie again. And soon. It's a matter of setting things up —"

"Supervised visit. He said supervised."

"That's not unusual. Focus on this. You will be holding your daughter in your arms soon. Think about that, will you?"

I was more than happy to.

***

There are, they say, five stages in an actor's life.

In stage one, the casting director says, "Who is Mark Gillen?"

Stage two: "Get me Mark Gillen."

Stage three: "Get me a young Mark Gillen."

Stage four: "Get me a Mark Gillen type."

Stage five: "Who is Mark Gillen?"

The great fear of actors is that they'll go from stage one to stage five without those other steps in between. What's that line from the Dionne Warwick song about San Jose? Years pass so quickly, and the actors who thought they'd be stars are parking cars or pumping gas.

That fear is a little ferret in the belly of actors, and the only way to keep it quiet is to do something.

Well, I did something, all in the grip of this elation over Maddie. That emotion does funny things to your mind, especially after you've been hammered. You start to feel that the momentum is changing, like in a basketball game. Not something you can measure, but you have the feeling you're about to go on a roll, can't be stopped.

Sure it was only a small victory, getting supervised visits, but it was huge to me. I wanted to see Maddie again, hold her, laugh with her, more than anything in my life. And soon I would get to.

But this sort of mind-set can create a false sense of confidence, too. So I took my giddiness, mixed it with the fear of failing as an actor, and went out and did something really stupid.

I drove from the courthouse over to the Burbank Studios. I told the guard it was Mark Gillen to see Lisa Hobbes. He made a call, then gave me a temporary parking pass.

I was in.

Lisa met me outside the office of DiBova Productions. She did not look happy. "What are you doing here?"

"I came to see Barbara."

Lisa's nostrils flared in what was her characteristic gesture of disbelief. "Without an appointment?"

"I need an appointment?" I said with mock surprise.

"Idiot," Lisa said. "What do you want?"

"Really. I just want to ask her a question."

"But you can't."

"Why not?"

"She's in a meeting."

I folded my arms. "That's the oldest one in the book."

"She really is in a meeting, Mark."

"I can wait."

"I shouldn't have let you on the lot," Lisa said. "This is about Number Seven, isn't it?"

"Ding ding ding."

"You can't change that, Mark."

"I just want to know why. Is that so unfair? I had the thing and then it's pulled out from under me. Maybe you can you tell me."

Lisa shrugged. "Things happen. Decisions get made. You know the drill."

"But I killed the reading." I tried not to let desperation make my voice all squeaky. "Barbara was hot to get me, my agent says. I want to know what changed."

"You know how this business is. Sometimes it just doesn't make sense. I'm really sorry —"

"What happened, Lisa? You know, don't you?"

She did not answer.

"You do know why." I almost jumped down her throat.

"Mark, don't." She put up her hands and took a step back.

"Why, Lisa?"

"Just let it go, Mark. You'll have other chances."

"I want to know about this one."

"I need to get back —"

She started to turn but I grabbed her arm. She jerked it away. "Don't."

"Please," I said.

"I can't tell you anything." But from her look I knew she could. There was more here and she wasn't letting me in on it. Which only made me crazy.

"You can't do this!" I shouted.

"I'm not doing anything."

"I thought you were a friend."

"Mark, don't put that on me."

"Why shouldn't I?"

Before Lisa could say another word a security guard with a shaved head seemed to appear out of thin air. He looked like he chewed bones.

"Problem?" he said, glaring at me.

"No," Lisa said. "He was just leaving."

I told myself it had to be the publicity angle. Barbara DiBova and the powers that be decided my profile in the papers made me too, what, unstable to work with?

But part of me argued that in a world full of Sean Penns and Russell Crowes, having negative publicity didn't really matter. In fact, it might even raise ratings.

At the same time, I knew that wasn't really it. There was something else going on, beneath the surface.

Or maybe I was just losing it, becoming another paranoid actor who ends up old and unemployed, muttering lines to himself on the corner of Hollywood and Vine.

The bone-chewing security guard made sure I found my way to my car, and watched me drive off the lot. I sort of lost track of time after that.

– 4 –

Maddie had a spell there where she had frequent nightmares. She'd wake up screaming. I'd jolt out of my sleep like someone getting a cattle prod in the back and run to her room to calm her down.

One time, when Paula was off shooting her movie, Maddie screamed for me around midnight. I ran into her room and she made me get in bed with her. She buried her head in my arm.

"He's in the closet," she said.

"Who?"

"The bad man."

"What bad man? Was he in your dream?"

She nodded, keeping her head buried.

"Why is he in the closet?"

"He wants all our Cheerios," Maddie said.

That made me crack up.

"It's not funny," Maddie insisted.

"Why does he want our Cheerios?"

"I don't know. He wants to eat them all up."

"Do you want me to get rid of him?"

Nod.

"Wait here," I said. I slipped out of the bed. Maddie put the pillow over her head as I went and opened her closet. A little part of me wondered if there really might be a Cheerio bandit inside. "You have to leave now," I said to the little dresses. "And don't ever come back again."

"No, Daddy," Maddie said in a muffled voice. "He's in the hall closet."

"Oh, sorry."

I tromped out to the hall, opened the closet, and picked a mean-looking jacket. "You hear me? Get out! Don't come back, ever!"

Maddie was out of the pillow when I got back.

"Was there really a man in there?" she asked.

"What do you think?"

She thought for a long moment. "If he wasn't, who were you talking to?"

I cradled her in my arms. "I was showing you what I'd do if

there ever really was a man who wanted our Cheerios. Or anybody else who tries to scare you. I'll always protect you, okay?"

Her little head went up and down on my chest, happily. I loved that.

I was thinking about that moment eating my own bowl of Cheerios the next morning. Ron Reid called to tell me his new address. I wrote it down, though I still didn't know what to do about this guy. He did not seem like my father, and I was sure he never would. That hole in me was going to stay.

After breakfast I walked to Samuel French to pick up a couple of fresh paperbacks of Hamlet, the scene I decided to do with Nikki. It was good to be in there, surrounded by plays. Made me feel like I was still an actor. Out of work, without pay. Still hurting from betrayal. But hey, I could still say lines. I could still act.

Around noon I got a call. From Lisa Hobbes.

"This is a surprise," I said.

"You free to meet?"

—~—

"What are we doing in the back of a used bookstore?"

"Looking for The Complete Idiot's Guide to Being an Idiot," Lisa said. "By Mark Gillen."

"Thank you."

"Don't mention it."

Lisa had asked me to meet her at Book Central in North Hollywood, a big used-book store that does a heavy trade. It was housed in a two-story building off Lankershim, near Blockbuster Video. Inside it was all wood and musty smell. So the meeting with Lisa seemed clandestine and mysterious, something out of a forties film noir.

I found her in the back corner of the first floor, actually wearing dark glasses.

The first thing she said when she saw me was, "You almost got me canned."

"Nice to see you, too."

"You hear what I'm saying?"

"What did I do?"

"Barbara saw you."

"DiBova?"

"No, Bush. Of course DiBova."

I slapped a shelf of books, hitting, I think, a volume of Victor Hugo. "I'm sorry. All I was looking for was a reason."

"Yeah, with this big chip on your shoulder. So Barbara asks me what you wanted. More to the point, she asked me what I was doing out there talking to you."

"What, did she think I was packing heat or something? Going in to shoot up the place?"

"You never know. You're the actor. You're one of the crazy people."

"So what did you tell her?"

"I told her you'd left your SAG card with me and came to pick it up."

"Why did you do that?"

Lisa put her hands on her hips. "To save your sorry butt, that's why. You are on thin ice right now. You can't afford to make things worse."

"What do you mean thin ice?"

"The whole Paula thing. You're not exactly smelling like a rose."

"Is that the reason they decided to stab me in the back? They were so afraid of bad publicity?"

"That's part of it."

"Excuse me. Didn't Barbara DiBova do time at Betty Ford? That didn't seem to hurt her any."

"She's a name. She's a player. Drug rehab can be a career boost if you've got game. But who are you?"

"Thanks again."

Lisa sighed. "Look, sorry. I'm blunt. You know me. I always have been. But I like you, Mark. Would I be here if I didn't?"

"You said that was only part of it, the publicity. What else?"

Lisa ran her finger along the spines of some books. "Don't say anything about this, okay? Don't tell anybody, ever, we had this conversation."

"This is starting to sound very All the President's Men."

"If this ever gets back to Barbara, I'm toast."

"You're really serious."

"Yeah, genius, I am."

"What's wrong?"

An old man with a crooked, wooden cane and smelling of Old Spice and older wool, shuffled to the shelf next to us. He put his nose near the titles and started scanning. He was obviously going to be awhile.

Lisa motioned for me to follow her to the staircase at the back of the store. They creaked like a haunted house as we went up. We were in paperback fiction now, mysteries. Which seemed appropriate.

I was busting at the seams. "So what is going on?"

Lisa spoke in a low voice. "I hard-copy Barbara's e-mails, the ones she marks. And then file them by date. Other ones she marks for trash. Usually, she trashes them herself. Sometimes not. It depends. I'm supposed to go through the trash at the end of the day and make sure nothing was put in that wasn't marked for it. Doesn't take long. Just a quick scan. Last Monday I did that and saw one in the trash with the subject line Seven. Which obviously meant Number Seven."

"And?"

"I read it. Barbara has a special file for Number Seven, and I thought she'd put this in by mistake. Turns out this e-mail was about you."

My throat started to close. "From who?"

"Leonard Remey."

No way. Remey was a big-time agent at AEA, one of the top three agencies in town. Paula's new agency, in fact. "Remey was talking about me?"

"I have to assume."

"So what was in the message?"

"All it said was, 'Re: our conversation. Yes, has to go. Non-negotiable.'"

"How do you know that was about me?"

"Who else from Number Seven was let go?"

The sea of books around us actually started to undulate in my vision, like some old movie effect where a guy's about to pass out. "But why? Why would Leonard Remey be sticking his nose in my life?"

"I have a theory."

"Tell me."

Lisa sighed. "You know who he represents?"

"Yeah, Paula and a lot of big names."

"Including Antonio Troncatti."

Boom. I felt like I'd been jabbed in the face by a heavyweight. "You think Troncatti is behind my getting axed?"

"Look at the way it's worded," Lisa said. "It sounds like DiBova checked with Remey on whether you really had to go."

"And he said yes, nonnegotiable. And DiBova caved." My voice slammed into the shelves.

"Of course she caved. It goes back to what I've been saying. In the pecking order, Remey is up here—" Lisa put her hand up high—"and Barbara is here." She put her hand about shoulder level. Then she dropped it to her side. "And you're here. Remey has a lot of people Barbara wants to work with, so she's not going to fight him when it comes to an actor who has yet to break into the big time."

Emotions flared around inside me, like random fireworks. If this was all true, and it sounded too smarmy not to be, it was Antonio Troncatti himself who had cut the legs out from my career. My head started to feel real tight.

"I had to tell you." Lisa put her hand on my arm. "I think it stinks. But I wanted to tell you so you knew what you're up against. If you want to keep acting, you need to walk away from this thing with Paula as quietly as you can."

- 5 -

"Calm down," Alex said.

"Don't I look calm to you?" I held two fists up in the air.

"I want you to practice keeping that anger in check. You're going to be sitting in front of another evaluator and the judge, and I don't want you to come off as Genghis Khan on steroids."

"At least he had the satisfaction of killing his enemies."

"You don't know for sure what happened."

"It all makes sense." Pacing up and down in front of her desk, I felt like a panther or some other beast of prey — say, a Hollywood agent? I wanted some raw meat to tear apart.

"You got some secondhand report that is easily deniable," Alex said. "It's not going to do us any good."

"I can't believe you're saying that! Troncatti calls up his agent and has the agent sabotage my career. What are we talking about here?"

"We're talking about a very rotten deal, but one that the court is not going to consider."

"How can that be?"

"Because unless you have some evidence to back it up, this will fall under the category of depraved vituperation."

I just stared at her.

"What that means," Alex explained, "is that so often in divorce proceedings one side accuses the other side of some big, nasty thing in order to gain the upper hand. Much of the time it's just made up, and judges know that. They don't want to sit up there and listen to accusations flying back and forth unless they can be backed up somehow."

"What if Lisa testified?"

Alex shook her head. "She doesn't want to lose her career, does she? Even if we force her on the stand, she might deny the whole thing. And even if she didn't, you know what Bryce Jennings will do to her on cross?"

My mind conjured pictures of Lisa sobbing uncontrollably, in true TV-lawyer-show fashion.

"What I'll do is shoot off a letter to Jennings," Alex said, "that tells him in perfectly vague legalese that we know something's been going on and it better stop. Yakkety yakkety yak. No threats, just a little wake-up reminder. And it'll become part of the file. Meantime, you concentrate on being a model citizen and be ready to stay perfectly calm when you see Maddie on Tuesday, and the evaluator sometime next week."

"It won't be the same one, will it?"

"It might."

"She looks like a teenager. How can I talk to her without thinking about zits?"

"Like the cool, calm, rational person I see before me now." She looked at my hands. "Unclench your fists, please."

⌁

I had to keep visions of my hands around Troncatti's neck from consuming me. Once more, acting was my way out.

Nikki met me at the church, where we could rehearse in the little theater. She came in looking like she'd just had makeup put on by the staff at Max Factor. Beautiful.

"I was reading for a mascara commercial," she explained.

"Looks like you got the part."

"We'll see. You know how it goes."

Did I ever.

We sat in the audience seats and I threw her a fresh copy of Hamlet. She smiled. "Boy, you are ambitious. Why Shakespeare?"

Because I fell in love with my wife talking Shakespeare.

"They don't do much Bill Shakespeare around here anymore," I said.

"We do," Nikki said. "We're planning a production of As You Like It for next season."

"No way."

"Way." She laughed. "Why is that so astounding?"

"It's not. It's just sort of a coincidence." I didn't explain that that was the very play Paula and I talked about on our first date. Some things are better left unsaid.

I flipped open my copy of the play. "I thought we could do the 'Get thee to a nunnery' scene."

"Ah yes. So you think Hamlet's insane?"

"The way I play him? Definitely yes. Typecasting."

Again she laughed and opened her book. "Where are we starting?"

"I promise I won't do 'To be or not to be.'"

"What a silly question."

"Right. Page 35. Start with 'Soft you now! The fair Ophelia! Nymph, in thy orisons be all my sins remembered.'"

And off we went, reading the scene. No acting, just the lines. That's always how you start. Let scene and character come to you gradually.

All went well until I got to Hamlet's line, "I say, we will have no more marriages." My face must have changed like a traffic light.

"You doing okay?" Nikki asked.

"Yeah. No. Hanging in there."

"You didn't want the divorce?" She said it so simply I was not at all offended. It did not seem like prying. It was more like a friend asking me to talk it out. Actors tend to do that. Peel away the emotional layers to get at something real inside.

"No." I shifted in my seat. "I wanted to stay married. I wanted us to be a family and all that. I keep looking for something I may have done, or not done, that ruined things. Honestly, I can't. But now it's happening. I hate the whole thing."

"You're on the right side," Nikki said. "God hates it, too."

"Excuse me?"

"Hates divorce."

"So what does that mean? Does he hate me?"

"Of course not. Although some churches might make you feel that way."

I shrugged.

"Divorce is sometimes treated as the unforgivable sin. I'm a preacher's kid, remember? Though my dad didn't do it, some people over the years managed to elevate divorce to the level of murder and child molesting."

"Are you kidding?"

Nikki shook her head. "What was so sad about that is since there is no-fault divorce law, a party can be perfectly innocent and still get the scarlet letter—in this case a D—stitched on his shirt."

"Great. Get the tar and feathers ready."

"You're not that far off. Many Christians would actually say you are just as guilty as your wife. That's so stupid it's not funny."

Her mind seemed crisp and alive, like she'd thought this all through deeply and it meant something to her. "So you're really a preacher's kid, huh?"

"Yep."

"Know your Bible pretty well?"

"Oh yeah. You want me to tell you the names of the Bible books, in order?"

"Some other time, maybe." I paused, feeling like she and I were together for a reason more than just doing a scene. "So what would you, as a Christian, advise me to do now?"

Nikki paused for a long moment, treating the question seriously. Then she said, "Forgive."

The word blasted out at me like mace spray. "Forgive? Paula? For having an affair?"

"I know it sounds crazy."

"Yeah, it does."

"But God has a reason for it."

"And that would be?"

She patted her chest. "To keep you from being eaten up inside."

I shook my head. "That does not make sense to me."

"Me neither," Nikki said. "But I finally figured out it's better to obey God than wait until you've got it all straight in your mind. Remember what Jesus did on the cross? He asked God to forgive those who were executing him."

"Let's get back to the scene," I said.

VISIT

- 1 -

Thursday finally came, and with it a new player in my little drama. His full name was Renard J. Harper, and he was a robust African-American social worker assigned to monitor my visit with Maddie. Middle-fifties, I guessed. We sat on a bench at a Studio City park. At least I got to choose the location for the visit.

"This is very uncomfortable for me," I said.

"I can relate," Harper said.

"I mean, this whole security thing." I waved my hands around. "Like I'm going to do something to my daughter."

"Happens all the time." Harper had a deep voice, kind of soothing. Like somebody's favorite uncle. "Doesn't mean there's anything to it, but we have to walk carefully when a child's involved."

"Yeah, but what about the parents?"

"What about them?"

"Don't they have rights, too?"

"That's what court is all about. Better if the two of them can get together and talk it out."

"Right." Bitterness dripped off my tongue. "What if the other party doesn't want to talk?"

"Then you end up with me." Harper smiled. At least he was trying to be pleasant.

"What gets me is that anybody can say anything, and we end up with you. I mean, this whole thing is so stupid. Paula knows I love Maddie and I'd never try anything."

"What about the beach thing?"

"You mean when I took Maddie to Ventura?"

Harper nodded.

"You know about that?"

"I got the whole file, of course. All I'm saying is, the littlest things can come back at you."

I looked him right in the eye. "You think I'd ever do anything to my daughter?"

"Not for me to say. I'm just doing what the court tells me to do."

"And I get to pay you for the privilege. That's another thing that bites."

"Mr. Gillen, you want some free advice?"

"Sure." I slapped my thighs. "How much will it cost me?"

"My football coach in high school used to gather us around before a big game and say, 'Gentlemen, show me what you're made of.' And we'd all go out and pound heads for him. Well, this is a big game for you, seeing your daughter. Show her what you're made of. I'll see it. And when I report back to the court I'll be able to say something good about you. I'd like to, you see."

"Thanks for that." I almost choked up. Somebody in the system was showing a little humanity. I needed that.

"No problem. You played baseball, right?"

I nodded.

"Who's your team?" Harper asked.

"Dodgers."

"Too bad."

"Why?"

"I'm from the Bay Area."

"Oh no, you're not a Giants fan."

"Going back to Willie Mays, my friend."

"Oh great!"

Harper let out a big laugh. "Now, let's see. How many times did you steal the pennant from us?"

And I couldn't help laughing, too. I knew what he was doing. Trying to get me relaxed, get my mind off things until Maddie got here. A good man, Harper.

We talked baseball for another ten minutes or so. Harper told me he'd once tried to sell a country song about baseball called "You'd Be So Nice to Slide Home To," but it never made it. He even sang a verse or two. What I remember was the line, "I've been in right field so long, missin' you, I feel like The Babe's old mitt."

Then the limo pulled up.

All the relaxing I'd been doing shot out of my head, replaced by a twisting of nerves and a stomach doing flips.

The same driver I'd seen up at Troncatti's—the one I called Igor—exited and opened the rear door.

And Madeleine Erica Gillen got out.

My heart started pumping something fierce. A sweat drop came out of my armpit and slid down my side.

"Game time," Haper said, encouragingly.

That helped only a little, because I immediately saw something that turned my stomach into warm clay. The limo driver was holding Maddie's hand as they walked toward us. Her hand in his. Like it belonged there. Still, I stuffed my feelings down as deep as I could and put on a smile.

"Maddie!" I jumped up and started toward her.

The driver stopped, putting up his hand. And Maddie slid behind his leg, like he was a protective fence and I was some sort of animal.

The move froze me.

"You Mr. Harper?" Igor looked right past me.

"Yes, sir," Renard J. Harper said.

"Can I have a word with you, please?"

Harper gave me a glance.

"What's going on?" I asked him.

"Hold on, Mr. Gillen. I'll find out." Harper went over to Igor and Maddie and started talking. I stood there like the stupid statue on the Island of Idiots.

A minute or two later, Harper walked back to me. "There's been a request for no physical contact."

"What?"

"This happens. The mother has requested that you not touch your daughter."

Heat ran up my face. "No way! If they think I'm going to just sit here and not touch Maddie—"

"Mr. Gillen, listen to me. If there's a request like this, I have to honor that, unless you want to go back to court and convince the judge to allow it."

"This is unreal."

"It seems the child is a little upset about this visit," Harper said.

"Please, you can't let them do this to me."

Harper spoke calmly, a veteran of many battles like this. "I understand what you're going through, I really do. Some advice again?"

"What?"

"Talk to Maddie. If she makes a move toward you at any time, wants to hold your hand, anything, I'll allow that. If she doesn't, just remember this is all only temporary. You'll have your day in court soon enough."

Maddie was peeking from behind Igor's leg.

"This is killing me," I told Harper. "How could she be afraid of me?"

"I can't answer that," Harper said. "So come on and sit down and we'll do this thing."

I sat on one side of the picnic table. The bench was cold and hard. Igor coaxed Maddie to come along and sit down opposite me. She did, but her eyes avoided mine.

What was going on?

"Hey," I said to my daughter.

"Hi," she said, still not looking at me. I had my hands on top of the table, hoping she'd put hers out and touch me, so it would be all right. But her hands were in her lap.

"How's it going?" It was like talking to a stranger. I could hardly stand it. It felt like Maddie was on drugs or something. I sensed Igor glaring at me from several feet away, and it was all I could do not to scream at him to get out of my face. But I fought for control. I knew I had to, for Maddie's sake.

Maddie shrugged in answer to my question.

"What have you been doing?"

She shrugged again, still not looking at me.

"Maddie?"

She kept her gaze on the tabletop.

I looked at Harper for some help, knowing there was not a thing he could do. He nodded at me to try again.

"I've missed you," I said. "I miss story time."

"Tony reads me stories."

If an ice pick had been jammed in my heart it wouldn't have hurt more.

"Do you miss me?" I said.

Maddie didn't answer.

"I sure miss you, pumpkin."

Suddenly, I felt like a prisoner, getting a visit from a reluctant relative. Nothing much to say. Small talk that goes nowhere. And a big screen between us. No human contact.

I looked at Harper. "Something's not right here."

Igor huffed.

"Starting with him." I pointed my finger at Igor's face. He didn't like that. I didn't care. If I hadn't been sitting down I don't know what I might have done.

"Go ahead," Harper said. "We'll stand over here." He got up and motioned to Igor.

"No," Igor said.

"Come along," Harper said, his voice with just the right amount of official insistence.

Igor shook his head.

Maddie looked at her hands.

"You don't want to be here, do you?" I said.

Maddie shook her head.

"All right, baby," I said, my voice wavering. "You don't have to."

Without any hesitation Maddie slipped off the bench and ran to Igor. Out of everything that had happened in this nightmare, that was the worst part. It reminded me of the time Maddie was four and I took her to a birthday party. There were some older kids there as well, and one of them jumped out from a corner and screamed, scaring the little kids. Maddie was one of them, and she turned and ran directly for me, throwing herself at my legs. I was her protector.

Not anymore. And it killed me.

- 2 -

I was desperate with Alex over the phone as I told her about Maddie's behavior at the visit.

Alex tried to calm me. "This is not uncommon."

"You've got to be kidding me."

"Kids Maddie's age are very susceptible to influence from the custodial parent."

I thought about that a moment. "You mean Paula's messing with her head about me?"

"Like I said, not uncommon. I've seen cases where in a matter of days a child has been turned around."

"But Maddie and me." My voice was hollow. "She loved me."

"I know."

"She wouldn't even look at me."

"Mark, I'll put this in the file—"

"File? We've got to get Maddie out of there."

"We're working on that."

"Meanwhile, Maddie's stuck up there? With Troncatti and Paula? And they're feeding her lies about me? And we can't do anything about it?"

"We are doing something about it. We have to do it the legal way."

"Not enough. I can't just sit here."

"Mark, don't do anything—"

"Good-bye, Alex."

I disconnected and turned off the phone. Then I burned rubber onto the San Diego Freeway.

The offices of AEA, American Entertainment Artists, Inc., were in a new glass building on Wilshire in what was known as the Power Corridor of Beverly Hills. It was halfway between CAA and William Morris. Fully 90 percent of the big players in the movie and television industry had their reps in these buildings, all within a half mile of each other.

I was not even in the other 10 percent. But that didn't stop me from walking up and down Wilshire, across the street from the place, waiting for someone to emerge.

That someone was Leonard Remey, and he loved sushi for lunch. You pick up those facts by reading the industry trades and assorted media. Most of the time it's about actors. But Remey was a superstar agent, the biggest kahuna since Ovitz ruled the roost, and he was news.

He liked Ito Sushi, a very upscale place within walking distance of the AEA building. I'd been in there once, with a small group after an acting class. The sushi was good and expensive, the atmosphere alive with power talk. How many stars had been made or broken there over a plate of raw fish?

What I was about to do was a high-wire risk, but I didn't care. I was beyond caring about my reputation. This was about protecting Maddie, and whatever might happen to me came in a distant second.

It was shortly after twelve when Remey finally came out. He was coatless, but in a crisp white shirt and blue tie. A couple of other men in similar attire were with him. I thought to myself, if a car hit all three of them, the town would probably have to shut down for a month while they figured out what to do with all the A-list stars who suddenly had no agents.

The trio strolled to the corner, waited for the light, crossed. They yakked it up, but as they got closer I saw that they were not speaking to each other. All three of them had cell phone ear-pieces inserted in their heads and were talking into the little mikes.

Perfect, I thought. All human contact cut off. Business as usual.

The three power mongers walked and talked another block or so, me strolling along behind. They turned left at the next corner and, as predictable as the night, entered the gold and burnished walnut doors of Ito Sushi.

I waited a minute or so, then walked in.

The place was already doing a brisk trade. A few young turks — black shirts, short goatees, earrings — sat at the bar, talking to each other and a couple of impossibly blond women in dresses that hugged their silicone. An older couple, probably citizens of Beverly Hills since the Lucy-Desi era, seemed out of place in the corner. It was as if they had been stuck there purposely, so as not to intrude on the important schmoozing now under way in the prime sushi-bar seats.

A hostess asked if I had a reservation, and I said no, I'd sit at the bar, and there was a chair open. As I made for the chair — between one of the turks and a guy who looked like his jaw had been chiseled by Michelangelo — I spotted the three agents at a table near the back.

Still talking into their little wires. To be hip in LA you have to have a busier-than-thou attitude. You have to believe there is

simply not enough time in the day, and so on the eighth day God
created cell phones and PDAs to prove your indispensability to the
universe. Staying hip is almost a full-time job for Angelenos. And
the three major cheeses at the back table were in frantic pursuit
of their calling.

A nice-looking waitress handed me a warm, damp cloth and
asked if I'd like anything to drink. I asked for a very un-hip glass
of ice water and continued to watch the three stooges.

Was I nuts? My thought had been to just walk over to Remey
with a surprise attack. An in-your-face to tell him I knew exactly
what was going on.

Too public, too desperate, I decided.

Which meant I could accidentally-on-purpose follow him into
the men's room and let him have it with a threatening cool.

But to what purpose? Did I really think one of Hollywood's
most powerful agents was going to care what I had to say?

This was beginning to feel like another of my fool's errands.

A sushi chef with a bright bandana on his head asked me what
I'd like to start with, so I ordered shrimp.

I remembered Maddie liked sushi. We couldn't afford it very
often, but every now and then, for a treat, I would take her out.
Shrimp was her favorite.

And thinking of that only made me angry. Maybe I would go
over to Remey right now, while the feeling was with me.

What stopped me was the sight of one person I never expected
to see.

Paula's mother, Erica Stanton Montgomery, was making a bee-
line for Remey's table.

I almost choked on some ginger root.

Erica was tall, statuesque, perfectly groomed, and dressed to
the nines. She looked like old money and new surgery.

Yet here she was, in the land of warm beaches.

Remey stood up to greet her. They shook hands like old friends.

She did not sit down. She spoke to Remey for a couple of minutes—as the other two agents spoke into their wires—and then she turned to walk out.

Without a thought I got up, tossed a ten on the counter, and followed her.

Erica was strolling down the street, casually looking in windows. She could have been going anywhere. There were tons of upscale stores in the vicinity. I followed her.

She did not go far before ducking into a place called Maria's, which was, from the look of it, a woman's apparel place.

I waited a moment, then went in.

The place looked like it was designed in gold. Maybe it was. All I knew was that I was a fish out of water in there.

Erica was looking at a dress display near the window. It was some sort of strapless number. I made my way to her side.

"Not your style," I said.

Her look was startled at first, then furious. When the Montgomerys get mad, it's like something out of Nature's Savage Fury on The Discovery Channel.

"What. On. Earth."

"Hi, Erica. Longtime."

Suddenly she looked around, as if afraid someone would see her talking to me. "How did you—"

"Find you? Serendipity. Sometimes things are just meant to be." I slapped my hands together. "So, what are you doing out here on the coast?"

"I don't have anything to say to you, Mark."

"Maybe you'd like to explain to the judge what you're doing meeting with Leonard Remey?"

I wondered if her heart was beating as fast as mine. Certainly blood was pumping to her face. I could even see it through the industrial layer of makeup.

"You were spying?"

"I was sitting in a public place, is what I was doing. Leonard Remey has taken a bit of an interest in my career, though not in a way that's very flattering. You know anything about that?"

"I am not going to stand here and let—"

"Chill, Erica. You owe me."

"I owe you nothing."

"Oh really? Let me hazard a guess then. Meeting with Remey has something to do with Paula, obviously. Why else would he give you the time of day? I figure you're getting some money, maybe you're managing her career. What's that, fifteen percent?"

Erica stiffened, and I knew I had her on the run. "I don't have to stand here and—"

"Your daughter and her boyfriend are trying to keep my daughter away from me. You all right with that? You think that's right?"

Erica said nothing.

"And Remey's part of the plan. You probably know all about it. You know he made sure I didn't get the role that was going to save my sorry acting career." The outrage was still fresh in me, and my voice was getting higher. "He called up and—"

"Is there anything I can help you with?" A saleswoman—all pearls and stiff hair—was behind us.

"The gentleman is leaving," Erica said.

"I'm just browsing," I said, nodding toward the dress on display. "Do you think it's my color?"

Apparently, the sense-of-humor fairy had flown over Beverly Hills without stopping.

"Is this man annoying you?" the saleswoman said.

Erica looked me up and down. "As a matter of fact, yes."

"Sir, I'll have to ask you to leave."

"Are you the one who put Remey up to it?" I leveled my eyes at Erica.

"Sir," the saleswoman said.

I ignored her. "You the one who's pulling the strings?"

"Sir!"

"Answer me, Erica."

"I'll call the police." The saleswoman marched toward the counter.

"See what you've done now?" Erica said.

"I'll find out," I said. "I will."

"You're a pitiful man. It's a good thing you won't have Madeleine anymore."

My chest spasmed, like I'd been given a shock from a live wire. "How do you know that?"

She looked sheepish all of a sudden and completely turned away. I grabbed her arm and spun her back.

Her chin dropped like a stone. "Don't you touch me!"

"What do you know? What sort of scam is going on?"

There were about half a dozen women in the shop, all looking at us.

"What you're doing," I said, "is wrong." That's all I could think of to say. It was wrong, but did that matter to her? Had it ever, her whole life?

Erica said nothing. She looked behind me. Before I could turn I felt a hand like a bear trap clamp down on my shoulder.

Igor. He had me and was pulling me toward the door.

"Hey man!" I tried to whirl out of his grip but couldn't.

So, with all my might, I jammed my elbow into his stomach. It was like hitting a wall. The guy was in shape.

My blow, such as it was, did nothing but make him mad.

Igor threw me out the door of the shop.

I went sprawling on the hot sidewalk, head hitting hard.

Something took hold of me then, and I knew what I would do if they ever tried to keep Maddie away from me.

God forgive me, I knew.

Next day I was in Nancy's office. She'd called me in. More bad news.

"Are you seeing anyone?" she asked me, almost before I was in the chair.

"Seeing someone?"

"A shrink."

"No."

"Maybe you should reconsider."

"That why you called me in here?"

"No, but it's a good idea, don't you think?"

"Why did you call me, Nancy?"

"You have some decisions to make. I have some decisions."

"Such as?"

"Such as whether to keep you on as a client." Her face was as cool as November. Gone was any of the warmth she used to toss my way when I faced troubles.

"You're actually saying ... Are you dropping me?"

"That's what we're here to discuss, yes."

I could see a thin layer of Valley smog outside her window—a dull, grayish haze that kept the mountains from view. Nothing was clear out there. Or in here, for that matter.

"Why would you do that?" My palms were starting to sweat.

"There comes a time, that's all. A time when it looks like it might be in the best interests of both parties to pursue other avenues."

"But why now? I got on a big series. Until Leonard Remey got involved."

"Are you sticking with that story?"

"Story? It happened."

"You can't go around town telling people Len Remey sabotaged your career. You know what that'll do to you? Ever hear the expression 'You'll never eat lunch in this town again'?"

"What about truth?"

"Truth is not the currency of the moment, Mark."

"Great. What is it then?"

"Relationships. People returning your phone calls. That's what this business runs on. When that's jeopardized, you're finished. I don't want to see that happen to you, or to me."

"Are you saying having me as your client is harmful to your career?"

Nancy said nothing, letting her silence answer for her.

"So that's it? You want me out of here? Never darken your door again?"

Finally, a little thaw showed through. "Here's what I'm saying, bottom line. You have to decide something, Mark. Once and for all. You have to decide if you want to make it as an actor. I know you have the talent. But you have to have the want to. It has to be the most important thing in the world, and you have to be willing to put everything else aside. You have to be willing to shut up if it's hurting you to talk. There is no other way to do it, my friend. You know that. And those are the terms for our future together. If you can assure me that you're going to put your career on the front burner, then we can move on. That's what I want to hear from you."

For a long time I sat there, a swirling in my belly. And I knew she was right. It was the only way to make it in the business. You had to make it A-number one on your life list. I gazed out her window as I thought about it. The smog was still there, but I thought I could see, way off in the distance, the peak of one of our local mountains, just barely visible in the muck. Once, a couple of years ago, we got some rare snow on the tops of those mountains, and I'd taken a day to drive Maddie up there. It was like Wonderland to her.

I stood up. "That price is too high, Nancy. I can't do it."

She seemed shocked. "You're giving up?"

"No," I said. "I just figured out what I want to be more than anything else."

"And what's that?"

"Maddie's father."

— ❧ —

Paula is stroking my hair as we sit entwined on the sofa, her legs over mine, watching Maddie perform her dance.

Maddie has taken ribbons and wrapped them around her ankles. She has used Scotch tape to hold the ribbons in place. The ribbons go round and round until they disappear into her slippers, which are fuzzy and have rubber puppy-dog faces.

These, Maddie announces, are her ballet slippers.

And now she dances, arms swirling in the air as she spins, then stops and leaps. It is not an abridged dance. It is the long, uncut version. It seems like she will dance forever.

"She has talent," Paula whispers to me, not wanting to disturb the genius.

"Gets it from me," I whisper back.

"Not."

"You haven't seen me in tights?"

"Nice image." Paula hits a phantom computer keyboard with her fingers. "Deleted."

"No, watch me!" Maddie twirls.

— 4 —

Sutton Hallard was his name. He was a licensed psychotherapist and avid golfer. At least that's what his office made it look like. There was a huge, framed photo of a gorgeous golf hole on one wall. It had an oceanscape and clear blue skies.

"Pebble," Hallard said when he saw me staring at it. "You ever play Pebble?"

I shook my head. "Don't play golf."

"Too bad." Hallard chuckled, but it sounded forced—like a man who thought anyone who didn't play golf could not possibly be a fit human being, let alone father.

Hallard sat behind his desk—a mini-golfbag held his pens and pencils—and regarded me. He was trim, about fifty, with perfect, steel-colored hair.

"This is your time," he said. "I want to be clear on that. I'm here to listen, maybe ask a few questions. But the most important thing for me is to get to know you. I have to make a recommendation to the court about custody for your daughter. That's a hard thing to do, I want you to know."

Hard for him? What about me?

"Sure," I said.

"So why don't you start. Just tell me anything that's on your mind." He leaned back in his leather chair.

I reminded myself to keep calm. I didn't want a repeat of the Sheila Bonner interview. Hallard seemed a little more human, and maybe the fact that he was a man was a good thing.

"Well, I love my daughter. That's pure and simple. Since she was born I've been a different person. I didn't realize just how different until she was taken away from me."

"That hasn't happened yet."

"But it has. I mean, that's why we're sitting here. I gave Maddie to Paula in good faith, and she refused to return her to me. In my book, that's a taking. And it hurts. It hurts bad."

"But you've had a visit with her—" he looked at a paper on his desk—"on the twenty-second, isn't that right?"

"Hardly a visit. They brought her to a park, and I had to pay for a social worker to be there with me."

"As per the order of the court."

"That wasn't the bad thing, though. It was Maddie. She didn't want to be there at all."

"She is, after all, five years old."

"Yeah, but this was something else. When she was with me, she loved me. We had a great relationship. Somebody has been messing with her."

"Are you accusing your wife of that?"

"I don't know who, I only know that Maddie wasn't herself, and that concerns me. What if they're trying to poison her against me?"

"If they are, they will be in deep trouble."

"Meantime Maddie suffers. And I suffer. And who knows how bad it is?"

"But you haven't any actual proof."

Calm. Stay calm. "It comes from years of knowing my daughter. I mean, living with her and doing all of the things a father does. You get to know a person."

"How well do you know your wife?"

"I thought I knew her pretty well. I guess that was naive."

"You're saying, then, you don't know her?"

I shrugged. "It's all messed up now."

"Do you really think she would do something to hurt your daughter like this?"

Did I? I did not want to. But hatred was starting to well up in me and I didn't care to deal with it. "There are all sorts of things people do when this sort of thing is going on. Divorce and child custody. It's not unheard of for a mother to try to keep kids from the father."

"Nor the other way around."

"I don't know. It seems as if most of the time it's the fathers who get the shaft."

Sutton Hallard tapped his lower lip with the eraser on his pencil. "Are you a sociologist, Mr. Gillen?"

"No, but—"

"Where have you been getting this information?"

"I just came across it."

"Did someone share this with you?"

He sounded like a man homing in on me. I suddenly felt I had to hide the fact I talked to Joe Pfeffer of the fathers' rights group. I also felt like Sutton Hallard knew I was hiding something. And that my next response was crucial.

"When I was looking for a lawyer," I said, "I did some talking to people, yes. Do I need to go into details?"

"It's entirely up to you."

"I don't know what it will accomplish. All I'm saying is that I don't have Maddie with me, and it's possible she's being influenced. I don't think that's right."

"It is not right, Mr. Gillen, but again, facts are the only things that matter. Otherwise, we would be flying back and forth with accusations alone. My concern, if I may, is that if you think this way, then if you were to get custody of Maddie, you might try doing something similar, out of spite. That would not be a good situation either."

Stay calm!

"Mr. Hallard, I don't know what else I can tell you except that I've never done anything to harm my daughter, or even put her in a place where harm would come to her. I mean, willingly. I would never do that. And doesn't a child need both parents around? For the best shot in life, I mean?"

Hallard lightly sucked on the eraser. "Are you saying a mother who brings up a child alone can't do a good job?"

"No, I wasn't saying that at all. Just that all things being equal, both parents should be involved."

"Yes, that's the ideal, and the courts seek to do that when there are no circumstances that militate against it. That's part of this evaluation process."

"Is she being evaluated?"

"Excuse me?"

"Paula. Is she going to have to go through this same deal?"

"Of course. I will be interviewing her, just as I am interviewing you. And I will talk to Maddie as well."

"Alone?"

"Yes. For part of the time, anyway."

This excited me. "Then would you do one thing for me?"

"What would that be?"

"Would you ask her a question?"

"Maybe."

"Ask her about the moon dance."

"What is the moon dance?"

"She'll know. Ask her if she remembers dancing with me, by the light of the moon. Just ask her that and look in her eyes. Please."

Sutton Hallard jotted something on his pad.

—◦—

I decided Hamlet was crazy-in-love.

Nikki thought so, too. But his obsession with avenging his father's murder makes everything else pale. Even Ophelia. And so he has to drive her away. Because he loves her so much.

"I think that lends a lot of colors to the scene," Nikki said. We were rehearsing at the house in the Hollywood Hills she was renting with two other actresses. There wasn't much furniture in the place, in keeping with the actors' life. But potted plants and some funky artwork made the house feel homey.

Nikki was wearing a sweatshirt with UCSD on it and light blue jeans. She offered me a soda, and we sat across from each other and read the scene together.

Then we decided to try it on our feet, to see what emerged.

What did emerge neither one of us was prepared for.

Hamlet begins by teasing Ophelia, and I did that by remembering the times I used to tease Paula—she didn't like it, but usually I could make her laugh after a while.

"Are you honest?" I—Hamlet—said.

"My lord?" Nikki answered in character.

"Are you fair?"

"What means your lordship?"

I began to circle her. "That if you be honest and fair, your honesty should admit no discourse to your beauty."

Nikki stood still, as Ophelia might, wondering what Hamlet was up to. "Could beauty, my lord, have better commerce than with honesty?"

"Ay, truly; for the power of beauty will sooner transform honesty from what it is to a bawd than the force of honesty can translate beauty into his likeness." I looked at Nikki/Ophelia as if she were a statue. "This was sometime a paradox, but now the time gives it proof. I did love you once."

"Indeed, my lord, you made me believe so." Nikki/Ophelia had eyes wide with sadness, confusion.

"You should not have believed me," I/Hamlet said, but I did not move away. "For virtue cannot so inoculate our old stock but we shall relish of it. I loved you not."

Nikki's eyes began to mist. She was crying already! Totally into the scene. Amazing.

"I was the more deceived," she said.

Following our improvisational format, I felt moved to grab her by the shoulders. Nikki went with it. Her eyes were filled with fear.

The feel of her shoulders was soft and warm. She was delicate, as I imagined Ophelia would be. And smelled like orange blossoms.

That's when I kissed her.

Was it part of the scene? I, as Hamlet, doing what the moment demanded? Or was it something I just wanted to do?

She went with it again. Was she just an actress?

When I pulled back and looked at her I knew neither one of us was acting.

Her face got red. There was a long pause. She looked at the hardwood floor.

"Interesting choice for Hamlet," I said.

She laughed defensively but did not look up.

"Do you want to start from the top?" I said.

Before she could answer her roommate, Deborah, walked in carrying an Entertainment Weekly and eating a peach.

"Hey guys," she said. She stopped, getting that sense of interrupting something secret. "Oh, sorry."

"No, Deb, it's okay." Nikki waved her in. "This is Mark Gillen, an actor friend."

"Oh, hey," Deb said. She wiped her hand on her shirt and shook mine. She had short curly hair and a lithe body.

"Nice to meet you," I said.

"You guys doing a scene?"

"Hamlet," Nikki said.

"Cool," Deb said. "Which scene?"

"Get thee to a nunnery," Nikki said.

Deb laughed. "That's exactly what I was thinking today. Nunnery. Beats Hollywood, don't it? You dudes go ahead." She whisked out of the room.

Leaving Nikki and me in an awkward silence.

Finally, I said, "If we do the scene again, it's going to go the same way."

Nikki nodded. "I think it will. Maybe that's why we shouldn't do it."

"You want to postpone until tomorrow?"

"I mean, maybe we shouldn't do it at all."

"No," I said, "I want to do it."

She shook her head. "Let me call you tomorrow."

"Hey, I'm sorry. I was out of line. I shouldn't have—"

"No," she said. "I wanted you to."

"What?"

"Can we talk later? I'm feeling a little irrational at the moment."

Go ahead, I wanted to say. Be irrational! Irrational is good! But it's bad, too! What was I doing?

"All right," I said. "I'll call you tomorrow."

"Thanks," she said.

I exited, like Hamlet leaving Act III—confused, needing to do something to keep the ghosts away.

—◆—

I almost yelped when I saw Ron Reid sitting outside my apartment building.

"What are you doing here?"

"Came to see my son, man." He was dressed in jeans and sandals.

"I'm not into seeing anybody right now."

His face got a hangdog look. He was my father. I didn't want him to be.

"All right, all right." I started to unlock the front door. "You want to come up for a minute?" Ron followed me in.

I made up some instant coffee, and we sat at the dining-room table.

"So how's the job working out?" I said.

"Ah." Ron waved his hand. "It'll do for now."

"You have to work. You have to settle down now. Don't blow this thing."

"I don't know, it's just not a good fit."

"You're drawing pay, right?"

"Well, yeah."

"Then it's a good fit. You're a convicted felon. You don't have a lot of choices."

Ron shook his head. "Enough about me. How are you doing?"

I shrugged. "Getting by."

"What's the latest on Maddie?"

"There's an evaluator dude looking at me, at Paula. He makes up a report and gives it to the judge. Then we'll see."

"How do you think it's going?"

"I don't know." I ran my thumb along the rim of the coffee cup. "They can't think I'm a bad father. No way."

"No way," Ron echoed. At least he was trying to sound supportive. "So where you been?"

"Huh?"

"I was out there a long time."

"Oh, rehearsing. Doing a scene."

"The old acting thing."

"I can pretend."

"What kind of a gig?"

"Not a gig, just a scene. To try and get into an acting company."

"Oh yeah? Very cool."

It was still unnerving to hear my father, now in his fifties, talking hip. But it was a mild diversion.

"So what's the scene?" Ron said.

"You really interested?" If he was, I wouldn't mind talking about it. Acting discussions were fun for me.

"Yeah, really."

"I'm doing a scene from Hamlet, where he confronts Ophelia."

"Hamlet, huh? Cool guy in tights?"

"Funny. Maybe I'll look as good as Mel Gibson did."

Ron laughed. "Who's the chick?"

"Chick? Did you really say chick?"

"Babe?"

"Ron, the woman is named Nikki, and she's very nice."

"How nice?" His eyebrows bobbed.

"Come on."

"You like this ... young lady?"

"Like I said—"

"No, I mean really like?"

It almost seemed like I was fifteen and Dad was asking about my first crush. "I don't know."

"But maybe?"

"Maybe. Who knows? My life is a little unsettled right now."

"But if the opportunity came up, would you ... ?"

His eyebrows danced again. I didn't like it. "Would I what?"

"You know."

"Sleep with her? Is that what you meant?"

"Don't get bent about it."

"First, what business is it of yours? Second, the thought hadn't crossed my mind."

Ron squinted at me.

"Other than what's normal," I said. "She's a Christian girl, I'm not going to try and get her into bed."

"Why not?"

That snapped it. I put my cup down so hard it splashed all over the place. "Shut up, Ron, just shut up."

He put his hands up. "Whoa—"

"Grow up, will you?" That sounded odd coming from me, but I went with it. "Quit acting like some teenager. Quit talking about not working. Get your life together, man."

"Look who's talking," he said, with an edge.

"What's that mean?"

"You can't even keep your family together."

I recognized the familiar grip of rage inside me. It was almost as if I was standing outside, looking in, watching myself lose control. The outside part was passive, didn't even try to intervene. Didn't want to.

In my mind I saw my fists driving into Ron Reid's face. I don't know what stopped me, but looking back it seems a voice was whispering to me. Don't don't don't. Was it the voice of God? I think now it was.

If only I had continued to listen for it.

– 5 –

I woke up the next morning thinking of Nikki McNamara.

She was there in the fading landscape of my dreams, hanging on despite the onrush of consciousness. As I showered and shaved, I kept replaying the scene from Hamlet and wondering what she was thinking today.

I wanted to call her. Now. But I sensed she needed room to breathe, so I put it off until later.

What I needed to do now was salvage the rest of my life.

Acting had been everything to me for the past ten years. Becoming a star was what I was about. Every year I'd watch the Oscars and see myself up there someday. I thank the Academy for this honor, and all the people who helped me along the way.

There would be dinners at Spago and interviews on E! network and major movie deals the rest of my life.

Somewhere in there was a real love of acting, too. Because you could assume a role, play somebody else. For some reason, I found that appealing.

But now I wanted nothing more than Maddie in my life. And I knew that being a struggling actor was not the best profile for a soon-to-be single father.

So where did that leave me?

As I sipped morning coffee, I made a mental list of options. Baseball coach maybe, at some high school. Not real glamorous, but it could get me back in touch with the game. Maybe I could look up the coach at Cleveland High and offer my services as an assistant.

Or maybe I could reach higher. What about being a lawyer? Do what Alex did. Help fathers with their custody battles.

Only problem. I needed to go to law school. And to do that, I needed to go to college. I'd gone straight into baseball after high school. I was not a great student to begin with. From where I sat now, at thirty-four years old, actually doing the whole college thing seemed like a huge mountain to climb.

But challenges were part of sports, and I'd never backed away from those.

So I finished my coffee and drove over to Cal State Northridge and picked up some admissions information. What the hey? The journey of a thousand miles begins with a single step. I'd made it half a step anyway.

Shortly before noon I called Nikki's cell phone.

"Hi, Hamlet here." Trying to sound as positive as I could.

"Oh hi. How are you?"

Very much in limbo. "Fine. You want to have lunch?"

Pause. "I would like to see you, but you don't have to —"

"Done. Let's pick a spot."

"I really don't think lunch is a good idea."

The air was suddenly heavy with intrigue. "You have to eat."

"Can we maybe meet at 1:30 at the church?"

Not the place I had in mind, but ... "Sure."

"Thanks."

—◆—

I arrived at 1:15, and waited in the courtyard. A gardener was cutting some shrubs with big clippers. Shick shick shick. Made me think of the death of a thousand cuts. The only other sound was the

101 Freeway and the traffic rushing by the church grounds. Sunlight dappled the courtyard through the tree leaves. The church seemed to be straining to be an oasis in the city wilderness.

Nikki arrived looking so good I almost fell off the bench.

"Sorry I'm late," she said.

"Are you?" I had lost all track of time.

"A little. Been waiting long?"

"No, just watching the clipper do his work."

She gave a quick glance at the gardener, then sat down on the bench. "Thanks for coming out here."

"No prob. I've been thinking a lot about what happened last night."

"Me too."

"Want me to start?"

"Maybe I should."

"Okay."

She paused a moment, took in a deep breath. "Mark, I don't think it's a good idea to do the scene together."

My stomach knotted a little bit. "Why not?"

"We got a little too involved in it."

"That's Method acting!"

My attempt at humor brought only a polite smile from Nikki. "It was more than that."

You're a man, you try to read a woman's face. You try to pick up signals in voice and tone. Sometimes you just plow on through, doing what you want to do, hoping it's the right thing.

I took her hand. "I know it was more."

She gently but firmly pulled her hand back. "Wait. This is like a train, things are going so fast."

"Hey, let's enjoy the ride."

"I can't. We can't."

Shick shick shick. The sound of the clippers filled the silence.

"Why can't we?" I said.

"You're married." She looked at me as if that were bad but undeniable news.

"But my wife is divorcing me."

"It doesn't matter," Nikki said. "You are still married."

"Not for long."

"It isn't right for us to get involved."

"Why not?"

"I just told you."

"That doesn't make sense to me. You like me, I know it."

"Yes, that's what's hard about this."

"It doesn't have to be."

She shook her head. "Mark, God looks at marriage as sacred. You're married, we just can't see each other."

"Not even to do a lousy scene?"

"It won't be for just the scene. We both know that."

Boy did I. "I want to keep seeing you."

"I know. But we can't."

"What if I won't stop?"

"Please, Mark."

"I mean it."

"What do you mean not stop? Even if I want you to stop?"

Shick shick shick.

"I'm sorry," I said. "I'm being a real jerk here."

"No."

"Can I still come to church and the Bible study?"

"Of course. I'd like us to stay friends."

For a short moment, the sound of the clippers stopped.

"Why do you have to be so mature?" I said.

She laughed.

THE SETUP

- 1 -

"Let's talk about your anger for a while," Sutton Hallard said.

Great. It was Friday, and I was in for another interview with him — I felt like the proverbial dog jumping through hoops — and now we were on my weakest point. What I was busting to ask him was whether he'd talked to Paula or Maddie. I knew he had. I also knew he wouldn't tell me boo about it.

"I know I have a problem with anger," I said, being up front and confessional. I was going to be so even tempered that Sutton Hallard would want to put me up for a humanitarian award when we were finished. "But I feel I know about it and can manage it."

"What makes you say that?"

"Just what I've seen in myself the last few weeks."

"Can you give me an example?"

"Sure." I tried to think of one and ran with the first thing that popped into my mind. "The other night I was talking to my father."

Hallard looked at the paper in front of him. "That would be Mr. Reid?"

"Right. He came over, wanted to talk or something, so he came up to my apartment and I made some coffee. We talked for a while, then he said some things that I thought were out of line. We got into sort of an argument, and I told him he needed to get his act together."

"In what way?"

"Just plain old growing up. He's still acting like a kid. Not being responsible about his job and stuff like that. Well, I told him that, then he says to me, 'Look who's talking.' And I start to get hot and ask him what he means. He says I can't even hold my own

203

family together. That was below the belt, and my first thought was to take a punch at him. But I didn't. And that's what I'm saying."

"Why don't you think you took a punch at him?"

Should I tell him about the voice? Or would that put me in a whole new category in Sutton Hallard's eyes? N for nutcase.

"I just didn't. I held back. I could feel myself holding back, not wanting to do it."

"And you have no idea why you didn't?"

For some reason I'll never fully understand, the next voice I used was Peter Lorre's. "Who knows the depths of the human mind?"

Sutton Hallard stared at me like I was, in fact, a nutcase.

"That's my Peter Lorre imitation," I explained. "Just to show you my acting side."

"Very amusing." Hallard tapped his pencil on the fleshy part of his palm.

"No, but seriously," I said, using the familiar segue, "I truly think I'm becoming a better person. I'm not just lashing out."

"People don't simply change, out of the blue. There is some sort of stimulus and, if you look hard enough, you can usually find it. If we can do that now, it may play an important role in this aspect of the case."

Important role? I wondered what he meant. It sounded like a verbal clue, almost like he was prompting me to give him something he could work with. Maybe like he was on my side a little bit. Feeling sorry for me? I didn't care. I'd take any bone Sutton Hallard wanted to throw my way.

"Maybe there is something," I said.

"Please."

"Church. I've joined a church. I'm really trying to look at things from that perspective."

"A Christian perspective?"

"Yeah. I mean, the Bible and all that. I'm in a Bible study group; we meet on Wednesday nights, a lot of actors in it. Good people. I feel like I can talk about anything with them."

"What church is this?"

"Gower Presbyterian, in Hollywood."

Hallard jotted a note. "Tell me more."

That had to mean I was on the right track with him. Good. Ride this train to the end. "For instance, the other night we're all talking about how frustrating the acting business is. And I say, 'Amen, brother.' And the guy leading the study, who is doing pretty well I might add, says, 'How do you handle it?' And I say I have no clue. And then he opens the Bible and reads about not having any anxiety, but by praying to God and being thankful for what you do have, you can have peace. That really helped me a lot."

"You pray regularly?"

"I'm trying to get in the habit."

Hallard scribbled another note. I wanted to see what he was writing so badly I almost snatched the paper.

"Are you seeing anyone?" Hallard asked when he was finished.

"What?"

"Anyone romantically?"

That was a bolt out of the blue. But I guess he had the right to ask, and I had to wag my tail and jump through the hoop. "No," I said.

"No dating?"

I thought of Nikki McNamara and was glad now we hadn't gotten into anything. I felt it was better for me if I played the role of spurned husband, wanting to keep the marriage together.

Did I? If Paula suddenly called it quits with Troncatti, would I even want her back? I didn't know at this point.

"Do you have any plans in that area?" Hallard said.

"No," I said, truthfully. "What I want is my daughter. And it was my wife who started fooling around with another man. I didn't do a thing."

"Not anything? You are claiming this is all a one-sided situation?"

"All I know is things seemed pretty good until Paula left to do that movie. Meanwhile, I stayed back here and took care of Maddie while she got to go and make herself into a movie star."

"Let's talk about that part of it for a moment. Your wife has done exceedingly well in the last few months, has she not?"

"Yeah, she has. She's being made into this major star."

"While your career has not exactly gone upward."

What a great psychologist this guy was. Knew how to make me feel like absolute dirt.

"No," I said. "But that's another thing."

He raised his eyebrows in a signal to continue.

Should I tell him what I knew? Or what I thought I knew?

"You were about to say?" Hallard blinked at me.

"Just that my career was set to have a major boost. I got cast in a new show with John Hoyt, on NBC. But then it was yanked out from under me. And I know why."

Sutton Hallard waited.

"The producer got pressure to drop me," I said, trying to sound as objective as possible. "I found out about it through a friend who works at the company. I did a little snooping and found out it was Antonio Troncatti's agent who put the pressure on. Coincidence? I don't think so. Especially after I saw Paula's mother meeting with him."

"Meeting with whom?"

"The agent, a guy named Leonard Remey."

Hallard tapped the end of his pencil on the desk, making dull thud thud sounds. "Do you have any corroboration of this?"

"I only know what I saw and heard."

"What you saw and heard?"

He wasn't buying this. And I knew what it must have sounded like. The paranoid ravings of a spurned husband. Grasping at straws. Flinging mud at my wife.

"No, there's Lisa, my friend at the production company. She ..." I stopped. I had promised her I wouldn't say anything.

"Can you get a letter from her, addressed to me, setting forth these facts?"

"I just don't know. I told her I'd keep it confidential. She has a job ..."

Sutton Hallard's face became vaguely skeptical.

"I'll do what I can," I said weakly.

"Please. Until then, I can't consider this in my report. What I need are facts and supporting documentation. You understand that, I'm sure."

"Yeah. Sure."

"But getting back to your acting career—"

"Look, I've been doing a lot of thinking about that lately, and I want to tell you that my number one concern is Maddie, being able to be a good father and support for her. I've been looking into going back to school, getting my degree, getting something more stable going."

"You're thinking of leaving the acting profession?"

"If that's what it takes to be a good father, then yes. I don't care about acting more than I do my own daughter."

"If you go back to school, money will be tight, will it not?"

How was I going to deny that? "But people do it all the time."

"Who would watch the child when you're in class?"

"I'd work that out, like other people work it out."

"You would need money to pay for daycare then, wouldn't you?"

"Yeah, I suppose."

Hallard wrote something on his paper.

I couldn't stand it anymore. "Dr. Hallard, did you talk to Maddie yet? Did you ask her about the moon dance?"

He stopped writing. "You know I cannot answer that."

"You can't tell me anything?"

"It will all be in my report."

"When is this going to end?"

"Soon."

~ 2 ~

I went home and decided to get a little more acquainted with my friend, Antonio Troncatti. Having no idea what Hallard was getting on him, I thought I'd better do my own research project.

Starting with Google, I did a search for anything with his name in it. I got over a thousand hits. So I added the words "career" and "biography." That narrowed it down some, but I still had a ton of material.

After a couple of hours, I'd cut and pasted a nice dossier on Troncatti. What I had made me hate him all the more.

He'd been the protégé of Bertolucci and Lina Wertmuller, working on several of their films. His first film, as a twenty-six-year-old wunderkind, featured Giancarlo Giannini as an aging hit man who has an encounter with a small child that changes his life. I never saw it, but it captured an award at the Cannes Film Festival, and Troncatti's career was launched.

His next film was the one that set him up as an international directing star. It was a remake of The Count of Monte Cristo, only this time done as a modern tale of corporate greed. It starred, of all people, John Hoyt, and really reactivated his career.

What got the attention of the critical set was the fact that Italian cinema is not generally known for its action. Most of the time, in fact, it's like watching paint dry. But Troncatti became the "Italian John Woo" and soon moved to the U.S. for his directing chores.

Three major hits followed in succession. The guy was a movie god.

Also, from what I read between the lines, quite the ladies' man. Have to admit, from the pictures of the guy, that he was good looking. A Roman nose above thin lips and a jaw that might have been chiseled marble; olive skin that grew naturally darker in the Southern California sun; long black hair of shoulder length. I mean, he could have been the cover boy on some romance novel.

Which didn't do a lot for the old self-esteem.

He'd had affairs with three actresses, all of whom you'd know. One, who was somewhat older than Troncatti but still considered a queen of glamour, almost got him to the altar.

What kept them all away, apparently, was Troncatti's volcanic temper.

There were stories of Troncatti tearing up hotel rooms, wrecking cars, beating up people in bars, and generally carrying on like a large, petulant child. (I was thinking all this time how I'd love to be the one to give him a whipping with the thing they used in Mutiny on the Bounty. What did they call that? The cat-o'-nine-tails? Perfect.)

I found one item of particular interest. Back in the nineties, around the time of the O. J. Simpson murder trial, there had been a domestic violence incident. One of the actresses whom he'd been living with had summoned the cops. The case went to the D.A.'s office, which was particularly sensitive to these things in the wake of Simpson, and was close to being filed.

But the actress withdrew her complaint. She said it had all been a mistake, that she'd just been mad at him for making eyes at some other woman.

It was all swept under the rug. I thought it would be a good thing to whip that rug away at the custody hearing.

I felt a new wave of disgust. And fear. This was the man who was around Maddie. What might happen to her sometime if he lost it? What sort of example of adult behavior would he be? (I admit I was not thinking of my own anger. It was all focused on Troncatti.)

Then I decided to do a search for pages with both Troncatti's name and Paula's. That brought up thirty-one hits. Most of them were references to the movie they'd shot. But one item was from a gossip page in an online entertainment site:

Taming the Bad Boy of Cinema?

Has Antonio Troncatti finally met his match? The former wild child of the film business seems to have settled into a bit of domestic bliss, sources tell us. Falling head over Amore shoes for Paula Montgomery during the shooting of Conquest, Troncatti is becoming a real homebody. He's particularly fond of Montgomery's daughter, Madeleine, who has had an almost hypnotic effect on the Italian auteur.

Montgomery, who is engaged in a custody battle with her soon-to-be ex, sometime actor Mark Gillen, has settled into home life with the director. Maybe his next film will be a paean to wedded bliss, rather than another blow-'em-up. But don't bet on it!

That was the last thing I read. I couldn't take any more after that. Funny thing was, I didn't mind the part about being a "sometime actor." Maybe a year ago that would have been the hard part.

Now, I was somewhat surprised to learn, that didn't matter a bit. What mattered was that Maddie was apparently bonding with the jerk who had stolen my wife.

Why was Paula with him, if he was such a jerk? Well, he was major league powerful for sure, and such Hollywood power was a turn on. No doubt the guy was charming and magnetic and all of that. And maybe there was a part of Paula that was drawn to the wild thing in order to tame him.

And I was powerless to stop her from trying.

I said that was the last thing I read. I meant about Troncatti and Paula. Feeling like I was about to rip my computer out of the socket and throw it out the window, I went back into Google and searched for a Bible.

———

Jesus said something about asking and getting, I remembered. A couple of search terms later, I found what I was looking for in the New International Version, Matthew, chapter 7:

> Ask and it will be given to you; seek and you will find; knock and the door will be opened to you. For everyone who asks receives; he who seeks finds; and to him who knocks, the door will be opened.

I looked for a loophole in there and couldn't find it. I decided to check another version, the King James, for the same passage.

> Ask, and it shall be given you; seek, and ye shall find; knock, and it shall be opened unto you: For every one that asketh receiveth; and he that seeketh findeth; and to him that knocketh it shall be opened.

My tongue twistethed as I read it out loud, but the effect was the same. Jesus really did say it, and I was being taught to trust the Bible.

So I asked.

God, give Maddie back to me. Please.

– 3 –

I went to church on Sunday, hoping to see Nikki there.
She wasn't.

Which made the service a little lonely to me. I tried to do my duty though and mouthed the songs along with the words on the screen. I even tried to believe all of what they said—about the glory of God and the love of Jesus being all we need.

The pastor, Scott Stephens, was in his forties and gave a good sermon. Only today I found myself answering him in my mind. I kept saying, No way, José.

Pastor Scott—as he insisted on being called—was preaching on the subject "The Heart's Radical Makeover." Basically, he said, living the Christian life begins with a surrender of the heart, the will, to God.

"When Jesus said you must be born again," Pastor Scott explained, "he did not mean that you become some sort of baby, although in a spiritual sense that is true. Rather, what he means is that your heart must be changed, cleansed of all the muck that's grown around it over the years. Muck that this society keeps throwing on it."

Muck is right, I thought. Try the family law system sometime!

"The Bible says in 2 Corinthians 5, 'Therefore, if anyone is in Christ, he is a new creation; the old has gone, the new has come!' This is a radical makeover. It is a complete change in our nature. But the strange thing, the unfortunate thing is this—many Christians don't live any differently in their day-to-day lives than they did before they were saved.

"You remember that bumper sticker many years ago? It said, I'm not perfect, just forgiven. Well, the theology may be correct, but the message to the world is lost when the car carrying that bumper sticker cuts somebody off in traffic. Or honks in anger. Or when the driver bends the truth, or acts out of self-interest only."

The image of the kid in the truck—and my road-rage reaction—came charging into my mind. He deserved worse than I gave him, I thought. And realized I was arguing with the preacher.

"To become a Christian who walks the way Jesus did requires more than good intentions. It requires a decision, followed by action. Listen to the words of Paul from Romans, chapter twelve. 'I urge you, brothers, in view of God's mercy, to offer your bodies as living sacrifices, holy and pleasing to God—this is your spiritual act of worship.' Do you hear that? Unless you are willing to offer all of your life to God, you are not worshiping him.

"And further, 'Do not conform any longer to the pattern of this world ...' We live by habits, and most of us have grown up with the habits of the world pounded into us: Do your own thing. Get all you can. Look out for number one. Do it to him before he does it to you."

If I could do it to Troncatti and Paula, I sure would.

"But the Bible tells us to cultivate habits different from the world and only then will we begin to actually be salt and light."

Salt? Light? What's up with that?

"Where do you start? May I suggest one place that hits very close to home in all of us. If you will do this one thing, I believe it will do more to cleanse your heart of the muck we've been talking about than just about anything else."

Okay, doctor, give it to me.

"We find it in Ephesians, chapter four, beginning at verse thirty-one. 'Get rid of all bitterness, rage and anger, brawling and slander, along with every form of malice. Be kind and compassionate to one another, forgiving each other, just as in Christ God forgave you.'"

In the morning LA Times they had a picture of a possum on a residential wall with an arrow sticking through it. The homeowner was tired of the creatures around his house and shot him with a crossbow.

I felt like that possum. The arrow was this stuff about anger and forgiveness and there was no way I was going to be able—

"Friends, if you have anything against anyone, you must learn to forgive, or a root of bitterness will take hold in you and block your fellowship, not just with each other, but with the Father. The

Bible is very clear about this. You have been forgiven in Christ, therefore you must forgive ..."

Forgive Paula? Troncatti? No, José, there is no way. They don't deserve it. You don't go around forgiving people unless they deserve it.

" ... even if you don't think they deserve it."

I almost slid off the pew. But not before remembering that Nikki had said something to me about forgiveness, too. It was getting to feel like a conspiracy around here.

"Because you did not deserve the mercy of God. I say, forgive, and you will feel a burden lifted from your spirit. And you will feel what it is like to become new."

⌒⌐

I waited around after the service to see if I could catch Nikki. Maybe she was coming to the next service.

But I didn't see her.

I did, however, see Mrs. Hancock.

"How is that little girl of yours?" she asked.

"As far as I know, fine."

She looked confused.

"It's a bad situation right now," I explained. "My wife wants a divorce."

"Oh, I'm sorry—"

"And Maddie. She wants full custody of Maddie."

Mrs. Hancock put her hand on my arm. "If there's anything I can do."

"Thanks, but ... You know, maybe there is. Would you be willing to write a letter? I need every friend I can get."

She said she would.

I hung around a little while longer. Still no Nikki. So I went to Tommy's for a burger and thought about what Pastor Scott had said. I thought about trying to forgive Paula and Troncatti, but it didn't make sense.

They were in the wrong, not me. They were up in Brentwood, laughing it up, with Maddie around.

No, I couldn't let go of my anger and hatred. It was about the only thing I had going for me.

– 4 –

Maddie had this thing when she was four. All kisses had to be rubbed in.

I couldn't just take a little peck on the cheek from her. She'd kiss me and then say, "Rub it in."

The first time I sort of laughed and said, "What?" Then she put her hand on my cheek and rubbed it, hard.

"It has to stick," she said.

And when Paula or I kissed her, Maddie would rub that in herself.

I started wondering if Maddie remembered when I kissed her, and how she rubbed it in.

I wondered about that for the next two weeks of my life, which came and went with numbing routine.

I worked Josephina's.

I went home.

I went to church on Sunday. Saw Nikki and waved, said hello, but that was about it. At least Ron Reid wasn't coming around.

The person I saw the most, in fact, was Sutton Hallard. Two more follow-up visits went just like dentist appointments, only less fun. Hallard was as easy to read as the Washington Monument. I had no idea what his report was going to be like.

Then came the day Alex called me and said I should come in. She had the report.

"Better for you to see it with me," she said.

BAD TO WORSE

Alex was subdued. I was like a terrier puppy hearing the dinner bowl sound. Tell me tell me tell me!

"Sit down," Alex said.

"What did he say?"

"Please sit down, Mark." She went behind her desk and waited until I parked myself in a chair.

"I'm going to give you a copy to read along with me," Alex said. "I want to go through this with you."

You know what this sounded like to me? A doctor about to discuss the various options for treatment of brain cancer.

That's why my hands were shaking as I took the thick report from her. I guessed it to be about sixty pages. I looked down at the cover page.

Sutton J. Hallard, Ph.D.
Clinical and Forensic Psychology

Declaration of Sutton J. Hallard, Ph.D.

I, SUTTON J. HALLARD, PH.D., a Psychological Child Custody Evaluator, hereby declare as follows:

I have completed a sixteen (16) hour Advanced Domestic Violence Training Program as required under Section 3111 of the California Family Code, as described in Section 1816.

I have also completed a four (4) hour Domestic Violence Update Program for the current calendar year, as required under Rule 1257.7.

I declare under penalty of perjury under the laws of the State of California that the foregoing is true and correct.

It was dated and signed.

I looked up at Alex. "Meaning basically the guy knows whereof he speaks?"

"Just read," Alex said.

I turned to the next page and saw this:

CONFIDENTIAL. DO NOT DUPLICATE FOR DISTRIBUTION. ALL INFORMATION CONTAINED HEREIN SHOULD BE KEPT FROM CHILDREN.

"This sounds horrible," I said.

"The page you're reading is boilerplate. Turn to the summary section, which starts—" Alex shuffled through the report—"on page forty-eight."

I did as ordered and started to read.

Pursuant to Stipulation of the parties and the court order, I have conducted a Psychological Evaluation in the custody and visitation matter of Madeleine Gillen, aged five years, the daughter of Mark Gillen and Paula Montgomery.

I received and reviewed from counsel and the parties numerous documents, including, but not necessarily limited to, Letters, Pleadings, Declarations, Court Orders, and the report of Sheila Bonner, Marriage and Family Counselor, as per previous order of this court.

DISCUSSION

This case presents a situation where the court ordered monitored contact between Mr. Gillen and Madeleine, and the results thereof. Mr. Gillen also has a previous history of abusive behavior.

"History!" My eyes were stinging with outrage. "Of abuse?"

"We'll get into that," Alex said. "I want you to read the rest of the section."

I tried, my face boiling all the way.

> Mr. Gillen represents that he has been unfairly denied visi-
> tation with Madeleine, and further that the monitored visit on
> August 17 was deliberately sabotaged, a charge not supported
> by documentation received by this evaluator.
> He denies all accusations of abuse, either physical or verbal.
> There appears to be an envy factor at play as well. Mr. Gil-
> len's career as an actor has been on the opposite trajectory as
> that of Ms. Montgomery. Mr. Gillen made certain allegations to
> this evaluator suggesting a bit of paranoia at the circumstances
> against him.

"Paranoia! Alex, this is so unfair."

"Tell me about it."

"I don't want to read any more."

"Read it, because you need to help me understand it."

"I'll help you understand it. It's all a lie."

"All of it?"

I threw the report on the ground. "Whose side are you on?"

Alex kept cool. "If you react this way in court, the judge is going to conclude that the report is all true. Can you see that?"

> Ms. Montgomery represents that she is fearful of Mr. Gillen's
> anger, and what that might mean for her safety and that of Mad-
> eleine. While Mr. Gillen has expressed an interest in religion as a
> way to deal with his anger, he has not as yet taken any specific
> steps toward anger management. He does appear aware that he
> needs such counseling.

"Wow," I said. "He threw me a bone."

Alex said nothing.

> Madeleine has been reluctant in her responses concerning
> her father. She expresses that she does not wish to visit with him

unattended by a monitor, but that she would prefer there be no visitation.

My heart, broken in half, was now shattering into smaller bits. Tears came to my eyes. I tried to stop them, but there was no way. I threw the report on Alex's desk. "I can't read anymore."

Alex said, "Mark, I need you to—"

"No! Not now." I turned toward the door.

"Mark—"

"Please. In God's name. Do something."

I left before she could say another word.

- 2 -

"You look bad," Roland said.

"Thanks."

"No, I mean Freddy Krueger bad. Ugly bad."

"Thanks again."

"Meaning what's up?"

I was at Roland's NOHO club again, sitting at a table with my piano-playing friend, trying to get out of myself. I told him about the report issued by Sutton Hallard.

"Bad," Roland opined.

"It's like I'm in this nightmare I can't wake up from." I was working on a Coke, wishing it had a heavy dose of rum in it. But no, I was determined not to get back into the drinking thing.

"What's next?" Roland said.

"The hearing. Comes up in a week."

"What happens there?"

I shrugged. "The lawyers duke it out."

"So will Maddie be there?"

"Probably not."

"Paula?"

"For sure."

"Troncatti?"

I lifted a glare. "If he is, I may do something I'll regret."

"Don't talk that way."

"I mean, it's all slipping away from me."

"Your lawyer okay?"

"She's not in the same league as the other guy. Money buys you certain things."

"It'll work out." Roland patted my arm. "You'll see."

But I didn't see. "What makes you such an optimist?"

"He's watching."

"Who?"

Roland pointed upward.

"God?"

Roland nodded.

"His eyesight isn't so good."

"God plays jazz."

"Right."

"No, think about it. God's the ultimate jazz man. Bible says the universe was chaos till God starting playing. A riff on light, and there it was. Light! Plays a little with the ocean—fish! I mean, where'd that come from? Fish? Jazz. So he gets hot, keeps jamming, makes a man."

"Big finish, huh?"

"Only he's not finished. Man keeps messing up, doing bad things, hitting all the wrong notes. But God still plays so man can hear the music. And the great thing is, we can jam with him if we want to." His face brightened. "This is good stuff. You writing this down?"

"Sorry."

"Thanks a lot, man. I'm tossing out genius and you just sit there."

"I heard you."

"I hope so." Roland stood up. "I gotta go play. Wait around, huh?"

I had another Coke as Roland got ready to play. Then Milo Ayers, the owner, came over to my booth. "Hey, good to see you, my friend."

I shook his hand. "You too, Mr. Ayers."

"How's things?"

"Hanging in there."

"You ever get a lawyer, like we talked about?"

"It's been in all the papers," I said.

"Never read 'em. Too depressing."

"Yeah. I couldn't afford your friend, but I found another one. I'm in the middle of things right now."

Milo Ayers, like a concerned uncle, slid into the booth next to me. "She's not cooperating, your wife?"

"No."

"Going to court?"

"Soon."

"You let me know how it turns out, eh?"

I looked at him, wondering why he should be so concerned about my little problems.

"I mean it," he said. "Consider me a friend. Who can get things done." He winked, patted me on the shoulder, and left.

And then Roland started playing a nice rendition of the old Billie Holiday song, "Ain't Nobody's Business If I Do."

— 3 —

When I got to the courthouse on the big day (without the benefit of a sound sleep for at least a week), I could see there was a media camp set up on the walkway between the two main buildings. Word had gotten around that Troncatti and Paula were going to show up at the hearing together. I'd seen that report on a cable program, as if it were the opening night of some rock concert. These two were the new darlings of the paparazzi.

I, on the other hand, was the news equivalent of chopped liver. None of the eager reporters recognized me as I made my way from an overpriced downtown parking lot toward the security doors of the Los Angeles Superior Courthouse. As anonymous as an unproduced screenwriter, I ambled past the reporters, who had the look of circling sharks in their eyes. I just wanted to get inside with the real sharks—the lawyers who would be doing battle for my future.

But along the way, I changed my mind. In Los Angeles, live media events are not to be avoided. I was half an hour early anyway. So I bought an LA Times from the machine and waited to catch the show like everyone else.

I also knew, but didn't want to admit, that I wanted to see Paula, live and in person. I wanted to watch her body language as she made her appearance. Maybe I was just a glutton for punishment.

There was no mention in the Times of the hearing, or Troncatti and Paula. Not that I could find, anyway. Instead there was the usual spate of bad news from the Middle East, our own inner city, along with today's special guest disaster area, Tennessee, which was experiencing massive flooding.

The world, in other words, was spiraling along as always, and for a fleeting moment I forgot about my troubles. Who was I, in the grand scheme of things? With people being slaughtered over barren strips of land, or losing their homes and, in some cases, lives, under the grinding forces of nature?

Who cared what happened to me?

The answer came like a cliché: God. God was supposed to care. That was what I was told in church, in Bible study, by friends. So maybe there would indeed be a party of One who gave a rip about what became of Mark Gillen after today.

Can you hear that, Lord? Consider it a prayer, will you?

I turned to the sports section. The Dodgers were in the wild card hunt, half a game behind the Giants. Then I noticed the reporters suddenly start to mill around like anxious sheep. Camera lights flicked on, making it seem like a small, artificial sun just erupted. People on the outside got the message something was up and angled in for a closer look. I was one of those people.

And suddenly, there they were.

Troncatti was taller than I thought he'd be. He wore the obligatory shades and had some sort of furry thing around his neck — either the carcass of a weasel or a fashionable item from some Italian men's store. His hair was longish and stylishly unstyled. His bearing was roguish and bad-little-boy. Along with plenty of money.

Paula was also in dark glasses along with a thousand pounds of jewelry. I could hardly believe it. She'd gone from being a good, working actress to some sort of Brentwood diva. I remembered reading about Elizabeth Taylor and Richard Burton back in the sixties. How they hooked up and became jet-set icons and "stars" more than real actors who cared about the craft.

Was that what I was observing now? The ruination of Paula Montgomery? We used to talk about how we wanted to be real actors, do Shakespeare together, maybe start a theater company someday. Dreams. Everything fades in the green light of money and the crush of media attention.

Troncatti started making some statement. Bryce Jennings, shorter than the director, was almost obscured by the thrusting microphones. He'd do his talking in court, of course, but right now he seemed more like a puppet master. Did he have his hand up Troncatti's back, controlling the whole deal?

I edged closer, trying to catch some of what Troncatti was saying. Like most Italians, he was doing a lot of talking with his hands. And I could tell, even from this distance, that this guy had a personal magnetism that would be hard to resist.

The reporters weren't resisting at all. They were eating up his every word. And I had a quick, stomach-churning thought that I wasn't in this guy's league, never would be, and no wonder Paula was attracted to him.

Paula was standing by his side, holding his arm, but looking subdued. No smile on her. I thought for a second she was going to turn and run toward the courthouse. That would have been news.

But she didn't move. She kept her lips pursed and her gaze forward while Troncatti kept flapping his yapper.

I strained to hear.

" — to all of our friends," he was saying in his accented voice, "and their support, we cannot say more. We are grateful for what is being shown to us. But we remember, always, this is not about the two of us alone, but of Maddie, beautiful Maddie, and what is best for her."

My heart was really pumping now and the air felt hot and sticky. I was starting to sweat under my arms. But still I couldn't turn away. It was like watching a car wreck; the car wreck was me.

Voices shouted more questions. Troncatti started to answer, but then Jennings stepped in and took over. He pulled Troncatti forward, parting the Red Sea of reporters. From where I was standing, near a brown trash can, the Israelite army would pass within a few yards.

I waited, hoping to get a closer look at the happy couple.

Paula glanced over and saw me, through a crack in the reporter mob. Very clearly and directly, her dark glasses looked at my face. I knew she saw me, because her mouth dropped open a little.

The power of surprise.

What surprised me was how I felt. I didn't know I was capable of such depths of hatred and rage. But the surprising thing, the shocking thing, the thing that almost sent me screaming into the street, was the other part of the feeling — longing.

You're so sunk. You still love her. Even while she and Italy Boy are sticking the spikes in you!

And then, just as quickly, she had her back turned to me. The reporters, amoeba-like, moved almost as one organism, after the couple du jour. And I almost lost my breakfast. I realized I was hugging the trash can to keep from doubling over.

- 4 -

"Remain seated and come to order," the bailiff said. "This court is now in session. The Honorable Harold J. Winger presiding."

The judge, his robe sweeping along with him, hotfooted it to the bench. He looked all business today. And like he'd already made up his mind.

My neck started to itch, in part because my shirt collar was too tight. I hadn't bought a new shirt in years, or worn a tie in months. Sweating outside during the little press conference didn't help. It was just past nine on a hot morning and stains were already appearing under my arms. The air conditioning in the courtroom was a little too cold. I'd probably come out with a case of pneumonia. But that was the least of my worries.

My biggest worries were sitting on the other side of the courtroom. Paula was enthroned, like a queen, next to Bryce Jennings. Troncatti was in the gallery section, near the slatted wood wall. He still had his dark glasses on. His limo driver, who I had somehow missed on the outside, was seated next to him, all brooding and Vin Diesel-like. Troncatti's bad boy bodyguard. There were a couple extra deputy sheriffs in the aisles, no doubt to keep autograph hunters and troublemakers at bay. A whole bunch of reporters, ready to scribble, were in the other seats.

"This is a custody hearing in the matter of Montgomery versus Gillen," the judge said. "State your appearances."

The reptile representing my wife stood up. His suit was perfect. Some men just are born to wear expensive clothes. Jennings was one of them. I wanted to stuff one of my nice T-shirts into his mouth.

"Good morning, Your Honor. Bryce Jennings for the petitioner, Paula Montgomery."

My lawyer, raring to go, got to her feet. "Alex Bedrosian for the respondent, Your Honor."

"Parties are present with counsel," Judge Winger said. "Very well. Mr. Jennings, call your first witness."

Jennings swept his arm toward the gallery. "Petitioner calls Dr. Sutton Hallard."

Like a rabbit appearing out of a hat, Sutton Hallard stood and ambled down the aisle. Reporters craned their necks and wrote in their little pads. The drama was about to begin.

Hallard stood like a bedpost as the clerk swore him in. Then he took his spot on the witness stand. He looked fresh and composed, as if he'd done this a thousand times before. Which he probably had.

"Good morning, Dr. Hallard," Jennings said, as if this were some tea party.

One lump or two? I thought.

"Good morning," Dr. Hallard said.

"You are the court certified evaluator in this matter?"

"I am."

Jennings snagged some papers from his table. "May I approach the witness, Your Honor?"

"You may," said the judge.

Jennings placed the papers on the rail of the witness box. "Is this the report you prepared and submitted to the court?"

Hallard gave it a quick glance. "Yes, it is."

"Is that your signature on the cover of the report?"

"It is."

"Thank you. I am not going to go over all of the ground you covered here, Doctor. The court has read the report. I would, however, like to have you expand upon a few matters."

"I'd be happy to."

I just bet you would, I thought. In your completely objective and unbiased fashion, right? And what right do you have to be happy about it?

"Dr. Hallard, on page seven of the report you reference Mr. Gillen's charge that his monitored visit with Madeleine on August 17 was sabotaged. You also state that the evidence for any interference with this visit was not forthcoming, and further that Ms. Montgomery denies any such charge. Do you recall that?"

"I do."

"Is it uncommon for one party in a custody dispute, such party being challenged on his or her parental competence, to react with charges against the other party that may, in fact, be completely fabricated?"

"Objection," Alex said. "Assumes facts not in evidence. The report of Dr. Hallard is only his opinion."

"It is merely a hypothetical, counsel," Bryce Jennings said with a condescending smirk. He looked at the judge. "I am entitled to ask a hypothetical question. This witness is an expert. The court has approved him in that regard. Further, the evidence code permits facts or data which are reasonably relied upon by experts in their particular field, to be considered in a hypothetical question. Such data is in the report."

"Whether this data is reasonable is what is at issue," Alex said. "Much of what is in this report is bogus."

"All right," Judge Winger said. "I'm going to overrule the objection. You will have the chance to cross-examine the witness, Ms. Bedrosian. Go ahead, Mr. Jennings."

Bryce Jennings repeated the hypothetical.

"No," Sutton Hallard said, "it is not uncommon for this to occur. It is, in fact, all too frequent. When one party perceives that evidence is mounting against him, resorting to false charges may be the last, desperate ploy."

The good doctor was calling me a liar, a desperate liar willing to say anything to win. Funny, but I thought that was what Bryce Jennings was. Why don't you psychoanalyze him, Sutton? There's one for your medical journals.

The assassination of the character of Mark Gillen continued. Jennings asked, "Does it sometimes happen that the party making the allegations actually comes to believe they are based on fact, when they are not?"

"Sometimes, yes."

"In which case, the party is somewhat delusional?"

"Or perhaps completely delusional. But, I must add, this is rare."

"But it does happen?"

"Yes."

"Do you have an opinion as to whether it has happened to Mr. Gillen?"

Sutton Hallard's beady eyes — at least that's how they looked to me, Mr. Delusional — bore in on me for a second.

"I would not like to speculate on that," he said.

How big of you, I thought. But you'll speculate on everything else.

The witness added, "Although ..."

"Yes?" Bryce Jennings prodded.

"There is an aspect to Mr. Gillen's behavior that may point, in a small way, in that direction."

My hands were squeezing the sides of my chair now. Was I hearing right? Was he going to say I really was delusional, crazy, a wild-eyed danger to society? If he was, I thought I might prove him right by jumping into the witness box and pulling his tie extra tight.

"What aspect would that be?" Bryce Jenning asked.

"Mr. Gillen has made a sudden leap into religion," the good doctor explained. "This coincides with the timing of this custody dispute. Now, religion can be a perfectly healthy way for people to deal with problems in their lives. But under certain conditions, it can be an escape from reality."

I had this terrible feeling that Hallard had rehearsed this little speech, and he and Jennings had set it up to appear spontaneous. My anger was flaring, but if I was going to be painted as a religious nut, I thought it might be good for some Old Testament action to happen right here in court. Maybe a pillar of fire to consume Hallard and Bryce Jennings, right in front of everyone's eyes. Is that admissible enough for you, Your Honor?

Hallard continued. "In this instance, from what I have gathered from Mr. Gillen, he has gone rather quickly into a constricting form of Christianity. It offers him the sudden and comforting appearance of black and white, good and evil, and makes it easy for him to separate himself from Ms. Montgomery in this fashion. This, of course, raises concerns for—"

"Objection!" Alex's voice rang out, louder than I'd ever heard it. "Is this court seriously going to entertain the religious bigotry we are hearing from this witness?"

Winger drummed his fingers on the bench. "Do you have grounds for your objection?"

"Relevance to start with. Materiality. Competence. This witness is not an expert in the field of religion. Furthermore, we have First Amendment implications here. The right of free exercise. To make my client's religious affiliation grounds for denying custody is unconstitutional."

"If I may?" Bryce Jennings said.

Judge Winger nodded at him.

"Ms. Bedrosian's impassioned speech notwithstanding, there is a line of cases which makes religious affiliation one of several factors to consider in custody matters. The court must always seek the best interest of the child, and how religion may affect the child is of critical importance. It is quite true that religion alone has not been held dispositive. However, it has certainly been considered along with all other factors. If the court wishes, I can prepare points and authorities."

"I am aware of the cases," Judge Winger said. "What about Ms. Bedrosian's argument that Dr. Hallard is not an expert in the field of religion?"

"If Your Honor please, I can qualify him in that regard."

"Go ahead."

Jennings turned back to Hallard. "Doctor, what is your background with regard to religious studies and its psychological impacts?"

"As part of my doctoral program at Johns Hopkins, I took a seminar in comparative religion with Dr. Simon Stuart, of Princeton Theological Seminary. That resulted in a paper in which I compared the religious teachings of Judaism, Christianity, and Islam with regard to the mind's place in monotheistic moral systems."

If this was gobbledygook, it was sure impressive sounding. I could feel the heat emanating off Alex. She wanted to get at this guy. But did she have the weapons?

"I also contributed a paper to the Journal of Theological Studies on the impact of religion on various mental states."

"Is one of those mental states relevant to this case?"

"Yes. I have concluded that Mr. Gillen has a problem with anger, and that is one of the mental states I explored in this paper."

"Your Honor," Jennings said to Judge Winger, "I submit that Dr. Hallard is qualified to offer an expert opinion in the matter of religion, when it has a direct bearing on the question to be decided, namely, the competence of Mr. Gillen as a parent."

With hardly a second to think of it, Judge Winger said, "I agree."

Alex objected again, the judge denied it again, and Bryce Jennings smiled as he asked his next question.

"How do anger and religion play a role in the matters at issue?"

"It is quite common for the sudden adherence to a fundamental religion to result in the subject's attempt to sublimate, rather than deal openly with, perceived personality problems. In the case of anger, the subject may attempt for a time to keep from expressions of anger and may even be successful in the short term."

"What about the long term?"

"Inevitably, the suppression results in an explosion. A fit of rage may result with attendant violent manifestations. The subject, feeling massive guilt, may then go to the opposite extreme in his religious life."

"Expand on that, if you will."

"There will be a tendency to become something of a fanatic in religious exercise. And this is where I am most concerned about the child in this case."

"Tell the court."

Sutton Hallard, all professional dignity and with the calm of a professional hit man, half-smiled at the judge. "I am concerned that Madeleine would be subject to the more harmful effects of religious fundamentalism with Mr. Gillen. His religious sensibilities are still quite new, and until there is a record of his being able to deal with those, I fear harm may come to the child."

"What sort of harm?"

"It runs the gamut, from psychological harm in the form of thought control, to physical violence in the form of corporal punishment."

Alex couldn't contain herself any longer. "Your Honor, I object in the strongest terms possible to this testimony, ask that it be stricken, and that you do not consider it in any way in your decision. This is patently unconstitutional and outside the purview of this witness's alleged expertise."

The entire courtroom seemed to take a collective breath. The judge thought about it for about two seconds.

"Overruled."

I felt like I'd been socked in the mouth, and I know Alex felt the same. We were both reeling as Bryce Jennings finished with Sutton Hallard.

Alex requested a short recess.

– 5 –

"Can we rip his lungs out?" I asked Alex. "Is that legal?"

"Moral maybe," Alex said. "But I don't think the D.A. would look kindly on it."

We were on a bench outside the courthouse. We had half an hour before court started up again. Sitting in the shade of the municipal trees was actually pleasant. But my mind was too consumed with visions of Sutton Hallard buried up to his neck in sand to take any pleasure in it.

"How can he sit there and lie like that?" I was having trouble getting my breath to stay below hurricane level.

"He's Jennings's hired gun, is what he is. He wants to be used by Jennings in the future because he knows he will be well paid. And while it's not uncommon for evaluators to be biased, it is odd that Jennings would call him to the stand after a favorable report. He really wants to bury us in front of the judge."

"Is the judge buying it?"

Alex shrugged. "He's hard to read. I'm going to try and make sure the words are very plain when I cross-examine."

"What are you going to do?"

"Go for the jugular."

That brought the first smile of the day to my face. Maybe the first in a week. "You know, I love it when you talk like that."

"Shut up and finish your coffee."

As I took a sip I glanced to my left. What I saw made me almost spit my coffee out like a bad comedian.

Ron Reid, in an ill-fitting shirt and tie, was making his way toward the courthouse.

"What's he doing here?"

Alex gave a look. "Who?"

"My wayward father."

My lawyer watched Ron amble toward the doors. She shrugged. "Public's entitled to hear what's going on. Except ... your father doesn't normally dress that way, does he?"

"No."

"Hmm."

"What do you mean, 'hmm'?"

"I mean he's dressed for court. Like a witness."

I looked at her. "You think Jennings is going to call him as a witness?"

"I wouldn't put anything past Bryce Jennings."

Ron was sitting in the hallway outside the courtroom. When he saw me he stood up and put his hands out, as if to say, I'm as mystified as you are.

Not likely.

"Hey," he said, "I got subpoenaed by the other guy."

"What for?" I asked. Alex was standing next to me, wanting to hear for herself.

"I don't know. I just—"

A young woman with tight blond hair and a dark blue suit tapped Ron on the shoulder. "Please don't talk to anyone, Mr. Reid. Come this way, please."

Sheepishly, Ron shrugged at me and then followed the woman down the hall.

"What is that all about?" I asked.

"She's an associate of Jennings's," Alex said. "They're going to put him on the stand if they need him."

"What's he going to say about me?"

"You don't know?"

I tried to think. "There's nothing he can say either way. He never saw me with Maddie. Maybe I got ticked off at him. It could be my anger."

Alex nodded thoughtfully.

"Will they put him on?" I asked.

"If they don't think Sutton Hallard makes enough of a case."

"He's doing pretty good so far," I said, the despair thick in my mouth.

"He hasn't gotten by me yet." Alex started for the courtroom.

———

Alex took her notes to the podium in the middle of the courtroom. This was it, the showdown at high noon—her cross-examination of Sutton Hallard. My best hope for a chance to get custody of Maddie.

And where was Maddie? I suddenly wondered. Who was she with at this very moment? Not Paula or Troncatti. Erica? That thought spilled ice cubes in my veins.

I pictured Maddie in that big house. Was she, even now, crying for some reason? Had she skinned her knee or stubbed her toe or lost Bonson, her stuffed ape? Why wasn't anyone there? Why wasn't I allowed to comfort her? Why wasn't—

"Dr. Hallard," I heard Alex say, "how long have you been a clinical psychologist?"

"Twelve years," Hallard said.

"And how long have you been giving evaluations in family law cases?"

"About seven years, give or take."

"Give or take what, sir?"

Hallard looked momentarily confused, like he'd misplaced his cuff links or something. "A few months, I suppose."

"Dr. Hallard, we are going to be covering very specific questions regarding a highly sensitive matter. Rather than supposition, I would like to—"

"Objection!" Bryce Jennings was on his feet. "Ms. Bedrosian's lecture, I am sure, is of little interest to this court. I would remind Ms. Bedrosian that there is no jury present to play to and that we are all here on a matter of much more—"

Judge Winger put his hand up. "All right, counsel. For the record I'll overrule the objection. We're just getting started here, so we all might as well take a deep breath. The witness is experienced, and I'm sure understands the need for specificity. I'm going to give Ms. Bedrosian some latitude, since she bears the burden of persuasion. Continue, Ms. Bedrosian."

Score a round to us, I thought. Or maybe it was just one punch. But I was willing to take anything at this point. At least Alex was showing both Jennings and the judge she was not going to back down one bit.

She took a white piece of paper out of a manila folder. "According to your curriculum vitae, Dr. Hallard, which is quite extensive, you were in partnership with two other doctors for five years?"

Hallard nodded. "That is correct."

"And you left the partnership in 1996?"

"Correct."

"What part of 1996? For specificity."

Sutton Hallard looked up at the ceiling a moment. "That would have been—the early spring, I believe."

"And then you opened your own office in that same year, is that correct?"

"Correct."

"What month was that?"

As I watched Sutton Hallard, the cool and collected clinical psych-dude, I thought I noticed his eyebrows twitch. Or maybe I was just hoping I saw it.

"I believe it was September," Hallard said. "Yes, September."

"Early, middle, or late?"

"Your honor," Bryce Jennings said, "how is this relevant?"

"Good question," Judge Winger said to Alex.

Alex said, "Indulge just a couple more questions on this, Your Honor?"

"A couple," said the judge. "But then let's move it along."

Alex looked at the witness. "Your answer?"

"Yes, I believe it was in the latter part of September. I remember because my lease began in the beginning of September and I was trying to get everything up in the new office, but things kept happening."

I threw a quick glance at Bryce Jennings, sitting at the other table. He had a concerned look on his face. What was Alex up to? Whatever it was, it was making Jennings sweat a little, and I loved it. Paula, on the other side of Jennings, was clasping and unclasping her hands.

"Things do happen, don't they?" Alex said.

Hallard seemed mystified.

My lawyer stepped to the side of the podium. "So between the spring of '96 and late September of the same year, you did not have an office, is that correct?"

"That is ... true."

"Why not?"

The question rang out like a shot. The way Alex asked it, she was telling everybody in the courtroom, including the witness, that she very well knew the answer. And suddenly Sutton Hallard's poker face got a serious case of the jitters.

Bryce Jennings got the message. "How is this at all relevant, Your Honor? I must object. When Dr. Hallard took residence in his office? How he spent his summer vacation? I don't understand."

"You will," Alex said.

The courtroom was suddenly stone silent. The reporters seemed to lean forward as one.

"May we approach the bench?" Jennings said quickly.

The judge motioned them forward, which only heightened the tension in the room. And with both lawyers striding toward the bench, there was no human obstruction between Paula and me.

I looked toward her. She looked at me.

For one second our eyes locked. My breath left me. She was so beautiful, even with the exhausted look she had. For a split second I almost felt sorry for her, thought I'd let her off an embarrassed hook by looking away. But steel came back to me, and I knew I was not going to be the one to look away. In fact, I kept right on honing in with my stare until she looked down at her hands.

A minor victory. I felt hollow.

Jennings was motioning wildly in front of the judge. Alex stood by calmly, listening. When the huddle broke, I couldn't tell from the looks what had happened, who had come out on top.

"Back on the record," Judge Winger said.

"The question is," said Alex, "what happened between your leaving the partnership in the spring of 1996 and opening your own office in late September, that interrupted your professional life?"

Sutton Hallard breathed deeply. "I experienced some personal setbacks, and was taking steps to deal with them."

"By personal setbacks, what do you mean?"

Bryce Jennings was tight lipped. The judge had ruled in our favor. Had to be. Why else was Jennings sitting there like a dumb Buddha?

"I went through a divorce," Sutton Hallard said, "and was drinking more than I should."

"You sought treatment for the abuse of alcohol?"

"Yes. But may I add—"

"Thank you. You've answered the question."

"Your Honor, please," Jennings said. "The witness wishes to expand upon his answer."

"The question has been answered," Alex repeated.

"I'll allow the witness some latitude, just as I've allowed you, Ms. Bedrosian." The judge nodded to Hallard. "You may complete your answer, sir."

"Thank you." Hallard assumed a prouder pose. "I have never allowed anything in my personal life to interfere with my professional duties. I have never had any disciplinary action taken against me by the governing boards of my various associations, nor the state of California."

Good answer, I thought. But Alex had managed to make a good point, too. Was it enough to shoot down this guy's testimony? That remained to be seen.

– 6 –

Alex grilled Dr. Sutton Hallard for two hours. She attacked every part of his report. She bit into Hallard like a Doberman chomping a mailman's leg. She was magnificent.

But so was the witness. He fought back hard. It was like the Ali-Frazier fights. One fighter went down, got up, knocked the other guy into the ropes. For fifteen rounds.

Then, somehow, Alex kicked into a higher gear.

"Dr. Hallard, I want to read to you a portion of your report. This is from page twenty-seven if counsel wants to refer to it. You state: 'Madeleine has been reluctant in her responses concerning her father. She expresses that she does not wish to visit with him unattended by a monitor, but that she would prefer there be no visitation.' Did you write that, sir?"

"Yes, I did."

"You choose your words carefully, don't you?"

"Of course I do."

"Every word here is important, because this is a matter of the utmost importance, the future of people's lives, is it not?"

"I take this all very seriously."

"But there is a word in here that is not very specific. Negative, yes, but not specific. That word is reluctant. It is ambiguous, is it not?"

"Ambiguous?"

"Yes, that means it is open to several nuances of meaning."

"I know what ambiguous means." Sutton Hallard looked like the kid on the playground who just got teased for an answer he missed in class. "The word seems clear enough to me."

"Does it now?" Alex left the podium and approached Hallard. He stiffened. "Do you refuse to answer my questions, sir?"

"No, of course not."

"Would you rather be back in your office now?"

"I'm not sure I know what you mean?"

"Rather than testifying here in court."

"Well, certainly, all things being equal, who'd rather be grilled by an attorney?"

There was a ripple of laughter in the courtroom.

Alex nodded. "Then I take it there is a degree of reluctance here?"

Hallard narrowed his eyes. "I wouldn't say that."

"Did I use the word incorrectly? You just said you'd rather not be grilled by an attorney."

"If you're going to get technical, sure, you might use the word that way."

"So there are a number of ways to use that word. That makes its use in your report ambiguous, does it not?"

"I can explain what I meant."

"I'm not interested in what you mean now. You filed a report, you used this word, and you have no facts to back it up. You offer it as an opinion, but there is nothing in this report that explains the basis of that word, is there?"

"I think the report is clear."

"That's the problem, Doctor. Your definition of clearness is different than mine."

Bryce Jennings objected and the judge sustained it, but Alex did not even pause for a breath.

"There is nothing in your report on the basis for Madeleine's so-called reluctance, is there?"

"Her visits with her father," Hallard snapped back. "She doesn't want to see him."

"I asked you about the basis of that opinion, sir."

"It's what I picked up from her responses to my questions."

"Did you include any actual questions and any actual responses in this report?"

"I don't believe so."

"You don't know?"

"No, I did not."

Alex swept back to the podium and looked briefly at her notes. "Do you recall testifying on direct that it is a frequent occurrence for a party to resort to false charges as a desperate ploy?"

"I believe I said that is likely to happen when one party believes the evidence is mounting against him."

"And by him, you of course mean him or her, don't you?"

"Depending on the case. In this case —"

"Thank you. Isn't it also true that false charges may be made based upon ill feelings alone?"

"That can happen, yes."

"So if one side bears enough animosity toward another side, this ploy of false allegations may be resorted to."

"I've seen it done."

"And isn't it also true that this may be a trial tactic used by overzealous attorneys?"

Bryce Jennings lurched out of his chair. "This is an outrage, Your Honor! If Ms. Bedrosian is accusing me of unethical behavior then I demand the basis for the charge."

I think Alex's eyes twinkled. "It is merely a hypothetical, counsel."

Judge Winger almost laughed, like a parent would at two siblings fighting over the TV. "I'll allow the witness to answer."

Hallard seemed surprised. "I cannot speak to that. I don't interview the attorneys."

"Lucky for you," Alex said. "I have one more area I want to discuss with you, Doctor. You have held yourself out as an expert on religion as it relates to mental health, is that right?"

"That's a somewhat broad description, but yes."

"And on direct, I believe you used the term constricting form of Christianity. Do you recall that?"

"Yes."

"What did you mean by that word, constricting?"

"Well, I meant to say that Mr. Gillen has accepted the teachings of that wing of Christianity which is very harsh in its treatment of personal expression."

"Harsh?"

"Yes."

"Do they use whips?"

"Of course not. I mean they teach a very black-and-white doctrine of right and wrong."

"That's terrible," Alex said. "Imagine that."

"Objection," said Jennings. "Argumentative."

"Sustained."

Alex acted like she didn't even notice. "So your assessment of a religion which teaches right and wrong is that it is harsh?"

Sutton Hallard cleared his throat. "It can be, especially for a child. It can become a fearful experience."

"I see. Tell me, do you agree with the following statement: The fear of the Lord is the beginning of knowledge."

"No, I don't believe that's an accurate statement. God should be an object of love, especially for a small child."

"If I told you that statement came directly from the Bible, what would you say?"

Again Bryce Jennings objected, but Alex was ready. "Your Honor, Mr. Jennings qualified Dr. Hallard as an expert in religious studies. If I wish to explore that subject, he can hardly bring about an objection."

"My only question would be relevance," Judge Winger said.

"If you'll allow me to continue, Your Honor, I expect to show an unprofessional bias in this witness, which calls into question his entire report."

If this had been a TV movie, the courtroom would have gasped at that point. The silence that followed had almost the same effect. It felt like a ticking bomb had just been placed in the middle of the courtroom.

After what seemed like a ten-minute breath, Winger said, "All right. I'll let this go a little further."

Jennings was steamed as he sat down. For the first time I thought he looked a little shaky. Go Alex!

My lawyer opened the briefcase on her table and took out a leather-bound Bible. She held it like a weapon. Opening it, the pages riffled like little gunshots.

Alex stopped turning the pages. "Please answer the question, Doctor. I just quoted a passage from the Bible for you, the book of wisdom, Proverbs. Chapter one, verse seven. Do you disagree with the statement that 'the fear of the Lord is the beginning of knowledge'?"

"I believe the Bible teaches that God is love," Hallard said.

"How about this passage?"

"I'd have to see it in its context."

"Do you believe the Bible teaches that it is a sin to have rage?"

"That may very well be."

"So if a person, let's say Mr. Gillen, believes the Bible to be the Word of God, and believes that rage is a sin, and devoutly tries to overcome that sin, wouldn't you say that's a good thing?"

"My opinion is that a person has to deal with who he or she is, and that attempts to sublimate parts of the personality may result in an explosion later on."

"I believe you said sublimate as opposed to dealing openly with. Is that right?"

"I don't recall saying that."

"Would you like me to have the reporter read the answer back to you?"

"Yes." Hallard was now openly defiant.

"Your Honor, may I have the reporter read that back?"

The judge said, "All right. The reporter will do a word search for dealing openly with."

The reporter, a rotund woman with flying fingers, stood up from her transcribing machine and went to a computer terminal on a table near the judge's bench. She keyed something in, waited a moment, made a few clicks with a mouse. Then she hit a key and waited. She returned to her station with a piece of paper from a printer.

"The witness gave the following answer," the reporter said. "'It is quite common for the sudden adherence to a fundamental religion to result in the subject's attempt to sublimate, rather than deal openly with, perceived personality problems. In the case of anger, the subject may attempt for a time to keep from expressions of anger and may even be successful in the short term.'"

"Does that refresh your recollection, Dr. Hallard?" Alex asked.

"Yes."

"And is that still your opinion?"

"Yes, it is."

"Do you know what Christians mean by confession of sin?"

"Of course."

"It's something like when clients open up to you in your office, isn't it?"

I thought I saw Hallard's cheeks getting rosy. "In some ways, I suppose."

"Please don't suppose any more, Doctor. Yes or no?"

"Yes."

"And when people tell you intimate things, they are seeking to deal with them openly, aren't they?"

"Yes."

Alex flipped a few pages in her Bible. "Quoting now from the book of James, chapter five, verse sixteen. 'Therefore confess your sins to each other and pray for each other so that you may be healed.' Does that sound like failing to deal openly with problems, sir?"

"Ms. Bedrosian," Hallard said, "you can quote chapter and verse all day long. What I was concerned with is the actual out-working of this form of Christianity with regard to the child."

"Just what is that concern? Are you afraid Madeleine might actually come to believe in Christianity?"

"No, that's not it."

Alex answered with a shout. "Then just what is it, Doctor!"

The whole place seemed to rock back at the sound of her voice. Sutton Hallard looked like a man slapped. And when he jumped back at Alex, I knew she'd gotten him right where she wanted.

"It is the threat of physical harm," he said. "This type of Christianity believes in corporal punishment of children. I've seen it time and time again."

"Oh, you're one of the progressive doctors who knows that a spanking can never be good for a child, is that right?"

"Corporal punishment is antithetical to the best interests of the child."

Alex had a file sitting on the counsel table. She opened it and took out some papers, then put them on the podium. "Are you aware of the study conducted by Dr. Diana Baumrind, a psychologist at the University of California at Berkeley?"

"I have heard of Dr. Baumrind."

"Do you agree or disagree with her findings, which she summarizes as follows: 'Occasional spankings do not damage a child's social or emotional development. These results call into question claims that any physical punishment hurts children psychologically and damages society as a whole.'"

"I happen to disagree."

"Have you conducted any such study?"

"No. I've read several, however."

Alex looked at her notes. "Have you read 'Familial and Temperamental Determinants of Aggressive Behavior: A Causal Analysis'?"

"I don't recollect at this moment."

"Wherein it was concluded, 'Childhood aggressiveness has been more closely linked to parental permissiveness and negative criticism than to physical discipline'?"

"I would have to read it."

"Obviously."

Jennings's objection was sustained.

"It is inappropriate to hit a child!" Hallard said.

"Not in the opinion of the Ninth Circuit Court of Appeals," Alex said, pulling out another paper. "You are familiar with the Calabretta case, I'm sure."

"Which one was that?"

"A Christian family that dared to spank a child? And based on an anonymous tip, a social worker showed up with a policeman and forced the mother to pull down a three-year-old child's pants. Does that refresh your recollection?"

"I think so."

"What did the court hold, sir?"

"I don't remember."

"I'll read it. 'A social worker is not entitled to sacrifice a family's privacy and dignity to her own personal views on how parents ought to discipline their children.' Do you agree or disagree?"

"In that case, I would have to disagree."

"Let's see then. You disagree with the Bible, other psychologists, and the Ninth Circuit Court of Appeals, is that about it?"

"There are always areas of disagreement in my field."

"Precisely," Alex said. "And what you have presented is a one-sided, biased report which justifies your personal opinions."

"Object to the speech, Your Honor," Jennings said.

"Noted," the judge said.

Alex flipped to another part of Hallard's report. "You did not interview Antonio Troncatti, did you?"

The name hit like a balloon popping.

"No, I did not. He is not a party to this action."

"He is, however, Ms. Montgomery's live-in boyfriend, is he not?"

"Yes."

"That didn't factor into your opinion?"

"That Ms. Montgomery is living with Mr. Troncatti?"

"That Ms. Montgomery is an adulteress, yes."

Well, you could have set off the fire alarm in the building after that, and no one in the courtroom would have moved. The reporters acted like kids at a birthday party when the piñata erupts. Candy for everybody! Big ol' pieces, too.

Jennings, of course, put on a show of outrage. But it was Troncatti who became the perfect sideshow. His shout of what I took to be Italian wrath was both pitiful and theatric, sort of a Verdi aria as sung by Jackie Gleason on The Honeymooners. His arms were flapping around, like some landlocked crane honking at intruders. I almost laughed.

Judge Winger was not laughing. He was pounding his hand on the bench (he didn't have a gavel for some odd reason) and shouting, "Enough! Enough!"

Meanwhile, Alex leaned casually at the podium, her arms folded.

Finally, some order was restored. Judge Winger's face had a slight, crimson glow. "Ms. Bedrosian," he said, "your use of inflammatory language is not needed."

"Excuse me, Your Honor," Alex said, in a way that made me think contempt of court. "What word would you have me use? Paramour is a bit dated, don't you think?"

"You do not need to cast aspersions on the petitioner."

"Just so I'm clear, Your Honor. You are saying that the fact that Ms. Montgomery is engaged in a sexual relationship outside of her marriage is not of any relevance here?"

"It isn't to me," the judge said.

"I want that noted, on the record."

"It is already on the record. Now move on."

"Clarification. Does the fact that Ms. Montgomery's boyfriend has a violent temper have any relevance?"

"Object to that as well," Jennings said.

"Sustained."

Alex looked ready to jump up and literally hit the ceiling. "Your Honor, I take exception to that. I have numerous reports from news sources that point to Antonio Troncatti's own anger problems, and thus call into question his fitness to be around a young child and—"

"I have ruled, Ms. Bedrosian." The judge looked at Hallard. "Sir, do you think there is any danger, any at all, in the girl's living where she is, with her mother and the mother's boyfriend?"

Hallard didn't hesitate. "Not at all. In fact, the home and amenities provided are quite good. I did not witness anything to indicate any risks."

"Thank you," Judge Winger said. "That covers that, as far as I'm concerned. Do you have any other areas to go over, Ms. Bedrosian?"

"Your Honor, you are cutting off a relevant line of inquiry."

"I take it then your answer is no. We will take a recess."

~ 7 ~

The press was all over us outside the courtroom. Funny, now we were the stars. Alex's cross-examination and the fireworks over that word—adulteress—had met all the requirements of drama for the evening news.

Alex did the talking, and she was like an actor that handles the big moment in a play with a Tony award-winning performance.

"The report in this case is a bogus piece of psychobabble that is biased and unprofessional. When the best interests of a child are at stake, this simply cannot be allowed to go unchallenged. The attacks on Mr. Gillen's character are without foundation. I believe that was shown through the testimony of the other side's own witness."

"Will your client be testifying?" a reporter shouted.

"We'll see," Alex said.

"How has this affected him?"

"How do you think? His life is being trashed for no other reason than vindictiveness. But that's how some people practice law in this city."

As if on cue, Bryce Jennings walked out of the courthouse doors, Troncatti and Paula next to him. As soon as a couple of reporters saw them and scampered over, the rest followed suit.

Like hogs at feeding time.

Troncatti was livid. He was doing that same wild stuff with his hands. I hoped they got a good dose of that and would report it again.

"Let's get out of here," Alex said.

We drove a few miles away to a Quiznos. My stomach wasn't accepting food, so I sipped a Sprite while Alex munched a sandwich.

"You want to go on the stand?" she asked.

"Want to or need to?"

"I think Jennings is going to put on more witnesses. How they do will answer your question. Regardless, I don't want to do it if you think you'll ..."

"I'll what?"

"Not be able to handle it." She looked me square in the eye. "I'm sorry to say it, but Jennings will do whatever he can to get you to lose your temper."

"So if I kick him until he's dead, that's a bad thing?"

"I mean it."

"I know. I can do it. I want to do it."

"Think long and hard," Alex warned.

"For Maddie," I said. "I can do this for Maddie."

∽

Alex was right. Jennings called Ron Reid to the stand.

It was a surreal experience, seeing my biological father step up to testify for the other side. The big question was what possible relevance he was to Paula's case. It didn't take long to find out.

After a few preliminaries, Jennings asked Ron about his reasons for making contact with me after all these years.

"I just thought it was time," Ron explained. "And I found out I had a granddaughter."

When he said that I looked over at Paula. I wondered what she thought about that aspect of this whole thing. Ron Reid was not the sort of person she'd want seeing Maddie.

"How did you find that out, sir?"

"I saw something in a news story. About the divorce and custody thing and all."

"Which prompted you to contact Mr. Gillen?"

"Yes."

"And was that contact successful?"

"Sort of."

"What do you mean, sort of?"

"I mean it wasn't exactly a warm family reunion."

"Can you explain that?"

Ron shrugged. "I can understand. Father comes to you, after all this time, you're not exactly gonna take it like Christmas. But we talked it out, and he let me stay in his place."

"He invited you in?"

"Yeah."

"And what can you tell us about that experience?"

With a little twitch of the lip, Ron said, "It wasn't the greatest. We had a fight."

"What was the fight about?" Jennings asked.

I leaned forward.

"Do I have to say?" Ron Reid asked.

"You are under oath, sir," Jennings snapped.

"Well, I came in one night and he was doing something I thought wasn't a good idea, for him or for his daughter, if she ever came back to live with him."

Now I was coiled tight, like I might snap. What was he talking about?

Jennings knew already and asked with a calm voice, "What was this something you didn't think a good idea?"

Reid swallowed. "Smoking dope."

My voice exploded. Words came out by themselves, like horses from a flaming barn. "No way! That's a lie!"

It was one of those TV moments, where the innocent accused screams out just before the commercial break. Up to that point I always thought those moments a bit contrived. No more.

"Mr. Gillen!" The judge said. "You are not to talk in open court, is that understood?"

"He's a liar!"

Alex put her hand on my arm, trying to calm me. I jerked it away.

"That's all, Mr. Gillen." The judge's face was getting red.

"Do something!" I shouted at Alex.

Judge Winger pounded his fist on the bench. "Last warning, Mr. Gillen. Sit down and be quiet."

Alex took my arm again and pulled me down, generating laughter from some in the courtroom. "Be quiet," she whispered sternly.

"But Alex—"

"Be quiet."

Finally, a modicum of sanity prevailed in my mind. I clammed up and let my hatred of Ron Reid warm my body.

Bryce Jennings, who had been smiling at the podium, continued as if nothing had happened.

"Mr. Reid, how did you know that Mr. Gillen was smoking a narcotic?"

"I'm not proud about it, but I know what grass—marijuana—smells like, because I used to do a lot of it."

"You have drugs in your background?"

"Like I said, I'm not proud about it. But I'm clean now."

"No longer use drugs?"

"No, sir."

"What did you tell Mr. Gillen, if anything, about the use of drugs?"

Ron Reid swallowed once, the liar. "I told him he shouldn't be doing that around his kid, my granddaughter. I told him that was about the worst thing he could do."

"And what was his reaction, if any?"

"Nothing. He told me to mind my own business if I wanted to stay around."

"What did you say to that?"

"I told him I was going to move out. And the next day, I did. I didn't need to be around that stuff."

With a nod, Bryce Jennings smiled at Alex. "No more questions."

I don't know what Alex was thinking when she got up to question my lying father. I did see the back of her neck, though. It was fire-engine red.

"Mr. Reid," she said, "you have a criminal record, isn't that right?"

"Objection," Bryce Jennings said. "Improper impeachment."

Judge Winger looked at Alex. "Only felony convictions can be considered for impeachment, Ms. Bedrosian. Do you have a foundation for this?"

"I do," Alex said.

"Then I'll allow it."

Alex turned back to Reid. "Sir, do you have a criminal record?"

"I'm not proud of that."

"Apparently you're not proud of a lot of things, are you?"

Bryce Jennings mouthed an objection, more for show, I think, than anything. It was like a halfhearted attempt to give his witness a few moments to think about things. But the judge sustained it, calling the question argumentative.

Big deal, I thought.

Alex didn't pause. "You served time for dealing drugs, right?"

"Yeah." The slightest bit of fear snuck into Ron Reid's eyes. He glanced over at Bryce Jennings. I got the feeling he wanted to say something like Hey, I didn't sign up for this.

"And you served how long for that?"

"Six years, give or take."

"What comes next on your menu of crime?"

Jennings objected again, calling the question argumentative again. Of course, I thought. This is court, you jerk.

Alex sighed. "Your Honor, I'm sorry that Mr. Jennings is so sensitive to the English language. But he is the one who put this witness on the stand, he is the one who brings Ron Reid's criminal record into this proceeding. If he does not care for the way I ask questions, tell him he is free to step outside. But allow me to cross-examine."

The judge said, "All right. The question is colorfully phrased, but there is nothing objectionable in it. Overruled."

"Tell us," Alex practically spat at Ron Reid.

Reid said something I couldn't hear. Neither could the court reporter, who said, "Please repeat that."

"A little louder, please, Mr. Reid," said Judge Winger.

"Battery," Reid said.

"Whom did you batter?"

"A guy who provoked me."

"Oh? Are you easily provoked?"

"I don't think so. I try to get along with everybody."

"But not this man you battered, is that right?"

"He was drunk. We were in a bar. He was coming at me."

"What did you use as a weapon?"

Ron Reid's chest went up and down in a cautious heave. "A glass."

"What kind of glass?"

"Beer glass."

"One of those heavy kind?"

"I guess."

"Don't guess while you're under oath, Mr. Reid."

"It was pretty heavy."

"Did you draw blood?"

"Yes."

"Mr. Reid, isn't it true that the police took a statement from you at the scene?"

As I watched Ron squirm I could see, out of the corner of my eye, Bryce Jennings lean forward. I leaned a little, too. How had Alex gotten all this information?

"Yeah," Ron Reid said. "Of course."

"And isn't it true that this report was admitted into evidence during your trial?"

Ron's eyes got a little wider. "Yeah."

I half expected Alex to whip out the police report right then and there, but she couldn't have. We hadn't known Ron was going to be put on the stand.

"And isn't it also true that the statement you gave to the police was contradicted by witnesses at the scene? Isn't that true, Mr. Reid?"

A flash of anger shot out from the mellow follower of the Wheel, which was crushing his toes at the moment. "So what? They were friends of this guy."

"The jury did not believe you, did they?"

"I didn't take the stand."

"They didn't believe your story in the report, did they, Mr. Reid?"

Bryce Jennings almost cried out in pain. "Objection to this line of questioning. How long are we going to have to go down memory lane here?"

As long as your witness, my loving dad, is bleeding in the corner.

"I think the point has been made," Judge Winger said. "Let's move on."

Alex did not even pause for a breath. "Mr. Reid, you have also lied in this proceeding, haven't you?"

"What?"

"Am I speaking too fast for you, Mr. Reid? I'll slow it down. You. Lied. Under. Oath. Right?"

"No!"

"You claim you found my client smoking dope?"

"That's what I said."

"It's a lie."

"No, it isn't."

"Anyone else see this?"

"I don't know."

"Anyone else report this?"

"Not that I know of, I only know—"

"So all we have is what you, a perjurer, tell us."

No surprise that Jennings objected and the judge sustained it. I didn't care. Alex was doing with words what I wanted to do with a sharp weapon. The sense of outrage and betrayal in me was almost more than I could stand. I'd taken this guy in, given him money ...

Money.

I scribbled the word on a piece of yellow legal paper and slid it toward Alex. She saw the motion, came over and read it. Nodded, then returned to the podium.

"Mr. Reid, how much money are you getting for your testimony?"

That's when the place went crazy. Jennings started shouting, Alex started shouting, and Troncatti, his Italian hands waving in the air, shouted too. Just to join in the fun, some reporters started shouting questions, at who I don't know.

The judge started pounding on the bench with his gavel and when he finally got a word in he ordered a recess. And the lawyers to get their behinds into his chambers now.

- 8 -

"Why won't anybody help him?" Maddie asks me.

"Some of them are afraid," I explain. "Some of them are ungrateful."

We're watching High Noon on TV. I'm trying to share some of my favorite movies with Maddie, but she's not old enough for a lot of them yet. She gets squirmy.

But for some reason she likes this one. There's something about Gary Cooper's face, I guess. It's etched with a devotion to duty, but also a deepening sorrow. The killers are coming into town soon, and no one will sign on to help the marshal, played by Cooper.

Maddie's always had a soft spot in her heart for injustice. When she sees something that's unfair — like a big kid at pre-school snatching a toy from someone — she gets very upset.

"What's 'ungrateful'?" she asks.

"Well, when somebody does something nice for you, you say thank you, right?"

"Right."

"That's being grateful. When you don't say thank you, that's being ungrateful. And in this town, see, the marshal did a lot of good things for the people. He helped make the town safe. But now that he needs help, nobody will help him."

"That's not fair!"

I am about to tell Maddie that life is not fair. But she is only five and that lesson can wait. Hopefully, for a long time.

"What is he gonna do?" Maddie says.

"Let's watch and find out."

"I'm scared for him. He's all alone."

~——~

I was alone on the corner, pacing behind a bus stop bench, when Alex found me.

"What are you doing out here?" she asked.

"Calming down. What happened with the judge?"

"He is plenty ticked off. Mostly at me."

"Why?"

"He thought my question about money was improper. He's probably right. There's no basis for it."

"It just makes sense," I said. "Why else would he lie like that?"

"Point is, the judge does not want this thing turning into a hockey game. My sense is that he wants to get it over as soon as possible. Which leaves us with a decision to make."

It sounded serious. "What is it?"

"Jennings said he has no more witnesses to present. He's made his case, in my opinion, even though we've tried our best to blow some holes in it. We went into this thing with the weight of evidence against us. So we have to decide whether to put you on the stand."

"I'll do it."

"Not so fast. You're very emotional right now. That can blow up in our face if it continues."

"No," I said. "Put me on. I won't blow it."

"You understand Jennings is going to hit you with everything he's got. He may well have held back some things he knows just to use them when you testify. It's called sandbagging."

"What else can he know? Everything's out there."

"You didn't know he'd call your father."

True. But that was his big weapon, it had to be. I could handle anything after that.

"I want to tell my side," I said. "I'll be good. I promise."

What an easy word to say, promise. What an easy thing to break into a million pieces.

– 9 –

"Mr. Gillen, please tell the court how you feel about your daughter."

The question was so simple, but it hit me like a 350-pound lineman. Where do you even begin? How do you get it out so it made sense? This was like my one moment, the big one, the only chance I'd get.

If I was too emotional I'd seem unbalanced. But the emotion was so strong in me I wanted to jump up on the bench and grab the judge by the robes and shake him until he understood.

But Alex had prepped me and told me to take a few deep breaths before answering.

Which is what I did. And it helped. For about two minutes.

I looked at the judge, who seemed like Thomas Jefferson on Mount Rushmore. Rock hard, expressionless. "Words can't really do justice to what I want to say, Your Honor. I could say I love my daughter, and that would be true, but it would also be something you've heard before, and it's just words. I don't know how to say that it's more than that, so much more than that."

I glanced at Paula. She was looking at the floor.

"I've pretty much been on my own ever since I was a kid, had to make my own way. And I thought I was pretty good at it. But when Maddie was born it was like—it was like being born myself, in a way. My life was just starting then. I felt like this was my life being born, because there she was, and then I had a reason for not being on my own, ever again."

The courtroom was dead silent, but my pulse was pounding in my ears. This was when I began to lose that fragile control the few, short breaths had given me. A heat was rising up from my chest and taking over like a wildfire in the hot, dry California hills.

"What I guess I mean, judge, Your Honor, is that Maddie is more important to me than anything, and that's coming from a guy who's only wanted two things in his whole life. To be a major league baseball player, and to be an actor."

When I said actor I looked, by reflex, out at Troncatti. He rolled his eyes. That's when it all left me, the self-control. The bad reality of it hit me then, the nightmare part, the worst part of the nightmare, right before your brain wakes you up.

The words literally stuck in my throat. I always thought that was a dumb cliché, but it's not after you feel it. My skin started tingling like I had a fever.

The next few seconds were like slow motion. There's that scene in Sam Peckinpah's The Wild Bunch where the entire population of Mexico is shot and dies in slow time, blood pouring out. That was the scene I was in.

I looked from the judge to Alex, who was starting to look concerned. She must have known I was in trouble.

I looked over at Bryce Jennings, weasel lawyer, sitting with what looked like a grin.

And then I saw Paula—smash cut to close up. Paula. The only woman I'd ever really wanted. Beautiful, but also somehow lost now.

I found my words. "Paula, don't do this. Why are you doing this? Paula, why? Don't, don't—"

"Mr. Gillen." It was the judge's voice, from a far-off place.

"Paula, please, you can't do this. Why—"

"Stop, Mr. Gil—"

I stood up. "Paula, look at me. Call this off, will you? Don't do this to Maddie—"

"Ms. Bedrosian, tell your client to—"

"Mark!" That was Alex.

I was in a tunnel now, just looking at Paula like she was at the other end. "Paula, look at me, will you?"

She didn't.

Next thing I knew this beefy deputy with a red face was at the side of the witness box, looking up at the judge like some obedient Doberman, waiting for the cue to bite.

The judge was slamming his hand on the bench and looking at me with all the understanding of Hannibal Lechter.

"That will be enough, Mr. Gillen!" He sounded like Moses, as played by Charlton Heston, rebuking the Israelites.

My face felt like it was going to melt right off me. It was Alex's face I couldn't bear to look at. She seemed at once to be full of pity for me and about to implode with professional embarrassment.

I clunked back down in my seat, like a condemned prisoner who just got turned down for a pardon from the governor.

"I'm not going to let this happen in my courtroom," Moses said to me. "Do you understand that, Mr. Gillen?"

"Yes," I said.

"I'm not sure that you do. I'm going to take a ten-minute break. Ten minutes exactly. You can confer with your lawyer and decide what you want to do. But if anything like this happens again, I'm going to disallow any further testimony from you. Are we clear on that?"

"Yes."

The judge left the bench.

"You've done enough," Alex said when we were alone in the hall.

"I couldn't help it. You want me to lie?"

"Calm down." She was gun-shy now, looking around for reporters. "There's nothing more we can do. Nothing you say is going to add or detract from what just happened in there. You can go back in and be contrite, and it will make your outburst look more like some out-of-control episode. Or you can go in and say nothing and look belligerent. What we're going to do is go in there, and I will make a statement of apology to the judge on your behalf. I don't think he wants you to say anything at this point, but if he does you get on your feet and say you're sorry. Right?"

"You know what a blimp feels like when it's deflated?"

"Mark, this was the Hindenburg. My only hope is that the judge will pick up your sincerity and not your instability."

"Thanks."

She put her hand on my shoulder. "We are long past the point where I patronize you, Mark. You are not doing well on this whole thing. We have no more evidence to put on. We leave this to Judge Winger."

"Throw ourselves on the mercy of the court?"

"If it helps to think of it that way, yes. And start praying now."

Making News

- 1 -

"Your Honor," Alex said, "my client is apologetic for his outburst on the stand and wants the court to know that he regrets his feelings for his daughter became so—obvious. We trust the court will take his testimony into account on its merits."

"You can trust the court, Ms. Bedrosian," the judge said. "Do you wish to question your client further?"

"No, Your Honor."

"Mr. Jennings, do you wish to cross-examine?"

The lawyer stood, like a man about to start demolition. "Most definitely."

"Mr. Gillen," Judge Winger said, "please retake the stand. I will remind you, you are still under oath."

My knees were doing a rumba as I walked back to the witness chair. I was, frankly, scared out of my shoes. Alex had said she'd do everything to protect me, if Jennings crossed the line. Whatever that meant.

But the look on his face was something between a surgeon's seriousness and the maniacal glee of a serial killer.

"How are you feeling, Mr. Gillen?" Jennings asked with fake concern. A nice way to remind everybody how I'd lost my cool half an hour ago.

"I'm fine," I said, and out of habit added, "thank you." It was like we were at a tea party.

"Good. We were a little concerned there."

I'm sure you were. Like an aardvark is concerned about ants.

"Mr. Gillen, you're an aspiring actor, are you not?"

What a great question, slipping that little word aspiring in there. But I was ready. "I'm a professional actor, yes."

"Professional?"

"Yes."

"How much did you make from acting last year?"

Not much. "I did all right."

"Can't recall a figure?"

"Not right now, no." And that was true.

"Would it be fair to say that the majority of your household income came from Ms. Montgomery's paychecks?"

"She had a recurring role on a soap."

"Do you have a recurring role in anything?"

I saw Troncatti was smiling widely, the way a beer-guzzling gambler must smile at a cockfight when his bird is humiliating the opponent.

"Not at this time."

"Have you ever had a recurring role?"

"I've done stage work."

"Paying?"

"Minimum."

"You also work as a waiter, is that right?"

"Yeah. I have a recurring role at Josephina's."

"You make more money as a waiter than as an actor, is that right?"

Alex objected. "Irrelevant."

"Sustained," the judge said, but it was clear Jennings was satisfied with his opening salvo. My right leg was jerking up and down, the way it gets when your nerves are snapping through it. I put my right hand on my thigh to stop it.

Jennings said, "Do you consider yourself a good actor, Mr. Gillen?"

Again Alex objected, but Jennings convinced the judge this was a different line of questioning. The judge gave him some room.

"Yes," I said.

"Feel like you're good enough for a series or movie role?"

"Yeah. If I didn't, I'd quit."

"Take acting classes and the like?"

"Sure. I work hard at the craft."

"So it wouldn't be hard for you to make a scene, say in a court-room, to try and sway a judge?"

"Objection!" Alex almost blew papers off the counsel table with her voice.

"That's argumentative, counsel," Judge Winger said. "Sustain the objection."

But Jennings was unfazed. It seemed to me he was more than willing to ask the occasional improper question, just to get into my head. So if it was acting he wanted, I'd give it to him by acting as calm as I could. Only my right leg didn't want to cooperate.

"Let's turn to the matter of your church, Mr. Gillen."

Alex told me this was going to come up. How a parent intends to educate the child, what religion, if any, he wants the child to be raised in — these are all things a court will take into consideration. So I had to sweat it out.

"You attend this church, Gower Presbyterian, correct?"

"Yes."

"And you have taken your daughter to church there?"

"Of course. She likes it."

"They have a Sunday school, something of that nature, for children?"

"Yes."

"Are you aware of what they teach?"

"Yeah," I said. "The Bible."

"Their interpretation of the Bible, correct?"

"They teach Bible stories. Maddie loves Bible stories."

Jennings flipped to another page on his legal pad. "Are you aware this church has a program of child rearing called, I believe, Raising Godly Children?"

"Yeah, I've seen that."

"Ever attend any classes?"

"No."

"Intend to?"

"Maybe."

"Do you endorse this program?"

"I don't know much about it."

"You do know it is sponsored by your church, do you not?"

"Yeah."

"Do you know, for example, that this program, Raising Godly Children, advocates corporal punishment with a stick?"

"Objection," Alex said. "Foundation."

"I am only asking if the witness knows," Jennings said. "If counsel likes I can introduce into evidence a copy of the curriculum of this program, which we have obtained."

"I also object on grounds of relevance," Alex said. "As I mentioned during my cross-examination of Dr. Hallard, the Ninth Circuit Court of Appeals, in the Calabretta case, held that the use of a token rod for disciplinary purposes did not violate California law."

"It did no such thing," Jennings remarked.

Alex went to her briefcase and snatched some papers. "I took advantage of the break to make copies of Calabretta. I will hand one to Mr. Jennings and one to the court. The relevant language is as follows: 'The social worker plainly expressed the view to the mother that use of any object to spank a child, such as the "rod" (a nine-inch Lincoln log) was illegal, and she did have reason to believe that such an object was used, but appellants have cited no authority for the proposition she was right that California law prohibits use of any object to discipline a child. The statutes we have found prohibit "cruel" or "inhuman" corporal punishment or injury resulting in traumatic condition. While some punishment with some objects might necessarily amount to cruel or inhuman punishment, a token "rod" such as a nine-inch Lincoln log would not.'"

Judge Winger motioned for a copy of the case. Alex handed it to him. For what seemed like an hour, but was more like five minutes, the judge went through the copy. During the silence I kept my head down, not wanting to look at anyone. I think I was praying. Only once can I remember looking up, at Paula. She was not looking at me.

Finally the judge said, "In the best interest of the child, I am going to consider the curriculum Mr. Jennings has obtained. Regardless of what Calabretta holds, and it is a narrow holding, I believe I am duty bound to consider the consequences of a particular form of discipline on a particular child. Counsel's objection is overruled."

"Exception to that," Alex said, "on First Amendment grounds."

"Exception noted. Continue, Mr. Jennings."

Paula's lawyer, unflappable, in quiet and deadly tones, went on. "Would you describe yourself as a person who has to deal with anger, Mr. Gillen?"

"Deal with it?"

"Yes."

"I don't know what you mean by that."

"That's confusing to you?"

"I just don't know what you mean." Easy. Easy.

"Do you have an anger problem?"

Now what do I say? "I get angry sometimes, like everybody."

Jennings raised his eyebrows. "Not everybody throws glass bottles at people, do they?"

Someone cackled in the audience. I looked over. It was Troncatti.

"I threw a bottle of water on the sidewalk next to Paula," I said, keeping myself in check. "I lost my temper."

"Do you often lose your temper?"

Alex stood. "Objective. Vague as to often."

"Sustained."

No stop from Jennings. "Have you lost your temper this week?"

"I don't know."

"Can't recall?"

"Right. Can't recall."

"Throw anything?"

"No."

"Stayed pretty calm?"

I shrugged. This wasn't getting any of us anywhere. "I'm not this out-of-control freak," I said. "I'm no danger to society."

"Pretty normal, you feel?"

"Sure."

"Have you ever hit your daughter in anger?"

The question was delivered softly, but it had the impact of a smart bomb — the kind that kills people but leaves buildings intact. Looking back, I'm sure Jennings had asked all of his previous questions just to set me up for this.

The setup worked. My body jerked and my face flushed. I was sure it was a neon sign to the courtroom, flashing guilty guilty guilty.

"I never ... I only ..." I stopped to regroup, catch a breath, which must have made me look even worse. "There was one time in the car, she was screaming and wouldn't stop. I hit her on the arm. Once."

"You dealt with her behavior by striking your daughter, isn't that correct?"

No getting around it, nowhere to hide. "One time."

"You did not spank her, did you?"

"No."

"You did not, with deliberation, lay her over your knee and use a Lincoln log to discipline her, did you?"

Alex was silent at counsel table, and I knew there was nothing she could do to stop the bleeding.

"No. But I was sorry I did it, I told her how sorry I was."

"Were you sorry when you let your daughter get kicked in the head at a park?"

I tried not to let my face light up with shock. How did Jennings get that information? It was like he had a video camera on my whole life.

"I did not let my daughter get kicked," I said. "It was an accident."

"She suffered a concussion, isn't that right?"

"Mild concussion. I brought her home."

"You were at a park, let her wander away—"

"She was playing. That's what kids do at parks. Ever heard of that?"

Jennings smiled slightly, and I knew he was doing this to get me to lose it again. With all my strength I calmed myself down.

"The fact is," Jennings said, "that your daughter was injured at a park while under your care, that is the truth, isn't it?"

"It was an accident."

"That's not what I asked you."

I just shook my head. "I'm telling you what happened."

"I think we have enough of an answer here." Jennings tugged at one of his cuffs. A gold cuff link glimmered in the harsh courtroom light.

"Do you have anger toward your wife?" Jennings said.

Another quick shift in the questions. I was starting to rock back and forth on the swivel witness chair. It squeaked. So did my voice.

"Paula?" I cleared my throat.

"Do you have another wife?" Before Alex could object, Jennings said, "Strike that last remark, Your Honor."

"Stricken," Winger said.

"Do you have anger toward your wife?"

His snide little remark had given me a moment to regroup. "No, I wouldn't say that. Maybe at first there was. Now it's just ... hurt. I don't understand why she's doing this."

"Do you think your hurt might affect how you act around your daughter?"

"No."

"No chance of that?"

"No."

"What is it that hurts you, Mr. Gillen?"

Was he serious? Or setting me up again? I just stared at him.

"Did you understand the question, Mr. Gillen?"

"Sure." I paused. "Wouldn't you be hurt if your wife took up with another man?"

Jennings didn't flinch. "I'm not on the witness stand, sir. You are. So the fact that Ms. Montgomery fell in love with Antonio Troncatti is what hurts you?" Every time he said hurt he pounded it, like a boxer hitting a heavy bag.

I looked at Paula, who wouldn't make eye contact. "Of course it does."

"How does that hurt manifest itself?"

"You really want to know? I'll tell you. I wake up every day feeling like I've lost something I'll never get back. I wanted us to be a family, and now that's not going to happen."

Jennings paced a moment. "Does your hurt manifest itself by your involvement with other women?"

"What? Are you kidding me?"

Judge Winger said, "Please answer the question, Mr. Gillen."

"Of course not," I said.

"Do you know a woman named Nikki McNamara?"

Stunned, I stopped rocking. My face — must have been flashing neon again — felt hot.

Alex objected. "What is the relevance?"

"Veracity," Jennings said. "Catching the witness in a lie."

"I object to the characterization!"

"Hold on," the judge said. "Let's just take a step back here. The witness has asserted that he has a certain emotional state toward Ms. Montgomery —"

Emotional state? What was I, a lab rat?

"—and that included an assertion of fact that he was not, I think the word was involved, with other women, and now counsel has asked about a woman I assume he is going to link to Mr. Gillen. Doing so would have a bearing on Mr. Gillen's veracity. So I will overrule Ms. Bedrosian's objection."

I felt bad enough, but now Nikki's name was dragged into this thing. A complete innocent.

"That is unfair," I said. "Nikki McNamara is a friend, someone I know from church. That's it."

Jennings snatched something from the podium. He put it in front of me. It was an 8-by- 10-inch photograph, in full color. Taken with a telephoto lens. Me, embracing Nikki in the courtyard of Gower Pres.

My mind blew up in a million pieces. I glared at Jennings. His smug face glared back. "You slime," I said. "You hired some guy—"

"Mr. Gillen," the judge said. "No question has been asked."

"How can you allow this?" I said to him.

"Mr. Gillen, please wait for a question."

What a farce.

"Who is pictured in this photograph?" Jennings asked.

"How did they ever let you practice law?" I said.

Troncatti snorted in the gallery. That was, as they say, the final nail in the coffin. Or my heart. I was dead.

Jennings took the photograph away. "Your Honor, I don't think I can get anything more from the witness that will be of use to the court. We are ready to submit this matter to you."

"Anything else for this witness?" Judge Winger asked Alex.

"No, Your Honor," my lawyer said.

What more could there be? Every time my lips moved I dug a deeper hole.

"You may step down," Judge Winger told me.

My body moved out of the witness box. As I walked by Paula I thought she had a little look of sympathy there. The way a hunter looks at a wounded lion right before he finishes the job.

"Any further evidence?" Winger said.

"No, Your Honor," said Alex.

"It has been a long day for all of us," Judge Winger said. "I understand that, having been on this side of the legal fence for twenty years. I will take the matter under submission."

~ 2 ~

We are at the arcade in the mall because Maddie wants to see me shoot baskets.

It is not as easy as it looks, even to a former jock like me. The rim is smaller than regulation and balls are extra bouncy. So you have to put the ball perfectly through the hoop or else clunk it in off the backboard.

I choose clunk.

The balls come fast off the canvas that catches them. The unforgiving clock ticks down.

Maddie is cheering. "Come on, Daddy! You can do better! Come on!"

Her voice is practically begging me.

I drop about five bucks' worth of tokens into that stupid game, but manage to win enough tickets to get us something from the lower-end shelf.

Maddie doesn't care. I am her hero. Ticket man.

She presses her nose against the glass, quickly scanning the items. She finds no attraction in the Chinese finger trap, or the loudly colored plastic geckos, or the giant wax lips.

No, for some reason she chooses a red kazoo.

"You sure you want that?" I say.

"Yes! You can toot with it."

"What about a nice gecko?"

She looks at me like I'm weird.

"Okay," I say, "get the kazoo."

Which is a mistake. All the way home, it is kazoo time. Only Maddie is not playing any tunes. She's talking. Talking through the kazoo.

ZIZIZZMOBZZZZIZBUBZIZZIZWUBZIZIZIZ

"Maddie, take the—"

ZIZZYMUBOOOIZZYZABBOOZOOOY

"I can't understand—"

ZIZZYZOOOBOOIZZYOOO

All the way home, and into the apartment. And finally I lose myself in laughter, pick her up, turn her upside down, and say, "Oh yeah? Oh yeah? Then ZIZZYOBBYZIZZYOZIZZY to you, too!"

We fall on the sofa, laughing our heads off.

It was not a good night, beginning with the evening news.

Local channels 4 and 7 made me their lead story. Lead story! When they had several choice murders to choose from and a high-speed chase down the Harbor Freeway.

This town sure has its priorities straight.

I flipped back and forth, but watched channel 4 first. The talking head who was reading the news—Mr. Mousse, I called him, for his helmet of hair—had a smirk on his face when he announced the next story. Behind him, the pop-up graphic shows my own, undignified kisser in an attitude that is a mixture of bug-eyed rage and a sort of Kathy-Bates-in-Misery insanity.

"Some major testimony today in the Paula Montgomery custody dispute," Mr. Mousse said.

They pulled back to a two shot that includes the female portion of this tag team, a gorgeous blond who seemed to be having a great time in the studio tonight.

"We finally heard from Paula M's ex, didn't we?" she said.

"Oh boy, did we," Mousse chuckled.

I didn't expect they would get it right. Our divorce wasn't final yet. But as far as the news media was concerned, that was all over. This was a fight between the woman they were starting to call by her initials, and some crazy, angry former husband who couldn't contain himself.

I turned off the TV and tried to pray. But it wasn't happening. Maybe, in some small way, I didn't think I deserved to have God listen to me.

And I thought of Nikki. I had dragged her into this thing. I needed to call her. But weird thoughts kept intruding. Like maybe my phone was tapped. I was going bughouse.

It was seven o'clock when I realized it was Wednesday. The Bible study at church. She'd be there. I could do this thing face-to-face, and maybe that way she'd be in a more forgiving mood.

And I needed to be around some people. So at 7:30 I was there.

Nikki wasn't.

Which almost made me get up and get out. But Tom Starkey made a big deal out of welcoming me. He'd seen the news (who hadn't?) and was full of concern. He convinced me to stay.

He got everybody together—the group was about fifty or sixty people—and we sat. Then he opened up with a prayer. When that was over, he asked how people were doing, if anybody had anything they wanted to share with the group. He looked at me, and when he did I thought everybody else was looking, too.

So I jumped in. "I just have a question."

"Shoot," Starkey said.

"About prayer."

"Okay."

"It says ask and you'll receive?"

"Yes."

"Where does it say that?"

"In the Sermon on the Mount."

"Pretty big promise."

"It is."

"So how come I've been asking and not getting? What's up with that?"

Tom Starkey nodded, like some sage from a hilltop in India. I got irritated. I know it was wrong. These were good people. Maybe I wanted to be irritated. It helped dull everything else. But I was also really interested in the answer.

"There are times when what we ask for may not be good for us," Tom said. "We have to find out what that condition is."

"Why?"

"Because God's first concern isn't to give us things. It's to make us more like Christ."

"I don't want to be like Christ," I said. "I just want some answers. Isn't there something in the Bible about having faith, just a little bit, and you can throw a mountain into the ocean?"

"Yes."

"So?"

"There is also this, from the book of 1 John. 'This is the confidence we have in approaching God: that if we ask anything according to his will, he hears us.'"

"What's that mean?"

"It means that God's will comes first. Jesus even prayed a prayer that wasn't answered with a yes."

"Yeah?"

Tom flipped a few pages in his Bible and read. "'"Father, if you are willing, take this cup from me; yet not my will, but yours be done." An angel from heaven appeared to him and strengthened him. And being in anguish, he prayed more earnestly, and his sweat was like drops of blood falling to the ground.'"

"What's this about a cup?"

"Jesus was praying that he wouldn't have to go to the cross. The cup was figurative, meaning a cup of suffering."

"So what was going on? He prayed not to be killed?"

"But he says to God, not my will, but yours. That's the key to prayer. If it is not God's will, it's not good for us."

"That's very convenient."

"How do you mean?"

"Well, you ask and it's supposed to happen. If it doesn't happen, you can say, oh, not God's will. Sorry."

"It also says, in 1 John ..." Tom flipped more pages. The guy was good with pages. "'Dear friends, if our hearts do not condemn us, we have confidence before God and receive from him anything we ask, because we obey his commands and do what pleases him.' So there's a condition there, about obedience. If we need to be taught something about what pleases God before our prayer requests are given to us, then we have to bite the bullet and learn that. Sometimes God has rough hands."

I frowned.

"A potter's hands are rough," Starkey added, "from working with all that clay. Loving and rough at the same time."

This time I shrugged. It wasn't coming through loud and clear. Or maybe I didn't want it to.

To Starkey's credit he didn't press me on this. The Bible study continued. I tried to listen but my mind was all over the place.

Until Nikki walked in. She took a chair on the opposite side of the circle. We locked eyes for a moment. I didn't move. She nodded at me. If I was a nod reader, I would have read that as being shocked or dismayed. But I wasn't, so I waited to see if she'd talk to me after the study was over.

She did. Walked across the room.

Her face was full of knowing and that much I could read.

"You look like you heard about it," I said.

"My dad called me. It was on the news in San Diego."

"I'm sorry."

"Not your fault."

"I don't want this to hurt your career."

"Such as it is?"

"I mean it."

"I'm not worried. What about you. How are you getting along?"

I shrugged.

"I'm glad you're here," she said.

"Yeah, it's fine. Everybody's been great."

"But?"

"There's some things you just have to work out for yourself."

"I don't believe that."

I put my hands up. "Nikki, don't tell me to pray or think about God right now. I know all that. I just—have to work it out."

She nodded. Smiled. And that's when I said, "Can you come outside a second?"

We went out into the night, near the same courtyard where a snake hired by Jennings had taken our picture. I didn't care now if they had a video camera on.

"I want to see you again," I said.

She looked at the ground, like this was bad news. "I knew you were going to say that."

"How did you know?"

"Because I was thinking it, too."

"I want to see you."

"I know. But nothing's changed."

I put my hands on her shoulders, wanting to kiss her. "But how do you feel?"

"Mark, please don't press this right now. Please."

I hesitated a moment, feeling suspended in midair. Then took my hands down. "Okay."

She breathed a sigh of relief. "Come on, let's go back inside."

"I need to go."

"Mark—"

"Keep praying for me."

— 3 —

No sleep.

There's a scene in the old Dick Powell film noir, Murder, My Sweet, where Powell, playing detective Philip Marlowe, is drugged by the bad guys. Hopped up, as they used to say. He can't see anything straight. The world is all webby and fuzzy and off-kilter. He starts to wonder if he's ever going to see things straight again. And he's alone.

That's what I felt like. Alone and in a fuzz. Didn't want to see anybody, talk to anybody.

Except one guy. And that became my obsession.

I drove over to Atlas Auto Body and walked into the first bay. Some guy with a shaved head and tattoo on the back of his neck—I think it was a fish or an eggplant—gave me a look.

"Ron Reid around?" I said.

"Not here," Fish Neck said.

"When's he coming back?"

"Never. If he does, I'll wrap some cable around his neck."

"I'd appreciate that."

Fish Neck stared at me. "Who are you?"

"Somebody who wants real bad to talk to him."

"You and me both. He left me doing double time."

"You have any idea where he might've gone?"

"None. Wait. You're his kid, right?"

"Yeah."

"He talked about you."

"Oh yeah?"

"Said he was gonna make some money off you."

A white light flashed behind my eyes.

"Wasn't he on parole or something?" Fish Neck said.

I left without answering, drove immediately to the federal building downtown. Ron had been in on a federal rap, so this was the
place to start looking for him, I guessed. I wasn't going to tell them
why I wanted to find him, of course. That was my business. But I
could say I was his son and really needed to contact him. True.

My plan was all mucked up with red tape once I walked in.
Guys in blue blazers with earphones gave me the twice-over even
before I checked through the metal detectors. The suit at the front
desk gave me a Can I help you that was larded with suspicion.

I explained my business as best I could. Long-lost son looking
for paroled father and all that. The suit told me to wait and got on
the phone. Then he told me someone would be right down.

That someone was a young-looking woman who introduced
herself as Stephanie Wong, marshal. I got the immediate impression she was running interference for everybody else, maybe got
the short straw when they said some guy looking for his father was
downstairs.

I put my best face on. "My dad is on parole, I think he was in
Terminal Island. I'm looking for him, but he's gone. I'm wondering
if he's in trouble or something." He was in trouble. With me.

"If he is under our jurisdiction," Stephanie Wong said, "I'm
afraid that information is not something we can give out."

"Even to a family member?"

She looked at me, making me wonder if she believed me. "I'm
afraid so."

I wished she'd quit saying she was afraid.

"So there's no way you can help me?"

"You could fill out a JN–30 form."

"What's that?"

"Request for confidential information. You'd have to provide a justification, and then the matter would be reviewed. It happens sometimes."

"How often?"

Marshal Wong shook her head. "Not often."

"So what do I do?"

"You really want to find your father?"

"Oh yeah."

"Can I ask you why?"

I told myself to stay calm. "There are just some things I haven't had a chance to say to him yet."

"Have you thought about a private investigator?"

"No."

"Sometimes they have resources and contacts. I can't promise you anything and this is off the record, okay?"

"Sure."

"That's what I would do if I were you."

I wanted to say You can thank your lucky stars you're not me.

~ 4 ~

I didn't know any private investigators. It's not like the movies, where you can find them in an office building, and some guy looking like Bogart comes out to help you. I didn't know where to turn.

And then I did.

I headed out to Club Cobalt. But it wasn't to see Roland. He wasn't appearing tonight.

But Milo Ayers was there. Like always.

"Hey, Markie, how are you?" He gave me a firm handshake and a slap on the shoulder. "Rolie isn't here."

"I know. I just came by."

"You want a table? Sit at the bar?"

"Mr. Ayers, could I talk to you a minute?"

His eyes, rigid and warm at the same time (I imagined a hit man looking at a puppy), looked deeply into mine.

"Sure," he said. "Come on over, I'll get you a drink."

"Just water."

"Bottled," he said.

When we were settled at a table in the corner, me with my San Pellegrino and Milo Ayers with his scotch, Ayers rubbed his hands together. "Now what can I help you out with?"

"You gave me some good advice once," I said. "About finding a lawyer. You gave me a name."

"Gregory Arsenault."

"I couldn't afford him."

Ayers shrugged and stuck out his lower lip. "Not a problem. I hope you like who you got."

"I think she did her best."

"But that wasn't good enough?"

"Not when the other side got a lying witness."

"Who?"

"My father."

"Your father lied against you?" His tone was one of complete disbelief, like that wasn't a possibility in his world.

"The other side got to him somehow."

"And this lie hurt in court?"

"Big time."

Milo sat back, drumming his fingers on the table. His gold bracelet jangled. "Markie, I like you. You been a good kid, a good customer. I help you out, you keep it between us, huh? Like a favor I'm doing and you don't want to spread it around, hey?"

"Yes. Whatever help you can give, I'll take. I'm at the end here."

"I'll call you. Now what you do is, you go home. You do what you do and don't let anything anybody does to you get you. You know what I'm saying?"

"Yes, Mr. Ayers."

"Then you'll be okay."

Sure. Okay and alone.

– 5 –

There was a structure to my loneliness.

Like the arc in a good play, I went through the acts, wandering through what actors call the "through line." That's the thing that holds the drama together, the string that penetrates through each beat of the play.

Act one began when I woke up, wishing I hadn't, seeing the light and knowing there was a long act two to come, knowing I had to live through the day wondering if the court would let me see Maddie again.

Somehow I'd pull myself out of bed and begin the living of it. Moving forward was the hardest thing. I felt like I had on one of those lead aprons, the ones the dental assistants plop on you before they take the X-rays. It was like it was permanently attached, and that's how my life was going to feel from now on.

So I'd go through the motions of the day. Not helpful to anyone. Hearing people talk to me like they were disembodied ghosts. Life was a haunted house. Act two seemed interminable. The minutes, as they say, seemed like hours, and the hours go so slowly. Wasn't that from some song in West Side Story? I didn't care. This was my play, and it wasn't a musical.

Then I'd come on toward night, and act three. The curtain came down as I tried to go to sleep, sometimes crying, sometimes numb. And always in the back of my mind a little critic saying maybe we should close this show. Maybe tomorrow the theater could be dark, and that wouldn't be a bad thing.

And then I'd wake up again.

For a week I was like this.

Mrs. Williams tried to pull me out of myself. She stopped me once in the laundry room, where I wasn't doing any laundry. I was just listening to the machines.

"Don't do any good to stew," she said. "Come on and let me fix you a meal."

"Thanks, but I have plans."

"What? You gonna go down to the bus stop and listen to the traffic?"

"Passes the time."

"Time heals all wounds."

"Wounds all heels," I corrected. "Groucho Marx said that."

"Never liked Groucho Marx. Now Phyllis Diller, there was a funny lady."

Somehow, I went to church on Sunday. Maybe it was a life raft thing. I'd been having a recurring nightmare. It went like this:

I am on board a luxury liner making its way across the Atlantic. The Atlantic Ocean is the scarier ocean, of course. Pacific meaning "peaceful" and all. It is much too placid for a nightmare.

Also, the Atlantic seems colder. I grew up sloshing around in the Pacific on hot, Southern California days. It is the type of ocean that embraces you; the Atlantic couldn't care less.

Anyway, it's night on this cruise and everybody is dressed up in evening clothes, like Cary Grant and Deborah Kerr in An Affair to Remember, and there's a party going on. I seem to float through it, looking for someone. No one sees me.

I am like a ghost, and I am looking for my daughter.

She is not here among the guests. In my dream-mind I reason that, of course, she should be in bed. It is late at night, after all. And in the way you shift locations in dreams, I find I am going through the door to my stateroom, the stateroom I share with Maddie, sure that I will find her soft, brown hair and calm face on the pillow on the bed.

She is not there.

I begin to panic. Where is she? Has she just wandered off, sleepily? Or has something more sinister taken place? Has someone, in fact, stolen into this room and taken her?

My dream takes me through the stateroom corridors, up the steps, deck by deck, until I am outside in the chill, running a complete circle around the ship.

No one pays me any mind. There is light fog on the deck, and the upper-crust people strolling around — it always seems like a 1930s black-and-white movie at this point in the dream — give me rebuking looks.

I stop to ask a man, in top hat and tails like Fred Astaire, if he's seen a little girl tonight. He huffs, does not answer, and my panic expands.

Maybe she's fallen off!

I try to scream for help, but only manage a low moan (I am sure that is what comes out of my throat as I dream).

I run to the stern and look over into the dark, churning ocean. Leaning over, desperate to see something, anything, I fall off.

Down into the black nothing of the sea.

Flapping my arms, I scream. And now it is full-blooded, desperate, dying.

No one hears.

I scream again. Only the sound of the wake slapping at my ears comes back in answer.

The stern of the ship is getting farther and farther away.

Please! Somebody!

And then I see her.

Maddie.

She is looking over the stern, looking for something. Or someone. Me! She is looking for me. I am lost to her, and she is looking.

Maddie!

She does not hear, and then twin shadows appear next to her. I know one of them. Her mother. The other is a man, and it is not me. I know who it is.

The two of them enfold Maddie in their arms. She falls into them with comfort and joy.

The lights of the ship become pinpricks in the death shroud of night. Farther and farther away it goes, then disappears altogether.

Now all that is left is darkness and night and me treading water, and knowing that there is nothing to be done. I am lost in the middle of the freezing ocean, not a lifeboat in sight.

There is no one to save me, no one to hear me.

I had this dream five times in one week.

So I went to church.

I saw Nikki but didn't talk to her. I'm sure she took it as embarrassed silence. I took it as not wanting to have anything to do with anything human. The sermon that day droned on like commercials on the car radio during a long commute — you hear the noise but none of the message stays with you.

Then one night things changed.

I forget who it was who said if a story starts to drag, just bring in a guy with a gun. That means a sudden change in the plot.

In my own sorry story line the sudden change was a shoe box in the back of my closet. I was looking for an old pair of boots. I found them, dusty and black, in the rear corner. As I pulled them out I saw a pink shoe box. Clearly not mine or Paula's, because of the size.

Maddie's.

I grabbed it. When I got it out into the light, I saw it had a rubber band around it and something written in crayon. In the unmistakable hand of my daughter, it said: DADYS BEREED TRESER.

I did everything I could to keep my heart from bursting. I removed the rubber band carefully, so it wouldn't break, because I didn't want anything that Maddie had touched to break. Slowly, I removed the top of the shoe box.

The first thing I saw was a little kush ball, red and yellow rubber strings together in a sphere. She loved those things, so it was no small gift. I picked it up, smelled it, and rubbed it against my cheek.

There was a nickel in the box. Treasure indeed. I decided I would tape that nickel to the refrigerator.

Last of all was a paper, a piece ripped off a yellow legal pad. I turned it over and saw the crayon drawing. Three stick people. A man, a woman, a little girl. Holding stick hands. A building in the background, roughly the shape of our apartment complex.

And above the building, where the sun would have been, a heart. With light rays coming from it, down toward the three stick people holding hands.

I lost it then. I was thankful I was alone in a closet.

— 6 —

Even before she said anything, I knew Alex had bad news. It was the look in her eye, like her cat had been run over by a cement truck. I was the cat.

"Sit down, Mark." Alex looked trapped in her own office. She'd called me that morning and said I needed to come in. Try as I might I couldn't get her to talk to me over the phone.

"Give it to me." I made no move to sit or even move.

"Please, sit. We need to talk."

"She gets Maddie, right? All Maddie, all the time."

"Yes."

The word hit like one of those anvils that drops on Wile E. Coyote in the cartoons. Now I sat, pushed down by the weight of it. And then I got that feeling, the one that comes with my nightmare, when I'm in the sea at night as the ship pulls farther and farther away. Gets me in the pit of the stomach and stays there, even after I wake up.

"Why?" It sounded like a stupid question, considering how I'd messed up in court.

"That's the way the judge decided. We can appeal."

"What did it? What was the thing that did it?"

"He looked at the totality of the circumstances, which is what he's supposed to do. We both know it didn't look good."

"What about the lying witness? That didn't help."

"It was not emphasized in the decision, but certainly that hurt."

"And what if he admits he lied?"

"How is he going to do that?"

"I might convince him."

Alex cocked her head at me. "Are you not telling me something again?"

I put my hands up. "Relax. I don't know where he is. But I'm going to find him."

Sighing, Alex said, "Mark, listen. You have been through an ordeal, a bad one. There is still hope. There's still more we can do within the system. If you start doing dumb things, I won't be able to help you. And you may not get to see Maddie at all."

"At all?"

"If you'll just listen. You still get monitored visits, Mark."

"Oh yeah, and we know how great those things are."

"It's better than nothing."

"I don't know if it is. I couldn't stand it happening the same way again." I looked at the ceiling for a moment. "I'll take it."

"But there's a condition."

I looked back at Alex as if she were Torquemada ready to twist the rack again.

She said, "You are to enroll in an anger management program before you see Maddie again."

"Anger management?"

"That's right. There are programs that are court approved that—"

"I have to go through some stupid program to see my daughter?"

Alex closed her eyes, then opened them again. "The sooner you start, the sooner we can set up a visit."

Oh yeah, I was going to start all right. I was going to kick the life out of something before the night was through, and then I'd worry about managing the old anger.

I thought if God was in front of me, say like a burning bush, I'd kick that bush, too.

"You have not responded well to setbacks," Alex said.

"Thank you."

"You want it straight, or do you want it namby-pamby?"

"Namby-pamby."

"Sorry, you're not going to get it from me. I didn't get to this point, advising clients, by short-shrifting. You have got to get yourself together."

Her words reminded me of that scene from Tootsie, when Dustin Hoffman is told by his agent that he has to get some therapy because he's too difficult for anyone to work with. So Hoffman puts on a dress.

I considered that option, too.

Managing

Anger management. It sounded so eighties, so Richard Simmons. Get all touchy-feely and you're a model of calm. You come out wearing a leotard and passing out flowers at the airport.

But it was what I needed to get a shot at seeing Maddie. It took me a couple of days, but I finally accepted that. So I was going to do it. In fact, I was going to be the best manager of anger the world had ever seen, because nothing was going to keep me from my daughter. I was going to become the best father the world had ever seen, the kind of guy Maddie would love again, forever.

And I knew I had an anger problem. I wasn't anxious to dig too deep about it, but I'd take it as it came.

Turns out what came was some advice. Which hit me like a truck doing seventy.

The first class I went to met, wouldn't you know, at a church, a Methodist in North Hollywood.

There were ten of us that first night, not counting the facilitator. His name was Stanley; he was about fifty, and looked like a commercial for mellow. He had a salt-and-pepper mustache, and his voice was calm as a pond.

We sat in a circle in metal chairs. Stanley kicked off the evening with a welcome, then said, "We have a new member tonight. This is Mark."

Everybody said Hi, Mark.

"We don't make anybody talk here," Stanley said, "if they don't want to. If you want to share anything about yourself, Mark, we'd all be happy to hear it. What we say in here, stays here."

Fair enough. "Well, I'm here because I've been told I have an anger issue — isn't that the way you're supposed to put it? And a judge says I need to deal with it if I want to see my daughter. Custody fight and all that."

Several heads nodded. I was among friends.

One guy on my left, whose name I would later learn was Rick, said, "I'm trackin' ya, bud. Been through that sweatbox myself."

From the look on his face, it was a painful experience, but he seemed ... resigned. Did I even want to feel resigned? Not at the moment, but I'd work my way into it. I just kept thinking about Maddie.

"The way we like to start," Stanley explained, "is to go around the circle and see how people handled situations this week, things that might have made them angry, or did in fact make them angry, and how they handled it. Our big saying here, Mark, is 'In your anger, do not sin.' Anger is an emotion, it comes of its own volition. It's what we do with the anger that counts."

And so around they went. Each of the guys was open about their struggles and victories, and by the time it got to me I was feeling pretty good about this crowd. It was like there was nothing phony about them.

So when it came back to me I let them know the whole story. Everything. And it felt good, like letting a big sack of rocks off my back.

When it was over, we helped ourselves to some Famous Amos chocolate chip cookies and coffee from a big urn. Stanley let me know that I'd just given a very promising first session and said I'd made good progress.

It all was positive, upbeat. Until I got outside the door.

Rick stopped me. "I'll walk to the parking lot with you."

He was a big guy, did construction work. Looked, in fact, like he could tear a mattress in half with his hands. Or teeth.

"You're here under court order?" he said.

"Yeah. You?"

"Oh yeah. My old lady dragged me in. Domestic violence. They let me off with a fine and community service, and this deal." He jerked his big thumb back toward the church.

"What do you think of it?" I said. "Stanley and the whole thing?"

Rick shrugged. "Good as anything, I guess. Won't do jack squat for your case, though."

"What?"

"Listen, my friend, once they've got you going to this, it's like admitting you're a child molester or something. No way a judge is going to change his mind on the custody deal. They're too afraid somebody like us is going to end up killing the kid or the spouse, and then they're up for reelection with that hanging over their heads. Nope, we're up a creek, pal."

"So what's the point?"

"There is no point, that's the whole thing. The system's set up to squash guys like you and me like bugs. We're here because the court makes us, and it's better than getting time in the cooler. But it's all over."

Suddenly, LA at night seemed like a giant vacuum, sucking my ribs out.

"No," I said. "This is going to work. I'm going to get to see my daughter."

He shrugged again.

"You believe in the God part of all this?" I said.

"Like the higher power deal? Nah."

"Well I do. I have to. It's got to work."

"Just keep telling yourself that, man."

———

I did keep telling myself that. Over and over, for the next several days.

I told myself that at Josephina's. I told Roland.

God was going to get me through this, because I was in the right. God was going to overrule the judge. I'd wait them all out, Paula and Troncatti and the judge — and Maddie, too. I'd earn her trust back, one visit at a time.

She'd have to remember the good times. The moon dance. The buried treasure. You couldn't just rip those out of a child's head, if that's what they were trying to do.

Even though a little voice, sounding like Linda Blair in The Exorcist, kept suggesting they could, oh they could. Day after day they could feed her whatever line they wanted about me and the acid of that would coat Maddie's mind, burning away all of the good things.

It was enough to drive a guy with an anger problem into kicking a baby seal. What kept me sane was knowing that a visit with Maddie would be coming soon.

Meanwhile, my only job was to keep it together, check in with my group, show the court proof of attendance and all that. Ruff ruff. See Mark jump. See Mark jump through hoops.

I didn't care if the hoops were on fire. Just as long as I got to see my daughter.

— 2 —

"Daddy, I can't sleep."

"What's the matter?"

"I miss Mommy."

"So do I."

"I'm scared for her."

"Scared?"

"What if she falls in the ocean?"

"She won't. And even if she does, she'll have a floatie."

"How do you know?"

"Because Mommy's smart, like you, and she'll think of that."

"You're smart, aren't you, Daddy?"

"Sure I am. I'm smart enough to be your daddy, aren't I?"

"Then if you're smart, tell me how to go to sleep."

"You crawl right up here with me. I'll sing to you until you sleep."

"Please don't sing, Daddy."

"All right, no singing. What would you like me to do?"

"Just be with me."

***

The day before the monitored visit I went to Ralph's and bought a bag of chocolate chips and all the ingredients needed to make cookies—butter, flour, eggs. I could have snagged Pillsbury premade dough and slapped them on a cookie sheet (which I also bought at the store), but that would have been cheating. In my mind at least.

I wanted to make these cookies from scratch, for Maddie, to be able to tell her I did it all by myself—what she used to say when she first tied her shoes or did her own braids.

No one will mistake me for some guy on the Food Network, but I whipped up some pretty good dough. I ate a couple of scoopfuls myself, and it tasted right. I preheated the oven, following the directions on the bag of chocolate chips, and spooned out the dough on to the sheet.

The first batch came out smelling as sweet as you please, a party in my nostrils. I couldn't wait and picked up one of the warm beauties before it was cool enough, and put the sloggy thing in my mouth, chasing it with milk. Heaven.

I made another batch, let them cool. I poured another glass of milk and had about six of them. Then I put the rest in a big baggie and secured it with a twist tie.

I was ready to meet my daughter.

But not ready to sleep.

I just couldn't, so I paced around the apartment, TV infomercials softly playing in the background. At various times I could have been a real estate millionaire, sculpted my body using a machine made mostly of rubber, become a master chicken chef with the touch of a button, or emerged wrinkle free after subjecting myself to weeks of some new goop from Sweden.

None of that appealed to me. Instead, I tried to appeal to God. I tried to pray, but the words kept failing me. My mind was all over. I think I know what it must be like to be in a cell in solitary confinement.

I needed help and knew who to call.

"Hi, Nikki."

There was a pause on the other end of the phone. "Mark?"

"Sorry it's late."

"That's okay. Is everything all right?"

"I'm going to see my daughter tomorrow."

"Oh, that's fantastic. So does that mean you have—"

"It's a monitored visit. I'm still on notice with the court. There's stuff my lawyer is working on. I thought you might pray. There's something wrong with Maddie."

"What is it?" Her voice was full of concern. I wanted to be with her. It was good I wasn't.

"I think Paula and Troncatti are getting into Maddie's head."

"How?"

"I don't know, but the last time Maddie was so different. I've heard stories about parents who try to turn their children against the spouse they're divorcing. When a kid is Maddie's age, it's easy, I understand. I need Maddie to see that I'm the same father she once couldn't get enough of."

"Of course I'll pray."

I didn't say anything for a couple of seconds. "I don't have many friends left in this town."

"You have a family. Here at church."

Family. Was that even possible?

"Thanks," I said.

"Try to get some sleep," Nikki said.

Fat chance.

When I got off the phone I went out on the balcony. The moon was almost full and I could feel the memory of Maddie in my arms. And I just looked up at the sky, and in my head some words flashed.

Okay, God, I don't want to be a star. I want Maddie. I want to be part of her life. I don't know why you let the Troncattis of the world have all the success and never take them down. I don't care anymore. I don't know why you took Paula away. I know I'm not supposed to hate anybody, but I do. But I'll give that all up if you'll just get me back with Maddie. Just please, please, give me my daughter back, and let her remember the way things were and make her want to be with me, God. Is that a deal? Just make it happen. Please, please, please.

– 3 –

Seeing Renard J. Harper again was like a family reunion. He greeted me with a warm handshake and a smile. Called me Mr. Gillen.

"How you doing?" I said.

"Better'n most, not as good as some," Harper said. "How you been?"

"Model citizen, baby."

Harper laughed, the way a friend does when he wants to encourage you. We were in the parking lot at Woodley Park, where they have a man-made lake and ducks. Maddie loved ducks.

I was anxious to tell Harper what I'd been up to. "Been doing anger management, cleaning up my act. No driving wild. No smashing bottles."

"All right!"

"I mean, you've got to look at the positive, right?"

"Always."

"And that's what I'm doing. I know it's not going to be easy, but I'm doing it for Maddie."

"That's the way."

"Going to let her take it slow with me, I won't force anything. Just sit and listen. Won't even say anything if that's the way she wants it. Just being with her, that's the first step, right?"

"You're gonna be all right, man. I know it."

I showed him the bag of chocolate chip cookies I'd made. Opened it up so he could smell them.

"Take one," I said.

"You sure?"

"Come on. See if I passed the test."

He smiled, took a cookie. A moment after the bite he nodded his approval. "Good job. Oh yes. My mama used to bake all the time. Cookies. Cakes. That's why I'm in such good shape." He patted his tummy, which was round in a comforting sort of way.

There was a little bit of wind today, making tiny whitecaps on the lake. A couple of paddleboats were out there. And the ducks, of course. Maddie and I would crumble up a cookie or two and feed them. Real duckie treats.

We took a bench near the parking lot. "You think it'll be better this time?" I said. He wouldn't know, but I had to hear somebody say it. I was so nervous my hands were shaking.

"I'm sure it'll be," Renard J. Harper said. "All you have to do is relax."

"Yeah. Right."

"Take a deep breath. Think about happier times."

"When were those?" I said with a laugh.

"Oh, I can remember." Harper smiled. "Radio days. Back before rock took over everything. I remember my mom listening to the radio, and the DJs saying simple things like, 'Here's Nat King Cole singing "Stardust."' And then you'd hear Nat King Cole, and then the DJ'd say, 'That was Nat King Cole and that great old number, "Stardust."' You're too young to remember."

"I've heard of Nat King Cole," I protested.

"You had real groups back then, too. Frankie Valli and the Four Seasons. Sally Jesse and the Raphaels—"

"Sally Jesse ... you're messing with me!"

"Just wanted to see if you were listening."

And I was, and I wanted to kiss Renard J. Harper. He was playing with me, helping me forget my nerves, setting me at ease. The guy was a saint. He even sang me a little more of his country song, "You'd Be So Nice to Slide Home To."

When I looked at my watch, I was surprised to see twenty minutes had passed. It was now 11:40. Maddie was ten minutes late.

"What happens if she doesn't come?" I said.

"Don't worry. She'll be here. If they don't bring her, that'll look bad. You haven't done a thing, and I can see what it's doing to you. Just relax."

But I couldn't. I kept fiddling with the twist tie on the bag of cookies.

"Tell me about your acting," Harper said.

"I don't think acting's for me anymore," I said.

"No way."

"Yeah."

"What makes you say that?"

I shrugged. "The business, I guess. So much of it now is based on plugging in the right look. There's not much respect for acting anymore. I mean, actors who wanted to make it in Hollywood used to go to New York and train on the stage. Or the studio would make them take acting lessons. Now some guy who looks like he had his jaw cut for Mount Rushmore walks off a soap and into the movies because he's got some fan base made up of teenage girls."

"Not like you have an opinion or anything."

"Did I run off at the mouth there?"

"I like a man with opinions."

"Funny, when I was first with Paula, she said the same thing." I stopped a second, feeling transported. "I told her the same thing about acting and she agreed, and we used to talk about doing some stage work together, but of course realized there's no money in that. Pretty soon, it always comes down to money. And now she's got it."

The wind was all I heard for a long moment. Then I looked at my watch.

"Could be traffic," Harper said.

But the knot in my stomach was telling me it wasn't traffic. It was telling me Maddie wasn't going to be here. Period.

It was at 11:55 that Harper gave in. He took out his cell phone and made a call. I couldn't listen to that. I walked to the edge of the lake and started tossing a few cookie crumbs to the ducks. I became instantly popular. There was so much delighted quacking I didn't hear Harper walk up to me.

When I turned around and saw his face my soul dropped.

"Bad news," he said.

- 4 -

Alex's receptionist looked at me, eyes wide, and said, "She's with someone. If you can call—"

"Get her," I said. "Now."

The poor girl must have thought I was strapped with a bomb or something. She looked at me that way, got up, and sort of backed into Alex's office.

A moment later Alex herself came out, took one look at me, didn't say a word. She went back into her office and walked out a middle-aged woman who seemed confused but understanding.

"I'll call you with the details," Alex told the woman, who gave me a look before she went out the door. I could only wonder what she thought.

"Come in," Alex told me.

The moment I stepped in the office I couldn't stop shuddering—shaking wildly like a man caught in the Arctic in his underwear. The rage was so intense behind my eyes I couldn't focus. For a moment I couldn't even speak.

"I got a call from Jennings," she said.

"What—"

"Please have a seat, Mark."

"No way."

"Are you going to just stand there?"

"No, I might walk around a little."

"I know what you must be feeling, believe me."

"I don't think you do, Alex. I was sitting there waiting for Maddie. Waiting for her with all the ducks. You know what happened? I stepped in duck doo. It was perfect. I was standing there rubbing my shoe on the grass as Harper tells me they're not coming. They're not going to let me see Maddie anymore. They think they can pull this—"

"Mark, please—"

"I'm sick of this! What are they trying to do?"

"Wear you down."

Yes. Exactly. The words rang true. Wear me down emotionally and financially. They were certainly doing a great job.

"What can I do?" I said. "I'm running out of money to pay you, Alex, and I'm not going to be able to afford you from my tips."

"Don't worry about money. I can still petition the court."

"Petition?"

"They may award reasonable attorney's fees."

"And may not?"

"Maybe."

"I can't ask you to take that risk."

"Forget that for now." There was something in Alex's eyes that told me she was not being completely level with me. Not that she was deceptive, just not willing to give me the whole nine yards.

"Alex, what's going on? Did Jennings tell you —"

"Why don't we schedule a hearing date, then you and I can —"

"What aren't you telling me?" I hit the edge of her desk with my fist. It hurt but the pain didn't matter to me.

"If you sit down, I'll tell you."

The words were ominous in her mouth, like an executioner taking an order for a last meal. I threw myself into a chair.

Alex paused a moment and took a breath. "You've got to understand something, Mark. This happens in more cases than I care to think about. Most often it's a desperate lie."

"What is?"

"Paula is accusing you of sexually molesting your daughter."

– 5 –

There's a long stretch of asphalt in the rural part of Orange County called the Ortega Highway. It meanders along an old Indian trail, past dark green oaks and golden grasslands, up into the Santa Ana Mountains where you can still glimpse the occasional mountain lion or a red-tailed hawk circling around in the sky. As the highway climbs up into the hills you have rock walls on one side and steep canyon drop-offs on the other.

It's a narrow snake of road, and some say it's the most dangerous road in the state of California. Sections of it have catchy nicknames like Dead Man's Curve, Ricochet Rim, and Blood Alley.

That's where I drove after Alex gave me the news.

Alex told me this was a desperate ploy, this sexual molestation charge. That it wouldn't hold up, that we had remedies. But I no longer believed her. I no longer believed anything. If you couldn't trust God, if you could pray and not get anything in return, how could you trust a lawyer?

I drove. I had to drive, and I was drawn to the road where there are more accidents every year. It's one of only two main arteries connecting homes in Riverside County with jobs in Orange County, so the highway lures more and more lunatic commuters every year. They speed, drift over the center line, pass illegally — even on blind curves — to advance their place in the string of cars, trucks, and big rigs.

Sexually molesting my own daughter?

My insides were exploding as I gunned the Accord. Drive, drive, drive, figure out what to do.

I finally reached the crest in the grade and thought for a moment about plowing through the guardrail, over the side. Compromising, I stopped at a turnout, got out of my car, and looked over the side. Scrubby pines stuck up like spears. It didn't look like lovely nature.

I started to think thoughts that scared me. Would anybody care if they found my body, bloody and bruised, at the bottom of a gorge? What would it do to Maddie? It couldn't be any worse than what Paula and Troncatti were doing to her. No doubt they had her convinced she had been molested. And they probably had some quack doctor to say whatever Bryce Jennings wanted him to say.

I was history. The allegations would go out over the news, and whatever scrap of reputation I had left would be like gum on the bottom of a shoe.

Then I remembered something Nikki told me. It was the word hope. She'd said that the one thing Christians had that atheists didn't was hope. If you were convinced that the universe was a great big void, and when you died you became worm food, hope was a pipe dream, a deception, a ruse.

Yeah, I thought as I stared down at the gorge, but maybe hope was not enough to live on anymore.

What kept me from jumping was an old familiar feeling. Good old hatred. And a picture of Troncatti feeling satisfied, the great director directing his greatest scene: the death of a jerk.

I got back in my car and drove to the ocean. And that's where I gave God my ultimatum.

Standing in the sand, looking at the water that Maddie loved so much, I just cranked out a prayer.

I don't know what you want from me. I don't even know what to say to you. Why won't you make it stop? Why won't you give me some sign that you're there, that you'll help me out a little here? What's going on, I want to know—I have to know, so tell me. Or I'm just going to go on by myself and forget everything. It isn't worth it if I can't have Maddie. Is that clear enough? Then be clear back to me, will you? Finally?

I stayed at the beach till the sun went down. I didn't hear any voice from the sky. The only thing I felt was the wind, and it got cold out there.

But on the way back to the apartment I found myself behind a slow-moving car, an old Chrysler, one that had seen its best days when George Bush the elder was president. What caught my eye was the faded bumper sticker it had stuck on its old chrome:

I Still Miss My Ex—but My Aim Is Improving.

From some dark, dim corner of my mind, came this laugh. The only thing I can compare it to is that famous laugh from Boris Karloff's The Mummy, where Bramwell Fletcher goes screamingly, laughingly crazy at the sight of the walking dead. My laugh was just like that—maniacal, all consuming. For about one minute I laughed, until I realized cars were honking behind me. I sped up, knowing I'd crossed over some line I had never quite seen, never wanted to see.

And I started wondering, Is that the sign, God? Is that it?

THE EDGE

Alex called me the next morning, checking up on me, telling me to hang in there. And pray. I was way ahead of her, though I didn't tell her about my ultimatum to God.

I also didn't tell her that I hadn't slept all night and was, in fact, feeling like another person. Like some big part of me had been yanked out and twisted too much to get back in.

Roland knew something was wrong when I sleepwalked through the lunch shift at Josephina's. He tried to get me to talk but I wouldn't. It was like I didn't want anybody talking to me. No personal contact. Roland invited me to come hear him play that night and I think I only grunted.

After the shift, though, I got some contact I did want.

My cell phone chimed as I was driving home. The voice on the other end was smooth and dark, like black honey. "I'm the guy Mr. Ayers told you about."

"Mr. Ayers?" I said. "I don't recall—"

"Maybe he didn't tell you."

"Tell me what?"

"About me."

A Hummer nearly cut me off with a lane change. "Hold it," I said. "Who are you?"

"The guy Mr. Ayers hired."

"To do what?"

"Find things out."

My hand started to sweat as I held the phone to my ear. I remembered that Milo Ayers said he would help me out. I guess this was it. "Are you like a private investigator?"

"Like that," he said. "Yeah."

"And what have you found out?"

"A couple of things. You were looking for Ron Reid, right? Your old man?"

"Yes."

"Give me a couple of days on that. I might have an address for you."

The thought made me anxious, as if I wasn't that already.

"The other thing is that Italian and your wife."

Now I almost rear-ended the Hummer, which was still in front of me. "What about them?"

"His house is on Dakota up by—"

"I know where it is."

"I was watching the place last night. There's a big slope down the street, another guy's house but it's way back, I could scope the Italian's place from there." He pronounced it Eye-talian, which I found odd and amusing at the same time. "You can see right into the pool area and into a big window of the house."

"Did you see anything?"

"I'm getting to that. I think I saw your wife, or is she your ex-wife?"

"Ex, I guess, though it isn't official yet."

"Bummer. Anyway, I saw her sit in a chair and it was like she was talking to somebody. Then she stood up and clenched her fists and started screaming at whoever it was. That's all I could see."

"How could you see this?"

"Nightscope. No big deal. But it just looked to me like there was a little trouble in paradise."

A scene played out in my mind, of Paula screaming at Troncatti, and it was vivid. I could almost hear the voices shouting.

"Is that all?" I said.

"Yeah. I'll call you about your old man."

He cut out before I got his name. But that wasn't heavy on my mind at the moment. What was heavy was Paula. And Maddie. In a house with Troncatti. And something bad was going on, I was sure.

But what could be done about it? The police? Tell them to go out there because some PI had told me he was snooping and saw Paula upset about something?

Sure. In a case where I was being accused of sexually molesting my own daughter.

No. I had to do something. The Lord helps those who help themselves kept going through my mind. That's not in the Bible, I know that now. I should have known it then.

∼——∼

Instead of going home I drove down to Jamy's Optics and picked out the best scope they had. LN–24 Night Vision. Set me back $1,200. They took Visa.

A sweet scope, the LN–24. Computerized proximity sensor, digital control, long-range infrared illuminator. You can see a bug scratch itself in total darkness from three hundred yards away. The guy at the store gave me a half-hour seminar on how to use it. By the time he was through I was a black belt in light amplification and infrared magnitude.

"You doing some PI work?" the guy asked me.

"Just for myself."

"You could go into business with that thing."

"I just may do that."

I poured myself into my car and took the freeway to the 405, taking the loop toward the west side. I got off at Sunset just under the looming gaze of the Getty Museum. It was up there on its perch, looking down at the city, me especially. I wondered if there were other people there, taking a break from the masterpieces of European art, to care about what went on below.

The traffic on Sunset was backed up. The sun was beating down and made the car feel like a kid's lunchbox left on the playground. My air-conditioning wasn't working and the flow through the open windows was nothing more than hot breath. There was even an accident — a bumper thumper around Roxbury — that gave me no choice but to take my sweet time.

It also gave me the opportunity to think a little bit about what I was going to do once I got near Troncatti's house.

Like driving the car right through the gate. Ram that baby like it was those big battering rams they used to break down castle doors with. I'd smash in and drive through the front door, lay down some rubber in the living room, hop out and say, "Hey, guys, nice to see ya."

Then Maddie would come running through the living room, giggling loudly like she always did when I came home, and jump into my arms and say, "Daddy, let's go for a ride."

"Sure honey," I'd say. "But before we do I have a little business to attend to." I'd go over to Troncatti and I'd grab him by the lapels of his imported shirt and throw him through one of those big plate glass windows that surrounded his house like vanity mirrors.

And then I'd turn to Paula and I'd say, "Are you ready to forget all this and come home?"

And she would quietly nod her head, give me a kiss on the cheek, and then all of us would get back in the car and drive away from the Troncatti house once and for all.

That's the way you dream of revenge in LA, I guess. With real audience appeal and plenty of shattering glass.

Traffic opened up a little bit past Roxbury, but it was still a long, slow drive until I got to Dakota. As I turned the steering wheel, it slipped in my fingers. I could feel the sweat stains in my armpits. If a cop would have stopped me, I'm sure he would've thought I was some lunatic who'd forgotten to take his meds but had, somehow, stolen a car.

I continued to climb up the curving road. Every house I passed seemed to be an immaculate example of how perfect people live. I saw a gardener, a Latino, hunched over a clump of yellow flowers in front of a huge, Tudor mansion. He looked up at me when I passed, and his eyes seemed to say I know you're an intruder but what am I going to do about it?

When I got near Troncatti's house I almost slammed on the brakes. What if Paula and Troncatti and Maddie were outside the gate? What if they were in the limo with Igor at the wheel?

And what if my daughter saw me, her eyes meeting mine, and she turned away in disgust? I don't think I could've handled that.

But with my pulse pumping, I drove on. I had to. This was the only thing left for me to do. No exit, no turning back.

I heaved a little sigh of relief when I saw there was no one out on the driveway. Place was as closed up as a bankrupt theater. The gates were shut and some thick, visual barrier had been put up, keeping gawkers from being able to see inside.

I drove on, looking for that slope the guy had told me about. I found it at the bottom of another private driveway that coiled up a hill. There was a fancy mailbox at the bottom of this driveway — a smaller version of a mansion set atop a twisting chain.

Stopping my car, I got out to take a quick look. That's when a dog started barking.

I couldn't see the house where the sound was coming from, but it sounded like a house further up the road. It was a big dog, too, and from where we were in this canyon, his woof echoed around like a big, pounding Salvation Army drum.

I wondered if the dog barked all the time anyway, or if it was just me. Because if I got up the hill at night and no one saw me, but this dog kept beating the drum, there'd probably be a 9-1-1.

Hey God, I thought. Maybe you can at least take care of a dog for me, huh?

– 2 –

And what a night.

I drove up there again and it was like Oscar night at Troncatti's. Major party going on. Cars and limos driving up to the big gate where a couple of burly guys with earpieces would motion them in. There was even a paparazzo flashing pictures as fast as he could with no one making any effort to stop him. I figured this was part of Troncatti's publicity machine at work.

My Accord was definitely out of character, and I drove on by the gate, catching a quick peek of the inside. For a quick second I thought about jumping out and just running on in. Surprise.

Instead, I drove on, well down the street, then parked. If I kept my eyes open I could get to Checkpoint Charlie—my name for the hillside where I was going to watch the house—without being seen.

I was all made up in my ninja gear, which consisted of black tennis shoes, black Levi's, and a complementary black T-shirt I'd gotten from watching a taping of That '70s Show. I even wore a black knit hat, the kind OJ reportedly wore when he went out after his ex-wife. Yep, this was going to be a real Hollywood story.

The rest of the street was relatively quiet. But from Troncatti's I could hear the strains of classic rock. I think it was the Stones, who I never liked. Fitting.

The big dog wasn't woofing. I wondered if that was a sign from God.

Then, with my scope around my neck, I scurried up the hill.

From where I was positioned, headlights from oncoming cars would not illuminate me. The only thing that could find me would be an LA police helicopter shining its high beams down, not an unlikely scenario. That is, if someone reported something strange happening in their neighborhood.

I had a good view of the swimming pool that was lit up in a light blue shade. All around in the yard were torches set off with flame. It looked like the Tahiti set in Mutiny on the Bounty.

And all sorts of people were milling around. A bartender in a fancy red coat had a setup near the pool house. Guests were swilling booze and laughing it up. And why not? This was a Hollywood party. At the home of the hottest director in the world. Exclusive. No outsiders allowed. Except I got to watch everything.

There was no sign of Paula or Troncatti for the longest time. I was beginning to think they left the house to an army of lackeys for a weekend without them. And I kept wondering where Maddie was.

Please God, let me see Maddie.

Troncatti finally made an appearance, walking out of the main house and throwing his hands up in the air to every guest that approached him. It was like he was greeting some long-lost brothers. Or maybe it was more like the pope receiving supplicants crawling on their bellies to kiss the great man's ring.

For a few moments I fantasized that the scope I was looking through was attached to a high-powered rifle. I felt a chill. Had I really been reduced to thinking like this? Something like a voice in my head, whispery but strong, was telling me not to do this, to get out of there, to keep from slipping further into the hole I was digging. Was it the voice of God? I shook it off and just kept watching.

Paula came out a few minutes later. My throat clenched. It felt like she was five feet in front of me. She was in a form-fitting dress, bare shouldered in the warm night. Stunning.

But I noted she did not attach herself to Troncatti. That was surprising to me. I thought they were like trophies to each other, so it was strange they didn't make the rounds together. I thought they would be the perfect Hollywood couple, strolling arm in arm around a party greeting visitors.

But Paula and Troncatti did not come together. Not once.

Paula looked like she was in a good mood. Maybe too much of a good mood. She was laughing more than was normal for her, almost like she was putting on an act. But I thought I understood that. She was in a throng of real power brokers. That's what being Troncatti's squeeze brought her. Who could fault her for trying to make an impression?

I could. Why wasn't she miserable, like me?

And where was Maddie? Was she inside that house right now? Alone, perhaps, watching TV? Could I slip in and quietly take her now?

My eyes started to feel heavy, so I turned my attention to Troncatti for a while. He was acting hyper, like he was on drugs or something. The guy never stopped moving. And another thing—he kept planting big old kisses on all the women. Not a friendly, nice-to-see-you kind. More like the hope-to-see-you-after-the-party variety. No wonder Paula wasn't hanging around with him. I almost felt bad for her.

Paula went back inside the house a couple of times. She also made several appearances at the bartender station. Paula had never been a big drinker, maybe a glass of wine with dinner sometimes. Now she was throwing the stuff down like Elizabeth Taylor in Who's Afraid of Virginia Woolf?

An hour and a half went by. I was feeling more than exhausted, but I willed myself to keep watching, because the party was in full swing. Some people fell into the swimming pool, fully clothed. That generated a great round of applause from the other guests. Yes, Hollywood is an entertaining town.

Some salsa dancing, very nineties, broke out. I could hear the music. And I could sure see Troncatti grinding against some shapely starlet types. Now I was not just tired; I started feeling sick.

I rolled on my back and tried to keep myself from crying out to the whole neighborhood.

The big dog barked.

I closed my eyes and just breathed. Breathed. And, at some point, I fell asleep.

I had no dreams.

When I woke up the dog wasn't barking anymore, and the moon had skipped over half the sky. And something was crawling on my face.

I sat up with a gasp and brushed whatever it was off. My neck was kinked and I was cold. And for a minute I didn't know where I was. Then I grabbed my scope and looked down. The party was largely over. A few people were still scattered around, but the bartender was gone and the music was over.

No sign of Troncatti or Paula.

The guards were gone from the front gate, which I noted was slightly open now. Maybe they were around somewhere, but for a moment or two it felt like I could have walked right in.

Then I saw some movement in the house.

It was Paula. She had her back to the big front window. She stood, with fists clenched at her sides. And she was screaming something at somebody else in the room.

It was just like what the PI had described, happening all over again. My skin erupted in a million pinpricks.

Troncatti came into the picture, like an actor entering a scene. He grabbed Paula by the shoulders and shook her.

I squeezed the scope so hard my hands started hurting.

And then Antonio Troncatti slapped Paula across the face.

~ 3 ~

Even now I can't remember exactly how I managed to get in. My mind was like a volcano, one thought flowing into the next, a hot mess. I half remember charging through the gate and running past a man who was staggering near the pool. He may even have said something to me.

But everything came into focus when I opened the big white door and found myself standing in the same room with Paula and Troncatti.

I still had my expensive night scope around my neck. It kept thunking against my chest, stopping only when I did, a few feet from the happy couple.

Troncatti was speechless, his eyes filling with rage.

Paula was in shock. "Mark!"

Before I could say anything, Igor charged into the room. We made eye contact, and I reveled in his look. It was outraged, no doubt because I had managed to get into physical proximity with Troncatti.

He grabbed my arm. I yanked it away.

"It's all right, Farid." Troncatti waved his hand at Igor. "Leave him with us."

Igor looked almost injured, and he backed out of the room very reluctantly.

"Time we had a talk," Troncatti said. "One talk. You understand?" The last word sounded like unnerstanna.

I looked at Paula, who was now strangely silent. I say strangely because she was never one to back down—on screen or in real life. My nerves were crackling. For a moment we all stood there, like we were holding guns on each other.

Then Troncatti walked in a big semicircle around the room, looking at me, like he was sizing up a shot in one of his movies.

"You are not a pleasant man," he finally said. "Things go so much better if you are a pleasant one."

"You need a new writer," I said.

"You are in a lot of trouble, being here."

I looked over at Paula. "Am I in trouble?"

"You shouldn't have come here," she said.

"You are talking to me," Troncatti said. "Leave her out."

"You want to be left out, Paula?"

"Over here!" Troncatti hit his chest.

Paula looked a little scared. That made me angry. "I want to see my daughter."

Troncatti shook his head. "That has been decided already."

"You two can let me."

"No way," Troncatti said.

"I'm no threat to her. Paula, you know that."

"You shouldn't have come," she said.

"Why are you turning her against me? Why are you making up lies about abuse? What did I do, Paula?"

She didn't answer.

"There is no reason with you," Troncatti said. "I will call the police you don't get out."

I wasn't afraid of him. Foolish, yes. But there was nothing more anybody could do to me. I didn't care what happened. All I wanted was to say my piece to Paula. Even as Troncatti fished for his cell phone, I didn't move.

"He tell you what he did?" I said.

Paula was still silent, but this time she frowned.

"Or were you in on it?"

No answer. Troncatti was barking into his phone.

"You know about the part I was supposed to get?" I didn't take my eyes off Paula's. I didn't just see the beauty in them, I saw something else. A darkness. Like somebody had just shut off the lights.

"I was all set to get a lead on a new show at NBC." My voice was calm but strong. "They wanted me. They picked me. It was going to make me a star. And your lover had his agent get hold of the producer and ax me. He did that. Did you know?"

I couldn't tell from her face and dark eyes what she knew. All I knew was she was listening. But that wasn't enough for me. I took a step closer. "Did you know?"

There was a flicker in the eyes, like she might want to say something.

"Did you?" I was feeling tears stinging my eyes. "And you went along with it?"

We looked at each other. Her lower lip quivered a little, like there was a heavy word teetering on the edge.

And then Igor was back, grabbing me by the shirt.

"Farid will take you outside to wait for the police," Troncatti said.

I tried to jerk away, but the limo-driver–bodyguard held me fast. I was considering what to do next when I sensed someone else in the room.

Maddie.

She was standing on the upper level, looking down into the room. She had a robe on and her big eyes stared at us, like we were hyenas at the zoo.

"Maddie!" I screamed.

She turned quickly and ran away.

"Maddie!"

"Shut up," Troncatti said.

I put everything I could into an elbow to Igor's midsection. It was rock hard. But it got me loose for a split second.

I ran toward the stairs yelling, "Maddie! Maddie!"

I made it to the first step when my feet went out. Igor had me by the legs. My head thudded against the banister and my chest detonated in pain as I fell on the stairs with my scope under me.

For good measure, Igor let me have a fist to the left eye. Red opened up on my mind's screen like a special effect from a World War II movie. My head shot back to the hard edge of a step.

"Stop it!" Paula's voice came from across the room. "Let him go."

"Shut up!" Troncatti spouted.

"Just let him go," Paula pleaded.

"Farid, get him to the gate. Wait for the police."

As I was jerked to my feet, my head buzzing, I heard Paula say Please and Troncatti say Shut up again. What was left in me wanted to run over and grab the guy by the neck for talking to her like that, but what was left in me wasn't too strong. Igor had no trouble getting me out into the night.

"You try to run," he said, "I will break all your fingers."

– 4 –

"You want to tell me what you expected to do there?" the cop asked. He was a uniform, a sergeant, and we sat at his desk at the Santa Monica station. They'd given me Insta-Ice for the side of my face, which felt like a football after the extra point.

"Not particularly," I said.

"You want to be difficult?"

"Aren't you supposed to read me my Miranda rights or something?"

"You watch too much TV."

"What if I want a lawyer?"

"Do you?"

"No."

"Then why don't you tell me what you were doing in Troncatti's house."

"Trying to stop him from hitting my wife."

"You were trespassing."

The officer's name was Ruchlis. I wondered if he was a reasonable man.

"You have any children?" I asked.

He looked at me a little disappointed. "We're here to talk about you, not me."

"Look, I'm sorry I was on that scum's property. I didn't damage anything. In fact I'm the one with the black eye. But I'm not a criminal."

"What are you, Mr. Gillen?"

"Just a guy who's ..."

"Go ahead." He seemed to want to listen.

"I just wanted to help her."

"Who?"

"My wife. And my daughter was in there, too."

"Is this a custody thing?"

"Yeah."

"You're supposed to go to court for that. You take things in your own hands it ends bad."

"It can't get any worse."

Another uniform walked over to the desk. "I need you for a second," he said.

"Just sit here," Ruchlis told me. He got up and walked a few steps away from the desk. I watched them talk and knew it had to do with me. Ruchlis looked over at me a couple of times while the other cop talked to him.

When he came back to the desk he sat down, looking almost upset. "You'd better call that lawyer after all," he said.

~ 5 ~

The Men's Central Jail in LA is not the place to plan a vacation. It's meat storage, a holding pen for as many accused as they can stuff into it. That results in more than a few disturbances among the inmates. But there's also a marketplace. Drugs are sold, deals made, even lives are occasionally traded.

I was booked, showered, garbed, and given a cell. It was the weekend, so I got to sit there for two days, waiting until Monday to go before a judge.

I did get my one phone call, and used it for Alex. She said she'd show up for the arraignment and bail hearing. But she did not sound happy about it. I couldn't blame her. It wasn't bad enough having a client who had permanent foot-in-mouth disease. Now he was a criminal.

I got the shakes getting shown to a cell. They got a little worse when I met my cell mate, a very large person named Ignacio. He had muscles in places where I don't even have places, and a face that had been on the business end of more than one fight. He told me he was in for beating up a guy in a bar who had dissed the Oakland Raiders, Ignacio's favorite team.

I decided to leave football out of our conversations. And we did have conversations. Or rather, Ignacio did. He loved to talk. He gave me an earful, especially when he found out why I was here.

"Trespass? You in here for that? Man, you getting the dedo grande."

When I told him about Maddie, Ignacio actually got kind of brotherly. He said he had a daughter too, with his girlfriend. The girl's family took her back to Mexico to keep her away from Ignacio. Maybe just as well, he said, until he learned how to keep from hurting people who ticked him off.

"Got to get rid of the hate, man." Ignacio shook his very large head. "If I got hate, I use it. Got to get rid of it. So how'd you lose your daughter?"

Nervously, but then warming up, I gave him the story, warts and all, and he gave me another earful. "Man, you are stupid. You know how stupid you are? If there was a school for stupid people, you'd be the teacher, man."

I let him have his opinion.

"You let the system beat you up. You got to know how to play it." He went on to tell me all about how to beat an assault rap. Maybe that would come in handy if I ever came face-to-face with Troncatti.

That night I didn't get much sleep. There was a lot of noise in there, but mostly I couldn't sleep because I kept thinking about Maddie and Paula. And Troncatti.

And a lot about what Ignacio had said about hate. Got to get rid of it.

I didn't want to get rid of it. That was absolutely the last thing I had going for myself.

― 6 ―

I woke up on Sunday with Ignacio talking to himself. Actually, I think he was singing, something about birds and guns. And he kept it up even while we were walking in the long line toward what they call breakfast in this place.

"You stay with me," Ignacio said. "I don't want you hurt."

That was a relief.

I was halfway through cold eggs and limp toast when they made the announcement that if anybody wanted to talk to a chaplain—and they had different kinds for different religious preferences—then you could sign up. And, after breakfast, I did.

Maybe I was halfway curious what a jail chaplain would have to say to somebody like me. Maybe I really wanted to hear some words of wisdom. Or maybe I just wanted to be relieved of Ignacio's rat-a-tat talk for a while.

Whatever the real reason, I was glad to get out of the cell and walked by a deputy down to an interview room. Inside I saw another inmate, only this one was dressed in civvies. I wondered how he'd gotten those clothes.

Then he introduced himself. "Chaplain Ray," he said.

He was the Christian chaplain? He was a muscular Latino, had a tattoo on his forearm and a shaved head.

"You're not the type we usually get in here," he said. "Mostly they look like me."

"How did you ... ?"

He smiled. One of his front teeth was gold. "You believe a sweet face like this used to bust heads? When I got saved, I told God I was gonna do whatever it took to get back in here and talk to my people. Ten years ago. And now I'm talking. But like I said, you don't look like the type. So why don't you tell me how you find yourself in this place?"

For the second time in two days, the first being with my roommate in the cell, I told the story—of me and Paula and Maddie, of Troncatti, and everything I did about it. I sounded even more stupid this time around. I was glad Ignacio wasn't here. When I finished, I asked the chaplain, "So how stupid do you think I am?"

He shrugged. "About as stupid as David. Dude couldn't keep his eyes off the pretty girls. Brings one into the palace, gets her pregnant, tries to cover it up by killing her husband. And the guy is one of the heroes of the Bible. If God didn't use stupid people, he'd have a pretty tough choice about finding anybody."

"But I made a real mess of things, I mean, bad."

"Yeah, you did. Only question now is what're you gonna do about it?"

"What do you think I should do?"

"You told me you were going to a Bible study and church. What happened to that?"

"I tried it with God. I even prayed that he'd let me have my daughter. It didn't work out."

"So you walk away? Listen, you don't try it with God, like he's some cafeteria line and you don't get the dessert you wanted so you don't come back to the place. You got to grab hold with everything, like your life depends on it, which it does."

"But what does that even mean? I poured out my heart to God and got hammered."

"Pouring out your heart is a good thing, but it's not the only thing. It's not the place you stop. It's the place you start. You move on to where God wants you to be, which is in Jesus Christ."

"What do you mean, in?"

"It's what the Bible says. Listen." He reached for his leather Bible—which was as worn as any book I've ever seen with the cover still on—and flipped through it. I could see the pages marked up with different colored inks and highlighter pens. Every page was like a child's rainbow.

"'Therefore, if anyone is in Christ, he is a new creation; the old has gone, the new has come!' You see that? In Christ."

I remembered that passage. Pastor Scott had used it in one of his sermons. Was this a telegram from God?

"Not outside," Chaplain Ray continued, "not looking in, not messing around, but making the big dive with your whole life into Christ. You give it up for him, and you don't look back, you don't keep things to yourself, you don't make it halfway. You spill out everything and admit that you can't make it on your own and that you want Jesus to be making it for you, and you don't mess around with sin anymore, which means trying to have everything your own way all the time and running around hating everybody, like your mother-in-law and this Italian dude. You make a decision and you ask Jesus to forgive you and make you right. And if you want to know how to do it, take a look at Psalm 51, which is the one David wrote after he murdered the guy and took his wife. And if you can say those words and mean them then you're going to be home free, understanding that Jesus is the one who died in your place on the cross."

"Whoa."

"I can keep talking, man. I'm just getting warmed up. But I don't want to talk to the wall. I want to know if you're gonna do anything about this."

My last line of defense flew up like a ragged cobweb. "I haven't got a Bible."

He reached for his coat, which was laid across a chair, and pulled out a brand new hand-sized Bible. "Now you do. Want to walk through it with me? I got time."

"I guess I'm not going anywhere, either."

I don't know how to explain what happened next. After we read a bunch of the Bible together, all of a sudden Chaplain Ray was praying over me and with me and I was praying to Jesus and it felt like a washing of my body, inside and out. And when we were done, I was still in jail, still in the jailhouse jumpsuit, I still didn't have Maddie, I still had a string of stupid things behind me—but I felt like there was a hand on me pulling me up from where I was to where I had to be.

Ray said, "When you get out of here, I want you to get your rear back in church. Got that?"

I nodded.

"You trust God. For everything. Your daughter. Your life. You ask him what to do. You get your face in the Bible. You trust God. You hearing me?"

"I'll try."

"No, man. You do it. I don't want to hear no excuse."

After all the ways I'd messed up, I knew I was full of excuses. And I knew the people I cared about, and who cared about me, could look at this and see only a thin jailhouse conversion.

But the trust thing hit me hardest. Chaplain Ray was right. I had to trust God this time, all the way, no matter what people thought.

And that's the way it was going to be, for Maddie's sake.

– 7 –

On Monday, Alex got me released O.R. after the arraignment, where she asked for a continuance. The deputy D.A. went right along with that, which seemed strange. Didn't they always fight for bail on Law and Order?

A few hours later, after I was officially sprung, I found out why.

Alex told me to come to her office, which I did.

"I've been talking to the D.A.'s office," Alex said. "They're ready to drop the filing."

Stunned but feeling a tiny glimmering of hope, I could only say, "Why?"

"Because there's a catch."

That brought me back to earth, but quick.

"I've got some papers here from Bryce Jennings," Alex explained. "I'm obligated to tell you about it. So I'll just come right out with it. Bottom line, there will be no complaint against you if you agree not to fight for custody of Maddie."

Suddenly it all made sense.

"You don't have to do it," Alex said. "We can still—"

"They've worked it pretty good, haven't they?"

"Mark, like I said, I'm willing—"

"You've been around this type of thing. Nasty people fighting over a kid. What's that do to the kid?"

Alex treated the question seriously. "It depends on the child, but most of the time it's not good, obviously. But Maddie—"

"And it can be worse if the kid's the emotional type."

"That depends, too, on a lot of—"

"Maddie's emotional."

Alex looked at her hands.

"If I sign the papers, she won't have to deal with this whole mess anymore, right?"

"You don't have to sign. I can still—"

"I know. But I'm saying, if I did, she wouldn't have to go through anything. I mean, we fight the abuse charge and she's going to have to go on the stand. You're going to have to question her."

"At some point."

"And doctors probing her."

"Yes."

I couldn't let that happen. There was this time when Maddie and I were out walking and went past a chain-link fence. Suddenly, this little dog appeared out of nowhere and ran toward us, barking its head off. Maddie got scared, grabbed my leg, held on tight.

I patted her head and said, "It's all right. Watch." I put my hand near the fence, letting the dog smell it. The pooch stopped barking and wagged its tail.

"See?" I told Maddie. "You want to say hi to the dog?"

Maddie, (I could still feel her trembling) peeked out from behind me and said, "Hi doggie."

I was there to protect her from the barking dog and to show her she didn't have to be scared. But now if I went forward in a fight over Maddie and child abuse, I wouldn't be able to protect her anymore. In fact, I would be the barking dog.

I looked at Alex. "Can I tell you something?"

"Of course."

I recounted my jail experience, then added, "It seems like climbing a mountain, and after all this struggle you get to a plateau and know that you're not going back again. You are higher and safer than you were just a little while ago. I want to stay here."

Alex listened closely.

"I can't give up fighting for her, Alex. But I can't see her hurt, either. What do I do?"

Alex waited a long time before answering. "I'll stall Jennings. Do you have any job opportunities?"

"I've been thinking of coaching baseball. Would it matter if it was in Arizona?"

"Why there?"

"I have a friend, a guy I played with in the minors, who coaches a high school team in Phoenix. About a year ago he said if I ever want to assist, give him a call. I want to get out anyway. I'm through with LA.

"You still get monitored vists —"

"I'll never miss one. I'll make the drive. Ride a bike. Crawl if I have to."

"Meantime, we get you a good criminal lawyer. I know a few."

"Whatever it takes."

"At the right time I'll go back to Jennings with our own offer. I can't promise anything will change but—"

"Go for it, Alex."

She nodded. "And you and I, we pray, right now. We pray for that trust you were talking about. Even lawyers need it. Maybe especially lawyers."

So we prayed. I gritted my teeth as we did. I kept seeing Maddie's face in my mind.

FINDINGS

~ 1 ~

I gave notice at the apartment that afternoon. And started wrapping up my affairs, if thin threads left blowing in the wind can be called affairs.

The idea of moving to Arizona and starting all over again felt right. Any place that was not Los Angeles was fine with me.

I'd only be a six- or seven-hour drive away and could get back for the monitored visits with Maddie. It wouldn't seem like a bad drive if I knew she was on the other end. And my getting it together as a baseball coach or some other job would look good to the court down the line. The criminal case was hanging over my head, but I decided to believe it would work out. Somehow.

The first person I told about my move was Mrs. Williams. In many ways she'd been like a mother to me and a grandmother to Maddie. One of the last few decent people in LA, I say.

She almost cried when I told her, standing in front of her open door in the hallway.

"Will you call me from time to time?" she said.

I hugged her. "Count on it."

When evening came I went over to the Club Cobalt, to see Roland. How was I going to break it to him? Part of me sensed he already knew. I hadn't called him, I'd quit waitering with him, I'm sure he knew something was up.

Roland was in the middle of a set when I came in. Man, he could play. I'd miss that, but I had heard a rumor that jazz had made it to Arizona. There would be other venues.

I sipped a Coke in a booth while Roland played and for a little while felt musical relief. Roland finished off with a rousing update of "Take the A Train." It was like he had sixteen fingers. Piano doesn't get much better than that.

When he joined me I apologized for not having been in touch and told him I was moving out, good-bye.

"Can't believe it," he said. "There's no way."

"Way."

"You're just giving up?"

"Moving to a different location, that's all." I tapped a little tune on the table with my fingers. "You remember that thing you said, God playing jazz?"

He nodded.

"Well, I'm trying to listen for that now, see? I'm really trying to listen."

A long silence passed between us.

"You keep in touch," Roland said.

"Not just that. When I come back into town, maybe I can take up some room on your couch."

"If you shower first."

I put out my hand and we shook. "Deal."

Roland went to play another set and I ordered another Coke. Halfway through the first number, Milo Ayers came into the Cobalt. He made a few rounds, then came over to my booth.

"Markie! You don't answer your calls?"

"Hi, Mr. Ayers. I haven't listened to my messages today."

He sat down. "The guy, looking for your father?"

I'd almost forgotten about that. "What about him?"

"Wants to talk to you. I think he has something."

My skin pulled tight on the back of my neck. "Found him?"

"Don't know. Call him." He took out a pen and wrote something on a paper napkin, then handed it to me. It was a phone number. "You call, huh?" Milo said.

– 2 –

It was a Motel 6 off Highway 15, just outside of Barstow. That's where the guy said he was. Ron Reid, on his way to who knew where.

There was a Denny's next door, separated by a block wall and some dusty oleander. I parked in the Denny's lot and found a place near a couple of pea-green Dumpsters where I could look over the wall and watch the motel parking lot.

The Dumpsters gave off a lovely scent — industrial stink, rust, and rancid food. It blew toward me on a soft wind.

I ignored it, because I was focused on finding a way to get into room 107. That was the number the guy Milo hired gave me.

Your Motel 6's don't get the BMWs or the Benzes, the ones with the most sensitive alarm systems. My best guess for what I was about to do was a new Acura, which was only a few yards away from the door to 107.

Worked like a charm dipped in chocolate. All it took was me sitting hard on the hood, and the alarm — a real nasty one — tore up the quiet of the evening.

I ran down to the end of the row and waited.

Doors began opening, light from inside rooms flooding out on the walk. A husky voice cursed, shouting that the owner — whose legitimacy the shouter was questioning — better take care of this situation now.

My hope was that the owner of the Acura would be the last one to respond. In a bath or something, or maybe at Denny's grabbing a cup of coffee.

The alarm kept going. Room 107 stayed sealed.

I edged a little closer, right in front of the window of 108, which was dark. Sound sleepers.

The WAW WAW WAW WAW of the alarm was like an ax to the brain.

The shouter was out on the walk now, a hairy man in boxers and a T-shirt, holding a Dr. Pepper like a grenade.

And then a crack in 107.

I waited half a beat, then pushed it open.

Ron Reid shrieked, but the Acura worked its magic and no one could hear it.

"Mind if I come in?" I said over the noise.

"How'd you find me?"

"Are you going to leave me standing out here?"

"You don't understand —"

I pushed past him and walked inside the room. He closed the door quickly, as if someone outside might be spying on us. For all I know he could've been right.

The car alarm continued, though now we were able to talk in a more normal tone. He had on a Hawaiian shirt, red, with pictures of little surfers and fish.

"How did you find me?" he repeated.

"I just want to know one thing — how much did you get?"

"Mark, listen —"

"How much did Troncatti give you to lie in court?"

Ron Reid gave me a long look and sighed. "Ten," he said.

"Ten thousand?"

"Yeah."

"Who gave it to you? Who made the drop?"

"Look, they're gonna hurt me, I say anything. I gotta get out of here."

He looked like a lost and desperate mutt. Where I should have felt something hard and hot inside me, I now felt this black, cold hole. I sat down on the edge of the bed.

I looked at him. "You've got to come back and talk about this."

He paced toward the window. The alarm died outside. "Mark, maybe I wish I could, but I can't. I'm afraid of these people."

"You can be protected."

"You don't believe that."

He was right. "You're just going to leave then, take off?"

"I've been on the road most of my life now. I'll find a way to get along."

"You know I have to tell this to the police."

He nodded. "I don't think they'll believe it."

"They just might."

He cocked his head.

"Look, I'm going to be moving to Phoenix. If you want to talk, you can find me. I'll be listed."

He swallowed hard, like his throat was parched. "Why would you want me to do that?"

I wasn't sure myself, but I told him about being in jail and Chaplain Ray and what that all did to me. It must have gotten through a little because Ron Reid nodded and said, "Heavy duty."

I got up. "Just tell me one more thing. Who handed you the money?"

Ron Reid paused a moment, then said, "Troncatti's driver, I think his name's Farid. You know him?"

"Yeah, I do."

"Gave it to me in a gym bag and showed me the gun he said he'd use if I talked."

One more try. "Come back with me, please. Turn this over to the police. Let them—"

He shook his head. "I'm getting out." He looked at his feet. "I'm sorry, Mark. I know I messed things up pretty bad for you."

"You did."

"If it means anything, I'm pretty messed up, too."

"That Wheel isn't so hot, is it?"

He looked up at me and a small glint of realization flickered in his eyes. I went to the motel dresser, pulled out the top drawer, and there it was—a good old Gideon Bible. I took it out and tossed it on the bed. "Read that," I said. "Read that like your life depends on it, because it does."

I started for the door.

"Mark."

I turned back.

Ron Reid's voice quavered. "I wish things had been different. You know, between us."

"Me too, Dad."

I left the room. A desert breeze cooled my cheeks, because they were wet. I wiped them with the back of my hand. I was shaking a little when I got to my car, but managed to unbutton my shirt and take off the cassette recorder I'd strapped to my body with duct tape.

– 3 –

I had to wait an hour at the Santa Monica station before Ruchlis came in. From the look on his face he probably would have expected to see Winona Ryder with a bagful of stolen clothes before he saw me.

"I need you to hear something," I said.

Maybe it was the seeping desperation in my voice that convinced him. He didn't ask for any explanation but showed me to his desk where he took out a small cassette player. We loaded the tape and listened.

It was a pretty good recording with the usual muffles associated with a shirt over a torso. But the stuff I wanted him to hear came out clear.

Ruchlis sat back in his chair and folded his arms after it was finished. "You know this is not admissible evidence."

"I don't care what it is as long as you believe it and get the D.A. on it."

"Suppose I did believe it. The D.A.'s gonna say, what can I do with this? Unless the guy comes in and is willing to testify about what he knows, I can't use this."

"Can you go talk to him then? He's probably still at the motel, or if he isn't you can find him. I did."

"Then you're talking about resources," Ruchlis said. "I got to tell you I don't think this is going to fly. Who's to say this isn't a doctored tape? You're an actor, right?"

"What's that got to do with it?"

"You get one of your friends to play Daddy and out comes this little tape."

I just looked at him for a second. How could he think I would make up something like this? My hands were like claws as I touched my forehead. In my mind I was crying out to God for help.

"Look," Ruchlis said, "you've got to see it from my standpoint. I'm a cop and my feelings don't matter. I think you may be telling me the truth. But I also know you were spying on Troncatti's house, you broke in, you're desperate, and maybe even a little nuts. Who knows?"

"I know."

"Does anybody know if they're nuts or not? I may be a little squirrel food myself. Point is, I can't do anything for you, except maybe give you a lead."

I looked at him.

"You forget we had this conversation when it's finished, got it?"

I nodded.

"Call Harrison Ellis at channel 7. Say the stripes from Santa Monica sent you over. He'll listen to what you have to say, but from there I can't promise you anything. My advice, don't get your hopes up."

— 4 —

Harrison Ellis was well known to LA audiences. He'd broken quite a few stories, including one that brought down the head of a major studio. Ellis had the reputation of being a straight shooter and a good reporter.

We met at a little restaurant on Argyle. It was out of the way but sort of LA tony. That meant a lot of people who pretended like they didn't want to be seen ate there, hoping to be seen.

Ellis was about forty and didn't have an anchorman's good looks. That was a point in his favor. He was a guy who had to make it on his reporting skills and not on the fact that he could read a teleprompter with a straight face over a square chin.

The hostess knew him and showed him to what I took to be a regular table. It was near the kitchen out of the way. We were not among those who wished to be seen.

I told the story as quietly and objectively as I could. I didn't want him thinking that I was what everybody else seemed to think I was — a slightly off-kilter child abuser with an ax to grind. Fifteen minutes later I ended my tale, which was only interrupted a couple of times by the waiter who wanted to do his job.

Then I handed him the cassette and told him what was on it. His eyebrows went up at that. He seemed to be smelling a story.

"You have a copy?" he asked.

"Of course," I said.

"Don't say of course. I've seen smarter guys than you make the stupidest mistakes. Like this lawyer who liked to make videotapes of his, shall we say, conferences with female clients. He digitized the tapes and put them on a CD-ROM. Then one day he was in court presenting a final argument to a jury, and using the CD-ROM on his laptop to project some graphics about the evidence — "

"Don't tell me."

"That's right. Instead of a picture of the accident scene up came a nice shot from one of his private consultations. That was the end of his legal career. I hear he's making two hundred grand a year now making adult films. America, what a country."

He laughed.

"Personal note," he said. "Let's say all this is true, what you went through, which I'm judging it is, looking at you. How're you keeping it together?"

It was strange how quickly and surely the answer came. "I'm just hanging on to God, Jesus, hope."

Harrison Ellis smiled. "Throw in good ratings and I might just be with you on that."

— 5 —

That old cliché about the quiet before a storm is true. Aren't all clichés based on fact? In my case, it should be modified a little. Because what happened next was worse than a storm. A storm's something you've been through before, so you think you can handle it. What hit next was something I could never have been prepared for.

It happened three days after I left the tape with Ellis. I had a week left on the apartment and was cleaning it up, hoping to get back the security deposit. There was even a small beam of light at the end of my tunnel. Garner Charles, my coaching friend in Arizona, said there was a spot on his staff for me. It wasn't much money, but it was more than I was making now, which was zero.

I gave in and called Nikki. I felt like I could finally talk to her. I thanked her for all she'd done, for getting me into the Bible study, for being one of those people God uses to point someone in the right direction.

I also thanked her for reminding me what real acting was all about. "I hear there are some good regional theaters near Phoenix," I told her. "Maybe I'll give it a shot."

"You should," she said. "Because you're really good."

That meant a lot, coming from her. I said I'd keep in touch.

That evening I went down to the Cobalt to hang with Roland. In a way, it was like a going-away party. He played some of my favorite jazz, just for me. It made me feel happier than I had in a long, long time.

It was around nine and I was still at the club when my cell phone rang. It was Ruchlis on the other end. I almost fell off my chair.

"Paula's in the hospital," he said.

My heart froze. "What happened?"

"I'll tell you when you get here. We're at St. Stephen's, Santa Monica."

I made it in record time. At the desk they told me she was on the third floor.

As soon as I got out of the elevators I saw Erica Montgomery. She was pacing in the hall, as if she were waiting for me.

"Oh, Mark," she said, without any animosity in her voice. That in itself was strange. There was defeat about her. Every other time I'd seen Erica, she had this air of invincibility, like she was made of cold granite. Now there were chips and cracks, and a confusion in her eyes. The world she had tried to control was no longer under her influence.

She started, very slightly, to shake. Without a word I took her arm and pulled her into the waiting room and sat her down on one of the vinyl chairs. She did not resist me a bit.

"Where's Maddie?" I said. "Who has Maddie?"

"She's —" Erica cleared her throat — "with a woman, a social worker."

"Where? What happened?"

And then the granite shattered. Erica put her head in her hands and quaked with sobs. There was one other person in the room, an older gentleman on the other side. He looked at me with a sort of weary wisdom, as if he had been through this scenario countless times and was telling me what to do.

I did something I never thought I'd do in my life. I put my arm around Erica's shoulders. More amazingly, she did not pull away.

"He cut her with a knife," she said, into her hands, so it was muffled. But I knew what she said and felt paralyzed — I don't know, with fear of the awful implications. Was Paula hanging on to life by a thread?

"My beautiful Paula," Erica sobbed. "He cut her beautiful face."

That was more shocking, more horrible. I knew exactly what she meant. There was an infamous case out here some years ago, where an actress's face was scarred by a crazy stalker. He couldn't have her, so he was determined to punish her. And I knew that fit Troncatti's profile. He considered himself a god among men, an impression reinforced by all of the bootlickers that hang on to a good Hollywood ride. Paula must have threatened to leave him.

It fit with what I'd seen that night at Troncatti's, when he'd hit Paula. She was so much like Erica, not a woman to take anything lying down. Was this the result?

I kept my arm around Erica as she fought against her tears and lost. I just held her for a while.

"I'd like to see her, Erica," I said. "May I?"

I did not have to ask. I could have left her and gone straight to the room. But I asked anyway.

She stopped crying—well, stopped gushing—and looked up. Her eyes were red and wet and tired. She opened her mouth but did not speak. Then she nodded her head.

"Wait here for me," I said. I went outside the waiting room and found a water fountain with paper cups. I filled a cup and took it back to Erica, lifting her hand to put the cup in it.

"I'll be back," I said.

The nurse at the station told me Paula was in room 504. I followed the wall around until I found it. I went in the open door and saw Ruchlis.

He was standing midway in the room, which held two beds. The one nearest me was empty. A screen obscured the second bed, which held Paula.

Ruchlis put his finger to his lips and motioned me outside the door.

"I want to see her," I said.

Ruchlis put up his hand. "I know. You will. I just want to have you talk to me later."

"What happened up there?"

"Troncatti apparently sliced your wife's face."

"Apparently?"

"Well, that's what she says."

"Where is he? Did you get him?"

"Not yet."

That news made me want to jump out of my skin and scream. Troncatti was still out there. "And where's my daughter?"

"Down at the station with a very nice lady from child services."

"I want her."

"One step at a time."

I shook my head. "I want her, and I want her right after I talk to Paula."

"Don't fight me on this, huh? I'm going to have a man come up and keep the press away. There's going to be a circus when the news hits, and I'm going to try to keep it from hitting as long as I can. You blundering around isn't going to help."

He was right, of course. "Can't you get Paula to some secret location?" I said.

"I can't. Maybe she has friends, family. You."

The prospect of me having anything to do with Paula's future hadn't entered my brain. Ruchlis provided me an odd little jolt, like the snapping of static electricity.

"Why would he do that?" I said. "Cut her?"

Ruchlis shrugged. "Paula says she didn't know about the payoff to your father, that Harrison Ellis got to her by phone and asked her about it, played the tape over the phone. She says she confronted Troncatti and they had a blowout and she said she was leaving him, and that's when it happened. Troncatti may have been under the influence at the time. Drugs."

I nearly dropped to the floor. It was almost too much for my mind and body to handle.

"Come down to the station after you talk to her," Ruchlis said. "I'll see what I can do."

"Thanks."

As I walked into the hospital room, two waves of emotion hit me simultaneously, like I was some hapless surfer in storm-tossed waters. The first emotion was a growing elation that I was going to get to see Maddie soon, down at the police station.

The other emotion was a burning dread in my stomach as I got closer to the curtain and Paula's bed. It wasn't just what I thought I'd see, though the pictures in my mind were bad enough. What was I going to say to Paula? Or she to me?

What was I going to feel?

I stepped slowly around the curtain and there she was. Her eyes were closed but they were barely exposed anyway. Her face was wrapped in gauze. Two large bulges stuck out, one on each cheek. I could only imagine what was underneath the bandages.

For a full minute I stood there, just looking at her. I tried to imagine her face the way it was, and saw it—not the last time, at Troncatti's, when it was full of dark confusion. But the first time I saw her, at Roland's party, when I'd been knocked over by her beauty. The way she smiled when we ate peanut M&Ms together. That was the face I saw.

Some low sound came out of my throat, and she opened her eyes. I took one step closer.

Her eyes got big and then she shut them again, turned her head toward the pillow. Then she shook it a little, like someone saying No with a tone of regret.

"I came as soon as I heard. The cop. I know him."

Paula didn't say anything, but her breath came out in a slow, labored way.

"I mean, he knows me. I won't go into it. He says Maddie is okay. Down at the station. Maybe you know that. I saw your mom out there, we actually talked a little. Can you believe that?"

Still not a response from Paula.

"You want me to go, I will," I said.

She did not turn her head. She put her hand over her face, like she wanted to hide from me.

"We don't have to say anything," I said. There was a chair near the bed. I sat in it and stayed there for a long time.

Sometime in there Paula fell asleep. She was peaceful finally, and I imagined it was the most peace she'd had since, well, since getting involved with Troncatti.

How could she have known all this awaited her? She'd gone to Rome for a big break, the thing that all actors hope for. You get into that whole whirlwind and don't think about much else. Don't think about a director who gets high on power and manipulation, and what he might do if you don't let him have power over you.

That he might go nuts and scar you.

In a way that made me sick, I thought about my own bouts of craziness. Throwing glass bottles. Losing control. Not caring what other people said.

Was I that different from Antonio Troncatti? Only by a miracle of grace was I going to be better than I was. And I wanted to be better. For Maddie. And for Paula.

I leaned over her and whispered, "I'm sorry."

A nurse swept in, all business.

"The police," she said. "They're not here?"

"Not right now."

That seemed to disturb her. "And you are?"

I didn't hesitate, the answer flowing out of my mouth without doubt or question.

"I'm her husband," I said.

SIGNS

Arizona is everything they say. The Grand Canyon State. Landscapes to take your breath away—mountain ranges, winding rivers, grasslands, sand dunes, and sunsets that stick to your heart.

It's also hot. Hell's stove. Especially right outside Phoenix.

How do people make it in the summers? I suppose I'll find out. I plan on sticking here for a long time.

The nights are what I love best about the place. Sometimes the moon is so big you can poke lunar dust with a stick. And the stars—well, let's just say the same sky doesn't flicker over LA.

Nights here are what give me hope, and what I hang on to with a grip that would make a bear trap weep with envy.

I hope a lot of things. I hope they'll catch up with Troncatti someday, hiding out in Europe, get him back here to stand trial. At least I won't be. The D.A. had to drop the criminal charge, their chief witness being a slasher on the run.

And I hope they nail Bryce Jennings as an accessory to fraud on the court. Ruchlis keeps me posted on this. The tape I made of Ron Reid was played on a TV news report and a legal firestorm broke loose in town. Alex called me a week ago to say that Ron had been located and might even be willing to cooperate.

In a strange way, I hope that Ron will do the right thing and that I'll actually talk to him again. That part of my life has yet to be written up.

There's also the chance that Paula and I will do some theater work together, if she ever gets the desire again. She'll always have two jagged white scars on her cheeks, but makeup will suffice for a theater performance. There are a couple good regional theaters here and one that does a lot of Shakespeare. With Paula's name recognition, she'd be a shoe-in to be cast as Rosalind in *As You Like It*. I'd be happy to be a spear carrier, so long as I got to be in the show with her.

We'll see. The fact that she's here with me is miracle enough for now. Even Erica seems to be for us. I guess we've all been through enough to see that none of us are made of granite.

But what I pray for constantly is that I get Maddie back.

Oh, Maddie is with us here, physically, in the new apartment just outside Phoenix. Getting her out of protective custody, even with Paula's consent, was a two-week nightmare. We did it, though the system wanted to keep putting the screws to us. Alex was a big help. It took an emergency court appearance and sworn testimony from an unexpected source — Renard J. Harper testified on my behalf.

The LA part of the nightmare was finally over.

But Maddie is not the same little girl I knew.

A very nice psychotherapist in Phoenix, someone we now go to church with as a matter of fact, is giving us a reasonable deal on therapy for Maddie. She was definitely messed with by Troncatti and Paula. Dr. Nelson deals with Paula's guilt, which is almost as bad as Maddie's distrust. But both of them are tough. They got that from Erica.

As for me, when we were alone, Dr. Nelson told me what I can do, and it's what I've already done a hundred times over — forgive and seek God's healing in all things. When I do, I can't help thinking of that thing Tom Starkey said one night, about how the most important thing we may need, before anything else, is to be shaped by God's rough hands. I still don't quite get it. I'm not a saint in the forgiving part. But then I'm beginning to realize you don't have to get everything before you trust.

Which helps with the guilt I sometimes feel. If I hadn't given the tape to Harrison Ellis, if he hadn't played it for Paula over the phone before he ran with the story, maybe Paula wouldn't have been cut up.

Paula told me what happened. When she heard the tape she confronted Troncatti. She said she'd tell everything to the police about what they'd done to Maddie unless he left her and Maddie alone and didn't do anything else to hurt my career. Troncatti had been drinking heavily that night, and the threat of exposure, coupled with the threat of a woman leaving him, made him snap. That's when he grabbed a knife and did it.

All I know now is that Paula and I are somehow finding our way back to each other, both of us broken, both of us helping each other glue pieces back together. Maddie does not trust me fully yet. But I think time will overcome that. I pray hard to God every day. And look for signs.

– 2 –

Last night I went out on the balcony of our apartment. The moon was big and silvery, like in the storybooks. I sat down on a plastic chair in the warm air and watched the sky for a while.

Then the sliding door opened. I thought it was Paula coming out. But it wasn't. It was Maddie.

This was a little shocking, as Maddie had not wanted to be alone with me since we'd all gotten back together. She would cling to Paula, of course. And as long as her mother was in the room I was welcome. I didn't push anything. Dr. Nelson said I should just let things happen naturally. Even though Paula had explained about the bad things she and Troncatti had made up about me, there was a wall between Maddie and me that had to be taken down a brick at a time. That project was only just beginning.

Maddie didn't say anything to me at first. She sat in the other plastic chair and looked at the sky, too. Her feet, dangling from the chair, did not quite reach the ground. She swung them back and forth slowly. Still so little.

Finally, I said, "Hi."

"Hi," Maddie said.

"You like it here in Arizona?"

She nodded.

"Where's Mommy?" I asked.

"Lying down."

"Good."

We shared a silence for a long moment. I wanted to be so careful.

"Maybe we could all go get some ice cream tomorrow," I said.

"Okay."

I looked back at the sky. "Big moon, huh?"

"Yeah." Maddie's eyes reflected the moonlight as she looked up. Then she started to hum something. I wasn't sure at first what it was, maybe just an embarrassed tune to fight the discomfort of our moment. But as it went on I could hear it clearly. She was humming "Buffalo Gals."

"You remember that song?" I said.

"Uh-huh."

I stood up, slowly, so as not to scare her. But there wasn't any stopping me. It was like I was being pulled up by a string from the sky. Facing my daughter then was like an actor's horrible moment, when the casting director is about to announce who made the cut and who didn't. Who would be called back for more auditions, and who would be sent home to lick their wounds and wonder whether they'd ever make it in the business.

What would Maddie tell me when I said what I just couldn't hold back?

"Would you let me pick you up, Maddie?"

It was pushing it, I know. But I couldn't stay silent.

Maddie looked into my eyes, like she was searching for a memory, one that was smudged and unclear but sitting back there in her mind as real as the dark hills off in the distance.

Then she stood up and came to me, raising her arms a little. I reached down and lifted her to me, being very careful not to squeeze too hard.

I shifted her so she was against my chest and she put her head on my shoulder, just like she used to. I smelled her hair. The scent of shampoo was on it and it was silky soft against my cheek.

And then we swayed, swayed, swayed. Time went completely away as we danced by the light of the moon.

Acknowledgments

As usual, I owe thanks to several key people who helped in the writing of this book.

Ronald Gue, attorney-at-law, was wonderfully generous with his time. He shared his expertise in California family law with me and gave me helpful comments on the novel as a whole.

Dave Lambert, my editor, once again helped me shape a better book. Karen Ball was insightful and encouraging in so many ways. What a blessing it is to have them on my side.

Many thanks to Heather Wilke, Eileen Clubb, Lisa Samson, Colleen Coble; also to Alan Perkins of Journey Christian Church, Westlake, Ohio, for allowing me to reproduce a portion of his sermon, "A Commitment to Prayer," in these pages.

And to my wife, Cindy, my first editor and encourager throughout the writing process—I can't thank God enough that you're my partner in all things.

PRESUMED GUILTY

For E. and The Chaz Man

PROLOGUE

My life is marked by contrasts—then and now, light and darkness. Heaven and hell.

Marked too by memory.

I remember the exact moment it started.

In fact, in a perverse recollection of detail, I even know what I was wearing—Dockers slacks and a blue golf shirt with the Wailea Emerald Course logo on it. My shoes were the brown slip-ons my wife had bought for me online a couple of months earlier. No socks.

I was in my office, looking out the window at the stunning view of the valley. The church occupied twenty of the most valuable acres in Southern California, prime property we bought when we outgrew our smaller space in Northridge ten years before.

And I can remember my thought patterns that day, leading up to the moment she walked in. I was thinking of Moses, another mountaintop man, and how his human frailty kept him from the Promised Land. He struck the rock, and water flowed, but he had disobeyed God.

As I was about to do.

And that is why I am here.

A jail cell is smaller than it looks in some old James Cagney movie. When you're in one it doesn't seem possible for life to continue, for the paper-thin fragility that is human existence to sustain itself.

But since my life has ceased to exist, I suppose nothing is lost.

Do I suppose I can regain my life by writing down these confessions? Or am I writing just so I can eventually place another volume on my shelf?

Yes, even within these walls, my ambition bares its teeth and grinds through the lining of my guilt. Maybe that's why I'm here. Maybe that's why God put me here after all.

Maybe that's why I did the unthinkable.

Unthinkable, at least, if you were to look at me ten years ago. Even five. Then you would have seen a star. Not a comet, flaming out, a fading tail of cosmic dust in its wake.

No, a real star set in the evangelical heavenlies.

Then I fell, let it all slip away, that day in my office overlooking the valley.

How did it happen? All I know is that, somehow, it began.

It began with a plea.

PART I

Other men's sins are before our eyes;
our own are behind our back.

Seneca

ONE

1.

"Help me. Please."

A note of hopelessness vibrated under the girl's voice, a soft trilling like a night bird's cry. Ron Hamilton felt it in his chest—an electric snap, a static in the heart.

"I'll do anything I can," he told the girl. She must have been around twenty, though he had long since given up guessing ages. When he turned fifty a year ago, he was certain selected segments of his brain went into meltdown, like a kid's snow cone on a hot summer day.

"I've done a terrible thing, I don't know what to do." The girl looked at the floor, and when she did, Ron couldn't help noticing her shape under the snug dress. It was a red summery thing, with thin straps over the shoulders. Before he could stop it, his gaze lingered, then he forced himself to look away. His focus landed on his seminary diploma, hanging on his office wall. Doctor of Divinity. But he couldn't keep looking at it and give her the attention she deserved.

How was he going to avert his eyes if this interview continued?

Best thing he could do was put her at ease, then ease her out of the office. The interview would be over and he'd pass her off to someone else, maybe the professional counseling team the church had an arrangement with.

"I'm sorry. Let's back up." He looked at the Post-It note on his desk, the one where he'd scribbled her name: *Melinda Perry*.

"How long have you been coming to church here, Melinda?"

"Little less than a year."

Ron didn't recognize her face. But then, with the church at roughly eight thousand members, it would have been easy for her to blend in. So many others did.

"What attracted you here?" he asked, putting his marketing hat on. He couldn't help himself sometimes. Seventeen years of good marketing sense had built up Hillside Community Church.

She looked at him. "You."

Another electrical snap went off inside him. And this time it tripped an alarm. *Danger here. Remember last year . . .*

Yet he found himself wanting to know exactly what Melinda Perry meant. What could that hurt?

"I listened to you on the radio," she said.

Made sense. His sermons were recorded and played on L.A.'s second largest Christian radio station. Three times throughout the week.

"Well, I'm glad somebody's listening." He laughed.

She didn't laugh. "You don't know what it meant. You saved my life."

Now he was hooked. "Really?"

"Oh, yes. You preach from the Bible, right?"

"Always." Well, he attached Bible verses to his favorite topics.

"You were talking about something to do with heaven. Do you remember that?"

He fought the temptation to smile. "I talk about heaven quite a bit—"

"In this one, you said heaven was going to be a place, a *real* place, where we'll live."

"Yes, what the Bible calls the new earth."

"And streets made out of gold and all that?"

"All that, yes."

"And I was thinking of snuffing my candle, Pastor Ron, I really was. You don't know what I've been through." She paused. "Anyway, I was flipping around the radio stations and I heard you. I heard your voice. I thought what a nice voice. You really have cool tones, Pastor."

"Thanks." Heat seeped into his cheeks.

"And what you said about heaven made me cry, it really hit me, and that's why I started coming to Hillside. I sit in the back mostly. I don't want people to get too close to me."

"But why not?"

"That's part of the reason I'm here. To tell you why."

Did she have a boyfriend? She looked like she could have many boyfriends.

"But I'm afraid," she said.

"Of what?"

"Talking about it."

He wanted to know. "Would it help to talk to a professional counselor? I can arrange for you to have a free session with a—"

"No. I want to talk to you. You're the only one who can help me."

"There are others who are trained—"

"No." She almost sounded angry. "You have to tell me first."

"Tell you what?"

"If God can ever forgive me."

Without so much as a beat, he ran off a familiar message. "That's what God does best. He forgives us. Anything."

"Anything? Even something so bad ..." She looked down.

There was no way he was going to let her go now. He almost got up to put a comforting hand on her shoulder, but the alarm sounded again, and he stayed in his chair.

"Go ahead and tell me. Take your time."

He watched her chest rise with breath.

"All right," she said. "It started this way."

2.

Dallas Hamilton put her hand over her left eye and said, "Whoop-de-do!"

The boy looked at her, confused, then shook his head. "That's not a pirate."

"You think all pirates have to say *argh*?"

The boy, a six-year-old named Jamaal, nodded tentatively.

"How boring! You can be any kind of pirate you want. That's the thing about the imagination. And this ship can be as big as you want it to be."

Dallas picked up the square of Styrofoam from the craft table, took a straw, and stuck it in the middle of the square. The boy and his mother watched Dallas as if she were a diamond cutter.

"See that?" Dallas said. "That's the mast."

"What's a mast?" Jamaal said.

"The place where the sail goes. We're going to put a sail on the straw, see?" Dallas held up a square of construction paper. "And that's how you get a sailing ship. And here's the best part." Dallas took a couple of thumbtacks and a rubber band from the clear plastic box on the craft table. She'd carved out a square section from the stern of the foam boat and now secured the rubber band across that span with the tacks.

"This is where we're going to put the paddle. You wind it up in the rubber band, and it'll make the boat go in the water. No batteries required."

"That's nice, huh, Jamaal?" the boy's mother said. Her name was Tiana Williams. She was twenty-three, but to Dallas she looked ten years older. The ugly puffiness around Tiana's right eye was part of the reason. It marred what was otherwise a pretty face of smooth, dusky skin.

"That's your ship," Dallas said, "and you don't have to be like any other pirate. You can say *whoop-de-do* or any other word you want."

Jamaal smiled. It was what Dallas had been looking for all along. Smiles rarely occurred inside the women's shelter on Devonshire. Six years ago, the church board at Hillside Community gave Dallas the go-ahead to start Haven House, a place where abused women could find safety. The board appointed her to oversee the daily operations and fund-raising. She also taught classes in child rearing and women's self-defense.

On a couple of occasions, she'd given a room in her own home to one of the women, for a few days anyway, when Haven House got overcrowded. Ron, good husband and Christian that he was, supported her all the way.

Her favorite place, though, was right here in the craft room, where the kids could imagine and create. So many of the women had children with them.

"Would you like to color some?" Dallas asked Jamaal. The boy looked at his mother. Tiana nodded.

Dallas got a fresh coloring book and a box of crayons from the cabinet and set Jamaal up at one end of the craft table. There was a little girl there, hunched over her own book. Jamaal grabbed a red crayon, opened his coloring book, and took to his work with an optimism that made Dallas want to weep.

"You got kids?" Tiana asked as they watched Jamaal.

"Two," Dallas said.

"How old?"

"My daughter, Cara, is twenty-seven. Jared, my son, is twenty-four."

"They turn out all right, don't they?" The anguish in Tiana's voice was familiar. Dallas had heard the same anxiety in countless voices over the years. "I want Jamaal to be all right. I don't care about anything else."

Dallas had no doubt about Tiana's sincerity. It was her choices that mattered most, and she would have to make one right here and now. "Tiana, you can't go back to where you were."

Tiana looked at Dallas with sunken eyes, cavernous with dread. "I've got nowhere else to go."

"We have a network of places, rooms. We can find something."

"Got no way to pay for it."

"We can help get you on your feet. Maybe look for a job with you."

"What do you know about it?"

Dallas put her hand on Tiana's arm. "Don't go back, Tiana. Let me help find you a place."

Tiana pulled her arm away. "Jamaal needs a father."

"He's an abuser, he—"

"I can talk to him. I know how."

"No, you can't, not someone like that."

"You don't know him."

"I know about abusers."

Tiana slapped the table with her open palm. "I can talk to him! He loves me and Jamaal, and you don't know what you're talking about." Tiana paused. "You don't know anything about me."

"Maybe I know more than you think. I was down pretty low once, had someone who took it out on me, but God was there to pull me up."

Tiana shook her head. "I used to go to church. With my mama, before she died."

"Our church isn't far from here. My husband's the pastor. We'd love to have you and Jamaal come."

"Your husband preaches?"

"He's wonderful. Has a radio program. You may have heard him sometime."

"Don't listen to the radio much."

Jamaal's voice broke in. "Look, Mama!" He was holding up the coloring book, which was now a madcap swirl of multicolored lines.

"That's good, baby," Tiana said, as if willing herself to believe it. "That's real good."

"It's a pirate ship," he said.

"A big one, huh?" said Dallas.

Jamaal nodded and said, "Whoop-de-do."

Dallas's heart melted into a mixture of hope and uncertainty. *Oh, Lord, let these two make it. Please, let them make it.*

3.

"I was just this dumb kid from North Dakota," Melinda said. "Ran away and I was gonna make it in Hollywood. You know the story."

Yes, Ron thought, like countless other teenagers who flooded into Hollywood. A lot of them did come with hopes for stardom, and every now and then one of them had what it takes. Melinda, on looks alone, could have been one of those exceptions. Her face held the mix of beauty and girlishness that Marilyn Monroe had early in her career.

Ron remembered watching *The Asphalt Jungle* with Dallas a couple of years ago, and how striking Monroe was in her brief appearance on screen. Almost as striking as Melinda was in person.

"I thought I could get a waitressing job or something to tide me over, but it's rougher than it looks out there. I ended up on the street. I didn't know what I was going to do. I thought I might have to start, you know, selling the goods."

Ron noticed his right hand trembling. He put it in his left hand and put both hands in his lap.

"I saw this ad in one of those free papers they have down in Hollywood. Open auditions. Made all these promises, like they'd get a tape to agents and producers. I figured I didn't have anything to lose, so down I go to this dumpy-looking place, and they have a camera set up, and when they told me to take off my clothes I figured that's what it takes these days. I'm going to have to show myself onscreen sometime. They kept saying all these nice things and then all of a sudden they call in this guy and ..."

Her voice trailed off in a muffled sob and it was everything Ron could do not to get up and go to her. He wanted to hold her. He wanted to hear the rest of her story. He was suddenly very afraid, but not enough to open his office door.

"They told me I could make five hundred dollars that day, right there, and all I had to do was ... Five hundred dollars. Only I didn't know it wasn't five hundred all at once, until after. They said they'd give me the rest over the next couple of weeks, but that I could make more, and if it worked out and I was good enough, a lot more."

Melinda looked at Ron, her eyes savagely probing. "I want to get out of this life. I need to get out. But I'm in so deep. I want God to save me, but I don't know how to ask."

Ron felt suddenly lacking, as if all his years of study and preaching and writing amounted to exactly nothing at this particular moment in time. But there was something more disturbing, he realized, muddying the counseling waters. No, polluting them. In his mind he kept seeing her, Melinda, in scenes his imagination was firing at him with involuntary vividness.

Call this off right now. Set her up with a counselor. Open the door. Get her out.

Suddenly she was up, turning her back on him and walking toward a bookcase. Her red dress hugged her form, and the form swayed—

Melinda put her fingers on the spine of a book, delicately. And then her head slumped forward and her shoulders began to shake.

Ron got up.

Open the door.

He went to her, her cries rising up, anguished. He touched her shoulder.

4.

The phone rang the moment Dallas stepped through the door. She took it in the kitchen.

"Hey, kiddo!" Karen, Ron's literary agent, chirped in a good-news sort of way. "You sitting down?"

"No."

"You got pillows under you?"

"What is it, Karen?"

"That book deal we've been working on? It came through. And it's a monster. A million for three books."

Dallas nearly dropped the phone. "Is this for real?"

"Honey, would I kid about this?"

Joy filled Dallas to the brim. What a confirmation from God this was. Dallas had always believed in her husband and his ministry. She had prayed long and hard for it to prosper, and now God was opening doors, windows, and floodgates.

His last book was a surprise bestseller. It tackled the dangers of pornography, a subject suggested to him by Dallas. She'd seen her share of girls trying to escape what was euphemistically called "adult entertainment." It was a hell on earth is what it was.

She also knew firsthand what a porn addict could do to a woman. It had happened to her once, long ago.

But that was in the past, God had covered it, and now Ron's new series on prayer had sold for a million dollars. More money than they'd made in the past ten years, counting all the speaking Ron was doing now, his church salary, and the book sales to that point.

"Dallas? You there?"

"Karen, I don't know what to say."

"Say praise the Lord."

"Praise the Lord."

"Is Ron at the church? I don't like to call him at work, but this—"

"Oh, Karen, let me tell him." Dallas and Ron needed something to celebrate, an excuse to put all the strains aside and laugh and be joyful. "I'll tell him when he gets home. I'll put some sparkling cider on ice, make it an event."

"Do it. I'll be getting the contract in a week or so and then we'll go over it. Don't go spending it all right away now."

"Well, there is that small island I've had my eye on."

Karen laughed.

"I don't know how to begin to thank you," Dallas said.

"Just give me one of your imitations saying it."

"Who do you want?"

"How about Katharine Hepburn?"

Dallas always thought it was God's sense of humor that gave her the ability to do impersonations. She couldn't sing, draw, or play the piano, but by golly she could do Bette Davis and a whole bunch of others.

"Here it comes," Dallas said, switching to Kate Hepburn. "I am so, so thankful. Rally I am."

Karen cracked up. "Perfect, dahling! I'll call Ron tomorrow. Enjoy."

Enjoy. Yes. *Oh, God, thank you for sending this at just the right time.*

Just the right time to beat back the fear hissing at her from an inner cave, the fear of growing older and becoming less attractive to her husband, the fear that sometimes clutched her when she'd nuzzle up to him at home and ask, "Love me?"

He always said yes. Or stroked her cheek. Or shook his head at her and said, "How can you ask me that?"

Never did he say, "I love you so much, I can't even begin to tell you."

He would never cheat on her, of course. She knew that. She trusted him completely. But she feared worse—a seepage of neglect, building up over time until it calcified into something impenetrable.

Dallas put a bottle of Martinelli's sparkling cider in the fridge. And waited. Yes, they would celebrate. It had been so long since she and Ron had actually spent time together, intimate time. Maybe the good news would be just the thing.

It was later than normal when Ron came through the front door. Darkness was already falling over their home two miles from the church.

Dallas jumped up to greet him, throwing her arms around his neck and kissing his mouth.

He sighed and said, "I'm really tired. What's to eat?"

Dallas tried to conceal the excitement in her voice. "Come in and sit down."

"Huh?" Ron was already heading toward the kitchen.

"Come into the living room and sit down."

Ron stopped, turned. "Is that an order, Captain?"

Her smile dropped. "Of course not. I just want to tell you something."

"Can it wait? I want to grab something and go for a swim."

"I think you'll want to hear it."

"Is Jared in trouble?"

"No, no. This is good news."

"Just tell me then."

"I want ... how about a glass of sparkling cider first?"

Ron frowned. "Dallas, will you just tell me what the news is?"

Not the reaction Dallas was looking for. She wanted a buildup, a production. But she'd come to the point in their marriage where she could, like a master chess player, anticipate several moves ahead. If she kept up the pretense of getting him into the living room, sipping cider, she could foresee disaster. She capitulated to reality.

"Karen called," she said. "Your deal has come through."

"When did she call?"

"Around two."

"Why didn't you call me? Why didn't she call me at the church?"

"Because I asked her not to call. I wanted to tell you myself. I wanted to make the announcement a little special. That's what the sparkling cider was for."

"Well, what is it? What are the details?"

"Ready? A million dollars!"

"For how many books?"

"Three!"

Ron looked at the ceiling. "Don't you think I would have wanted to know that?"

"I wanted to tell you—"

"You should have had her call me at the church." He looked at his watch. "It's too late to call her now. I wanted to talk to her."

"You can call her in the morning."

"Thank you. That's not the point."

Dallas bit down on the insides of her cheeks. "I thought the point was going to be that you and I could celebrate some great news together."

"When it comes to the books, let me handle the business part of it, okay?"

He turned around and started walking down the hall toward the bedroom. Dallas followed him. "Can't we just consider this a blessing from God and be happy about it? We can call Cara tonight."

Her husband did not stop. He pulled off his shirt and threw it on the floor near the bedroom door.

"Ron?"

"Let me just go for a swim."

"Did something happen today? At church?"

He spun around. There was an anger in his eyes, a cold fury that Dallas had never seen before. It froze her.

"Yeah, something happened at church. I didn't get a phone call I should've gotten."

That hurt as much as a slap in the face. "Please don't do this, Ron."

"What am I doing?"

"Being angry."

"I'm going for a swim."

He started to get out of his pants. She tried to understand. He'd been under a lot of stress lately with things going on at church, some fallout from the antiporn book. They were just a few miles away from the porn capital of the world, Chatsworth. But the book deal should have made him happy.

She sat on the bed and shook her head slowly. "Why didn't we see this coming?"

"See what coming?"

"This . . . hardening."

He slipped on his swimming trunks. "Dallas, look. I know things have been stressful the last couple of months—"

"Stressful! We make coffee nervous."

"Very funny."

"Oh, Ron, can we just go away for a while and—"

"I'm going for a swim."

He turned quickly and strode out of the room.

5.

Jared Hamilton took a long hit on the glass pipe, held the smoke deep in his lungs, let the music play on. Combination was everything now. A high would calm muscles and mind, while urban bass from the radio pounded his brain and kept memories at bay.

The combo was the only ritual in his life, so he treated it with a gentle reverence. It came on Fridays around four, because on that day Scott would let his crews off a little early. Scott worked them fifty plus and paid them for it. But there was nothing like a jump start to the weekend to keep up morale.

Jared had been working for Scott almost six months now. Good, steady work. Painting houses. It was a routine, and he needed routine.

So when he finished on Fridays he said good-bye to Carlos and Guillermo, the two he usually worked with, and headed off in his beat-up but running red Chevy pickup for Bautista Market on Fourth Street. It was a small, family-run operation, and they knew him there. He liked being known by them and not too many others.

He would buy a six-pack of Dos Equis and a bag of Doritos and a small jar of salsa. It was, he would sometimes think, his communion. That thought was always accompanied by an ironic smile. If his dad were to see him now . . .

He would then drive to the park on Lake Avenue. In his pickup he had a camping chair, the kind that folds into a cylindrical shape for an easy fit under the arm. He always kept a tent and bedding ready too, for he was not sure from one day to the next if he'd have a roof over his head.

He would set the chair on a nice patch of grass, in the shade of a pine tree, with the sun behind and the fields in front of him. The fields where the children played.

The games were organized, mostly. Soccer practices, baseball, volleyball. The little ones were his favorite. They still did what the adults said and were eager to please. Like he'd once been.

He would open a beer and the bag of chips. He'd set the chips on his lap and put the bottle of Dos Equis in the cup holder of the camping chair. He'd open the salsa and place the lid on the arm of the chair.

He would sip and eat until the nameless guy came with the weed. He was a friend of Guillermo's and sold him a nickel bag. Jared would pay him and the guy would sit on the ground for a minute and want to talk.

Jared never talked.

The guy would leave and Jared would fold up his camping chair and throw it into the back of the pickup and take his beer and salsa and Doritos and grass and drive to a new place each night. Listen to music, loud.

The combo.

He was convinced it kept him from blacking out, the way he had a few times since coming back from Iraq. Yeah, keep the mind lit up and the music playing.

This night he was sitting on the hood of his truck in an empty parking lot without lights and feeling it, eyes closed, the music loud in his head and—

"... down, will ya?"

Jared looked up at the sudden appearance. It was dark and cold this night, and in all of Bakersfield there had to be this one guy who looked like he wanted to make trouble and looked like he could do it too. Big and beefy, with a faded Lakers jersey over his shirt.

"Look, man," Jared started to say loudly. Yeah, the music was blaring from the stereo—the only good piece of equipment in the whole truck—but that was the right of a guy sitting in an empty parking lot off the highway.

"It's pounding through the walls. Will ya turn it down?" The guy was big, no doubt about that, about Jared's age, twenty-four. Bigger, even though Jared was six-one and not exactly flabby of muscle. The Marines didn't go in for flab.

Jared put it together that the guy had come from the AMPM across the street.

Jared made no move off the hood.

"You gonna turn that down or what?" The Laker dude was wide, yes, but his belly showed the effects of a few too many breakfast burritos.

"I'm just sittin' here, man." Jared raised his hands in protest, all the while sizing up what it would take to put the man down. One jab to the jugular would probably do it, followed by gouging the eyes.

"If you could turn it down, that'd be cool," Laker guy said.

"You know what else'd be cool?" Jared said, just loud enough to be heard. "I could take your head off and spit down your neck."

At that moment Jared had a vision of it, of ripping the fool's head right off and leaving a wound he could look into and see the lousy messed-up soul inside Laker dude.

"I'll be calling the cops now," the guy said, turning.

"Wait, wait, okay." Jared slid off the hood, feeling light, reached in through the window, and turned the key. The music stopped. The silence of the night was like a blow to the head.

"All right," the guy said. He started back toward the AMPM. Jared, without thought, went to the back of the truck and grabbed a crowbar. It was heavy and nice in his hand. It would make a major dent in the guy's head, or his kneecap.

There was nobody in the store that Jared could see. Maybe he could lay the guy out and take a few things. Sure—

Then it was like a beautiful scene in a movie playing in his mind, the guy lying on the floor with blood all around, bright red, living color. Jared Hamilton, hero, Tarantinoesque—he'd have made a difference. To himself.

The scene was vivid.

Stuff like that kept showing in his mind ever since he got back.

The crowbar heavy in his hand.

What would his father say?

No. Who cared? It was Mom. What would she think?

In his head: *Do it anyway. That's the combo. That would really put the bad thoughts away.*

TWO

1.

Resistance is futile.

Dallas smiled as she drew herself a bath, threw in some salts from the Burke Williams spa, and settled in for a good, rejuvenating, sweet-smelling soak. One thing she had not tried lately was the venerable art of marital seduction. She knew that was one thing their relationship needed, and the one thing that was almost entirely up to her.

Last night Ron had come home and avoided her, gone swimming, disappeared into his study, and slept there.

Tonight would be different. She would make him remember.

She would make him remember how they were when they first married. She was the one with experience, a remnant of her past, and he had taken her gentle guidance and been transformed by it. But the change in her was no less intense. She was in love for the first time, really in love and not just drawn physically to a man. She loved Ron's character, his faith, his authority. She trusted him completely. Giving herself to him was as pure a thing as she had ever done in her life.

Part of the reason she felt that way, she well knew, was that she was fleeing an abusive relationship with a true lowlife. Chad McKenzie was a real piece of work—the devil's work. She barely escaped him, running from L.A. to San Francisco and living the street life.

She'd met Chad when she was seventeen. He was twenty and had a nice little business selling dope to the rich kids on the west side. It enabled him to ride around in a red Corvette and convince her that if she really wanted to get somewhere, it would be with him.

And Dallas was ready to go. Life at home was intolerable, she and her mother fighting all the time. Dallas knew it wasn't her mom's fault. Dallas had bad stuff going on inside. Without a father—he left when Dallas was three—there was just no way Mom could keep Dallas in check.

Those first couple of months with Chad McKenzie were exciting. The danger was a turn-on, as good as getting high.

Then the high turned into a nightmare. Getting kicks sexually was, for Chad, a matter of pain. Hers. He was a porn addict, the S and M variety.

She had scars on her soul, carved with the harsh blade of Chad McKenzie's sadism. He managed to make her feel like all the dirt and scum and trash of the world was, if not all, at least in large part due to her pointless existence.

And she took it. She took it for weeks, because she thought she'd never be worth anything to anybody again.

She was sure that she would be dead by now had she not run away to San Francisco.

Later, when she entered that revival meeting where the young Ron Hamilton was preaching, she knew without doubt that God had brought them together. Here was the thing she wanted most in the world—something that would *last*.

Their daughter, Cara, was conceived on their honeymoon, on a cruise down the Pacific coast to Mexico, a gift from his mother.

Three years after Cara's birth, Jared came along. And the rearing of children combined with the building of a ministry sent their lives on a different course. Their love was as strong as ever, but their energy was tapped by a thousand new demands.

Ten-year-old Cara developed a neuromuscular problem that would require three solid years of mentally draining attention. At the same time, Jared was displaying signs of ADD and a certain steely rebelliousness that Dallas was sure came from her. On more than one occasion she thought of Jared's behavior as God's revenge for the pain she'd caused her mother.

Cara healed and even became a top high school tennis player. Jared also displayed some athletic ability, and that calmed his inner waters for a time. When Dallas and Ron were finally able to peer above the troubled waters, they saw they were no longer the kids who'd met at a Jesus rally in North Beach, San Francisco.

She was a mother who had poured all her creativity into her children. From would-be hippie poetess to suburban mom—and a minister's wife, with all that went with it. Not all of it to her liking.

Ron was rising in the ranks of pastors and speakers. He was on the road more, most often without Dallas and the kids. He developed a more formal bearing, perhaps as a defense to all the people who were starting to want a piece of him.

But their love and friendship was never a question in Dallas's mind. Even though physical intimacy occurred less frequently, they managed to find time to get away together. Yet even those occasions had somehow dried up over the last few years. Dallas pledged to get them back.

Most of the strain was because of Jared, of course. Their son hung between them like a veil of division, sheer and unmentioned but present in every moment. Jared, the second born, the son. Ron had been so proud when he was born. His face lit up the delivery room. A son!

Jared was this perfect thing, an innocent baby glowing with unlimited potential. Those first few years, Ron could not stop talking about what a blessing their family was. A cute and loving daughter, a smart and curious—though somewhat serious—son. "One of each!" he would often say in those days.

But then came the growing pains and the realization that Jared had in him some traits that were not in line with what Ron had envisioned. And then came the war and Jared enlisting without a word, not a word to either of them.

Then, worst of all, his returning from Iraq a different person. Dallas prayed for him daily, intensely.

But tonight, it would be Ron she would think of, Ron she would bring back to the fold.

As she soaked in the water, Dallas thanked God she was still healthy. She worked at it. She kept in shape, went to the gym. Though her body was changing, developing knocks and pings and obeying the inexorable laws of gravity, she still weighed in at only five pounds above her wedding weight. That was something to be proud of. She enjoyed going to functions with Ron, hanging on his arm, looking good for him.

When she got out of the tub she put on a little body lotion and just a touch of Ron's favorite perfume. What to wear? She had a lacy white blouse that accentuated the positive, and some tight jeans that nearly eliminated the negative. Seemingly casual, but designed for the male eye. Deadly.

Resistance is futile.

She pulled back the covers of the bed, then went to order dinner from Stonefire Grill, Ron's favorite eatery. Dallas requested whole barbecued tri-tips, slaw, and mashed potatoes.

She would be the dessert.

At five thirty, the meal came. Dallas set the table, popped a Larry Carlton CD into the Bose.

At five forty-five the call came.

2.

"Dallas, honey, something's come up. I won't be home till late probably."

Strange, but Dallas had almost sensed he would say that when she picked up the bedroom phone. It was all too perfectly dreadful. She had made all these plans, and they simply had to be dashed, didn't they? Wasn't that the trajectory of their lives? Wasn't this going to be some bad soap-opera moment?

"Is there some trouble?" she said.

"I have to talk to someone is all."

"Why so late?"

"I have to take a drive. Not too far. But I just can't predict ..."

She waited for him to explain. He didn't.

"So I'll call you later," he said.

"What about dinner?"

"I'll grab something."

"I got Stonefire."

Pause. "Put mine in the fridge, huh?"

And then he was gone.

Dallas sat on the edge of the bed. Was that a hint of avoidance in his voice? Or was there something more, something like her husband not telling her the whole truth?

Feeling ridiculous in her sexy outfit, she kicked off her shoes and pulled off her jeans. She could breathe again. She unbuttoned her blouse and threw it against the wall. Putting on her robe, she went downstairs, grabbed the Stonefire bag, and stuck the whole thing in the refrigerator, slamming the door. The clock on top of the refrigerator fell to the floor, and a huge chunk of the face broke off.

"Perfect," she said.

3.

The motel had a sickly sameness to it and looked like a thousand others along a thousand freeways and roads. The parking lot was about half full. A couple of Hispanic men in undershirts leaned over the rail of the second story taking in the view, which consisted of the parking lot, an Applebees restaurant, and an auto-parts store.

I drove to the end of the parking lot, as Melinda had instructed me. I pulled into one of the last spaces near a cinder-block wall. She would be in room 105. It was around on the other side of the motel, facing north. At least from there you could see some mountains.

I gave three quick knocks, as she requested. I waited a moment, heard nothing inside. Then I saw the peephole darken.

She opened the door. "Come in, quickly."

She closed the door and put her arms around me, burying her head in my chest. I very properly patted the middle of her back with one hand and said, "It's okay. I'm here, you're going to be fine."

She didn't let go of me. I could feel her chest heaving. I could smell her hair. It was vaguely scented, hinting of spice.

I guided her to the bed and sat her on it. The only other furniture in the room was a stark functional chair and a desk with a lamp. I stayed standing, and that's when I noticed she was wearing something very sheer and revealing. It did not surprise me, because that's the world she lived in. But I backed up three steps and tried not to look at her below the neck.

"Now tell me who is after you," I said.

"The people. The people I work for." She was lacing and unlacing her fingers as she spoke, looking down at them. "They beat up one of the other girls. I saw it. They were laughing about it. I couldn't stand it. I screamed and ran out. One of them ran after me, telling me to come back or I was going to be sorry, and I better not think of going to the police or I was going to be dead."

She looked at me and I fell into her eyes. She said, "I was so scared I couldn't stop running. I thought they were going to come after me in a car. I had my coat on and a few dollars and I hopped a bus and then the Metro Link, which is how I got here. I used a credit card for the room. But now I'm afraid they'll trace the transaction somehow and find me. What do I do?"

"You have got to go to the police."

She started to say something, but I cut her off. "It's the way things work. We can't do this alone. You can't deal with people like this by yourself."

"No police!"

I thought of Jared then. The way Melinda said No was a lot like the way he used to say it when we were fighting the battles at home.

I paced in front of the curtained window, thinking. "What about getting out of town?"

She looked up.

"I can give you some money," I said. "You could start all over again somewhere."

The idea seemed to strike a chord with her. "Where?"

"Almost anywhere. I know some great churches and ministers around the country. I could tell one of them about you, and he would help get you set up in a new community."

"You really think so?"

She suddenly looked so young. All that hope in her face, like a child who's just been told her lost puppy was found.

"It's perfect," I said. "It'll be a chance for a fresh start."

Tears were starting to form in her eyes. If she had not stood up and come to me, I do believe with all my heart that none of this would have happened. That was the moment, the key, the breaking point. At least that's what I tell myself on nights I can't sleep and the memories play, unbidden, in my mind.

When she put her arms around me this time it was softer. I made no move away from her.

When she put her head on my chest it was gentler, almost a caress.

I put both my hands on her back and kept them there. I don't know how long we were like that, but when she turned her head up toward mine everything exploded, and I knew things would never be right again.

THREE

Dallas awoke, calling her husband's name, reaching for his body in the dark.

She realized in the blackness that her nightmare was over, chased away by her desperate waking. A shimmer of what she deemed hope flashed across her mind, like a sliver of distant lightning in a storm-swollen sky.

She reached for Ron again, felt only the cold, empty spot on the bed.

No, he would not be there. He had not shared their bed for a week. He slept in the study, wouldn't tell her why. Just holed up, mumbling excuses.

Even more troubling, Ron had asked Bob Benson to preach for him yesterday, Palm Sunday. Ron always preached both Palm Sunday and Easter. Something was terribly wrong, but Ron wouldn't say what.

She looked at the clock by the bed. Four thirty-seven. Too early to be awake.

Sleep was out of the question.

Her head was full and heavy, a bag of nails. The throbbing behind her eyes that started last night began again.

Then she saw red lights flashing. Outside the window.

It wasn't just in her dreams.

Police car, she thought. Why? Next door, the teenager, Craig. He was in with some pretty questionable people, and who knew why the cops were here? Drugs? Stolen property?

A loud knock on the door. A pounding that was not friendly.

The red lights . . .

Another knock. Full, loud, relentless.

One of the kids. Something happened to one of the kids. Accident? Death?

She got up, heart accelerating. In the dark she reached for her robe. She rushed out the bedroom door, bits of awareness popping up like the lights of a city as night falls. Halfway down the stairs she saw the front door open and a police officer standing there.

"What's going on?" she fairly screamed.

She reached the bottom of the stairs and saw, on the porch, her husband. In handcuffs, with another police officer holding his arm.

"What is this?" Dallas heard her own voice, felt herself plunge forward.

The first cop put his hand up. "Ma'am, stay where you are, please."

"Ron!"

Ron turned to her. "Call Jeff Waite," he said.

Dallas looked at the cop inside the house. "Please tell me what is going on."

"Call a lawyer, ma'am," he said.

2.

Jefferson Waite returned her call a little before nine in the morning. She'd left two messages on his cell phone, knowing he would be asleep like the rest of the normal world. Knowing, too, he would call just as soon as he could.

"What is it, Dallas?"

"It's Ron. They arrested him."

"Arrested? What for?"

"They didn't say. They didn't tell me. Aren't they supposed to tell me?"

"When was this?"

"A few hours ago."

"Do you know where they took him?"

"No."

Dallas clutched the phone. Jeff said, "All right, don't worry, I can find him. Is there anything else you can tell me?"

"Nothing. I can't believe this, Jeff."

"I'll find out what's going on." His voice was warm and calming. "If he calls you, tell him not to talk to anyone."

"Will he?"

"Did you hear what I said?"

"Yes."

"Tell him he's not to say anything, and I mean anything, to anybody. I'll see him as soon as I can."

"But—"

He clicked off. Dallas sat back in a chair in the gray of the morning, paralyzed.

3.

"You crazy, man," Guillermo was saying. "You gonna get lightning on your head, you keep talkin' that trash."

The three of them—Jared, Guillermo, and Carlos—were working a church, a little white Catholic number northeast of Bakersfield. A new coat of white on the inside, around the stained-glass windows, patching cracks.

Guillermo and Carlos had the radio blaring that salsa crud, and at every break Jared had to listen to somebody spouting Spanish.

At least it muted the voices in his own head.

So yes, he was crazy. Jared agreed with Guillermo on that much. But not crazy for talking trash.

"That's what I said." Jared pointed with his brush at the crucifix. Jesus hanging on a cross and set on the little altar. "He's no help to anybody. He's hanging there. It's just a stupid statue."

"You're the stupid one, man." Guillermo didn't say it viciously, but Jared could sense a bubbling beneath his surface.

Didn't matter. Jared felt a compulsion to speak. The thoughts were like bile wanting to burst out of him of their own accord, and he would let them.

"What's with people looking at statues, huh? Thinking there's anything there?"

Carlos, who was forty or so and smaller than the other two, dipped his brush in a paint can and said, "Shut up and work."

"You want some?" Jared put his hands out, challenging.

"Crazy," Guillermo said. "In a church, talkin' trash about Jesus."

Jared walked a few steps on the drop cloth toward his coworkers. "Listen to what I'm saying, genius. People are better off not knowing anything, instead of coming into a church and worshiping Jesus statues."

A voice on the radio shouted something in Spanish.

"Come on," Guillermo urged. "You bring down bad stuff on everybody, you keep talking that way."

Jared let the words fly. "You afraid of God? That what you're afraid of? Because of a stupid statue?"

"Hey—" Carlos pointed at Jared.

Now it wasn't the radio noise rattling around in Jared's head but something else, voicelike, pounding. He didn't know what this was, but it was urgent and angry. Spitting angry, and something had to be done to show these stupid—

"Get back to work!" Carlos yelled, but Jared was already going down the aisle, the noise beating inside his head, and he had his brush up.

He heard Guillermo say, "What's he doin'?" but it barely registered in the chaos of his brain.

Now Jared focused in on Jesus, on his face, looking down. Jesus nailed, a statue. Was this what they were afraid of?

With one swipe of his brush, Jared covered Jesus's face in white paint.

"No!" Guillermo shouted.

And Jared thought, *I know how to bleed too, Jesus.*

When he turned around, he saw his two coworkers staring, but not at him. At the door.

Jared looked over and saw a priest standing there, shock all over his face. And next to him Scott, the boss man, about to go ballistic.

4.

"Cara, it's me."

"Hi, Mom. Guess what? I'm getting a promotion at the bank. Today I—"

"Cara, listen to me."

"What's wrong?"

Dallas tried to make her hand relax its grip on the phone but couldn't. "Your dad's in trouble."

"Trouble? What do you—"

"He was arrested."

Cara's gasp jabbed through the phone. "Why?"

"I don't know, but the police came to the house this morning. They took him away in handcuffs. They wouldn't even tell me."

"Mom, Mom, are you all right?"

Dallas swallowed hard. "Will you start praying—"

"Mom, I'm coming over."

"You don't have to—"

"I'll be right there."

Dallas felt trapped in a fog, seeing little, hearing nothing, until Cara came and threw her arms around her and held her. Dallas returned the embrace around Cara's taut body. Her daughter, at twenty-seven, still looked like the tennis player she'd been in high school. But her face, under the short blond hair, was worried.

"Mom, you have got to tell me what's going on. I can't believe Dad would be arrested for anything."

Dallas shook her head. "All I know is what I told you. They arrested your father, just took him away like a common criminal. Why would they do that?"

"Have we got a lawyer?"

"Yes. Jeff Waite. He's going to see your father this morning."

"Is he good? Because we have got to have the best."

"Oh, yes, he's good. He's done pro bono work for the church."

Out of habit, Dallas patted her daughter's shoulder. It was the calming move. Cara had always been a bit of a control freak, an imposer of order. Dallas had spent more hours than she could count settling her daughter's nerves. Now Cara was here to return the favor.

Cara said, "Have you talked to Jared?"

Dallas shook her head. "I don't know where he is."

"Does he have a cell phone?"

"The old number doesn't work. He must have let it go."

"Probably didn't pay his bill."

"Do you know any of his old friends? People who might be in touch with him? I'm afraid of how this is going to hit him."

"I can try to think of someone."

"Please do."

Cara took her mother by the arm and sat her down in her favorite chair. Dallas felt lumps in it. It was getting worn.

"How about some lunch?" Cara said.

"I can't eat."

"Yes, you can," Cara insisted, echoing the words Dallas must have said a thousand times to her daughter during her bouts with sickness or distress.

It was a disquieting juxtaposition. Cara was the mothering one now, and Dallas the little girl. But she did not want to be little, or helpless, or paralyzed. She wanted to help Ron. Now.

And couldn't.

5.

Jefferson Waite arrived just before noon. He hardly had a foot in the door when Dallas asked him what was going on.

"Let's go into the living room," Waite said.

Dallas stood still. "Tell me now. Please."

Cara, who had been making sandwiches in the kitchen, came to her mother's side.

Jeff closed the door. He wore a powder blue dress shirt, sleeves rolled halfway up his forearms, and a burgundy tie perfectly knotted. He was in his midforties with a full head of brown hair flecked by wisps of gray. He exuded confidence, which was exactly what

Dallas needed at that moment. "I don't want you to worry the first time you hear it. These things—"

"What happened?"

"They say it's murder."

Dallas felt something flow out of her head, a sucking away like the sand under a receding wave. Cara grabbed her left arm, and that's when Dallas knew she had almost fallen.

Jeff helped Cara get Dallas to the sofa. Cara sat next to her and put an arm around her shoulder.

"It's a huge mistake," Jeff said. "I saw Ron, I talked with him, he's scared but he's staying strong. It's all a major misunderstanding."

"Who was it?" Dallas said.

"The victim is a young woman named Melinda Perry. That's all I could find out."

Young woman? "Can I see him?" Dallas said. "Where is he?"

"They've got him at the men's jail, downtown."

She looked at the lawyer. "What's going to happen, Jeff?"

He sat on the coffee table so he could take her hand. He was muscular and trim, with intelligent blue eyes. "Tomorrow he goes before a judge. I'll be there with him and get the formal charge and the arrest report. Then I'll go talk to the DA and see what they've got."

Panic burst through her. "They've got to have something. They wouldn't arrest him if they didn't have anything. What could it be?"

She heard screeching outside. The sound of tires.

Jeff went to the door and pulled back the curtain.

"Man, that was fast," he said.

"What?"

"TV people."

Pinpricks stuck her skin. Publicity. She hadn't even considered that. In her singular focus she thought only of Ron, and of this problem as one they could solve together, quietly. That's the way they handled things between them, wasn't it?

But now she realized this accusation would not be kept quiet, couldn't be swept under their private rug. Ron was a big-time pastor with a national platform. He'd been on radio and TV, once on *The O'Reilly Factor* talking about the scourge of Internet porn.

He was a media darling, with his good looks and eloquence. Now he was a target for the press—a family-values pastor accused of murder.

"Stay calm," Jeff said. "I will do the talking for you. All right? Not you, not your daughter, not Ron. Is there anyone else in the family they could get to?"

Dallas shook her head. "Only our son, Jared, but he's out of the county."

"Don't sell these people short," Jeff said. "Now stay here."

He went outside, closing the door behind him. A few moments later Dallas heard his voice, firm and resolute.

"Mrs. Hamilton will not be commenting on this matter. I will be speaking for the family ... No, we have no comment at this time ... There has not even been a formal charge yet ... No, there will be no further comment ... And by the way, any entrance on this property will be treated as a trespass. So I advise you to clear out and direct all inquiries to my office."

The muffled shouts of several voices shooting questions came next. Cara squeezed Dallas's hand.

Dallas closed her eyes. She remembered someone telling her once that the most effective prayer on earth was *Help me help me help me.*

That is what Dallas prayed now. She prayed for a sign from God, something to tell her that it wasn't true, that this whole nightmare was going to go away.

At twelve forty-five a police tow truck showed up, much to the delight of the media circus, and towed Ron's car away.

6.

How do you look at your wife from the inside of a cage?

Do you fake it? Do you put on a happy face, like that old song says?

Do you do it so your wife, who loves you, who has known only your stability and strength, won't freak?

Do you smile and give a little wave through the Plexiglas barrier and make some joke through the handset about your orange jumpsuit? "Like my new style?"

Do you do everything within your power to hide the clawing, voracious fear that is working your insides?

Or do you let go of your face? Let it all hang out?

Most important of all, do you let the truth, the whole truth, and nothing but the truth flash like neon in your eyes? Do you drop all pretense and all deceit and let her read your expressions like the front page of a tabloid?

The woman who loved me with a solid, dependable love came to see me. And I could hardly look at her.

7.

The men's jail was downtown, on Bauchet Street, just east of Chinatown and Union Station. It housed the county's ever-increasing population of criminal defendants, those waiting for trial as well as cons serving less than a year.

It had been the temporary residence of several high-profile defendants the last few years.

Like Ron Hamilton.

Dallas was shaking when she got to the visitation room. It was smaller than she'd expected, with two rows of stools in front of glass partitions. A deputy sheriff told her where to sit.

The stool was hard and cold.

What was it going to be like to see Ron for the first time? In here?

Worse, what was it going to be like for him to see *her*? She knew she looked terrible. The shock was still fresh, had been pressing down on her for the last twenty-four hours. No sleep. She felt like bags of cement were under her eyes. Eyes that fell on her husband being led in on his side of the Plexiglas. Dressed in an orange jumpsuit. Not the blue of the regular jail inmate. Orange marked him as high security.

He sat opposite her, his features gnarled in confusion. She grabbed the handset, waiting for him to pick up.

"Ron," she said, then found she couldn't coax another word out of her mouth.

His voice came through the wire thin and distant. "Dallas, I'm so sorry you have to see me like this."

"Are you all right?"

His eyes were darting around, not staying on her directly. "It's jail. Not a place I ever thought I'd be."

She put her hand on the Plexiglas. She wanted to push her hand through and stroke her husband's cheek. She wanted to break through and hold him and drag him out of there and keep the world away.

"What on earth happened?" she said.

Ron pursed his lips and shook his head. "It's not true, what they're saying."

What *they* were saying was that her husband had been "involved" with an actress in what *they* referred to as "adult films." She first heard the report on the radio news as she was driving to the jail. She almost ran into another car.

But she knew it couldn't be true, couldn't be. She fought the information with all her will.

"How then?" Dallas said, needing to know.

"Listen to me, Dallas. I was stupid. I made a stupid mistake."

She waited.

He looked up toward the ceiling. "I was counseling this girl, the one they found. She was in with some pretty bad people. She was scared. I was trying to help her."

Dallas said nothing. She watched her husband's face twitch around his eyes. He was the scared one now.

"Why didn't you call the police?" Dallas said.

"She didn't want the police. She was scared if she called them these people would find out and they'd do something to her."

"Why didn't you send her to Haven House?"

"I don't know," he said. "There's just so much I don't know."

A large woman sat on the stool next to Dallas. She had on a sleeveless dress. Her arms jiggled as she adjusted herself. Dallas caught a whiff of body odor. The woman swore as she fiddled with her handset.

"What happened, exactly?" Dallas said.

"Jeff says not to talk. This could be monitored."

"But you didn't *do* anything." And then, like a cockroach in the kitchen, distrust skittered across her mind. Dallas shook. Never had she experienced anything but complete faith in her husband.

Even in their worst times, when he could put on the big freeze and not talk to her for hours, she had never questioned his integrity. He was absolutely without fault in that department.

But now ... She refused to give the thought credence. It was the stress, the surroundings, the nightmare circumstance.

"Dallas, I didn't do anything but be stupid. They got to her, the guys she was afraid of. That had to be it." He paused. "They'll use this, you know. The porn people. They'll use this to show I'm a hypocrite. All our work will be called into question."

She couldn't deny it. She and Ron were actively fighting the spread of the porn industry by pushing for new zoning restrictions in the city. Ron, as the front man, had been called many things by his enemies. *Hypocrite* would now be added to the list.

"I'll keep the pressure on Bernie," Dallas said. Bernie Halstrom was their city councilman, the one they had worked closely with on the zoning issue.

"Thank you," Ron said, with what seemed heartfelt gratitude.

"How long do you have to be in here?"

"Jeff'll move for bail, but he told me they might not give it. This is what they call a high-profile murder case. Me, imagine ..."

"Are you all right?"

"They've got me isolated. That's the way they do it. I can take it if you can ..."

She saw his hand shake and then drop the phone. Then his head was in his hands and he was sobbing. Sobbing uncontrollably.

"Oh, Ron." Dallas jumped to her feet, pressed her forehead to the window, hit it with her open hand.

A deputy sheriff was at her side instantly, pulling her away.

"No!" she shouted. "No, please!"

"Sit down, ma'am. You can't touch the glass."

She sat. Ron kept sobbing. Then he whirled away and stood.

"Ron, don't go!"

Apparently he couldn't hear her. Or chose not to.

"Ron!"

"Keep your voice down, ma'am," the deputy said. "Looks like your visit is over."

Over.

No. Dallas steeled herself against the thought that more than this visit was over, that life as they all knew it was over and would never come back together again.

She would not let that be.

8.

Jared looked at himself in the mirror behind the bar and almost spat.

You have no job now, pal. Your little game with the crucifix didn't really do it in the eyes of the ol' boss. And the good Father? Well, he was about to consign you to the fires of hell right then and there.

You thought men of the cloth were supposed to be reverent in church, didn't you? At home, didn't your father wait to unload on you until after church, when Mom was making up the lunch?

So now it doesn't matter when you drink, because you've got no job, and the only question on the table is when will the money run out?

Jared listened to himself inside his head, laughing because he was having a little dialogue up there between himself and—who knew? Somebody who knew how to drink, that was for sure.

He sat at the end of the bar this time, right by the bathrooms. He came to this little place on occasion, when he wasn't out trying to dull the ache with items of illegal pedigree.

Nursing a double shot of Daniels was just as good tonight, and it was cold outside anyway.

Tomorrow. Maybe tomorrow he'd give another run at the VA hospital. They were giving him the big-time runaround on post-traumatic stress disorder. He knew why too—because there was a whole new wave of it.

What was the number he read? Like three hundred thousand homeless vets, about half from Vietnam. But it was growing, the numbers. Guys coming back from Iraq and Afghanistan. And Jared kept hearing through the grapevine that the Iraq vets had it worst of all in the head.

But not according to the VA. To them it was illness as usual. Even when some of his buddies had to take meds that could knock out a seriously ticked-off elephant.

Self-sedation with Jack Daniels was about the best he could do under the circumstances. What did that country song say? Something about when it rains, I pour? Jared smiled and shook his head. *Good one, boy, go ahead. And tomorrow you can wake up tight and early.*

There was a pool table in the center of the barroom with a couple of guys shooting, and a TV tuned to ESPN. Not as good as rap, but almost. The obnoxious sports heads who screamed clever phrases provided a little anesthesia.

Maybe I'll just buy a bottle and go back to the room at the rat hotel. He'd have to clear out of there in a week if he didn't land something to get some more money and not spend it on weed or alcohol.

He ordered another JD, worked it, looked occasionally at the TV. The images blurred into colorful splats on the screen, uniforms and graphics bleeding together, formless.

Then he saw his father's face.

What? Couldn't be. But there was no mistake.

Some words flashed below the face. *Crime of Passion.*

A squib for another cable channel, he realized.

His father was a news story.

Then, suddenly, the face was gone.

Whoa. Jared wondered for a moment if he really saw it, or if maybe it was a trick of the mind and alcohol. Maybe the voices in his head were becoming more sophisticated now, giving him altered realities, using visuals.

But then he realized he wasn't so drunk after all, especially not after the jolt of adrenaline that blasted through him the moment he recognized his father.

Crime of passion?

He called to the bartender, a woman with a look of thirty years' hard experience as a mixer.

"Can you get the news for me?" he said, pointing at the TV.

She looked at the tube. "We got people want to watch the game."

He was aware of anxiety clutching him. The weirdness of it all, having a father on the news, even if it was a father he hated. It was like the whole world had a pipeline into his life now, only he didn't know what the pipeline was connected to.

"Just change it to the news for a second, will you?"

"I got more than you in the bar," the bartender said.

"Just *do it.*"

She gave him the look she must have given a hundred thousand surly drunks over the years. "Relax. You want another drink?"

Jared stood up and raised his voice to the whole place. "Does anybody know what's going on with this crime-of-passion story on the news?"

People stared at him. The guys playing pool looked annoyed. The three other barflies looked singularly uninterested.

"Come on, anybody?"

"Settle down, will you?" the bartender said. "You talking about that preacher?"

"Yeah, that's the one."

"Why didn't you just ask me instead of making a scene? Sit down. I'll get you another drink."

"Tell me what's going on."

"Guy's some minister down in L.A. He had a porn actress on the side, then he offed her."

Flares of disbelief shot through Jared.

"Yep," the bartender said with a laugh, "you gotta love that town."

9.

Wednesday morning the Ron Hamilton "Crime of Passion" story was front page in the *Times* and *Daily News*. A small media camp was set up on the street outside the Hamilton home, waiting for Dallas to emerge.

And the phone in the house wouldn't stop ringing. There were at least twenty messages in the voice mail now. Dallas didn't bother to listen. Cara had her cell-phone number, and that's all Dallas cared about.

But life had to go on, and she was not going to let the media make a prisoner of her. There was the church to look out for.

So, dressed in business casual and with all the makeup skill she could muster showing on her face, Dallas got into her Nissan Pathfinder, locked the doors, and clicked the garage-door opener.

As soon as she made the driveway she was swarmed.

Though she'd prepared herself to ignore them, it was unsettling to see cameras aimed at her and microphones poking at the window. Behind the microphones were anxious faces shouting questions at her. She nearly ran over a woman in a blue blazer and was almost sorry she didn't.

Dallas prayed for peace and strength all the way to the Hillside parking lot, where more news vans were gathered. This was absurd. She wanted to get out and yell at these hounds to get a life and cover something newsworthy, not just some false allegation that—

False. Please oh please be false.

She was stunned that she could think such a thought. Of *course* it was false!

Dallas pulled around to a rear entrance and used her key to get in, unseen by the reporters.

She found the office in a tizzy. The first one to see her was Dave Rivas, their head of security. Dave, a former cop, volunteered his time. He and Dallas, in fact, had done the research that resulted in the church's state-of-the-art system.

"Been like this all day," Dave said. He was around fifty and always wore a black baseball cap with LAPD in white letters on the front.

"Any incidents?" Dallas asked.

"Depends what you mean. I had one guy from KTTV try to bring a camera in, but I yanked a few cords and that was that."

"Thanks, Dave. Hang in there."

"You too, Dallas. We're praying hard for you."

Dallas continued to the reception area. Three of the church secretaries were in various stages of harried activity—answering phones, peeling faxes from the machine. They didn't even look up to see Dallas.

But Lisa Benson did. She was on a phone, waved at Dallas, said something, and hung up.

She came to Dallas and gave her a hug. "Dallas, how *are* you? It's been a zoo here."

Dallas was glad Lisa was here. Though twenty years younger than Dallas, Lisa was a true friend. And a remarkable woman. Charismatic, and a perfect complement to her husband, Bob, Hillside's associate minister. This couple was going places, just like Dallas and Ron when they'd first come to Hillside.

Which was why Dallas always felt that Lisa could understand her own problems better than anyone else. Nothing like being a minister's wife to give you laser-sharp insights into life, the universe, and everything.

"My head is spinning," Dallas said. "I had to come up here to figure out what we should be doing for the church."

"Good," Lisa said. "Bob's been working on that. He'll want to see you, I'm sure. Come on."

As she walked with Dallas toward Bob Benson's office, Lisa said, "When the dust settles a little bit, let's get together and do something, huh? Just you and me."

"That sounds good."

Lisa rapped on her husband's office door, then opened it.

"Come in," Bob Benson said. Lisa kissed Dallas on the cheek and closed the door behind her.

The young associate stood and welcomed her into his extremely neat and orderly office. He was, as he had always been to her and Ron, impressive. Only twenty-seven, he was clearly a gifted minister. Educated, witty, and above all, able to communicate.

When they were settled, Bob asked how Dallas was.

"Not real good," she said. "News trucks outside my house. I'm under a microscope."

"We all are, I'm afraid." Bob wore his brown hair in an understated spiky style, just haphazard enough to give him credibility with the younger crowd. But he could preach a great sermon to all age groups.

"We've got to get a message out to our people," Dallas said.

"Already being done."

That surprised her. "How?"

"I drafted a statement for the website. And I'm working on one for the media."

"Can I see it?"

"I'm still tweaking."

"What about Sunday? Who's—"

"Dallas, don't worry. These are things you shouldn't have to stress over, okay?"

"It's Ron's church! Of course I'm going to stress."

The moment she said it she realized how desperate she must have sounded. Hillside was not *Ron's church*, even if he was the senior pastor who had overseen its growth. It was God's church.

Bob kept his voice calm. "I don't want you to worry, because things are being looked after. I've got an Easter sermon ready for Sunday, then I'll continue to preach the same sermon series Ron was on. That way there'll be a feeling, at least a little bit, of continuity. But I plan to address the issue full-on in all our services."

"Some great Easter, huh?"

"I'll be careful, Dallas. You know, 'You've all read about this tragedy in the paper, or seen it on the news—'"

"It's not a tragedy, Bob. It's a mistake."

Bob picked up a notepad and moved it to the opposite side of his desk. "Yes, of course. And I'll mention that we do still have something called the presumption of innocence. And I'll call on everyone to pray for the church."

"And Ron."

"That's a given."

"I'd like to be part of the planning too," Dallas said. "Decisions will have to be made affecting the church."

"Sure. I'll keep you in the loop."

"When can we talk?"

Bob looked at his watch. "I have to leave tonight. I'm speaking at a conference the next couple of days."

"That's right, something about reaching Gen Yers?"

"Right. But I'll be back late Saturday."

"What are we going to do about the media out there?"

Bob spun around in his chair and looked out the window. "I'm going to go out and deliver my statement."

"May I see it?"

"Like I said, I'm still working on it."

"May I see what you have so far?"

Bob hesitated just long enough to make Dallas uncomfortable. Dallas chalked it up to anxiety, hers and his. They'd all have to pull together and heap mounds of grace on each other.

Bob took a paper from the printer on his credenza and handed it to her.

> As associate minister of Hillside Community Church, I have had the privilege of working alongside Ron Hamilton for three years. During that time I have come to know him as both a friend and a boss, as a brother in Christ, and as a fellow worker in this community. We are holding him up in prayer and trust that the media will remember the most important principle of our justice system: that a man is presumed innocent until proven guilty beyond a reasonable doubt. We also would ask the media to respect the privacy rights of the worshipers here at Hillside, and not to interfere with our operations. Thank you.

She set the paper on Bob's desk.

"You look disappointed," he said.

"No, Bob. It's good. It's just …"

"You would have preferred an outright statement that we know Ron is innocent?"

She nodded, impressed by the young minister's insight.

"That was my first instinct, until I thought how that would look to the media. Naturally they've heard all that before, the protestations of innocence from family members. And we are Ron's family, right? In my mind, that would only make them dig in deeper. But by putting it out there as objectively as possible, by saying what the law says, that Ron's innocent until proven guilty, we show we're being as objective as the law. I don't know, maybe I'm wrong, but I had to consider Hillside's reputation."

Dallas sensed his defensiveness. She reached over the desk and put a hand on his arm. "Thanks, Bob. I know you have the welfare of the church, and Ron, at the top of your thoughts."

"And you, Dallas. Lisa and I want you to remember you can count on us for anything."

"I know."

"And I'd like to do something right now. I'd like to pray with you, Dallas. Will you join me in that?"

10.

Back home again, Dallas felt like her head was finally emerging above the waters of adversity. She was able to look around, think a little bit, and remember that she had duties to people that didn't go away because Ron was in jail.

She called Haven House and spoke to Danielle, her assistant there. "Have you been able to place Tiana and Jamaal yet?"

"No luck," Danielle said. "She said she's going back to her boyfriend."

"No! Don't let her do that."

"What can I do? She's getting ready to go."

"Let me talk to her."

"She hasn't come down yet."

"I'll wait."

As she did, she peeked out the front-door sidelights at the persistent news crews. There were only a couple of diehards left. They'd rushed her as she pulled into her garage. She let the door down fast hoping it would clonk one of them on the head.

This would soon be over. Jeff Waite was going to get to the bottom of things. Ron was innocent, and when they found out, there would be egg on the face of all the major news outlets. She would demand some apologies. She was starting to get really ticked off at the smug looks.

Didn't these people know about the presumption of innocence? Of course they did, but it didn't matter, because sex sells papers and advertising. Who was going to let a little thing like the truth, or legal rights, get in the way?

Tiana's voice interrupted her bitter musings. "Yeah?"

"Tiana, this is Dallas Hamilton."

"I know."

"Danielle said you're about to leave."

"Yeah."

"Don't do it. You can't. He'll only beat you up again."

"Don't worry anymore about me."

"Tiana, listen to me, Jamaal could be beaten up too. For his sake, don't go back there."

"I've got nowhere else!" Tiana's voice was rife with anger and desperation.

"You could come here."

"Huh?"

"Come stay with me. Just for a while, till we figure out what to do. You can stay in my daughter's room. Jamaal can have my son's room."

"His own room?"

"That's right."

"Why?"

"Why what, Tiana?"

"Why are you opening up your own house?"

"I do sometimes. Please let me come get you and Jamaal. At least for a couple of days. Will you do that?"

Long pause. "Okay."

"Thank you. I'll be down there by three."

She hoped Tiana would still be there. Women in Tiana's situation could change their minds on a whim, so fragile were their psyches.

Now all she had to do was get the house in order. Good. Nothing like some old-fashioned housework to get occupied with something other than the things she had no control over.

She started with the family room and was about to go upstairs when a pounding at the back door, off the kitchen, startled her. Her heart spiked. She was certain it was a reporter.

Another knock at the door.

She thought about calling 911. But then, like a convict in an old prison movie, Dallas put her back to the wall and moved to a place where she could glimpse the door.

She saw the top half of a head over the curtain on the kitchen door.

And nearly jumped out of her skin.

11.

"Jared!"

She threw open the door.

"Hey, Mom."

Dallas threw her arms around his neck, kissed his cheek, held her face against his.

Jared said nothing. He felt rigid in her arms. She stood back and looked at him.

His dusky hair was still shoulder length. What was new was the goatee and a small ring above his left eyelid. He was wearing an old leather jacket, jeans, and dirty work boots spotted with white paint.

"Why didn't you call?" Dallas shut the door behind him.

"Maybe you wouldn't have wanted me around," Jared said.

"What!" She embraced him again and held him close, as if he were eight years old again and had come home from school crying because some older kids had made fun of him.

Jared pulled away. "So they got cameras out there in the front yard."

"I guess we're the story of the month."

"That's why I came in the back. Don't think anybody saw me hop the wall."

Dallas practically pushed him into a kitchen chair.

"Where've you been?" She sat across from him.

"Bakersfield. Painting houses."

"Good work?" she asked.

"Used to be."

"What does that mean?"

He sat back in the chair. "Did he do it?"

The directness of the question and the coldness of it hit Dallas like a blow. "No, of course he didn't do it."

"How do you know?"

"How can you say that?"

He drummed the tabletop with his fingers. "Anybody's capable of anything."

"Not your father."

"Come on, Mom. Why not Dad? He's human, isn't he?" His eyes, cool and aloof, seemed to catch a vision. "We can do bad things—"

"But not what they're accusing him of. I know he couldn't have done that."

"Did you know this girl?"

"No, she was someone your father was counseling. She had a troubled background. Anybody could have killed her."

"Right. Anybody but Dad."

Dallas looked at her son and hardly knew him. She supposed she hadn't known him since he returned from Iraq, but now he seemed even farther away.

"Listen to me, Jared. Carefully. I've seen your dad, looked in his eyes. He's confused and scared. He tried to help a girl in trouble, that's all, and then he wakes up accused of a horrible crime. And now he's in a jail cell and everyone is writing about him as a criminal. He's been convicted in the papers, the tabloids, and with oh-so-much glee. Can't you give him the benefit of the doubt?"

"When did he ever do that for me?" Jared stood up, almost knocking his chair over. He turned his back on her. She felt the onrush of bad memories from the many times Jared and Ron fought and screamed at each other.

Suddenly Jared laughed. It was a short, disturbing chuckle. He faced her. "It's funny. I remember a sermon Dad did once, about going through trials. I remember he said that sometimes God hits a Christian with suffering in order to get his attention, if he's been sinning. And so that's how suffering can be a good thing, la-di-da. I remember that, Mom, because it scared the juice out of me. Because I knew what a rotten kid I was and—"

"Jared—"

"Listen! I knew what a screwed-up case I was, so I was just getting ready to get hit with it, get God's freaking wrath poured all over me. Well, I'm over that now. Whatever this world is about, it's about getting garbage all over you. So maybe Dad was off doing something he shouldn't have, and now he can say God's getting his attention."

Jared sat down again, looking halfway conciliatory. "Look, Mom. I don't know what I'm talking about. Forget it. If you saw Dad and don't think he did it, that's good enough for me. I just don't want to see you hurt, you know? That's the only reason I'm here. It's not because of him. It's because of you."

"Will you see him?" Dallas said.

"No."

"He's still your father."

"Don't remind me."

"Stop it!" Dallas stood up. "I know you're hurt, Jared, and I know you've been through an ordeal. But don't disrespect your father. He doesn't deserve that."

"Relax, Mom, I'm not going to—"

"Do you understand me?"

Jared looked away from her. "I'm not a little kid, Mom."

But he was her kid, no matter what. Dallas embraced him again.

He said nothing but at least made no move to break away from her.

"Do you have to go back to Bakersfield?" she said. "Can you stay?"

"I sort of lost my job up there," Jared said. "You know, if I ran a mortuary, nobody would die."

"Jared—"

"So if you have any painting needs, I'll swap you for a bed."

"You don't need to swap anything," Dallas said. "This is home. Remember? The peas in the pot?"

When he was little, maybe five, he heard the expression *just like two peas in a pod* and somehow got it in his mind that the four of them—him, his mom and dad and sister, Cara—were four peas in a *pot*. He kept saying it that way, until the family adopted it.

Jared closed his eyes and nodded.

"All right then," Dallas said. "Let me get you something to eat."

12.

It's the silence that kills.

The theory of the penitentiary was that it would be a place of penitence. Stick a man in a cage and make him think about his black soul.

It works.

Of course, many of those held in isolation in the old days went crazy.

It's the silence that kills.

They built this jail back in the sixties. It's a big concrete block. Inside, a labyrinth of corridors, rows of cells, and metal gates. Garbage bags and sheets hang from cell doors to keep inquiring eyes from looking in. Shouts, curses, and clanging doors echo through the facility, which is penetrated here and there by a few shafts of sunlight.

But the silence remains for the celebrity inmates, like me. And in the silence, faces haunt you.

Faces. I see the faces of those I love.

Cara. My lovely daughter. She came to see me today and cried and I couldn't hold her. So I see her face now, wet with tears even as she told me she loved me, and the vision torments me.

Jared. Wherever he is. His face is troubled, and so it troubles me.

Dallas. I see her face all the time. I can't reach out to it; it just hovers over me. Hurt look. Accusing eyes. She tries to hide them. Can't.

Yet these are not the only faces I see.

Melinda.

Even since her death, I see her face. It screams at me.

Like a demon.

FOUR

At least he was doing something other than wallowing in self-disgust. Still, Jared felt stupid behind the wheel of his mother's SUV. He was not a soccer mom. But he was, for the moment, a delivery service.

Delivering people, one of them to his own bed.

His mother—cleverly now, he realized, to get him moving—had asked him to pick up this woman and her kid and bring them home.

Now this was going to be strange. Here was a woman with a face that had been through things. Her kid, only six. Jared thought of all the children he'd watched in the park. That crack in his heart that ached for them throbbed again now. What chance did a kid like this have with a father who beat up on his mom? What chance did any kid have these days?

On the way to the house, the woman named Tiana said, "Your mom's a good person."

"Yeah."

"I mean, she didn't have to do this."

"That's my mom. Always taking in stray ... looking out for people." He wondered what Tiana's boyfriend was like, and why a girl stayed with somebody who slapped her around. He'd been with women. He didn't quite get them.

"You were in the Marines?" she said.

"My mom tell you about me?"

"A little. Jamaal wants to be in the Marines."

The boy was belted in the backseat. A six-year-old wanting to be in the Marines. How quaint.

"Tell him to go into football instead," Jared said.

"Mama, is he in the Marines?" The boy's voice was tissue-paper thin.

"Yeah, baby."

"In war?"

Tiana asked Jared, "You been in war?"

"Can it, will you?" Jared snapped, though pulling the punch a little. "Tell me how come you stay with a guy who knocks you around."

"You don't know anything about it."

"I know it doesn't make sense."

"You got a woman?"

"Not at the moment."

"Then you don't know."

Jared realized he was gunning the SUV too fast down Devonshire. He let up a little. *If you're going to crash, do it when nobody's in the car with you.*

"You seen your dad?" Tiana said.

"What are you talking about?" He knew what she was talking about.

"He's in trouble."

"Yeah, well, that's what you get, isn't it? You live, you get trouble. I shouldn't have to tell you that."

"I just asked if you've seen him. A son ought to see his father."

"That's kind of weird, coming from you."

"I was talking about you."

"Yeah, well, don't talk about me."

"Real friendly."

Oh yeah, he thought, *it's going to be great having these two in the house. Mom and her charity projects.*

"I wanna be in the Marines," Jamaal yelped from the back.

"No more talking," Jared said. "Just let me drive."

"Real friendly," Tiana said.

2.

The next day, Thursday, Dallas drove to Jeff Waite's office in Encino, summoned by Jeff himself. His voice on the phone sounded troubled, which only added to her already overcharged nervous system.

She'd picked up tension between Tiana and Jared the moment he brought her and Jamaal home yesterday. And she knew why. It was becoming clear to her that Jared's ability to relate to people was wounded, a casualty of war. She had to face the fact that this was no passing phase. He was out of it. Something had happened to him in Iraq. He was nearly gone, and she had to try to get him back before it was too late.

But how could she, when God dropped Ron's arrest on her? Or allowed it to happen, or whatever the correct theology for it was. Yes, he was sovereign, she knew that. And she knew God did things that defied human explanation. That didn't quell her hunger to know. This was her family at stake, and if she had to wrestle God like Jacob did, she would.

When she finally got to Jeff's office building, Dallas realized she couldn't recall any details of her drive there. She didn't even remember what streets she'd taken.

Jeff's unsmiling face did nothing to relieve the pressure.

He closed the door to his office.

"Ron's arraignment is tomorrow morning," Jeff explained. "I just got the arrest report from the DA's office."

"And?"

"Not good. Sit down."

"I don't want to."

"It'll be better if you do."

Dallas allowed herself to sink into a chair in duet with her sinking spirit. How much worse could this news be?

Jeff sat on the edge of his desk, facing Dallas with no obstruction between them. "How you doing, Dallas?"

"You have to ask?" She held up her hands. They trembled. "Don't put me around the nuclear button."

"You're a lot steadier than you think. I know that."

"Don't fool yourself."

"Your faith is what will get you through this."

"Tell me the news."

"All right." Jeff folded his arms. "Melinda Perry, the decedent, was being counseled by Ron. She was involved in, basically, porn movies. Went under the name of Melinda Chance."

"That's been all over the news," Dallas said bitterly. "They love that angle."

"Did Ron ever tell you he was counseling this girl?"

"He hasn't been too communicative this whole year. I just chalked it up to all he had going on. So, no, he never told me about her until I saw him at the jail. But that doesn't mean he killed her. He didn't."

Did he, Jeff? Did he? Tell me flat out he didn't do it.

"Let me tell you what the sheriff has," Jeff said. "A deputy found the girl's body early on the morning of the seventeenth, a Thursday, at a place in Pico Rivera called the Star Motel. She had Ron's card in her purse. On Friday they interviewed Ron. He went in to the Pico Rivera station. Did you know about that?"

"No."

"They asked him if he knew Melinda Perry and he said he'd been counseling her. They asked when the last time he saw her was, and he said either the tenth or the eleventh. They asked him where he was the night of the sixteenth, and he said he worked late at church. No one else was there, he said."

"He sometimes worked late there." At least, that's what he told her. *Don't let it be a lie!*

"They asked him if he'd ever been to the Star Motel. He said he'd never heard of the place."

Don't be a lie.

"Dallas, hang on. They found carpet fibers in Ron's car. They match the carpet in the room where the murder took place."

Something hard and vicious scraped Dallas's insides.

"Ron lied to the police, Dallas. That's something we can't avoid."

"But *why*—"

Because he did it.

No!

"He was scared," Jeff said. "That's what he told me. He went to the motel because she had called him on his cell phone. The police have a record of that call, on the night she was murdered. But Ron insists he just talked to her and left."

"Yes. I remember something he said. This girl was scared that some bad people were going to get her. That has to be what happened. They followed her, or followed Ron, or ..." She paused, trying to think. "Maybe they set him up."

Jeff said nothing.

"Doesn't it make sense?" Dallas slid to the edge of the chair. "This girl was in porn films. Ron's a big enemy of the industry. He's been working with our councilman, he's been vocal."

"Dallas—"

"Jeff, that has to be it."

He put his hand up. "Let me tell you the way it's got to play out. We have to deal with the evidence as it is. No judge is going to let me argue a conspiracy theory unless we come up with something to show there is at least a shred of possibility."

"Then let's find it."

"Believe me, Dallas, I have one of the best investigators in the city who'll be on this. But right now you have to be prepared for some very bad days."

And what's it been until now, a cakewalk?

Jeff sighed and looked at the floor.

"Is there something else?" she asked.

"Yes. Some detectives went over to Hillside earlier today."

"Detectives?"

Jeff nodded. "And they had a search warrant. They took Ron's computer and a bunch of his papers."

"But he's got all his stuff on there, his programs, his work."

"They have to preserve it all, under the law, but they can look at whatever they want."

"Jeff, this is unbelievable. It's so wrong."

"It's the way the law operates, Dallas. Sometimes it protects us, sometimes it invades us. Right now, it's invading. It's my job to get it all straightened out."

But what if it doesn't get straightened out? What then?

"What's going to happen next?" Dallas asked.

"Ron's entitled to a prelim within ten days of arrest. I'm not going to waive time. I'll hold their feet to the fire and try to smoke out what the prosecution thinks it has. The sooner we force it the better. This is now a big, fat media case. The DA is out there on a limb claiming Ron is the murderer. They'll fight every step of the way to make this stick. I just wanted you to be prepared. Don't talk to anyone. Refer all questions to my office."

Questions? She herself had a ton of them. Like, what really happened at the motel? And if Ron lied to the police, could he be lying to them all?

3.

My life was changed by fire.

It was like that famous account of Pascal's conversion. I mean, there he was, living a worldly life in Paris in the 1600s, confused. What was life all about? he wanted to know. Is the sensuality I experience all there is to existence?

There he was, this genius in mathematics, founder of probability theory and advanced differential calculus. (I never even took calculus, I was too afraid.) His physics experiments led to the invention of the hydraulic press.

But he couldn't figure out life.

One night he picked up his Bible and began reading the gospel of John. Suddenly, he was filled with a sense of God's presence, so extreme and rapturous that he felt as if he were on fire. He grabbed a parchment and tried to record what he was feeling. When he died at the age of thirty-nine, they found this parchment sewed up in the lining of his jacket, where he'd kept it close to his heart:

FIRE

"God of Abraham, God of Isaac, God of Jacob,"
*   not of philosophers and scholars.*
Certainty, certainty, heartfelt, joy, peace.
God of Jesus Christ.
God of Jesus Christ.
"My God and your God."
"Thy God shall be my God."
The world forgotten, and everything except God.

It went on, but I know how he felt. I know because it happened to me.
I was seventeen, alone in the house, watching Billy Graham on TV.
I'd listened to Billy Graham before. Mom and Dad, even though
they weren't Christians, said he was one of the best speakers around. I
was interested in acting, so I liked listening to good orators.

Billy Graham was one of the best, I agreed. But I had never
responded to his message.

Until this night.

I can't remember what his subject was, but when he started speak-
ing about death, I got attentive. Even at seventeen, I realized I would die
someday. Maybe this was something I needed to hear.

Then Billy Graham said that, for Christians, there is no fear of
death. He pointed to the sky. "We're going to heaven!" he said.

At that moment, instantly, my body got hot from head to foot. I knew
nothing about the Holy Spirit or the call of God. All I knew was I was
brimming with an inexpressible joy and longing, the fire of it, the blaze
of it, and I wanted that heaven Billy Graham was talking about.

When Billy offered the invitation, I dropped to my knees and prayed
to the TV.

That was the fire of my own conversion, and it burned away
everything else I thought was important to me. Basketball, hot cars,
cheerleaders.

I gave my life over to him that high school year, and I knew I was
going to be a minister.

Mom and Dad were shocked.

So were my friends and teachers.

But there was no going back. The fire had burned it all up—my
sins, my plans, my life.

I never doubted my conversion or my choice. But over time, the
memory of the fire faded.

Now I want it back.

FIVE

1.

The first Monday in April was hot in L.A. The usual snarl of morning traffic choked Temple Street as Dallas, clinging to Cara and following Jefferson Waite, approached the criminal courthouse.

Immediately, the pack of waiting reporters descended on her, barking questions at the new hot story—Dallas Hamilton.

In the last several days she had become the focus, the media star, the Garbo of wronged wives. Wanting nothing more than to be left alone, her resistance excited brute passions. She knew nothing worked the media beast into a frenzy like the pursuit of one who wished to avoid them.

Especially where sex and murder were the two angles, the salacious twins of tabloid headlines.

"No comment. No comment," Jeff repeated. He did not wear dark glasses. He smiled for the cameras. Dallas was not so naïve as to believe Jefferson Waite should want to shun media scrutiny. He was a lawyer, after all, and in Southern California, one case with publicity like this could make an entire career. But she also trusted him implicitly, knew he was good, knew he would fight to the last to prove Ron's innocence.

They followed closely, this organism of publicity, like a cloud of gnats swarming on a hot morning. Dallas kept her head down all the way to the front doors, holding Cara's arm, and was thankful when she finally passed through the metal detectors. Safe at last in the place that was the most forbidding. At least the deputy sheriffs would keep order, keep nosy reporters from getting in her face.

Ron's preliminary hearing was to begin this morning in Department 27. Judge Clifford Bartells was fair but tough, Jeff had explained. And a prelim was not generally where a case was won. The prosecution had only to provide minimal evidence, just enough to convince a judge to bind a defendant over for trial. With Bartells, that would be a low threshold indeed.

"But I'll be looking for the haymaker," Jeff told her. "Every now and then the prosecution messes up. If it does, I'll be ready."

The prosecutor, one Mike Freton, was a tall, silver-haired man with narrow eyes. The sort of man, Dallas thought, who has seen his share of evil people. How could he think that of Ron? How could anyone think that of Ron?

She and Cara were given seats in the front row, near the wall. It was on the jury-box side of the courtroom, which meant she was closest to the prosecution table. Ron and Jeff Waite, and Waite's investigator, Harry Stegman, were miles away on the other side.

Ron wore one of his suits, not the orange coveralls. He gave her one look before Judge Bartells entered. It was a look of inscrutable sadness. She wanted to go to him, hold him, reassure him. At the same time, she wanted to scream, shake him, make sure all the bad stuff was out.

Cara patted Dallas's arm and whispered, "Hang in there." Dallas nodded. She wished Jared had come too, to show support for his father. But he'd refused even to talk to her about it.

After a few words with the judge, legalese Dallas couldn't quite comprehend, Deputy DA Freton called a deputy sheriff named David Barnes to the stand.

He was a clean-cut young man who might have stepped off the beach at Santa Monica, been handed a badge, and told to catch bad guys.

After the swearing in, Freton began. "Deputy Barnes, you are with the Los Angeles County Sheriff's Department?"

"Yes, sir."

"How long have you been so employed?"

"Six years, come August."

"Turning your attention to the morning of March 17, can you tell us what your assignment was?"

"I was working out of the Pico Rivera station. I was in a cruiser."

"And did you receive a dispatch at around ten o'clock that morning?"

"Yes. I got a 911 report of a possible domestic disturbance at the Star Motel in Pico Rivera."

"Who were you told placed the 911 call?"

"The day manager of the motel, a Mr. Franze."

"What did you do next?"

"I proceeded to the location. I went to the front office and talked with Mr. Franze. I asked him if he had reported a disturbance and he said—"

"Objection," Jeff said. "Hearsay."

"It's the basis of the deputy's belief," Freton said.

Judge Bartells nodded. "Overruled."

"You may answer," Freton said.

"He said there was always something disturbing going on at this place."

The spectators and reporters in the courtroom laughed. Dallas felt a warm chill, hot ice, up and down her back. Like a fever. They were laughing at this now. At Ron.

"What did you do next, Deputy?"

"I asked him why he called, and he said somebody in room 103, a man named Knudsen, said that he'd heard—"

"Same objection," Jeff said.

"Overruled."

Deputy Barnes continued. "This man Knudsen had heard an argument the night before in room 105, some screaming, and then there was nothing. Silence. He thought about leaving it alone, but the next morning he just had this concerned feeling and felt he had to tell Mr. Franze about it. Mr. Franze went to room 105 and knocked, got no answer. He thought it best to give a call to 911."

"Did he give any reason why he thought to do that?"

"Yes. He said he was afraid of being sued."

More laughter in the courtroom. Dallas gripped the arms of her seat and shook her head. Cara took her hand and squeezed it.

"What happened next, Deputy Barnes?"

"I asked Mr. Franze to look up the registration on room 105. He told me the name was Melinda Perry. I then asked Mr. Franze to accompany me to room 105. We proceeded to the room. I knocked on the door and announced that I was a Los Angeles County deputy sheriff. There was no answer. I knocked and announced again. Still no answer. So I requested Mr. Franze to unlock the door, which he did."

"Why did you request Mr. Franze to unlock the door?"

"It was my belief that there might be someone injured inside the room, based upon the 911 call."

"What did you see when you entered room 105?"

"A young woman on the bed. Not moving. I went to the bed and said, 'Ma'am?' I said it three times. When she did not respond I checked her wrist for a pulse. There was none."

"What did you do next?"

"I secured the room and contacted the sheriff's department homicide division."

"When did they arrive?"

"Approximately twenty minutes later."

"Did anyone enter or exit room 105 before the homicide division arrived?"

"No, sir."

"No further questions."

Freton was direct, confident. And from the moment he started, a blistering dread thickened inside Dallas, nearly choking off breath. It was happening. Really happening. Her husband was really a defendant in a murder trial.

2.

Jefferson Waite stood up, buttoned the coat of his dark blue pin-stripe suit, and approached Deputy Barnes.

"Just a few questions, Deputy. You say you received a dispatch about a 911 call?"

"Yes."

Dallas noted that the witness did not add *sir* when addressing the defense attorney.

"You did not hear the 911 tape, did you?"

"Nope. I merely responded to the call."

"And the call was for a possible domestic disturbance at the Star Motel, isn't that correct?"

"Some sort of disturbance, yes."

"The dispatch told you that someone had reported screaming, correct?"

"Yes."

"That person, in fact, was the manager of the motel, Mr. Franze?"

"Yes."

"But Mr. Franze was relying on the statement of a Mr. Knudsen, correct?"

"Yes."

"And you proceeded to the scene?"

"Yes."

"Did you at any time on the way to the Star Motel receive any further information on the factual basis of the 911 call?"

"Factual basis?" Barnes said this incredulously, as if everyone in the world would know that was an absurd question.

Jeff did not flinch. "Yes, Deputy. Factual basis. As opposed to mere speculation or opinion. I'm sure they cover that at the sheriff's academy."

"Objection," Freton said.

The judge half closed his eyes. "Sustained. Continue, Mr. Waite."

"So the answer is, you did not receive any further information concerning the 911 call, is that correct?"

"No, and that's the way it always is. There is no —"

"You've answered the question. Next question. When you got to the motel and contacted Mr. Franze, did you question him about who this man Knudsen was?"

"No."

"Instead, you made him walk down to room 105 and open it up."

"Objection," Freton said. "Misstates the evidence."

"Ah, yes," Jeff said. "There was the token knock on the door. By the way, when you knocked and announced, there was no answer inside, was there?"

"No."

"No sounds from inside, right?"

"That's correct."

"Then you instructed Mr. Franze to open the door."

"Yes."

"And you went in."

"Yes."

"No more questions."

Dallas could not see that the cross-examination of the deputy had made any dent in the prosecution's case. What was Jeff after? A deputy sheriff answered a distress call, went into a motel room, and found a dead body. Hard facts indeed.

The prosecutor placed some papers in front of Jefferson Waite and was saying something to him. Jeff was looking at them with a concerned expression. Dallas saw him in profile, then he gave her a quick look. The next thing she knew he was standing and saying, "Your Honor, may we take a ten-minute recess?"

"Very well," the judge said.

What was happening? Dallas looked at Jeff. His eyes practically burned with neon, a sign spelling out *disaster*.

3.

Jared found the cardboard box at the back of the hallway closet, under the Christmas wrapping paper. He'd been looking for a fresh toothbrush, and his mother usually kept such items in this closet.

At least she had five years ago.

But the box didn't contain what he needed. It held, instead, a bunch of old stuff from his room.

Weird. Like going back in a little cardboard time machine. But it wasn't a fun trip. He was tense. His jaws were locked and hurt. His insides were screaming for some combo, but he'd stayed away from weed and beer and even loud music for his mother's sake.

He wondered how long he'd last before the inevitable fall.

On his knees in the hallway, Jared picked through his past. A couple of old Chip Hilton books. Trophies from his Little League days. Pictures of his teams—the Orioles, Royals, and Cubs. One year his dad was in the picture as an assistant coach. The season with the Pirates. That was an embarrassment. He and his father did not get along one bit that year—

"What're you doing?"

Jared looked up. Tiana was standing there. "What I'm doing is my own business in my own house."

"Just asking."

He went back to rummaging through the box, fishing out a couple of old Little League mitts. Why had his mother bothered to save these?

"I don't really want to be here, you know," Tiana said.

Jared stifled the urge to say, *That makes two of us.* But a quiet nudge not to be such a jerk interrupted the insult. He sat back against the wall.

"What's going to happen to you?" he asked.

Tiana shrugged. "Jamaal and I can't stay here forever."

"But you can't go back to your boyfriend." He looked at her closely. The ugly bruise that had marred her face was mostly gone. So was the puffiness. Tiana was really very pretty, he thought. He wanted her to stay that way.

"He's Jamaal's father. He loves Jamaal. Jamaal wants him."

"Even though he hits you?"

"Not all the time."

"I say once is too much. Don't be stupid."

"I'm not stupid." She had some attitude in her voice.

Jared started to get angry. He clenched his teeth. "Stupid's putting yourself where you and your kid are gonna get hurt. So don't—"

"Who are you to give me advice?"

"What's that supposed to mean?"

"Means you got a father in trouble and you don't even go to court, don't even talk to him. You got no cred with me."

Jared got up from the floor. His head was tight. "You don't know what you're talking about."

She put her hands on her hips. "And you do? Get over yourself."

"Hey, I don't need anything from you, okay? I'm minding my own business."

"Your mom needs you to go with her to court—"

"Shut up."

"—so get off your—"

"You want to go back? Get your stuff. Get your kid. I'll drive you."

She hesitated, then a steely resolve came to her face. "That's good by me."

And she left the hall.

Jared let her go. *Good one. Mom's gonna love you for this. But that's the way it breaks.*

Fifteen minutes later, Tiana and Jamaal were in the cab of Jared's truck, heading toward Pacoima. This was one of the most run-down, gang-infested areas of the Valley. Jared almost turned around. Forget the boyfriend. What chance would Jamaal have of even making it out of his teens here?

That's the breaks.

They rode in silence. Once, Jamaal tried to ask Jared a question, but Tiana put her finger to her lips and quieted him.

The only words spoken were Tiana's directions to the apartment building. It was a prop-up job on Dorado Avenue, within shouting distance of the rail line running along San Fernando Boulevard. What little grass there was in front of the place was brown and patchy.

"Good luck," Jared said.

Tiana said nothing as she got out, unstrapped Jamaal, and fished her trash bag of clothes from the bed of the truck.

Then she stuck her head in the window. "I hope you find what you're looking for," she said.

Jared watched as she and Jamaal shuffled toward the apartments. Suddenly Jamaal stopped and turned around.

And waved.

Jared just looked at him.

Then Jamaal saluted. He stood at attention for a moment, then turned and ran toward his mother.

4.

Jefferson Waite walked Dallas to the end of the corridor. Cara was down in the coffee shop on the first floor, waiting for Dallas to join her.

"How you holding up?" Jeff asked.

"I don't know. I'll tell you at the end of the day."

He looked back down the long hallway, like he was avoiding her all of a sudden.

"What is it?" Dallas said.

He sighed. "You need to be strong. I have to tell you something."

Strong? She felt like warm Jell-O. "What is it?"

"The next witness is the deputy coroner, the one who performed the autopsy."

"And?"

"Freton just gave me a copy of his report."

"What does it say?"

"Dallas, I will always be up front with you."

"Please talk to me."

"They found seminal fluid in Melinda Perry."

The walls of the courthouse began to close in on Dallas, even before he said what she knew he'd say.

"They did a DNA analysis. It's a match with Ron."

Fireworks behind her eyes, a momentary blindness to every-thing around her.

"Dallas—"

"No." She put her hand up. "Just let me alone."

She turned and walked the other way, down the corridor, a long dark tunnel now. Even with the lights, the people, the elevators, the sounds—even with all that, she was alone in a blackness that went on and on.

Thought smashed against thought. She was unaware of what she was doing. She knew she was walking, then entering the restroom. There may have been another woman in there, she wasn't sure. She saw only the first stall with its door open, and that is where she fell to her knees and retched.

5.

"Mom, what on earth?" Cara took Dallas by the shoulders and sat her down on the plastic bench in the coffee shop.

"I'm sick."

"Let's get you home."

"No. I'm staying. Your father ..." How to break this to her daughter? How to soften the blow?

"What about Dad?"

"Cara, they have evidence, that your dad and the girl ..."

"Not sex."

Dallas nodded.

"Oh, Mom, no."

Dallas was still nauseated and took a long breath. "Jeff's not finished. We don't know everything."

"Let me take you home."

"I'm staying."

"Then I am too."

Dallas held Cara's hand during the entire testimony of Dr. Edward Varaki. The deputy DA put him through a clinical, step-by-step recitation of the autopsy. Asphyxiation. Suffocation. Lack of oxygen to brain. Evidence of sexual intercourse.

And the DNA match with Ron.

She could sense the reporters working overtime, scribbling notes or clacking on tiny keyboards. They had the good stuff now, the guarantor of ratings and circulation. *It used to be about the news that's fit to print,* Dallas thought. *Now it's all the sex that fits, we print.*

She had been betrayed.

Jeff cross-examined. "Dr. Varaki, the evidence of sexual intercourse and the cause of death have nothing to do with each other, do they?"

"I offer no opinion on that."

"It's entirely possible to have sexual intercourse with someone and not kill them, isn't it?"

"Objection," Freton said.

Jeff nodded and said, "No more questions."

Freton had one more witness, a sheriff's detective named Powell Dennison. He was paunchy and graying. His hairstyle was a buzz cut, like the cops in TV shows of the sixties.

"You questioned the defendant on the morning of March 18, is that correct?" Freton asked.

"Yes, sir."

"Did you record that interview?"

"I did."

"And do you have the written report in front of you?"

"Yes."

"Referring to your report, Detective, can you tell the court if Mr. Hamilton was advised of his Miranda rights?"

"He was."

"Did he request a lawyer?"

"No. He said he would like to answer questions, to clear this all up."

"Did he sign a waiver?"

"He did."

"Did you ask if Mr. Hamilton knew the deceased, Melinda Perry, also known as Melinda Chance?"

"He said that he did know her. Said he had been counseling her at his church on occasion."

"Referring to your report, at page eight, will you please read into the record lines six through sixteen?"

"Sure." Dennison flipped a couple of pages and began to read. " 'QUESTION: When was the last time you saw Miss Perry?

" 'ANSWER: Oh, I'm trying to think. It was probably last Thursday or Friday.

" 'QUESTION: That would be the tenth or the eleventh?

" 'ANSWER: Yeah, I guess.

" 'QUESTION: There is no way you've seen her in the last two days?

" 'ANSWER: None.

" 'QUESTION: Have you ever been to Pico Rivera, Mr. Hamilton?

" 'ANSWER: Pico Rivera? I don't think so.

"'QUESTION: Ever heard of the Star Motel in Pico Rivera?

"'ANSWER: No.

"'QUESTION: Did you ever have sex with Melinda Perry?

"'ANSWER: No. No way. I would never do that.'"

Mike Freton cast a quick glance at Jefferson Waite. The hint of a smirk crossed Freton's face. Dallas thought she might get sick all over again.

Freton sat down. Jeff said he had no questions for the witness.

The last witness for the prosecution was a forensic technician from the sheriff's lab. He testified to the presence of the carpet fibers from the Star Motel in Ron's car.

Jeff cross-examined with some technical questions Dallas didn't understand. But it was obvious Jeff was trying to lay a foundation for a later challenge to the gathering of this evidence.

When Jeff finished, Freton announced that the prosecution's case was over.

Judge Bartells nodded. "Mr. Waite, do you have witnesses to call?"

Jefferson Waite stood ramrod straight. The way he did it made Dallas think of a gladiator.

"No witnesses, Your Honor. But I would like to ask for a recess until Wednesday."

"The purpose being?"

"I would like to supplement my points and authorities on my motion to suppress. I believe that what we've heard today from the prosecution leads only to one conclusion, and that is all the evidence gathered from the Star Motel is inadmissible."

Dallas thought she heard a snort from the prosecutor. The judge made no sound, but his eyes lit up with surprise.

"All of it?" the judge said.

"Every last fiber," Jeff said.

The judge looked at his wall calendar. "Very well. We'll address this on Wednesday afternoon, at one thirty sharp. We're in recess until then."

Everyone stood as the judge left the bench. Then a deputy sheriff took Ron by the arm to lead him out of the courtroom.

Ron did not turn around to look at Dallas.

As Jeff gathered his notes, Dallas tried to make her way to him. She was immediately confronted by several reporters angling for a comment. She waved them off, but still they came, like sharks to chum.

Only the bailiff, a broad-shouldered deputy sheriff, restored order with a verbal threat to the press. They shrank back with sour looks all around.

Dallas got to the rail, where Jeff saw her.

"What's going on?" she asked.

"I've got some work to do on my motion to suppress. We'll be back here Wednesday afternoon."

"What if the judge doesn't go along with this motion?"

"Let's cross that bridge when we come to it."

"What do I do now?"

Jeff put a hand on her shoulder. "Just try to get some rest. This has been a traumatic day, I know."

Rest? Out of the question. Her body and mind wouldn't allow it. Not, at least, until she looked her husband in the eye again.

SIX

1.

"Look at me, Ron."

He did. Reluctantly. His forehead was furrowed and his eyes uncertain. It was nearly four thirty in the afternoon, and Ron was back at county jail. This would be his world for at least another two days, until Judge Bartells issued his ruling.

But at the moment Dallas wasn't thinking about judges or lawyers or courtrooms.

"You lied to me," she said, letting the hurt vibrate her words.

Ron nodded, looking at the scarred table in front of him.

"I said look at me." Dallas was gripping the phone so hard her forearm ached. "Have you ever lied to me about … about women?"

"Dallas, believe me, I—"

"Why *should* I?"

"Because I'm telling you, I'm telling you the truth with every ounce of my being. Yes, I did a terrible thing. And lied to you about it. But I'm not lying now. I did not kill that girl."

She looked at him and wondered if her instinct was right. That her husband was not a killer, could never be. He could lie to her about a sordid affair. He could lie to her about loving her, about a great many things. But not about this.

"You believe me, don't you?" Ron asked.

"You've hurt me. You've hurt your family, your church."

"I know that. Don't you think it's ripping me apart?"

"Good."

"Good?"

"Because that's the only way God is going to get through to you."

His eyes cooled. "You're telling me what God is going to do?"

"Why shouldn't I? Are you going to deny that sin has consequences?"

Ron looked away, silent.

"I see you in there and I know you're not a killer, you're just a man. You're not the man I thought you were, and maybe that's my fault. Maybe I should have come out of the fog a long time ago."

"Dallas, don't." He hesitated, then spoke again. "Is Jared going to come see me?"

"I don't know."

"Will you please tell him I need to see him?"

"Yes, I'll try." She started to get up, feeling that if she stayed another moment she'd burst a blood vessel in her brain.

"Please stay for a little while," Ron said.

"I'll be in court Wednesday." Dallas put down the handset before he said another word.

2.

That was the worst part, her going away. The palpable hurt on her face. I never wanted to hurt my wife, but of course no man does when he falls to temptation. He just has part of himself take over without thought of hurt or consequence.

There is a slash in the fabric of our marriage now, a fabric I always thought would remain whole. But a lie is a razor. It cuts quick and deep.

And what of my son? The son who turned his back on me? Or was that me doing the turning?

I was so proud when he was born. The second child, a son. Something happens to a man when his son is born right before his eyes. He receives an infusion from on high, a divine current that reshapes and remolds what is inside him.

That new shape remains until something devastating warps it.

Like now.

I am misshapen.

3.

Dallas sighed with relief as she pulled into the garage. No media at the curb today. At least they'd figured out the Hamilton house was dry ground. They'd have to suck marrow from some other set of bones.

Her marrow was seriously depleted. Confronting Ron was not a happy event. Confronting herself about how she felt was even worse. She did not take kindly to being the thing she'd never thought she'd be—the betrayed wife.

Adultery. Betrayal.

Let him sit in jail. Let him sit there a long time and feel the punishment.

She gasped at her own thoughts. But they did not stop, and she did not try to stop them. Like steam coming out of a boiler, it was keeping her from blowing.

It good to be home, a place where people were. People who were not Ron or reporters or prosecutors. She was starting to grow fond of Tiana and Jamaal. And Jared, at least for the past week, had been civil, if distant.

But the house was silent when she came through the door. And she knew something was wrong.

"Hello?" No answer. She heard a scuffing sound in the hallway and went there. Jared was leaning against the wall.

"Why didn't you answer me?" Dallas said.

He shrugged and looked at the floor. What was he up to?

"Where's Tiana?"

"Home."

"What do you mean, *home?*"

"I took her home. Drove her. And the kid."

"Jared, look at me."

He looked. Dallas saw such a faraway aspect in his eyes that she wanted to forget everything else and hold him. She was also getting ready to scream.

"You're saying you drove her back to that abuser?"

"Mom, she wanted to go home. She wasn't a prisoner here."

"She wasn't going to go!" All sorts of terrible images came to her mind now. "I almost had her convinced. What did you say to her?"

"Nothing."

"Don't lie to me, Jared! I don't want to be lied to anymore!"

"You want the truth?" The chill in his voice nearly froze her.

"Yes. I want the truth."

"Then I'll give it to you. The truth is you can't save anybody, and it's driving you crazy. Dad's up for murder, and even if he didn't do it he probably did something he ought to be in jail for. And you can't save me. So you picked some poor woman who's going to end up dead anyway, and you made her a project."

"No—"

"Another Dallas Hamilton feel-good project, because it's a sure thing her family isn't feeling good."

"Stop it!"

"This woman doesn't want your charity. She doesn't want us, doesn't need us."

"Stop, please." Dallas sank down until she sat on the floor.

"Mom, I'm sorry."

Jared got down next to her and wrapped her up in his arms. Her tears started falling.

"No, Mom, don't do that."

She shook in his arms. He kept holding her. Like she had held him when he was sick or scared or hurting. Once when he was twelve and sick with a fever, trying to be brave, saying he didn't need anything, she lay next to him on his bed. He let her, put his head on her shoulder. Just before he drifted to sleep he said, thick of voice, "I'm glad you're here."

Dallas stopped crying and sat up. Jared started to say something, but she raised her hand.

"Things have to change," she said. "You and I have to come together on this. Your dad. He's going to lose everything. He's made a horrible mistake. He didn't kill this girl, I know it. He did wrong. He knows it. He's paying for it. Don't make him pay anything more, Jared. Go see him."

"Mom—"

"Please. He needs you. Go see him."

"I'll think about it."

"He needs you to forgive him."

"I'll try, okay?"

"Just do it, Jared."

"Mom, let me do it on my own. You want something to eat? Want me to make you some eggs or something?"

"No." She couldn't eat. She'd been losing weight.

Jared leaned back against the wall and looked at the ceiling. "It's all so messed up."

She got on her knees and faced him. "Jared, you used to believe in God when you were a kid. You can again."

"It's not that simple anymore. I mean, look at the world, Mom. Look at TV. Look at the people on *Cops*. Why would a good God allow that?"

"I know it's not simple. But, Jared, I know you used to believe, and—"

Jared shook his head. "You don't really know me, Mom."

"I do!"

"Yeah?"

He stood suddenly and pulled his T-shirt off over his head. His chest was pale under a patch of dark hair. Over his heart she saw the tattoo, USMC, with the marine insignia. She'd seen it before he'd shipped over to Iraq.

Then he turned around.

And Dallas gasped.

In the middle of his back, from neck to waist, was a blue-black tattoo of a sword. On the blade was written *I Come To Bring You Hell*.

4.

Her son's body, desecrated. The same body she had birthed and nursed and held and healed. Scarred now with this image.

Jared did not move, as if he wanted her to get the full effect of the shock.

"Pretty, huh?" He finally turned around and looked down at her. "Want to hear why I got it?"

She did not. She wanted it to go away, disappear right before her eyes, restore her son's skin to its purity. But she knew she had to hear just the same. She nodded slowly.

"I'll tell you," he said, "but you must not interrupt me. Understand that? Don't interrupt me because I'm only going to say this once, and once I get started I can't stop or it won't come out again. Got it?"

With effort she said, "Yes, Jared."

He nodded once, then lay down on the floor, facing up, and closed his eyes. For several minutes he breathed, rhythmically, his chest rising and falling like a soft swell in the ocean.

When he finally spoke, his voice was calm yet distant. "It was the end of the battle for Fallujah. Our squad was mopping up. We followed a column of infantrymen heading east just below the main highway between the northern and southern sections. It was like a science-fiction movie about the end of the earth. Rubble everywhere. Every house had at least one hole through it. We went inside houses, ready to shoot if we had to. And then, from the south side of the street, fire. And grenades. There were insurgents in a house, and they were trying to kill us."

Dallas listened, her heart falling.

"I felt a sting in my arm. I got hit in the bicep. But I didn't say anything because I could keep going. I could be one-handed if I had to. A buddy of mine got hit in the back, just below his flak jacket. They hauled him off to the big bus. That's the medical vehicle. I thought that's where I was going to end up eventually, only I was sure it would be by way of a body bag."

Jared's voice was almost a monotone. This, as much as the story itself, filled Dallas with dread.

"We kept going. Every step we had to watch. There were all these improvised explosive devices rigged. It was like they were waiting for us, just waiting. And every house we went into had some sort of weapon. Grenades. Whatever. We got to one house, empty, and some of the Iraqi special-forces guys assigned to our unit found some rice and vegetables and made lunch. We had some warm chow. But halfway through there was an explosion outside and a window shattered, throwing shards of glass into the food."

He paused, his eyes still closed, his breathing rhythmic.

"When that happened, I screamed. I screamed with anger and maybe fear, I don't know what all it was, but it didn't even seem like me. But I started to have thoughts I never had before. I won't even bother telling you about those, because it's not really the thing I want to tell. We got up and kept going, house to house.

"We got to one about two blocks from a staging area. We were almost out. It had been about five hours of this. I thought we'd make it out, and I'd get my stupid arm taken care of, get out of this hell town. And then we went into this house, full of rubble, full of . . ."

He stopped for a long moment. Dallas, silent, watched him. His breathing, for the first time, quickened.

"There was something about this place. It smelled more like death than any of the others we'd been in. Like it had been down the longest, like it was leading the death parade. I was the one who went around the last corner. The last look. That's when I heard something move."

Dallas watched his chest rising, falling.

"I lifted my weapon, trigger ready. I wish it had gone off. I wish it had exploded and killed me. I saw a little girl, maybe eight, nine. Dead. Spread out dead. She wasn't moving. There was a dog on her. It was chewing her body, it . . ."

Dallas felt inner wiring ripping out of sockets, shutting her down. Blacking out would have been a relief.

"I shot the dog. Just blew him away. And that's sort of the last thing I remember for a long time. I did wake up in a hospital and I do remember cursing. I cursed God because he hadn't seen fit to put me in that body bag. That's when I let go of the last of whatever beliefs I had. And that is what I wanted to tell you."

He slowly opened his eyes and raised to a sitting position.

"Jared . . ." Dallas leaned forward, and the moment she did, Jared put up his hand.

He pulled his shirt back on and said, "Don't say anything. Don't do anything. Just stay here."

He stood and walked away. Dallas heard the back door close.

And immediately she thought, *He's going to kill himself.*

She ran to the door and threw it open. "Jared!"

He was getting into his truck.

"Jared, wait."

He slammed his door shut. The window was rolled up.

"Jared, please!"

The truck started and burned rubber out of the driveway.

Dallas clutched her throat. *Dear God dear God don't let him do it restrain him God keep him from it dear God dear God.*

She dropped to her knees on the concrete, closed her eyes, made fists. *Dear God dear God protect him . . .*

5.

Jail has its own postal system.

It's more efficient than Uncle Sam's. There's a lot prisoners get done this way. Like making a jailhouse drink called pruno. They get a plastic bag and save up all their orange rinds and fruit bits and put them in water to ferment. It's powerful, I'm told.

But mostly they talk to each other through written messages, sometimes with the consent of the jailer.

I got one such message yesterday.

When my lunch was shoved through the door at me I saw on the tray a bit of tin foil. About the size of a marble.

That was definitely out of the ordinary. I knew immediately something was inside it.

Something meant for me.

I sat on my bunk and unraveled the foil.

Inside was a wad of toilet paper.

This I unraveled as well.

Someone had written on the toilet paper, in blue ink: "So then because thou art lukewarm, and neither cold nor hot, I will spew thee out of my mouth."

6.

At 11:42 p.m., Officer Jennica Brune of the Los Angeles Police Department, on routine patrol in Hollywood with her partner, spotted an illegally parked pickup on Franklin Avenue. She pulled her black and white parallel to the truck. She heard loud music blaring from inside. The engine appeared to be idling.

Her partner, Officer Jeffrey Benkert, got out and directed his flashlight into the cab. A male Caucasian was sprawled on the seat. Benkert knocked on the window. No response.

The truck was unlocked. With Officer Brune taking the sidewalk position, Benkert opened the door.

"Whoa," he shouted above the music. "We got ourselves a dewey."

Officer Brune knew he meant DUI—driving under the influence.

Benkert shut off the stereo and tried to rouse the occupant. He was out.

"I'm guessing this guy's gonna be over two-point-oh," Benkert told Brune.

"What's he been drinking?" Brune said.

"Beer. Talk about your open containers. There must be eight, nine bottles in here. Looks like Dos Equis is his preferred label." Benkert sighed. "Let's take him in."

SEVEN

1.

After a fitful sleep in a holding cell, Jared was informed he was at the Hollywood station on Wilcox, that his truck was impounded, and that he would get one free call. He used it to call Cara. He wasn't ready to spring this on his mother.

When his sister came for him, he felt embarrassed and dirty, and it didn't help that Cara was silent all the way to her car and all the way out to Hollywood Boulevard.

Finally Cara said, "So what are you going to tell Mom?"

He shrugged.

"She's been sick with worry. I won't let you stab her in the heart."

"Thank you so much. You ever thought about going into psych?"

"Shut it, Jared."

"Much better."

Cara shook her head. "You think you can dance away from this?"

"Quit trying to play big sister, will you?"

"I'm just your sister then, and you know what that means? I love you, dork."

"Sounds like it."

"Why don't you listen to your family?"

"Like Dad? Great role model he is, huh?"

"That's real forgiving of you, Jared."

"Here it comes."

Cara jammed the brakes. Tires shrieked as she turned the car to the curb in front of a Chinese restaurant.

Jared lurched against the shoulder strap. "Are you nuts?"

"You're not the only one with problems, you know."

"What are you doing?"

"I want you to come back to church," Cara said.

"What's that going to do?"

"At least you won't be drinking."

"For two hours maybe."

"It's a start."

"Just drive," Jared said.

"Promise you'll come to church. You still have friends there."

He sat still, eyes directed out the window. A man in a Dodgers hat stood outside the Chinese restaurant, yelling at someone through the door. Jared couldn't tell if the guy was angry, high, or a combination of both.

"Cara, I'm messed up," he said. "I know that. The VA says it's PTSD, but I don't know. It's like my genes got messed up and I'm this totally new person, and nobody knows who I am."

"Somebody knows," Cara said.

He glared at her. "God? Is that what you're saying?"

"Yes."

"Have him send me a memo," Jared said.

"He will. In church. Say you'll come with us."

"I'm not going to—"

"Promise or I'll get out and take you down, right there on the sidewalk."

A laugh poked through Jared's anger. He remembered when Cara could actually do that to him, back when he was scrawny and she was in a tennis champ. It got him mad back then and he swore to himself he'd become a Marine someday. Just so he could wrestle his big sister to the ground.

"I'll think about it," he said. "Now drive on."

2.

Still no word from Jared.

It was past nine in the morning and Dallas paced the family room like a big cat in a cage. She prayed but kept looking at the phone. If she didn't hear anything in a few hours, she'd call the police.

That reminded her about the strange message she'd had on her cell phone last night. A male voice, a whisper. *Call me. Very important.* He gave a number with a 310 area code.

Terrific. No doubt some reporter seeking an exclusive got her number!

How?

Somebody gave it away.

No, that couldn't be. That would mean someone close to her was leaking information. Maybe someone from the church. She couldn't allow herself to think that. She had enough to deal with without cooking up conspiracy theories. *Maybe it was Oliver Stone.*

Stop it!

It was probably just some sleazy reporter who had a way of finding out these things.

But she wasn't going to call, no way. She did jot the number down on a pad just in case she had to tell the cops about this.

She had to do something besides stew. She fired up the computer in the study and went to Google. She wanted to read more about posttraumatic stress disorder, especially as it related to the soldiers coming home from Iraq. In seconds she had a slew of links and started to check them out.

She came across the account of a Marine soldier whose profile sounded eerily like Jared's. A kid raised in a Christian home in the South, who came back covered in tattoos.

Soldiers like this signal that a crisis is unfolding, mental-health experts say. One out of six soldiers returning from Iraq suffers from a severe type of posttraumatic stress. Experts say they have not seen its like.

The Pentagon, which did not anticipate the extent of the problem, is scrambling to find resources to address it.

A recent study found that 15.6 percent of Marines and 17.1 percent of soldiers surveyed after they returned from Iraq suffered major depression, generalized anxiety, or posttraumatic stress disorder — a debilitating, sometimes lifelong change in the brain's chemistry that can include flashbacks, sleep disorders, panic attacks, violent outbursts, acute anxiety, and emotional numbness.

Army mental-health experts say there is reason to believe the war's ultimate psychological fallout will worsen. The army survey of 6,200 soldiers and Marines included only troops willing to report their problems.

"The bad news is that the study underestimated the prevalence of what we are going to see down the road," said Dr. Frederick J. Matthews, a professor of psychiatry and pharmacology at Johns Hopkins School of Medicine. "And there is some aggravating factor underneath the surface of all this that we need to more deeply explore."

Aggravating factor.

The words stuck in her mind. What could that be? She jotted the phrase on a pad and determined to follow it up.

She switched to the Google news site to see what was being written about Ron. More sensationalized stuff with the sex angle. There wasn't going to be any getting away from that.

One squib with the term "Melinda Perry" in it caught her attention. She clicked on the link. Dallas couldn't get past the gut feel of the woman scorned. Melinda Perry, though dead, was a rival. What had drawn Ron to her? What had she done to seduce him?

She read desperately for answers.

Melinda Perry, the deceased, was also known as Melinda Chance. She was, by the account of industry insiders, a rising star in adult films. Producer/Director Vic Lu, one of the industry's top moneymakers and principal owner of LookyLu Productions, said Ms. Perry was on the verge of stardom.

"I discovered her and knew she had what it takes to be a superstar," Lu said in a phone interview. "I mean, she had it all."

She had it all. Apparently Ron thought so too.

She skipped the rest of the sex-themed stories and found some covered locally. And then, at the *Daily News* site, she found a quote that was apparently being readied for the next day's edition:

Councilman Bernie Halstrom, who was working with Hamilton on possible regulations of the adult-entertainment industry in Chatsworth, mentioned the case.

"I know Ron Hamilton to be a good, decent man. I cannot, of course, comment on a pending criminal matter."

"Why not?" Dallas whispered out loud. "What's stopping you?"

And then it hit her. There was something bigger than Ron going on here. It wasn't just about him and his ministry. The overarching issue was the one they both cared passionately about — the evil of pornography.

This case was going to be used to try to destroy that work. She was not about to let that happen. She'd promised Ron she would keep the pressure on Bernie Halstrom, and she would.

She heard a key in the front door. She jumped up from the desk and nearly ran to the foyer.

Jared was standing there, head slightly down, with a serious-looking Cara behind him.

"I'll let you take it from here, Mom," Cara said.

3.

Cara entered the sunlight of her apartment and went immediately to the window. This was her favorite place to kneel before God and pray.

Prayer, she'd come to believe, was her particular duty, a calling. She'd been called the hard way, but that was fine with her.

When she was ten, the neuromuscular disease she had trouble pronouncing threatened to take away all the things she loved most —running, playing, keeping up with the boys. She took treatments and therapy for three years before the doctors said the disorder would stay with her for life.

That's when she really started praying. Before, she prayed in obedience to her parents and Sunday school teachers. Now it was from a scared heart.

Alone in her room, she had underlined passages in her Bible about prayer. She especially loved something Jesus said in Luke. "Which of you fathers, if your son asks for a fish, will give him a snake instead? Or if he asks for an egg, will give him a scorpion? If you then, though you are evil, know how to give good gifts to your children, how much more will your Father in heaven give the Holy Spirit to those who ask him!"

She asked. For a whole year she asked, clinging to the promises. And she was healed.

Now, almost fifteen years later, she still prayed the promises, even when the answers weren't what she expected or God seemed silent.

She didn't care that some of her friends teased her about it. One, Susan Farmer, called her "praying Cara," which was a riff on the Stephen King novel *Carrie*. Cara looked it up.

> Tommy Erbter, age five, was biking up the other side of the street. He was a small, intense-looking boy on a twenty-inch Schwinn with bright red training wheels. He was humming "Scooby Doo, where are you?" under his breath. He saw Carrie, brightened, and stuck out his tongue.
> "Hey . . . Ol' prayin' Carrie!"

Even though Susan only meant it in fun, it did strike Cara that she must have seemed as odd as Carrie White to those who didn't believe in God.

For Carrie, of course, the ultimate answer came in the form of murderous, telekinetic powers. For Cara Hamilton, the answers came from God.

Her apartment was on the third floor of a security building in Encino. A place she could call home and feel safe in. She still displayed her love of sports in the décor. Posters of some of her favorite athletes, like Serena Williams and Annika Sorenstam, were framed on the wall. A small case held some of her tennis trophies.

She vaguely recalled that a tournament she wanted to attend was coming up, but just as quickly the thought left her.

She had Jared on her mind now.

She'd been in prayer for her father and mother, and now her burden shifted to her little brother. This was a spiritual battle for his soul.

At the window she knelt and closed her eyes. She was going to stay on the front lines for Jared until the enemy's power was broken.

4.

After getting Jared's truck from police impound, Dallas suggested they grab a Papa John's pizza. The two of them, just like old times.

Before the storm-tossed seas of his teen years, Jared had been open and demonstrative with affection for his mother. Some of the best times they had were when Ron was on the road and Cara was in her room, talking to friends on the phone.

There would be eating and talking, a giant pepperoni pizza with extra cheese between them, sometimes watching a British mystery on television. Jared especially loved Miss Marple and liked to sit on the sofa next to Dallas, watching the intrepid Jane solve the latest to-do in her village.

Here they were again, under quite different circumstances. Dallas knew beyond question now that Jared was on a dark slide that had to be stopped. She had no idea how, except by prayer and by keeping him close.

They brought the pizza to the table out back, where once upon a time the four of them dined during the summer months. When they were settled, Dallas said, "Would you say a blessing for the food?"

"You do it," he said.

She prayed out loud for the food, adding a silent prayer for Jared at the end.

"You doing okay, Mom?"

Dallas nodded. "I've got a little bit of callus developing, I think. I hope."

"We all do, maybe."

"Why don't you go see your dad? I know he'd love—"

"How is he?"

"Scared."

"They going to let him out?"

"No bail yet. Jeff's going to ask for a new hearing."

"Funny, isn't it?"

"Funny?"

"Him in there and me out here. Shouldn't be that way."

"Shouldn't be that way for either of you."

"Maybe I'll be in soon enough."

"Don't talk that way, Jared."

He took a bite of pizza but didn't look like he tasted it. They ate in silence for a while.

Jared said, "Try not to worry about me, Mom."

"How can I do that? I've always worried about you. You're my son, that's what I do for a living."

"I bet you don't worry about Cara."

"I do. Just in a different way."

"Yeah, she's normal. And she doesn't get drunk. She's the good one."

"Jared, don't say that."

"Why not? Didn't you and Dad always tell me to be honest? Isn't that what a Christian is supposed to be, totally honest? Confess the old sins. Well, I've got a trunkful."

"Good."

"What?"

"It's good that you've got a trunkful, and that you told me about it, and now you can go to church and talk to God about it."

"Why do I have to go to church to talk to God?"

"Do you talk to God?"

"No."

"Then come to church and just listen for a while."

"I've been listening all my life. Do you know I hear Dad in my sleep sometimes? I hear his voice. He's usually telling me something that I don't want to hear. So I make myself wake up. I've lost a lot of sleep that way."

Dallas looked at the pizza box, grease stains on the bottom. *God, help me reach him. Give me the words to say.*

"Got an idea," Dallas said.

"What?"

"Remember the way we used to watch mysteries on TV?"

"Sure."

"See if one's on."

Inside, Jared turned on the TV while Dallas brought in the dishes. When she got to the family room, it was no mystery on TV.

Jared was looking at the Hank Dunaway show.

Dunaway was the hottest interview show going on cable news, sometimes featuring a celebrity or newsmaker, other times a panel discussing current events.

This night, the guest host was that blond woman, the former prosecutor who always assumed the worst about any current case. Dallas always thought she was a little too zealous, a little too show biz. And truth seemed to be the real victim whenever she clamped her jaws on a case.

"Tonight," she droned, "the Ron Hamilton murder trial. Our panel of experts will analyze what will go on in court tomorrow, and what we can expect in the months ahead. All that and more on *Hank Dunaway Tonight.*"

"You want me to turn it off?" Jared said.

"No. We might as well see what everybody's saying."

The blond looked at the camera with her liquid sincerity and in her superior tone explained what "everyone" already knew. Ron was guilty. The pretrial motions were just smoke and mirrors. Then she handed it off to a guest, some lawyer in Florida, a guy with hundred-dollar hair.

"No surprises," he said. "Jefferson Waite will make a motion to suppress, and it will be denied. Then Ron Hamilton will be ordered to stand trial. Remember, the threshold at a preliminary hearing is very low, so it doesn't take much to convince a judge to bind a defendant over."

"But the evidence is overwhelming," the blond insisted. "I mean, you have the DNA, the sexual contact, the lying to police."

"We don't know that he lied," hair boy said. "We know that he didn't volunteer everything."

"That's a lie in my book, and a pretty stupid one. It was bound to be exposed."

"Turn it off," Dallas said.

Jared clicked the remote and the tube withdrew into blessed silence.

"See if you can find a DVD or something." Dallas's phone chimed. She recognized the number. Karen, Ron's agent.

"Oh, my dear sweet Dallas, how are you? I just watched the Dunaway show."

Dallas leaned against the kitchen wall. "Some fun."

"You doing okay?"

"Hanging in there. The way those circus guys used to hang by their teeth way up in the air."

Karen chuckled. "Tell me about it. I've had days where my clients were all ..." There was a pause, and Karen said, "I'm sorry. There's no comparison to what you're going through."

This time there was a longer pause, and Dallas knew there was more to this call than an expression of concern.

"Dallas, I'm afraid I've got some bad news regarding the contract."

Dallas closed her eyes. Her mental wheels turned and locked in place. It made sense and seemed so inevitable. "Canceled, I suppose."

"Withdrawn, actually, since the contract never went out. I'm just sick about it."

"So the publishers have assumed his guilt, have they? What wonderful people."

"I know it doesn't help, but if you see it from their perspective, they—"

"Why should I? Are they sitting around seeing it from my perspective?"

"You have every right to be hurt."

"Thank you for that permission."

Silence. Then Dallas added, "Karen, I'm sorry. It's just that this is another—"

"You don't have to say it, Dallas. I understand completely. I'm not going to give up fighting for this project. And if there's anything I can do, anything, I want you to call me."

"Sure."

Dallas clicked off. And threw her cell phone across the room.

5.

It was nine thirty the following morning before Dallas felt sufficiently calmed down to turn up a little heat on Bernie Halstrom.

Halstrom's chief aide, Clark Thoms, tried to give Dallas the administrative runaround when she showed up at the field office.

"The councilman's schedule is just packed, Mrs. Hamilton," he said. Thoms was a bushy-haired grad-student type, with wire-rimmed glasses framing ambitious eyes. "But I know he wants to talk to you."

"No time like the present," Dallas said. "I won't be ten minutes."

"I wish I could, but—"

"Just ask him." Dallas made it sound like *tell him.* "And remind him that the reporters want to talk to me in the worst way, and I don't want to have to say anything negative about anybody."

Thoms's forehead made little rows. "Let me see what I can do."

Predictably, Thoms could do what was expedient, and a few minutes later Dallas was in the office of Councilman Bernie Halstrom.

Dallas knew his history. Bernie was elected to the city council in the late nineties after a twenty-year career with the Los Angeles County Sheriff's Department. He was fifty-two, married, with two successful sons. One of them was a Wall Street lawyer. The other was a graduate of the famous USC film school and was slowly climbing the Hollywood ladder.

Bernie greeted Dallas with his usual gregariousness. "Dallas, I'm so glad you came over." He took her hands in both of his and held them warmly. "I've been thinking about you and Ron almost nonstop."

Dallas wanted to say, *Then why aren't you supporting him?* Instead, she said, "Thanks," with little enthusiasm.

"Been meaning to come to Hillside soon for services," Bernie said. He was a true Los Angeles politician who did not practice any single religion but walked among them all. Voters, after all, were in synagogues and mosques as well as churches and cathedrals.

"I'm sure this whole thing is going to be straightened out. Jeff Waite's a great lawyer." He offered Dallas a chair, then took the one next to it.

She started to feel a little foolish. What was she to expect from a man who had more than just the Hamilton family problems to worry about?

"Bernie, I'm sorry for imposing on you like this."

"Nothing of it. I'm happy to have this chance to talk to you."

"It's just that this has become such a high-profile case now."

"Tell me about it." Bernie shook his head. "It's something you can't control. It's arbitrary what the media decides to clamp down on. If it wasn't Ron, it'd be somebody else. I've been there, believe me."

Bernie became a huge target three or four years ago when a female aide in his office accused him of sexual harassment. It was front-page news in the *Times* for about a week. As usual, the *Times* took the side of the accuser, slanting all their coverage against the councilman. They even brought up a fifteen-year-old accusation from his time on the police force, one that had been summarily dismissed by an administrative proceeding.

The *Times* never questioned the female aide's story. When a *Daily News* reporter discovered she had a lurid past and had lied on her official employment documents, the *Times* waited two days before making a tepid admission that the case against Halstrom was going nowhere.

"One of the things you have to do," Bernie said, "is hang onto your faith that the truth will come out eventually. I know Ron couldn't have done what they say. Murder, I mean."

Bernie cleared his throat. What was left unsaid, Dallas realized, was that the other part, Ron's adultery, *was* something he had done.

Quickly, Halstrom added, "Ron is as decent a guy as I know. We're all human around here. Even me." He laughed. "We make mistakes. But that's all they are, mistakes. Sins, you would say. Isn't God in the forgiving business?"

Dallas half smiled. That's exactly what Ron used to say. And then she realized why Bernie was so good at what he did. He knew, really knew, about the people he worked with. He knew enough to quote one of Ron's own expressions.

"You're right," Dallas said, even as she wondered if she could forgive Ron. That hadn't happened yet. "I was just hoping that maybe you'd keep up the pressure on the porn regulations you and Ron were working on."

Bernie's district included Chatsworth, which was by all accounts the center of the pornography business in the United States. Dallas had never understood how it could be allowed to prosper like a legitimate enterprise. Nor had Ron.

When Ron's book became so popular, it was Bernie who called on him with the idea of hammering out a new set of regulations for the city that would severely limit, if not eliminate, the manufacturing of pornography in Los Angeles.

It was admittedly an uphill battle. So little had been done over the years. Politicians had shown all the backbone of soufflé against the porn that enveloped neighborhoods and polluted souls.

"Believe me, Dallas," Bernie said, "I'm as determined as ever. This setback is not going to stop me from trying to put the brakes on the porn business."

"It's flesh trade, not business." She thought a moment. "What do you know about this guy Vic Lu?"

He blinked. "How did you come across that name?"

"I read about him on the Internet. He's apparently one of the bigwigs in pornography around here. He was the one who discovered Melinda Perry and put her in his movies."

Bernie scratched underneath his chin. "Yes. LookyLu Productions. Nice double meaning there, huh? Cute. But he's well known around here. He's one of the more successful adult-film producers."

"You mean pornography, don't you? Calling these *adult films* seems too respectable."

"Agreed."

"Let me just ask you, Bernie. Straight out. I've never really gotten a square answer on this. How can the law allow sex acts to be filmed and sold? I mean, prostitution is illegal. Why isn't this?"

With a bemused smile, Bernie said, "The courts have given this some strange thought. They have held there is a distinction between people being paid to have sex as actors, but not as individuals in a free exchange."

Incredulous, Dallas asked, "What on earth is the difference?"

"You've got me. Lawyers pretend to understand this stuff."

"Incredible."

Bernie nodded. "What it all comes down to, Dallas, is that we have the kind of society we want. If enough people want porn, they're going to get it. The courts have not been helpful. Over the years they've allowed more and more stuff to be produced, protected by the First Amendment. I doubt our founding fathers would be pleased."

"Give me a flamethrower and some addresses," Dallas said. "I'll take it out of the hands of the courts."

"I believe you would. Heck, I might even join you. Until flamethrowers become legal, though, rest assured, I'll keep pushing for tighter controls. And, Dallas, try to get some rest. You can't carry all this on your own."

6.

At one thirty, Dallas arrived back at the criminal courts building for Jeff Waite's argument to suppress evidence. There was a massive press presence outside, with news vans and camera lights and scurrying talking heads holding microphones.

Dallas got in, feeling sick. But she refused to let it show. She walked inside without a word to the screaming press or to anyone else and found refuge in the elevator.

Jeff Waite was already in the courtroom, sitting at the counsel table, going over notes. The friendly bailiff showed her to her reserved seat. As he did he wagged a finger at some reporters. The warning was clear. *Keep away from her unless she talks to you first.*

Seated, Dallas took a moment to pray. She found herself praying for wisdom, which surprised her. Why wasn't she praying for Ron's outright release?

Because I have doubts.

Before she could argue with herself, the side door opened and Ron was led in by a deputy. He looked pale. And thinner.

He gave Dallas a cursory glance before sitting down next to Jeff.

At one thirty-five, Judge Bartells entered the courtroom and called the case.

"Mr. Waite, you may address the court on your motion to suppress."

Jeff stood up and went to the lawyer's podium. Without notes. "It's really quite simple, Your Honor. Deputy Barnes testified that he arrived at the Star Motel without probable cause to search. All he had was a 911 dispatch."

"Which certainly gives a reasonable suspicion to investigate."

"Investigate, yes. Break into a motel room, no."

"But it was the motel manager who let him in."

"That is irrelevant, Your Honor. It's true that Mr. Franze is a private citizen, and normally a citizen does not trigger the Fourth Amendment. But it does trigger when the citizen is working at the behest of law enforcement. It was at the request of Deputy Barnes that Mr. Franze unlocked the motel room door. As you know, Your Honor, a motel room is as protected as any residence, which means the police must have a search warrant before they can enter. And Deputy Barnes did not have a search warrant."

"What about exigent circumstances? Didn't Deputy Barnes have reason to believe a victim of a crime might be inside room 105?"

"To qualify under the exigency exception, there must be a factual basis for that belief. Which brings us back to the uncorroborated tip of an anonymous informer."

"That would be Mr. Knudsen," Judge Bartells said. "Not anonymous."

"For the purposes of this preliminary hearing, Judge, he is. He was not called. We don't even know if he exists. All we have is Mr. Franze's testimony about him. And Mr. Franze's recollection about a hearsay statement from this Mr. Knudsen that there was trouble in room 105. Even that is not enough to establish a factual basis. All we have is a hearsay report that there was some screaming going on in room 105. But that screaming may have been in the nature of a loud argument, or it may have been in the nature of screaming in ecstasy."

"Ecstasy?"

"We don't know. All we have is an opinion that was phoned in. No case has ever allowed that to be the basis of a warrantless entry, Your Honor."

"What about the DNA evidence?" the judge asked. "That would have been discovered during the autopsy, no matter when the body was found, or by whom."

"But my client would not have been in custody as a suspect. The connection was only made because of the illegal entry and the subsequent evidence that was gathered as a result. This, Your Honor, is the fruit of the poisonous tree. It must be suppressed."

The judge paused, thinking about it, and Dallas felt a tenuous reed of hope spring up in her. Could it really be possible? Suppress the evidence? She'd seen Court TV a few times. Didn't suppressing evidence mean the case was tossed out? Over? That Ron would walk out of the courtroom a free man?

She looked at the prosecutor again and saw him sit up straight in his chair. Jeff's sword had drawn blood.

"Mr. Freton," the judge said, "do you have a response?"

Freton stood and buttoned his coat, as if formally rising to lead a flag salute at a chamber of commerce luncheon.

"I must say I admire Mr. Waite's creativity. But I must also remind the court of the notice requirements. Our office received no notice of these grounds."

"And I would remind my colleague," Jeff said, "that it was evidence adduced on the stand, from his own witness, that gives rise to these grounds. Where there is a warrantless entry, it is the burden of the prosecution to prove an exception."

The judge put up his hand, then lowered it slowly like a sage. "I believe Mr. Waite has the right to make his motion. What have you got to say on the merits?"

That seemed to throw Freton a curve. He bent down to confer with his colleague, a woman in a dark burgundy suit. She was the one doing most of the talking. She flipped through a book on the table and pointed to something.

The prosecutor addressed the judge. "Your Honor, there is the question of standing. It was not the defendant's motel room. The defendant was not present when the search occurred. The Fourth Amendment is personal, Your Honor, and the moving party must have a proprietary interest in the place searched. The defendant does not have this. No standing, no motion."

Dallas was not following all the words. It was a legal fight. But Jefferson Waite did not look fazed.

Jeff said, "Your Honor, it is the prosecution's theory that my client was having an affair with the victim. If that is so, he was in that motel room as an invited guest. The Supreme Court, in *Olson*, held that an invited guest has standing to challenge the search of a premises."

Now there was a long pause from the judge. He was thinking about it. Dallas felt her heartbeat quicken.

She also felt something strange and disturbing. It was about Ron. His betrayal was heavy upon her. She wanted to ask the judge to stop the proceedings before he granted the motion. Stop so she could go over to Ron while he was still in custody and make sure he was feeling the torment and consequences of his actions. Look in his eyes, maybe, and see if they still held love for her, any at all. Because if they didn't ... what would she do?

The judge said, "I have considered your points and authorities, Mr. Waite. Your motion asserts that the defendant has standing because of his status as an invited guest, based on an assertion that he was having an affair with the victim. But the People have not made that essential to their case. I don't know of any case that holds the defense can base a motion on a theory yet to be made by the prosecution. In view of that, the court denies the motion to suppress."

Even though Jeff had prepared her for this, Dallas still felt the defeat personally, almost as if she herself were on trial. Maybe she was. Certainly in the court of public opinion her every move was being monitored.

"I further find that the People have presented sufficient evidence to bind the defendant, Ronald Hamilton, over for trial. Shall we set a trial date, gentlemen?"

7.

And so I go to trial, up there for the world to see and flay. Oh, Dallas. What's this going to do to her?

Got them to get me a Bible. At first my guy, my keeper, my chief jailer —Deputy Dawg, I call him; his name is Daugherty—said I couldn't have one. I reminded him of my rights under the US Constitution and that this was a very public case and it would not be good press if this ever got out.

Deputy Dawg is not a bad sort. He said he'd see what he could do.

Came back an hour later with a paperback King James. Good old King James. Hadn't cracked one of those in years.

I opened to the passage I wanted to read. Revelation 3. I scanned down until I found the key word, Laodiceans, and read:

> And unto the angel of the church of the Laodiceans write; These things saith the Amen, the faithful and true witness, the beginning of the creation of God; I know thy works, that thou art neither cold nor hot; I would thou wert cold or hot.
>
> So, then, because thou art lukewarm, and neither cold nor hot, I will spew thee out of my mouth.
>
> Because thou sayest, I am rich, and increased with goods, and have need of nothing, and knowest not that thou art wretched, and miserable, and poor, and blind, and naked,
>
> I counsel thee to buy of me gold tried in the fire, that thou mayest be rich; and white raiment, that thou mayest be clothed, and that the shame of thy nakedness do not appear; and anoint thine eyes with eyesalve, that thou mayest see.
>
> As many as I love, I rebuke and chasten; be zealous, therefore, and repent.
>
> Behold, I stand at the door, and knock; if any man hear my voice, and open the door, I will come in to him, and will sup with him, and he with me.

I tried to remember what my prof said about this passage in Bible college. Revelation was always a mystery to me, and I never got heavy into prophecy and end-times stuff. All I remembered was that luke-warm was something not to be. Being spewed out of Christ's mouth was not a good prospect.

I have grown lukewarm over the years of my success.

Was it even success at all?

I had a church of eight thousand. In the eyes of my peers and the church world I was a rousing success.

I.

The word that crept into the center of my unspoken vocabulary.
How did it happen? How did I drift away?
Questions. More questions.
Who was my interrogator, the toilet-paper prophet?

8.

"Dallas," Jeff Waite said, "we have a very important decision to make. Not an easy one."

Once again he had graciously come to the house to talk to her. It was the day after the decision to send Ron to trial, so there was a fresh media encampment out on the street. That was another reason she was grateful for Jeff's presence. Someone to run interference.

"It's going to be Ron's call," Jeff said, "but we're family here. I want you to know everything, because you may need to help Ron make the decision."

"What decision?"

"Whether to plead guilty."

"But he's not." Dallas searched his eyes. "Is he?"

"I can only tell you what the evidence is. You heard it. You know what we're up against. They've got Ron caught in a lie, and they've got the forensic evidence to prove he had sexual relations with the victim. It's what the prosecutors call a slam dunk."

"He didn't kill her. I know he didn't."

"All that matters is what the jury will be allowed to hear, Dallas. No one will care what we think about Ron. If I had something, anything I could put on in Ron's favor, I would. Stegman, my investigator, tracked down this guy Knudsen and interviewed him. He's not going to be of any help. He didn't see anything, only heard some voices he can't identify."

"So we're just throwing in the towel?"

Jeff shook his head. "If you and Ron want to go to trial, I will do everything in my power to create a reasonable doubt about every aspect of the prosecutor's case. That's my job. But it's also my professional obligation to inform you of what we're up against and what the options are."

"Are there any good options?"

"If Ron pleads to second-degree murder, he'll be looking at fifteen to life, but with the possibility of parole. To be quite frank, this victim does not appear likely to have anyone who will appear at a parole hearing to argue against Ron's release."

"That we know of."

"This isn't one of those cases where a nice girl from some well-to-do home in a nice neighborhood gets brutally murdered and someone from the family shows up every time there's a hearing."

"That sounds harsh."

"I'm just giving you the reality. You need that. Now, if Ron elects to go to trial and is convicted, he's going to get the max. He'll die in prison."

She tried to let that picture pass over her, but it stayed. "How long do we have to make a decision?" she asked.

"All the way up to trial. Stegman and I will keep looking around for something, but this case seems pretty straightforward."

"Except for the fact that Ron didn't do it." Her voice was louder than she'd expected.

Jeff folded his hands together as if trying to be patient. "If we could find some exculpatory evidence, pointing toward innocence, we'd have something to hang a trial on."

"Then we have to find it," Dallas said. "Oh, one other thing. Jared was picked up for drunk driving."

Jeff nodded, almost as if he'd expected the news. "Did you get an appearance date?"

"Next month."

"I'll handle it."

"Jeff, I can't ask—"

"I'll handle it, Dallas. Let's wait and see what the arrest report says. Meanwhile, is there anything else I can do for you?"

She folded her arms. "Reverse time?"

"Hey, there are some things even lawyers can't do."

Dallas tried to smile.

"One more thing," Jeff said. "Ron doesn't want bail."

"What?"

"I tried to talk him into it, but he said he absolutely doesn't want me to move for bail. That means I can't."

"Did he say why?"

Jeff shook his head. "I have a feeling he wants to punish himself. If you can talk him into reconsidering, I've got a bail motion all ready."

But Dallas wondered if she wanted to talk him out of it after all. Maybe some jail time was just what Ron needed to get his life straight.

EIGHT

Sunday morning Dallas shook Jared awake at seven-thirty.

"We're going to church," she said.

He grumbled something vaguely negative.

"Rise and shine. Cara's meeting us."

"Mom, I said—"

"I know what you said." She drew the covers halfway off him. He was facedown. She saw the vile tattoo. "We are going to the house of the Lord together, and I don't want to hear any more about it."

He turned his face toward her. "I'm not seven, Mom."

"Listen to me, Jared. I don't care how old you are or how old I am, or what's happened to you in the past. All I know is that we need to go worship God and that's what we're going to do, and I have access to ice water and I will use it. Don't think I won't, because I'm not completely rational at the moment, if you get my drift."

An hour later, Dallas and Jared were on their way to Hillside.

This was her first Sunday back since Ron's arrest.

It felt a little like coming home, and a little like stepping into the spotlight on a bare stage. There were plenty of well-wishers and hugs, and double the number of curious, probing eyes.

She didn't blame Jared for standing off to the side, leafing through the visitor pamphlets with his head down. At least Cara joined him there, looking protective.

When the worship band started in, they made it to a row in the back. A few more hellos and hugs and even a hand or two for Jared.

Who did not sing any of the worship songs.

At least he's here. At least he came. Witness to his spirit, Lord.

The order of worship was the same as always, with a beautiful solo by Priscilla Potts, who was a member of Hillside and a recording artist.

Then Bob Benson took to the pulpit.

"Welcome to Hillside," he said, his voice full and vibrant. "We hope this is a place where you can settle back and be comfortable for a while. We're glad you're here."

Behind him, on the big screen, a video appeared. A dour-looking man walked along a busy sidewalk.

"I'd like to introduce you to a guy I know. Negative Ned is a guy you've seen around. Probably pass him on the street all the time. He usually has his head down. Probably just kicked his dog too."

On the video screen, as if on cue, the man looked directly at the audience, frowning, and that's where the image froze.

Ripples of laughter around the church. Though it was harder than she'd expected to see someone besides Ron up there, Dallas had to admit Bob had *it*. The charisma, delivery, and timing that put an audience into the proverbial palm of his hand.

"What would you say to ol' Ned if you met him on the street? Go home and kick the dog again? Or would you try to tell him that God has a better way? Would you tell him we all go through tough times, but we all have a choice how to handle them?"

If only it were that easy.

The video started up again, this time with an actor smiling and practically dancing down the street. It was over the top, and the whole church laughed.

"That's my other friend, Positive Pete. He's the guy with the perpetually sunny disposition. You don't see him as much, do you?"

Jared leaned over to Dallas and whispered, "Are we in third grade here or something?"

"Shh."

"But Positive Pete has learned to trust God and make the choice to be positive about his circumstances."

"Why doesn't he crack open a Bible?" Jared said.

"Quiet."

Bob did use a few Bible verses, shot up on the screen for all to see. But mostly it was an entertaining and uplifting sermon. Dallas couldn't help feeling some tension, though. Part of her didn't want the people to be uplifted or entertained. She wanted them to be sad about Ron. Were they so quick to forget?

At the end of the sermon, as if reading her mind, Bob changed to a serious tone. "As we leave today, let's remember to keep praying for our brother Ron Hamilton. Pray for justice to be done. For his protection. For his recovery."

The last word rankled her a bit. But she couldn't argue with it. Ron did need to recover.

More well-wishers approached her after the service. Lisa Benson was last of all, with a warm embrace and an invitation to have coffee the next day.

Cara said good-bye in the parking lot and kissed her brother. "Be good."

He looked at her, plastered a huge grin on his face, and jumped up in the air. "I will! I'm Positive Pete."

"Nice sarcasm," Cara said.

"I'm trying to be good at something," Jared said.

Dallas took Jared's arm and started him toward her car at the far end of the lot. "Your sister loves you," she said.

"That makes two of you."

"And your father."

"Sure."

"Jared."

He was about to say something, then stopped. He pointed. "Look at the car."

Dallas saw that her front left headlight was smashed. "Just great! When did that happen?"

"There's a note."

A piece of paper under the driver's-side windshield wiper. Dallas removed it and read: *Why don't you return my call?*

"What's it say?" Jared said.

Dallas couldn't speak.

"Let me see." She handed it to him. "It's got to be a joke," he said.

"A sick joke, if it is. But who would do that? And who would know this is my car? Someone at church?"

Jared shrugged. "I think we should call the police on this."

"Wonderful. Just what I need to cap a fine day at church."

"Don't be a Negative Ned, Mom."

"Be quiet."

2.

All night Dallas kept jerking awake, thinking about the headlight, trying to find some way to believe the vandalism was just random. She knew it was not. Somebody was out to mess with her mind. But who?

In the morning she took a long bath. At nine o'clock she felt just human enough to meet Lisa for coffee.

Dallas wore a broad-brimmed hat and dark glasses and drove out to a Starbucks in Agoura, making sure no newshound followed her.

When she got there she found Lisa similarly attired. It was Lisa who had suggested the disguises and the location. Agoura was far enough away from the Valley that Dallas felt she could walk around without hassle.

Still, she was glad for the hat and glasses.

"This is all so cloak and dagger," Dallas said as she and Lisa took their lattes to an outside table that afforded a fair degree of anonymity.

"But fun, you have to admit." Lisa fairly giggled. "Don't you think half the fun in the world is putting the big runaround on the know-it-alls? Like the stupid media that's hounding you?"

Dallas smiled in agreement. She couldn't help feeling swept up in Lisa Benson's youthful exuberance. The girl was so full of life and energy.

Putting on her Bette Davis voice, Dallas said, "Fasten your seatbelt. It's going to be a bumpy morning."

Lisa shook her head. "You crack me up. Where did you ever learn to do that stuff?"

"It's a gift."

"You should be on Leno with that act."

"Thanks. And thanks for asking me out."

"I just wanted to spend time with you," Lisa said. "For support and prayer."

"I appreciate it."

"Bob and I are just like you and Ron, in a way. I absolutely know what you're going through."

Did she really? She and Bob were in the spring of their marriage, and it was still fresh and clean and vital. And she did not have a husband who was an admitted adulterer.

"How did you and Bob meet?"

Lisa leaned back, her flaxen hair framing her face. "Oh, wow. I was the one who pursued him."

"Really?"

"We were in the same youth group at church. He was mister big shot. All the girls had their sights set on him. It was pretty funny."

"He fought them off with a stick, huh?"

"He had a big head too. Had to be taken down a peg. That was my job."

Dallas took a sip of coffee, enjoying the tale. "How'd you do it?"

"I ignored him. Totally. Just to get his goat. I knew it'd make him crazy. I knew eventually he'd make his move. And sure enough, he did. One night after youth group I was walking slowly to my car, knowing he'd been scoping me, and he called my name. I pretended not to hear him."

"You're a stinker."

"Oh, yeah. So he calls out again, louder, and I slowly turn around. I give him a look, like, why are you bothering me? And it stops him cold. For a couple of seconds he doesn't say anything. And then, finally, he goes, 'So, how come you never talk to me?'"

"Just like that?"

"Just like that. And I say, 'Who are you again?' And his mouth just drops open. I keep a poker face as long as I can, which was about five seconds, then I just started cracking up. And he starts laughing, which is why I decided I liked him. And the rest is our little history."

"That's a cute story."

Lisa said, "How did you meet Ron?"

"It was a God thing. I was running away from a very bad situation, ran up to San Francisco. This was '77 and I thought maybe I'd try to become a hippy poet. But all the hippies were pretty much gone by then. I was a day late and a flower short."

Lisa laughed.

Dallas searched her memories. "I stayed in North Beach with a friend who had her own little marijuana operation going, which caused me to lose track of about a week of my life. But I do remember walking along Columbus Avenue this one night, in a stupor, when I heard music coming out of a place, rocking and rolling. I went inside. All these smiling faces looked at me. I thought I was tripping. Somebody showed me to a seat. It was a little theater. I thought that was cool. Or *groovy*."

"I got it."

"I was into the music, and then it stopped, and then this guy comes out and starts talking. He's got all this energy and he's good-looking too. Pretty soon it breaks through to me that he's talking about Jesus. And he's holding a Bible. And pretty soon I really *was* tripping, but it was on what he was saying. I know now that was the Holy Spirit doing his work in me. When he gave the invitation, I walked up to the front and asked for Jesus to save me. It was Ron, of course."

"Revival Ron?"

"You wouldn't have known him then. He was really into street preaching, and he was good at it." *When did he lose that zeal?* "Anyway, we were two completely different people. How we ended up together is really something God did." Dallas said it and wanted to believe it.

After a pause, Dallas said, "If you ever found out Bob had an affair, and lied to you about it, what would you do? Would you forgive him?"

The half smile that Lisa had on her face faded. "My first instinct would be to kick his loving you-know-what. My second instinct, and I'm being totally honest here, would be to divorce him."

"Wow."

"Wait a second. I said instinct. That's just a knee-jerk reaction. I think ..."

"Go ahead, Lisa, if you want to."

Lisa looked away.

"Lisa, what is it?"

Lisa looked like further words might crush her.

"Please," Dallas said. "Maybe I can help."

"It's not about me." Only then did Lisa look at Dallas again. The look was a bridge to a cold, dark place.

"What is it then?" Dallas said, wishing she hadn't been insistent.

"I didn't think I'd ever have to say."

"Say what, Lisa?"

"This is so hard." Lisa lowered her voice. "All right. I guess I have to say it, because it's something Jeff Waite needs to know about."

"Jeff? What's he got to do—"

"Because the prosecutor is probably going to find out."

"The prosecutor? How—"

"They want to interview me and Bob."

"Interview?"

"That's right," Lisa said. "They want us to come in. I told Bob to tell them to take a flying ... Well, I don't know if we're going to be able to get out of it. I think it stinks."

"What could he possibly hope to accomplish?"

Lisa took a long moment to answer. "That's what you need to tell Jeff. There's something, if they ask me, I'd have to tell them."

"Tell me now, *please*."

Lisa inhaled deeply. "This woman, this Melinda whatever-her-name-is?"

"Yes?"

"She's not the first woman Ron had an affair with."

3.

How does it begin?

In innocence, I tell myself, as if that makes a difference. In ignorance too, as if there were no danger involved, and no consequence.

You tell yourself that you can handle it, that you are an adult and therefore beyond the juvenile temptations to associate with this kind of stuff. And you tell yourself that it is merely research, as if by labeling it that way you remove the sin from it.

You also know, without admitting it to yourself, that you like the power. You like the idea that with the touch of a button, the click of a mouse, you can control a veritable universe of forbidden fruit.

I wanted to see just how easy it was to access pornographic images on the Internet. I could have answered that question quite easily one hundred miles from a computer. Everyone knows it's easy. Everyone knows the skin trade and the pedophiles and the sick and the bored control the vast majority of territory in the electronic cosmos.

But I told myself it was research as I typed the word into the search engine, a word I would never use in public or even privately. And in a microsecond I had it all before me.

I was sweating, I remember that. Sweating and trembling. I was not praying, nor was I thinking about God at all. Or if I did, I shoved those thoughts far back into the dark alleys of my mind, stuck them into abandoned warehouses with boarded-up windows and firmly locked doors.

The images literally took my breath away. My research was done. It was easier than getting a Coke at the 7-Eleven or channel surfing at home. Indeed, it was easier than almost anything, and that was the lure of it.

That, and being all alone in my office, no one to look over my shoulder, no one to call me in to dinner.

My "research" lasted almost two hours.

And when I was done I knew the images would always be there waiting for me.

Always.

And when they weren't on my screen, they would be in my mind. Always.

4.

Jared sat in the truck across from the apartment complex and waited. What was he doing here? What possible good was going to come out of this?

He had no ready answer, but that wasn't strange. He didn't have answers to a lot of things.

But this was something to do, something besides stew in his own juices at home, feeling like a total loss.

For an hour that morning he'd tried to get to someone at the VA, a human voice. He wanted somebody to tell him what he could do to stop the bad things, what pill he could take, what injection to the brain would stop the memories.

No human voice. And his next appointment wasn't until August.

August! He wondered if he'd even be breathing in August. He wondered if he could stand it until then. There were other ways out. There were guns, and he could get one and—

He saw Jamaal run into a fenced front yard. Or what was a bad excuse for a yard in this fallen suburbia.

Jamaal was alone, holding a football that was as big as his chest. He cradled it, looking like he didn't know what to do.

Jared got out of the truck and walked to the fence.

"What's up?"

Jamaal looked at him, then smiled. "Nothin'."

"Your mom around?"

He shook his head.

"Dad?"

Shook again.

So what's he doing in a yard all alone? Jared told himself to leave. This was a stupid idea. A desperate reach. What was he looking for? He shouldn't have come.

But something about being with the kid, one of the innocents. For a moment at least it soothed the burn inside.

"Why you here?" Jamaal asked.

"Hey, came to see how you were, you know? So … how are you?" He looked closely for any marks on Jamaal. Saw none.

"Good," the boy said.

"Cool."

An older woman shuffled down the walk and gave Jared a suspicious look. A long look. Like she was remembering his face. Then she went on.

He couldn't blame her. The way things were these days, a stranger talking to a boy was something to note. She was a one-woman Neighborhood Watch.

"You a football player?" Jared pointed at the pigskin in the boy's arms.

"You said."

It took Jared a minute to figure that one, but then he remembered. The kid wanted to be a Marine. Jared had suggested football instead.

Amazingly, the kid had apparently listened, taken it to heart. Jared could hardly believe it.

He went around to the gate and let himself into the yard. Jamaal ran up to him.

"Toss it," Jared said.

Jamaal made an attempt to throw Jared the football. The ball was so large in Jamaal's hands he had to use both for the throw. The ball went nearly ninety degrees sideways, hitting the fence.

"Oops," Jamaal said.

"Looks like we got a little learning to do." Jared picked up the football. It was all rubber. He held it up to Jamaal. "See these white things here?"

Jamaal nodded.

"Those are the laces. Let's see your hand."

Jamaal put his right hand out. Jared turned it palm up and placed the football in the middle of it. Jamaal's hand disappeared under the ball.

"No problem," Jared said. "You'll grow into it. You feel the laces on your fingers?"

Jamaal concentrated. "Uh-huh."

"Okay. What you want to do is keep your fingers on those laces when you throw. Pretty simple, huh?"

Jamaal shrugged.

"Give it a try."

The boy paused, then started to lift the ball. It teetered. He put his left hand on it.

"Hold it," Jared said. "Try it one-handed."

Jamaal took his left hand off. And then was motionless. "I can't."

"Yeah, you can. Keep your fingers where they are and just move your hand toward me. Go ahead."

The boy gave it a try. The ball went about a foot. But it went forward.

"Yeah, man," Jared said. "Good one. You see that?"

The kid blinked.

"Wanna try it again?"

"Yeah," Jamaal said.

Jared put the ball back in the kid's hand, then took two large steps backward. "Okay now, all the way to me."

With a determined look, Jamaal reared back with his arm and flung the ball. It made it all the way to Jared, who caught it over his shoes.

"Yeah, baby!" Jared put his hand up. "High five." Jamaal ran over and slapped Jared's hand.

"Let's do another," Jared said, and Jamaal nodded.

Then a voice said, "Hey."

Jared turned and saw a man walking toward them from the east side. And then he saw Tiana, right behind him, her eyes wide with surprise.

Jared knew this was the boyfriend, Jamaal's father. Jared sized him up. He was about Jared's height, but his shoulders were broader and he was older, maybe thirty. He wore a tight black T-shirt and he had packed muscles.

Jared noticed that Jamaal did not run toward him. Didn't move, in fact.

"What's goin' on?" the man said, hard and quick.

Jared looked at Tiana's face. It virtually begged him not to say a word.

"Just doing a little football," Jared said. "Kid's got quite an arm."

"Who are you?"

"Just passing by."

The guy stepped up to Jared, closer than was comfortable. "I said who are you?"

Jared felt the heat, his muscles tensing.

From behind, Tiana said, "Rafe, he's the guy brought us home."

Rafe gave her a snap look, then came back to Jared. "So what are you doin' here?"

"I was driving by and—"

"Why?"

"Why what?"

"Were you drivin' by?"

"Rafe," Tiana said, "drop it, okay?"

"I ain't droppin' nothin'." He pointed at Jared's face. "Don't come around here no more."

"Rafe, he's just—"

"Shut up."

Tiana closed her mouth.

It was all Jared could do not to grab Rafe's throat. He was conscious of Jamaal watching everything.

Jared looked at Tiana. "Is this what you want?"

Before she could say a word, Rafe was in Jared's face. "You don't be talkin' to her, you got that?"

"Go, please," Tiana said.

"Yeah," Rafe said. "Now."

There was something else here, not just the four of them. Not another person, but a presence. Jared felt it as fully as he had sometimes in Iraq. He always thought it was just the circumstances, the obvious stress, a thing stirred up by the acids in the stomach when the heat was on.

Now he wasn't so sure about that.

He gave a quick look at Jamaal before walking back to his truck.

5.

When Dallas got to Jeff's office, he did not greet her with a smile. His normally crisp white shirt was wrinkled and his desk a mess of files and papers. He looked more like a law student stressing over finals than a successful trial lawyer.

Which was only going to make it harder to trip the land mine that Lisa had revealed a couple of hours before.

"I saw Ron," Jeff said immediately. "He doesn't want to plead out. Says he did not kill the girl and that it would be a lie to plead guilty to anything."

"So what does that mean?"

"It means . . ." A pained look flashed across Jeff's face. "Please sit down, Dallas."

The heavy weight of her heart forced her into a chair.

"There's no easy way to tell you this," Jeff said.

Him too? "Just tell me. Straight out."

Jeff closed his eyes. "I'm thinking of withdrawing from the case."

"What?"

"Dallas, listen carefully. I am obligated to represent a client with zeal. That's what the code of ethics says. That requires a certain trust, on both sides. When things happen that destroy trust, the zeal that's supposed to be there fizzles. I won't be doing Ron any favors by continuing to represent him."

"What happened? What did he say to you?"

"It's what he didn't say. I have the feeling he's holding back something, not being up front with me."

Dallas stared at him. *Just wait.*

"Ron originally lied to the police, and he lied to you and me about whether he had sex with Melinda Perry."

"Yes, he did, and he's sorry for that. I really believe he is and—"

"I think he's still lying."

"How?"

"I don't know. But I have a terrible feeling he's lying to you too, Dallas."

Dallas clenched her teeth. She couldn't fight it any longer. "He is holding back, Jeff."

He sat on the edge of his desk. "What do you know?"

"I had coffee with Lisa Benson today. She told me the prosecutor wants to interview her and Bob."

"Did she say why?"

"Boy, did she." Dallas rubbed her right temple, which felt like an earthquake's epicenter. "She found out that Ron had an affair."

"Someone other than the victim?"

Dallas nodded. "About a year ago. I remember the woman. Her name was Amy Shea. Does that name ring a bell?"

Jeff shook his head.

"You'd probably remember her if you saw her. She was a striking woman. I never got to know her real well. It's easy to come and get lost at Hillside. But that's that. Will this hurt the case?"

"It may. If the prosecution finds her, she could be called as a witness to establish a pattern in Ron's life. Regardless, this is another example of Ron's not being up front with us."

Dallas took a couple of deep breaths, and they felt like the last gasps of a drowning woman.

"Jeff, won't you stay on? I can't imagine getting another lawyer."

He hesitated, then said, "All right, Dallas. For you I'll do it."

She almost cried then but managed to make it out of the office with her eyes dry. And then she drove to the ocean.

She parked along Pacific Coast Highway near Point Dume, then walked down to the sand and sat and just looked.

She'd grown up in California, always lived near the coast. She couldn't imagine not having the ocean near her.

At least until now.

Now she thought what she might do. Sell the house and buy some place in the South. A place that was not California, where she could start over, out of any limelight.

She had no husband now. She was not married to Ron Hamilton after all, but a phantom, a liar, a shadow man.

He was sick in a deep, spiritual way. Well, she didn't have to share that sickness.

Divorce. Everyone would understand. No one on earth would accuse her of selfishness or abandonment. Not after this.

She thought about praying but decided not to. Right now she didn't want to hear the voice of God. That was tiring. She didn't want to pray for herself, or Ron. Let him pray for himself, if he had any faith left.

It was almost noon. She could sit here all day, watch the waves, let the world go on without her. No Jared, no Ron. Give up and not fight it anymore.

She remembered another beach, near Big Sur, where she'd stopped after thumbing out of L.A. to get away from Chad. It was twilight and she was wearing a long cotton dress and she kicked off her shoes and waded into the water, toward the gentle waves.

There'd been a split second there, as her dress got soggy with brine, that she thought she might just keep going, get beyond the waves and let the current take her out, then under. Give it all up to a beautiful cleansing and rest and absorption into peace. Chad had made ground meat of her soul, and this seemed a perfect place and time to dump the whole mess.

And then she began to weep.

She didn't know how long she wept, but suddenly a man, an older man in a bathing suit, was in the water next to her asking if she was okay. He had gray hair on his chest, a gray moustache, and a nice smile.

Stammering something, nodding, she returned to the shore and sat on the dry sand and cried some more. When she finally stopped she looked around, and was completely alone in the oncoming darkness. She ran to the road and caught another ride, this one all the way into San Francisco.

Now, looking out at her beloved ocean, hearing waves hitting sand, she wept again, and thought about the heaviness of water.

6.

As I got busier, as my writing and speaking invitations grew, as Hillside began to burst and began a new building program, as I started on the radio, as I spent more time in my office than at home, how could I not have expected my spiritual life to atrophy?

*I did not read the Bible much, except to find verses to pin on my
sermons. My sermons were no longer about the power of God, the good
news of redemption. When people came to my services—MY!!—I
wanted them to feel that I—I!!—was giving them words of comfort for
their "felt needs."*

*I was not searching the Word so it could search me, nor was I pray-
ing as I ought, with a passionate longing.*

*Not like when I was preaching on the streets of San Francisco, when
I had no choice but to depend on the power of God, on the power of his
Word.*

*When I first came to Hillside, the pastor I was replacing, Roger
Vernon, took me aside and asked me what the most crucial thing to do
was, and I said, "Pastor the people."*

"More crucial," he prodded.

I said I didn't know what was more crucial than that.

And he said, "Where does the word crucial *come from?"*

I shrugged.

"It comes from the word cross. *That is what you must do. Preach
the cross of Christ, make it the center of everything you do, first and
foremost in your own life."*

7.

"What is it, Dallas?" Ron, on the other side of the Plexiglas,
frowned. He looked like he'd aged five years. "Why don't you say
anything?"

"I'm trying to gather my thoughts," she said. She'd been trying
to gather them for the past three days, since learning about his
other affair.

"What is it? Something's wrong. Jared?"

"Jared is a topic for another time."

Ron shook his head. "You seem so distant, Dallas."

"Do I?"

"I don't understand."

"No, I don't think you do."

How like a little boy he looked now, knowing he was in trouble but not knowing the details. "Please talk to me, Dallas."

"Before I do, I want to lay down some ground rules."

"Rules? What are you—"

"Just listen. If you want me in here again, you will listen now, okay? Nod if you understand."

He nodded.

"Good. The first and most important rule is this. You will not lie to me. Ever again. And I mean ever. Do you understand that?"

"Dallas, I wish you'd tell me—"

"*Do* you understand that?"

"Of course I do. If you're still angry about what I did, I thought that—"

"Quiet. You're still listening to me. The second ground rule is that you are to speak to me directly and not try to hide behind words. I want direct answers and admissions. Is that understood?"

"I guess so." He was looking worried now, and Dallas felt a pang of sympathy for him. She had never talked to him this way. He had always been the leader, the authority in the family. He looked truly pained that she was talking like this.

Tough.

"Here it is, Ron. And I want you to think very carefully before you answer. Because if I sense any evasion whatsoever, then I am out of here. For good."

Ron blinked, then nodded his agreement.

"I know about Amy Shea," Dallas said.

For at least ten seconds, Ron did not move, didn't even twitch. Dallas kept her eyes trained on him, not giving an inch. She was not going to soften. Not this time.

Ron looked down. "She came to see me once. She was going through a divorce and said she needed spiritual counsel. I tried to give it to her. I honestly tried to tell her to keep her marriage together."

Dallas almost snapped at him but stayed quiet.

"She asked me if I'd meet with her again, and I agreed. Only she said she wanted to meet at her place of business, and could I do that. She was running a pretty successful boutique in Malibu. So I went. I thought seeing a little more of her life would give me good insight into her problem. Stupid mistake."

Dallas felt the heat of humiliation in her, pushing upward toward her tear ducts. Still, she remained silent.

"She insisted on taking me to lunch, to show her appreciation. I told her I didn't think that was a good idea. Honest, I did. I knew it wasn't. But ... I just went."

What wasn't I giving you, Ron? Why did you feel the need?

"We had lunch at this place by the beach, looking out at the ocean. She was, I guess, in her element. I was the fish out of water. But then she started talking about my preaching, about how she thought I was a natural for television, about this and that, and I just got caught up in it."

Nothing like the power of flattery from a beautiful woman. Men, in some fundamental ways, are so weak.

"We went back to her boutique. She told the other girl there that she wanted to close up early. Amy locked the place up. And that's when it happened."

"In the *boutique?*"

Ron nodded, looking down.

"How long did it go on?" Dallas said.

"A few weeks. Then I stopped it."

"Why?"

"Because"—he looked into her eyes—"I couldn't handle the guilt. And because I love you."

The words did not melt her heart, and that was surprising. For so many years Dallas had fed hungrily on those words, which came less and less frequently from Ron's lips. Now they were nearly unpalatable.

"One more question, Ron."

He waited.

"Were there any others?"

"No. I give you my absolute word."

"Was it me?" she said. "Was I lacking in some way? Did I—"

"No, Dallas, no. Please believe me."

She tried to.

"Now I have a question for you," Ron said.

"What?"

"Will you forgive me?"

She stared at him, wondering if she could.

NINE

Saturday morning and her head was about to explode. *I'm a Hindenburg waiting to happen,* Dallas thought as the walls of her house crowded in around her.

She'd already turned away one reporter who'd come knocking at the door like a Jehovah's Witness with three thousand questions.

She had to get away. And in Los Angeles that always meant hopping in a car and driving as far as you wanted. Alone.

She grabbed her purse and went.

She got to the freeway and was relieved that no news vans were following her. She headed east toward Pasadena with the radio tuned to the classic-rock station. A nice blast from her past. She'd always liked the music of the seventies. She didn't want to think about anything but driving and listening and being anywhere but home.

At least the day was clear. The San Gabriel Mountains on her left were looking fine. Nothing ever bothered them, except a few brushfires now and again. Or floods sometimes, which caused the mountains to shed muddy skin, sloughing it into the yards and swimming pools of the homes foolishly packed below.

She remembered the first time she'd seen these mountains as a little girl when her mother had moved them here. They drove over the Sepulveda Pass and looked down on the Valley where the San Gabriels merged with the Santa Susanas. And it seemed like a wonderland then, a land of adventure, a place where she would meet wonderful friends and where, one day, she'd become a famous singer. All this was years before meeting Chad McKenzie and learning that dreams were kid stuff, and sometimes deadly.

She'd had a different dream when she moved back here with Ron. A dream of new beginnings and a marriage that would be a permanent and glorious thing. Moving back to Los Angeles then was a way of recapturing hopes and sharing them with a man she finally loved and trusted and would stay with forever.

Dallas merged onto the Foothill Freeway, and as she did she found she was crying. She wiped the tears with the back of her hand. The rock station was playing "Love the One You're With." She punched the *off* button. This time, the music was no help.

Maybe it's me. Maybe I wasn't a good enough wife or mother. Maybe I just blew it. And maybe all that stuff from Ron about loving me and wanting forgiveness is just the last gasp of the dying man who really doesn't care. Maybe we're better off without each other.

She drove on, through Pasadena, and then past Sierra Madre and Duarte. Towns where normal life was happening, to people who weren't her.

She saw the 605 Freeway coming up, and her inner geography kicked in. The 605 south would take her to El Monte, La Puente.

And Pico Rivera, infamous of late as the town with the Star Motel.

Don't do it. Leave it alone. Keep driving. Find a movie theater. See a comedy. But don't torture yourself by—

She took the 605 south.

When she got off in Pico Rivera she pulled into a Shell station next to a pay phone. She got out and looked in the Yellow Pages and found the address for the Star Motel, which didn't do her a lot of good, not knowing where the streets were.

But the nice young man at the counter told her, in his New Delhi accent, that the street she wanted was just two blocks away.

2.

The Star looked like it had been built in the fifties, the golden age of motels in Los Angeles County. But the years had not been kind to it. The exterior was done up in weather-beaten white with a muddy aqua trim. The letters spelling out *Motel* on the roof were red and accented with neon lights that, in the sunshine, looked superfluous and ugly.

Dallas turned into the driveway and noticed only a few cars parked in the lot. The lot itself appeared to form a horseshoe shape. She followed it to the far end and saw there was another driveway in the back.

And she saw the room. Number 105, at the very rear of the building, the dull silver numbers easily readable from the car.

She almost drove on. What good was this? What did she hope to accomplish?

To find something, anything, that would show Ron didn't kill Melinda Chance. Jeff said they needed some evidence, and it wasn't forthcoming. But maybe her eyes could see something here others had missed.

Didn't that happen on the TV shows? Some CSI person would find a shell casing or carpet fiber or ... who was she kidding? This was reality, and she was no trained forensic specialist.

But she could at least say she tried everything she could think of.

She pulled her car into the last spot in the lot, facing the street in back of the motel, and let the car idle. Finally she turned it off and got out and faced the building.

There was no car in front of the room, and no one appeared to be around. The news hounds had taken their fill of pictures. Curiosity seekers had no doubt driven by in the first few days after all the publicity.

Maybe this place would end up on a map someday, the kind sold by street hawkers in Hollywood, which showed tourists movie stars' homes or famous crime scenes. *See where Charles Manson did his thing! See the room where Ron Hamilton offed that girl!*

Dallas shivered then, even though the day was hot. There was evil here. Bad things going on behind closed doors.

She was vaguely aware of a grating sound, turned, and saw it was a boy on a skateboard, coming into the parking lot from the back street. He was Latino, around twelve. The lot was big enough that it probably made a nice track for skateboarders.

But instead of heading toward the lot, he came right up to her and stopped.

"That's where it happen," he said.

"Excuse me?"

"The killing, you know? Right there."

He pointed at room 105.

Dallas nodded. "I know."

"Lots of people come by to look."

"Sure. Do you live around here?"

He jerked his head over his shoulder. "There. So you want me to tell what happen?"

"I already know."

"She was hot."

"What? Hot?"

"Lady that got killed."

Dallas almost jumped. "Did you see her?"

He shook his head. "My friend."

"Your friend saw the lady that was killed here?"

The boy started to look a little nervous.

Easy. Back off a little. "Go ahead. What else can you tell me?"

"Nothing."

"Wait, you said you had a friend—"

"I don't know nothing."

"But you said—"

He turned and pushed off on his skateboard.

"Wait!"

He didn't wait. Dallas took two steps after him, but he was fast. The sound of skateboard wheels on pavement was all he left her.

"Please!"

She watched helplessly as he disappeared around the cinder-block wall.

Something had scared him off. She had to know what it was. She ran to her car, started it, backed out of her space. A car horn blared at her.

She slammed on the brakes. She'd almost backed into a Lexus. The driver, a man in sunglasses, yelled at her, gesticulating with one arm.

Dallas gunned her car forward, almost scraping the wall. She actually burned rubber out of the driveway. She stopped at the road and looked both ways. No sign of the boy. There was a strip mall to the left and some housing to the right.

She chose right, drove, then caught sight of the boy a fair distance down a residential street. She stopped, backed up, and turned down the street.

What on earth was she doing? Chasing a kid on a skateboard? A scared kid at that.

It didn't matter. He was a thread, a chance.

And what would she do when she caught up to him? Money. Give him a five or a ten, get him to tell her something, anything, to get her to the next step. Whatever that was.

She was only vaguely aware of the topography of the neighborhood. The homes were smallish, probably built around the same time as the Star Motel. There were manicured lawns next to fenced yards. Spare trees, testaments to faded glory, leaned against cracked curbs.

The boy disappeared up what looked to be a driveway. She followed into what turned out to be an alley. A wooden fence on one side, block walls on the other. City garbage cans lolled against the fencing.

And the kid had stopped and was talking to someone.

A group of someones.

Dallas stopped, saw the boy pointing at her. The one he was talking to was older, wore a white wifebeater and black jeans, and had a blue bandanna tied around his head.

He was about thirty feet away from her, but when he looked directly at her she saw everything she needed to know in his eyes.

It was more than enough to get her to put the car in reverse and start backing out the way she came.

Only now she couldn't. Because a car had somehow come up behind without her noticing, and it was blocking her way. Purposely, she knew.

A moment later four doors flew open and young men who might have been wearing neon GANG signs poured out.

And started slowly walking toward her.

3.

Jared stopped and looked at his reflection in the dirty window, darkened on the inside so the early drinkers could be shielded from sunlight. In the window he saw the same dumb face he'd seen for the last couple of years, staring back with eyes as dark as the pane of glass, as bereft as the hopes on the other side.

What were you thinking? You think you matter to a kid and some woman whose life is shot because that's the way she wants it? What're you after, idiot? Quit pretending that it's going to get better. Go in, have a drink, get some cheap bourbon down your throat, feel the nice warm glow that comes out your nose when you knock it back neat, and maybe later you can grab some weed and get high before you decide where you're going to head off to so you don't bring your mom down anymore and make your sister crazy.

You gave it a shot, but let's face it, boy, you are damaged goods, no use.

He turned back to the boulevard and thought maybe a fast-moving truck would be the best solution for everybody. All he'd have to do is jump in front and take a good thumping and that would be that. Unless he lived, of course, in which case things would be worse than ever and Mom would have way more to deal with than he would wish on anyone.

No solution, then, after all. Which spun him right back to the bar.

Go get that drink, fool, what're you waiting for?

He started to go in when he heard someone call his name. He turned around and saw Joe Boyle walking toward him. Joe. They'd been in youth group together at church. Jared hadn't seen him in years, hadn't kept in touch.

"Thought I recognized you!" Joe threw his arms around Jared and gave him a hug. Jared let him but didn't return the favor. "How you been, man?"

Joe looked a little more prosperous than he had in high school. He wore khaki slacks and a knit shirt and looked like he could be getting ready to go to the golf course and actually play golf, not get high like they used to, sneaking out at night.

"I'm fine," Jared said.

"You just get back? From the Marines?"

"I been back a while."

"Bummer about your dad." Joe shook his head. "I don't believe it, you know."

"Thanks."

"What are you doing now?"

Getting drunk at 11:00 a.m. How about you? "Not a whole lot. You?"

"Vista Ford. You know what? I really like selling cars. I mean, I'm good at it."

"No doubt." Joe had always been good at anything.

"Married too." He held up his left hand, showing a gold wedding band.

"Who'd you end up with?"

"You mean who took my sorry self? Remember Rona Conroy?"

"Oh, yeah." Very nice looking, as he recalled.

"Yeah, baby too. Little girl."

Was he rubbing it in or something? "Cool. Congratulations."

"Hey, I'm just stopping over at Wendy's. Can I buy you a burger?"

"No, thanks. I got some things to do."

"Well, let's get together." Joe took out a snap case and pulled out a business card. It had raised gold lettering on it. Joe was a *Sales Executive*.

Jared took it. "Sure."

"I mean it." Joe pointed his finger at him, gun style.

"Right. You bet."

Joe gave him a slap on the shoulder. "See you. Call me."

And he turned and walked back along the sidewalk, toward the Wendy's a block away. Jared watched him, waited until he was out of sight, then went into the bar, crumpling the card as he did.

4.

"What you want?"

The kid with the blue bandanna was standing at her window now, the boy on the skateboard behind him. The others were around her car, two of them directly in front. She was going to have to talk, so it might as well be now.

"I was looking for ... I don't want anything, I just wanted to ask a question."

"You scared or something?"

"Yes."

"What, you think this big bad banger, he gonna mess you?"

She nodded. She could hear blood pulsating in her ears.

"I look like a banger to you?"

She nodded.

He smiled, showing perfect white teeth that fairly gleamed. On his neck were tattooed the words *Mi Vida Loca*. He slapped the top of her car, creating a popping sound that entered her ears like ice bullets.

Loca turned to the boy with the skateboard and said something in Spanish. The boy looked at Dallas and nodded. Loca turned back to Dallas. "So you come to see the place, huh, the place where the guy smoked her?"

"Yes."

"Why?"

She could fudge around it or tell him. She could try to finesse her way out or lay it on the line. Something told her fudging could only lead to worse trouble.

Dallas opened the door so she could get out and face him. He let her. He was not very tall. She was eye to eye with him.

"My husband is the one they think did it."

He gave her a long look, then said, "He musta been on something, huh?"

"He didn't do it."

"Yeah?"

"He didn't. The boy said he had a friend who saw the woman."

The gangbanger slapped the back of the boy's head. The boy yelped.

"You got money?"

"Yes."

"Give it to me."

Dallas reached into the car and got her purse. She had twenty-two dollars and some change. She handed it over.

"Okay," Loca said. "You did good. You come with me now."

5.

He led her down the alley, the others following. Was she being a complete fool to go with him?

Yes.

But two things kept her going. Instinct and faith. She had the idea that she could trust this guy, and being in the daylight helped. But she also had faith that she was protected and she had to step out in that, had to at this moment in time because she'd come this far.

Near the end of the alley was an open garage. Only this was done up like a room, with posters and shelves and secondhand carpet over the cement. At the back of the garage was a mattress, and on the mattress sat a rotund teenager. His white T-shirt was too small for his frame, and an ample portion of stomach protruded out over his jeans. He held a comic book in one hand and looked up nonchalantly as Loca entered the space.

"Hey, this lady wanna talk about the lady you saw at the motel, huh?"

The kid slowly looked at Dallas with a dark moon face.

"You don't got to be afraid, man. Talk to her."

Dallas sat on a crate, tried to speak calmly. "Will you tell me what you saw?"

Loca kicked him, half playfully, half rebukingly. "Go on, Ratón. Tell her."

"She was hot." The words came out of Ratón slow and childlike. Coupled with the detached look in his eyes, Dallas concluded that he was mentally challenged.

"Where did you see her?" Dallas probed.

Ratón was silent.

Loca said, "He hangs over there at the place. He likes to watch the people. It's like his TV. Crazy, huh?"

"He watches the motel?"

"And the 7-Eleven. That's how he changes channels." Loca laughed.

Ratón laughed, looking at Loca as if taking his cues from him.

The strangeness of the scene coalesced around her. Gangbangers, a kid on a skateboard, a handicapped kid on a mattress who may have seen something, may not have. But why stop now? "Please tell me what else you saw."

"The man." Ratón looked at Loca. "Should I say about the man?"

"What man?" Dallas said.

"Yeah," Loca said, sounding like this was news to him too.

Ratón licked his lips. "He was fast. He ran fast. Went into that place."

Dallas said, "You saw a man go into a room?"

Ratón nodded.

"What did this man look like?"

"Black."

"He was a black man?"

Ratón frowned and shook his head, then rubbed his hands on his T-shirt. "All black."

"You mean he was dressed in black clothes?"

Ratón nodded quickly.

Dallas considered the information. A fast man dressed in black. That did not sound like Ron. He wouldn't dress that way if he was just meeting with Melinda.

"Did you see this man go into the room?" Dallas asked.

Ratón squinted. "I think. And then he came out, ran away."

This was such a thin thread, even if she could believe what he said. But it was the only thread she had in hand.

"What else?"

"Huh?"

"What else did you see?" She couldn't temper the desperation in her voice.

Ratón's eyes widened, and he made a little squeaking sound in his throat. He looked at Loca.

Loca said, "He's getting a little nervous. Maybe you should go now."

"Please," she said. "I have to know everything."

"That's it."

"No, tell him to tell me. Please."

Loca shook his head, took hold of her arm, and pulled her up. "You can go now. And don't come back."

She pulled her arm away. "You don't seem to understand."

"Oh, yeah?"

"I'm not an enemy."

Loca shook his head. "You're not a friend, neither. Now get in your car."

6.

She drove immediately to Jeff Waite's office in Encino. She knew he often worked on Saturdays and took a chance. It paid off. The security guard in the building called him and then sent her up.

Jeff was in casual clothes when he met her coming off the elevator. "What brings you down here?" he said.

"Jeff, listen, where can we talk?"

"Come on." He walked her into the suite of offices on the fourteenth floor. They went into the library, which had a table in the middle of the room. Papers and open books were spread out there.

"Just doing a little research on the admissibility of a victim's past. We need to show that Melinda Perry was not exactly running with a good crowd. Meaning there were others who could have done this."

"Can you show this?"

"It's iffy. What we'd be saying is that we have an alternative theory, and the courts have held we need to provide some factual basis for it."

"Can we?"

"Not yet. We need something that connects Melinda and her background to something in this case, like the motel."

Dallas's breath accelerated. "What if you had a witness who could do that?"

"Witness?"

"That's what I came to tell you. I was just in Pico Rivera, I went to the Star Motel, a kid was skateboarding there, and I followed him"—she didn't care how wild this sounded—"and, long story short, I was talking to another kid who saw someone at the motel that night, someone who was not Ron, and when I—"

Jeff put his hands up. "Whoa, slow down. First, who is this guy?"

"His name is something Spanish, Ratón."

"Mouse?"

"That's what this other guy called him."

"What other guy?"

Dallas huffed. "It's a little involved, a gang member—"

"*Gang* member? Dallas, what the heck—"

"Listen to me. This kid I was talking to, he saw something. He's just a little ..."

"A little what?"

"Mentally slow. But he knows what he saw, he—"

"Dallas! First of all, what are you doing going around investigating things? I have people who do that for a living."

"I know. It was spontaneous. I just had to do something."

"Yeah, and if you do the wrong thing it could blow Ron's case up, did you consider that? Did you consider you might chase away information?"

"I'm sorry, Jeff."

"And this alleged witness, you're telling me he's got mental problems. You know he might not even be competent to testify."

"You should at least talk to him."

"You've got a very unreliable witness here. The DA will take him apart."

"But what about the truth?"

Jeff dropped into a chair. "Dallas, that's what I've been trying to tell you. It's not the truth that matters. It's the evidence. It's what the jury is allowed to see. If we thought trials were about the truth we'd hook everybody up to lie detectors and let the judge sort it out. But it's not. It's about who's got the best evidence and who can bluff the other side into the best deal. If the evidence is roughly equivalent, we go to trial."

"So now we have evidence."

"That doesn't make it equal. Like I said, the DA will kill this witness's credibility. And he has all the physical evidence he needs."

"Jeff, I can't give up on him. Maybe I should, but I can't. He's still my husband, and he's still not guilty of murder."

"I want to believe that."

She looked at him hard. "You don't? Jeff, you honestly don't?"

He said nothing, and that was answer enough.

"I don't know what to do," Dallas said. "But it's got to be something."

"We'll try."

"There is no try. Only do."

"Huh?"

"It's an old saying."

Jeff smiled at her, then nodded. "You're quite a doer when you put your mind to it. All right. I'll have you talk to Harry."

7.

Late Monday morning Dallas met Harry Stegman at Jerry's Famous Deli. Jerry's was an overpriced hangout for young movie turks and the old-money crowd who lived in the hills south of Ventura Boulevard. These people had bought homes in the fifties and sixties, and were now sitting atop the mushroom cloud of the real-estate boom.

Harry was sitting in the waiting area and got up when he saw her. He was about sixty, with a laurel wreath of white hair surrounding a bald pate. His suit was beige and rumpled. Every time Dallas saw Harry, in fact, whatever suit he happened to be wearing seemed to be the final resting place of all the wrinkles in the Western world.

His lack of spit and polish was oddly comforting, though. A bit round in the middle, Harry Stegman seemed more like somebody's competent accountant brother than a criminal investigator.

"Thanks for seeing me," Dallas said as Harry pumped her hand.

"Nothing of it, we're all part of the team."

They were shown to a booth, and Harry ordered coffee for them. Then he folded his hands in front of him on the table. "You holding up okay?"

Holding up? She was just thankful she could walk around. "Every day is its own adventure, it seems."

"You have got that exactly right." Harry smiled. It was an easy smile, smooth and calming. Dallas realized he must have comforted countless people over the years in his professional capacity.

"I been doing this a long time," Harry said, "and every time I think I've seen it all, something throws me for a new loop. At least it keeps me young. You wouldn't think to look at me that I'm only twenty-five."

"Never would have guessed. You don't look a day over twenty."

"Bless you, my child."

The server brought coffee and asked if they'd like to order any food. Dallas declined. Harry ordered a "sky high" corned-beef sandwich.

"Stuff'll stop my heart," Harry said. "But I figure we ought to enjoy our stay, you know?"

"You have family, Mr. Stegman?"

"Harry. Please. I have a daughter. In Oklahoma. She works with horses. She's got a gift." He smiled and his eyes seemed to be looking at a memory. "Wish I could see her more." He came back to the present. "Now, let's see what we can do here." He put on some reading glasses and took a pad and pen from his coat pocket. "Jeff says you think somebody else killed the girl?"

"I think Ron was set up somehow. Do you think that's possible?"

"Like I said, there's always something new. But there are some things that always stay the same. Like in murder. There has to be a reason, a motive. A strong one too, if it involved a plan to frame Ron. Let's think that one through a bit. Who might possibly entertain such a motive?"

"Ron was outspoken about pornography. He was working with Bernie Halstrom on trying to crack down on the porn industry here in the Valley. The girl was a porn star." Dallas was struck with a new thought. "What if she was part of this plan to ruin Ron?"

Harry tapped his lower lip with the pen. "Why would she have to be murdered? If they were trying to ruin Ron with an affair, she could have just come out with that story and played it to the end."

"What if she got some other ideas along the way? Maybe she was playing both sides against the middle. Maybe she was trying to get more money out of whoever hired her."

"You're pretty good at this," Harry said. "I like the way you think. Still, we have a lot of maybes. Let's see if we can link them up. We'd be talking a conspiracy here."

"Does it have to be a conspiracy?"

"It only takes two people in agreement on a criminal scheme, and that's what we're supposing here. We have the girl, Melinda Perry, and a somebody else. Maybe a few somebody elses. But as for linkage, right now we only have an untested CI."

"CI?"

"Citizen informant. The other problem is he also happens to be a gang member."

"I don't think he's a member, really, he's sort of ..."

"Mentally challenged?"

Dallas nodded, feeling her hopes starting to drain away.

Harry scribbled some notes on his pad. The server came back with one of the largest sandwiches Dallas had ever seen. Harry's face lit up. "You sure you don't want part of this?"

"I'm sure," Dallas said.

"Because I'll just have to eat the whole thing."

"You could take half of it home."

Harry shook his head. "Good corned beef never tastes the same half an hour later. I don't know why that is, but it's one of the most important things to know in this life."

Life. Would it ever be normal again? Would she ever again be able to take pleasure in simple things, like a good sandwich?

She sensed that Harry, seasoned pro that he was, immediately picked up her vibe.

"Try not to worry," he said softly. "It's Jeff's job to look at the evidence and tell you the score. It's my job to dig and dig and find everything I can that'll help. That's what I get paid the big bucks for. That's why I can afford to buy sandwiches the size of Nebraska."

A single tear coursed down Dallas's left cheek. She grabbed her napkin and dabbed her eye.

"Let me have one bite here," Harry said, "and then you give me all the names you can think of, all the people Ron may have had connections with, places he used to go, anything at all. How's that sound?"

"Thanks, Mr. Stegman."

"Harry."

She watched him savor a bite. It almost made her want to order one for herself. They spent an hour together, and Dallas gave out all the information she could think of. Just before she rose to leave, Harry extended his hand.

"Try not to worry," he said again.

She nodded. He was looking at her closely.

"You remind me a little of my daughter." He seemed sad when he said it. "You've got the same eyes. A little vulnerable, but tough."

Dallas smiled. "I think I'd like to meet her sometime."

"That," he said wistfully, "would be nice."

8.

On her way back from Jerry's Deli, Dallas stopped off at Ralph's for some groceries. Life had to go on. No matter what she was feeling about Ron and the whole mess, she had Jared and Cara to think of.

She suddenly remembered a scene from her San Francisco days. She'd gone over to see Alcatraz and was walking up a steep ramp at the old abandoned prison. At the top, perched on a wall, she saw a large seagull. The gull had its wings spread out, resisting a stiff wind.

Dallas approached, fascinated. The gull didn't move, but watched her closely. She smiled at it and cooed a little to settle it down. But when she was about five feet away, the gull squawked threateningly, eyes riveted on her. Dallas stopped. And then she saw the reason for the bird's defiance—two small, fuzzy chicks stuck their heads out from under each of the mother gull's wings.

She was protecting her young against the elements, approaching strangers, and anything else that might do them harm.

Though she had no children of her own then, Dallas knew that's what it would be like to be a mother. Instinct would kick in, and nothing dangerous would get close to her children without a fight to the finish.

She knew this even more now as she thought of Jared and Cara and all the events swirling around them. She would keep her wings over them, defying the dread winds, and nothing would move her from her maternal duty.

In the market she selected a man-sized rib eye to cook for Jared. She hadn't fired up a steak in a long time. It would be good to do it again. A reminder of better times.

It would be a way to break through the fence he seemed to be erecting.

As she got to her Pathfinder with her cart, she heard a man's voice behind her say, "Can I help you with that?"

"No, I've got it." She didn't want to look at him. She wanted to get in the car as quickly as possible and lock the doors.

She saw him out of the corner of her eye, just standing there. That's when she knew he was trouble.

Don't panic. There are plenty of people around.

She unlocked her door, put the first bag in. Turning for the next, she noticed the man was closer.

Security guard. There's one at the store entrance. Should I call out?

"You really look like you could use some help."

No way to avoid it. Heart kicking, she looked the man in the face.

And her heart nearly stopped.

Chad McKenzie hadn't changed much in, what was it, nearly thirty years? That was scary. Age had only added to his malice. His charcoal hair was shaved down close. He wore a black knee-length coat.

"Hi, Dallas."

His voice sliced her. How easily and eerily it all came back to her, flooding her with dark memories. Her legs started shaking. She wondered if she could even move.

"You look great. Better than on TV." He made no move toward her, but she felt cornered just the same.

"I have to go," she managed to say.

"Whoa, wait. That's all you can say to me after all these years?"

This was too surreal. How did he find her? This wasn't a coincidence.

"How come you didn't return my phone call? A guy could get a real feeling of rejection from that."

Thoughts tumbled into place. The note. The smashed headlight. The strange message on her cell phone.

Chad.

Go. Now. She looked down, as if doing so would make him disappear, and reached for her last bag. Chad snatched it out of the cart.

That was it. The breach, the physical act. He'd gone too far, but he always had. Trembling, she could sit there and take it. Or do *something.* But what?

The one advantage she had was being in a public place. "I will scream my head off if you don't give me that now."

"No need, no need. I'm not out to hurt you."

"Like I believe that."

"Why would I pick a public parking lot, huh? I just want to talk to you."

She sensed the smallest hesitation in his tone of voice and told herself not to back down. "Give me the bag."

"Just talk."

"We have nothing to say to each other."

"Now I'm hurt. After all we were together?"

"Give me the bag."

"I saw your face on the tube. Isn't that a wonderful thing? You see somebody who shared her body and soul with you, right up there on the TV, and she's in trouble. How could I not come?"

"Bag."

He didn't move. "You know, I thought about you in prison. Maybe the same way good old Ron is thinking about you right now, missing your warmth, your—"

"Stop it."

"How'd you end up with a guy like that? A preacher man? You weren't exactly into being religious when we were doing our thing."

"I will scream, I swear, if you don't give me the bag right now."

He smiled. "I was just helping." He held the bag out to her. "I'm a helpful guy."

She took the bag.

"And I want to help you," he said.

Just turn and drive away. Don't listen.

"I want to keep your sad family story from getting worse."

"What are you talking about?"

"That's better. That's nicer. How *are* you, Dallas? I really missed you."

Master manipulator. All abusers were. But he knew something, had some leverage. All right, she would manipulate him right back.

"You were in prison, huh?"

"Hey, what can I say? You make a mistake, they catch you, they make you pay. Kind of like Ron."

"You don't know anything about Ron, so just drop it."

"You ever tell him about us?"

"Of course I did. I told him everything."

"Everything?"

"I told him what mattered. About the way you beat up women."

He winked at her. "I'm what they call *rehabilitated*."

"If you have something to say to me, say it now. And say it once."

"Sure, Dallas, sure. I don't want to see you hurt any more than you have been. That guy, Ron, he ought to be taught a lesson. But your whole family doesn't have to suffer."

Her hands tightened on the shopping bag.

Chad patted the pockets of his coat. "You happen to have a smoke? I'm out."

"What about my family?"

"Hey, for old times' sake, maybe you could spot me a twenty. What do you say?"

"Good-bye."

She made a half turn as Chad snapped his fingers and said, "That's right, we were talking about your family. That daughter of yours. What did the paper say the cutie's name was? Cara?"

Dallas went cold.

"And a son who served in Iraq? Jared? Must be a fine boy."

He paused, his face congealing into smugness. "Do I have your attention again?"

"Say it!"

"The way the papers have it, you're a fine, honorable wife, holding a family together in the face of this very embarrassing turn of events. Must be hard on you and the kids. I wouldn't want to see it get any worse for them."

She knew he was leading up to something, so she waited.

"The way these reporters are hanging on every shred of story, what if they got the whole story of our passion from way back? I have pictures too. You remember the pictures, don't you?"

The pictures. She'd nearly forgotten he once hid a camera and took pictures of ... them. Awful, disgusting. If her children ever saw them ...

"They wouldn't run those," she said weakly.

"You kidding me? You know how much some of those tabloids pay? Which brings me back to my little problem. Twenty bucks ought to cover it. Call it a first installment."

The scheme was now clear. "How much do you want?"

"Like I said, a twenty."

"I mean altogether. To make you go away."

"Two zero." He put his hand out. Kept it there.

She knew he had her. Well planned and played by a con without conscience.

She fished out a twenty-dollar bill from her purse and practically threw it at him. "Now will you leave us alone?"

"We'll talk again, Dallas." He put the bill in his coat pocket. "Just make sure you answer my calls, huh? I get kind of impatient with the phone-tag deal, you know? And let's just keep this between us, because if the cops come sniffing around, that would be bad." He smiled one more time. "Hey! Great to see you again, Dallas. You look prime."

9.

Dallas drove in the grip of anger to a quiet residential area, pulled over, and called Jeff Waite. She left a voice message for him to call *immediately.*

She waited.

And as she did something was illuminated in her head, like when the high beams of a car hit a road sign at night. The sign told her there were two directions she could go.

One was to continue in the way she was already headed, dragged on by a limp but real faith to which she would occasionally respond. She needed something basic right now. Something her tenuous hope could easily grip. Not changing the status quo was easy. On the other hand, one more blow might permanently cripple her trust in God. She might never respond again.

Or she could cast off everything she could—every fear, every betrayal, every unknown—and dive into God. She could go to

God with her whole self, heart and hands and head uncovered, and scream, *Is this what you want?* and then wait for the tearing away of anything that wasn't truly his.

Do it, God, tear it all away and take me and show me and do whatever you want, because it's all over if you don't.

She had her eyes closed and her hands clamped on the steering wheel when Jeff returned her call.

"Are you okay?" he said. "You sounded desperate."

"I am."

"What's the matter?"

She told him about Chad. When she finished there was a long pause.

"At this point," Jeff said, "you've got the first step toward a criminal complaint. Write down exactly what happened—date, time, location. Keep a record. At some point he's going to cross the line. Do you have any protection?"

"You mean like a gun or something?"

"That's what I mean."

"No."

"Get a stun gun. You can carry it in your purse. The guy ever comes at you physically, you can give him a jolt."

She sighed. "I don't want to have to carry a weapon around."

"Who does? But it's an evil world we live in, Dallas."

With that she couldn't argue. *Evil world.* That was it, really it. The thing she'd not fully faced.

When she clicked off with Jeff she called Danielle at Haven House, to make sure all was well there. It was. Then she called the Hillside church office and had them look up the current number for Hillside's retired pastor, Roger Vernon.

TEN

1.

On Thursday Dallas went to see Roger.

Now eighty, Roger was living in Palm Desert. He had been the preacher at Hillside when Ron was called. At that time, in the quaint old church building, the membership was around 300, good people, examples of Christian charity and discipleship.

Roger and his wife, Betty, were mentors for Ron and Dallas. Then they moved to Palm Desert, and over the years the contacts were limited to Christmas cards and one long letter Roger wrote a few years ago informing them of Betty's passing.

Roger greeted her in the front yard of his home. "It's been so long, Dallas. I'm very happy to see you." He gave her a hug. "What do you think of the place?"

She looked around at the sandy yard, which was like the yards of the other modest homes in the neighborhood. No grass out here. "You spent your life preaching warnings against hell. Now you live there."

He laughed. "It only gets up to about 120 in the summer. Child's play. Come on inside."

His home was done in a Southwest style. Roger was originally from New Mexico, where he pastored a church before coming to Hillside. He had some iced tea ready for them in the living room, which was decorated with a collection of multifaceted rocks.

"I hope you know I've been praying for you and Ron," he said when they were settled. "I can't imagine how you feel."

"Did you ever see *Braveheart*?"

"The Mel Gibson movie? One of my favorites."

"Remember what they do to him at the end? Well, that's what it feels like. Tearing out the insides."

Roger nodded. His face was full of understanding, as she knew it would be. He got up and took a rock off a shelf. "I collect these things," he said. "This one's interesting."

He handed the dark rock to Dallas. "What is it?" she asked.

"Gneiss."

She looked at it. "Nice enough."

"Not *nice*. G-N-E-I-S-S. Pronounced the same way. It's a metamorphic rock. The minerals that compose gneiss are the same as granite, but only after intense pressure and heat." He paused. "Think you can relate to this rock?"

"You saying I'm a very gneiss girl?"

Smiling, Roger said, "You got the picture. You'll come out of this stronger. So will Ron. I'll go see him."

"Would you?"

"Certainly. What about your kids? How are they taking it?"

"Cara's managing, but Jared ... Oh, boy." She told him about Jared. Everything. And the helplessness she felt because the medical experts didn't seem able to do anything for him. When she finished her eyes were wet.

"I'm sorry," Roger said quietly. "I'm not surprised, though."

"Why not?"

"There's an angle here the VA isn't considering, because if they did the ACLU would be all over them."

"What sort of angle?"

"Spiritual. It's spiritual battle being waged, so if they don't recognize it, how can they help?"

"You mean demonic?"

Roger nodded. "We don't know how demons influence us. How they get into our thoughts, how they suggest things. We only know they do it. In Ephesians we read about the prince of the power of the air, the spirit that now works *in* people. Then there is the horrible account of the Gerasene demoniac, in whom was Legion, many demons."

"And you think that's what's happening here?"

"I have something in a file." He got up and went to a file cabinet by his bookshelf. He opened a drawer and rifled through it. "Yes, here it is. It's something that was in the *New York Times* over a year ago. A psychologist from Stanford, reflecting on what happened at Abu Ghraib. Listen. 'I believe that the prison guards at the Abu Ghraib Prison in Iraq, who worked the night shift in Tier 1A, where prisoners were physically and psychologically abused, had surrendered their free will and personal responsibility during these episodes of mayhem.'"

"No free will?"

"*Surrendered* free will. There's more. 'These eight army reservists were trapped in a unique situation in which the behavioral context came to dominate individual dispositions, values, and morality to such an extent that they were transformed into mindless actors alienated from their normal sense of personal accountability for their actions—at that time and place.'"

Dallas could only shake her head at this.

"It's our ignorance of the demonic that is at issue here," Roger explained. "Demons are territorial. They control areas. When the people in those areas worship the demon, the demon feeds. Gains power. Gains control. And there is every reason to believe that the stronghold of all demonic forces in the world resides in southern Iraq."

"Babylon," Dallas whispered.

"Precisely. Ancient Babylon. Also known as Shinar and the land of the Chaldeans. The presumed location of Eden, now Eden corrupted. In Revelation we are told that Babylon is the habitation of devils, the hold of every foul spirit. That's quite a claim."

"Still?"

"Why not? In Babylon, the chief god was Marduk, also called Bel. I firmly believe that Marduk is real, and is another name for Satan."

"This is starting to blow me away."

"It should."

"This Marduk is Satan?"

"Listen to the development: In the beginning, God creates the heavens and the earth. He creates man and places him in Eden. The serpent, Satan, begins with Eve, and the first thing he does is call into question God's Word. 'Ye shall not surely die,' he tells her. He is a corrupter of God's truth.

"The Babylonian creation myth is a corrupted version of the truth. In this story, Marduk becomes chief god by defeating the goddess of the sea, Tiamat. Marduk, Satan, rewrote the truth for his benefit, and Babylon fell to worshiping him."

"I've never heard this before."

"It's not surprising. Let me show you something." Roger went to his bookcase, which was packed, and pulled out a heavy volume. He leafed through it until he came to the page he wanted, then laid the book on Dallas's lap. She looked down at an image of some sort of monarch.

"This," said Roger, "is a drawing of Marduk, taken from a carving dating to ancient Babylon. Notice that he's wearing a crown studded with fine stones. His garment is equally resplendent, and he holds a rod and ring, symbols of authority."

"And what's the creature at the bottom?" A terrible-looking head popped out from behind Marduk's robe.

"That is a serpent, but it is not a separate entity. It is the bottom half of Marduk himself."

"This is so strange ..."

"Now, who was the original inhabitant of Eden?"

"Adam."

"Before that."

Dallas frowned. "Satan?"

"Precisely." Roger opened his Bible, turned pages. "Listen to this, from Ezekiel chapter twenty-eight. 'Thou hast been in Eden, the garden of God; every precious stone was thy covering, the sardius, topaz, and the diamond, the beryl, the onyx, and the jasper, the sapphire, the emerald, and the carbuncle, and gold.' I'm with the scholars who say this is a description of Lucifer before his rebellion. Lucifer is Latin for *light-bearer*, which is what we find in Isaiah 14, when Satan is described as 'son of the morning' or 'morning star.' He is also equated with the king of Babylon."

"It fits, doesn't it?"

"Cut to today. Marduk, Satan, rules in the place where your son was fighting. The demons are strong. They infect, they invade. Soldiers come home affected. It's as if you were to go swimming in a polluted lake. You think you're doing fine, but all along you're being infected. Sometimes the bacteria incubates, only asserts itself later.

Outside of Christ, that's what happens to us, especially when we enter strongholds of demonic presence. And no stronghold is more formidable than Babylon."

Shaking her head, Dallas said, "Are you saying that demons have followed Jared back here?"

"There is so much we don't know about demonic activity," Roger said. "Except that it's real. You've read accounts of people coming into contact with some mysterious stranger who has helped them in times of trouble and then disappears?"

"Angels."

"Right. Sometimes in a time of terrible crisis, with death imminent, an angelic presence offers deliverance. Why then would we be surprised that fallen angels, demons, don't also operate in this world?"

"It's scary."

"For those outside of Christ, certainly. But in Christ all of the power of God is on our side. Greater is he who is in us than he who is in the world."

"What do we do?"

"The Bible tells us: Put on the full armor of God. All of it. Leave out one piece and you're vulnerable. Of course, this first requires that we be in Christ. That we have the new birth. That we are a child of God. Otherwise, we're vulnerable. Your son, is he a Christian?"

"He confessed Christ and was baptized, back when he was ten."

"Then you and I, we'll pray against the powers of the air that are seeking your son's destruction."

"And for Ron." She was relieved to have said it. In that moment she made her decision. She was going to fight for Ron and for her marriage.

Roger nodded. "And for Ron. He's a target too, because he went after pornography, a powerful weapon of the enemy. But the name of Jesus is more powerful than all the host of hell. I believe that, Dallas. Do you?"

"I do."

"That's all we need."

2.

When she got back home, around four o'clock, Dallas found Jared on the sofa, his leg draped over the arm, watching TV.

"Jared, we have to talk. Now."

"What about?"

"God."

"Not now, Mom, okay?"

"When?"

He shrugged. "Look, I've been thinking of going back to Bakers-field, to—"

"You can't go anywhere. Not yet."

"Why not?"

"First of all, you have to deal with that drunk-driving arrest."

He made a James Cagney voice. "They'll never catch me."

"I'm serious. But there's something else. Jared, I know your faith isn't strong right now, but I had a long talk with Roger Vernon today. Do you remember him?"

He thought a moment. "He was the pastor before Dad took over. He taught my Sunday school a couple of times."

"Then you remember that he was always a good man of the Word."

"I guess."

"He laid something out for me, something that you need to know. It's about demonic activity."

"Mom—"

"Listen, please. You can't fight this battle on your own. You need the power of God." She told him, in abbreviated form, about Roger's Babylon theory.

When she was finished Jared thought about it for a long time. "If you were into that sort of thing, I guess it might make sense."

"Then call on God."

"What I'm saying is that I'm not into that sort of thing."

"Why not? What's changed?"

He shook his head. "We had a chaplain over there, and I went to him one day and asked him why God was allowing this to happen. He said God is just as upset as we are about it, but he's not really able to stop it. He's growing right along with us."

"That's crazy."

"Is it? I think it's a pretty good explanation."

"It's not what the Bible teaches."

"Who cares? Nobody uses the Bible anymore."

"If I believed that I'd have no hope at all."

"Welcome to my world."

"Jared, please give God another try. Put him to the test."

"It's all right, Mom."

"Don't just try to mollify me. I'm serious about this. You either believe in God or you don't. You believe in the God of the Bible or you don't."

"I don't."

Dallas flopped back in a chair.

Jared sat up straight. "Mom, you've given it your best shot. Time to cut your losses."

"Losses? What are you talking about?"

"Dad. Me."

"Stop it, Jared."

"Why?" He jumped up. "It's true, you know it. Face it! I'm gone, there's something wrong with me. It's not going to be straightened out by God or anybody else."

"Jared—"

"And Dad's been lying to you, for years probably. To both of us, to Cara too. You're too good for us, Mom. Move on with your life."

"I'm not giving up on you, Jared. Or your father. He's come clean to me, he asked me to forgive him."

"He's come clean?" Jared's voice was skeptical.

"I saw him. He told me a lot of things."

"How do you know he's not lying again?"

"I know because I was looking right at him."

"You're so naïve."

That brought Dallas to her feet, cheeks burning. "You think that? You really think that?"

"Yeah. I love you, Mom, but you're not in the real world sometimes."

"And I suppose you are? In the stinking mess you call a world, that's real to you?"

His eyes were cold. "You know it is."

"I don't know. You're the one who's naïve, Jared. You deny God. You deny the truth. You're wallowing in your misery. Well, it's time to snap out of it."

"You think I want this?"

"Maybe you do. If you don't turn it over to God, it's over."

"Then it's over. This whole idea was stupid." He turned his back on her and started toward the door.

She followed him. "What idea?"

"Coming home," he said.

"Don't go."

He faced her. "You go back to your world, Mom, if that makes you happy."

Then he opened the door and left.

Dallas didn't call after him.

3.

When you spend twenty-three hours a day in a box by yourself, you have time to think.

I was thinking about irony today.

I used to do a prison ministry when I first got to Hillside. Each Wednesday evening I'd take a little group out to Sylmar and preach to the inmates. That was before the membership at Hillside started to build, and I started putting all my efforts toward growing the church.

As I think about it now, the prison ministry, like the street preaching I used to do, made me depend on God, kept me on the edge, in a good way. The more popular I got, the less sharp the edge.

A. W. Tozer said something about preachers who seek comfort. It's easy to do in the ministry. Popularity becomes an opiate.

And that dulls the mind and even the moral sense. That helps explain Amy Shea and Melinda Perry.

Explains, doesn't excuse.

I am saying the twenty-third Psalm, over and over, out loud.

4.

That night, Dallas dreamed of something just beyond her reach. It was dark in the dream and she had to get this thing, or whatever it was, or she and her whole family would be lost or dead.

Dread, the substance of nightmares, infused her sleep. She tried to will herself to wake up, but not before transport to the edge of a cliff, looking down into dark waters. There. The thing was in there, but she was too high to reach it.

If she jumped, she might die. If she stayed, she might die. And behind her, something approached.

She woke up breathless, as if she'd fallen on her stomach. She fought for air. She was alone in the bedroom and it was still dark outside.

For a moment she sat in the silence, steadying her breathing.

And then she heard the floorboard squeak downstairs.

Jared. He'd come home.

But was he all right? She listened to the cadence of the footsteps, wondering if she could tell if he was drunk or drugged.

She couldn't. And the sounds ceased.

Which could have meant he was passed out. Or lying on the couch watching TV.

Dallas thought about going back to bed. Maybe he just wanted to be alone. But she couldn't. She had always checked on Jared, ever since he slept in a bassinette.

Throwing on a robe, she went downstairs.

It was dark. All lights out.

Then she saw the flickering glow of the TV screen.

"Jared?"

No answer. And no sound coming from the set. Just the flicker.

She went into the family room expecting Jared to be on the couch.

No one was there.

"Jared, where are you?"

The lights came on. And Dallas almost screamed.

Chad McKenzie was leaning against the far wall.

"Evening."

A hundred thoughts ripped through Dallas's mind. At the top of the heap was the one that reminded her she had not secured a stun gun as Jeff suggested.

"Get out of my house." She tried to put menace in the words, but they sounded flat.

Chad smiled. "A nice house too. You've done very well for yourself, Dallas."

"What do you think you're going to accomplish here? You've broken into my home. That'll send you back to prison."

"I didn't break anything. Did you hear anything break?"

"Then how . . ."

"You invited me in, remember? Oh, you may change your story later, but since there's no evidence, there's no problem."

Had he picked the lock? No, she'd left the back door open for Jared. Stupid!

Chad took a step away from the wall. "See, what really happened was I came to see an old friend, and you let me in and we had a nice talk."

"We are not going to have a nice talk."

"Sure we are." He was still wearing the dark coat. He held his hands out in an innocent gesture. "And when it's over, you'll understand a few things."

Dallas shook her head. "I have nothing to say to you, and my son is going to be home soon and he is an ex-Marine."

The news didn't faze him a bit. "About that. I'm sure he's a good kid and all, but he won't be coming home for a while."

The horror of the unspoken filled her. "What have you done to him?"

"Maybe we should sit down like good friends and discuss this."

"Tell me you—"

"Easy there, Dallas. I wouldn't want you to fall into sin. Wouldn't that be a fine how-do-you-do?"

She could fold, do what he said. But then she wouldn't find out if he was all bluff or not.

The power is not in me. It's in the armor. She mentally stepped behind the shield of faith.

"Don't worry about the boy," Chad said. "He'll sleep it off. He's got a bit of a drinking problem, doesn't he? Too bad. Some of our boys who served never get over it."

"Wherever Jared is, God is watching him. He's watching you too, Chad."

"I'm really worried about that."

"You should be."

"Trying to rattle the old Chadster? That's not like you."

"You don't know me. You don't know anything. You're a loser, Chad. You always have been."

His left cheek twitched. Enough for Dallas to know she'd landed a blow.

In the lull she weighed her alternatives. If she could get to her cell phone, which was charging in the kitchen, she could lock herself in the bathroom and call 911.

"That's not a very Christian attitude, I must say."

Or she could grab the hammer from the tool drawer and go for the head.

Chad looked at her, long and lingeringly. "You've really kept in shape there, Dallas."

Now the serious creeps were running all over her. "Tell me why you're here," she said, "and then go."

"You work out?"

"Chad—"

"I pushed a lot of steel in the slam, kept in pretty good shape myself. And I'm still a very loving person."

He was going to attack her.

She took a step back. If she made a break, he'd be on her in a second.

The armor ...

She blurted the first thing that came to her mind. "In the beginning was the Word, and the Word was with God, and the Word was God."

Chad squinted. "What?"

What indeed. But at least she'd stopped his advance.

"Your name is Legion," Dallas said. "For you are many."

"You've gone bye-bye," Chad said.

"Every knee shall bow and every tongue confess that Jesus Christ is Lord."

"Shut up."

"Do not tempt the Lord your God."

He jumped. It was quick, hard, and he was at her before she could even think.

His hands grabbed her robe. He pushed. She slammed against the wall, her head hitting last with a jarring thud.

His face was in front of her and she could smell his breath, a noxious mix of beer and cigarettes. She fought not to gag.

She raised her arms and went for his face. He anticipated the move, locked his hands on her wrists, and pulled her arms behind her back.

Her arm sockets filled with fire.

Chad McKenzie smiled.

And then he put his face to hers.

5.

Tonight I feel the need, the urge, the call to pray as I haven't prayed in years.

I am praying now, even as I write, even as I don't know how to pray. Only that I must.

The Bible says that the Spirit intercedes for us, with groans words can't express. That's what I need right now, Lord. Intercession from the Spirit, because I don't know how to pray.

The dinner just arrived. Burrito. I find I am looking forward to burrito night. It is one of the more palatable items on the fancy menu here. They like to keep the food laden with starch and carbs, to keep the prisoners happy. The burrito is their crowning achievement, and it comes as a small oasis in this desert of a cell.

The ravens brought meat to Elijah. I am almost positive that the burrito contains meat of some sort, but I do not ask for details.

Tonight, another message in a tin foil envelope came with the burrito. It was once again in King James: "Take heed, brethren, lest there be in any of you an evil heart of unbelief, in departing from the living God."

No Scripture reference, though it sounded familiar enough. The book of Hebrews, I thought, and looked it up. Sure enough, right there in chapter three.

Someone was playing with me, someone who was following my case. Maybe it was even one of the deputies who watches this cage.

Whoever it was, he was pressing a hot iron into my soul.

Yes, I feel the need to keep in prayer. I'm stopping now and getting on my knees.

6.

"Yo!"

Jared heard the word through a thick wall of brain matter.

"Yo, you better get up and get out, now!"

A kicking in the ribs. Jared opened his eyes. It was not easy. They were heavy and tired.

Cold. It was cold and he didn't know where he was. Hard ground. The sound of cars, an echo chamber. Dark. Some time of night.

Now a string of swear words from the voice and another kick in the ribs. Jared tried to focus. He looked up and saw a face staring at him.

It was not like any face he had ever seen.

The eyes were feral and fiery. Superior. The guy's face was distorted, not by expression but by some permanent force that had twisted bone and skin.

Around his head was a dirty blue bandana, and a stained coat covered the rest of his body. Jared caught a whiff of whisky and sweat.

"Gonna stomp your head to Jell-O, you don't get out now. Anywhere you go, I'll know where you are ..." And more foul language poured out of the man's malformed lips.

Jared's head was pounding like an industrial crusher. Fear shot through his body and got him to his feet.

The face did not move. "You're dead. You don't know it. Make it real, baby."

What?

His head was mush. He had no idea where he was. But he had to move or he had the feeling his insides would be torn out.

He began to stagger down the walk. He had no idea what direction he was going.

The voice of the man echoed off the walls of the underpass. But he didn't speak words. Now the guy was howling.

And Jared tried to run. His feet were cinder blocks, his legs hot rubber.

The howling was like a mad wolf at the sight of a harvest moon.

The world vibrated around him, swirled and gyrated. What was wrong with his head? The same smell—whisky and sweat—hit him again. Was the guy behind him?

No. Jared realized the smell was coming from him.

Drunk. I got drunk and passed out here.

Headlights from oncoming cars shot beams of blinding light through his skull. He was in the street now. A horn blared and tires squealed as the lights went around him.

Another voice, another shout, another obscenity. And then the car drove on.

Why couldn't he focus his eyes? Where had he been before this?

Get out of the street!

He sucked in a huge gulp of night air and made for a streetlight. A fixed point in this sea of uncertainty. He'd grab it. He could hold on.

It became his point of reference. By concentrating, he could keep the rest of the world from spinning out of control. If he could make it to the pole, he could hold on, hold tight.

He remembered something. A story. About the Asian tsunami of '04. He'd read the accounts, one about a fisherman in a little village. His house was completely washed away; the only thing left was a pole embedded deep in the ground. The man hung on, with his three children, to the pole. He lost two of the children. But four hours later they rescued the fisherman and his daughter, then found the other two kids alive.

A miracle, the fisherman said.

This would be like that, Jared managed to think. *Don't get washed away. Get away from the guy in the underpass.*

Another car blared a horn, went around him. He kept his eyes on the light pole. Wasn't that the way they used to show drunks in newspaper cartoons? Clinging to a lamppost?

Why wasn't his head clearing?

Where had he been drinking?

At last, the pole was within reach. Jared almost fell down getting to it. But he kept enough balance to get to the standard and throw his arms around the pole.

It was rough and cold against his cheek.

No, I wasn't drinking.

The thought cleared a path in his brain. Other thoughts followed, plowing the field.

He remembered storming out of his mother's house. They'd argued. About God. Yes, and other things. He was going to move back to Bakersfield, right?

He had his truck back, and he'd driven down to the little strip mall off Rinaldi. Went in the liquor store. What did he buy?

Jim Beam. A fifth.

Where was it? Where was his truck? He couldn't remember drinking anything. But his smell.

The light pole was keeping him up, helping him clear his head. He kept one arm draped around it.

He'd bought something else.

Gum. He bought some gum at the liquor store. He checked his right front pocket then. A mashed pack of Big Red. Cinnamon gum covered the smell of alcohol best. If he drank and drove and was stopped, Big Red would help him hide the fact.

But he did not drink. He was going to the park on Reseda to do it. He remembered getting out of the truck, taking the bottle with him.

The park. Something happened to him in the park.

7.

"You're still so fine," Chad said.

Dallas could not move. Chad's arms were like steel beams.

"Your man's been messing around on the side," he said. "Don't you think you deserve a little action?"

He's just talk. He wants to see you sweat.

But she could not deny that his talk always turned into physical abuse. Just before she left it had been the worst. He used duct tape to bind her, then beat her for an hour with a wire coat hanger.

No, he was not just talk.

He brought his face to her again. She turned hers. He licked her cheek.

Her mind flashed back, her body took on the full remembrance of how she'd felt when she finally worked up the guts to leave him. She'd thought seriously of killing him in his sleep.

She felt that way now.

"Listen, suppose we start all over again," Chad whispered. "I'm going to be getting a steady job real soon. Good future. Your man'll be sitting in the joint for the rest of his life. Fine woman like you shouldn't be alone."

He smiled and, once more, leaned toward her.

This time Dallas did not turn her head. She relaxed.

Chad ran his tongue over her lips.

She let him.

His grip lessened. Slightly.

With a quick jerk she thrust upward with the heel of her hand and smashed his nose.

She felt the crunch of cartilage.

Chad shrieked and stepped back.

In another defensive move, one she'd taught many women, Dallas smacked Chad's ears with her cupped hands. He screamed again. His eardrums would be damaged and his equilibrium upset.

She pushed him hard in the chest with both hands.

He staggered back, hands on his face. She saw blood seeping through his fingers.

She ran.

An onslaught of obscenity erupted from Chad, and she knew she had to get out of the house or she'd be dead.

She was aware of her robe flapping and pulled it tight. She was barefoot. How far could she get that way? He'd catch her.

Outside, she could scream. But would anybody hear? Were all her neighbors blissfully asleep?

Chad's voice, behind her, guttural and foul, getting closer.

She knew then she wouldn't have time to unlock the front door, throw it open, get outside. She knew, too, that getting outside would not bring freedom.

I have to get to a phone. No, no time to call.

Lock myself in a room.

How long would that last?

Dear God, help.

She charged up the stairs. *Stupid.* But there was no turning back.

There was, however, a heavy table at the top of the stairs. Her grandmother's oak table, given to Dallas shortly after her marriage. Not the flimsy kind the furniture warehouses sold by the bushel. This wood had substance.

Halfway up the stairs Dallas heard Chad charging around the corner. She didn't have to turn and look.

She had to get to the table. Throw it down on top of him.

But was she strong enough to move it?

"Got you now, baby." Chad's voice mocked her. Dallas sensed that he'd stopped to gloat. She was at the top stair and looked back.

He was smiling, his hands out wide, his face grotesquely smeared with blood. "Come to papa!"

The fear and rage in her practically lifted her off her feet. She knew, simply knew, that she'd have no trouble with the table. It was squat, with a doily on top. And a drawer. In the drawer were some old pictures and papers she hadn't looked at in years.

The past surrounded her.

"Alone again . . ." Chad was singing!

Her back was to the stairs, the table against the wall. *Leg muscles. Use your leg muscles to lift.*

". . . naturally . . ."

She lifted. And the table was slightly off the floor.

It was heavy, like holding a sack of cement. Leaning back, she let the weight of it produce momentum.

One shot at this. One.

Chad had stopped singing.

When she whirled around and let the table go, she knew she'd been perfect. It took a bounce, then hit him.

Table and man fell down the stairs, leaving a bloody streak on the beige carpeting.

And then Chad's body lay at the bottom of the stairs, motionless.

Dallas, aware of her own breathing, watched. She hoped he was dead.

Then she ran to the bedroom, locked the door, grabbed the phone, and dialed 911.

A woman's voice answered. "Dispatch, how may I help you?"

"There's someone in my house. He wants to kill me." She was sure that was his intent.

The 911 operator, calm of voice, began to ask a question. Dallas didn't wait. She gave her address. "Get someone out here right away."

"We are notifying the police right now. Can you hang on?"

"I don't know, I—"

"Are you safe, ma'am? Are you in a secure location?"

"Just hurry."

She put the phone on the bed and considered her options. Maybe she'd better get out of the house, but that would mean going past Chad's body. But what other choice was there?

She quickly threw on a workout pants and jacket, and a pair of Nikes, not bothering with socks.

She heard a siren in the distance, getting closer.

She reached under the bed for the big flashlight, the kind the police carry, which she kept there in case of earthquake.

Now she was glad she had it for another reason. It was a perfect club.

If he broke in, she'd be ready for him.

◊

Jared was finally getting his bearings. The freeway was the 405. He saw the sign for the onramp.

He was remembering what happened in the park.

Blackout.

One moment he'd been sitting on the top of a park table, feet on the bench, the bottle of Jim Beam beside him, the dark trees his only company.

The next moment he was out.

And now he was in a different location, not knowing how he got there.

But there was something strange here.

His mouth, for one thing. His tongue was not thick, nor his throat dry, the way they would be if he had too much to drink.

He looked up at the light, blurry to his eyes. He tried to focus on it.

But there was still a fuzziness in his brain.

Why was this happening? It was like a hole had opened up in his head in Iraq, and darkness poured in, something foreign and vicious. It wasn't PTSD, like the VA kept saying. It was a whole lot scarier.

But now what? He couldn't stay here all night.

His truck. Back at the park.

Could he make it? How far had he walked?

More to the point. What would he do when he got to the truck?

And then, he knew.

9.

Dallas tried not to breathe loud enough to be heard.

The sirens were close now, and she was still alone upstairs.

She hoped.

She listened at the bedroom door. If Chad was indeed out there and tried to break in, she'd have a slight advantage. She'd planned it out in her mind. She'd throw the door open, then knock a homer with the flashlight.

She was amazed at how anxious she was to do it. Chad McKenzie was back, and he'd done something to Jared. She wasn't going to turn the other cheek at that.

Threaten my family and you're toast.

No sound outside her door. The sirens stopped.

Half a minute passed.

A knock at the door.

She had to go down. The front door was locked.

Holding the flashlight at the ready, she threw open the bedroom door.

And saw pieces. Four pieces of a photograph.

It was a wedding photo, the one of her and Ron looking at each other adoringly, the one she had selected above all others to be framed and hung in the hallway.

Now it was removed, torn and quartered, and placed like a mocking curse in front of her bedroom door.

ELEVEN

1.

The police officer took a half hour to get the story from Dallas. A tech arrived, and the officer suggested Dallas find another place to stay while they finished gathering evidence.

Dallas remembered that Cara was up in Santa Barbara with two girlfriends for a couple of days. So she called the Bensons and got Lisa.

"I know it's late," Dallas said. "But something's happened."

"What is it?"

"Can I come over?"

"Of course, but—"

"I'll be right there."

Bob and Lisa Benson lived in Canoga Park, about a fifteen-minute drive from the church on a low-traffic day.

Lisa was waiting for her outside the house.

"I'm so sorry to get you up," Dallas said.

"No worries," Lisa said. "Come on in and tell us what's going on."

Bob, his eyes a little red, looked concerned. Lisa brought her into the living room of the little "starter" home. In the Valley, where the median price of a home was over half a million dollars, young couples like Lisa and Bob had to start out on the lower end of the spectrum.

That meant less house in an older neighborhood.

But for its very smallness, it was homey and put Dallas just the slightest bit more at ease as she sat.

"I was attacked tonight. In my home."

Lisa put a hand to her chest. "Attacked?"

Dallas told them the story. She found she was trembling at the end, as if Chad were right there in the room with them.

"Are the police doing anything?" Bob asked.

"They came to the house and I told them what happened. They said they'd look into it, but I know Chad. He's toyed with the law before. He knows what he's doing."

"Would you like to stay here tonight?" Lisa asked.

Gratefully, Dallas accepted. Lisa made up the bed in the small guest room of the two-bedroom house. When she was finished, she sat on the bed next to Dallas. "This is all going to pass," Lisa said. "You're one of the strongest women I know. You're holding up under a lot of strain."

"I don't have any other choice."

Dallas's cell phone beeped. She looked at the screen. A number she did not recognize. Her entire body shuddered with a deep chill.

What if it was Chad?

"You going to answer?" Lisa whispered.

"I don't know."

But then she decided to take a chance, for only one reason.

"Hello?"

"Mom?"

She'd been right. "Jared, where are you?"

"I'm somewhere in North Hills, I think. I just wanted to tell you not to worry. I'm not going to make your life any worse."

"Jared, wait—"

But he was gone.

"No, please."

Lisa put a hand on her arm. "Where is he?"

"North Hills is all he said. I'm afraid he's going to kill himself." Not just afraid. Practically certain.

"Maybe we can find him."

"How could we possibly?"

"Let me see your phone."

Dallas gave it to Lisa. She flipped it open, hit a couple of buttons. "Come on."

She bounded out of the room like an excited schoolgirl. Dallas followed to the dining room, which for the Bensons was also an office. A laptop was on the dining-room table.

Lisa sat in a chair and patted the empty one next to her. Dallas sat in it.

"I'm going to show you an awesome search site," Lisa said, her fingers already on the keyboard. Dallas watched with a feeling of admiration and unease. She was as far removed from this generation as her own mother had been from Dallas's. For her, computers were complex and barely tolerable. Oh, she could do common things and even surf the Net, but for Lisa it was like second nature. In no time she had called up a site with little phone graphics all over it.

"I'm going to type in the phone number where Jared was."

She did. Then hit *return.*

In two seconds a result came up.

"We can find out where that phone is," Lisa said. "All it'll cost is $14.95. You want to?"

"Yes! I'll pay."

"We have to put in a credit card."

"I'll get mine." Dallas retrieved her Visa card from her purse in the guest room, brought it to Lisa.

"You trust me with the number?" Lisa said. "I can order lots of cool stuff with this."

"Hurry."

Lisa typed in the card number and expiration date. Hit *return* again.

"Here it comes," she said. "It's a pay phone."

"Pay phone? Does it say where?"

"It sure does. The intersection of Lassen and Sepulveda."

"Can you drive me there?"

"Let's do it."

They drove to Lassen and Sepulveda in Lisa's Camry, but there was no sign of Jared by the battered pay phone. The sidewalks were deserted. Lisa took the car through some strip mall parking lots, past bus stops and mini-marts.

"Maybe we should call the police or something," Lisa said.

"Based on what? That I want to talk to my son? He's an adult. They wouldn't help."

"I suppose not."

"But you have," Dallas said. "Thanks anyway."

"Let's go home. Get some rest." Lisa turned the car around.

It was good to be going back with Lisa, good to have a friend taking the reins, at least for this night.

2.

I remember vividly my first fight with Dallas.

She was mesmerizing to me. When I baptized her in the ocean, her face was the most radiant thing I'd ever seen. I kept thinking of that story where the sinful woman anoints Jesus's feet and cries over them, wiping his feet with her hair. Jesus told the Pharisee that because she had been forgiven much, she loved much.

That's what Dallas's face reflected, and I was a little jealous of her.

I admit that now. It was wrong, but I was.

Because I had never experienced what I saw reflected in her face.

Later, we fought about that. It was before we were married.

I should say, I fought about that. Dallas was doing volunteer work with our evangelism team, and she could not stop talking about Jesus. She was flush with the enthusiasm that overtook converts in those days. I don't see it happening that much anymore.

At least not at Hillside.

But one day I told her she needed to cool it a little.

"Why?" she asked.

"Because, well, you're coming off as a little bit fanatical."

"And that's bad?"

"A little."

"Why?"

"It just is."

Without any hesitation at all, without any realization that she had no training or knowledge in matters theological, she said, "That seems a little bit strange, coming from someone trying to keep people from going to hell."

Maybe it was the word strange *that got to me. But I proceeded to tell her she was making it all too simplistic, that she was missing the bigger picture.*

"What's bigger than showing people how to get to heaven?" she said.

"You're a little young in the faith yet."

"Stop trying to control me."

"I'm not—"

"You are. And don't tell me you're not, because I've been with a pro, baby, the big leagues. Don't play that game."

I unloaded on her for that. And she just looked at me with these eyes that said she understood more than I did.

Now I know she brought something of her worldliness to her new faith and was more on fire than I had ever been.

I knew I had to have her for my wife. I did not mean to put out her fire.

3.

Jared's first thought was that this was not his father. It was some actor, cast in a TV movie about Ron Hamilton. A good likeness, but not the man who raised him, whom Jared had idolized, then run away from.

His eyes were not familiar. The assurance and certainty of purpose they once held was gone. He had wounded eyes now, red-rimmed with affliction.

Why had he even come? Last night, after calling his mother, he drove to the top of Chatsworth, a place he'd gone to many times to get away. He slept in his truck, trying to figure out if he wanted to see his dad one last time.

He did know he was going to get out. Leave L.A. He didn't care about the DUI or anything else. He was messed up, and hanging around here was just making life worse for his mom.

Time to cut the cord. And that, in the end, was what brought him to the jail. Two cords needed to be severed.

"Hello, Jared." His father's voice was tinny coming over the wire.

Jared nodded.

"Thank you for coming. I didn't think you would."

"So how you getting along in here?"

"Oh, not so bad, considering."

There was a taut formality between them, which Jared grasped lightly as a protective covering, like an awning against rain. Who would be the first to take it down, dare to get wet?

"I really came here to help Mom get through this thing," Jared said.

"That's good. That's really good. How are *you* getting along?"

"I been working. Up in Bakersfield." He decided not to go into any greater detail. What his father didn't know about his recent past was best left hidden.

"That's good," Ron said.

But Jared heard the subtle disheartenment in his father's voice. It stretched out in a ribbon of silence.

"Don't believe what the papers are saying," Ron said. "I did not do this."

Jared shrugged.

"You have to believe that, Jared. I couldn't stand it if I thought you didn't believe me. I couldn't do such a horrible thing. Ever."

You have no idea what horrible things you, what anybody, can do.
"Sure."

"There's just no way."

But Jared did not believe him. There was a desperation about him now. He would say anything. In a way, Jared understood. His father was a man who put great stock in appearances. How could Jared expect him to come clean in front of his son?

Lies. He'd been taught his whole life that lies were sin. Now his father used them for his own sanity. Jared couldn't really blame him for that. Sanity was something hard to keep hold of.

"I really wanted to see you again," Ron said.

"I know."

"Jared, please pray for me."

Jared said nothing.

"Will you do that for me, Jared?"

"Just don't hurt Mom anymore."

"No, I don't want to. Jared, please tell me you believe me, will you? Can you tell me that?"

Jared looked at the table.

"You do believe me, right?"

Jared started to stand.

"Don't go yet. There's so much I want to know about you."

"No. You don't want to know, Dad. I'll see you."

"Wait!"

4.

He did not wait. My son.

Why?

Why didn't it all work out as planned? My family was supposed to be my big achievement.

I remember being embarrassed about Jared. When he started to show signs of rebellion, I didn't want it known. It would have hurt my reputation.

When he got in trouble at school, I sent Dallas down to do the dirty work. I didn't want anybody to see me show up.

I wanted to sweep Jared under the rug.

He knew that. Kids always know.

I tried to reach him. But I did it with that stupid concept called "quality time." He needed time, period.

I found that out too late.

5.

Jared sat in the truck in front of his mother's house, wondering if he should continue waiting for his mom.

Maybe it would be best to forget the good-byes and just go. He could always call later and not have to face her. There would be tears and it would get all complicated.

He didn't need that.

As he gripped the steering wheel he knew he'd never be back. The last good time he could remember in his life had been in that house. It was when Cara came to his room one night and they didn't fight. Instead she'd confided in him about boyfriend troubles and asked for his advice. For once he was the one who had the wisdom, and she'd actually listened.

After, she kissed him on the cheek and hugged him, and he felt loved by his sister, and that was good. The last good time.

A tap on the window startled him.

Tiana was standing outside his truck, Jamaal behind her.

Jared got out. "What is this?"

"Hey," she said.

"What are you doing here?"

"Came to find you."

"Me? Why?"

"I wanted to tell you something."

"How'd you get here?"

"Bus."

Jamaal stuck his head out from behind his mother and smiled at Jared.

"How you doin'?" Jared said.

"Good," Jamaal said.

Tiana knelt down. "Jamaal, go over and sit on the steps there, will you, baby? I need to talk to Jared."

"I wanna stay."

"Go on."

"I wanna *stay*."

Jared looked at him. "If you go do like your mama says, I'll toss the football with you some, huh?"

"You will?"

"Sure."

"Deal." And he ran off toward the front steps of the house.

"So what's going on?" Jared asked.

"Something's up with Rafe. Something that has to do with you."

Jared shook his head.

"After you came to see Jamaal that day, he whaled on me good. He said something was going on with you and me."

Jared put his hands on her shoulders. "You're not going back, you hear me?"

She closed her eyes. "I just came to tell you he said he's going to do something to you. Mess you up."

"I don't care about that. I don't want you and Jamaal going back."

"What have you got to say about it?"

"I don't want you back there."

"Who cares what you want? I've got nothing else."

"You've got me."

The words stunned him. But he knew he meant them.

Tiana shook her head. "What're you talking about?"

"The three of us are going to figure it out together, and you're not going back. Stay with me. I'll take care of you."

"How?"

"I'll figure it out. First thing we do is get a place. I know where we can go. You coming?"

She paused, then looked past him. Jared turned around. Jamaal was looking at him.

"Can we throw the football now?" Jamaal said.

Tiana said to Jared, "What have you got in mind?"

6.

"I've got two things to talk to you about," Jeff said as he closed his office door. He did not look pleased.

Dallas took in a labored breath. "Bad news?" Of course it was bad news. That's why he hadn't told her anything over the phone. Instead, he told her to come to his office even though it was nearly six at night.

Jeff smoothed his tie — red with understated palm trees on it, very L.A. — and sat on the corner of his desk.

"I got the arrest report on Jared's DUI," he said. "And I think I can get a dismissal."

"You mean completely gone?"

Jeff nodded. "There's a little thing called a driving requirement for a DUI. The person actually has to be driving. Even if it's only an inch. But according to the report, Jared was passed out in the car. That's not going to cut it."

"Any good news at this point is welcome," she said. "And I have something to tell you."

Jeff waited.

"Chad, the guy I told you about, he came to my house last night. He attacked me."

"What?"

"I managed to call 911. The police came, but he got away."

"This is terrible." Jeff walked to the window of his office, which looked out on Ventura Boulevard and the Valley beyond. The tone in his voice was so ominous it made Dallas think of horror movies. She was about to be lowered into some sort of pit.

"Jeff, what is it? What's the other news? Did Mr. Stegman talk to that witness I found?"

"He tried."

"Tried?"

He turned back to face her. "Dallas, I've always been up front with you about this case, and I don't want to stop now. Are you with me on that?"

Fighting back a jitter, Dallas said, "Yes. I want to know everything."

"Then I'll tell you. First of all, that witness you found, like I told you before, is not going to be very helpful. There's a gang connection, and the issue of mental competence."

"But it's *something*."

"Less than that, Dallas, believe me. I've been doing this a long time. But yes, it was the one thing that had any sort of connection."

"What do you mean *was*?"

Jeff paused as if looking for the right words.

With all the strength she had, Dallas fought against the anguish trying to open a hole inside her. "Tell me, Jeff. Tell me right now."

"It's going to hurt."

"Tell me."

"Dallas, this morning I received several reports from the prosecution. Evidence they intend to introduce in a trial."

"What sort of evidence?"

"They completed an inventory of what they found on Ron's computer."

"And?"

Very slowly and deliberately he said, "Dallas, it's loaded with pornography."

A momentary darkness hit her behind the eyes, as if someone smashed out the lights with a club. Air rushed from her lungs.

"Pornography?" She could barely say it.

"I'm afraid so."

Dallas fought to keep coherent. *This can't be happening.* "You said *loaded?*"

"According to the report, there are over seven hundred images."

Seven hundred!

Dallas conjured an image of Ron in her mind, sitting in front of his computer with a devious grin on his face. She scratched it out of her brain. That couldn't be right. The deception involved. She would have known. She would have—

"Where are they?" she said.

"Where are what?"

"The reports. I want to see them."

"Dallas, don't go there—"

"Show me!"

Jeff pursed his lips and reached for something on his desk. It was an inch-thick sheaf of papers. "Don't punish yourself," he said.

"Give it to me."

It was page after page of thumbnail pornographic images. At about the fifth page she dropped the report on the floor, fell from the chair to her knees, and sobbed uncontrollably—huge, lung-collapsing sobs.

She felt Jeff's hands lifting her like deadweight. But that was the only sensation outside of her manifest grief and shaking body that she was aware of.

The sobs melted into audible gulps, full of more despair than she could ever remember.

She had entered the office clinging to a safety line. She'd begun
to think there would be a change in trajectory soon, that God would
not allow more than she could bear.

Now this. No more clinging, no more line. She was falling.

Jeff handed her a tissue and she stabbed at her eyes with it.

"I'm so sorry, Dallas. We'll talk about the case later."

"What case?" she said bitterly. "He's guilty. He did it."

"Dallas—"

"He lied to my face. Again. He's never stopped lying! There's no
way he's not guilty."

"He insists—"

"I don't care what he insists! I don't care what happens to him.
Let him rot in prison."

"Dallas, let's give this a day or two—"

She stood up. "I don't need a day. I don't need another second.
What you do with Ron is up to you. I want no part of it anymore."

Jeff looked at the floor. "I can't say that I don't understand. Listen, if there's anything you need, call me."

"There is something I need."

"What is it?"

"The name of a divorce lawyer."

PART II

Meanwhile the passions rage like tyrants,
and throw into confusion the whole soul and life of men.

Augustine

TWELVE

1.

"Tonight, an exclusive. The first interview with Dallas Hamilton, wife of Ron Hamilton, the minister accused of murdering Melinda Chance at the Star Motel. She speaks out publicly for the first time on *Hank Dunaway Tonight*."

Dunaway's trademark theme music—synthesized trumpets with a military air—played. And Dallas tried to swallow. Her throat was dead dry.

But she knew Dunaway was a master at putting people at ease. She hoped he was on his game tonight.

Dunaway looked into the camera.

"Ron Hamilton, a minister from Los Angeles, sits in jail tonight awaiting trial on a murder charge. The case has been all over the news since his arrest two months ago. But no one has heard from Ron Hamilton's wife, Dallas. Until tonight."

He looked at her now, his blue eyes crinkled at the corners. "How have you been holding up the last few weeks?"

She forced a smile. "Holding. Thanks."

"Where were you when your husband was arrested?"

"In my bedroom."

"What were you thinking when it happened?"

"That there had to be some mistake."

"And when you found out it wasn't a mistake, how did you feel?"

She thought a moment. "A two-by-four to the head."

"You hired a lawyer?"

"Jefferson Waite, yes."

"And the trial has been set for August?"

"Yes."

"You have children?"

"Two."

"How are they taking it?"

Dallas blinked. "Different reactions."

"How old are they?"

"My daughter is twenty-seven. My son is twenty-four."

Dunaway glanced at a sheet of paper in front of him. "I understand you had an incident in your home last week."

"I was attacked by a man named Chad McKenzie."

For a moment Dunaway seemed taken aback. But he kept his cool. "You knew the man?"

"He was someone I was involved with when I was a teenager. An abuser. He apparently thought he could use my trouble to his advantage. I hope the police will discuss that with him soon. He has threatened to go to the press with some sordid stories about me and claims to have photographs of me when I was with him, doing things. He wanted to extort money from me in return for his not giving the photos to the press. Well, I have a message for him. He's not going to get a thing from me, ever. What I did thirty years ago is over. I was not a Christian then. I am now, and whatever I did has been forgiven and forgotten by God."

Dunaway paused for what seemed like dramatic effect, then announced a commercial break.

"You're doing fine," he told her during the break. "You feeling all right?"

"Surprisingly, yes." And she was. It was cathartic, finally being able to talk.

When they started up again, Dunaway asked, "When was the last time you saw Ron?"

"I don't remember the date."

"You haven't been talking to the press. What prompted you to come forward now?"

This was the moment. "I wanted to talk about the bigger picture here, the bigger problem. And that is the pornography business in this city, in this country. That, I believe, is behind what's going on."

"Behind the murder of Melinda Chance?"

"She was a porn actress. She was employed by a pornographer named Vic Lu. How he and his ilk are allowed to operate I don't know. Prostitution is illegal, but this kind of filmed prostitution is not. It doesn't make sense, it's wrong, and it has to be stopped."

"Your husband wrote an antipornography book, didn't he?"

"Right."

"So you can't blame the press for picking up on that angle."

"I'm beyond blaming the press. They follow what sells. I'm more concerned about the blight of pornography in our communities, and what it does even beyond the people who make it and the people who buy it."

"What do you mean, beyond?"

"I believe there is a spiritual component to this, Hank. Evil is real, and it emanates."

"You're not calling people who buy adult videos evil, are you?"

"They're playing with a fire they don't understand."

"But evil?"

"Hank, I believe evil is real. Don't you?"

Dunaway raised his eyebrows. "Some TV critics maybe."

"I wouldn't disagree, but I also think the truth goes deeper than that."

"You said you're a Christian."

"That's right."

"What would you say to people who reject your views as merely personal and religious?"

She relaxed a little more. She and Ron had discussed this objection many times. "We're all citizens, and we can all look at our society and see if it's the kind we want to live in. And a society that condones pornography by labeling it 'adult entertainment,' that turns a blind eye to the garbage that keeps pouring out, that's not the kind of place I want to leave to our children and grandchildren."

"What can anyone do about it?"

"Get mad, for one thing. Quit sitting on the sidelines about it. And get involved. Get in line with good politicians like Bernie Halstrom, and tell them your concerns."

"Bernie Halstrom is in the studio with us tonight."

"Yes, he is. He is one of the few politicians who actually puts action behind his words. I heard someone say that evil wins when good people do nothing. Let's all do something and maybe we can start to get rid of the flesh merchants."

"We'll be right back," Dunaway said to the camera.

2.

The wind was whipping up dust in the Chatsworth hills. It was funny, pitching a tent up here. Jared had pitched camp in a lot of places, but not within a rock's throw of the 118 freeway.

Down below, the lights of the San Fernando Valley started to blink into life. In the tent, Jamaal slept soundly on top of a sleeping bag. Jared could only imagine what the kid had probably been through.

"It's kind of pretty, isn't it?" Tiana said. She and Jared sat on the dirt, looking into the Valley.

"I guess."

"Why are you doing this for Jamaal and me?"

"I don't know. I just don't want you to get hurt anymore. I don't want you going back to that guy."

"I don't know why I even went back in the first place," she said.

"Hey, we're all dumb in some way. I don't know why I do most of the things I do either."

"I'm scared though."

"What of?"

"Taking care of Jamaal. I've got no way to make money."

"Everybody can do something."

"I'm not talking about working at McDonald's. I can do that. But that's not going to be enough for Jamaal."

"You love him, right?"

"Of course I do."

"That's the most important thing." He thought of his own mother then, the way she always stood by him. Was he doing the right thing by going away now?

"What do you like to do most in the world?" Jared asked.

"I don't really know."

"Well, think about it this way: When you were twelve years old or so, what was your favorite thing?"

She grew quiet for a long time. "I guess I liked to make pretty things. Didn't have much around, but I was always trying to make things look nice. I remember once I had this dress, the one I wore to church whenever my mom took me, and I found some tinsel in a trash can, you know the kind you put on Christmas trees?"

"Yeah."

"And I took it and I took some of my mom's sewing stuff and I sewed this tinsel onto my dress. A whole bunch of it. I wanted it to look like the kind of dress I saw on TV when the movie stars'd go out and be all glamorous. When my mom saw it she about fainted. But she let me wear it to church."

Jared could hear the cars on the 118, a steady rush like a river flowing. "Maybe you can make things pretty again. I think there's got to be a place for that in this world."

Tiana said nothing.

"What happened to your mom?" Jared asked.

"Died when I was fifteen."

"How?"

"Homeboys shot up the wrong place."

Jared shook his head. "I'm sorry."

Tiana put her arms across her chest. "It's getting cold."

"We're gonna have to huddle up in there." Jared nodded toward the tent. "Hope you don't mind." Then he added, "You can trust me."

"Hope so. 'Cause I've had enough of the bad stuff."

Bad stuff. Jared closed his eyes. For this brief moment the bad seemed miles away. Down there, in the Valley. Along the freeway corridor, where angry drivers hunched over wheels. In the neighborhoods, where tempers flared and guns went off. The bad stuff was all out there in this moment, not here with the air and boulders and brush, and the three of them together.

He would not be the one to hurt them. As far as he could help it, he would not be the one.

3.

"You were terrific," Bernie Halstrom said as they pulled out of the studio on Fairfax where the Hank Dunaway show was broadcast. Dallas had met him at his office, and Bernie had brought her to the studio in his Town Car, complete with driver. She didn't turn down the luxury. It was nice to be taken care of.

"Might have to hire you to be my personal PR maven," Bernie added.

Tired but wired from the interview, Dallas said, "Maybe I'll take you up on it."

"Anytime. I want to tell you I think you've got tremendous courage. I don't know many women as strong as you, Dallas."

"I'm running on fumes here."

"No, you did great."

"Thank you for setting it up."

"Hank's an old friend." Bernie looked at her. "And a good one to have on your side."

"I need all the help I can get."

"Have you heard from Jared?"

"One message. To tell me he's all right." But he wasn't all right. He'd skipped his DUI appearance, and Jeff said he was now subject to arrest.

She leaned back against the headrest and agonized silently. *How long, Lord, before you answer my prayers? I'm worn out.*

"How about a bite to eat?" Bernie said.

"No, thanks. Being on TV takes something out of you. How do you do it?"

"I went to Ireland last year and kissed the Blarney Stone."

"Really?"

"No. But it's a good story."

He let the ride continue in silence, which was nice. Dallas closed her eyes. She prayed for Jared then and thought of Ron and Jared together. Reconciled. No matter where they ended up individually, they were father and son after all. They needed each other.

Her thoughts drifted back to happier times, which seemed a century ago. The four of them, the whole family, at Disneyland.

Cara was healthy again and Jared had not yet lapsed into sullenness. They all got soaked on Splash Mountain, but Ron and Jared got the worst of it, and they laughed and hugged each other, a couple of soggy maniacs—

"What's the matter?" Bernie Halstrom's voice, directed to his driver, Derek, jerked Dallas to the present.

Derek had stopped short of the lot. "There's somebody standing there."

Dallas looked out the front window. Illuminated by the headlights, a man stood in the middle of the drive. He wore a Hawaiian shirt and jeans.

"Shall I back away?" Derek said.

"Wait a second." Bernie leaned forward. "No. I know who that is." He turned to Dallas. "How would you like to meet Vic Lu?"

4.

Have mercy upon me, O God, according to thy loving-kindness; according unto the multitude of thy tender mercies blot out my transgressions.

Wash me thoroughly from mine iniquity, and cleanse me from my sin.

For I acknowledge my transgressions, and my sin is ever before me.

Against thee, thee only, have I sinned, and done this evil in thy sight: that thou mightest be justified when thou speakest, and be clear when thou judgest.

Behold, I was shapen in iniquity, and in sin did my mother conceive me.

Behold, thou desirest truth in the inward parts, and in the hidden part thou shalt make me know wisdom.

Purge me with hyssop, and I shall be clean; wash me, and I shall be whiter than snow.

Make me hear joy and gladness, that the bones which thou hast broken may rejoice.

Hide thy face from my sins, and blot out all mine iniquities.

Create in me a clean heart, O God, and renew a right spirit within me.

Cast me not away from thy presence, and take not thy holy Spirit from me.

Restore unto me the joy of thy salvation, and uphold me with a free spirit.

Then will I teach transgressors thy ways, and sinners shall be converted unto thee.

Amen.

5.

Vic Lu had an exotic look, what Dallas thought used to be called Eurasian. His black hair was nearly shoulder length and slicked back. His casual clothes could have been worn by any number of beach-loving, laid-back Angelenos.

In his midthirties, he didn't look like the multimillionaire the reports said he was.

"I caught the show tonight," Lu said. "Man, I'm being hammered here." He smiled. His teeth were white, perfect.

The three of them were in Bernie Halstrom's office and, for all Dallas knew, alone in the government building.

"Is that what you came to tell me?" Bernie said. "That you're a Hank Dunaway fan?"

"Bernie, I'm right up the street here. We're neighbors. We never talk. I heard Mrs. Hamilton say you were at the studio with her. I figured you'd come back here. I didn't know Mrs. Hamilton would be with you. That's what you call a bonus."

"What is it you have to say?" Bernie said.

"That I'm not the bad guy here, all right?" He looked at Dallas. "Mrs. Hamilton, all I'm doing is making a living, okay? Just like anybody else."

"The flesh trade is not a living, is it?" she said.

"I'm in business. I'm a working man, all right? I came over here fifteen years ago, no money, no nothing. I used to clean up the bathrooms at the bus station downtown. You know what that's like? You have no idea. But I did it because I needed a job, and you know what? That's the best I could do at the time. I don't even have a high school diploma. I read books alone at night, trying to figure out how to better myself."

Bernie said, "Lots of people work their way up and don't go into your business."

"My business is legal, Bernie. I want to remind you of that. LookyLu may not be MGM, but it's legit. I know you're trying to do your thing, your political thing, and I accept that. But right now I'm as legal as the Ford dealer on Topanga. And I treat my actors like royalty. They get the best pay in the business, the best medical, the best HIV tests. I'm not twisting any arms to get them to be in my movies. And if I didn't hire them, they'd be working for some other dude who doesn't care half as much as I do."

"But it's what they *do*," Dallas blurted, unable to stop herself. "It's ..."

"Indecent?"

"That's a nice word for it."

"Sinful?"

"Yes."

"I know you've got religious beliefs, and I respect them. I really do. I believe in America. I believe in freedom of religion. And if a guy doesn't have religion, he's free too. And as long as he obeys the law, he's allowed to run a business. Bernie, tell her I'm legitimate, will you?"

Bernie allowed his desk chair to swivel. "That's not a word I prefer to use."

"Then at least stop the personal stuff," Lu said, looking at Dallas.

"I have the right to speak, just as you have the right to make pornography."

"Come on, Mrs. Hamilton," Lu said, spreading his hands wide. "What I'm doing is legal. What you're doing is a personal attack. Is that what Jesus would do, Mrs. Hamilton?"

"Let's not bring Jesus into this," Bernie said.

"Why not? She has."

He was right, of course. "All right," she said. "But that doesn't mean I'm going to stop trying to change the laws."

"Fair enough," Vic Lu said. "That's America too." He stood up. "I know you don't approve of me, Mrs. Hamilton, and I respect that. I respect the right of people to disagree. I also have feelings involved in this."

"Feelings?" Bernie said. He remained seated.

"Melinda Chance, she was one of my girls. Now she's dead. I've had a death in the family. Can you understand that, Mrs. Hamilton?"

She hadn't thought of it that way before, that he could in any way be running anything even remotely like a family. But in his world, maybe that's all the family he had.

"I'm sorry for what happened to her," Dallas said. "That shouldn't happen to anybody."

"I'm sorry it was your husband who did it," Lu said. "I know that must be very hard to take."

"Let me remind you," said Bernie, "that another one of America's better assets is the presumption of innocence. We have a trial to determine guilt."

Lu nodded almost imperceptibly. "Point taken. And I've taken up too much of your time. I'm glad we had this little chat."

6.

At Cara's apartment, Dallas almost fell asleep sitting on the sofa. But thoughts of meeting Vic Lu face-to-face kept her awake. There was something about him, beyond his slick persona and filthy industry, that needled her.

Yeah, a needle in a haystack.

"You looked good on TV, Mom," Cara said, coming in with hot tea. She set the tray on the coffee table. "Very cool and collected."

"Thanks. My nerves were like a cat after an earthquake."

"You came across fine."

"Thanks for the tea." Dallas picked her cup up and waited for Cara to do the same.

Instead, Cara slipped her hands into the pockets of her jeans. It was a gesture from her childhood. The preparation for uncomfortable words.

"What is it, Cara?"

"Are you really going to divorce Dad?"

So there it was. The elephant in the room, the thing Dallas had tried to ignore.

Cara kept her hands in her pockets. Her arms looked rigid. "It's kind of harsh, don't you think?"

Dallas sat back on the sofa. "Divorce is always harsh."

"Then why are you doing it?"

"You know why."

"Just because some other stuff has turned up?"

"Other *stuff*? Cara, I don't know if you realize what's been coming out, things your father ..." She paused. "I don't want to say things that will hurt you."

"What things?"

"About your father."

"What about him? Aren't you hurting him?"

"He's brought this on himself."

Cara took her hands from her pockets dramatically and slapped her sides, just like she used to do when she was little. "Oh, that's a fine thing to say."

"You don't think it's true?" Dallas tried to keep her voice low, but it rose anyway.

"Can't you just forget about what's in the past and go on?"

"Maybe once I thought I could do that. But the lies—"

"Now he's a liar?"

Yes, Cara, he is. "I know it's hard on you, really."

"No, you don't. What makes you think you really know what's going on, anyway?"

"Cara—"

Her daughter shook her head and, without another word, left the room. Dallas didn't have the energy to pursue her. Spent, she put her head back on the sofa and closed her eyes. *God, what is it you want me to do? Keep me from sinning against you—*

Her phone chimed. She didn't recognize the number. Maybe it was Jared again.

"Hello?"

"I'm real disappointed in you, Dallas."

Chad.

She couldn't speak.

"You know what my nose looks like now? I'm not going to be pretty for a long time. We're going to have to get together soon and—"

She clapped the phone closed, trembling. It was as if Chad were in the room. Had he found out where Cara lived? Followed her? Could he circumvent the security?

What could she do? Take Cara and run? No. If she did, she'd never stop, because Chad wouldn't.

"Cara!"

A moment later her daughter appeared in the doorway. "What's wrong?"

Dallas stood up. "Help me use the Internet. I want to find somebody."

"Who?"

"Chad McKenzie. The guy who attacked me."

"Mom, don't get yourself into—"

"Cara, please. He's out there. I ..." She hesitated, studying the concern on Cara's face. "I never told you about my involvement with him, did I?"

"Only that you did some things in your past that you really regretted."

"I felt so ashamed, and I didn't want you and Jared to know."

"Does Dad know?"

"Yes. I told him everything before we were married. And now I better tell you."

She did, holding nothing back. The confessions felt like scabs flaking off her soul. But once gone, there was a warm relief.

When she was finished, Cara said nothing.

"You don't think less of me, do you?" Dallas asked.

Cara took her hand. "No, Mom. No way."

Through sudden tears, Dallas enfolded Cara in her arms and held her.

"Now," Dallas said, "help me."

She had Cara use her laptop to connect to the Internet. Using the same website Lisa had shown her, Dallas typed in the number Chad McKenzie had used to call. She paid for the search and got an address on Cherokee in Hollywood.

Just like that.

"Now what?" Cara said.

"Now I give the address to the police."

"This better work."

"You're oh so right."

THIRTEEN

1.

"I'm hungry," Jamaal said.

"I figured," Jared said. "I got it covered."

It was a cool, crisp morning up in the hills. Jared already had the little Coleman going. Tiana was still asleep in the tent.

Jamaal sat down next to the little blue flame.

"Time you learned about Spam," Jared said.

"Spam?"

"I'm not talking computers, either. I'm talking this." He held up the can so Jamaal could look at it.

"What is it?" Jamaal said.

"People been trying to figure that one out for years. But let me tell you, on a cold morning, when you fry it up … baby!" Jared popped open the can, then slopped the brick onto the cold pan. Using his buck knife, Jared sliced up the army delicacy, thick and nice, then set the pan over the flame.

"You're gonna love this," Jared said.

"Love what?" Tiana was out of the tent, rubbing her eyes.

"Breakfast," Jared said.

Tiana gazed at the pan. "What is it?"

"Sam!" Jamaal said.

"Spam," Jared corrected.

"Spam! You can eat it."

"I never had it," Tiana said.

"Hey, I'm no famous chef from Paris and all," Jared said, "but I know my Spam. We'll eat and then hit the road."

"Where to?"

"I don't know. Anywhere. Camping here is technically illegal. The sooner we get out the better."

And then they were sitting, the three of them, eating Spam slices on crackers and sharing water from a gallon container Jared kept behind the driver's seat.

That's when a strange feeling hit him. Jared nearly shook his head at it, as if to rid himself of the unfamiliar. Was it happiness? No, that was a little too much. More a cessation of pain. A lifting, momentarily, of all the dark weight he'd been carrying around.

He wondered, too, for the briefest moment—wondered and even found himself hoping—that they, the three of them, would remain together, somehow, some way.

And then, as quickly as it had come, the thought was gone, chased out by his inner voice.

Stop it. You can't be with people anymore, you jerk. This is stupid. Get away from them before you hurt somebody.

"It's good," Jamaal said. "Spam is good."

"Yeah, real good," Jared said. "Now finish up and let's get out of here."

2.

Los Angeles Times

Preacher's Computer Had Pornographic Images

A computer seized from the office of accused murderer Ron Hamilton contains several hundred pornographic images, sources close to the case revealed.

Police took possession of the computer, found in Hamilton's office at Hillside Community Church, pursuant to a search warrant. Hamilton is awaiting trial for the murder of adult-entertainment star Melinda Perry, aka Melinda Chance.

Legal experts were divided on the significance of the evidence.

"It's highly prejudicial," said Los Angeles criminal defense lawyer Dave Danilov. "There's no way a judge is going to allow it in. If he does, he risks a reversal on appeal."

But Loyola Law School professor Levi Josephson disagreed. "If it's possible to show a connection between the images and anything having to do with the victim, then the evidence could come in. And that would be devastating to the defense."

Calls to Hamilton's attorney, Jefferson Waite, were not returned.

Trial is set to begin August 1.

Dallas put the morning paper down and closed her eyes, her insides twisted like spaghetti on a fork. Here was another level of distress. What would this publicity do to the witness of Hillside Community Church? The church at large? Every time an evangelical leader fell to scandal, the papers were all over it.

They hardly ever reported the good stuff. The daily sacrifices Christians made every day to help *the least of these* went unnoticed.

Cara came in, startling her. "Sorry, Mom."

"I'm a little jumpy, huh?" Dallas put the paper down, hiding the story.

"Coffee?"

"Thanks."

Her daughter paused. "Mom, I'm sorry about last night. I think I was kind of out of line."

"No, you weren't." Dallas took her hand. "You spoke up for your family, which includes all of us. You want it back the way it was."

"I want it even better. I want Jared back too. I can't stop thinking about him."

"I know."

"I pray for him, but sometimes it feels useless."

"Cara, remember the parable Jesus told about the unjust judge?"

Cara nodded. "The persistent widow."

"We think about how worn out the judge got. But what about that widow? She must have been worn out too, without even a hint of hope. Yet she kept coming back. That's how it is sometimes, isn't it? We just have to keep coming back. We have to storm the throne."

"Storm the throne. I like that."

The phone on the kitchen wall rang. Cara answered, then turned to her mother. "It's for you."

"Who?"

"Police, he said."

Jared. Dallas practically jumped to get it.

"Mrs. Hamilton?"

"Yes?"

"This is detective William Lacy of the LAPD. You called in an address on Cherokee last night and left this number."

"I did, yes."

"I'm at the location now. I wonder if you'd mind coming down here. I'd like to ask you some questions."

"About what?"

"About the guy we found at this address."

"Is he in custody?"

"No, ma'am. He's dead."

A rush of disbelief coursed through her. "Dead?"

"If you could come down, I'd really appreciate it."

3.

Detective Lacy was in his forties and lanky. Dallas met him outside the beat-up clapboard house on Cherokee. The house, maybe twenty years ago, was once sharp and homey. Time and the city had worn it down. A couple of uniformed policemen stood just outside the open front door, which had yellow police tape across it.

"Thanks for coming down," Detective Lacy said.

"What is this place?"

"Halfway house. Place for guys on diversion drug programs or parole."

She noticed a few men sitting off to the side, smoking and looking lost.

"I know this is a tough time for you," Lacy said. "Your husband's case is all over the place."

Dallas nodded. "Part of the deal these days, I guess."

"Right. I'm just old enough to remember when you had to go to the *Times* or the *Examiner* to get your news about a high-profile case. Now you can't turn on the radio or TV without something being piped in."

He reached to his inside coat pocket and pulled out a small tape recorder. "I need to ask you some questions about the deceased. We found a couple of items in his possession that you might be able to explain."

"That's fine."

"First, what was your connection to Mr. Bryan?"

"Excuse me?"

"The deceased."

She shook her head. "No, I called in about a man named McKenzie, Chad McKenzie. I thought that's who—"

"Mr. McKenzie isn't here, although he was. No, the deceased is a man named Raphael Bryan."

"But I'm afraid I don't know anyone by that name."

"He seems to have known you."

"I'm sorry, Detective, but I'm really confused."

He nodded as if this news did not surprise him. "Apparently he was also known as Rafe."

4.

"You're not ever going to think of going back to him, got it?" Jared said. The three were heading up the 5, past Sylmar now, heading for an undetermined destination.

"I don't want to," Tiana said.

"What about him?" Jared looked at Jamaal, who was sleeping on Tiana's lap.

"Never."

"Good."

"But now what?"

Jared thought about it. "You find another place to live. You get a job and you raise your boy. Simple as that."

"What're you going to do?"

"I don't know," Jared said. "I've gotta find a place too."

"You going back to L.A.?"

"People are better off if I don't. I'm pretty screwed up. Who needs it?"

"Maybe we could work together."

He looked at her. "What's that mean?"

"You know, figure things out together. Jamaal likes you. So do I."

"That's a mistake," Jared said, looking at the highway construction, at the attempt to put a new surface on a worn-out road.

"I don't think so," she said.

"Then don't think." Sensing his words had stung more than he intended, Jared said, "I'm not one to get involved with. I'm not anybody who can have anything permanent, okay? I might end up doing the same thing to you as Rafe."

"You won't."

"How do you know that?"

"I just do."

"You don't know anything. Your choice in men, that proves it."

"I think you're just feeling sorry for yourself."

"Maybe I am. I don't really care."

"That's your problem."

"No, it isn't."

"What is then?"

"Just let me drive," he said.

5.

Alarms went off in Dallas's head. "I know of a Rafe, an abusive boyfriend of a woman I was counseling."

"Tell me more," Lacy said.

"I never met him. I just remember the name. But what's he doing here?"

"That's what we're hoping to find out. There seems to be a connection that runs through you."

"How?"

"You filed a complaint about this guy McKenzie, who attacked you in your home."

"Yes."

"Then you phone in an address where you think he is. Turns out you were right. The pay phone is the one right over there." He pointed to a unit affixed to the house, near the northeast corner.

"But what does Rafe have to do with it?"

"He turns up dead in the backyard, and our boy McKenzie is gone. We found an item in the victim's wallet, has your name on it, and the name of a Jared Hamilton."

Fear gripped her. "That's my son. Where is he?"

"I don't know anything about that. Just want to know why your names should be in his possession."

"I can't tell you that. I have no idea. Unless Chad had something to do with it."

"What might he have had to do with it?"

"I don't know, except that he was out to get me and my family. Could he have given our names to Rafe?"

"That's what we want to find out," Lacy said.

"But that doesn't make sense."

"Things usually don't at the beginning." He paused and looked briefly at the notebook in his hand. "Does Gentri Land mean anything to you?"

Dallas shook her head. "What is it?"

"Something written on the back of the same paper that had you and your son's names on it. Just thought I'd throw that out."

"Do you have any idea what it means?"

"Not right now. If anything occurs to you, I want you to give me a call." He handed Dallas his card. "Now what can you tell me about this guy's girlfriend, the one you were counseling?"

"Tiana Williams. I didn't know her real well, even though she stayed in my house for a few days."

"When was that?"

"The end of March. Right after Ron was arrested."

"You brought her to your house to stay?"

"Her and her little boy, Jamaal. We do that once in a while."

"And the reason for that was?"

"I didn't want her to go back to her boyfriend, and she had nowhere else to go. I thought she could stay with me and sort things out."

"So you brought her home with you?"

"Actually, Jared picked them up."

Lacy registered a look, the kind that shows the gears meshing. "So there's a connection here to Jared, through this woman."

"Connection?"

"This work is all about connections, and you just hope some of them make sense."

Another alarm, this one intensely personal, sounded in the back of her brain. "You don't think Jared had anything to do with this." She tried not to sound too adamant, but her voice was firm.

"We have this guy, McKenzie, and the vic, Bryan, and you and your son, all coming together here. I don't know what it means, but I have a feeling it's going to mean a lot of shoe leather and coffee."

"I should tell you," Dallas said, "that my son is an ex-Marine and was in Iraq and has had some troubles back here. But he is not capable of killing..."

She stopped, suddenly aware of the harsh, unremitting pattern. The words were the same she used about Ron at one time, words she was less sure she could use about him now.

Lacy said, "Do you happen to know where he was last night?"

"No, he's not been at home."

"Know where I can reach him?"

"I can't reach him either."

Why did this sound so sinister all of a sudden? *Don't be Jared. Please, don't be Jared.*

As if reading her every thought, Lacy put a hand on her arm. "Well, if you think of anything, you have my card. I appreciate your coming down here. I'll be in touch."

As she walked back to her car, in the grasp of new uncertainties, she was aware that the men of the halfway house were watching her go and making some comments. One of them laughed, clearly at her.

It felt like the mockery of demons.

6.

Roger Vernon came to see me. Imagine that.

Here I am, sitting alone, not knowing whether I have a family anymore, not knowing if I have a life anymore, and I get the word that I have a visitor.

Roger looks younger than I do, even though he's thirty years older. I know what I look like. The slam, as they say, has not been great for my skin.

But Roger, there's a light in his eyes and a vibrancy in his voice. Even though he only had a church of two hundred, and I one of eight thousand, I know that it is his voice God honored.

When I saw him I broke down crying.

He waited patiently while I gained enough control to talk.

"It's good to see you, Ron."

"I'll bet."

"I mean it. I don't care what the circumstances. It's been too long since we've talked."

"My fault. I could have kept in touch."

"It goes both ways."

"Mostly my way, I'm sure. And look at me now. This road wasn't even paved with good intentions."

Roger shook his head.

I looked inside myself and determined I wasn't going to hold anything back. I wanted the whole house cleaned.

"I didn't want to hear from you," I said, "because I thought I was a better minister. It was obvious to me, because the church was growing. But maybe a part of me really believed that you had it right. That the idea is not the number of people in the pews, but the power of the Spirit in the people."

"I never thought that was your priority."

"But it was! I just didn't let it show. Now I've lost everything."

"I don't think so."

"How can you not?"

He didn't hesitate. "Because nothing is truly lost in the kingdom. Christians are inverse paranoids."

"Inverse what?"

"We believe that there is a massive force always working to bring about our good in the world. That's God working out his plan, his will for his children."

"I used to believe that."

"What's stopping you from believing it now?"

"Me."

He waited for me to explain.

"Roger, I'm thinking of changing my plea to guilty."

"But why?"

"Maybe by giving up I'll get out of the way long enough for God to work on me again."

"But you can't plead for something you didn't do. That wouldn't be right."

I looked at him and shook my head. "But I did do it, Roger."

"What?"

"I killed Melinda Perry."

7.

"Hello, Mrs. Hamilton. Jeff's told me some very nice things about you."

The lawyer, Rich Pelicanos, was about Jeff's age, with thinning brown hair moussed to the max. He looked competitive, the kind of lawyer most people would want on their side in a divorce.

The very word made Dallas's heart do little trapeze tricks. She didn't want to be here. She knew she had to be.

Rich Pelicanos's office was in Santa Monica, which meant he was one of the upper crust. To afford the rent here, you had to be good. Jeff had assured her he was.

Mr. Pelicanos had his assistant bring in cappuccino. It was a comforting gesture.

For Dallas, it barely worked.

"Today's just a preliminary meeting," he explained. "Nothing to feel any pressure about. I want to answer any questions you may have, explain a few things, give you some stuff to fill out at your leisure. The main thing I want you to know is that your interests will be protected."

"I'm not really concerned about that. I don't expect there's going to be a big fight, knowing Ron."

Mr. Pelicanos nodded halfheartedly. "Would that were true. You just never know in a divorce how the other side will act."

"I thought I knew Ron."

"I understand. We'll just get prepared, and I'm sure we can deal with all contingencies. Do you have any questions for me, anything I can clear up?"

"Will I have to go to court?"

"Only if there's a contest."

"I don't want a contest. I don't want anything."

"Mrs. Hamilton, you must protect yourself. That's part of—"

"I don't want anything. I don't want to punish anybody or—" She thought for a moment she was going to be sick.

"Can I get you something? A glass of water?"

Ron's face flashed into her mind then. But not the Ron of the last few years. It was his face the first time she saw him, at the Jesus rally in San Francisco. Innocent yet full of fire. Inviting, because he had something that was so certain and seemingly pure. Part child, full of wonder; part Christian man, ready to take on the world.

"I can't do this," she said.

"Take your time, there's no rush to—"

"No. I can't do it."

Mr. Pelicanos looked at her sympathetically. "It's natural to have second thoughts. But in order to protect yourself, you ought to continue with the paperwork, just in case."

She looked at the packet on his desk. "I'm sorry for taking your time. I'll pay for it, of course. But I can't do this."

"Does it have to do with your religious convictions? Because I've had many clients where this has initially been an obstacle, but once they thought it through—"

"Maybe I'm being stupid. I'm sorry, but I—"

"No, please. Why don't you think more about it? But while you're doing that, let's think about setting up a separate bank account for you, getting some ducks in a row—"

"No ducks," she said. "I just need more time."

"Of course you do," the attorney said. "Feel free to call me anytime. I'm here for you."

Here for you.

The words of a divorce lawyer.

They should have been the words of God.

But back at Cara's, alone in the apartment, Dallas found it difficult to believe God was really *there.* Oh, she knew it was true, the way she knew four plus four was eight. But the certainty of it, the kind of assurance that permeates the soul, she lacked that.

Maybe it wasn't there because of all the cul-de-sac thoughts she was thinking, questions that ran up to a curved barrier but could only turn back on themselves.

One question that kept repeating itself, over and over, had Vic Lu's name attached to it. She couldn't stop thinking about something he'd said.

I'm sorry it was your husband who did it.

There was something theatrical about his statement, as if it was delivered by a bad actor. He was selling her. Or trying to.

Why? Another question with no answer. There were only odd threads out there, dangling.

If only she could tie some together.

Like Melinda Perry. She'd worked for Lu, and now she was dead, and Ron was taking the fall for it. And Lu wanted to be very sure he expressed his condolences to her on that score.

But what if Ron didn't do it? As much as he had lied, she could not bring herself to believe he was a murderer. You don't live with a man for a quarter of a century and not know—

Then she remembered that case, where was it? Kansas? The serial killer who had lived an outwardly normal life for decades. He even had his wife fooled.

I'm sorry it was your husband who did it.

Why was Vic Lu emphasizing this? Control? Spite? Or was there something else going on, something connected to Melinda Perry's murder?

Using Cara's laptop on the kitchen table, Dallas ran a Google search on Melinda Chance. Scrolling through the hits, she saw a link with the term "Escort" in it. She clicked on that and was taken to a magenta screen with the words "Valley Night Escorts" on the top of the page, and an *Enter* button in the middle. Below the button was text in a large font: "Warning. You must be 18 years of age or older to enter this site. Contains adult content. By clicking the enter button you acknowledge that you are 18 years of age or older. Valley Night Escorts assumes no liability for misuse."

Dallas wasn't sure what to do. It was scary in a way. She had never been on any website like this before. It was so easy. And that was scary too. How easy it must be for kids to do this. The little warning was a joke.

Pulse quickening, Dallas hit *Enter.*

Almost immediately the screen was filled with a series of thumbnail photographs, all of beautiful women in various stages of undress. The images hit Dallas like flung garbage. A deep despair washed over her. Each one of those girls had a life, a life being wasted for this. Multiply these girls by a million, maybe more, and sadness could not be avoided.

Below each image was a small description. There were so many of them, all sexual in tone and distinguished by race, sexual orientation, particular fetish—just reading them made Dallas sick. But she went on.

Near the bottom she saw a description of private parties with film stars. The girl in the thumbnail looked like she was kissing the camera.

Dallas clicked on the kissing girl.

Another screen came up with yet another set of images. Below these images were names. Dallas scrolled down the names, looking for Melinda Chance. Then she realized that the site would have taken her off. Men don't usually pay for escorts who are dead.

Dallas sat back and just looked at the screen for a moment, silently praying, asking God over and over to do battle.

Just before leaving the site, Dallas stopped when she saw the name Gilda. That was all, just Gilda. Next to her name it said, "If you like Melinda Chance ..."

Dallas clicked on Gilda.

Half the screen was taken up with the photograph of a pretty woman with oddly colored hair—was it purple?—and her mouth pouty in a provocative, come-hither way. The other side of the screen was a text message. "Hi! My name's Gilda, and you may have seen me on some of the hotter selling DVDs over the last year. Acting is not all I'm into. I love to party! Are you into fun? Then give me a call! If you like Melinda Chance, you can double your pleasure, because we work as a team. VIPs only."

There was a phone number. Dallas jotted it down, wondering why the text hadn't been changed in light of Melinda's death.

Cara's phone rang and Dallas picked up.

"I'm glad I got you," Jeff Waite said. "Have you seen the paper?"

"Yes."

"I'm absolutely outraged the pornography stuff was leaked to the press." His voice was hard. "It had to come from the police or the prosecution. Either way, it's unethical. It could poison the jury pool. I'm not going to be quiet about this."

"Maybe the truth is supposed to come out," Dallas said. "Did you ever think of that?"

"I don't know what you mean."

"Trials these days seem to be about gamesmanship. Each side trying to keep the other from finding things out or letting the jury hear about it. What if a trial was actually about truth for a change?"

Jeff said, "Then you'd have to change the whole system. The one we've got works pretty well."

"But that doesn't change the fact. The fact is that Ron sinned." She paused. "Funny to hear myself use that word about Ron. But that's what it is. He sinned, and he hid it, lied about it, and now it's coming out. If that leads to his facing up to what he did, not lying anymore, then maybe God can do something with him."

"Well, I'm not God. I'm only a lawyer, and I don't like what's going on."

"Neither do I. Especially now. Something bizarre's happened."

"Like what?"

"Relating to Chad McKenzie." She told him about the call from Detective Lacy and the revelation that Rafe Bryan was found shot to death at the place where Chad was recently holed up.

"What does the detective say about it?" Jeff asked.

"Nothing yet. He's still making the connections, like Colombo."

"Good old Colombo."

Dallas put on her Peter Falk voice. "Just one more question, sir."

"That's pretty good."

"Maybe I should do voices permanently, keep myself occupied."

"They might put you in the mental ward."

"That's probably where I'll end up anyway," Dallas said.

"No, you won't."

"This guy Rafe had a piece of paper with my name on it, and Jared's. And also the words Gentri Land."

"What's that?"

"I don't know. But I'm hoping this Detective Lacy finds out before we get to the trial."

"That would be nice. Because we don't have anything else."

"What about the witness, the one I told you about?"

"Dallas, he's not going to help. Harry interviewed him."

"And?"

"At the kid's mother's house. First of all, he won't even be allowed to testify."

"Why not?"

"Competence. Every witness has to have a level of competence under the Evidence Code. From what Harry tells me, this kid's mental capacity is just one problem."

"There's another?"

"I don't know what you were told, Dallas, but this kid doesn't recall seeing anybody at the Star that night. Harry asked him six ways from Sunday, trying to figure out what he may or may not have seen, but got nothing." He paused. "Dallas, I wish I could give you better news."

Dallas looked at the ceiling, wishing it would open up and send down a message from heaven.

It didn't.

9.

Guillermo Padilla's mouth hung open.

"Hey, man," Jared said. "Need a favor."

His old painting partner stood in the doorway of the little house outside Bakersfield. He shared it with his mother, and it had a small shack out back where Jared had stayed a few weeks when he didn't have another place.

"What you doing up here?" Guillermo said, looking over his shoulder.

"This is Tiana and Jamaal."

Guillermo said, "This ain't no hotel."

"Look, we just need a place for a night or two, okay? Getting away from a bad situation."

"Guillermo?" a woman's voice from inside. Jared knew it was his mother.

Guillermo said something in Spanish and the woman said something back. Then she appeared at the door.

"Jared! ¿Cómo estás?"

"Bien."

"You come to stay?"

"Mama," Guillermo said in a stern voice.

His mother slapped his shoulder, then looked at Jared. "You are welcome. Come, I have food."

They all ate hot home cooking, then Señora Padilla made up a bed and two cots in the shack. She yelled at Guillermo to stop complaining, then left the three alone.

"I don't like it here," Jamaal said.

"What's not to like?" Jared said. The place was one room, small, with a water closet. Not exactly the Ritz.

"How long we got to stay here?" Jamaal said.

Tiana looked at Jared for the answer.

"This'd be a good place for you to get your bearings," Jared said. "Señora Padilla, she'll let you do some work around the place and you can stay, until you can get a job."

"Like where?"

"I don't know." Jared threw his hands up, then slapped his sides. "Go bang on some doors. Read the want ads. Do what you have to do."

"You're not staying?"

"Why should I?"

"Where you goin'?" Jamaal said.

"I don't know."

"Whyn't you stay with us?" The boy took Jared's hand. Jared pulled it away.

"Get in bed," Jared said.

"I don't wanna."

"Tough."

10.

Dallas had done nothing so strange since her days wandering North Beach.

But these were strange times, and something had to happen.

It was late afternoon, and she used her cell phone to call the number for the escort named Gilda.

She almost clicked off. But a recorded voice stopped her. It was melodramatically sultry. "Hi there. This is Gilda. I'm soooo glad you called. If you'll leave me a number, I'll get right back to you. I'm anxious to meet you, you know."

And then there was a beep.

Dallas had at least thought it through to this point. She put on a deep voice, her best one—Mel Gibson-ish—and threw in a Southern drawl to boot. "Howdy there. I saw yer picture and I'd sure like to see you. Call me back and tell me what to do." She left her cell number and closed her phone.

Are you completely nuts?

Yes.

Her call was returned in half an hour. Dallas saw Gilda's number on the LCD.

She answered in her deep Southern accent. "Howdy."

"Well, hi there." It was the same throaty voice as on the recording. "Is this the nice man who just called?"

"Shore is." Dallas's hands were shaking, but the deep voice was working on Gilda. So far.

"Well now, you sound like somebody I've just got to meet. What say you and me get together?"

"Yep."

"All you have to do is name the place."

Place! She'd forgotten about that. What was she expecting, that she'd ask a call girl to come to Cara's house?

"I'm, uh, a little nervous about this."

"Your first time?"

"Oh, yeah."

"That's so special! Oh, you sound sweet. And just because of that, I'm going to make you a special deal. I don't always do this. But for you, I will. I'll meet you for a drink at a place I know, and we'll talk a little. If you like me, I know a nice, quiet place we can go for a while. Sound like a plan?"

"Shore."

"Way cool! There's a bar called the Laurel, it's on Ventura. You just go on in and tell them you're meeting Gilda. Say eight o'clock tonight?"

"Okay."

"Don't sound so nervous, honey. We're just going to relax and have ourselves a great time. I guarantee it. Oh, and just so there's no surprises, the drink'll cost you fifty dollars."

"Huh?"

"You know, I love my work, but it is a job! I'm trying to save up for a Mercedes. Think of the drink like an initial consultation. And if you like me, we'll deduct the fifty from the rest of the evening's tab. See? Usually the first drink is a hundred, but like I said, you're special. I love showing first-timers around. What do you say?"

She could barely speak. "Eight o'clock then."

"Super trooper! I'll see you there."

11.

The Laurel was stuck on a strip of Ventura Boulevard in the rundown section between Laurel Canyon and Lankershim. It was next to an auto-parts store, not exactly the upscale draw the boulevard was desperately seeking a couple of miles east.

The last time Dallas had been in a place like this was back in San Francisco. The bad days. She almost turned around and forgot the whole thing.

But she was close to something. No, she *had* to be close to something that would explain what had happened to her husband. Willing it to be so, she entered the Laurel. It was dark inside, and she was immediately greeted by a man with a barrel chest in a blue T-shirt stretched to the max. A silver necklace the size of a bike chain hung from his neck.

"Help you?" He seemed suspicious, as if a normal person walking into his dive was cause for alarm. No doubt it was. The place had a criminal ambience.

"I'm here to meet Gilda."

The man looked her up and down, then shrugged. "Business is business, am I right? Come on this way."

He showed her to a table in the corner, by the window. "What can I bring you?"

"Oh. Just water."

"Hey, not here. You got to order something."

Was he joking? She decided not to ask. "All right. A diet Coke."

"That's it?"

"Is that all right?"

He shrugged. "To each his—I mean her own."

Dallas watched him go and say something to the young bartender, who had dark curly hair and a jaded face. Working in a place like this, how could he not be?

The man returned with a modest-size glass of diet Coke that he placed in front of Dallas. It didn't even have a lemon slice with it.

"That'll be fifty dollars," he said.

"What?"

"Expensive Coke. Bottled in Saudi Arabia."

A criminal comedian? But he didn't smile or walk away. He was serious.

"It's for Gilda," he said.

Of course. Dallas felt a blush rushing in and was glad the place was dark. She was so unsophisticated about these things. This was the way it was done, she supposed. She fished in her purse for cash and put two twenties and a ten on the table. The man snatched it up.

"No tip?" he said.

Dallas looked at him.

"Kidding. Enjoy. I'll let Gilda know you're here."

The Coke was watery. This whole thing was watery—unsolid, unpredictable. She looked around the place. It was empty except for an older woman at the edge of the bar, looking into a martini glass. The young bartender looked at Dallas as if she were a curio.

Dallas took a small New Testament out of her purse, one she'd carried around for years. She'd read it in many a circumstance, but never one like this.

Her ribbon bookmark was in the twelfth chapter of John's gospel, and she read to the end:

> Then Jesus cried out, "When a man believes in me, he does not believe in me only, but in the one who sent me. When he looks at me, he sees the one who sent me. I have come into the world as a light, so that no one who believes in me should stay in darkness.
>
> "As for the person who hears my words but does not keep them, I do not judge him. For I did not come to judge the world, but to save it. There is a judge for the one who rejects me and does not accept my words; that very word which I spoke will condemn him at the last day. For I did not speak of my own accord, but the Father who sent me commanded me what to say and how to say it. I know that his command leads to eternal life. So whatever I say is just what the Father has told me to say."

Jesus came so that no one should *stay in darkness*. But to those who reject his words, only judgment and condemnation.

Oh, the stakes were high! For Ron and Jared especially. Would they reject Jesus after all? Jared was far away. Where was Ron? *Do not let them remain in darkness, Lord!*

She looked up and saw a woman in a red jacket with fur collar and cuffs talking to the man at the front. The woman also wore a black miniskirt from which two long dark-nyloned legs shot downward, coming to rest in black shoes with stiletto heels. Her hair was a blazing shade of purple.

And then she was walking toward Dallas with a face that did not look pleased.

"What is this?" she said.

"Gilda?"

Her face, registering annoyance, was heavily made up, especially around the eyes. They were cat eyes, and Dallas figured they must drive some men to certain distraction. Or should she say, destruction?

"I was supposed to meet a guy named Dallas."

"I'm Dallas."

"You're not a guy."

Dallas did Mel. "Thanks fer comin', ma'am."

Gilda's mouth made a little O. "Well now, that's very clever." She slid out the opposite chair out and sat down. "What's your real name?"

"It's really Dallas."

"How'd you get it?"

"My dad. He was from Texas and he loved the Cowboys."

"Oh."

"What's *your* real name?"

Gilda said, "You don't think it's real?"

"Just asking."

"Clever again. You ever see that old movie with Rita Hayworth?"

"*Gilda.* I think Glenn Ford was in it too."

"I always wanted to look like her. But you play the cards you're dealt." A distant, mournful tune seemed to play in her head. Then she snapped back. "You didn't need to do all that posing. I go both ways, I just don't advertise it. You do voice-overs or something?"

"Or something. Only for fun."

"Fun's my middle name, girl. Like what you see so far?"

What did she see? A woman of about twenty-eight or nine, on the cusp of getting too old for what she did. And then what? *Damaged goods.*

"I'd like to talk to you," Dallas said.

"Sure. We got a few minutes here."

"Fifty dollars' worth."

"That's right."

"Can I make it a hundred, and get more time?"

Gilda narrowed her eyes, now looked even more feline. "More time here?"

"Right."

"We won't need it."

"Maybe we will."

"Why?"

"Because I just want to talk. Nothing else. Should be the easiest hundred you've ever made."

"You a cop?"

"No."

"Good. Because I've got a tape going in my coat. It's just a formality in case you pull a badge."

"No badge."

"And no tape." She reached into her coat pocket and pulled out a tape recorder. Ironically, it looked identical to the one Detective Lacy used. Maybe the cops and hookers in L.A. shopped at the same store.

Gilda clicked it off. "So what do you want to talk about?"

"Melinda Chance."

Gilda's hand, holding the recorder, froze. "You *are* a cop, and I'm walking out right—"

"I'm the wife of the man accused of murdering her."

Now Gilda's body froze. For a moment Dallas thought she was going to walk out without another word. But then Gilda thawed enough to put the recorder back in her coat pocket and say, "I got nothing to tell you."

"I haven't asked anything yet."

"You don't have to."

"How well did you know her?"

"That's my business."

"I need to know."

"You don't need to know anything." Gilda took a long breath. "Look, I'll give you a word here, since you paid. Don't go anywhere with this. Forget about Melinda. She's dead. She's probably happier too."

"But I don't think my husband killed her."

"That's not my deal. I'm just telling you, don't go any further with Melinda, you understand what I'm saying?" She leaned over the table and whispered, "It wouldn't be good for you."

"Why not?"

"Trust me."

"Why should I?" Dallas surprised herself with that one, but she was not in a mood to back down.

"Look, you seem like a nice lady. Nice, respectable. And if your man did it, you won't be the first wife whose husband lied to her. Believe me, ninty eight percent of the guys I see have a little wifey at home. But the circles I run in, me and Melinda, it's not for you."

"Bad guys involved?"

"They can be."

"Like Vic Lu?"

She looked startled. "You are on thin ice, lady."

"Is that who you work for?"

"I got nothing else to say." Gilda stood up, almost knocking over the contents of the table.

"Please," Dallas said. "I need help."

"You need to keep your nose where it belongs. And do not call my number again. Stay away from this." She turned quickly and walked to the front, pausing for a word with the big man, then was out the door.

Well, that worked like a charm. A real detective she was. She took one more sip of her diet Coke, the most expensive drink she'd ever bought, and it was even more watery now. Like her prospects of helping Ron.

She felt the perfect fool too, as she started out. She could feel the bartender's eyes on her, and goodness only knew what he was thinking. *Never again, girl. Leave the cloak-and-dagger stuff to Harry Stegman.*

She didn't even want to look at the big guy with the bike chain necklace, but she couldn't avoid it with him standing right in front of the door.

"So soon?" he said.

What should she say to him? *Thank you for your hospitality?* He was creeping her out and she just wanted to get to Cara's and take a shower. She felt dirty.

"Excuse me," she said.

"You're not mad about the fifty bucks, I hope."

"Excuse me."

He didn't move.

The creepy feeling inside her grew stronger.

"May I leave?" she asked firmly.

"Sure. In a couple of minutes."

"Now."

"No can do."

She realized again that she was alone in this place, except for Necklace and the bartender. And Necklace wasn't budging.

"Move," she said.

Necklace smiled. "I need to ask you a few questions."

"Absolutely not. I'm leaving."

She took one step to try to get by him. His hand whipped in front of her and snatched her purse right out of her hands. Quick as a blink he tossed the purse over her shoulder. The bartender, now five feet away, caught it.

"Find out who this chick is," Necklace said.

Dallas tensed and considered her options. They were all bad.

As if he could hear her inner gears grinding, Necklace said, "Don't make me hurt you."

12.

Jamaal was asleep on a cot.

Tiana lay on the bed. Jared sat on the other cot, nowhere close to being able to sleep.

Back in the Padilla shack. It was like a bad dream. He'd once heard that life was just a series of recurrences. You never really got anywhere. You always ended up just going over the same ground, arriving at the same place. You died and came back and lived through it all again. Like that movie *Groundhog Day*, only it wasn't funny and you didn't remember anything.

Around and around and that was it, forever and ever amen.

"Can't sleep?" Tiana whispered.

"No."

"How come?"

"Why don't you sleep?"

"I've been thinking."

"Great. Now go to sleep."

Instead, she sat up. "Your mom's right."

"What's my mom got to do with it?"

"You got stuff going on you can't handle by yourself."

"I do all right. Go to—"

"Doesn't look to me like you do all right."

"I don't really give a flying rip what it looks like to you."

"I want to take Jamaal to church."

"He's your kid."

"Come with us."

"You do sound like my mom."

"I've been thinking this all through. You're right about me needing to get some work, and starting over again. I want to start *all* over again. Because of Jamaal. I want to give him the best life I can."

"There you go."

"You got us out of L.A., so why don't you stay with us?"

"And do what?"

She didn't answer immediately.

"You think I'm money?" he said.

"Huh?"

"You think I'm a guy you can palm off of?"

"No."

"Yeah, you do. You got that look."

What am I saying? He was starting to see pain in her eyes. The room started to go dark on him. He closed his eyes, opened them, hoping to bring in more light.

He saw Tiana staring at him.

"Cut it out!" he screamed.

"What's wrong?"

"Shut up!"

"Don't talk that way."

"Shut up I said!" Without a thought, operating on something like instinct, but from a source outside himself, Jared made a fist and raised it.

The moment he did, the moment he saw her eyes widen with shock and fear, in that moment he knew he was no better than Rafe.

He ran out of the house, jumped into his truck, and burned rubber.

He welcomed night. He could drive into it, get lost in it, stay there. Maybe if he drove fast enough, outran the demons, he could drive over a cliff or into a wall. Then there wouldn't be a blot of Jared Hamilton on the earth anymore.

He'd fought and bled in Iraq. He believed in the cause he was fighting for. He got to know enough of the Iraqi people to know how much they craved true freedom. But there was a kind of freedom some people would never know. Freedom from fear and memories and events that haunted.

He would never have that freedom.

Somewhere outside the city limits, on one of the darker roads, flashing lights came into the rearview mirror.

Cops or highway patrol. Maybe a sheriff. Anyway, they had him in their sights.

Keep going.

He pushed the pedal to the metal.

The siren split the night silence.

Now it was a high-speed chase.

Maybe end up on the evening news.

That'd thrill his mother.

Or he could charge into a tree right now, get it over with.

End it. End it now.

Yeah, right now.

He considered the trees, eucalyptus lining the road, standing and waiting, illuminated by his headlights.

Would have to be a strong one.

End it.

His mom. He saw his mom. How would she handle it?

It doesn't matter.

Yes, it does. It does matter. He couldn't do this to her now.

He braked, letting the truck come to a stop on the soft shoulder.

The car pulled up behind him.

It was a chippie. He came up on the passenger side, knocked on the window. Did not look happy.

"You miss me back there?" the chippie said. He was of the ex-linebacker style of highway patrolman.

"I stopped, didn't I?" Jared said.

"License, registration, proof of insurance."

Jared reached toward the glove compartment.

"Slowly," the chippie said.

Jared opened the compartment slowly, slid out the registration, and remembered he didn't have insurance. He took his license out and handed it to the patrolman.

Then waited as the officer went back to his vehicle. No doubt to write him up.

So what? What's a ticket gonna do? Keep going. Drive north tonight. You can figure out a way to die later, and write a note to Mom explaining it all. She'll have to make do with that.

The patrolman came back on the driver's side. And he was holding his weapon.

"Out of the truck," he said.

"What?"

"Get out, sir."

Jared opened the door. "What is all this?"

"Hands behind your back."

"Hey—"

"Do it *now*."

Jared complied. The officer slipped plastic restraints around his wrists, pulled them tight.

"What am I being arrested for?" he said.

"They want you down in L.A.," the patrolman said. "You skipped out on a DUI. They don't like that, you know."

13.

"That's better," Necklace said. He had Dallas sitting in a metal folding chair in a room behind the bar. She complied without resistance. He was going to get his way, and there was little she could do about it.

The bartender came in holding her purse and wallet. "Her driver's license says her name is Dallas Hamilton. How come that sounds familiar?"

Necklace shot him a glare. "Stupid, don't you watch television?"

The bartender looked hurt. "She on TV?"

"This is the babe whose husband offed Melinda."

A small light went off in the bartender's head. "Oh, right, right. Now what's she doing here with Gilda?"

"That's my question," Necklace said. He looked at Dallas. "You kind of pulled a fast one on my friend Gilda. Nobody would ever accuse her of being the brightest bulb on the shelf, but one thing she's got is instinct. You're in her line of work, you develop that. So I kind of agree with Gilda that you could cause a lot of trouble if you got it in your head to do that. So why don't you just tell me what you're doing here, what your business with Gilda was, and we'll figure the best way to consummate our little relationship."

"What you're doing is illegal," Dallas said. "You can't keep me here."

"That wasn't the answer I was looking for."

"Why don't you just let me go now, and there won't be any backlash."

Necklace folded his arms across his chest and looked at the bartender. "Did she just threaten us?"

The bartender shrugged.

"Did you just say *backlash*?"

"I have nothing to say to you."

"That's not good." Necklace shook his head. He had a prominent vein that ran from the top of his nose up his forehead, and split into two directions at his hairline.

She hadn't noticed it before. Maybe because it was only now throbbing.

"Now let's be up front with each other, huh?" He pulled out a metal chair for himself and sat on it backward, facing her. "You see what happens here. I provide a nice, safe place for people like Gilda to come and do a little business. It's not strictly legal, but I'm sure you didn't have to pay us a visit to deduce that."

Dallas didn't move.

"Vice knows about us, and a hundred other guys who do the same, and they let things go. It's always been that way, right? The world's oldest profession? But when somebody from the community gets upset about it, starts reporting things, then the cops, well, they think they gotta turn up the heat for a while. And that just gets to be a hassle."

Necklace ran his hand though his hair.

"So what I gotta decide here is if you're gonna go out and start making a big deal. Because that would just be bad for business, and I got a mother to support."

"Not to mention a girlfriend," the bartender said.

"Shut up." Another sharp look at the bartender.

"I'm not going to make any trouble," Dallas said, "if that's what you're worried about."

"I gotta have some sort of guarantee."

"What could I possibly do?"

"Just give me your word."

Now that was a strange thing to ask for. Why would a guy like this think anyone's word meant anything when it came down to protecting his business?

"All right," Dallas said. "You have my word."

"On what?"

"That I won't talk about you to anybody."

Necklace heaved a labored breath. "Now give me your undivided attention here, 'cause I have a guarantee for you. This is what it is: If I ever find out that you talked about me to anybody, I will not be the gracious host who sits before you now, huh?"

She believed him. The guy may have been a Tony Soprano wannabe, but he sure did a good job of convincing her he was qualified.

"Then you have no worries," Dallas said. "May I go now?"

Necklace held her gaze for another moment, then looked at the bartender. "Hey, what are you doing with the lady's purse? Give it back and escort her out."

FOURTEEN

1.

When she finally got to sleep at Cara's, Dallas fell into a dark dream. She saw Jared standing on a lake. Standing, as if he could walk on water. She was on the shore without a light, yet she could see him out there, alone.

She tried to scream at him to come in, but in the dream she couldn't make a sound. Her mouth opened, her throat clenched, but there was only horrifying silence.

Jared started sinking, slowly.

She wanted to swim out to him. Her feet were stuck in muddy sand.

Jared did not resist his own drowning.

He called, "It's better, Mom ..."

His head was about to disappear.

Dallas could not move. In her dream she prayed for God to save him. *Now.*

A boat appeared, churning toward Jared, sounding a strange little alarm, tinny and weak. What sort of alarm was it? It—

Dallas awakened to her cell phone chiming. What time was it? Her blurred vision caught the digital clock: 8:32 a.m.

The phone persisted. She glanced at the LCD. Jeff.

"Did I wake you?" he said.

"Yes, but I'm glad."

"Glad?"

"Dreaming. What is it?" She pulled herself to a sitting position. Her head buzzed with a shot of mental adrenaline.

"Ron wants to see you."

The thought of seeing Ron again triggered a dull ache in her mind. "Why?"

"I had a long talk with him yesterday. He asked me if he could plead out."

"You mean plead guilty?"

"It's actually nolo contendere, no contest. Means he's not admitting to guilt, but he's not going to contest the charge. It has the same effect as a guilty plea, but he'll get a reduced sentence."

"How long?"

"I discussed it with the DA early on. He'd agree to fifteen years to life. But that means Ron will be eligible for parole. He can, with a good record, get out."

"But there's no guarantee."

Jeff paused. "No. But like I've said, there shouldn't be any opposition to parole."

"Not even from the district attorney?"

"I don't think so."

Dallas thought about it, the awful finality. Prison. For real.

"I spoke to him a long time about this," Jeff said. "He told me he just wants it all to end, to take away the pain he's caused everyone. Especially you."

She closed her eyes and tried to imagine what it would feel like to have all this ended.

"He wants to see you, Dallas. To talk about it. I'll do whatever you two decide."

"I know you will, Jeff. Let me just ask you, straight up. Is this the best we can hope for?"

"I've looked at every angle," Jeff said. "I've considered all the options. None of them is very good. In my professional opinion, this is the best."

There is no best. "All right. I'll see him."

2.

She did, the next morning at ten. Ron was skinny, much too skinny, but there was finally some resolution behind his eyes.

"Jeff told you?"

"Yes. Why are you doing this?"

"Roger came to see me again."

"He said he would."

"I told him what I'm going to tell you. I am responsible for the death of that girl."

Dallas's chest tightened. Did this mean that—

"No, I didn't do it," he added. "Maybe you don't believe me. I guess I can't blame you if you don't. But I'm responsible. If I hadn't let her get involved with me, she wouldn't be dead."

"But you can't—"

"Jeff says that if I plead I could eventually get parole. Maybe this is due penance for my sins, Dallas. I'm tired of fighting. I want to give up."

"Is that what Roger told you to do? Give up?"

"To God, yes. He didn't tell me to plead guilty. Or no contest. That's my own decision. And that will free you too."

"Me?"

"You can go ahead with the divorce."

The cool and calm way he said it indicated long deliberation. He was like a judge passing down a sentence. His words were the gavel.

"Is that what you want?" she asked.

"I can't ask you to stay tied to me."

She closed her eyes a moment. "That's the one thing I always wanted, more than anything. To be tied to you, to be married to you, to go on with you 'til death do us part." She paused. "I wanted our marriage to be the one thing in my life that would last. Maybe I wanted that too much."

When she opened her eyes she saw Ron's were filling with tears. She could not stop her own. How many tears had been spilled through the years in the visitors' room at the jailhouse? What was the sum total of misery?

"I hurt you, I know," he said.

"It was the lying, Ron. I think I could have taken anything else. How could you have kept so much from me. The pornography on your computer, the—"

"I don't know how that happened, Dallas."

"How what happened?"

"All those images." He took a breath. "What I mean is, I don't remember that many. I was doing research one night, and—I don't know how to describe it—I was caught up. I was looking and downloading. It was so easy. Scary easy. I lost track of time. I was ... crazy. When I came to my senses I felt so much guilt. I just couldn't tell you. But I deleted that whole file of images without looking at them again."

"Deleted them? Then how—"

"They have ways of recovering things on your hard drive, I guess, even when you think they're gone. Dallas, if there was any way I could go back and not have this happen to you ..."

And he wept again.

After a long moment of silence, Dallas said, "I don't think you should plead, Ron. No matter what you've done, the lies you've told, I don't think you're a murderer."

"I'm not admitting I did it. It's a no contest plea. A deal. People make deals. Why should I be any different than any other con?"

"Something may turn up. Jeff and Harry may find evidence that clears you."

Ron shook his head. "They're not miracle workers. Believe me when I say I'm at peace with this, Dallas. You have your freedom. You have the right to divorce me, and I am at peace with that too."

She gripped the phone hard. "If things were different, if none of this had happened, if we could go back to after Amy Shea and before Melinda Perry, would you have wanted to stay married to me?"

"Of course."

"No, I don't mean because of the Bible or your reputation or the church or anything else. I mean would you have wanted to stay married because you loved me?"

He thought a long time, then said, "Maybe it took all this for me to realize how much I did—do—love you. I do. I know that. But it's too late. I will pay for my sins, but I can't ask you to do the same. You're free, Dallas."

A deputy indicated that time for the visit was up. Ron hung up his phone before Dallas could say another word to him. He turned with a finality, as if judgment was already upon him. Upon them both.

3.

After being booked into Men's Central, Jared Hamilton nursed a bitter sense of humor about the whole thing.

Famous preacher from a large church and his only son, both in the same jail at the same time.

His dad had it easy by comparison. He had a room to himself. Jared was stuffed with five others into a cell originally built for two. It was the 4000 level, and the cell looked directly across at the sheriff's station, encased in thick glass. Jared thought it looked like a submarine passing by in this ocean of lost hopes.

His other cell mates were white. The jail, he knew, was purposely segregated. Too many gang rivalries to try and make this a color-blind lockup.

If the dark blue Aryan tattoos were any indication, four of his cell mates were white supremacists. All but one of the five were in their twenties. The exception was a guy who looked about forty. His hair was longer and his eyes more experienced. He was the only one who said nothing to Jared when he joined them.

The one with the most attitude, who called himself Pal, appeared to be the bull. Each cell had an unofficial head, usually the one who could do the most physical damage to the others.

"First things first, Fish," Pal said the moment Jared stepped through the cell door and heard it slam behind him. "I tell you to do something, that's what you do."

Pal, who was slightly shorter than Jared, gave him a direct stare with dark brown eyes.

Jared sized him up. He could take him if he had to. The problem was the other guys. They were Pal's boys. The old guy would probably stay out of things. Jared wouldn't stand a chance. He just had to take it. For two days. *Just two days.*

Pal pointed to the bare aluminum toilet in the center of the back wall, and then to a sheet secured to a corner of one bunk. "Second thing is, you want to use the can, use the sheet."

Jared said nothing.

"You understanding me?" Pal said.

"I got the picture," Jared said.

"I don't think you do. Let me show you." He took one step toward the toilet and motioned to Jared with his finger.

"Try it," Pal said.

"Try what?"

"The can."

"I don't have to."

"Just to show you how the sheet works."

"I don't have to go."

"Pretend you do."

Three of the inmates, all but the old guy, huddled around Pal and Jared. The cell, small as it was, suddenly seemed a lot smaller.

Jared shrugged and moved to the toilet.

"Have a seat," Pal said.

Without undoing his coveralls, Jared sat on the toilet.

"Now it works like this," Pal said. He took the sheet that was tied to one bunk and stretched it across to the opposite bunk. The sheet had a hole in the corner. Pal placed it over the bunk post.

Now Jared was looking at a sheet. Pal and his boys squatted on either side of him. Two grabbed Jared's wrists and twisted his hands. Excruciating pain shot up his arms. He couldn't move.

"Need to listen," Pal said. "Only gonna say this once. We got a real problem with the jigs and the wets. If it comes down to it, we gotta know whose side you're on. We gotta know whose back you got. You tell us, and we'll get yours."

Jared ground his teeth against the pain. "I'm not on any side."

The others did not let up on his hands. "You got to take sides."

"I'm not here long."

"Don't matter."

"Nobody's side." Jared's eyes were starting to water.

"You want a broken wrist? That'll get you out of the cell. You want that?"

Pain beat back Jared's voice and started to darken his vision. He expected to black out.

"I asked you a question," Pal said.

Jared sensed the darkness deepen and change, become a presence. That, more than the punks, brought fear.

"So what'll it be, Fish?"

The pain was reaching the point of unbearable.

Give it up, tell him you're in, just tell him and you'll be safe.

"Stick," a voice said.

Pal snapped his fingers and the two guys let go of Jared's hands, stood up, moved to the front side of the sheet.

Jared, his wrists aflame, stood up too.

The old guy was standing with his back to the cell door, looking at them all. Jared knew he was the one who had said *stick*.

Later, he would learn that a stick was a deputy who checked cells from the secure enclosure in the middle of the block.

"Don't want no stick in here," the old guy said.

Pal looked out the cell doors, then back at Jared. "Think about it," he said. "We'll have another talk real soon."

It was Friday. No action would be taken on bail or anything regarding Jared's case until Monday. There was no way he would be able to avoid another "talk."

The presence Jared felt intensified. And he was scared. More scared than he'd ever been in his life, more even than in combat.

He fought to keep from blacking out.

Then the old guy brushed past him and whispered, "Stay off the can."

4.

"Thank you for seeing me," Dallas said.

Deputy DA Mike Freton looked much more approachable in his office than he did in court. In that venue he seemed to be a living Rushmore, formidable and unbreakable. Here he seemed human, even warm.

But he was also a prosecutor convinced that her husband was a murderer.

"I represent the people of California, Mrs. Hamilton," he said. "You are one of the people, and if you have something to say to me about a case I'm involved with, my door is open. Even if it's a case you're very much involved with."

His delivery was sincere and smooth. He would make a good run at the district attorney position if he ever chose to go for it. In fact, he looked like he'd be successful at pretty much anything he tried.

"Does Jeff Waite know you're here?" he added.

"I don't think I told him. This is rather spur-of-the-moment. And I don't want to keep you." It was late Friday afternoon, and she imagined Freton wanted to get home like everybody else.

"You're not, Mrs. Hamilton. The office gets kind of quiet about now and I usually do some late work, especially when I'm in trial. Then I head over to a place on Temple for a bite before heading home."

"Where is that?"

"Pasadena."

"Nice."

"I like it."

He waited, punctuating an end to small talk. She said, "Mr. Freton, I know that you and Jeff have talked about Ron entering into a plea."

"Yes."

"Would that satisfy you?"

"I don't think *satisfy* is the word I would use. I do think it would be a just resolution to the case."

"Even though Ron didn't kill that girl?"

"Mrs. Hamilton, I have to look at the evidence. That's all I can do. In light of the evidence, I think a plea is the best thing for your husband."

"But what's your gut feeling, Mr. Freton? Do you honestly think Ron did this?"

"I don't use gut feeling. That would be a bad habit to get into."

But if you feel something's wrong—Dejection took over, sinking her words.

Mr. Freton seemed to sense it. "If you were to come to me with exculpatory evidence—sorry, that's legalese—evidence that would tend to show innocence, I would be interested. But I know Jeff

Waite and I know Harry Stegman, and if they don't have it by this time, it probably doesn't exist."

"I believe there is someone, or maybe more than one, who set Ron up. Because of the pornography connection. Ron is an outspoken critic of it and has been working hard to get some new ordinances passed."

The deputy DA nodded without conviction.

"You don't think that's possible?" she said.

"You know about the pornography we found in his computer."

Stiffening, Dallas said, "I know what I read in the papers. I also know it shouldn't have been in the papers."

"You're right. And I want to assure you that the leak did not come from this office."

She regarded him carefully. Perhaps his smoothness hid the truth.

"Then what are you doing about it?" she said.

"Following standard protocol for getting to the bottom of it. Meantime, I have to deal with the facts as they exist. And right now, I don't see a better resolution to this matter than your husband's plea."

"Even if that means the real killer is still out there?"

"We can't look at it that way. No one who prosecutes cases can ever see everything. Neither can a jury. The standard is proof beyond a reasonable doubt, not every possible doubt. We just have to do our best and hope things work out."

"What about the truth?"

"That's what the process is all about, as imperfect as it is."

"Forget the process. I'm sick of the process. All that's happened to me in this process is bad. I've been threatened and found people who know what's going on but aren't good witnesses and—"

"Whoa, what are you talking about?"

Should she even go there? What would Jeff think if she started telling Freton all this? Maybe it would hurt Ron.

"I'm just saying that you seem to want to convict on shaky ground, when there's people out there—"

"You keep mentioning other people, witnesses. Why hasn't Jeff produced them?"

Dallas looked down. *Quiet, motormouth.*

Mr. Freton said, "I understand completely a wife's desire to see that everything possible is done on her husband's behalf."

"Then find out who leaked the pornography story. Whoever did it might know more."

He paused. "That might not even be relevant to the crime."

"But it might."

"It's a very thin string, Mrs. Hamilton."

She stood up. "Very thin is all I have right now. So find that string, and pull it for all it's worth."

5.

"Dallas, I know where Jared is."

Dallas pressed the phone to her ear, as if that action could take her to her son through some sci-fi transference. "Is he all right?"

"He's in jail."

"What?"

"They found him up in Bakersfield, pulled him over for some rinky-dink traffic thing. They ran a check on him and found out there's a bench warrant for him for missing his court date. So they brought him here to the downtown jail."

"Where Ron is?"

"Sort of a weird coincidence, isn't it?"

Was it? Why would God have the two men in her life in the same jail at the same time? There had to be a reason, there had to be meaning, and she prayed that it would reveal itself.

"He'll appear before a judge on Monday morning," Jeff said. "I'll go with him."

Dallas looked at the clock in Cara's kitchenette. Six thirty. Past visiting hours.

"At least we know where he is," Dallas said. "Jeff, will he be safe in there?"

"It's only 'til Monday morning. Then we can bail him out."

6.

The eating area was segregated too, and staggered by time. Now it was the white inmates' turn. Jared parked himself at a metal table on a metal stool at the far end of the mess hall.

The meal tonight was some sort of macaroni and cheese. Jared wasn't sure it was even macaroni. The "cheese" was most likely made from some secret industrial powder also used for caulking ships.

He would be glad to get out of this place.

He hadn't taken two bites when someone said, "You're marked."

The old guy from his cell had slipped in next to him.

"What's that?" Jared said.

"Marked. Means you got something coming at you. And you don't know when it'll happen."

Little hot needles pricked Jared's skin. The guy was serious. Jared looked at him a moment, noticing as the guy chewed his food that one of his front teeth had a gold cap. "Can I get moved?"

"Not much time."

"Well, tell somebody, tell a deputy—"

"They don't care. They hear this all the time. You gotta watch your own back, Fish. That's it, that's all, the way of the slam. You don't look like you've done time before."

Jared shook his head.

"It's all over you, man."

"Why are you telling me this?"

"I have a reason."

Jared waited. "You want to tell me?"

"Sure." The old guy took another bite.

"So?"

"They want you in hell," he said.

"Excuse me?"

"Hell. The lake of fire."

Great. A crazy man. He was in a cell with four skinheads and a loon.

"Thanks," Jared said dismissively.

"Same as they want your old man."

Jared flinched, looked at him. "What about my father?"

"I know who he is. I know who you are."

Feeling exposed before a hundred prying eyes, Jared spoke low. "How do you know?"

The guy shrugged.

"Tell me."

The man said nothing. He shoveled a piece of bread in his mouth.

No, Jared decided, this was all crazy stuff, and all he was doing was encouraging more of it by listening. It was always possible too, that the old guy just liked messing with people's heads. Something to do to kill time.

"I don't care what you know," Jared said. "Just leave me alone."

"They won't leave you alone."

"Who?"

"The minions."

"What?"

"Of Satan. They're real." When he said this he set his jaw as if to underscore how serious he was. His gold tooth flashed like a warning light.

Certifiable nut. If he could survive another day he'd be clear of him, and the others. *Hell.* The old guy'd mentioned hell.

Perfect. Hell was just what Jared deserved.

You did it, boy. You got what you wanted. What was that illusion you had about Tiana and Jamaal? What were you thinking, man? This is the place for people like you, and no doubt whatever happens on the deuce you're going to end up here again, or a place like it. What does it matter if some guy punches your ticket now?

He looked around at all the blue-clad inmates in one big sardine can. They called him Fish—jail lingo for First In, Special Handling—and that was what he was, so the sardine comparison worked. Only nobody was going to give him special handling again. Everybody was better off with him out of the picture. His mom, his dad, his sister, and certainly that woman with a kid who couldn't catch a break. He wasn't going to be anybody's break.

The fear left him. His acceptance of death gave him a perverse hope that he wouldn't have to suffer anymore and wouldn't be the cause of anyone else's suffering.

And then chow was over, and he'd only eaten a few bites. It didn't matter. It was only an imitation of food here. He didn't feel hunger at all as he was marched back to his cell along with the other sardines. Nobody spoke—no one was allowed to speak—but he heard whispers. The whispers were directed at him.

Didn't matter anymore.

He got into his bunk and looked at the ceiling for a couple of hours, narrating moments of his life. They came on the big screen, like an ESPN video replay, complete with voice-over.

Jared Hamilton breaks his nose, ladies and gentlemen, when Freddy Van Horn throws him a baseball from the next driveway and he doesn't catch it. He doesn't put the mitt up there and ohhhh, that's gotta hurt, folks!

He remembered the stunning blow and the blood pouring out of his nose and the look of shock on his mother's face and the look of disappointment on his father's face because he had a mitt and couldn't catch a stupid baseball.

Yes, sir, and there he is trying to get Lisa Larson to like him, but she just laughs when he finally works up the courage to ask her out, and her boyfriend pushes him into the lockers, and that's when he decides he's going in the Marines someday so he can come back and deal with the boyfriend. You see that, ladies and gentlemen? You see that? Kind of sad, don't you think?

He skipped over Iraq completely, knowing those memories would come back soon enough. Over them he had no control. He thought of Tiana and Jamaal.

And there he is, folks, trying to save a woman, trying to be somebody in a kid's eyes, trying to make it seem like he's got a purpose around here. Give him a hand!

At lights-out the noise started up—the inmates came alive at night, because out on the street they were night crawlers, and in here night was their time to scream obscenities.

But he wasn't going to let the noise break him. He was going to sleep. And he did start to drift off, did start to fade away from voices and memories, when he felt something hard and sharp pressed against his jugular.

7.

They told me my son was in here!

Dear God in heaven, help him. I'm a K–10 and can't get to him, can't look him in the eye and tell him how stupid I was, how wrong, how blind, how unloving, how sorry I am now.

Jared, I let you down. I let you fall, because I was all mixed-up with … no, because I let myself get all mixed-up and I missed what was important for you.

God, let me see him again before they take me away. Give him another chance. Illuminate his heart toward you!

Protect him. I didn't. Protect him, Lord.

8.

"Don't move," Pal whispered.

He was standing over Jared, his back to the cell door.

"You move, you lose," Pal said. He pushed his weapon—probably a sharpened piece of metal—harder against Jared's throat.

Jared didn't move. He sensed the other three moving around, forming a human screen to cloak what was happening in the cell.

Pal put his face in front of Jared's. Pal's eyes sparked with a glint of virulent menace. Crazy eyes.

"You ready to pledge now?" Pal said.

Jared was silent.

Pal jabbed Jared's throat. It felt like it broke skin.

"Do you believe in Hitler?"

Jared said nothing.

"Answer me, Fish. And be careful what you say. Do you believe in the power and glory of Adolf? Do you, Fish?"

He glared at Pal.

"You better say something right now." Pal's weapon drew a trickle of blood.

"Do it," Jared said.

"What?"

"Do it. Now. Coward."

"You crazy ..." Pal hesitated, but his eyes widened, the color of hate filling them. "I'm gonna like this."

Jared closed his eyes. Waiting.

Then he heard the old guy's voice. "Put down the shank."

Time stopped. Jared opened his eyes and saw Pal's face flash with momentary confusion. But only a flash. "Shut up, old man," Pal said, still looking at Jared. "Unless you want some of this."

"In the name of Jesus Christ, and by his blood, I command you to turn around."

The old man spoke firmly but quietly, as if he trusted the words more than the tone.

Pal bared his teeth at Jared. Then he turned toward the old man.

9.

Cara jolted awake in the blackness.

It was night and she was alone in her bedroom.

But she knew she'd been summoned, without doubt.

Jared was in trouble.

She got out of bed and looked out the window. She could see the faint glow of the streetlights below. Her brother needed help.

Cara threw on a robe and opened her door. She was surprised by soft light coming from the living room. She followed it.

Her mother was on her knees at the sofa.

"Mom, what's going on?"

Dallas looked up. "I'm praying for your brother. He needs it."

"I know. I got the same message."

She took Cara's hands. "We need to cover him then."

Cara knelt by her mother's side. "Yes. Let's storm the throne together."

10.

"Told you to shut up!"

Pal approached the old guy. Jared saw the three others in the cell stepping away toward the back wall. What was happening? Did the old guy have a weapon of his own?

No. Nothing in his hands as he got to his feet. "In the name of Jesus Christ, and by his blood, I bind you."

Jared saw Pal's body go rigid.

"If you unbind me," Pal said, his voice lower now, "I will tear your eyes out."

"In the name of Christ," the old guy said, "what is your name?"

"Bel," Pal said.

Sweat burst out across Jared's palms. *Bel? What kind of name is that?*

"Will that statement stand for truth before the true and living God?" the old guy said.

"Yessss!" The voice from Pal answered, a voice unlike his own. It sounded like the answer was yanked out of him.

The other three inmates pressed themselves against the back wall as if pinned there. Freaked out, from the look of them. Just like Jared.

The old man leaned into Pal's face, and Pal just stood there, his arms at his sides. The man said, "In the name of Jesus Christ, and by his blood, you have no authority here. Jesus Christ is your Lord and conqueror. Confess it."

Jared could see Pal's back muscles flex, the skin rippling. The shank dropped out of his hand and hit the floor. That was the most amazing thing so far.

"Jesus Christ is my Lord and conqueror," the voice that was not Pal's said through Pal's mouth.

And then Pal screamed as loudly as any man Jared had ever heard. Jared practically jumped through the upper bunk.

The old man stood there, staring into Pal's screaming mouth, unflinching.

A deputy was at the cell, holding a club. "Hey hey hey! What's going on?" He pounded on the bars with his stick.

More screams rose from the cells along the module, screams of wild fury, like a chain reaction of otherworldly shrieks. What was happening? The evil that he'd felt earlier, the presence, he sensed now in the fullest force, in this place, focused.

"Get me out of here," Jared said to the deputy, rolling off his bunk. He picked up the shank and held it out. "He tried to kill me."

The deputy's eyes widened at the sight of the weapon. He drew his own. "Nobody move," he ordered, then called for backup.

Pal, or whatever was in Pal, looked straight at the old guy, who said, "In the name of Jesus Christ, I command you to go to Christ right now, to be dealt with as he sees fit."

"No!" the Pal-thing screamed.

"Now!"

The deputy's eyes were crazy wide as he shouted, "Shut up! Nobody move!"

The only one who moved then was Pal, as he fell to the floor of the cell.

FIFTEEN

Monday morning, after another night of little sleep, Dallas appeared in court with Jeff Waite. This time there was no press crowd, because this morning it was Jared Hamilton's appearance.

The judge was a woman, Maxine Novak. Grandmotherly, Dallas thought, if your grandmother packed heat.

"Mr. Hamilton, you missed your court appearance," she said. "We don't like that. We issue warrants when people do that, and we put them in jail. You don't want to go to jail again, do you, Mr. Hamilton?"

"No, ma'am."

"If it happens again, I'm going to have you put in jail and have you stay there, is that understood?"

"Yes, ma'am."

"Mr. Waite, does your client fully understand he can't do this?"

Jeff said, "He is fully informed, Your Honor. But another appearance won't be necessary."

Judge Novak put on her glasses, which hung by a beaded string from around her neck. "You have filed a demurrer."

"Yes."

The judge looked over toward the young DDA, a woman who looked to Dallas like she had just graduated from high school.

"Ms. Heilburn," Judge Novak said, "do you have a response?"

Young Heilburn cleared her throat. "We deny it."

"Deny what?"

"The demurrer?"

"Are you asking me or telling me?"

"Telling you?"

Judge Novak took her glasses off and rubbed her eyes. "Ms. Heilburn, I understand that you're new around here, but I can't make the arguments for you. The defense says that the facts as stated in your accusatory pleading do not constitute a crime. Specifically, the police report taken at face value leaves out the element of driving. As this charge is driving under the influence, you have a little problem there, don't you?"

The girl looked flummoxed.

"The engine was running, Your Honor," the DDA said. "The defendant was the only occupant of the vehicle."

"Not good enough," Jeff Waite said. "Under *Mercer* and several other cases."

Ms. Heilburn almost raised her hand. "I would like the arresting officer to testify."

"And do what?" said the judge. "Contradict his own report? Ms. Heilburn, you know that your complaint must be able to stand on its own four corners. You've left out a corner."

"Then I would like to move to amend the complaint."

"You would like to?"

"Yes, Your Honor."

"Then make your motion."

Ms. Heilburn looked around as if seeking a cue card. "The People move ... to amend the complaint."

"Motion denied," Judge Novak said. "Anything else?"

"Your Honor," she mumbled, "may I have a recess to confer with the head deputy?"

"No. Anything else?"

The young DDA was now rendered speechless.

The judge said, "There being none, I am going to sustain the demurrer and dismiss the complaint. Further, I find that the defect cannot be remedied, and so sustain without leave to amend."

"Public intoxication!" Ms. Heilburn interjected.

"Too late." The judge looked at Jared. "This action is dismissed, but I don't want to see you in here again, young man. And I certainly don't want to get even a whiff that you and booze are doing anything together in a motor vehicle, is that clear?"

"Yes, Your Honor," Jared said.

"Then you are hereby released," Judge Novak said.

Out in the hallway, Jeff explained to Dallas the sudden turn of events. "We were just lucky to get this judge at this time. She loves to put baby DAs through the grinder."

"Why?" Dallas asked.

"She used to be a prosecutor herself, in charge of training. She thinks the office has gone downhill in that regard since she left. Anyway, if a deputy isn't doing the job, she trains them from the bench. She's really pro-prosecution. She just sees herself as making them tougher. The next time Ms. Heilburn comes to court, you know she's going to be ready."

"Thanks again, Jeff."

The lawyer put his hand on Jared's shoulder. "No more beer in the car, right?"

"Oh, yeah," Jared said. "Or any other time."

Dallas wasn't sure whether she was more surprised by the announcement or Jared's apparent sincerity.

"Tomorrow morning," Jeff said, "Ron changes his plea. Try to get some rest tonight."

2.

In the car, Jared seemed about to erupt. He told Dallas to pull over.

"Now?" she asked. They were just about to pull onto the freeway.

"Now," Jared said. "Please."

She passed the on-ramp and drove down Grand to Cesar Chavez, where she pulled to the curb. "What is it?"

"Mom, I have to tell you something."

"Yes?"

"Something that happened to me in jail. You're not going to believe it."

"At this point, I think I can believe just about anything." She hoped it was good news this time.

"I was put in a cell with five other guys."

"Five? In one cell?"

"Yeah, unbelievable huh? Five white guys, and four of them were supremacist types."

"Oh, Jared."

"One of 'em wanted to scare me into making a pledge to him, and when I wouldn't he tried to slit my throat."

Dallas knew about the conditions at the L.A. jail, the overcrowding, the gangs. But throat slitting? Her own son? *Thank you, God, that he's alive!*

"I don't know if he was just posing," Jared said, "but it sure seemed real to me. He was going to do it, and I dared him to."

"You did *what?*"

"That's part of it, Mom! I was ready to die, I wanted to die—"

"Jared—"

"No, listen. That's what I was thinking, you have to know that. But there was this other guy in there, an older guy, and he warned me. He said he knew Dad, or knew all about him, and that these guys wanted me in hell. It was crazy sounding."

Dallas couldn't help thinking of Roger Vernon. Talk of hell was not so crazy.

"So this one skinhead holds a shank to my throat. He had this look in his eyes that was so freaky, Mom. I think I know why."

She waited.

"I think there was a demon thing going on."

"Jared, I'm certain of it."

"He's holding the shank to my throat and then this old guy orders him to turn around. And he does, and this guy starts saying, 'In the name of Jesus and by his blood' and the other guy says his name is Bel—"

"Bel?"

"Yeah. And now I am freaking out. He tells the guy to confess that Jesus is his conqueror, and the guy does! He admits it. And then he screams, Mom. He screams so loud! And the other guys, the guys who were part of his set, they're all standing against the back wall like they want no part of this. And me, I'm ready to run right through the bars and get the—get out of there."

Dallas could not speak. The torrent of his words covered her.

"And then a guard comes, and I tell him what's going on, and now he is looking freaked out and orders that nobody move, and calls for help, but the old guy and Pal, that's the guy with the shank, which he's dropped at this point, they keep looking at each other. And then the guy commands that this demon, Bel I guess, go to Jesus to be dealt with. And the guy screams *No!* and then falls right to the floor. Boom. He's out."

Jared took a deep breath. "Mom, it was the weirdest thing I've ever seen."

"I believe that, Jared." She put her hand on his arm. "Do you have any doubt God protected you?"

"I don't know what to believe."

"Last night, Cara and I were praying for you. We both knew you were in trouble. We had no idea this was going on. We just knew you needed help, and look what happened. It's time, Jared."

"Time for what?"

"To reclaim your position in Christ."

Looking at her, eyes searching, he said, "I feel like it's too late."

"That's a lie and you know it. You know your Bible. You were raised in it. 'If we confess our sins, he is faithful and just and will forgive us.'"

"'And purify us from all unrighteousness,'" Jared said.

She took his hand. "You do remember. That's God's Word, right?"

"I guess so."

"Don't guess. Believe it. Like you used to."

"I can't just turn it back on, Mom. Maybe in time—"

"Your time is now." She squeezed his hand. "Don't wait. Faith is a decision. Trust comes in when you're not sure. You've got something inside you that's never gone away. Now turn it back over to God, Jared."

She was shaking. Her prayers for him had been so fervent for so long she wasn't about to let him go. She'd wrestle him all day if she had to.

"What do you want me to say, Mom?"

"You know what to say. Just go to God, right now."

"Mom—"

"Try."

He sighed deeply. Then closed his eyes, still holding Dallas's hand. "Just do it, God," he said. "Just do it, okay? Whatever you know to do. I'm sorry. For everything. I really am. I been away from you so long and I want you back, I want ..."

Dallas looked at him. Tears were streaming down his face. And then he cried out, loud and mournful. She took him in her arms, held him close as he sobbed, the wetness becoming a baptism of forgiveness.

He kept his head buried on her shoulder until his crying softened and his breathing steadied. Dallas kissed his head and pressed her own wet cheeks on his hair.

They stayed like that for several minutes, Dallas stroking his back the way she used to comfort him when he was little.

Finally she said, "Through Jesus Christ our Lord."

Jared whispered, "Amen."

3.

Tomorrow, my life changes forever.

It has already changed.

Tomorrow, I take what is to come, whatever it may be.

I trust in the Lord.

I trust in the Lord for me.

For Dallas.

For Cara.

And for Jared.

Cover them all, Lord.

4.

Jared gunned his truck up Interstate 5, pushing the outer edge of the speed limit, staying within the spirit if not the letter of the law.

Spirit. That's what had changed. Maybe it wasn't too late for things to come out right.

In three hours he was knocking on Guillermo's door.

"What happened to you, dude?" Guillermo said.

"Where's Tiana?"

"She's gone, man."

"Where?"

Guillermo shrugged. "She didn't say nothin'. Took the kid and left."

"What did she leave in?"

"She walked. I don't know what she did after that."

"Why didn't you try to stop her?"

"I'm not no nanny, man. She said she was leavin'. What'm I supposed to do?"

"Did she say anything about where she might go?"

"Nothin'."

"Where's your mother, maybe she knows." Jared started to go inside.

Guillermo stopped him. "She doesn't know. She's asleep. What are you comin' around for, man? You're trouble. *Loco.* Leave us alone. Go bother somebody else."

"I got to say something, Guillermo."

Guillermo eyed him skeptically, but at least he didn't slam the door.

"I'm sorry, man," Jared said. "You're right, I was *loco.* You remember that time in the church, when I put paint on Jesus's face?"

"Oh, man, how could I forget that? I thought lightning was gonna come, man, fry all of us."

"I made peace with him," Jared said.

"Jesus?"

"Yeah."

With a narrowed gaze, Guillermo cocked his head slightly.

"I know," Jared said. "Coming from me it still sounds *loco.* But I did it, and I'm sorry for how I treated you."

"Hey, man, you were just a little whack, you know? I never thought you were a bad dude."

"I am a bad dude, but I got something working on the inside to change that. That's what I hope. I'm betting my life on it." He put out his hand. "Thanks for taking us in."

Guillermo shook it, smiled. "My mama, she woulda killed me if I didn't."

"Mama knows best."

Jared got in his truck and left.

He knew about a couple of homeless shelters in downtown Bakersfield. He checked them, but no one answering to the description of Tiana and Jamaal had been in either one.

He went to the bus station, but the cashier—who probably wasn't on duty at the time they would have purchased tickets anyway—wouldn't give out any information. Nobody gave out information anymore. It was too likely to result in a lawsuit.

Where would they have gone?

Maybe back to L.A.

He hadn't prayed in a long time, before that prayer of repentance in the car with his mother.

He sat in his truck outside the bus station, closed his eyes, and whispered, *God, help me find them.*

SIXTEEN

1.

Tuesday morning in court, with a buzzing press gathered in anticipation, Dallas watched as her husband's future was decided—where he would be housed and for how many years. Prison was a reality.

For her as well. Someone was about to get away with murder, and if that someone was never found, Ron would remain incarcerated for a crime he did not commit.

Ron was brought in, dressed in his orange jail coveralls, hands shackled. He looked at Dallas as the deputy unlocked his restraints. His face was peaceful, his body seemingly at rest.

Judge Harvey Carson entered the courtroom, and everyone stood. He looked fair but firm. He would have presided over the trial, had there been one, and Dallas thought he would have been a good choice.

"The court has considered a motion by the defendant to change his plea," Judge Carson said. "Is that still the defendant's wish, Mr. Waite?"

Jeff stood. "It is, Your Honor."

"Then I will advise your client. Mr. Hamilton, has your counsel talked to you about this change of plea?"

Ron's voice shook a little when he spoke. "Yes, he has, Your Honor."

Dallas bit down on her lip.

"You wish to withdraw your plea of not guilty?"

"Yes, Your Honor."

"And plead nolo contendere?"

"Yes, Your Honor."

"Did your counsel explain to you that a plea of nolo contendere has the exact force and effect as a plea of guilty?"

"Yes, sir."

"And that you will be waiving your constitutional right to a jury trial?"

"Yes, sir."

"And that you will also waive any evidentiary challenge to the truth of the underlying offense?"

"Yes."

"Do you also understand that a nolo plea to a felony offense *is* admissible in a civil action against you?"

"Yes, I do."

"Do you wish to waive your constitutional rights as I've described?"

"Yes, Your Honor."

"Very well. The court finds that the defendant understands the consequences of his change of plea. Withdrawal of the not-guilty plea is granted. Mr. Hamilton, to the sole count of murder in the second degree, how do you plead?"

"No contest," Ron said.

"All right. I find that the defendant has entered a plea of nolo contendere, knowingly and advisedly. Do the People wish to be heard?"

Mike Freton, the DA, said, "No, Your Honor."

"Is there any reason why sentence should not be imposed at this time?"

Jeff said, "No, Your Honor."

Mr. Freton said the same.

"Very well," Judge Carson said. "Mr. Hamilton, your plea is accepted by the court. You are hereby sentenced to state prison for the term of fifteen years to life. The facility will be decided by the sentencing authority. We are adjourned."

Judge Harvey Carson pounded his gavel on the bench. It exploded like a gunshot in the quiet courtroom.

Ron looked at Dallas one last time before he was ushered out. He mouthed the words *I love you.*

Before she could react the press was on her, several reporters seeking comment, shouting questions. This time she was ready.

Having appeared nationwide on Hank Dunaway's show, she was a public figure. God would use this moment.

"I will be happy to make a statement," she said. "I will make it outside on the street."

The press moved like a well-rehearsed army. In ten minutes she was standing in front of a knot of microphones and with the lights of several cameras directed her way.

"The decision made today by my husband is not an admission of guilt, though that is no doubt what many people will think. I can only tell you that I continue to believe my husband is innocent of murder, and that what's happening here is something far more insidious, and that the guilty party still walks the streets.

"I leave it to you to do your jobs. This story is not finished yet. But my husband and I have reached this decision together, because we believe that God is in control. I know that sounds like a cliché to many of you. Be that as it may, that is how we choose to live our lives. From this, our faith, there is no turning back. Thank you."

A flurry of shouted questions burst toward her. She shook her head and turned her back to the microphones, nearly bumping into a serious young woman.

"Mrs. Hamilton?"

"Yes?"

"I'm Tracy Harrington. I clerk for Mr. Freton. He sent me to ask if you'd like some help in getting your husband's things."

"Things?"

"I mean the evidence that was seized. Sheesh. I'm glad he didn't hear me say *things*. Usually this stuff—darn it, *evidence*—all goes back to the police station, but he has the box upstairs and wanted to save you the hassle of waiting."

"Where do I go?"

"Eighteenth floor. I'll take you."

Good. Someone else to usher her through the maze. She hoped she'd never have to be here again.

Just before entering the building, Dallas looked back at the dissolving swarm of reporters. It was like a fog clearing.

Then, through the fog, coming into clear focus across Temple Street, she saw an unmistakable face.

Chad McKenzie was looking directly at her.

He smiled. And clapped his hands.

2.

Mike Freton was already in his office when Dallas got there with Tracy. He had his coat off and was putting a file folder away in a metal drawer. Tracy left and closed the door behind her.

Mr. Freton offered her a chair. "I know that must have been hard for you, Mrs. Hamilton."

She didn't sit. "I know that my husband did not kill Melinda Perry."

The DA nodded wearily, as if he'd heard that particular line many times over the years, only with different names. "Can I offer you coffee or anything?"

"No, thanks. You ought to know that I was attacked recently by someone I knew over twenty-five years ago, a man named Chad McKenzie. And he's out on the street right now. He was looking at me just before I came up here."

Mr. Freton took a moment to process the information. "This guy is out there now?"

"Yes. Across the street."

"Did you report the attack to the police?"

"I reported it, yes. What do you suggest I do?"

The DA went to his window, which looked out on the south side of downtown. "Tell you what. I'll have courthouse security walk you to your car. If you can ID the man for the officer, he can call for LAPD. From that point on, it will be a police matter."

"Thank you."

He made a call. "It'll be just a few minutes."

"I appreciate your doing this."

He nodded. "I've seen many women in your position. None has handled herself as well as you have, especially considering all the publicity. I also want you to know that if any credible evidence is produced that would compel another look at this case, I'll take that look."

A few minutes later, a young man in a county safety police uniform entered Mike Freton's office. The DA gave the cardboard box containing Ron's computer to the officer and asked him to escort Dallas to her car.

She and the county officer took a special elevator to the ground level. That was nice. It definitely paid to know the right people around here.

3.

She called Detective Lacy from her car. After about a five-minute hold, he came on.

"Mrs. Hamilton, I was going to call—"

"I saw him. Chad McKenzie. Just now, at the courthouse—"

"Mrs. Hamilton—"

"Staring at me."

"I'm no longer on this matter."

"*What?*"

"I've been reassigned. The Rafe Bryan killing has been given to another team. That happens. I'll give you the contact information."

His voice trailed off in a way that indicated to Dallas he wanted to say more.

"Is there anything else you can tell me?" she asked.

There was a long pause. "There are some odd things. I really can't go into it all."

"Why not?"

"I wish I could."

Dallas pulled her car into Cara's apartment complex and parked. "Detective, please."

"I shouldn't do this, but I figure you deserve a break. I know you've been through a lot."

"What sort of break?"

"Gentri Land."

"Yes?"

"It turns out this is a corporation with quite a few real estate holdings in California, Nevada, and Arizona."

"What did Rafe Bryan have to do with any of that?"

"As far as I know, nothing. But Gentri Land owns certain commercial buildings in Chatsworth. And one of its tenants is LookyLu Productions."

Dallas tried to figure out what that all meant, but nothing clicked.

"Lu is clearly a factor here, but my money's on your guy McKenzie as the common denominator."

She shivered involuntarily. How would Chad be connected to Vic Lu? Well, other than by their salacious tastes?

"What should I do?" she asked.

"Not much you can do. Listen, if I hear anything that you need to know, I'll contact you. But for the time being ..."

"Yes?"

"Be careful."

4.

Jared turned his truck out toward Highway 99. As he drove around the perimeter of Bakersfield with country music playing on the radio—not the hard-core beat he used to play when getting high, but the twangy tunes about good-old boys in trucks like his—he felt both free and lost.

Free in the good way, the best way, the way that he'd learned as a kid from his mom and dad and the church he grew up in. But lost in another way, because he'd been getting used to the aimlessness of his old torment.

He knew that was partly an excuse, a reason he used to run away. But where would he run to now?

Just before hitting the highway he saw a billboard with a woman on it, a woman with a face and figure posed to stir the blood of any able-bodied male this side of puberty, and letters a mile high about a casino just a few miles up the road. What a great world it had become.

He'd fought for this world, this freedom, and it was worth it. Despite the naysayers and hate mongers, he would fight for freedom again. But when it was used for stuff like this, his throat ached. *Couldn't we do more with our most prized possession than this?*

He got on 99 and pointed himself back toward L.A.

5.

On Wednesday, Dallas went to the jail to see Ron for the last time before he would be remanded to the custody of the men's penal colony at Los Rios. All things considered, Jeff told her, it was a good place, not one of the harder places like San Quentin or Corcoran. Though it wouldn't be easy time, it wouldn't be hell on earth, either.

"I wish I could tell you how much I love you," he said. "I don't deserve you, but there it is. I want you to get on with your life without me, Dallas."

"Don't talk about that now. I'll be up to visit you."

"You don't have to."

"I want to. We're in this together. As strange as that may be."

"I also wish I could tell you what I've experienced in this place. Being in here has stripped away everything I was holding onto. I've been scraped. But free. Do you remember when we read the Narnia stories to the kids?"

"Of course."

"Remember that part where Eustace is being released from being a dragon? How painful yet freeing it was? Lewis had it right. That's exactly what I'm going through. And I'm grateful. I'm sure in eternity I'll look back and see this was the only way. And I'll give glory to God."

"He has worked in this, Ron. Jared has come back to the Lord."

Ron's eyes brightened. "How?"

She told him the story as Jared had given it to her, and of his prayer of repentance uttered in the car on their way back from his court appearance.

Ron broke down. Dallas couldn't keep her own tears from falling. When he was finally able to talk again, he said, "The guy who did this, who was in Jared's cell, you said he mentioned me to Jared?"

"That's right."

"Maybe he's the one."

"The one what?"

"Dallas, I kept getting messages delivered to me in here, Bible verses and the like. It was as if whoever wrote them knew me personally, knew exactly what to say."

"Ron, there's more to this. God's not finished."

He looked at her. "I have a long time to think about that."

6.

A long time to think . . .

That's what both of them would have from now on. She thought about it all day and into the night.

Naturally, she couldn't sleep. She was starting to get very tired of not sleeping, of the toll it was taking on her body. She recited the twenty-third psalm in her mind, in the King James, but even that did not help.

She reached over and flicked on the light. The clock said 1:47 a.m. This was nuts. Were sleepless nights going to be her own prison sentence?

Something was bothering her. Connections needed to be made, but they were elusive, like scattering rodents.

She swung her legs over the bed and saw, sitting on the floor, the evidence box Mike Freton had given her.

She opened it.

More than Ron's laptop was in there. The box also included a sheaf of stapled papers with a series of numbers on it, and a few letters and receipts. But it was the laptop that held her attention.

The laptop that contained the images Ron had downloaded.

What to do with it? Destroy it? Take a hammer to it and reduce it to bits?

She took up the letters. Nothing of particular relevance, as far as she could see. One letter saddened her, though. It was from Karen and included a copy of the publisher's letter, outlining the terms of the deal.

The deal that was pulled when Ron was arrested.

Her mind snapped back to the laptop.

Should she boot it up? In a way, it was like having a murder weapon in the room. It was ominous and dangerous and a threat.

The stapled papers. It didn't look like something seized from Ron's office. It was a list of a series of numbers that looked like a World War II encryption. But some of the numbers appeared to be dates. Random dates, in no particular pattern. At least, not that she could see.

What was it? She leafed through all five pages, her eyes crossing. She was about to throw it back in the box when she got to the very last page. The numbers filled only half a page.

Then, at the very bottom, was a notation:

Tomassi, L. 4903940/DASR45–4/13

Tomassi, L. Obviously a name.

She knew she wasn't going to sleep, so why not spend the morning hours trying to find out who this Tomassi was?

The answer could be in Ron's contact list.

On his laptop.

But it wouldn't turn on. No battery life. Now what would she do? Wander Cara's apartment like a somnambulant ghost? Instead, she padded down to Cara's study with the laptop. Cara had a similar model, with a power cord. In two minutes Ron's laptop glowed.

Dallas shuddered at what secrets she might find there.

Turn it off and forget about it. This is the past now. Nothing good can come from pursuing this.

But she kept looking.

She found his contacts list and opened it. Looked under the *T* tab.

No Tomassi.

She went to the *search* window and searched for *Tomassi* as a file name or part of the contents. She got the same message each time: *Search is complete. There are no results to display.*

Now she was fully awake, her mind engaged. She was going to look like a wreck in the morning. Wait, it *was* the morning.

Don't go nutty.

She logged on to the Internet. When in doubt, Google. She tried Googling *Tomassi* but came up with nearly 100,000 hits. Now *that* was a cure for insomnia. She tried to add the letter *L* to the search, but that only narrowed things down to 44,800. Sure, only take half the morning with those. She looked at the notation again. What if she tried typing in the number?

She typed in *4903940/DASR45–4/13.*

Nothing.

She kept staring at the code. Maybe the letters meant something. Some sort of organization maybe. What did she have to lose? It was getting on toward two thirty, and she was not going to sleep.

She typed in *DASR.*

And got 19,300 results.

That seemed strange. But she scrolled through a few and found it to be an abbreviation with several possible meanings, like Digital Air Surveillance Radar and Direct Access Service Requests.

Another dead end.

She almost logged off. But then she gave it one last try. She typed in DASR45.

And got one result.

She clicked on the link.

It took her to the website of the Los Angeles County District Attorney's Office. On a page titled "Press Releases."

An old release, from last year.

Now she wasn't just awake, her body was humming. She scanned the release, which was about a conviction being upheld on appeal. Then she got to the final section.

The court found that the error was harmless, and that introduction of internal reports from the District Attorney's office, like the DASR45 that was admitted in this case, were not inherently prejudicial.

Internal report from the District Attorney's office? That's what the form was. It must be a mistake that she had it. But what did it mean?

7.

Dallas presented herself at the DA's office at ten the next morning and asked to see Mike Freton. The receptionist made a call and asked Dallas to wait. A few minutes later, Freton's clerk, Tracy Harrington, came in.

"Hello, Mrs. Hamilton. Mr. Freton's in court. Is there something I can do for you?"

"If we could find a place to talk."

"Sure."

Dallas followed Tracy down a narrow hallway lined with filing cabinets to a little cubicle.

"My domain," Tracy explained.

"Nice."

"You're being kind. Someday I hope to graduate into a real shoebox. Coffee?"

"Do you have any that's really strong?"

"Always. We use it to reroof the buildings."

Tracy got two Styrofoam cups of coffee. And she was right. Definitely heavy-duty caffeine.

Dallas put the DASR report on Tracy's small desk. "I believe this was given to me by mistake."

Tracy picked it up, flipped through it. "Oops. You're right. This is ours."

"What is it?"

"District Attorney Summary Report. Subject number 45."

"I'm not in any trouble, right?"

"Oh, no."

"Can you tell me what it was for? The only thing I could figure out was that it's a report made out by someone named Tomassi for your office."

Tracy's face broke out into a huge smile. "Now that's funny."

"What is?"

"It's Lucas. Lucas Tomassi."

"You know him then?"

"He's my boyfriend."

"You're kidding."

"Nope. We're just one big happy family around here."

"He prepared that?"

Tracy nodded. "He's one of our IT guys. Computer whiz. Except when it's my computer, then he seems to take his sweet—"

"Could I talk to him?"

"You want to talk to Lucas?"

"Please."

Tracy frowned. "About this?"

"May I?"

"I don't know, I really don't—"

"Please. I've already looked this over. I just want to ask him about it. You can be here. If he's not supposed to say something, you can stop him."

Tracy smiled again. "I love doing that. Okay, Mrs. Hamilton."

Ten minutes later, a man of about thirty with stylishly unkempt hair and black-rimmed glasses popped into the cubicle.

"You rang?" he said.

"Lucas, this is Mrs. Hamilton."

He shook her hand. "I know. I recognize you from the news."

"That's my lot now, I guess," Dallas said.

"Bites, doesn't it?" Lucas said. "I mean, people who don't want to go public are forced to, while a bunch of people we'd rather not see more of are still out there."

"Mrs. Hamilton wanted to ask you some things about your DASR."

"Which one? I only do about a hundred a week."

"This one."

Tracy handed the report to Lucas. He flipped through it quickly. "How did you get this?"

"It was in the box that Mr. Freton prepared for me."

"This is internal. You shouldn't have it."

"It was a mistake, okay?" Tracy said. "But the case is officially over now. So don't get bent."

Lucas Tomassi issued an audible sigh, his response to Tracy. He looked at Dallas. "You sure you want to know?"

"Please."

"It's a log of all those images that we found on your husband's computer, okay? Sorry."

She had suspected it. "But what do the numbers mean?"

"They're just a collection of the dates the images were made, if they were part of the original download. And a code number for each image that I put in. For indexing purposes."

"Some job," Tracy said.

"Hey, I just work here." He looked down at his report. "And some other information like individual file size, a couple things I forgot about, yada yada—"

Dallas rubbed her temples.

"—files were downloaded, March 23, yada yada, April 11th I entered some of my own personal notations, in code of course, brilliantly conceived by me—"

"You're so brilliant," Tracy said.

With her head starting to throb, Dallas said, "Anything else besides the pornography report?"

"Nope. That's really all this is. My notations, sitting all day long and entering numbers. It's what I do all day. That's why Tracy, who makes about twice as much as I do, is taking me out to dinner tonight."

"In your dreams," Tracy said. She snatched the DASR from Lucas. "Now go back to your cage."

He bobbed his eyebrows. "I'm thinking Italian. *Ciao.*"

And then he was gone.

"Thanks for bringing this back." Tracy opened a drawer and put the report inside. "I know this whole thing hasn't been easy."

"You do know that somebody leaked this information to the press."

She watched Tracy's face carefully. The young clerk seemed stunned into silence.

"It had to come from this office, or from the police," Dallas added.

"You're not suggesting that Lucas ..."

"Maybe I'm just asking you for help, if you know."

"The case is over. I don't see how it's relevant anymore. If I did know."

"I'm not sure the case *is* over. At least for me."

Tracy took a long time before answering. "At this point, Mrs. Hamilton, I think it best that I not say anything further."

A heavy curtain fell. This scene was over.

"Thanks for the coffee." Dallas stood up. "I can find my way out."

8.

Dallas did not go to her car. Instead, she walked a couple of blocks to Los Angeles Street and entered Parker Center, home base of the Los Angeles Police Department. A large square white building, it was both solid and forbidding, the hub of all force and might in L.A. Which is what Dallas needed behind her.

At the front desk, she gave her name and asked to see Detective William Lacy. The uniformed officer who manned the desk picked up a phone and punched a couple of buttons.

"Dallas Hamilton to see Lacy," the officer said. He waited a few moments, then said, "Thanks," and hung up.

"Not in," he said. "You want to leave him a message?"

"Do you know where I can reach him?"

"You can leave a message, ma'am."

"Never mind," she said. She returned to the street, back to the public parking lot behind the courthouse. Dallas felt like a cork bobbing on a human sea. People were everywhere, and their movements all seemed random. That's what life was like now. No order. Questions, and no place to go for answers. Detective Lacy was a shot in the dark anyway. He wasn't even on the Rafe Bryan case anymore, so that probably settled it. No more help from the police.

Now what?

She got back to her car and paid the ten bucks it cost every time she came down here. The parking-lot business in Los Angeles, that was the business to be in. Maybe she could open one up and sit in a kiosk for the next twenty years, raking it in.

She thought about driving to the ocean again, finding a quiet spot for prayer. Instead she got on the freeway and headed toward Hillside. She would find someone to pray with her up there. Hopefully Lisa or Bob. He was her pastor now. Odd, but why not?

She listened to smooth jazz on the radio and tried to quiet her brain. The thoughts pinging around in there were more likely to drive her crazy than to the truth. She would find the truth at Hillside, at her church. That was the place she could get centered again.

She exited the freeway and noticed a flashing red light right behind her. To her chagrin, it was her car that had been targeted.

Terrific. What had she done? Speeding? No way. Broken taillight? She hoped the cop would show mercy. The last thing she needed in her life right now was a ticket to pay.

Then she noticed that it wasn't a black and white behind her, nor a Highway Patrol car. It was an unmarked vehicle.

Containing Detective William Lacy.

"I wondered when you were going to get off the freeway," he said when he got to her window.

"You followed me?"

"I didn't want us to be seen at Parker. We need to talk."

"You want to talk to *me*?"

"Yes."

"Then let's talk."

"Not here. Is there a place we can go, out of the way?"

She thought a moment. "Yeah, a little coffee shop called Benny's. It's a couple blocks from here."

"I'll follow you."

"You do that well."

Benny's was a diner Dallas used to take the kids to when they were little. It had a truck-stop feel to it, which Dallas liked. No pretensions. And the waitresses—they still called themselves *waitresses* here—never let coffee cups stay empty.

They took an empty booth in the back and ordered coffee. Lacy took his black.

"So what's going on?" Dallas said.

Lacy took a sip, put his cup on the table, and held it with both hands. "There's something very strange about Gentri Land Corporation," he said. "I did some follow-up information on it after we talked on the phone last. We have ways of getting information, of course. But I kept running into a wall with this Gentri Land."

"You said Vic Lu is connected."

"He leases property from them. But I looked into some of the other properties connected to Gentri Land. It's all over the map, commercial real estate and the like."

"Anything else?"

"I'm not sure at the moment. But I've got a hunch that there's more going on than we know."

"That wouldn't surprise me."

"I'm glad to hear you say that."

She looked at him.

"Mrs. Hamilton, what I am about to tell you needs to remain just between us, is that understood?"

"Yes, of course."

"I may need your help."

"*My* help?"

"Let me explain. I'm investigating a missing-persons case. We suspect murder. And the possibility that Vic Lu is involved."

"But what can I do?"

"I'm not at liberty to say anything else at the moment, but at the proper time I wonder if you would consider wearing a wire."

"You mean tape somebody?"

"Exactly."

"Like on television?"

"It happens in real life too."

She considered this for a moment, seeing herself in a dark room with all sorts of equipment on her body. "I don't know if I'm cut out for that."

"Believe me, I won't let you do it if I think it would in any way be dangerous for you."

Dallas thought about it again, a sip of coffee lubricating the mental gears. Finally she looked at Lacy and said, "Will you help me if I help you?"

"How do you want me to help you?"

"I want you to help me clear my husband's name."

Lacy frowned. "Isn't it a little late for that?"

"Not if he's innocent."

"You don't think he's guilty?"

"I know he isn't."

"Mrs. Hamilton, you know that as a police officer I don't have control over the cases assigned to me, and so I—"

"You have spare time, don't you?"

Detective Lacy smiled. "Oh, yeah. Tons."

"Then hear me out."

"Go."

At least he didn't shut the door entirely. "This possible murder. Is Vic Lu himself the suspect?"

"I can't say one way or the other."

"But that's why you thought about me, isn't it?"

"Maybe."

"Listen, what if Vic Lu was the one who murdered Melinda Perry?"

Lacy's eyebrows went up, and Dallas knew she'd struck something.

She pounced. "You know something I need to know. What is it? Please."

"You're very perceptive, Mrs. Hamilton. You'd make a good cop."

"I just want to get some sleep. Can you talk to me?"

Lacy stared into his coffee for a moment. "Lu is smart. We have to proceed very carefully. It's one of his girls who's gone missing. A girl by the name of Patricia Hood."

"Who was she?"

"Another one of the countless girls who come out here for fame and money and end up with some very bad people. I'm sure she had this fantasy floating out there in front of her and tried to grab it. She even took a stage name."

"A stage name?"

"Yeah. She called herself Gilda."

SEVENTEEN

1.

My cell mate, Ernesto Ruiz, killed two men in a bar fight in San Bernardino.

In the past, they would have had us segregated. The prisons, like the jails, did that to keep order. But the California Supreme Court came down with a decision that said they couldn't do that in state prisons anymore, so I get to be part of this grand experiment here.

The two of us didn't start out with racial reconciliation at the top of the agenda.

"You got somethin' against Latinos, bro?" That was the first thing Ernesto said to me.

"No way," I said. "If it wasn't for the Latinos, there'd be no California." I tried to say it with a smile, but my lips quivered.

Ernesto was twenty-six and, while not tall, solid as a bull. "That right?"

I gave him a short history of the California missions. "That's why that stupid decision in Los Angeles a couple years ago about taking the cross off the city seal was so misguided."

"You talk like college, man."

"Sorry."

"No, it's good. I been working toward my high school equivalent."

"Great."

"Doesn't mean I won't smoke you if you tick me off."

I looked at him, not feeling scared at all. For some odd reason.

Then he smiled. "Just messin' with you, bro. Did you really kill that chiquita?"

"Would you believe me if I said no?"

"Everybody in here's innocent, man, ain't you heard?"

"The answer is no," I said.

"Why'd you plead?"

"To get it over with. To get some peace."

"In here?"

"You'd be surprised."

"You gonna need somebody to watch your back."

"I got somebody."

His look was skeptical.

"Jesus," I said.

Ernesto shook his head. "Lots of guys got Jesus, and lots of 'em end up facedown. He don't seem like enough."

"What if I told you he was?"

"I wouldn't believe it, man."

"We got lots of time to talk about it, don't we?"

He put a finger in my face. "Don't push me, man."

2.

On Sunday they were in church together—Dallas, Jared, and Cara. Almost a complete family.

It would have to do. The rebuilding would begin here.

Here at Hillside.

Dallas allowed herself to fully engage in the worship and the singing. Quincy, the worship leader at Hillside, always did a good job with the music. What she liked particularly was that he sometimes included an old hymn. She loved the hymns, and Quincy did too. He was thirty-five, a former gang member, and everyone said he could have been a rap star. Instead, he gave his gifts to the Lord.

Today, just before the sermon, Quincy led the congregation in "It Is Well with My Soul," which had always been one of Dallas's favorites. The message of grace in it was, she thought, as deep as any. And it all came rushing over her as she sang.

> *When peace like a river, attendeth my way,*
> *When sorrows like sea billows roll;*
> *Whatever my lot, Thou hast taught me to say,*
> *"It is well, it is well with my soul."*

Dallas soared with the words. But then the most remarkable thing happened. She heard Jared's voice. Jared, who never liked to sing, who never did after age thirteen or so, was singing now.

> *And, Lord, haste the day when our faith shall be sight,*
> *The clouds be rolled back as a scroll,*
> *The trump shall resound and the Lord shall descend,*
> *Even so, it is well with my soul.*

Dallas praised God silently for the grace of the moment, the spiritual reunion that had come to her son at last.

Bob Benson came to the pulpit subdued. But his sermon seemed touched by the same Spirit that had moved the congregation. He was spot-on this day, giving a message of hope.

And he finished with words about Ron.

"As you all know," he said, "we have gone through what I would call a family crisis here. Our beloved pastor has been sent to prison. You well know the story, but we must also remember another story, the greatest story ever told, that any sin we commit can be forgiven. Ron Hamilton has been forgiven. His wife, Dallas, who is here today with us, has told me all about it.

"I remember back when Dallas came to see me at the church a couple of days after Ron was arrested ..."

Yes, Dallas remembered that day too. It was her first visit to the church after Ron was taken away by the police.

"... and we sat in my office and I remember there was a lot of media attention, and we even had some threats called in. I was glad we had Dave Rivas looking out for our security, I can tell you that ..."

Dave, who managed the security system that Dallas had helped select.

"... we sat in my office and prayed for Ron and for God to watch over this church during this troubled time and ..."

Trouble came in bunches, in search warrants and leaks to the press and—

"... we left it in his hands ..."

—Ron was arrested on Monday.

"... and that's what we're going to do here today ..."

Dallas didn't hear the rest.

Someone tapped her shoulder. Jared.

"Mom, are you all right?"

"Wait here," she managed to say. And then she got up and left the sanctuary.

3.

"Dave."

Dave Rivas looked up from the Bible he was reading. On Sundays Dave went to the early morning worship service, then spent time doing his Bible reading in the security office.

He got up to greet her. As usual, he wore his LAPD cap. "Mrs. Hamilton, it's good to see—"

"Dave, I have to ask you a question."

"Sure."

"How far back do you keep security tapes and records?"

"Everything's digital. We have archives back as far as when we set up the system."

"Can we look up a certain date?"

"Of course. That's why we got this bad boy. Remember when we did the system research? You liked that aspect, even though it cost us."

"Well, now we get to see if it was worth it."

"Okay, what date?"

"March 23." That was the date that shot into her mind at church, the date Lucas Tomassi had mentioned in passing at the DA's office, talking about his report. The date the files were downloaded, he said. One problem. The 23rd was a Wednesday, two days after Ron's arrest.

Dave tapped away at a keyboard in front of a large monitor. A series of thumbnail pictures came up showing various views of the church grounds.

"You can scan these first," Dave said, "and take a look at the time markers. Any time in particular?"

"After about seven o'clock at night. Can you isolate those?"

He did it. Another series of thumbnails. One of the parking lot. Dallas pointed to it. "Can we look at this view at various times?"

"Are beans good for your heart?"

"Huh?"

"Bad joke. Of course we can."

Dave brought up shots from the parking-lot cam, the time markers broken at fifteen-minute increments. The number of cars in the lot dwindled as time passed.

"Can we skip ahead?"

"Sure. Next set."

This set began with four or five cars in the shot and ended with only one car.

Dallas realized she'd been holding her breath.

"So," Dave said jovially, "is this system worth it or what?"

"Oh, yeah," she said, her heart dropping like a brick.

4.

Dallas sat in her car outside the Bensons' house for two hours, waiting for them to get back from church. She tried to talk herself out of what she saw, create a reasonable explanation. She couldn't, because there was only one conclusion, one thing that made sense.

When the Bensons pulled into the driveway Dallas got out of her car and met them on the lawn.

"Hey, girl, what's up?" Lisa said, concern etched on her face.

"You didn't come to rebuke me about my sermon today, I hope," Bob said jokingly.

"Can we go inside?" Dallas said.

They did, and Dallas sensed their awkwardness at her unannounced visit.

They went into the living room, but before Bob sat down Dallas said, "Would you mind if I talked to Lisa privately a moment?"

"I've always thought that whole girl-talk thing was a myth," Bob said with a forced smile. "But I know the odds are against me here. I'll be in the study."

Lisa sat on the sofa and patted it for Dallas to sit next to her.

"I'm so glad you came over," Lisa said. "I've been wanting to get together with you again. It's time for us to—"

"Lisa, were you ever going to tell me about the computer?"

"Computer?"

"Ron's computer."

Lisa's face froze.

"Lisa, I know what you did. I know about the porn on Ron's computer." She watched Lisa's reaction carefully. Her hope that Lisa would crack immediately faded.

"I'm sorry, Dallas, but you're going to have to spell this out for me."

"Ron's computer was taken from the church on the twenty-fourth of March."

"I sort of remember."

"Ron was arrested on the twenty-first."

Lisa said nothing. Her face remained impassive.

"I came to the church on the twenty-third. I saw you there, and I met with Bob. We prayed in his office. He said he was going off to a speaking engagement that evening."

"Sure, I remember that."

"Do you remember staying at the church and downloading pornography onto Ron's computer?"

Lisa's noncommittal expression morphed into cold steel. "That's a horrible thing to say."

"We have the security video. Bob drove off from the parking lot at exactly 9:17 p.m. You didn't leave until 11:33. There is a very clear shot of you getting in your car. I was at the DA's office. They have a report saying downloading was done on Ron's computer on the twenty-third. That would've been very hard for Ron to do, considering he was locked up. Shall I go on?"

Lisa stared at her for a very long time. Then, almost imperceptibly, Lisa began to tremble. But she tried to speak with conviction. "Ron had an affair and he didn't tell you about it. But I knew. I knew about Amy Shea. Do you know how hard it was for me to sit in church Sunday after Sunday listening to him? Knowing what he did to you? Knowing that you wouldn't do anything even if you knew? And then ..."

"And then he was arrested, and you thought you'd take the opportunity to make sure he was ruined."

"Dallas, he was living a lie."

"Like you are now."

Lisa shifted on the sofa, her body language stiff, as if gathering her defenses. "What do you intend to do?"

"Did Bob know?"

Lisa shook her head. "Please don't say anything, he's—"

"He's got to be told."

"Dallas, please—"

"You hurt more than just my family. You hurt the church."

"We can work something out."

Dallas stood. "I'll give you until tomorrow. Tomorrow I call Bob myself."

5.

Dallas was shaking when she got back in her car. Bitterness and pain were a lethal mix. The only note of relief was finding out that all those images weren't there because of Ron. She knew now his confession of downloading then deleting pornography was sincere. It has been Lisa who was responsible, sad Lisa whose act was driven by ambition. She wanted to seal Ron's doom in the eyes of the church and the public. Leaving a wide-open door for Bob to walk through and take over as Hillside's leader.

But Dallas was also certain that Lisa's desire to ruin Ron did not mean she had anything to do with Melinda Perry's killing. Melinda's real killer was still out there, and Dallas sensed that her opportunity to uncover the truth had not expired. But there was a connection she couldn't quite make. She was certain it had something to do with what Detective Lacy had told her.

She called him from the car and, surprisingly, he picked up.

"It's Dallas Hamilton," she said. "Can you meet me?"

"When?"

"Now."

A short pause. "Name the place."

She chose an isolated corner of a park in Chatsworth, as far west as you could go in the Valley without burrowing into a mountain. She'd often come here with the kids when they were little. It was secluded and still and dotted with oak trees. A natural spot for a game of hide-and-seek.

Dallas got there first and waited by one of the gnarly trees she actually remembered hiding behind on one outing. Jared was eight or nine, and when he couldn't find her, he got scared. He said it was because he thought he was being chased by someone. She remembered that clearly.

"Don't leave me alone!" he cried, clinging to her. She vowed she never would.

Detective Lacy walked across the large grassy area before the trees twenty minutes later, looking around. No one else was visible in the park. Dallas stepped out from behind the tree and waved.

"I like this place," he said. "Beats my office."

Dallas was in no mood for small talk. "If you want me to wear this wire, I need to know who and why. I want the details."

He nodded. "Let me tell you about it in a certain way, starting with Gentri Land. Are you ready?"

"Do I need to be sitting down or something?"

"You can lean against the tree if you have to."

She did. "I'm ready."

Detective Lacy looked around once, then back at Dallas. "Gentri Land is a legitimate corporation, at least from the outside looking in."

"And Vic Lu leases property from them."

"More than that. He's an investor. He pumps a lot of money into the corporation. Legally. In return, he shares in the holdings."

"So where's the illegal part?"

"We don't know yet if there is. But we're getting closer."

"How?"

"We've managed to identify a few of the principals. I have a list of names I'd like you to take a look at." He fished a paper out of his pocket, unfolded it, and handed it to Dallas.

There were five names on the page. She didn't recognize any of them.

"There is something that all these names have in common, besides Gentri Land Corporation," he said. "Each one of them was a major contributor in the last citywide election. And each one of them gave the maximum to one candidate."

She knew who it was even before he said it. "Bernie Halstrom."

The detective nodded.

"What's it mean?" she asked.

"Nothing yet. It's all perfectly legal. On paper. But it could be pointing to a fraud underneath."

"Fraud?"

"What if Gentri Land was a front to channel political funds into a campaign? In this case, Halstrom's. The contributions come from individuals, but Gentri Land compensates them for their contributions."

"I'm not sure I follow that."

"If Gentri Land has one principal investor, he could make a way around the campaign-contributions limit. He pumps money into the corporation, the corporation pumps it out to these individuals, the individuals hand it over to Bernie Halstrom's campaign."

She tried to ignore the sinkhole opening up in her chest. Disappointment, mostly. Bernie Halstrom was just like any other politician trying to skirt the rules. Maybe she was naïve to have thought it could be any other way.

"You want me to go in to see Bernie with a wire on?"

"If you'd be willing."

"I don't think I can do that. I'm not a very good liar."

"I'm not asking you to lie."

"In a way, you are. I would be betraying a trust."

"Just as Bernie has betrayed his public trust."

"I suppose that's true, but he's also been a friend."

"Are you sure about that?"

"What's that supposed to mean?"

Detective Lacy sighed. "I guess you trust me too. I haven't been completely forthcoming with you."

How many more disclosures were there going to be? She braced herself. "You can start now if you like."

He nodded. "There is one other name associated with Gentri Land, someone who is technically the chief executive officer. His name is Walter Channing."

"I don't know that name either."

"No need for you to know. It's not his real name anyway. His real name is Cheong."

"It sounds Chinese."

"Vietnamese. And he is the cousin of Vic Lu."

It was all a little too complex, a spider's web of sticky threads. "What do you think all this means?"

The detective leaned forward as if he didn't want anyone to hear him, even though they were alone. "It means that Gentri Land may be a way for Vic Lu to pay off Bernie Halstrom, hold his public antiporn campaigns at bay."

"When this all started," she said, "you told me Vic Lu had something to do with Gilda's disappearance."

"We don't know that for certain."

"But you think so. And maybe you think Bernie might be involved."

"That's why I've asked you to wear a wire."

EIGHTEEN

1.

Dallas set up a meeting the next day.

When she called Bernie, she made it sound important, which is exactly what it was. When he offered to pick her up, she accepted with trepidation. But meeting on his terms could get him loose enough to admit something that would help Detective Lacy make his case, which might lead to the answer on what really happened to Melinda Perry.

Lacy had her come to West Valley station, where a female officer rigged her with a wire that was a marvel of modern technology. It would record five hours on a digital media the size of a penny. She only had to be within five feet of Bernie Halstrom.

He picked her up in front of Cara's apartment. Derek, his driver, smiled and nodded as he opened the door for her.

Bernie shook her hand warmly as she slid in beside him.

"To the feed store, Derek," he said.

"Where are we headed?" Dallas asked.

"You'll see. Sit back and relax. I'm glad we have this chance to talk."

Talk away, as much as you want. She had prepared as best she could for this moment. Over and over in her mind she played out the scene: How Bernie would be the same old Bernie, glad-handing her, expressing concern. How she would have to pretend to believe it and keep her face from screwing up into a resemblance of a gargoyle.

This was going to be a lot harder in actual fact.

"I've been wanting to bring something up with you," Bernie said.

"Oh?"

"Now that Ron's case is off the front page," he said, "I thought you might like to have something to help carry on his work, a project."

"What sort of project?"

"I'm organizing a new citizens' committee to inform me on matters from a grassroots level. Everything from schools and parks to the cracks in the sidewalk. I feel like I need to have this network, and I want you to head it up."

"Me?"

"You."

"That's a lot of responsibility."

"I think you can handle it. I know you can. Will you at least consider it?"

I'll consider it before I reject it. "Sure."

"Good. I was hoping you'd say that. Maybe get Hillside involved in this. Bob and Lisa Benson."

Dallas closed her eyes for a moment. "I'm sure they'll be happy to hear from you."

"Are you feeling all right?"

She looked at him. "Just tired." Through the heavily tinted windows of the limo she could see they were heading south on Topanga, toward the canyon.

"Where are we headed?" she asked.

"My surprise. A little place in Malibu overlooking the ocean. You'll love it."

"Dinner?"

"You object?"

"No, of course not." A casual social setting might also serve her cause.

"Now," Bernie said, "what was it you wanted to see me about? You sounded very concerned on the phone, like it's something I should know."

Here it was. Detective Lacy had prepped her with the questions to ask. Now she had to make it all seem natural.

"Bernie, do you know a man named Walter Channing?"

"Sure, I know Walter. He's a great supporter of mine. You know him?"

"Not personally."

"What brought him to your attention?"

"The police."

"Police? Why?"

"They wouldn't say."

Bernie paused, his mind obviously working away. Finally, he said, "What was the nature of their questions to you?"

"Apparently he has some sort of connection with Vic Lu and a corporation called Gentri Land. Do you know what that means?"

That was it. Now was the time to watch his reactions. The tape would catch his words and, the police hoped, reveal something below the surface. Not an admission, that was too much to hope for. But statements that could be contradicted by physical records—phone calls, notes of meetings, computer files.

His face was clothed with concern. He couldn't hide it. But the wire could not capture visuals.

Bernie reached for a button on the side-door console. A black glass screen whirred upward, separating them from his driver.

"I want to keep this just between us," he said. "You must tell me everything that was said to you."

Dallas tried to remain calm. "That's really all. They asked vague questions on a lot of things."

"What other things?"

"I don't know if I'm supposed to say."

"Did the police tell you not to say anything?"

"Sort of."

"What do you mean, sort of? Dallas, please try to be clear."

"I don't know anything other than that, Bernie. Is there something wrong? You seem to be upset."

"I have political enemies, Dallas. You know that. Someone could be trying to manufacture something here. And you're being used."

"I don't think so."

He shook his head and put his hand on her shoulder. "We've known each other a long time, haven't we?"

Why was he touching her? Was this the gesture of an old friend, or something more?

"Yes, we have," Dallas said.

"And we trust each other, right?"

"Of course." She tried to sound as sincere as possible. Instead, her words rang hollow.

He kept his hand on her shoulder, patting it softly. "You know, I'm having to deal with so much. I feel I'm being accused of something I did not do. Some association with Gentri Land and Vic Lu, of all people. You don't believe that, do you, Dallas?"

She didn't know what to believe. She wanted to get out of the limo and hitchhike home.

"I'll listen to anything you have to say, Bernie."

"I'm sure you will. And who else?"

"Excuse me?"

His hand slipped down her back. "Who else is listening, Dallas?"

With a violent thrust, he pressed one hand on her mouth, pushing her head back into the seat. With his other hand he ripped her blouse. It tore away like paper. She was half-exposed now, but the shock of his attack froze her.

In one more second he tore the wire from her body and dangled the apparatus from his hand.

"Dallas, Dallas." He shook his head. "I can't believe you'd do this."

She was not going to put up any pretenses now. She let her voice give vent. "What about you, Bernie? All those years lying to my face? How could you do that?"

"Because I know you, and I know you don't get it. Politics is about compromise, and sometimes you have to do things to get the power to get things done. Good things. It balances out. But you and Ron never understood compromise."

"Lies, that's what I don't understand."

"You think I'm not doing good for the community? You think my record isn't something to be proud of?" His voice was rising. "I'll stand shoulder to shoulder with anybody for the benefits I've brought my constituents."

"Like Vic Lu." She gripped her blouse and held it together across her chest.

"Yeah, believe it or not, Dallas, he's a member of the community too. Get off your high horse. He's not a lawbreaker."

"You were supposed to change that. Instead, you used Ron and me to put up a front."

"Water under the bridge at this point. What matters now is what we're going to do about you."

She shuddered, her insides tensing like a fist. It was all so surreal, looking into the face of a man she thought she knew, thought was good, now speaking in a voice that froze her to the bone.

Bernie picked up the handset. "Derek, slight change of plans. Go back. We need to see our mutual friend. And make sure no one follows us."

He put the handset down and looked at Dallas. "Needless to say, dinner is off."

2.

Night had always been Jared's favorite time for driving. Especially on the quiet ribbon of Interstate 5. It was peaceful in its way, a place to think.

And he had plenty to think about after the visit to his father up north.

The prison at Los Rios was one of the older facilities in the California system. As such it had an almost nostalgic appearance, with its four corner guard towers right out of some old Warner Bros. movie, and a large water tower overlooking the razor-wire fence.

The visitors' room was a row of hard metal stools before wire screens. This time he would hear his father's voice for real, not over a phone line. And he wondered just how he was going to react to it.

Jared was drying his palms on his shirt when his father came through an inner door. He was dressed in denim pants and blue work shirt. He looked more like a farmer than a prisoner.

He sat opposite Jared, smiling. "You look well," he said.

"You look skinny," Jared said.

"It's a new thing—the felony accusation diet."

His father's attempt at humor went past his head like a stray bullet. "Why did you do it, Dad? I mean, plead guilty?"

"No contest," Ron corrected, then sighed. "I just chose not to fight anymore. And in a way I'm responsible for what happened to that girl."

"But you're not responsible. You didn't kill her."

"The evidence was going to convince a jury that I did."

"I don't want you in here." Jared felt a sudden burning behind his eyes. He fought for control. "I spent a lot of time mad at you, Dad. I guess I want a chance to work it out. Kind of hard when you're up here."

Ron didn't say anything for a long moment. He swallowed several times, his Adam's apple rising, falling. Finally he said, "Why don't we start with one step at a time. You know how to write. So let's do it that way and see what happens. Will you do that for me? Write letters?"

"Sure, Dad. I'll write up a storm."

And he would. As he drove back toward L.A., Jared thought about all the things he'd say in those letters, how he'd write and be totally honest and ask for forgiveness. How he wouldn't stop writing until he had his father back in his life again, because when he got right down to it, family was the only thing that really mattered in this world. Physical family, church family, any family where people came together because they needed someone to hang on to when the going got tough.

That included Tiana and Jamaal. Jared had to find them, had to resume the search. He wouldn't have any peace until he did.

A pale moon was in the sky ahead of him, partially obscured by clouds. But there was enough light to make the outline of the distant mountains stand out like sentinels. They guarded the way back home and would let him through only if he believed in the promise of reconciliations, a ton of them, laying beyond.

He believed, and drove on.

3.

Vic Lu's studio was a large cement tilt-up, a commercial building somewhere in Chatsworth. To Dallas, it might as well have been Pluto—foreign, cold, and forbidding.

This couldn't be happening to her. Bernie couldn't be this bad. But he had brought her here by force and stood by quietly as Derek the driver held her down on a hard chair.

Vic Lu, wearing a blood-red Hawaiian shirt, paced in front of her.

"How much you think you know?" he barked at Dallas.

Dallas said nothing.

"I'm asking you something, dear." Lu stopped, bent over, and looked her in the face.

"I know you're dirty," Dallas said. "And so is Bernie." It hurt her to say it.

"Hey, it's a loophole," Lu said, standing upright again. "A way to get our friend Bernie what he needs. Money is the mother's milk of politics, they say. What are you all upset by this for? This kind of thing goes on all the time, all over the place. We're not bad people."

Dallas looked at the councilman. "Bernie, how can you let yourself be used by this man?"

Bernie spoke to Vic Lu. "She's a romantic. She sees things in black and white and thinks God is going to come down and set everything right."

Lu shook his head. "That's called *deus ex machina*. It's not dramatically satisfying."

"We have to think this through carefully," Bernie said. "She had a wire, which means the police are in on this. I can pull a few strings and find out what's going on. Someone's obviously targeted me and the Gentri Land connection. Dallas, you'll save everyone a lot of pain if you tell me who it is."

She had no doubt there would be pain involved if she didn't talk. These were desperate men, a pornographer and a politician in bed together. Such a pairing could never produce anything but paranoia.

She'd seen it before. In the face of Chad McKenzie when he used to beat her. Part of the game for him was getting her to wilt in shame and fear, which she had. This was the same game. She would not play it.

Bernie sighed. "Not talking? Now we have a real situation on our hands."

"No sweat," Lu said. "You ever see *Wag the Dog?*"

"The movie?" Bernie said.

"Yeah, with Dustin Hoffman and Robert De Niro. That is one of the greatest movies of all time." Lu became animated, like he'd had too many shots of espresso. "It's a movie about taking real crisis situations and spinning them into a story that will sell a presidential campaign. Dustin plays the producer, and things keep going wrong, like planes crashing and crazy murderers getting loose, and he keeps saying, 'This is nothing. This is producing. I can take care of this.' That's all that's happening here, Bernie. This is what I do. I make up fantasies. I write, produce, and direct stories that people feed on. That's what we're going to do right now."

He paused, put his two index fingers to his temples, and closed his eyes.

"Bernie," Dallas said, "don't do this."

"It's too late, Dallas. I'm sorry. I really am."

"Quiet, please," Lu said, still concentrating. Then he opened his eyes, excited. "Got it! You two went for a nice ride, heading for a nice dinner. But Mrs. H got a headache driving through the canyon. So you brought her back home, only she never made it inside. You went home, Bernie. You are sound asleep. Tomorrow, she'll be reported missing. Naturally, the cops think you might be behind this, but she'll be spotted in Barstow. I'll get another supporting player for that."

"Then what?" Bernie said.

"Leave that to me."

"I don't want to hear any more about it."

A little-boy disappointment descended on Lu. "I'm just getting to the best part!"

"Forget it. Just take care of it. I don't want to know."

Bernie walked toward the door where Derek was now standing guard.

"So that's it?" Dallas called after him.

He did not answer. Derek opened the door, let Bernie through, then closed the door, staying inside.

Insurance.

When Dallas turned back around, Vic Lu was on his cell phone. She heard him say, "Right now," and then he clicked off.

"It won't be long," he said to Dallas. "You're gonna love the ending."

4.

Jared waited in his truck outside the dark apartment building, hoping he'd see Tiana or Jamaal go in or out.

Half an hour. An hour. No Tiana.

Then he saw a woman he thought he recognized. How? It came to him. When he'd first come to this place, she was the one who gave him a suspicious glare. The one-woman Neighborhood Watch. Tonight she was with another, younger woman. They were talking, illuminated by the bright lights on the front walk.

Jared got out of the truck and walked across the street.

The two women didn't pay him any mind until he was nearly within reach.

"Excuse me," he said.

They looked at him, the older woman examining him closely.

"Remember me?"

The woman looked at him like she did, but shook her head. "No, I don't."

"I'm a friend of Tiana Williams."

She narrowed her eyes, then slowly nodded. "I remember now. What're you doing around here?"

"I'm looking for her. And Jamaal."

The other woman joined in the glare. It was obvious they didn't trust him.

"I know all about Rafe," he said. "I helped them get away from him."

"He's dead," the younger woman said.

"Dead? How—"

"And maybe they don't want to be found," the first woman said.

"Do you know where they are?"

"I wouldn't tell you if I did. I don't know what you might do to them. Can't you just leave them alone? They been through enough."

"Then can you get a message to them? Please. I know you don't know who I am. My name is Jared. That's all you have to say. I'll give you my phone number and you can have her call me."

The woman gave him another hard look, only this time it had a dose of understanding in it. "You got a notion about the two of you, I mean the three of you?"

"Maybe. Maybe that's a crazy, stupid thing to have. The only thing I know for sure now is I want to see her again and just talk things through."

After a long pause, the woman said, "All right, young man. Wait here." She quickly added, "But if you go on and hurt that girl you're gonna have to deal with me, you understand?"

5.

"... think ill of me," Vic Lu was saying, still pacing and ranting. "I mean, come on. If it weren't for people like you and your ex-husband, we—"

"Not ex."

Lu shrugged. "Hey, who am I to get involved in your personal affairs, huh?"

"Holding me prisoner is pretty personal."

"You're not listening!" He stomped his foot, a petulant child. "I've got a point. Nobody gives me credit for a point, or for making art! I write my films, lady. Did you know that? I got nominated for an Eros Award last year. Does that matter? Why am I talking to you?"

He gave a wave to Derek, as if it was time for him to take over. In two minutes he bound Dallas to the chair. She prayed. She asked God to consume Vic Lu and Derek with fire. Why not? It was a prayer for protection, and God would work out the details.

The moment she was secured, the door to the studio opened.

Chad McKenzie came in.

"I believe you two know each other," Lu said.

Chad smiled. "Hey, babe, how are you?"

She glared at Vic Lu. "Him? How low have you sunk?"

"You hear that?" Chad said. "I used to get that all the time."

Lu pointed at Chad. "Shut up." Chad did as he was told. Then Lu looked at Derek. "Better tape her mouth," he said.

6.

"You reading that Bible again?" Ernesto's head hung down from the top bunk, looking at me.

"You know," I said, "I think I've discovered that the Bible is reading me."

"What are you talking about, man?"

"You really want to know?"

"I got nothing else goin' on."

I sat up. Ernesto dropped off his bunk and sat on mine. We had reached a point of mutual tolerance and even, on occasion, conversation. It usually happened like this, in the twilight time between chow and lights-out. Ernesto sometimes got downright chatty then.

"It's like this," I said. "I used to read the Bible just to get something out of it for me, like for my sermons or to back up something I was going to say in a book."

"Yeah."

"But the Bible is living and active, sharper than any double-edged sword."

"What's that mean?" He looked interested. But I must say he was a true example of a captive audience.

"It means it reads me. It cuts me up. But I have to let it."

"You sound a little out there, man, you want to know the truth."

"Yeah, it sounds a little nuts. But God is doing the cutting, see, inside me. He's cutting out all the stuff I don't need, that I used to let get in the way. Now I've got plenty of time to let God do his work."

Ernesto was quiet for a long time. Then he said, "My grandmother used to try to get me to go to Mass. I couldn't take it. I got bored. Guess I had some of that attention thing."

"Deficit disorder."

"You gringos are great with the labels. But I always thought when I was in church that there was something going on, something I couldn't see, but it was there. It was floating around. Think that was God?"

"Definitely. But then I'd go one step further and say there's a way to know all about that presence. And it's in this book."

Ernesto took the Bible from me and looked at it. "I never got into it. Lots of stuff I couldn't understand when I tried."

"We can talk about it if you want."

"You gonna try to convert me?"

"No. If that happens, it'll be because of the Word and the Spirit. But I'm thinking maybe there's a reason you and I were put in the same cell together."

"Yeah, so I can keep you from getting stabbed in the back. You are so white."

"Maybe I can return the favor."

"If I get bored, and I tell you to stop, you stop, got it?"

"Deal."

I took the Bible back and in that moment asked God what I should start with. The beginning. It didn't take a bright bulb to catch on to that.

So I started with, "In the beginning God . . ."

And for two straight hours Ernesto was not bored. He did not ask me to stop, and I felt for the first time in years that my preaching was anointed by God. Right there in a prison cell.

7.

Dallas lay in the backseat of the car where Chad had thrown her like a sack of laundry. The duct tape across her mouth chafed. Plastic restraints, pulled tight, held her wrists and ankles fast.

The night was black and she had no idea what direction they were going. She had a vague idea they'd hopped on the 118 Freeway, but she couldn't be sure.

About ten minutes into the ride, Chad lit a cigarette. Dallas could smell the smoke. She tried not to breathe deeply. She didn't want to cough against the tape. But he rolled the windows up, like he intended to torture her with the smell.

Then he started talking.

"Dallas, you have to know that I never wanted it to work out this way. I loved you. You think that's funny, but I really did. You think when I hit you I didn't love you? It was because I couldn't stand the thought of you walking out on me, that's why I did it. You know what I did the night you left me? I mean, the night I figured out you were gone for good? I could have come after you, but I didn't. I released you, like a butterfly. I bet you didn't know that. Instead, I went down to the beach and beat up a couple of guys, just because I needed to get it out of me, you know? That's something you never understood, that I had to get it out of me. If you really loved me you would have understood that. But you never did, so now it has to end this way. Man, this is hard for me. I mean, we had a lot of good times, didn't we?"

Dallas couldn't help answering him in her mind. *Good times? Perverse, ugly . . .*

"Just want you to know that we could have worked something out if you hadn't been so, I don't know, self-righteous. Pretty slick move, I must say, going on TV and telling about the photos and naming me right there in front of the whole world. You know that was bad for business? I couldn't even give 'em away. I tell you, you were a lot more fun back in the old days, back before you hooked up with that preacher and got all saved."

Save me now . . .

"I also want you to know you're not going to suffer. It's not going to hurt. I wouldn't do that to you. You believe that, don't you? I'll use the amyl nitrate on you, the way Rafe used it on Jared. You don't know about that, do you? They had your son marked from the start."

They. Vic Lu and Bernie Halstrom.

"When this Rafe dude found out who Jared was, he decided to get in on things. Lu hired him."

Rafe? Why would he care about Jared? And what were the chances of his random orbit intersecting with Chad's? And Vic Lu's? When had this universe she was trying to make sense of become so small?

Chad's voice dropped an octave. "Then that Rafe tried to strong-arm me. Big mistake. I'll tell you something, *he* felt it. When I did him, he felt it real bad."

He drove in semisilence for a time, humming softly, a rock medley. She recognized a couple of the tunes, then realized they were songs she had liked when they were together. Rolling Stones. Pink Floyd.

And then one tune that came to her in a flood of disgusting memories.

Meat Loaf, "Bat Out of Hell."

She remembered what they did to that song.

He was purposely taunting her.

It may have been two hours, maybe three, before the car finally pulled to a stop. Chad came around the side, opened the door, and yanked her out, pulling her by the plastic restraints. They cut into her skin.

She saw a darkened house. She smelled wet scrub and dirt and figured they were somewhere in the desert. She could not see lights anywhere else but in the sky. The night was alive with stars.

Chad put an arm around her neck and made her shuffle to the door. He unlocked it and pulled her inside, then flicked on a lamp with a yellowed lampshade. The soft orange light made only a slight dent in the darkness.

Dallas could see it was a small house, ranch style. Chad pushed her down on an old sofa. Musty, like it was from 1950.

"You believe they actually use this place?" Chad said, looking around. "They made a porno Western here. But some of the rooms are like little studios."

He appeared to be looking around for something.

And then found it.

From a table he took a large hunting knife, so large it looked like a small sword.

"After the amyl, you won't feel this, Dallas. And the good part is you'll get to be out in your God's creation. You'll just be lizard food, of course, but if it makes you feel any better, that's where you'll be."

Dallas looked at the knife and at Chad holding it, smiling. She had no doubt he was going to do it. He wanted her to suffer right now. He wanted her scared.

But she noticed, amazingly, that her heart was not beating wildly, nor was her breathing—through her nose—labored.

She was calm.

One thought raced into her mind, a confirmation of the sovereignty of God. He was ultimately in control, despite what men might do in rebellion to him. Evil men like Chad McKenzie and Vic Lu and, sadly, Bernie Halstrom, could not escape. Even if they killed her, God was ruler over all.

She would die now, but she was not afraid.

Chad was studying her face.

She looked right back at him, talking to him with her eyes. *Do this and you will be punished, and deep down you know it, you know it right now, don't you?*

Suddenly, anger seemed to engulf him. He cursed at her.

You are the dead one, Chad. You are the dupe.

"You make me sick," he spat.

You know it, you've always known it, and you're dead. Don't do this. In killing me you'll be killing yourself.

"Shut up."

His frenzy was almost comical. She hadn't said a word, couldn't through the tape. Yet he had heard everything.

He held up the knife and looked at the blade. "Maybe the amyl's a bad idea. Maybe you'd rather have the experience without drugs."

He brought the point of the knife down slowly, like he was drawing a picture in the air. With a slight flourish he stopped with the point just in front of her face.

"I can start anywhere I want." He examined her face like a butcher considering where to make the first cut.

You are the dead one, Chad.

"You want it done quickly, Dallas? Are you ready to meet your God?"

God, watch over my family always. Protect and keep them.

"If you want a chance to call God a liar, I might be able to let you go—"

Preserve Ron, bring justice, protect Jared and Cara, comfort them.

"—or I can just get started right now."

Let them live and know that I am with you.

"So if you want to curse God, just nod your head, Dallas."

She looked him in the eye, held the look, peering into his dark pupils. They were empty caves with no flicker of light inside.

He took a handful of her hair and snapped her head back. She couldn't see his eyes now, or the knife. She only smelled his breath, beer and cigarettes. He held her like that for a full minute.

Then she felt the tip of the blade on her throat. He poked her without breaking skin.

"You are so stupid," he whispered. "It's better for you to die."

Something creaked. A floorboard.

Chad released her head and whipped around to his right.

Dallas followed his look, saw a shadowy form ten feet away. A full second of time froze in the room, then came the flash of a muzzle and crack of a gunshot, and Chad fell backward. The knife fell out of his hand as he grasped his chest, already seeping red.

The form didn't move from the shadows.

Chad gurgled and thrashed. Blood smeared the floor as he struggled like a felled deer, his legs jerking outward to find traction.

Dallas expected the shadow to move forward and finish her too.

But it waited. Chad's movements slowed into an agonizing spasm of death. He turned his head toward Dallas, eyes terrified, as if he saw something horrible behind her head. His lips quivered as he opened his mouth in a long, excruciating, and silent scream.

And then he moved no more. His dead eyes stayed open, horror filled.

The shadow figure came into the light.

C.

"What?"

Tiana looked out the door of the little tract house in Eagle Rock, an expression of complete surprise on her face. The woman Jared took to be her sister stood by her side. There was a striking resemblance.

"Tiana," Jared said, "I—"

He heard scuffling feet, looked down, and saw Jamaal. The boy smiled up at Jared and said, "Where you been?"

"I had a few things to take care of. How's that arm?"

"Huh?"

Jared made a passing motion.

"Good," Jamaal said.

"Hold it!" Tiana said, hands on her hips. "How'd you find us? What are you doing here?"

"The neighbor lady from your old place gave me the address. I told her I had to find you, I—"

"After you ran out on us?" Her voice betrayed hurt mixed with the anger.

"Wait—"

She slammed the door closed.

A moment later it swung open again. This time the sister was alone with Jamaal. "Mister," she said, "what are you about?"

"I didn't run out on your sister. Or Jamaal."

The boy pointed at him and said, "You better not be lyin'."

"Believe me, kid, I'm done with that."

The sister gave him a hard, examining look. "I can't let you in here unless I'm convinced you're being straight. I'm not going to let my sister get hurt anymore, you hear me?"

"Give me five minutes," Jared said. "That's it. If you want me gone after that, I'm gone."

She considered it a moment, then stepped aside so he could come in. "My name's Lavonne," she said.

"He's Jared," Jamaal said.

Jared followed Lavonne inside. Tiana was on a blue sofa, her head in her hands. She looked up. When she saw Jared she started shaking her head.

"We can at least listen," Lavonne said.

"Five minutes," Jared said.

"I can't take any more of you," Tiana said. "You've got to leave us alone now."

"Three minutes, then I'm gone." Jared didn't wait for permission. "The night we argued up in Bakersfield, I went out and I was going to drive away, for good—you're right about that—but I got picked up by the highway patrol. They found my bench warrant on the DUI I skipped, and back I came, and I was in jail and a guy wanted to kill me, only this other guy in my cell talked Jesus to the guy and he stopped, and it freaked me out, but it woke me up and turned me around. I don't want to go back to the way I was again, no more booze, no more drugs, I'm gonna stay clean, but mostly I don't want to be away from you and Jamaal. And that's it, that's the whole thing."

The others looked at him as if he was slightly nuts.

Then Jamaal said, "Cool."

"That's a good one, all right," Lavonne said.

"All true," Jared said. "And that's why I'm here. And I want to know if you'll forgive me."

Tiana looked at him, thinking.

"Forgive him, Mom!" Jamaal said.

Slowly, a smile broke out on her face. "I do."

9.

If duct tape had not covered her mouth, Dallas would have gasped. The shadow was in full light now, and there was no mistaking who it was, though the face was terribly puffed up and discolored.

Gilda was shaking, gun in hand. Her eyes widened through the black and blue rings that were not makeup. The loud purple hair was unkempt. It looked like a handful had been torn out of one side.

She looked down at Chad and pointed the gun at him. Dallas thought she'd fire again, but instead, she kicked his side with full force. Chad McKenzie was very clearly dead.

Gilda turned her attention to Dallas, looking as if she didn't know what to do next.

Dallas tried to talk comfortingly with her eyes, but Gilda wasn't listening. She didn't look like *comfort* was in her vocabulary.

Still holding the handgun, Gilda examined Dallas's restraints, then slowly pulled the duct tape off her mouth. Dallas suspected a layer of skin came off with it.

"Why are you here?" Gilda said.

"He was going to kill me."

Gilda shook her head slowly. "Then we're both dead."

"Cut me loose," Dallas said.

Eyes wide, body still shaking, Gilda used the gun to point to her face. "Look at me! He did this to me!"

"I know."

"*What?*"

"He used to beat me up too."

"What are you *talking* about?"

"Cut me loose, Gilda, so we can talk."

"Talk now."

"All right. He was my boyfriend once. A long time ago. He tracked me down when my husband and I made the news. He somehow got hooked up with Vic Lu."

"You got that much right. I was a present. Vic gave me to him. Now look . . ." Gilda's words stuck in a short sob.

Vic gave me to him. The thought jarred Dallas, but it made perverse sense. Men like Lu and Chad were into total control.

"Gilda, I can help you."

"No way. It's over. Vic is going to kill me, and he'll get you too."

"How much do you know about Lu's dealings?"

Gilda gave a weak smile. "I've been here two days. Vic and Chad and a crew were coming up tomorrow for a shoot. Guess what? I shot first."

"You were going to kill Lu?"

"I messed that up, didn't I? The luck I have."

"Why, Gilda? It's because Vic Lu had something to do with Melinda's murder, isn't it?"

Gilda said nothing.

"You knew her. You were friends, you—"

"You don't make friends in this business," Gilda spat. "You do and you only get hurt."

"You know something. Tell me. We can stop Lu."

Turning her back, Gilda muttered something that sounded like *no way.*

"Cut me loose, Gilda. Then I can take you where it's safe. It's a place where women like you come to get away from the bad guys."

"No place is safe."

"Let me prove it to you."

Gilda seemed to be retreating into herself. In a few minutes, she might walk out. Or kill herself. Or both of them.

"Trust me, Gilda."

"Why should I?"

"Because I'm not like them. And neither are you."

For an extended moment Gilda just stared at her. Then she looked to the floor, bent over, and picked up Chad's knife.

"You better be right," Gilda said. And then she cut Dallas loose.

"How'd you get here?" Dallas said.

"My car's a half mile up the road."

"Let me get my purse. It's in Chad's car. Then we'll—"

"Do we have to call the cops?"

Dallas touched Gilda's arm. "I want to talk to my lawyer first. In the morning."

Gilda seemed relieved. "Where'll we go?"

"I have a place where we'll both be safe."

"But will you drive?" Gilda said. "I'm shaking all over."

NINETEEN

1.

Dallas drove Gilda's car back toward the Valley. On the way she called Cara, told her not to worry, that she'd explain everything later. She faked enough calm to get Cara to agree to wait.

Dallas got Gilda settled into Haven House around 2:30 a.m., then crashed in the office, on the sofa. She woke up, body buzzing with adrenaline, at eight.

She cleaned up in the small bathroom and then called Jeff. He was just arriving at the office. Dallas got there at 8:45.

She told him everything she knew about Vic Lu and Bernie Halstrom, the wire she wore, the Gentri Land setup, Gilda. And Chad's body in a house in the desert. When she finished she was exhausted but managed to conclude, "That'll mean Ron will get out of prison, won't it?"

Jeff's face was impassive. Not a good sign.

"What's the problem?" she asked.

"We would have to petition the court to allow Ron to withdraw his plea. And to do that, we have to have a factual basis for allowing it, like a clear indication of another's guilt or complicity."

"We have it."

"We have Chad's and Bernie's connection to Vic Lu, yes. What we don't have is the connection to the murder of Melinda Perry."

"We have Gilda. She knows things. She thinks Melinda was used by Lu as bait to catch Ron, that the murder was set up—"

"Thinks?" Jeff pursed his lips. Another bad sign. "Dallas, remember when we discussed that gang kid you found? The problems that a questionable witness presents? The DA is going to fight this, and we'd have to convince a court this witness really knows what she's talking about, can corroborate it."

"But I know she can."

"Do you really?"

644

She stopped. What did Gilda really know after all? And would it withstand scrutiny?

Softly, Jeff said, "As always, Dallas, I want you to be fully informed of what's going on. When Ron entered his plea, he waived his right to challenge the truth of the underlying offense. We would have to show the court good cause to lift this waiver. We would—"

"We have to go through with this, Jeff, we have to. Even though I don't have the wire on Halstrom, we have me. I can swear to what happened. Maybe that would force him to turn on Lu—"

"It's your word against his."

"Jeff! We have Detective Lacy working on this, we have—"

"There's a bigger problem, Dallas."

"What?"

"Ron."

She looked at him, wondering what he meant.

"He would have to consent to withdrawing his plea," Jeff said. "You remember, it was his idea to plead out in the first place."

"But the truth," she said. "Doesn't that matter to anybody anymore?"

"To us it does. It always will. And that's going to have to be enough."

With resignation rising like cold water inside her, Dallas heard her cell phone chime. She looked at the number. It was Cara.

"May I take this?" she asked.

"Go right ahead," Jeff said.

She spoke into the phone. "Cara, what's up?"

"It's Lacy. I'm at your daughter's apartment."

Something was wrong with Cara. "What is it?"

"Can you talk?"

She thought maybe she should call him back, but was too anxious to hear his report. "Yes."

"It's about Gentri Land. It's owned by a shell company. Called DatJam. Gentri Land is the only thing this shell company owns, as far as I can tell."

All very interesting, but it could wait, couldn't it?

"I looked deeper, and found out who the agent for service of process is."

"What's that?"

"A corporation has to have someone who can be served papers, in case they're sued, whatever. Dallas, the agent for DatJam is Jefferson Waite."

Every muscle in her body clenched.

Jeff.

Who had denied knowing anything about Gentri Land.

She tried to keep her face from blazing a neon sign of trouble.

"Mrs. Hamilton?"

"I'm here, dear."

"Excuse me?"

She looked at Jeff. He was scribbling something on a legal pad.

"I'm with your father's lawyer at the moment," Dallas said in a light tone.

"You're at Waite's office?" Lacy said.

"We're trying to see what we can do for Dad. I'll fill you in when I get home."

"Get out of there, Dallas."

"See you soon."

She put the phone in her pocket.

"Any trouble?" Jeff asked.

"No, no. Cara's such a worrywart. I guess I'd better go reassure her."

She stood up.

So did Jeff. He walked around his desk toward her. She watched his eyes, looked at his face for clues of his intentions.

Stay calm.

"Thanks for everything you've done, Jeff. Really. You gave it your best."

She looked at the office door.

"Something wrong, Dallas?"

She fought hard to keep her hands steady as she reached for the door. "Let's not give up."

"You look worried all of a sudden."

"All of a sudden? I've been in knots for months." She clasped the door handle.

Jeff moved close to her, smiling. "You know, a lawyer goes to court, argues cases to juries, looks witnesses in the eye. He does that enough, and he develops a sense of something going on. Is there anything wrong, Dallas? Anything you're not sharing?"

She pushed down on the handle. "I know how busy you are. Let's meet later this week."

"You sure?"

"I'll call you. Thanks for everything."

"Let me walk you to—"

"I'm a big girl, Jeff," she said with a lilt. "I'll find my way out."

She passed the receptionist, who gave her a nice smile. *Just how much does she know?* The woman was probably as deceived as everyone else in Jeff's orbit.

Dallas kept her pace slow and steady to the elevator. It felt like an hour before it came. She got on alone, punched the key for the parking garage, and only then began to breathe easier.

The elevator let her out in the deserted garage. She'd parked Gilda's car in the far corner. She'd feel completely safe only when she got out of there and connected with Lacy again. Fumbling for the keys, she realized how badly she was shaking. She was just about to press *unlock* on the key fob when she heard a voice.

"Don't move, Dallas."

2.

The look on the deputy sheriff's face was almost comical. "I didn't expect to see you walk in without cuffs," he said.

Jared smiled. "What can I say? It's not that I missed the place."

"You came to see somebody?"

"Yeah. I want to visit one of my old cell mates."

"What is this, old home week?"

"In a way."

"You're entitled to visit like anyone else. Let's get you a pass. Who was it you wanted to see?"

"That's just it. I never got his name. I thought maybe you could look him up for me."

The deputy thought a moment. "Let's go ask."

Jared followed him through a door on the right into an office where three other deputies sat at desks.

"This is Jared Hamilton, one of our recent guests," the deputy said.

The others gave him the same look as the first deputy had. Jared felt a little like a walking carnival exhibit. He nodded.

"He wants to say hello to one of his cell mates, if you can believe it, but he doesn't have a name."

One deputy, a woman with a nameplate that said *Sanchez*, motioned Jared over. She had a computer on her desk and tapped something on the keyboard.

"Okay," she said. "Hamilton, right? Jared?"

"Yes," Jared said.

"Yeah, here's your module and your cell number. Let's see, you only spent a weekend here."

"Quite a weekend."

"Looks like"—she peered at the screen—"you had four able-bodied companions. Pal Ingram isn't with us anymore. He was shipped off for trial in San Mateo. Good riddance to bad garbage. He wasn't the one you wanted to see, I hope."

"No. It was an older guy."

"Older?"

"Maybe in his forties."

One of the other deputies, a man in his forties, piped, "Way over the hill."

The other deputies, including Sanchez, laughed.

"And there were five other guys in there with me," Jared said.

Sanchez looked at the screen. "I only see four names here, and they're all in their twenties."

Jared leaned over and looked at the screen. He couldn't make out the codes. Sanchez pointed at a couple of numbers. "Only four assigned to that cell, until you came in. That makes five."

"But I know there were six of us. I can count."

"All I can do is tell you what's here."

"What if your records are wrong? Does that ever happen?"

"Never!" another deputy said. "Don't tell him any different, either."

More laughter.

"Sorry," Sanchez said. "You know, you come in a place like this, it's a little stressful. Maybe you don't remember."

"No, it's clear! He saved my life."

Sanchez looked at her fellows. "Haven't heard that one in a while."

"Call Oprah," another said.

And they laughed again, having a good old time.

No amount of cajoling could get Sanchez to search any further. Jared had come in hopeful and walked out mystified. Yet most of the recent events of his life were beyond his comprehension.

Like connecting with Tiana and Jamaal the way he did.

Like knowing God had watched over him all this time because his mother and sister and father all prayed for him.

Maybe that's all the comprehension he needed.

3.

"Harry, don't."

Dallas looked the investigator in the eye, willing him to relent, to move his hand from the door of the car.

"I'm sorry, Dallas. I can't let you go."

"You going to kill me?"

Harry's face twitched slightly, like he'd taken offense. "I don't want to."

"Kill for Jeff?" She put her hand on his arm. "I can't believe you'd do that."

Harry said nothing.

"Stop now. You can still do what's right."

"And what? Go to prison?"

"You only work for Jeff, you—" She stopped. "Did you kill Melinda Perry? Was it you?"

Harry's eyes showed strain and just plain exhaustion. "Just come with me," he said.

"I'm not going to," she said. "And you won't kill me." Why she said it just that way, she wasn't sure. But she was not scared.

"Dallas, please."

"Your life is at stake."

He shook his head.

"Do the right thing," she said. "For your daughter. For yourself. Don't—"

"Is there a problem?" Jeff Waite had come up behind Harry.

Harry looked at Dallas.

"Get her out of here, Harry."

Harry didn't move.

"Harry!"

The investigator whirled around. "Do it yourself," he said.

Jeff's face went cold. Seeing his expression, Dallas thought she saw the real Jeff Waite for the first time in her life.

"Harry, you're starting to make me nervous."

Harry Stegman didn't move. He was a human shield between Dallas and Jeff Waite.

Then a sound in the distance. Sirens.

Jeff's head cocked a little, and his eyes burned into Harry. "Get out of the way!"

Harry said, "Don't do it, Jeff."

"Move!"

Dallas couldn't see the lower half of Jeff's body but got the distinct impression he was holding something.

Harry's arm moved, as if he was reaching under his coat. It moved out again.

She heard three cracks, one after another. Harry's body fell back against her, pinning her to the car. And then he went down.

Jeff Waite looked at her, shock all over his face. Red wetness spreading on his white shirt, just below the left shoulder.

He opened his mouth, looking like he wanted to curse her, but no sound came out.

And then he dropped straight down, thudding on the concrete.

The sirens grew louder.

Harry's body was on her feet. But he was moving.

He rolled left, onto his side.

"Dallas ...," he said.

"Hold on, Harry. Hold on."

4.

Detective Lacy called Dallas the next day. "Stegman's going to be okay," he said. "Waite died early this morning. I'm at the hospital now to get a statement from Stegman, but he says he wants you here."

"Does he have a lawyer?" Dallas said.

"Waived the right. But he won't talk without you. Are you up for it?"

"I'll be right there," she said.

They had Harry Stegman in post-op at the Reseda Medical Center. A uniformed officer stood outside his room on the third floor.

The detective motioned Dallas to come in.

Harry Stegman lay in a bed by the window, the only patient in the room. A tube dripped fluid into one of his arms. His other arm was shackled to the bed by handcuffs. He looked pitiful, and even though he'd been two-faced to her, Dallas couldn't help feeling sorry for him. That he should have come to this.

"Hello, Dallas," he said, weak but determined. "Thank you for coming."

She nodded.

"I'm ready," Harry told Lacy.

Lacy took out a notebook and pen.

"It started out innocently enough," Harry said. "Vic Lu came to Jeff and told him about this idea he had for boosting campaign contributions. He wanted to know if it was legal. What he was really doing was setting himself up to grease the palm of whoever the city councilman happened to be. He wanted his life in the porn business to be as hassle free as possible, and buying politicians has been the best guarantee.

"He also promised Jeff considerable legal fees for his trouble in heading up the DatJam/Gentri Land scheme. So he was buying Jeff too. Once he got Jeff to be the front man, Lu had him hooked. Not that Jeff resisted him. It was Lu who suggested Jeff get involved in your church. A perfect cover for someone involved in, shall we say, less than upright dealings."

Dallas shook her head. "It's hard to believe."

"People do strange things when they get paid for it. Lu gave Jeff more than money. He also gave him Melinda Perry."

"Jeff was having an affair with her?"

"That's a nice way of putting it. Jeff was using her. Well, there came a time when she decided she wasn't willing to be used anymore. She wanted Jeff to get her out of the business and make her Mrs. Waite. When he said no, she threatened to go to the police and spill her guts about Gentri Land."

"She knew about it?"

"She was a very clever little girl. She knew how to get information from people in return for her favors. That's why she was perfect for the little plan to stop your husband. When Jeff told Vic Lu about Melinda's threats, Lu saw a great opportunity to use her seductive power. One thing about Lu, he casts himself as a visionary. Well, he is. And he can see some pretty grand things for himself."

Detective Lacy grunted and continued to take notes.

"What he wanted to do was kill two birds, so to speak. You and your husband were making trouble with Halstrom. Your husband was becoming too popular a voice for cleaning up the community, shutting down people like Vic Lu. So Lu came up with an idea to trap your husband in a sleazy murder situation."

"Why didn't he just kill Ron and be done with it?"

"Number one, that would have been too obvious. He didn't want people asking questions about who Ron's enemies might be. But the more important reason was Lu's ego. He saw this as an elaborate screenplay, a testimony to his genius. The guy is nuts."

"Did Jeff kill Melinda?" Dallas asked.

Harry nodded. "That was all part of it. Vic Lu wasn't about to get his own hands dirty. He had Jeff and Halstrom both across a barrel. He played his hand perfectly. That's how he got McKenzie involved. McKenzie shows up at Jeff's office, says he has some information he ought to know about. About you, Dallas. He wanted money to keep it quiet. The sap didn't know Jeff couldn't have cared less. So instead of kicking him out, Jeff recruited him. One thing Jeff could do was size people up. That's why he was so good in court."

"Unbelievable," Dallas muttered.

"Jeff was into control, so how convenient was it for him to be handling Ron's defense? He wasn't interested in getting Ron off. He wanted the whole thing disposed of as quickly as possible, and so he leaked the evidence about the porn on Ron's computer to the press to help things along."

Now Dallas couldn't even mutter. The depth of betrayal was fathomless. But wasn't that the way of the ancient enemy of God? Go after the families. Well, this time the plan hadn't succeeded. Her family was not what it once was, but God would knit it together again. She had to hang onto that.

"McKenzie killed a guy named Rafe Bryan," Lacy said to Harry. "Now that they're both dead, it's a little hard to figure. You know anything?"

"Not much, except that this guy Bryan may have been looking for your son, Dallas."

"I think he was," Dallas said. "My son and Bryan's girlfriend started seeing each other."

"When two sweeties like McKenzie and Bryan get together, something's going to pop. Bryan probably wanted in on McKenzie's cut."

"There's someone who can confirm," Dallas said.

Harry waited.

"Gilda."

"You know where she is?" Detective Lacy said, his eyes virtually lighting up.

"I know. And she can give you a bunch on Vic Lu."

"When we catch up with him," he said. "He has taken what they used to call a powder."

"Maybe Bernie Halstrom knows where he is."

The detective nodded, looked at his watch. "And right about now Deputy DA Freton is paying Halstrom a little call."

Harry seemed to relax a little, like he was finally glad to get all this off his chest. Then he said, "I'm sorry, Dallas. I really am."

"I know, Harry."

"I'm not a bad man. I just ... forgot."

"Has anyone called your daughter?"

"No."

"You want me to?"

"I don't know." He looked nervous.

Dallas put her hand on his arm. "Now's the time for family, Harry. Let me make the call."

After a pause, Harry nodded.

"I guess that's it for now," Lacy said. "Your cooperation will be duly noted, Mr. Stegman."

TWENTY

"Watch the paint there," Jared said.

Jamaal looked up at him, the roller in his hand almost as big as he was. White spots dotted his face, and his T-shirt and overalls were spattered as well. The roller was dripping with paint.

"Hold it over the pan." Jared pointed.

Jamaal complied. The wet roller almost pulled him over.

"Let me show you how to smooth it out," Jared said. "If you're gonna work for me you got to do it right."

"Okay." Jamaal was nothing if not excited about his new position in Jared's business.

They were in a house, a fixer on Plummer that was the first contract job for Jared and the fledgling house-painting business he'd started four months ago, a business consisting of himself and two employees—Jamaal, who was quite affordable, and Tiana, who was the head of the design team. She would make everything pretty. She'd started attending night classes in design at Valley Community College.

Jared got Jamaal squared away on the paint, then showed him how to make an X on the wall and roll the rest of the paint across the surface with easy strokes. Jared put on the finishing touches so Jamaal could watch. This process would take a little more time, but time was something Jared had a whole lot of.

Time with people he loved.

Jared handed the roller back to Jamaal. "Okay, now do it again."

Jamaal didn't move.

"What's wrong?"

"You gonna be my dad?"

"You want me to?"

Jamaal nodded.

"I have to talk to your mom about it."

"She wants you to be."

"Oh, yeah?"

"Then we could even live in the same house!"

"That sounds good to me."

Jamaal smiled like the morning sun. Jared knelt and put his hands on the boy's shoulders. He still couldn't believe how such a great kid could have had such a lowlife father, nor how Jamaal could have come out so fresh despite what he'd been through.

What a world it was. What a place Jamaal was being handed. That's why Jared wanted to be part of it with Jamaal. Help him make it through.

He looked the boy in the eye and said, "You can always trust your mom and me, okay?"

Jamaal looked totally serious as he nodded.

"Trust me about what?" Tiana had come in through the front door. She held a plastic bag from Subway in her hand.

Jamaal ran to her. "He said yes!"

The confusion on Tiana's face gave way to realization. She looked at Jared and smiled.

She was beautiful.

2.

The Wednesday night chapel service at the minimum-security men's colony just north of Lancaster always starts at seven o'clock sharp. That's one thing I make sure of. I know from my stint on the inside that these guys calibrate their lives by the minute. They look forward to any break from routine. I'm going to give them that break, and do it on time.

About twenty came tonight, almost double the number from last week. I've been coming each Wednesday for two months now. It's volunteer work, but it's the work God has called me to. Talking to the guys in the prisons.

Just before they bounced me from Los Rios, after the DA petitioned to have my plea withdrawn and charges dropped, Ernesto told me he wanted to keep in touch, said I had a way of talking about God that interested him.

And if I could interest Ernesto, I figured God had arranged it so I could interest others.

That's the way it's going to be.

The big news this past month is that Vic Lu has been arrested for conspiracy to commit murder, and Bernie Halstrom has been indicted on that and several other counts. The two of them are now blaming each other through their lawyers.

But it is a stake through the heart of porn and corruption in Los Angeles, and it's nationwide news. That's why I got a call from my former agent, saying I was "hot" again, and how about a new book?

I politely said no.

I will not go back to celebrity, or the paid ministry, unless God picks me up and literally throws me there.

Until that time, I will go into the prisons.

3.

After church, Ron and Dallas drove down to the pier at Santa Monica, just to be together and look at the ocean. They spoke very little on the way. For some reason, a reason Dallas couldn't quite fathom, words would have diluted the moment. It had something to do with the church service that morning. They'd sung one of Dallas's favorite old hymns, *Blessed Assurance.* When they got to *glory divine* Dallas thought that described perfectly the congregation, this body of Christ she and Ron called home.

After all the scandal, after Ron's fall and the resignation of Bob Benson over Lisa's duplicity—even after all that, Hillside had hung together. Sure, there was fallout. Several people left in disillusionment. But in the last few weeks others had come, filling the seats to hear the "new" preacher, the one unanimously called until a permanent pastor could be found.

Roger Vernon looked great up there, eighty years young and full of life, the kind that could only come from believing in the Word of God with every fiber of his being, and preaching it with utter conviction.

There was not one trace of discomfort for Ron in Roger's presence. Shortly after his release from prison, Ron had come forward to ask the congregation for forgiveness. It was given in an overwhelming wave of grace.

Now he was content to sit under Roger's teaching and let God deal with him as he would.

This morning, Roger asked the people to turn in their Bibles to the first chapter of 2 Corinthians. He read aloud, "'Praise be to the God and Father of our Lord Jesus Christ, the Father of compassion and the God of all comfort, who comforts us in all our troubles, so that we can comfort those in any trouble with the comfort we ourselves have received from God.'"

Ron had reached over then and taken her hand. She heard him whisper, "Amen."

Now, strolling along the pier, amidst the hustle of tourists and bustle of commerce, Ron took her hand again. They walked until they reached a place where they could gaze down at the blue-green water. It swirled and broke around the pilings. White foam churned then dissipated as it melted back into the sea.

Dallas realized then that in the very place where her spirit had been torn by Ron's betrayal, a healing had already occurred. This broken place had carried a scar, but it was stronger now and more resilient. That was God's way, she supposed. He didn't spare the scars, he transformed them. They melted into him, and that's how he made all things new.

"Let's go down there," Dallas said.

"Where?"

"The water. Let's take our shoes off and get wet."

Ron smiled at her. His eyes danced in the sunlight that flickered off the ocean. Then he put his arm around her shoulder and, in silent communion, they walked back along the pier to the stairs that led down to the beach.

ABOUT THE AUTHOR

JAMES SCOTT BELL is the bestselling author of *Breach of Promise, Sins of the Fathers, Deadlock,* and several other thrillers. He is a winner of the Christy Award for Excellence, a fiction columnist for *Writer's Digest* magazine, and an adjunct professor of writing at Pepperdine University. He lives with his wife, Cindy, in Los Angeles.

Visit his website at www.jamesscottbell.com.